Praise for
SILENT WITNESS

"Intense courtroom drama . . . As startling as the bang of a gavel."
—*People*

"This generation's best writer of legal thrillers . . . his strongest fiction to date."
—*Entertainment Weekly*

"Patterson hits the first line at a dead run . . . He never slows down . . . Everything is marvelously plotted."
—*Philadelphia Inquirer*

"Enthralling . . . the denouement is powerful."
—*Los Angeles Times Book Review*

"Chilling."
—*The Washington Post Book World*

"Hypnotic . . . [Patterson] is at his finest when he gives the emotions of [his] characters, who are connected by a lifetime of love and resentment, full rein in the courtroom. These are the scenes that his fans will anticipate most eagerly, and they are as explosive and revealing as anyone could wish."
—*Publishers Weekly* (starred review)

"An absorbing read."
—*New York Daily News*

More...

DEGREE OF GUILT

"A page-turner."

—*The New York Times Book Review*

"Compulsively readable."

—*People*

"One intense courtroom clash after another. . . An intelligent and gripping thriller."

—*The Washington Post*

"Flamboyant and entertaining."

—*Boston Globe*

"Electrifying."

—*Cleveland Plain Dealer*

"One of the year's best thrillers. . . Superb characterizations and intense dialogue make this utterly compelling reading."

—*Library Journal*

"Absorbing."

—*Publishers Weekly*

ECLIPSE

"Passionate . . . exciting [and] eye-opening, page by page."

—*Washington Post*

"Compelling and credible . . . guaranteed to rouse you to thought."

—*Richmond Times-Dispatch*

"Patterson has redefined himself as a writer willing to take risks." —*USA Today*

"Absorbing and suspenseful." —*Publishers Weekly*

"Required reading." —*New York Post*

"With verve, intelligence, passion, and humanity, Patterson tells an important story—and one that may find a place with *Advise and Consent* and *Seven Days in May* on the shelf of honored political thrillers."
—*Richmond Times-Dispatch*

"Absorbing . . . timely . . . a gripping read." —*Booklist*

"Will get your blood boiling."
—*Grand Rapids Press*

"A timely, fast-paced political yarn . . . Highly recommended."
—*Library Journal* (starred review)

"A slick, new entertainment. . . Frank Capra idealism meets Karl Rove reality."
—*Entertainment Weekly*

EXILE

"Torn from the headlines . . . *Exile* delivers."
—*The New York Times Book Review*

"Artful . . . compelling." —*USA Today*

"Astonishing, hugely entertaining." —Bill Clinton

Also by
RICHARD NORTH PATTERSON

SILENT WITNESS

Richard North Patterson

St. Martin's Paperbacks

Previously published by The Random House Publishing Group.

SILENT WITNESS

Copyright © 1996 by Richard North Patterson.
Excerpt from *In the Name of Honor* copyright © 2010 by Richard North Patterson.

Cover photograph © FUSE/getty images

For information address St. Martin's Press, 175 Fifth Avenue, New York, NY 10010.

Library of Congress Catalog Card Number: 97-94177

ISBN: 978-0-312-38164-6

Printed in the United States of America

Ballantine Books edition / October 1997
St. Martin's Paperbacks edition / February 2011

St. Martin's Paperbacks are published by St. Martin's Press, 175 Fifth Avenue, New York, NY 10010.

10 9 8 7 6 5 4 3

For Linda Grey and Clare Ferraro

PROLOGUE
TONY LORD

THE PRESENT

Gina Belfante murdered her husband at one-fifteen on a Tuesday morning. By Tuesday afternoon she had lied to the police; by Thursday, the police and the medical examiner had concluded that Donald Belfante, who had been shot to death while sleeping in his own bed, had not been killed by an intruder. The police did not find the prenuptial agreement—giving Gina a pittance should the Belfantes ever divorce—until Monday. The next day, after they charged Gina Belfante with murder, the lawyer she had consulted about a divorce posted bail and referred her to Anthony Lord.

Although San Francisco was a small city, and the wealthy society in which the Belfantes moved was smaller yet, Tony Lord did not know her. But, inevitably, Gina knew Tony Lord; she had seen him at the Oscars, she told him brightly, on the night that his exquisite wife, Stacey Tarrant, won an Oscar for Best Supporting Actress. Sitting behind his desk, Tony let Gina chatter nervously, without appearing to watch her as closely as he did. Finally, he asked a few questions; it was several hours later—well after Gina Belfante had tearfully admitted putting a bullet through her husband's brain—that Tony learned she was a battered wife and had doctors' records to prove it. That, he decided, would be his defense.

It was not simple. Given that Donald Belfante had died without waking, it was hard to argue that Gina had felt in imminent danger of violence. The prenuptial agreement made matters worse yet—in terms of money, it rewarded murder and punished divorce. There were almost no witnesses: like many abusive husbands, Donald Belfante had usually beaten his wife's body, often in ways both sadistic and intimate, while leaving her face unmarred; like many abused wives, Gina Belfante had lied to everyone save her doctor. And a society woman who stood to inherit twenty-five million dollars would not strike most jurors as so helpless that she had shot her sleeping husband in fear and desperation. His only choice, Tony knew, was to put her late husband on trial.

Donald Belfante had been a large man; like many entrepreneurs who retained absolute power over his own creation—in this case, a company that made computer disk drives—he was charming, egotistical, sensitive to slight, and a bully. If Gina was to be believed, he beat her often, and at random: he had beaten her four hours before his death, and had she not killed him when he stirred awake, he would have beaten her right then. It did not take much to anger Donald Belfante, and he enjoyed his anger; Gina lived in fear of each new beating, and of that final day—vivid in her imagination—when he would go too far and kill her. The prenuptial agreement, she insisted in tears, was not an incentive: it was the symbol of his unfathomable rage at the idea that she might leave him. Should she ever try, Donald Belfante had promised his wife, he would find and kill her; her belief that this would happen was both reasonable and heartfelt.

That was what she told the jury. That was what the defense psychologist told them. And, with all the empathy that he could muster, Tony Lord tried to make them feel what, in his best imaginings, Gina Belfante must have felt.

At forty-six, Tony retained the all-American look that seemed to invite confidence—blond hair cut to a moderate length, a youngish face that was strong but not threatening, candid blue eyes—and a jury persona to match. He was never arrogant, never overused his gift for irony, never took that obvious pleasure in his own skill that might cause some juror to dislike him.

The jury trusted Tony Lord. And, a few seconds earlier, to his profound relief, it had acquitted Gina Belfante.

The courtroom burst into sound—spectators turning to each other, reporters running for their minicams or computers, jurors embracing in sheer gratitude that this was over, and, from Donald Belfante's elderly mother, an involuntary moan of anguish. Gina Belfante collapsed in Tony's arms.

Her body was fragile, her frame slight. When a reporter called out, "Mr. Lord," he did not turn.

"Thank you," Gina murmured again and again. "God, Tony, thank you."

She was absorbing, Tony knew, the gift of freedom. She looked up at him with red-rimmed eyes.

"I think I love you," she said.

"A married lawyer?" Tony smiled. "I don't know which part's worse. You promised you'd start making better choices."

"Then I will." Gina's laugh was shaky, as if the sound of it startled her. "God, what do I do next?"

Tony stopped smiling. "Just sit quietly with this, Gina. After a while, you may want help."

"I *do*." Suddenly she burst into an ingenuous smile, which crinkled the corners of her eyes as it brightened them. "I'm rich, and I can do any damn thing I want."

Tony shook his head. "You can do *almost* any damn thing you want."

Gina looked around the stark courtroom, bleak with fluorescent light, and was pensive again. "All I want right now, Tony, is to leave this place and never come back."

Over her shoulder, Tony signaled to the bodyguards.

Moments later, they stood on the steps of the Hall of Justice. There was a cool spring breeze, but the sun was bright, and the camera lenses reflected its light like chips of mica. Tony would speak for his client; as he raised his hand, and reporters thrust their microphones to hear him, Tony admitted to himself that for a defense lawyer, the next best thing to a client whose innocence seemed certain was winning a case you were supposed to lose.

The questions went quickly; in some form or another, Tony had answered them many cases ago. When CNN asked if he thought Gina Belfante had won because she could afford him, he shot back, "Does that make Mrs. Belfante too wealthy to be battered? Or is it that because other defendants may effectively be deprived of the presumption of innocence, she should be too. Then this country would truly be a prosecutors' paradise—"

"Speaking of the DA," Channel Five cut in, "we've just had a statement from Mr. Salinas. He told us the verdict is 'emotional' and that there is 'no credible evidence that Mrs. Belfante was in reasonable fear of imminent danger.'"

Drawing Gina closer, Tony gazed at the young Asian woman who asked the question. Mildly, he said, "That's not a very gracious response, is it? And more than a little unfair to the jury. But then—unlike the jury—Mr. Salinas has been nowhere near this courtroom these past three weeks. Any more than he was there when Mrs. Belfante's husband was beating her . . ."

Enough, Tony warned himself abruptly—he had to keep doing business with Victor Salinas. He waved away more questions, saying, "Mrs. Belfante needs peace now, and I hope you can give it to her."

Quickly, he kissed Gina Belfante on the cheek. "Have a good life," he said quietly. She smiled up at him, and then two bodyguards hustled her away to a waiting limousine and whatever life she would have, while Tony Lord, feeling both loss and relief from this severance of their complex bonds, reclaimed the life that was his own.

At the foot of the stairs, Tony saw his black Lincoln, but not the driver. Snaking through the last of the reporters, he opened the rear door.

Concealed by the opaque windows, Stacey sat behind the wheel. It was so unlike her that, just as she had intended, Tony laughed aloud. Closing the rear door, he slid into the front seat next to her.

Blue-green eyes looking into his, Stacey kissed him. She took her time about it and then leaned back again, pleased at his surprise.

"Do you come here often?" she asked.

For a moment, Tony was content to look at her.

She was slim and honey blond, and the clean lines and angles of her face held several contradictions—a bright smile that did not erase a certain wariness in her eyes; an ingenue's fresh skin touched by lines at the corners of her mouth, which, when she smiled, reminded Tony that his wife was now forty-one. She wore little makeup: for a singer and actress whose face was so widely known, day-to-day indifference to how others saw her was both a luxury and an act of self-definition. But what made her presence at the Hall of Justice so surprising was that she made a practice of avoiding Tony's trials—she did not like courtrooms, and this building held bad memories for her.

Twelve years before, Stacey had given a concert to raise money for her lover, Senator James Kilcannon, a Democratic candidate for President in the California primary. As Stacey stood next to him, Kilcannon was shot and killed by a Vietnam veteran, Harry Carson, who was in the throes of post-traumatic stress syndrome. Or so had claimed Anthony Lord, who became Harry Carson's lawyer.

At the outset, Stacey had despised both men equally: even now, she could not fully account for how she had come to separate Tony from his client, and then to love him. But she had.

"Congratulations," she said.

Her gaze combined affection with a quiet inquiry. "Still," Tony said, "you're wondering what I've gotten away with, aren't you?"

Stacey smiled a little, though her eyes did not: while she had learned to accept, and even understand, the reasons for Tony's sometimes ruthless devotion to protecting his clients, she could never share it. "Not you," she said at last. "But Gina Belfante did kill him, after all. I understand battered woman's syndrome, but did *this* woman 'reasonably' believe that she couldn't leave him?"

Tony shrugged. "With a state-of-mind defense, all the lawyer can do is let the jury decide. In this case, I hope, the jury saw Gina Belfante as she really is. Or perhaps they just concluded that her next husband is safe enough, and the last one no great loss." This was not, Tony saw at once, the right thing to have said. "If it's any comfort, Stacey, I've never had a client I've walked on a murder charge go out and do it again. At least that's some comfort to me."

Silent, Stacey considered him. "Well," she said finally, "I'm just glad it's over. I missed you."

Tony pulled her close, burying his face in her neck. Her hair and skin smelled fresh. "Not good enough," she murmured. "Why don't we go home."

Their home in Pacific Heights was on a private block with a view of the bay. Like the car and driver, the house afforded both security and privacy. It was good, Tony had dryly remarked, that Stacey could afford it. Stacey had suffered stalkers, and some of Tony's clients were deeply unpopular: even had their lives not imposed on them certain lessons, both had genuine reason to worry for their safety and that of Christopher, Tony's son.

This was but one of the prices they paid for a celebrity that was, in the main, unsought: the gazes of strangers in restaurants; the careless gossip of people who barely knew them but pretended they did; the too-quick friendships of others drawn to "fame" for its own sake. But at least Tony and Stacey disliked all this in common, just as they disliked the assumption that they were somehow exempted from what would be stressful for any other busy couple—doubts as to their own careers; the need to keep their marriage fresh; the knowledge that both worked too hard; lingering questions as to whether, as Stacey was unable to bear children, they should adopt; their occasional worries over some change or another in Christopher. Most of all, they shared something that many people did not and that they understood in each other very well: an awareness that happiness was fragile, good fortune a gift.

True, they did not have to worry about money and, thanks to Stacey's success, never would. But if they were happy—and more often than not they truly were—it was less because of money than because they loved Christopher and each other, yet respected one another's separateness. This perhaps helped explain why they remained so close. Stacey had never asked Tony to turn down cases out of town, he just did; just as, on her own, Stacey had become more selective about what roles she considered—the Oscar was five years behind her, and she had grown less willing to accept the total removal from reality, and from their life, that shooting on location required. Lately she had returned to writing and recording her own songs—somewhat like Bonnie Raitt and Carly Simon, she had held her popularity—but now was reading an unusually good script of the kind, she had said to Tony wryly, suited to a woman her age: no nude scenes, car chases, dinosaurs, or child actors. Some of their fleeting dinners during the Belfante trial had been spent mulling this: Tony and Christopher had given Stacey's life a center, and she was reluctant to leave it.

When they entered the living room, Christopher was there, his Nike-shod feet flopped up on the couch, the rest of him looking somewhat like a clothes pile—baggy jeans, baggy sweatshirt, baseball cap. From beneath the cap, a face remarkably like a seventeen-year-old Tony Lord's regarded them with a pleasant smile.

"Hi, guys," he said without moving. "How're things?"

He was fresh from baseball practice, Tony knew, and this air of sloth amidst affluence was his current persona: Christopher viewed his fortunate circumstances as an elaborate joke, which might end by sunset. It was, Tony knew, a reflection of his son's inherent caution; though he never spoke of this, Christopher seemed to remember the conflicts of his first six years of life—his parents' fights over money, his father's ambitions, his mother's discontent—and of the three years, after the divorce, when his mother's insistence on raising him seemed less from love than a weapon aimed at Tony, the real constant in Christopher's life. Tony adored his son: he could never understand how Marcia could cede the pleasure and responsibility of raising Christopher by moving to Los Angeles to live, in Tony's view, a shallow life with her shallow second husband. But she had, and Tony was deeply thankful.

He stood next to Stacey, hands on hips, gazing at his mock-lethargic son. "Things," he informed Christopher, "are just dandy."

"Great," his son said cheerfully. "So do you think I

can borrow the car tonight? Aaron and I are studying for finals."

Eyeing her stepson, Stacey cocked her head. "Is that all? Weren't you about to ask why your father's home so early?"

Christopher gave her a blank look, and then Tony saw the comprehension dawn. "Oh, yeah—the *trial*. Sorry." He turned to Tony. "Did you win?"

"Yup."

"Cool." Now Christopher sat up. "Did she do it?"

"Of course she *did* it," Stacey said dryly. "But your dad informs me that's not the point."

Christopher looked from one to the other, amusement in his eyes. And then he got up, took three steps across the living room, and gave his father an awkward hug. "Well, congratulations, *padre*."

Tony took the opportunity to hold his son tight. Leaning back, he said with a smile, "Thank you for this spontaneous interest in my life."

Christopher grinned. "No problem," he said, and mussed his father's hair. "Anyhow, you're doing fine without me."

With that, Christopher Lord went looking for the keys to his father's car.

Tony made a pitcher of martinis and, sitting next to Stacey, poured a drink for each of them. Together, they looked out at the sailboats dotting the bay.

"Whatever will we do," he remarked, "when Christopher heads off to college."

Stacey checked her watch. "The same thing we're going to do in, I'd say, about fifteen minutes." Smiling over at him, she added, "I gave Marcella the night off."

Tony put down his drink at once. "You first," he said. "I like watching."

Stacey preceded him up the stairs to the master bedroom.

After five or six steps, she began taking off her clothes—sweater, then bra, then blue jeans. Watching her slim body climb the stairs, Tony saw her pause as she reached the top, not turning. With a single undulation halfway between sensual and mocking, Stacey let her panties fall to the floor.

"Cool," Tony said, and then no one was joking.

"I love you," he told her. Stacey smiled at him with her eyes.

They lay in the shadows of their bedroom, Stacey beneath him, sated, both of them, the moisture of lovemaking cooling on their skin. Tony still felt his warmth inside her, her breasts against his chest. His limbs had a pleasant lassitude.

"How many times," Stacey asked, "do you think we've made love?"

Tony smiled. "Not enough, lately."

She kissed him, then said, "During a trial, it's as if you're in another place. Like acting, I guess."

"At least actors know what everyone else is going to say. And how the story ends." Tony slid from inside her and down the bed, kissing her as he went, and laid his head on the hollow of her stomach. He saw her face turn to the window, absently gazing at the pastel sky of early evening.

"I've been thinking about that script," she said.

"And?"

"I don't know."

Tony raised his head. "I can't decide for you, Stace. I don't even want to vote."

She turned to him, raising her head from the pillow. "Not even for yourself?"

He shook his head, watching her. "You like this story. You don't, usually."

"I know, and they need an answer." She frowned. "It

isn't such a great time for me to give them one. I feel like you've just gotten back."

Smiling, he said, "I'll take off work for a couple of days. Then you'll be ready."

"If you did, I might never be ready." She turned to the closed door of the bedroom. "Maybe we can just raid the refrigerator and bring it back up here—wine, cheese—I don't really care. Whatever you want."

"Smoked oysters."

Stacey made a face, and then the telephone rang.

It was their private line, reserved for close friends and emergencies. Tony felt himself tense.

"Let it go," Stacey murmured.

"I can't. Not when we've got a seventeen-year-old running around in a car."

Stacey gave him a look of understanding and then nodded toward the phone. Tony got it on the third ring.

"Mr. Lord," a man's voice said. "This is your answering service. . . ."

"Jesus Christ," Tony murmured in irritation.

"We've had two long-distance calls," the man went on. "From a Sue Robb. It's an emergency, she says. . . ." Tony sat up on the edge of the bed, instinctively turning from Stacey. "I have her on hold, Mr. Lord. Shall I say you'll call back?"

Tony hesitated. "No," he said to the operator. "Put her through."

Tony stood at the window. From the bed, Stacey watched him.

"If you go back there," she said, "the whole thing will come up again."

He was quiet for a moment, feeling the truth of this. "I know."

"If I understand you at all, Tony, you've tried your entire adult life to put that time behind you. But you still have the nightmares, even now. And sometimes when I look at you, it's like you're *there*, not here."

Tony did not answer. "Sam and Sue were my closest friends," he said at last. "Part of me feels guilty about how I left it."

"As I recall the story, one of them was more than a friend." Stacey made her voice softer. "Leaving was a matter of survival, Tony. Sometimes I don't know how you got through it all."

Turning, Tony walked to the bed. "What's happening now could ruin them both. I needed a lawyer then, and they need one now."

Stacey shook her head in dismay. "This is eerie. It's too much like before. . . ."

"And that wasn't fair to me. This may not be fair to him. I know too damned well what that town can be like." He paused, fighting his own dismay. "I have to go, lover. At least for a couple of days. Even if there's no part of me that wants to."

Stacey looked down at the bed and slowly nodded.

He did not want it like this. "I can never explain. . . ."

She rose from the bed, putting her arms around his neck. "You never have to, Tony. The script can wait for a few days." Stacey paused a moment. "If it comes to that, I'll watch after Christopher. Real life has its demands, I know. And the one you lived before me *always* has."

On the flight that would take him to Lake City, Ohio, the home of his youth, for the first time in twenty-eight years, Tony Lord found himself remembering, like pieces of film, each moment of the night that Alison Taylor died.

The images were indelible—not just of Alison, or of Sam and Sue, whose crisis this was now, but of the months that had followed Alison's death. He owed this heightened clarity, Tony was certain, to what he had found in the grass of the Taylors' rear yard, and all that he had felt since that instant had bisected his life like a fault line. What was much harder to retrieve was who he had been in the hours before, still innocent of the knowledge that tragedy, like passion, could be summoned at random.

They were Christopher's age, seventeen.

PART ONE
ALISON TAYLOR

NOVEMBER 1967–AUGUST 1968

ONE

Tony Lord stood in a bowl of light.

The night air was crisp and cold: it smelled faintly of burning leaves and Bermuda grass, popcorn oil wafting from the bleachers. Beneath the klieg lights, the football field was a fluorescent yellow green, surrounded by darkness. The cheers and the stomping of feet in the wooden stands carried the energies of a town of thirteen thousand, a place unto itself, thirty miles from the rust-belt city of Steelton, where fathers might work but their families seldom went.

Half the town was here—parents and grandparents and other adults and most of the kids in high school, as well as their younger brothers and sisters, in search of an excuse for milling and talking and finding each other. But for the rest, bundled in coats and wool caps and leather gloves, the Erie Conference Championship was about school pride and town history and bragging rights at Rotary meetings and on business calls and in Elks Club smokers. Their raucous screams were etched with anxiety: Lake City was losing ten to seven, and Riverwood had the ball on the fifty-yard line, with a minute forty left. It was third and five to go; the Lakers' last chance was to stop this play.

Riverwood broke the huddle, seven kids in red jerseys and white pants coming toward the line, their shadows moving with them, the quarterback and fullback and two halfbacks settling in behind them. Their quarterback, Jack Parham, set his hands between the center's legs as the seven bodies bent over the chalk that marked midfield. Opposing them were four bulky players in Lake City blue—the defensive line—with the linebackers behind them and then, protecting against the pass or the ball carrier who might break away from the pack, two defensive halfbacks and two safeties. One of the halfbacks was Tony Lord; the other was Sam Robb, his best friend.

Jack Parham barked his signals. At the corner of his eye, Tony saw Sam edging forward, catlike.

The center snapped the ball.

Parham stuffed it into his fullback's stomach. As the fullback hit the line, Tony saw Parham pull the ball back and tuck it under his own right arm—a quarterback sweep, meant to gain the last five yards and run precious seconds off the game clock.

Sam was already headed toward Parham as Tony called out, "Sweep . . ."

Parham ran alone along the right side of his line. But Sam was sprinting all out; as Parham turned down the field, he spotted Sam coming for him from ten yards away.

Trailing Sam, Tony could see Parham hesitate, wondering whether to run out of bounds. But that would stop the time clock; in the moment of indecision, Parham slowed and stood up.

Tony knew Sam Robb far too well not to know that this was a mistake.

Three feet from Parham, Sam leaped. His body was a taut line, which ended in his helmet crashing beneath Parham's face mask.

There was a sickening crack; Parham's head snapped

back, and the ball flew from his hands. The crowd screamed as it flopped spinning onto the grass, five feet in front of Tony.

Tony dived. As his face hit the grass, Tony swept the ball in both arms and cradled it beneath his chest, bracing himself as three red-clad bodies hurtled into him, jarring his spine and rib cage and clawing at his arms and hands to steal the ball. Tony could smell their sweat.

The whistle blew.

Slowly, Tony stood amidst the sound of near hysteria, feeling the raw scratches on his arms, handing the ball to the referee with a calm he did not feel but felt obliged to feign. But Sam stood facing the Lake City stands, arms raised in the air, helmet in one hand so that his straight blond hair shone in the klieg lights. He did not seem to know that Jack Parham had not moved.

The crowd appeared to stand for Sam as one, their noise rising into the darkness. Only when Parham remained still, and the Riverwood coach and trainer ran toward him, did the cries die down.

Tony looked at neither the stands nor Parham but at the clock. Reading a minute nineteen, he wondered how to channel his fullback's aggression, what plays could win this game, how to keep Sam under control.

On offense, Tony was the quarterback. But the next minute, the last of their careers, belonged to them both.

They had been waiting for this moment since ninth grade, two weeks after Tony came to the public high from Holy Name—the parochial school where his Polish Catholic parents had sent him as long as they could—and the coaches had given Tony the job that Sam Robb thought was his.

At fourteen, Sam was already tall and fast, with a strong arm and an assertive manner that made most kids defer to him, a swift temper which made some a little fearful. It was clear that he expected no competition, least of all from this Catholic interloper.

For several days they drilled beside each other, barely speaking. Tony saw that Sam was the better athlete; what Tony had was quick reflexes and something he could not define but which the coach seemed to like. Among the team there was palpable tension; in the folkways of a small town with schoolboy sports at its center, everyone knew that Coach Ellis was picking not just the ninth-grade quarterback but the one who would be groomed to quarterback Lake City High.

At the last practice, George Jackson, who coached the varsity, watched from the sidelines.

Sam drove the team harder, favoring plays that showed his arm and running skills. At the end of the practice, Coach Ellis took Sam aside.

Tony was the quarterback.

In the locker room, he accepted the congratulations of some teammates but not Sam, who seemed to have vanished, and then Tony went to the stands and sat alone, puzzling over his good fortune. He heard heavy footsteps on the wooden planks; looking up, he saw Sam Robb, climbing toward him with the arrogant carriage that was all his own.

Silent, Sam sat next to him. Tony braced himself for the suggestion that he get out of Sam's way.

"These coaches don't know shit," Sam said at last. "You're still throwing off your back foot."

Tony turned to him. "How's that?"

Sam gave him a narrow look. "I've got a big back-yard. I'll show you."

After a moment, Tony nodded. "Okay."

Quiet, they walked the few blocks to Sam's house, carrying their books and binders.

At first hand, Tony knew little about Sam's life. But in Lake City it was impossible to know nothing at all: though the Robbs belonged to the country club, where Tony's parents were never asked, Sam's father's hardware store was widely believed to be failing. So Tony was not surprised that Sam's white frame house, set in a spacious, oak-lined yard, was large but a little dingy. Nor was he surprised that the Robbs' living room mantel featured several trophies earned by Sam's brother, Joe, Lake City High's Athlete of the Year in 1962, a year before he went to Vietnam and died there. Tony knew that Sam's tall but somewhat paunchy father, an athlete gone to seed, was past president of the Lake City Athletic Booster Club. What startled Tony was Sam's mother.

Dottie Robb was a blonde whose smooth face, snub nose, and china-blue eyes were very like Sam's, though the faint ravages of her own lost youth showed in the slight sag of her chin and upper arms. She lay on the couch in a bright, incongruous sundress, and her gaze seemed blurred. Ignoring Tony, she said to Sam, "You promised me you'd mow the lawn today."

Her tone was funny, slurred and demanding and a little pouty. Sam's body went stiff. "We were going out back, to practice."

Dottie Robb raised her eyebrows. "Oh," she answered in a somewhat derisive tone. "Football."

Shifting from foot to foot, Tony noted the half-empty tumbler of what looked like whiskey on an end table near the couch. He stepped forward. "I'm Tony Lord." Some cautionary instinct kept him from adding, "ma'am."

She gave him a slow look, up and down. Then she rose from the couch quite smoothly and extended a graceful hand. Her skin was cool and dry, her blue eyes direct and somewhat mocking. "I'm Dottie. Sam's mother."

Dottie Robb inspected him for another instant and then went to Sam, giving him a kiss on the cheek, which he neither fled nor accepted. As she hugged her son, his eyes were expressionless.

Sam was quiet as he led Tony to the backyard.

The grass was thick, the flower beds untended. Hanging

from the branch of a buckeye tree was an old truck tire on a rope.

Without preface, Sam said, "Watch my feet," and backed twenty feet from the tire. Sam danced on the balls of his feet; when he threw, Tony saw that his weight was on the front foot. The ball sailed through the tire.

"Your arm's not that bad," Sam said. "But like Joe said—my brother—if you don't have your weight right, you short-arm it. No zip, no distance."

Knowing that the words were those not of a fourteen-year-old but of his now dead older brother, Tony was struck by how much stake Sam's family must have placed in his success. For the first time, Tony sensed Sam's generosity; losing the quarterback spot would cost much more in this family than in Tony's.

"Your turn," Sam told him.

Tony began throwing, Sam standing by him with hands on hips, offering terse pointers. Tony went seven for ten.

At the end, Sam nodded without comment, tossing the ball underhand to Tony. "Sideline," he said, ran out a few feet, then sped toward a bed of roses along the left side of the yard.

Tony threw.

The ball sailed lazily over Sam's head. Sam picked up speed, trying to catch it, and then suddenly broke stride, leaping over the rosebushes as the ball thudded to the ground beyond him.

Behind them, a screen door squeaked open. Suddenly shrill, Dottie Robb's voice called out, "Watch the roses—those are my babies."

They turned. She faced them, leaning against the frame with both hands. Standing near the rose bed, Sam faced her, reddening in silent acknowledgment. Only Tony could hear him mumble, "Fuck you," under his breath.

Satisfied, Dottie Robb closed the door. Tony wondered how long she had been watching. Or drinking.

"Do it again," Sam said. "A little less arc on the ball, okay? And don't ruin her stupid roses."

With a mixture of solidarity and pride, Tony answered, "I'm at my best in the clutch." The next four passes were close to perfect.

"All right," Sam said abruptly. "We need a play. Someday in high school, some big game will be on the line and it'll be up to me and you." Sam paused, eyes on Tony, smiling for the first time. "I'm going to be the greatest pass-catching end in the history of Lake City High School. You'll need one."

Tony studied him to see if he was joking. Sam stopped smiling. "The other guys like you," he said bluntly. "They'll play for you. But you're going to need me."

Tony felt something poignant in Sam's admission, and in his desire to cover it with braggadocio. "Run a sideline pattern," Tony said at length. "Like we've been doing. Only hip fake the guy covering you and cut back over the middle, deep."

Sam flipped the ball back to Tony.

Tony paused, trying to visualize what he wanted. The day—the soft light of late afternoon, the deepening green of the grass and trees—faded around him. What was vivid was the moment he wanted to create.

He sensed Sam waiting patiently, as if he understood. "Go," Tony said.

Sam ran left toward the roses. Tony skittered back, light on his feet now, avoiding an imaginary tackier by running to his right.

Abruptly, Sam broke for the middle of the yard. Tony stopped at once, lofting the ball over Sam's head and to his right. Sam followed its flight, running as hard as he could as the ball slowly fell. With a last burst, Sam grasped the football in his fingertips.

He glided to a stop and turned, holding the ball aloft. For a moment, it seemed to Tony that Sam was no longer there but hearing an imagined crowd, which called his name. His eyes were half shut.

They opened abruptly. "Touchdown," Sam called out to Tony. "That's the play."

Their moment had come.

That Alison watched from the stands, or Tony's parents, meant nothing to him; Jack Parham's injury meant only the advantage of a time-out. As he ran to the sidelines, passing the cheerleaders, Tony was barely aware of Sue Cash's wave of encouragement, her curly brown hair and bright smile, the faint smell of her perfume as the cheer she led sang out. *We are the Lakers, the mighty, mighty Lakers . . .*

On the sidelines, Coach Jackson was pacing and staring at the clock, plainly dying for a cigarette. At forty-five, he had already suffered a heart attack, and only smoking kept the pounds off his thick-chested body. His narrow snake eyes stared at Tony from a red, sclerotic face.

"What do you want to run?" he demanded.

Tony told him.

Jackson's eyes widened, the look he used to intimidate. "Sam's been covered all night."

Tony shrugged. "So they won't expect it."

Something like amusement crossed Jackson's face, a bone-deep liking for the boy in front of him, his own pride in judging character. These were the moments, Tony realized, that Coach Jackson lived for.

"Just win the goddamned game," Jackson said.

As Tony led the offense onto the field, a Riverwood player and a trainer were helping Jack Parham to the sidelines. Trotting next to Tony, Sam said, "That felt good—a fumble and a time-out."

There was a primal joy in Sam's voice, adrenaline pumping. As the offense huddled, Tony paused to look at each of them—the offensive linemen; Sam; the muscular fullback, Johnny D'Abruzzi, Tony's friend from Holy Name; Ernie Nixon, the halfback, the only black in high school. Their faces were taut, anxious. Tony kept his tone matter-of-fact.

"We're gonna take this one play at a time. No fumbles, no penalties. No losing our head or trying to be heroes. We just do what we need to do, and the game belongs to us. I'll worry about the clock."

The team seemed to settle down. Tony called the play and they broke the huddle, taking their positions with an air of confidence. Standing behind them, Tony looked at the defense. The clock still read one-nineteen; it would not start until the center snapped the ball.

Tony stepped behind the center, aware of the screaming crowd only as a distant noise, feeling Johnny D'Abruzzi in back of him, Ernie Nixon to his right. He began barking signals.

The ball slipped into his hands. With the first pop of shoulder pads, the linemen's grunts of pain and anger and aggression, Tony spun and handed the ball to Ernie Nixon.

Ernie hit the line slanting to the left, then burst through a hole for five more yards until a Riverwood linebacker stuck his helmet in Ernie's chest and drove him to the ground.

The next play, a run by Johnny D'Abruzzi, gained almost nothing.

"Time," Tony shouted at the referee. Only then did he look at the clock.

Forty-four seconds. He had just used their last time-out.

The team huddled around Tony, Johnny D'Abruzzi screaming, "Give me the ball again. . . ." Stepping between them, Sam clutched Tony's jersey, his face contorted with panic and frustration. "I'm open. You've gotta start throwing—we're running out of time."

Tony gazed at Sam's hands, stifling his own anger. "There's plenty of time," he said. His tone said something else: *This isn't our moment.*

They stared at each other, and then Sam dropped his hands. Tony turned to the others as if nothing had happened. His heart pounded.

"All right." He looked into Johnny D'Abruzzi's fierce eyes and made his judgment. "We're running Johnny again, this time through the left side. Then I'll run an option."

He saw Sam's astonishment, Ernie Nixon's disappointment; ignoring them both, he called the numbers for the next two plays. But when the huddle broke, he grasped Ernie's sleeve. "I'm counting on you to cut down the left side linebacker."

"I'll do it."

Turning, Tony ambled behind the center with deceptive casualness. Then he suddenly barked, "Hut three," and the ball was in his hand, then in Johnny D'Abruzzi's arms as he ran to the left behind Ernie Nixon. Ernie shot through the liner; with a fierceness that was almost beautiful, he coiled his body and slammed shoulder-first into Riverwood's right linebacker, knocking him backward as Johnny ran past and then tripped, suddenly and completely, over the legs of the falling player.

"Shit," Tony said under his breath. The clock read thirty-one, thirty, twenty-nine. Still twenty yards to go . . .

The blue bodies scurried up from the turf to re-form along the line of scrimmage. Twenty-two seconds . . .

The center snapped the ball to Tony.

He ran along the line, with Ernie Nixon trailing him. His option was to run himself or flip the ball to Ernie.

As the crowd began screaming, a wave of blockers formed in front of Tony.

Ernie was behind him to the outside, in good position for a pitchout. But Tony could see the play opening up for him; ten yards down the sideline and then out of bounds, stopping the clock again. The screams rose higher as he crossed the line of scrimmage.

From nowhere a red jersey appeared at the corner of Tony's vision—Rex Stallworth, their quickest linebacker. Tony heard the crunch of Stallworth's helmet into the side of his face before the shock shivered his body and dropped him into darkness.

The next sensation that came to him was the smell of dirt and grass. Tony rose to his knees, time lost to him.

"Tony!" Sam cried out.

By instinct, Tony looked up at the clock.

Sixteen seconds, fifteen, fourteen. Tony staggered to his feet and loped to the center of the field. "Spike," he shouted. "On one."

Raggedly, the line took its position. *"Ten,"* the Riverwood fans started chanting. *"Nine . . ."*

"One," Tony screamed. The ball was only a second in his hands before he spiked it to the ground. An incomplete pass, stopping the clock.

Five seconds left.

Tony backed from the line of scrimmage, taking deep breaths. He was nauseous, dizzy. His head rang.

Sam was the first one to reach him. "You okay?"

"Yeah."

"Gotta pass to me, Tony. *Please.*"

The team circled him again. Tony shook his head to clear it, then said to no one in particular, "Screwed that play up, didn't I? Sonofabitch rang my bell for Parham."

Tony felt their quiet relief. Only Sam seemed too tight.

"Okay," Tony said. "We've got five seconds, twenty yards, no time-outs. Time to put this game away." He paused, looking at everyone but Sam. "Thirty-five reverse pass."

The huddle broke. Under his breath, Tony said to Sam, "It's ours now, pal."

Sam nodded, ready. For the last time, they walked to the line with their team.

Tony paused, taking it all in—the crowd, the light and darkness, the blue line of teammates, the red formation across from them shouting jeers and insults. And then he shut out everything but what he meant to do.

Time slowed for him. The cadence of his own voice seemed to come from somewhere else. But there was no other place that Tony wished to be.

"Hut two . . ."

The ball popped into his hand.

Tony slid the ball into Ernie Nixon's stomach. Bent forward, Ernie plowed into the line in feigned determination as Tony pulled back the ball, spun, and slapped it into Johnny D'Abruzzi's chest.

But only for an instant.

Johnny stood upright, crashing shoulder-first into a blitzing linebacker who was headed straight for Tony. And then Tony was alone, sprinting with the ball along the right side of the line.

In front of him, he saw bodies scrambling—two linebackers running parallel to block his path, believing he would run for the end zone, his own blockers forming in front of him.

Without seeming to look, Tony saw Sam break to the left sideline. Sam looked irrelevant, a decoy, so far was he from the sweep of the play.

Abruptly, Sam broke back across the center of the field, three feet ahead of the back who covered him.

Perfect, Tony thought.

All at once he stopped, cocking the ball to throw. The crowd cried out in warning.

From Tony's blind side Stallworth charged for him, head down.

Tony jerked back the ball, scrambling forward. As

Stallworth swept by, his outstretched arm grasped Tony's ankle.

Tony stumbled, losing his balance. Then he caught his fall, left hand digging into the grass.

Ahead of him, two more linemen charged forward. Tony had nowhere to go. He could not see Sam; if he tried to pass, he would be defenseless against the on-rushing tacklers.

Tony stood straight, cocked his arm, and threw, with his weight on his front foot, toward where he thought Sam's speed would take him. The ball left his hand an instant before the first defender hit Tony's unprotected ribs.

Tony felt his insides shift; the pain went through him as he hit the ground. By instinct he rolled on his side, sat up.

The ball arched above the players who turned to watch it, helpless. Its flight seemed to slow, a sphere sailing through light and shadow toward the rear of the end zone, accompanied by shrieks of hope and uncertainty.

I've overthrown it, Tony thought, and then he saw Sam Robb.

Seemingly without a chance, Sam sprinted for the ball as it fell to earth. Three feet from the ball, two feet from the back of the end zone, Sam timed his leap.

It took him parallel to the ground, feet leaving the grass as he stretched, arms extended, and clasped the ball in his fingertips. He fell beyond the end zone, feet trailing in a last effort to touch in-bounds. Tony could not see whether he had done so; he saw only, as Sam rose to his feet and turned to the referee, that the ball was in his hands.

Tony stood, pain forgotten as he gazed at the referee, a silent prayer forming in his head.

Slowly, the referee raised his hands aloft.

A lump blocked Tony's throat.

Touchdown. Mother of God, a touchdown. He began to run toward Sam.

Sam stood in the end zone, arms aloft, clutching the ball in his hand. Above him, the scoreboard registered six more points for Lake City. Sam's helmet was off; beneath the klieg lights, Tony could see the tears on his face.

Sam stood frozen. And then, suddenly, he saw Tony.

He turned, flipping away the ball, and ran toward him.

They met on the goal line. For an instant, they stopped there, then they threw their arms around each other.

Wordless, Sam held Tony close. In that moment there was no one Tony Lord loved as much as he loved Sam Robb.

"Touchdown," Tony said in a thick voice. "That's the play."

TWO

Their teammates pressed against them at the goal line, whooping and hugging and pounding each other. Nothing coherent was said: it was a moment they could share only with each other, and needed no words. At some unspoken signal, they broke away and headed through the exit gate toward the darkened tan brick building that had always looked to Tony more like a factory than a high school, the cheering fans who had poured from the stands forming two lines around them from the gate to the doorway.

Inside the door, Tony stopped in the narrow corridor as the line of teammates slowed to pass him, shaking their hands as he waited for Coach Jackson. As was his custom, the coach held himself aloof, trailing behind the team as if nothing much had happened. He would save his emotions for his players.

As he reached the door, Jackson found Tony waiting.

The coach gave him a look of mock annoyance, a man diverted from his business. "What you want, Lord?"

"Give him the game ball, okay?"

Jackson put one hand on Tony's shoulder, not smiling. "I'll do what I goddam want," he said, and headed for the locker room.

Why, Tony wondered, did the coach deny Sam the recognition he craved, even a thing so small. Sam played hard for Jackson and, beneath his bravado, feared the coach as much as most kids did. There was something skewed here: once more, Tony thought of the rumor that he devoutly wished Sam would never hear—that Coach Jackson was fucking Sam's mother. Tony hoped the coach's heart held up.

Turning, he went to the locker room.

The team sat on wooden benches in front of battered gray lockers, heads bowed, newly quiet as Coach Jackson—who Tony was confident had not seen the inside of a church for years—spoke a terse prayer.

"Thank you, Lord," he finished. Then his head snapped up abruptly, and he stepped atop a bench, his communion with the Almighty done.

"All right," Jackson said brusquely. "I won't tell you all that bullshit—that you're the greatest team I ever coached, that I'll think of you on my deathbed. 'Cause I hope to live long enough to forget about you all.

"The only thing that matters is what *you* take with you when you leave here.

"They don't keep score out there. This championship may be the last thing you ever win. But the most important job you did tonight was not to win but to *achieve*.

"You did your best. You worked with the other guy.

You respected yourself. Take that with you, and things just may turn out right."

The sweaty faces looked up as one to Jackson. In spite of himself, Tony was moved: Jackson had helped him learn that he could keep his head and make things turn out right. This was better than the game ball, because Tony could take it with him.

Jackson snatched the ball from an assistant and held it out in front of him.

Tony glanced at Sam. His friend sat gazing up at Jackson with a hope and need so naked that Tony looked away.

"Still," Jackson said, "there's this ball. There are a lot of guys that I could give this to. But some of you might fumble."

Some laughter now. But Tony saw that Sam did not laugh at all. His eyes were stuck on Jackson.

Jackson turned to Tony. "So I'm giving this to Tony Lord. I don't need to tell you why—you've played with him all season."

As Tony stepped forward, the team began clapping and cheering; when Johnny D'Abruzzi stood, and then Ernie Nixon, they all did. Tony did not look at Sam.

What to say. Quickly, Tony rejected some slop about sharing the game ball with Sam—this would slight the rest of them and, he decided, condescend to Sam.

Tony stood on the bench next to Jackson, looking out at them as he gathered his thoughts, and then began in solemn tones.

"I owe this ball to every one of you guys. So I want to share it with you." Pausing, Tony grinned. "Visiting hours are nine to five."

The team laughed in surprise.

Encouraged, Tony went on. "If you think about it, though, if it weren't for Sam Robb's catch, Jack Parham would be holding this game ball in some hospital, trying to figure out if it's a football or a world globe. So in honor of Jack Parham, Sam gets to sleep with the ball on weekends."

Amidst rising laughter, the young faces turned to Sam. *"All right, Sam,"* someone called. Sam grinned with pleasure and surprise. Tony waited until the laughter died, and tossed the ball underhand to Sam.

"Nice catch," he said. "Again."

The team turned back to Tony. His tone was quiet now.

"You guys are the best. Coach Jackson may forget you—he's got a lot on his mind. But I never will."

He stepped down from the bench before they could applaud, embracing the players who stood nearest him. But when he got to Sam, he said only, "Where are our girlfriends hiding?"

Half smiling, Sam spun the football on the end of one finger like a world globe, watching it with great concentration. "The parking lot," he answered, and flipped the ball back to Tony.

A half hour later, dressed in oxford shirts and khakis, they left the building together.

Outside, a few students and fans and a couple of local reporters still waited, milling about in the cold night air. Raggedly they applauded. Tony felt both pleasure and puzzlement: it was like celebrity, but only for a season, and it happened too young and passed too quickly to seem quite real. Already the heroes of two years ago were half ignored when they visited the team; often Tony sensed that they left without whatever they had come for, not knowing that they had only borrowed it in the first place.

But this was *their* season, his and Sam's: as the two reporters came forward, one young and one middle-aged, pads in hand, a certain pride entered Sam's face, which, to Tony, seemed close to innocence.

"Move closer, Tony," the young reporter called out, and snapped a picture of the two of them. "You know," he said, "you guys look like brothers."

They didn't, Tony knew: Sam's hair was close to white, Tony's caramel blond; Sam's smooth face was deceptively young, Tony's angular, his thin nose somewhat ridged; Sam was stronger and, at six feet, a good inch taller than Tony. But this season, Tony knew, people would see them as they wished.

The older man stepped forward, voice jocular. "So which one of you boys gets Athlete of the Year?"

Tony felt his goodwill vanish. "Who knows?" he said carelessly. "There are a lot of guys at this school who can play, and it's not even basketball season."

Sam stepped forward. "It's like that play tonight. We both made it up, back in ninth grade." He paused, smiling at Tony. "When I figured out this guy could actually get the ball to me. See, we've always worked together, so we don't care who gets the credit."

Sam was lying, Tony knew; he cared more deeply than he could say. But so did Tony. To lie was all they could do; to speak the truth felt dangerous.

"Thanks," said Tony. "We've got people waiting for us."

"Dates?" The younger reporter looked curious. "Who you guys going out with?"

Only in Lake City, Tony thought. He looked to Sam. "Sue Cash," Sam said, and shrugged. "Like always."

"How about you, Tony?"

Tony hesitated. "Alison Taylor," he answered.

The man nodded, almost solemnly. Alison Taylor, his look seemed to say. It was only fitting.

"Let's go," Tony murmured.

THREE

Sue and Alison waited beneath a tree at the far corner of the empty parking lot, talking quietly, Sue in her cheerleader's uniform and Sam's letter jacket, and Alison wearing a navy-blue coat, Villager sweater, and pleated skirt. When she saw Sam and Tony, Sue ran up to Sam. Alison hung back a little; as if to fill the void, Sue turned to Tony, giving him a tight squeeze.

"You guys were both so great, Tony. At the end I thought I'd die."

Looking down at her, Tony smiled. It was hard to imagine Sue Cash dying of anything; not with those lively big brown eyes, the compact body so full of energy, the expressive face that reminded Tony of the cute kid sister in a Hollywood musical—snub nose, strong clean chin, dimples when she smiled, the tight nimbus of brown curls. But unlike most girls Tony knew, Sue could almost be imagined as some lucky family's wife and mother: beneath her extroversion was something womanly and stable, the sense that Sue would always take care of whatever needed tending—at the moment, Tony himself.

"Sue," Tony told her, "you definitely beat a game ball."

They grinned at each other. Then Sue turned back to Sam, pressing her face against his chest as he held her close again, a couple.

Alison came forward, more tentative than the self-possessed girl she usually appeared. She gave him a fleeting kiss and smiled for the first time. "My hero," she said. "Is this where you drag me from the campfire?"

Her humor sounded a bit shaky—again, unlike Alison. Tonight she had a tensile quality; Tony was aware of Sue and Sam watching them.

"Maybe for a Coke," he answered.

With a hesitant smile, she gave a half shake of the head, too small for the others to see. Tony felt a tightness in his chest.

She was different from any girl he had known: smart and a little guarded, with an air of self-possession that implied that she accepted who she was or, perhaps, who her family was. That she was not like this tonight told Tony what he wished to know.

Softly, he said, "We'd better get going." Taking her hand, he turned to Sam and Sue.

"Come on with us," Sam said. "At least for a while. I've got some whiskey in the car—it'll warm you up."

Tony felt Alison's hand touch his elbow. "No, thanks. I think we need a little time."

Sam glanced at Alison and then gave Tony a crooked, somewhat sour smile. Guess you don't need whiskey, the expression said. Once more, Tony sensed Alison's discomfort.

"Just don't let the cops catch you," Tony said to Sam.

Sam laughed. "In this town, tonight? Who's going to throw either one of us in jail? Like Alison says, we're heroes, man. We can do anything we want."

For a night, Tony thought. There was something worrisome in Sam's elation; he had too far to fall.

"See you Monday," Alison said to Sue. She said nothing to Sam.

Turning, Tony and Alison walked to Tony's car. It was a '61 Ford Fairlane; Tony had bought it with his earnings from two summer jobs, and he kept it waxed and polished. But the most important thing was that the radio worked.

Inside the car, Alison turned to him.

She even *looked* different—like money, Tony sometimes thought, or a delicate sliver of steel. Her raven-black hair fell straight on both sides of her face, accenting the hollows of her cheeks, the cleft chin, the china complexion. Whereas Sue was vibrant, Alison was watchful and had a certain mettle. Sometimes when she smiled, it was with an air of secret reflection, but her black eyes had a quiet directness, and she seldom looked away. She appeared much like what she was: the class president, a girl other kids were more certain they admired than that they knew. The gift she had given Tony was to let him in.

Now he did not wish to rush her. "I guess we've still got things to work out."

She gave him a pensive look. But her voice had a quiet resolve. "No," she answered. "I know what I want now."

Silent, Tony kissed her. They would end what they had started, he thought, on the summer night that had torn them both apart.

The night had been warm, even for Lake City in the summer; wearing T-shirts and shorts, the four of them had cut through Alison's backyard, down the steps from the cliff to the Taylors' mooring, and then over to the public beach of the park that, like the old house that was now the library, had belonged to Alison's family before they gave it to the city, and years later still bore their name.

The beach was sandy, soft enough for sitting on or making out. Lake Erie was befouled; a somewhat fetid smell hung over the water, the sources of which did not bear close thought. But they were seventeen, and this was all the beach they had.

They built a campfire with driftwood and kerosene, cooked hot dogs. Sam had brought the beer; good-naturedly, he popped the tops off the cool brown bottles of Carling he had bought with fake ID and handed them each a beer. Once more, it struck Tony that they were a somewhat curious foursome: whereas Alison plainly liked Sue, she seemed to look at Sam with wariness, as if observing a natural phenomenon whose course she could not quite predict. Still, she was willing to admit that Sam brought to most occasions a sense of fun and a certain magnetism; Tony knew that Alison felt it too, even if Sam sometimes called her the "Ice Queen."

They sat back, drinking beer, in no hurry. The moon was large and full, its light refracting on the water that lapped against the shore. Beneath the quiet, Tony noticed Sam studying Alison, then him.

Tony could guess why. Though it was never spoken among the four of them, everyone knew that Sam and Sue had been doing it for months. With Tony, Sam was quite open about this, and expected reciprocity. But Tony had nothing to offer. Just the week before, he had said as much yet again.

Sam's eyes widened. "After six months?" he said with exaggerated amazement. "Come on, Tony, don't be such a fucking gentleman. Not with *me*."

"I'm not being a gentleman. I guess Alison figures she has some say in who gets to be the first."

Sam's eyes glinted with amusement. "She never has?"

Tony shook his head. "And if that ever changes, don't expect to hear it from me. . . ."

Now, Sam looked at Alison and said, "You guys want to go swimming?"

Alison gave him that direct gaze that seemed to be her property. "In what?"

Sam laughed. "It's dark out," he said carelessly.

Alison's slight smile did not change her eyes. "Not dark enough."

He looked at her a moment, then shrugged and turned to Sue. "Let's get in, okay?"

Sue did not answer. In the ethos of Lake City High, you weren't a slut if you slept with your boyfriend; or even more than one boyfriend, as long as the time between relationships was long enough to qualify both as love. What seemed to bother Sue was Alison—Sue turned to her, as if unwilling to compromise a comrade. With a certain patience, Sam waited: it struck Tony that

Sam treated Sue with more respect than he did anyone but Tony himself.

"We'll be back in a while," Sue said to Alison. Glancing at Tony, Sam took Sue's hand.

Silent, Tony and Alison watched Sam and Sue walk away, their shadows receding until they vanished in the darkness.

Gently, Tony kissed her. "Want to go in?" Tony asked. "They'll be tied up for an hour."

Face close to his, Alison regarded him with both hesitance and desire; although they had touched each other, sometimes to the point of torment, she had never been undressed with him. Then she stood and backed into the shadows, still watching him.

Tony waited, afraid to move. In the darkness, Alison was only a silhouette, arms raised above her head. Tony could sense, rather than see, her nakedness.

Her slender body appeared in the moonlight, skittering into the water. Tony thought of his confessor, Father Quinn; Alison was the "near occasion of sin," Tony knew, and the sin of making love with her would be a mortal one. He could feel his heart beat.

Stripping, Tony followed.

He saw Alison waist deep in water, her back to him, and then she seemed to kneel, turning to face him with only her head above the inky blackness. She had given him no permission, Tony knew; this was her way of covering herself.

He stopped a few feet from her, the water coming to his waist. Tony could imagine the hidden outline of her body, near enough to touch. He felt his own body stirring.

He moved toward her. She froze, stepped back once, stopped again. Her eyes were very still.

Reaching out, Tony lifted her by the waist and pulled her close to him, filled with months of wanting her.

Their mouths met, and then their bodies. Tony could

feel her small breasts against his chest, her hips thrust forward with her own sudden desire. Then she pulled her head back, twisting away.

"I can't." Her voice was strained. "This can't happen now."

Caught in his desperate need, Tony could not release her. "It can. . . ."

Her eyes shut; it was as though if she could not see him she would not want him anymore. Suddenly Tony felt hollow. He had come too close; this time the denial of passion seemed to have left a hole in him, as if they suddenly had nothing. In a low voice, he said, "Your parents have started in on you again."

Alison's eyes opened. Now she seemed incapable of looking away. "*Part* of it is my parents. . . ."

"Is it still because I'm Catholic?" In his anger and frustration, Tony felt his temper snap. "You can't be too careful, can you? Let 'them' in the club, and the next thing you know, your daughter will start having red-haired children with rosaries around their necks and a line straight to the Pope. . . ."

Abruptly, Tony felt a wall come down between them; on the other side, closed to him, was the world of shopping trips to New York City, vacations in Paris, and weekends with the sons and daughters of the Taylors' East Coast friends. All while Tony, whose grandfather Lord's Polish surname was once two syllables longer, tugged his forelock on the Taylors' porch.

Alison's eyes had never left him. "I don't defend them about that—"

"Defend them? Have you ever thought about *telling* them that I'm not the local equivalent of a car thief?"

"They *know* you're not, and it's not all about being Catholic. My parents are afraid we'll just keep right on going together. They think it's too young and too soon." She paused, voice quieter yet. "They're asking that we see each other one night a weekend and leave the other free."

Tony felt a stab of jealousy and, beneath that, a hurt that went much deeper. "And go out with other people, you mean? Just to keep your parents happy? I can't believe that's what you want."

For the first time, Alison looked down. "I said part was my parents. Not all." She drew a breath, sliding down into the water. "I'm *afraid*, all right? I'm afraid of how it will be for me and how I'll feel later. That somehow it will change things." She looked up at him again, tears in her eyes. "Sometimes I want you so much I can hardly stand it. But it's like putting you in charge of me, giving you a part of me. Don't you understand how confusing that feels?"

Tony shook his head. "*My* feelings aren't confused at all."

Now Alison's eyes took him in. Softly, she answered, "That's the last part, Tony. You weren't confused with Mary Jane, either. But how do you feel now?"

This time it was Tony who looked away. "What if it happened tonight?" she asked. "Like most of me wanted it to. Will you feel as good as you always tell me you would? Or will you end up feeling awful about what we've done, and have to confess me like I'm some kind of sin? Do you ever wonder how that would make *me* feel?"

She had never said this with such emotion. All at once, Tony lost the heart to argue.

Seeing this, Alison gently kissed his face. For an instant, their bodies touched; for this brief moment, Tony felt the electricity of renewed desire, the more painful because they might never satisfy it.

Slowly, Alison backed away. "They'll be coming back soon. We should get out."

Tony exhaled. "I guess so."

They walked to the shore together, Alison a little ahead of him. When she stepped from the water, she looked so beautiful that it hurt. Miserably, Tony said, "I can take you home."

She turned to him, a silver silhouette. "I'll stay for a while, Tony. I don't want you having to explain yourself to Sam."

They dressed in the dark and sat together, silent and unhappy, waiting for Sue and Sam to finish making love. It took them months to repair the damage; that night, Tony could not imagine that they would ever become lovers.

FOUR

Tony started the car. "I hated that night," he said to Alison.

Turning, she touched his face. "So did I."

In his headlights, Tony could see Sam in his own car, tipping a flask to his lips and then wheeling away.

Through the window, Alison watched the taillights of Sam's car recede in the darkness, her profile reflective. After a moment, she said, "I don't think I'd want to be Sue tonight."

Tony glanced at her. "He'll be all right. Most times, Sam's got a pretty good idea of where to draw the line."

"But not always." She turned to him. "Sometimes I wonder how you guys got to be so close."

Tony began driving toward Taylor Park. "We were just both there, the two best guys on almost every team we played for. We could have been friends, or we could have been rivals. I guess we both knew friends was better."

She gave him a curious look. "Sometimes I watch you two, and it's like Sam's your bad twin brother. The one who gets away with doing all the things the good brother wants to do but knows he really shouldn't."

"Like what?"

"Like at church that time. To me, it sounded scary."

Tony gave a short laugh. "It was. But I didn't want to be Sam. I was just glad to let Sam have the hangover for me and get out of there alive."

If Tony had seen it coming, he would not have been there in the first place. Mass had never looked so good.

It began at Sam's house, around one o'clock in the morning. Tony was sleeping over; they sat on the floor of Sam's room with the lights dimmed and the radio on, passing a bottle of whiskey back and forth. Sam had warmed up with a couple of beers; the effect was one of great self-confidence. But beneath this Tony sensed a certain volatility: the family hardware store had failed at last, and Sam sometimes seemed resentful of the town itself for the Robbs' declining station. And there was something Tony could not ask about—the stories about Coach Jackson and Sam's mother. "Good whiskey," Sam said, and took another sip.

"Rhapsody in the Rain" came on the radio in Lou Christie's near falsetto; as far as Tony could make out, it was about getting laid in the car to the rhythm of windshield wipers. Sam listened to the lyrics with a sardonic grin.

"So," he asked, "things any better with the Ice Queen?"

Tony gave him a look: the nickname annoyed him; the question depressed him. Coolly, he said, "The same."

Sam rolled his eyes. "You're gonna get hair on your palms, man. Maybe go blind. I can see you now, selling pencils outside the high school, 'cause Alison Taylor won't come across. You need my advice."

"Jesus, Sam, is that all you ever think about—sex?

Because Alison and me are about a whole bunch of stuff. Or don't you and Sue ever talk when you're alone?"

Sam assumed an expression of weary patience. "Help this man, O Lord," he intoned. "He is wandering in the darkness with a serious erection, and no salvation for it but his own."

In spite of himself, Tony laughed aloud.

Sam took a deep swallow of whiskey. "Speaking of our Lord, I've got a sermon to write. I think I'm gonna need you here."

"Sermon? For who? Horny Guys Anonymous?"

"I never told you? Christ." Sam took another swig. "Remember that Methodist youth group the old lady stuck me in 'cause I wouldn't go to church with her anymore? They elected me their president."

Tony looked at him in amazement. "I guess God must have spoken to them," he said at last. "I can't think of any other reason."

"Yeah, well, that's not the good part. The good part is our minister got this swell idea for an ecumenical youth service—skipping you mackerel snappers, of course. He drafted me to give the sermon. For my new flock and their parents, Sue's folks included."

Tony covered his eyes. "Has this guy ever actually met you?"

"You know me—I can fool anyone for a while. But you want to know the best part?"

"I was kind of hoping I'd already heard it."

Sam grinned. "Sermon's tomorrow."

Tony stared at him. "Shit," he said.

"Won't do. Has to be longer."

All at once, Tony realized he was a little drunk. "What are you going to say?"

"No clue." Sam was more than a little drunk, Tony realized; he gave off that weird sense of imperviousness Tony had seen before, just before Sam's judgment deserted him.

For Tony, the fun had gone out of this. "Maybe you'd better stop drinking."

Sam's eyes glinted with defiance. "Can't do that—I'd lose my edge."

Tony studied him, then looked at his watch. "When is this supposed to happen?"

"Six o'clock. It's outside—sort of a sunrise service."

Tony puffed his cheeks. "If I were you, Sam, I'd start praying right now. For rain."

Sam shrugged. "They'd just move the fucker inside. It's you and me, Tony. Want to see what we can make up?"

Tony sat back. With a certain irony, he noticed that on the radio Elvis had begun wailing "Crying in the Chapel." "Well," Tony said, "I guess it's good you're speaking to Protestants. As far as I can see, their idea of Hell is a year without golf. Church is where they go to sleep."

They went to the kitchen. Sam made coffee; Tony began scribbling in a spiral notebook. "If I were you," he murmured, "I'd say 'spirit of the Lord' a lot. When those guys raise money on TV, it looks like that works for them."

As Tony made notes, Sam drank coffee and whiskey; the result in Sam combined slurred speech with a certain crazy energy. Sam laughed a lot; Tony outlined a sermon.

"You're going with me, right?" Sam asked. "It wouldn't be fun without you."

"I've had enough fun. Besides, I'm not supposed to set foot inside a Protestant church."

"It's outside, remember? Don't you folks believe in the Good Samaritan?"

Sam looked a little shaky, Tony decided. "I'd better drive home first," he said at last. "Put on my suit and running shoes."

An hour later, walking to Tony's car, Sam looked pale. His hands were trembling as he stuffed the outline in the inside pocket of his suit. Tony guessed that he had drunk more whiskey.

Sam lay back in the passenger seat. "I'm gonna do Richard Burton," he announced. "He was terrific as the minister in *The Sandpiper.*" And then he promptly fell asleep.

They reached the church as the first light broke over the tree-lined street. To one side of the church Tony saw the folding chairs—already beginning to fill with people—set on the lawn facing a wooden platform with a podium and a cross. Sam was still unconscious.

Tony touched his shoulder. Sam blinked and then gazed at Tony with dazed incomprehension, like a child aroused from sleep. Tony could not restrain a bit of sadism. "Curtain time, Lazarus. Arise, and do the work of the Lord."

Sam burst out laughing. Tony found this so frightening that he got out and opened the car door for him.

Together, they walked across the dewy grass. In the fresh light of morning, Sam was nearly white; Tony, who had seen this before, knew that Sam was moments from throwing up.

The pastor—a slight, sandy-haired man with glasses—spotted Sam and started toward them with a ministerial smile, which did not show his teeth. "Take deep breaths," Tony murmured.

Sam did so, swallowing. "Good morning, Samuel," the pastor said. "Are you ready to lead us?"

Humbly, Sam bowed his head; missing the grin that this concealed, the pastor seemed to take Sam's posture for awe. "The Lord will help you," he told Sam, and introduced himself to Tony. "And where is your church home?"

"Saint Raphael's parish."

The pastor looked surprised, and then clapped him on the shoulder. "Good, good. I hope you enjoy our service."

As the pastor led Sam away, Tony saw that Sam's head was still bowed.

Looking around him, he saw Sue next to her parents, a brisk and amiable couple who both taught at the junior high school. Sitting next to her, Tony said hello to them. Sue was watching Sam. Under her breath, she murmured, "Is he okay?"

"He thinks he is."

Sue faced the podium again, her back straight, lips half parted. The service began. Both the pastor's prayer and his introduction of Sam were blurs to Tony. He knew only that the Sam Robb who the pastor implied stood before them existed nowhere in life.

When Sam stepped to the podium, Tony saw the sweat on his forehead, felt Sue's tense fingers curling around his. Sam seemed to swallow. "Last night," he said in a shaky voice, "I really wasn't ready for this."

Tony saw Sue's eyes close. Pausing, Sam seemed unsteady. "I was waiting to be filled with the spirit of the Lord. Instead I began feeling sick. . . ."

"What is he doing?" Sue whispered.

"Then I listened to some beautiful music, about the beauty of God's rain falling on God's creations, and found myself saying to my friend Tony Lord, 'Tony, you just can't do it alone. . . .

" 'Tony,' I said, 'you can't find life's joys without a partner. Someone you can feel deep inside . . .' "

Jesus fucking Christ.

" 'And that can only be' "—here Sam paused, giving Tony a small smile of moral superiority—" '*God.*' "

With a kind of fascination, Tony stared back.

"*God,*" Sam intoned, "is the way to fulfillment, to thawing the coldness around us, of realizing our deepest desires in the deepest possible way.

"God is the climax of our lives."

Tony recognized the hushed intensity—it was, to the life, the manner of Richard Burton's ultimate sermon in *The Sandpiper*. But he was not reading Tony's speech.

"God alone can touch us where we most need to be touched."

Tensing, Tony wondered when everyone else would get the joke. But when he glanced around, the congregation was attentive, unsmiling. Sam grew more vibrant.

"God alone can relieve our suffering.

"God alone can fill the empty places."

God alone, Tony thought, *can make our toes and fingers numb.*

"God alone," Sam said softly, "can give us what we really need."

Sam, Tony saw, was even more pale. He gripped the podium tighter and spoke in his own voice. "I should finish now, 'cause I don't want to go on too long. But I can't tell you what a comfort that feeling was to me—I hope to Tony too. Maybe even to all of you." He paused, as if in search of inspiration, and then finished. "Because I know what I need to do. What I think we all need to do. In the words of the old hymn, 'Rock of Ages, cleft for me. Let me find myself in thee.' "

He sat abruptly. The effect was one of extreme preoccupation; Tony guessed that Sam was close to becoming sick.

Moving behind him, a teen choir began singing.

Sue bit her lip, and then Tony saw the tears in her eyes. "You've got to get him out of here, Tony. Before something happens."

"I know."

The choir finished; mercifully, the pastor said a prayer and invited everyone inside for coffee and orange juice. As they stood, Sue's father turned and remarked to Tony affably, "That was pretty good. Actually, Sam surprised me some."

"Me too."

Quickly, he said goodbye to Sue and went to Sam.

Sam stood with his head bent over, listening to a husband and wife, who, in Tony's mind, were most notable for refusing to let their daughter date Catholics. "Sam," the husband said seriously, "I don't want to put pressure on you. But you may have a calling here. . . ."

"Excuse me," Tony cut in, and turned to Sam. "You promised to go to Mass with me, remember? I don't want us to be late."

The man's hawk-faced wife shot Tony a sharp look of irritation. Ignoring her, Tony grasped Sam by the elbow and hustled him across the lawn with such hurry that no one interrupted them.

They got in the car. Swiftly, Tony cranked down the windows and drove away. Sam leaned forward, breathing hard.

"Never again," Tony said. "Never again."

Sam did not answer. Tony drove quickly down Erie Road, past Alison's sprawling house, and veered abruptly into the empty parking lot in the middle of Taylor Park. The park was empty; the only sounds were birds chirping in the trees above them.

Hastily, Sam jerked open the car door and leaned over the asphalt. The sound of retching started before Tony jumped out the driver's side.

Propped up by his hands on the asphalt, Sam hung halfway out of the car, his white-blond head almost touching the pool of vomit. Though he still retched, nothing more came out. When at last he stopped, shivers ran through his body.

"Sam?"

Slowly, Sam turned over, head resting on the vomit-covered asphalt, and began laughing until the tears ran down his face.

"I fooled them," he said when he could speak again, and then grinned up at Tony, pale and wasted, eyes dancing. "I absolutely fucking fooled them."

FIVE

Tony and Alison pulled into the darkened lot of Taylor Park. Before he could turn off the motor, she said quietly, "I think we should be where no one can see us."

Tony felt the constriction in his chest. Without answering, he drove across the grass until his headlights caught a grove of oaks clustered near the cliff above the lake. Slowing, he edged the car forward until it was hidden among tree trunks and low-hanging branches. When he switched off the headlights, it was pitch black.

Alison took his hand. "Do you want to know," she asked, "what I told my parents?"

Though he could barely see her, Tony knew that he did not need to answer. Solitude, and emotion, seemed to soften her voice still more. "I told them that I loved you. And that they should get used to it. Because if that ever changed, it would be about something between you and me, not me and them."

The certainty in her tone surprised him. "What did they say?"

"A lot that you'd expect. Mostly that I'm too young to make decisions, for all of the reasons I'm still too young to understand. My mother cried."

"Over what? It's not like we're getting engaged."

Alison was quiet. "I think she's afraid," she said at last. "Not just of you and me, but that I'm starting on my own life, and that there are some decisions I'm going to make without her. Some without her even knowing." Her fingers tightened around his. "I know that's how this feels to me."

There was something new in her voice—at once wistful, fearful, and determined. Just as the decision she seemed to have made was not about her parents, Tony sensed it was also less about him than about Alison herself, resolving to share a moment of her life with him. It made him hold her close.

She leaned back, touching his face, and then kissed him without hesitation.

He did not quite know what to do. To kiss her passionately, as if trying to sweep away her senses, seemed foolish. What was happening felt too rational for Tony's comfort; he was not in charge, a seducer, but a partner in a rite of Alison's choosing. He felt both flattered and diminished.

As if sensing this, she stopped, looking into his eyes. "I had to be ready, Tony. It didn't matter what you did, or how much I might have wanted you. Can you understand that?"

Silent, Tony nodded. Alison leaned her forehead against his. He could feel her soft breath against his face: she was waiting for him, he realized. She knew what she wanted to do, but not how. This she would trust to Tony.

"I've got something in the glove compartment."

She shook her head. "It's okay, Tony. I just had my period."

There was a chill in the car. Turning on the heater, he saw that the clock read 10:55. Alison must be home in little more than an hour.

Tony took off his letter jacket and, reaching over the front seat, spread it to cover the back upholstery. Shrugging out of her coat, Alison said with a touch of humor, "I hope it doesn't itch."

They were in this together, Tony suddenly knew. He felt relief course through him.

Getting out of the car, Tony went to the passenger door and opened it for her.

She slid from the seat, knees and legs together, graceful even in her deep preoccupation. Something about this moved Tony so much that he pulled her to him and, for the first time that night, kissed her with intensity. He felt her tremor as she joined him.

"God . . . ," Tony murmured.

Hastily, he opened the back door and clambered inside after her. Kneeling on the back seat, Alison said, "It's *cold* out there. . . ."

Tony was suddenly aware that his hands were chill and numb, that their breath, the warmth they made, had begun to condense on the windows. Turning, he wrote on the window with the tip of one cold finger, "I love you."

Alison smiled. Beneath it, she wrote, "Me too," and added an exclamation mark. But her voice when she spoke was quiet.

"This won't be hard for me, Tony. Not with you."

Tony did not know whether she said this to encourage him or herself. Unbidden, Tony remembered his first time—remembered Mary Jane Kulas lying beneath him in this same back seat, her plump thighs open beneath him, a look of nothingness on her face. The first time had hurt her, and, although this went unsaid, Mary Jane had resented him for it. But not as much as she had when—after several more months had brought relief from pain but no real joy to Mary Jane, brief release and lingering guilt to Tony—he had broken up with her and so taken on the weight of still more guilt, which he now knew to have been unavoidable. Because he now knew that her cri de cœur—"You're dropping me for giving you what you wanted"—was the opposite of the truth: that only guilt had kept him from acting earlier on the realization that he could not really talk with her and that his own desire had concealed this from him just long enough to serve its selfish purposes. So that later he could not defend himself when Mary Jane, Catholic like Tony, had reacted to his dating Alison by calling him a social climber who had taken from her what was precious for mere sport. Nor was it much consolation that Mary Jane understood him so little that she did not know that Tony was unrelieved by the confessional and filled with self-contempt.

That had been a sin, Tony thought now. He did not wish *this* to be.

"Undress me," Alison asked softly.

Tony hesitated, and then said with equal quiet, "I love you." Said this half for her, half to reassure himself. He felt Alison sigh as he cupped her breast.

Distracted by his own past sins, Tony helped with her sweater, then the rest of it, until she was naked with him, gently shivering with her own desire. He closed his eyes in something strangely like prayer.

His savior was the touch of her skin.

Feeling the responsive stirring of his own flesh, Tony felt protective and aroused at once—for who was there to protect her from, save him? He kissed her neck, the firm tips of her breasts. The soft sounds she made were to encourage him.

Suddenly the car was a cocoon of warmth, shielding Tony from his other, guilty self. They had come here as partners: he must help make this a moment for them both to remember, perhaps for as long as they were alive. Her body beneath his was warm.

When he at last touched her there, she was as ready as she knew how to be.

He stopped, resting on his elbows as he looked at her in doubt and in desire, afraid of hurting her. He saw her eyes smile back at him.

"I want you," she whispered. As he raised his body, she opened her legs for him. He felt a current run between the two of them.

The slightest cry, and then Tony was inside her.

He hesitated. Alison cradled his face to her shoulder, murmuring, "I love you, Tony. You feel so good to me."

They were together in this.

Alison began to move with him. She was everywhere now: in the clean smell of her skin; the thick softness of her hair; the warmth of her hips and thighs and stomach. As they moved with one another, Tony forgot that

Alison Taylor had passed beyond the near occasion of sin, to sin itself.

Time stopped.

Tony felt the blood course through him, become a seizure that he could not control except to stifle his own cries. They were together no longer; alone in his shame and ecstasy, Tony shuddered and was still.

Alison looked up at him in inquiry and then smiled a little, as if with secret knowledge. Something about this made him feel embarrassed, yet closer to her.

"Did I hurt you?" he asked.

"Only a little. I don't break, you know."

This was said with a certain proud authority; she had things to teach him, the words implied, and yet they carried an undertone of relief—she was past something, and now it was beyond worry.

"I'm sorry," Tony said.

"For what?"

"That you didn't . . ." He hesitated. "Did you?"

"I don't think so." A pause of her own, and then another slight smile. "I think it's going to take a little practice."

Suspended between relief and embarrassment, Tony pondered her meaning. She raised her face to kiss him, and told him quietly, "I'm glad this was with you."

Touching her hair, he felt a wave of gratitude. "I want us to be together. Always."

"So do I. Always."

He smiled; beneath him, she wriggled slightly. "Can you move a little?" she asked. "Not off me, I don't want that. I just need to breathe."

He shifted on his elbow, and then she gazed at him more softly. "Did I feel good to you?" she asked.

"God, yes."

The small smile returned. "At the end, I could feel it happen to you."

All at once, Tony felt their deepening bond, like nothing he had felt with Mary Jane. *We did it,* he felt himself thinking, *and we're all right. This could not be a sin.*

He barely remembered to look at his watch.

It was 11:40. Tony held her closer, murmuring, "I never want this night to end."

They fell briefly quiet, darkness around them, complete within their world. Almost dreamily, Alison said, "Maybe I can come back out."

It surprised him. "Without your parents knowing?"

"I think so." She brushed the hair back from his face. "I want to be with you again. I hate this stupid curfew."

In the back of his brain, Tony felt his sense of sin resurface and, with it, prudence. "I don't want you to get in trouble."

Alison shook her head. "Once I'm in, they'll fall asleep. I can go down the back stairs, out the rear door, and through my backyard to here."

"Can you find your way?"

She gave a quick nod. "I used to play hide-and-seek here all the time. I could find you with my eyes shut. If you want me to."

Tony paused, ashamed of his cowardice. "I want you to," he said.

Hurriedly, they began to dress, newly giddy with defiance and conspiracy. Pulling on her stockings, Alison stopped. "I don't need these," she said with a decisive air, and stuffed them in her purse. "She'll never notice." The grin she gave him was careless and triumphant.

They scurried out of the back seat, each wiping condensation off the windows with their hands. But the glass was still too smudged to see through. The clock read 11:57.

"Don't worry," Alison said. "I can go home that way too."

"I'll go with you."

Together, they headed through the shadowy trees, tentative and a little scared. "Dark," Tony whispered.

She took his hand. "I know."

They reached the open field and began running across the park.

The night was overcast, close to moonless. A line of oaks separated the park from the Taylors' home; Tony could see the oaks only as a deeper darkness. All that he heard were their own running footsteps, ragged breaths.

They reached the trees. Through them, Tony saw the outline of the gabled house, looming as if a shadow, the faint glow of a light left on in back.

"We should stop," Alison whispered.

Tony brought her close. "I'll wait for you here."

She shook her head. "It's cold out. You can keep the car warm."

They looked at each other.

Without hurry, Alison kissed him, slowly and deeply. Tony did not want to let her go.

Alison pulled back. "We've just used my final minute," she said, and smiled again. "See you in about fifteen."

Before he could answer, she gave him a last brief kiss and was running toward the house.

Suddenly alone, Tony watched her vanish in the darkness, then reappear, wraithlike, in the light of the back porch. She turned, waving, and then the light went off.

SIX

Still parked where they had made love, Tony waited for Alison to return. The clock read 12:26.

It was cold. Tony turned on the heater, then the radio.

Time felt sluggish. As Bobbie Gentry sang "Ode to Billy Joe," Tony found himself silently counting, hoping that this would materialize Alison before he reached one hundred. It felt like part of him was missing.

The clock passed 12:40.

Restless, Tony strained to remember the feel of her, the way she had looked at him. When "Lucy in the Sky with Diamonds" came on the radio, he snapped it off in irritation.

Her parents must have stopped her.

He could imagine them waiting up for her, their older daughter and their favorite, to demand a further summit conference on the subject of Tony Lord; imagined her bare legs in the light of a living room lamp, her look of guilt and defiance as they asked her to sit down. Tony thought of his own parents, particularly his mother; without college or great expectations, Helen Lord peered suspiciously at a world she feared would snatch away her only child—this prize she had been given—as if to mock her for hoping above her status. Tony still struggled against her burdensome belief in his uniqueness; he both understood and disliked the Taylors' proprietary love for Alison. Once her parents started in on her, it might be impossible for her to leave.

It was one o'clock. But Tony could not desert her.

The house was close, perhaps a hundred yards. If his view were not blocked by the trees around him, he might see a light in Alison's window. With an instinct he could not explain, Tony knew that she would come to him. He did not want her to find her way alone.

Locking the car behind him, Tony stepped from beneath the trees. The night was even darker than before.

Slowly, he crossed the park toward the Taylors' house, listening for Alison.

Nothing.

Tony stopped. She could be somewhere near; on this night, it was possible that she might pass him unseen. The utter silence made the dark seem infinite.

Once more, he started toward the grove of oaks, guided

only by his senses. At last, he heard the chill wind stir their branches and, a few steps further, saw them.

Outlined against the sky, the leafless trees were skeletal. Through them he made out the roofline of the Taylors' house; no lights were on. Then he heard the brittle snapping of a branch.

The footstep that must have caused this was not his.

"Alison?"

There was no answer. Edgy, Tony walked toward the sound. His voice, low and muted, carried in the night.

"Alison . . ."

A second branch snapped, closer.

Tony froze. He sensed that whoever made the sound had paused at his approach.

Taut, Tony heard a second sound, fainter, perhaps the wind. Perhaps he imagined that it seemed plaintive, feminine.

Another branch snapped, nearer yet.

Tony's skin crawled. "Who is it?" Tony cried out, and then heard someone running toward him.

Unable to see, Tony braced himself. The thumping footsteps headed for him. Then, quite suddenly, the footsteps veered away. Heart pounding in his chest, Tony listened as their sound vanished in the endless dark.

Alone, he remembered the other, softer sound.

Turning, he ran toward the grove.

A branch lashed his face. The sting of it stopped him only for an instant, and then he crossed onto the Taylors' land.

Abruptly, he stopped, looking blindly about him. The house was concrete now, its peculiar shape dark against the sky; to his right, a deep lapping sound came from the unseen lake below. Only when the back porch light came on, casting yellow on the grass, did he see the shadow lying before him.

He walked toward it, fear growing inside him, not

wondering about the light. Curled on its side, the shadow was like a child sleeping.

Bending, Tony reached out to her. Felt the hair that hid her face, the cheek that was still warm.

His voice was hoarse. *"Alison."*

Her skirt was pulled up. As though to stir her, Tony touched her bare leg.

It was damp. Something smelled like urine. A cry formed in his throat.

The back door creaked open. The beam of a flashlight crossed the grass.

"Alison," her father cried out.

Stunned, Tony cradled Alison's face. At first, he could not see her, and then the flashlight found them.

Alison's face was flushed, her mouth contorted. The eyes that had held such love for him were wide and empty, pinpointed with red starbursts.

Mind reeling, Tony crossed himself, tears of shock streaming down his face.

Holy Mary, Mother of God, pray for us sinners now and at the hour of our death . . .

"Oh my God . . ."

Tony jerked his hand back. It took him an instant to realize that the cry of anguish was not his. "Oh my God . . . ," her father repeated.

Nauseous, Tony felt cold metal against his head, trembling with its own life. *"You animal—what have you done to her?"*

Turning, Tony faced a black revolver.

Behind it stood John Taylor, the white shock of hair faint silver in the light, his face sick with anger and incomprehension. Beyond him, the screen door framed the startled silhouette of Alison's mother. "Katherine," her husband's thick voice cried. "Please, call for help. . . ."

Tony felt himself trembling, unable to comprehend this. Gun in hand, John Taylor knelt beside his daughter, felt for her pulse. As the father's eyes shut, Tony blurted, "It wasn't me. . . ."

John Taylor's eyes snapped open. Like an automaton, he rose from Alison's side and aimed the revolver at Tony. In his disbelief, Tony could not move.

"Jack!"

Katherine Taylor ran from the house and knelt beside her daughter. She saw Alison's face, cried out. Then she threw herself across the slender frame, as if to protect it from hurt.

Staring at Tony across the two women, one still, one sobbing, John Taylor's eyes turned vacant. He raised the gun to fire; Tony covered his face.

"*Mama*—what is it?"

John Taylor blinked. In a nightdress, Alison's eleven-year-old sister called from the back porch.

Stiffly, Alison's mother rose to her knees, her gray-streaked black hair disheveled, her face ivory. In parched tones, she said to her husband, "Don't hurt him, Jack. Wait for the police."

John Taylor did not answer. Instead he turned, as if remembering his duties, and called out to his younger daughter with strained parental authority. "It's Alison, Lizzie. Please stay there." Shivering, Tony knew that Alison's mother had saved his life.

A siren whined. Tony saw the flashing red lights of one police car, then a second, tires squealing to a stop in the Taylors' driveway. A young cop came running, followed by the stocky chief of police, calling out, "What's happened, John?"

Slowly, John Taylor turned. In a toneless voice, he said, "This boy killed Alison—"

"*No*," Tony cried out. "I found her. . . ."

Breathing heavily, the chief stopped, looking from John Taylor to the body at his feet. He bent to Alison, hand covering her mouth and nose, then murmured, "There's an ambulance coming."

A hush surrounded him. Tony felt himself swallow. The chief gazed at him, his blue eyes astonished yet unspeakably sad. "I saw that game tonight . . ."

On the porch, Alison's sister began keening, thin cries of sympathetic fear. The chief looked up at Alison's father, then at his gun. "We have him now, John. You don't need to worry."

Stiffly, Alison's mother stood leaning against her husband. With a jerk of the head, the chief summoned the young patrolman to the Taylors' side. "It's better," the chief said to Alison's father, "if you step away a little."

Mumbling his consolation, the young policeman guided them away, Katherine Taylor gazing back at Alison.

Two more police officers stood behind Tony. The chief's mouth set. "Get him out of here." Standing, Tony found himself staring at Alison as if, dreamlike, she might rise with him.

Gently, the cops shepherded Tony across the lawn. It became the darkened landscape of a nightmare—the uniformed police, the dead girl he loved, her sister crying into her hands, hair black like Alison's.

They shoved him in the back seat of a squad car and started the motor. At the foot of the drive, Tony saw Alison's parents—her father staring fixedly at the car, her mother's head against his shoulder—through the blur of his own tears.

"It wasn't me," Tony repeated. "It wasn't me."

SEVEN

After that, no one spoke.

Tony stared out the window at the quiet streets, half suburban, half small town—the white frame houses of the twenties, the red-brick bungalows and postage-stamp lawns of the fifties, the spired city hall with its iron clock face and, next to that, the incongruous severity of the tan brick police station, completed the previous year amidst much controversy. Lake City seemed at once familiar and strange, a place he had half forgotten. He ached for Alison to be with him.

They got to the station.

The two officers led him to the basement. He accepted this without question—it was part of the logic of his nightmare—just as he obeyed the request by a third cop, given with the politeness of a doctor performing a physical, to strip. The man took blood from his arm; slid a needle beneath his fingernails; snipped a sample of pubic hair; swabbed the tip of his penis; snapped photographs of the welt on his cheek, which Tony supposed the branch had left. For however long this took, Tony asked nothing. All that he could think about was Alison.

They gave back his clothes and put him in a cubicle with yellow cinder-block walls. The room was claustrophobic, hardly larger than a closet, with a bare table and chairs beneath a bright fluorescent light. Tony slumped at the table, exhausted.

She had died for him, in a state of mortal sin. He could think of nothing else. It felt like the aftershock of a blow to the head, his memory a void, pain the only fact that he could grasp. His skull pounded.

Forgive me, Father, for I have sinned. . . .

He did not know how long he was alone. He did not

care: his parents, his friends, were nothing to him. Only Alison.

Two detectives entered the room. Dully, Tony recognized the young one, greyhound sleek, his brown hair slicked back—Sergeant Dana, the police liaison to Lake City High, whose job it was to sniff out drugs and theft. The older man was red-haired, slit-eyed, with the high color of a drinker. His freckled hands on the table seemed restless, twitchy. He lit a cigarette.

"I'm Lieutenant McCain—Frank McCain. You know Doug Dana from the high school, right? Used to play quarterback, like you. But nowhere near as good."

Tony rubbed his eyes, unable to process what was happening. McCain took a deep drag of the cigarette, as if to force himself to go slowly. "It's a terrible thing, Tony. A terrible thing. I'll bet you're as sad to be here as we are to be with you like this. I'm real sorry about having to put you through that physical stuff. But it's just routine—we have to do it." As he took another drag, McCain's hand seemed to tremble. "We've got a big responsibility here, Tony. A beautiful girl is dead—someone I know you cared about. Like you, her parents will have to live with that forever. We need to help them understand what happened. For whatever peace that brings."

Tony stared at the table. "It's my fault," he mumbled. "Tell them it was my fault."

McCain became very still. "How was that, Tony?" The cigarette burned in his hand.

"I wanted her to come back out. To be with me." A lump formed in Tony's throat. "If I hadn't wanted her to, he wouldn't have killed her."

Dana's eyes were keen now. "Who would that be?"

"I don't know. I heard someone in the park. . . ." Tony stopped; beneath this pitiless light, footsteps in the dark sounded foolish, hallucinatory.

The two police watched him. "Just tell us about your night," Dana said. "Everything after the football game."

Tony's lips were parched. Miserably, he tried; meeting Sam and Sue, taking Alison off alone, deciding to meet her again, the footfalls in the dark, the soft cry that led him to her body. Even as he spoke, Tony prayed that he could go back—stay with Sam and Sue, or tell Alison to remain inside, safe with the family who loved her. But the one fact that he omitted, her desire to make love with him, was the only way he could still protect her.

Dana was frowning. "How'd you get that cut on your face?"

Tony tried to remember. "From a branch . . . running through the trees."

"Why did you leave the car?"

"She was late to meet me. I went to look for her, and heard him in the park—"

"How would he know she was out there—the guy who killed her?"

Tony shook his head, bewildered. Quietly, Dana asked, "Did you have sex with her last night?"

Tony's eyes shut. "No."

"We think someone did, Tony." With an air of melancholy, McCain shook his head. "Alison may be dead, but her body will tell a story. So will yours, when the samples come back from the lab."

Tony felt guilt overcome him. "Could Father Quinn be here . . . my priest?"

McCain watched his eyes. "I'm Catholic, Tony, like you—we know that confession is good for the soul. But what you tell Father Quinn won't help anyone but you. *This* is your chance to help someone else, like the good Father would tell you to. To keep the trust of people in this town." His voice slowed for emphasis. "So let's start by telling me if you had sex with Alison Taylor."

Suddenly Tony had to urinate. "No," he said.

"Did you fight with her last night?" Dana prodded. "I mean, you were having trouble, right? For a while you broke up."

Tony's temples throbbed. "Who told you that—"

"So what was the trouble last night?" Dana cut in.

Tony's bladder hurt. "Nothing."

McCain put down his cigarette. "Work with us, Tony. Tell us what happened with you and Alison."

Tony did not answer. Dana's voice was soft again. "I think maybe I *know* what happened."

Tony felt something in the room change. "How?"

Dana sat back, regarding him without expression. "Sometimes women like to tease you. Or maybe let you think they like it a certain way, then figure out they don't." His look became confiding. "Is that why you wanted her to come out again? To do something a little different for you?"

"I just wanted to be with her—"

"Maybe you had a disagreement about it." Dana's tone was cool now. "Maybe *that's* what her body will tell us. That you forced her to do that for you."

Tony shook his head. *"No."*

"So what you want us to say to her parents is that she was fooling around with someone else."

"No . . . we were *going* together."

"Then let's be kind here. You say Alison had no other guy. You say Alison wasn't sleeping around. You want to be fair to her, don't you? You want to honor her memory. The only way to do that is to tell the truth about what you did to her."

All at once, Tony understood. Horror left him speechless.

McCain covered Tony's hand with his. "Did you love her, Tony?"

The surprise of this brought tears to Tony's eyes. "Yes. I loved her."

McCain nodded slowly. "To me, this looks like a cold-blooded killing. But I can't believe you'd kill in cold blood a girl you were in love with."

"No . . . I wouldn't."

McCain patted his hand. Maybe, Tony thought, this man believed him after all. "So how do you think," the detective asked, "the person who did this is feeling now?"

"I don't know." The pressure on Tony's bladder felt unbearable. "I need a bathroom—"

"Do you think he really wanted to kill her?"

The detective's voice was soothing. But now some intuitive part of Tony, listening through his shock, heard what lay beneath. Softly, he answered. "I know he wanted to."

Something flickered in McCain's eyes. "How do you know that, Tony?"

Tony took a deep breath. "Because I saw what he did to her."

Across the table, McCain leaned closer, forehead a foot from Tony's. "Then what do you think should happen to him?" he asked. "Surely there could be some mercy, if we only could understand."

"No," Tony answered. "I think whoever killed her should die. The way she did."

McCain's hand squeezed Tony's. "I don't think so. Not if he didn't mean it to happen. Not if things just got out of hand." The detective's eyes locked his. "It's time to be a man, Tony. Last night, you were a hero in this town. You can be a hero again. It's not too late for you."

Tony made what reasoning part of him remained focus on his own survival. "All I have to do is tell you what really happened, right? Then I can go to the bathroom?"

"Right." Tony felt a tremor in McCain's hand. "You didn't mean for her to die, I know that. No matter how bad this looks."

Slowly, Tony removed his hand, then looked at the detective dead on. "Okay. I didn't kill her. I found her like that. So you can quit being my friend." He stood, voice trembling with loss and fear and anger. "I want you to call my parents, right now. And tell me where the bathroom is."

McCain stared up at him, face turning red. For a moment, no one spoke.

"It's down the hall," Dana said.

His parents came. His mother's eyes were red; without makeup, hair too blond, her face looked pallid. She ran to Tony, hugging him desperately. "I didn't kill her, Mom."

"It's all right, Tony. It's all right."

Tony looked over her shoulder, at his father. Stanley Lord stood straighter. For an instant, his chin looked firm, his face more commanding. Somehow it reminded Tony of the wedding picture Helen Lord kept on the mantel; Stanley's hair, swept back, was darker, his Slavic features were thinner and keener. "See how handsome he was," Tony's mother would say, as if speaking of another life.

For the first time in years, his father took Tony by the hand. Looking from McCain to Dana, he said, "We're taking our son home." Tony felt the gratitude of a child who had been found.

Passing another office, they saw the chief speaking softly to John and Katherine Taylor. John Taylor stared up at Stanley Lord with terrible bitterness. Stanley Lord's eyes held compassion but no apology: he would take care of his own, the look said, no matter who John Taylor was. Then Helen Lord plucked at her husband's arm, and they left.

In the thin light of dawn, his mother leaned against their blue Dodge. Hands to her face, she wept. "You should have stayed away from her. I always knew it. . . ."

The words hit Tony hard. For once, it did not help him to perceive the superstitious fearfulness of a woman still defined by the Polish neighborhood they had left behind. Shaken, Tony turned to his father. "I'm sorry, Dad. I think I need a lawyer."

Tony saw Stanley Lord shrink from what this tragedy could do to them. Then saw his father come to terms with his new reality: a girl was dead, the son he loved in trouble.

Stanley Lord drew him close. "We'll find one, Anthony."

EIGHT

As he faced Saul Ravin, it struck Tony that the lawyer was someone who, in the life he had led until now, he would never have met.

In his first two days of grief and sleeplessness, Tony found that acceptance of Alison's death came slowly, inexorably, like drops of water on stone. The Saturday paper had seemed unreal: Alison's yearbook picture, the color drained from it, looked like a hundred other pictures of teenagers whose lives were cut short by tragedy. The headline read: "Lake City Girl Slain," and beneath that: "Boyfriend Questioned in Death of Popular Student." Tonelessly, Tony had asked his mother, "Who brought this?"

"Mrs. Reeves, from down the street. With a tuna casserole."

Something about this had made Tony laugh. The bitter sound froze his mother's face. "Next time I murder someone," he had told her, "ask her to bring lasagna."

Her hands had flown up to cover her mouth. From beside the window, where he watched the reporters who had gathered in front, his father had turned and said softly, "Son, we have to be good to each other. Especially now."

His father's skin looked sallow, the pouches beneath his eyes like bruises. As if in penitence, Tony had sat on the couch across from Helen Lord. "There's only us," she had told him. "Your uncle Joe and aunt Mary Rose wanted to come out. But we couldn't let them, with these people outside."

Tony had looked around him at the only home he could remember. The tiny living room with his parents' wedding photo, his own school picture, the porcelain bust of Saint Stanislaus, the figurine of two costumed peasants, dancing a polka. To him, the room reflected the borders of his parents' narrow lives: his mother's fears; his father's small diversions—bowling, church activities—his patient, hopeless serving of time in the cramped cubicle of a corporate bureaucrat. How many times had he imagined leaving this behind—his home, now his prison. Tony had wished that he were dead, like Alison.

Now it was Monday afternoon. Three days before, Tony would have expected to be in school, accepting more congratulations for beating Riverwood. Instead the school was closed for Alison's funeral; Tony and his parents found themselves in the office of this criminal lawyer, who was, they had been assured, the best in Steelton. At odd moments, Tony gazed through Ravin's window at the rust-belt city below, seemingly all cement and steel: gray buildings; gray highways; the polluted Steelton River a gray ribbon filled with gray ore boats and flanked by gray smokestacks. Even the smoke was gray.

Ravin put the facts of the Lords' new lives directly. This was a serious matter: Ravin would need a ten-thousand-dollar retainer, and if Tony was charged with murder, his parents would have to mortgage or sell their home. But today he was pleased to meet with Tony free of charge.

Regrettably, the lawyer concluded, he must do this

without Tony's parents, who could not be Ravin's clients and therefore should not ask Ravin or Tony about anything said between them; further, as prospective witnesses, his parents should never discuss that night with Tony at all. It was not that Tony was guilty, Ravin was quick to add, but that a clever prosecutor could twist small differences in what the three of them might recall. Mystified, the Lords listened to this as if to a strange new catechism. Then Ravin shepherded Tony's parents to the reception area and closed the door behind them. Tony and Saul Ravin were alone.

Ravin sat back in his chair, hands folded across his stomach. He was a paunchy man in his early forties, with curly gray-black hair, a prominent nose, a double chin, and eyes that were lively and lethal by turns, yet somehow sad. Tony guessed that the lawyer was Jewish—"Saul Ravin" had a somewhat exotic sound to it—but could not be sure: to his memory, Tony had not met a Jewish person before. But there was something avuncular about Ravin; he managed to convey that he knew that Tony was disoriented and that they would take their time. Tony sensed that Ravin had excused Tony's parents for yet another reason—that without them, it was more likely Tony would be honest with him.

"Well, Tony," he said at length. "Here you are with a total stranger, who also happens to be the one person in the world who you can absolutely trust. Nothing you say here leaves the room. So I want you to tell me everything.

"See, I won't know how to handle this if you start by holding out on me. Just remember telling God's honest truth is easy—it's the one story you never have to think about. All right?"

For an hour, Tony answered questions about his life: his family; his friends; his grades; his athletics and activities; his church; how long the Lords had lived in Lake City; why they had moved there from Steelton; where Tony planned to apply to college; his lack of prior problems with the police or school or anyone in the town. As he spoke, Tony understood that Ravin was trying to put him at ease while creating a picture for himself.

"You're a novelty for me," Ravin said after a time. "A client whose only prior offense consists of being seventeen." His face turned serious. "We need to talk about Alison, Tony. Not just what happened but who she was."

Softly, Tony began. At last, Ravin led him through the night of the murder, pausing as Tony needed. They concluded with the police; with polite insistence, Ravin picked at Tony's memory of their questions, even phrases. When Tony was finished, Ravin said, "There's something they're not telling you."

"What?"

"I don't know." Ravin steepled his hands beneath his chin, as if about to offer something more, then said almost dismissively, "The cops always hold back something. Sometimes to trip you up, sometimes so cranks don't start confessing murders they didn't commit. Sometimes just to protect the feelings of the victim's family." His voice softened. "But then you held back something too. From the cops, and from me."

Tony flushed. "What's that?"

"That you were sleeping with her."

Silent, Tony stared at him, shame and defiance warring within. Ravin began studying his gold cuff links with an unimpressed expression. "And like the cops, Tony, my question is, why? Their answer is that maybe you raped her. That maybe you squeezed a little too hard, trying to keep her quiet. You can't really blame them." Abruptly, Ravin looked up at him, eyes suddenly penetrating. "So which is it, Tony? Rape? Murder? Rape *and* murder? Or plain old consensual sex? And don't leave anything out this time."

Tony stood abruptly, walking to the window. But all that he saw was Alison, lying naked beneath him as she looked into his face. Only his resolve of the night before prevented him from crying. Without turning, he said, "We made love in the car. It was our first time."

"And you both wanted to."

"Yes." Pausing, Tony added dully, "That's why she came back."

"Why didn't you tell the police that?"

Tony expelled a breath. "Because it was between the two of us."

He heard Ravin rise from his leather chair. "She's *dead*, Tony. The way you describe her, I don't think she'd need all this chivalry from you." He placed one large hand on Tony's shoulder. "If I remember right, in your religion sleeping with Alison was a mortal sin. But I don't believe you killed Alison Taylor by making love with her. In my theology, only the person who killed her killed her. That's also the way the law works. So tell me one more time—did you kill Alison Taylor? Whatever your answer is, I'll work with. But it has to be the truth."

Tony turned to meet his gaze. "I didn't kill Alison, Mr. Ravin. I loved her."

Ravin looked at Tony steadily. Then he smiled a little. "Saul," he corrected. "Mr. Ravin sounds like my father, the rabbi, to whom I'm somewhat of a disappointment. Please, sit down."

As Tony did that, he felt a certain trust. Ravin sat back. "Let me tell you a few truths of my own, Tony.

"First, other than about you and Alison, there's no glaring problem with your story. The police and the Taylors may think it's unbelievable, but they'll need something more than that. What they think that must be, I don't know yet—some physical evidence from Alison's body; something they took off you, like fingernail scrapings; someone else who claims to know something bad.

"We can't do anything about the physical evidence, except tell the cops that you really *did* sleep with her and that it was consensual." Ravin paused. "Because if it *was*, I think the coroner will agree. Rape causes trauma to the tissue—even the first time won't do that kind of damage." Ravin paused for a moment. "Unless," he added softly, "someone else got to her later. In which case the coroner might not be able to tell—even with only one source of semen, they can't say whose it is. Only blood type."

Tony felt several emotions hit him at once—the anguish that Alison must have felt; his own hatred of the murderer; distaste for discussing Alison as if she were a piece of evidence; the weight of his own guilt. "Which brings us," Ravin went on, "to the something else we have to think about. When this happens to a woman, Tony, you have to consider that it may make more sense than you know. Who could be out there—anyone at all— who might have that kind of feeling about Alison . . . ?"

"No one. She wasn't some slut, running from boyfriend to boyfriend to turn herself on." Tony felt his voice rise. "*I* was the one who found her, not you. *I'm* the one the cops think killed her. If I knew someone who could do this, I'd have told them. Unless I killed him first."

Ravin gave him a cool look. "I'd skip any mention of murder. And until pretty recently, she was dating other guys. If *you* had feelings for her, they could have too. She might even have had some feeling about *them*. Or maybe they thought she did and got let down." Ravin's tone became crisp, factual. "Which gets us to a few more truths.

"If you go to trial, your folks' finances are ruined. If you get charged, your reputation is ruined—at least with some people—for the rest of your life. We need the cops to believe that someone else might have done this. For that I need your help."

Tony stared at him. Then, in a monotone, he named anyone that Alison had dated. Ravin wrote this down. "Thank you," he said politely, and looked up from his pad. "I'll give this to the police. When I go to enlighten them about Alison and you."

Tony straightened in his chair. "I want to go with you."

Ravin put down his pen. "What I was about to tell you is never to talk to the cops again. That's why you're hiring me. To know what's happening, and to not make any mistakes . . ."

"I thought the truth was the one story you never have to think about."

Ravin studied him. "Under these circumstances, I'd never let *any* client talk to the police. The risk is, something gets said that doesn't help. However innocent."

"I lied." Tony sat straighter. "I have to look them in the face again, say I didn't do this. I have to say that to everyone."

Ravin folded his hands, face softer now. In his eyes there was something sad again, infinitely weary. "There's one more truth I have to tell you, Tony. It's the harshest truth of all.

"You're the only person alive who *knows* you didn't kill her. Everyone else has to choose what to believe. And nothing that you seem to know is going to help the average Joe in Lake City believe you're not a murderer.

"Only the cops and the county prosecutor can do that for you, and only if I persuade them not to indict you. In the meanwhile, you're going to have to look to yourself for proof of your own innocence. All I want you to say to anyone—your parents, coaches, friends, even this Sam and Sue—is that you didn't do it, that you're counting on the police to figure out who did, and that you're helping them by keeping quiet. Nothing more."

Once more, his new isolation began to dawn on Tony. He had lost Alison forever, and there was no one to help him bear the sadness of this, his horror at finding her, his anguish that others might believe he had killed her. Gazing out the window, he spoke as if to himself. "Her funeral's going on right now. School's closed, and half the town is there—a lot of them hardly knew her, only want to think they did. The Taylors' minister called me to make sure I wouldn't come. It was what the Taylors wanted; he hoped I'd respect their wishes.

"Just to be fair, he encouraged me to pray for Alison in my own way, in my own church. I guess he figures we have a special pagan ritual for Roman Catholic murderers."

Watching him, Ravin for once looked out of his depth. Tony faced him directly. "All of our friends are going. But what's so hard is that her parents and I are the people in Lake City who loved Alison the most. And I can't even tell them that."

"Or share in the communal grieving." There was understanding in Ravin's eyes. "But stay away from the Taylors. They're terribly wounded, and seeing you would make it that much worse. In Lake City, the Taylors could do you real harm."

The advice compounded Tony's fear of what he had lost. "If I believe you," he told Ravin, "there's no one I can talk to."

"What about your priest?"

Tony hesitated. "I don't know yet," he said softly. "About Alison, he didn't approve."

Ravin studied him without expression, as if buying time for his own thoughts. "I'll make you a deal," he said at last. "Keep quiet for now, and you can come with me to the police. That way you can speak your piece to the folks who matter most." Rising from his chair, Ravin stuck out his hand across the desk. "Deal?"

Tony hesitated, then shook Ravin's hand. "Deal."

"Okay," the lawyer said. "I'll be in touch."

Tony headed for the door. It struck him that he was about to face a world he no longer knew.

"One more thing," he heard Ravin say.

Tony turned, hand on the doorknob. "What's that?"

"You can call me, Tony. Anytime you need to talk."

Tony paused. In his relief and gratitude, all that he could manage was, "Thanks, Mr. Ravin."

For the first time, Ravin's smile reached his eyes. "Saul," he said.

NINE

On the drive home, the Lords passed Saint Barnabas Episcopal. The street was jammed with cars. A black hearse was parked at the rear of the church.

Quietly, Tony said, "I need to see Father Quinn."

His parents, pale and silent, dropped him at Saint Raphael Church.

Though the parish was not wealthy, the church itself was spacious, filigreed, soothing in its shadowy quiet. Slipping into the rear pew, Tony sat alone.

It was three o'clock. Three days before, the football game was not yet played; Alison Taylor, not yet his lover, was waiting for their night together.

Tears running down his face, Tony prayed for the repose of her soul.

He knew where he must go.

At the side of the church, in a darkened corridor, was the confessional booth. Each afternoon, Saturday and Monday, Father Quinn heard confessions: the ritual had been part of Tony's life since childhood. Tony would recite his sins, venial or mortal. Father Quinn would hear him out and then prescribe a penance, the recitation of Our Fathers and Hail Marys, directing him to make a good act of contrition. *"Ego te absolvo,"* the priest would say—I absolve you—*"in nomine Patris, et Filii, et Spiritus Sanctus.* Go in peace." Tony would return to the church, kneel before God, and recite his penance. And then he would leave, his soul unstained again, his heart unburdened.

On this unfathomable day, it was his only hope of redemption, for Alison most of all.

As Tony approached the corridor, two women emerged, a mother and daughter. Seeing Tony, they stopped abruptly, backing away to let him pass. Whether this was out of deference to his loss or fear of what he must confess, Tony could not tell.

In the darkness of the corridor, the floorboards squeaked beneath him.

The confessional booth was at the end, an empty chair inside it. Entering, Tony sat. Behind the screen was the shadowy ascetic profile of Father Quinn.

"Father, forgive me, for I have sinned. . . ."

He sensed the priest's stillness. After a moment, the Irish voice asked softly, "What are your sins, my son?"

"Mortal, Father." Tony paused, the words catching in his throat. "I made love with a girl."

The priest hesitated. "Sex before marriage *is* a mortal sin. . . ."

"She's dead, Father."

Through the screen, Tony heard the intake of breath, but not from surprise. "How did she die?"

"I caused it."

This time the priest was silent. Tony bent forward in the attitude of prayer. "For months I pressured her, knowing it was wrong. Finally, she gave herself to me because she loved me. She wasn't Catholic; it wasn't a sin to her. . . ."

"Yes," Father Quinn said softly, "I know. And that in itself was a sin."

Tony felt himself tremble. The priest's voice became lower. "You haven't told me how she died. Only that you caused it."

Tony closed his eyes. "After we made love, I wanted

her again. I waited in Taylor Park for her to sneak back out. When she didn't come, I went to look for her. I found her in her own backyard, murdered." Tears came to his eyes once more. "I know that she died in pain. That she would never have been there except that I wanted her. That she died because of me."

There was a long silence. Then the priest asked, "Is there more you need to say?"

It was a long time before Tony could speak. "She died after we made love, Father. I need to believe . . ."

The priest bent forward, his voice parched. "You wish to know what has happened to her soul."

"Yes."

For a moment, Father Quinn was quiet. "But you cannot know," he said at last.

Tony felt sick. He had learned the dogma from his own parents: that non-Catholics, let alone a girl who died in sin, could not reasonably hope for salvation. "But our doctrine is changing. . . ."

"Perhaps. But not, I think, for this."

In bottomless grief, Tony covered his face. "Please, Father . . ."

More gently, the priest said, "I cannot tell you what is not so, even for the sake of a poor dead girl for whom your acts had consequences, and whose salvation is now between her and God. You may come here only to confess your own sins and to make penance for the sake of your own immortal soul." His voice hardened. "So I must ask you, have you told me everything . . . ?"

"*Yes,*" Tony said with sudden passion. "Father, forgive me, for I committed a mortal sin and sent a girl I loved to Hell for it."

"*Listen to me.*" The priest's voice rose. "You are speaking not to me but to God, the ultimate judge, and there is no statute of limitations on eternity. He can grant absolution only to you, and only for the sins you have confessed to Him. Are there any others . . . ?"

"I didn't kill her, Father. I just sent her to Hell." Tony felt himself fill with a hopelessness and fury he had never felt before. "You can absolve me now. Make me feel better. . . ."

Behind the screen was a sharp intake of breath. "You're in an emotional state, my son. Maybe you should consider this. . . ."

With a force of its own, torment jerked Tony from his chair. "Maybe I should go to Hell with Alison. That way she'll have company. . . ."

"Anthony," the priest cried out, "this is my obligation to you. Without absolution, you cannot receive Communion. It's *you* I want to help. . . ."

"You can't, Father. Not in this life."

Blind with despair and sleeplessness and abandonment, Tony Lord turned and walked away from his church.

A little past five o'clock, sitting alone in the basement, Tony heard footsteps coming down the stairs.

For a moment, Sam and Sue stood in the dim light. Then Sue hurried to where Tony sat, hugging him around the neck. "Tony, I'm so sorry. . . ."

Eyes shut, Tony put his arms around her. For a long moment, he held her like that, oblivious to anything except relief at seeing her, the comfort of this sudden warmth. "I'm so damn glad that you guys came. . . ."

She pressed her cheek against his forehead, then stepped back. Tony stood, embracing Sam. No one needed to talk.

After a time, Sam and Sue sat on the plaid couch, feet planted on the linoleum. Tony did not ask where they had been; in his charcoal suit, Sam looked awkward and ill at ease; Sue's somber navy outfit was one she wore only to church. Stripped of her vivacity, Sue looked smaller. Softly, Tony asked her, "How was it?"

Sue seemed to consider what answer to give. "Hard," she said at length. "Alison's father tried to speak, and couldn't. Her mother looked like someone else." For a moment, she stared at the gray linoleum. "I'm glad that you weren't there."

"I wanted to be, Sue. Their minister told me not to."

Sue looked up at him. "I know."

The simple phrase resonated with unspoken meaning. Steeling himself, Tony asked, "People think I killed her, don't they?"

Sue did not flinch. "People weren't talking much," she answered, then seemed to decide that this was not enough for a friend. "The ones who know you don't think that. I guess some people don't know what to think. I mean, it was just last Friday. . . ."

"It's unbelievable." Sam broke in, and Tony saw that his eyes were suddenly moist. "I keep thinking about that night. That we were at the maple grove, safe, while this was happening to you. That if I'd just made you two come with us, it never *would* have happened. . . ."

Sue gave him a look of silent remonstrance. But it did not matter: for hours on end, Tony had imagined himself and Alison safe in a parked car with these friends. So recently, he thought, there had been four of them; without Alison, it seemed that the organism that had been two couples had been maimed beyond healing.

"It's like a dream," Tony said at last. "Like maybe tomorrow I can talk to her about it . . ."

Sam folded his hands in front of him. At length, he said, "The papers say you told the cops you found her like that. . . ."

Tony touched his eyes. "Yeah."

"Was she . . . dead?"

"Yes."

Sam watched him, hesitant. "The cops came out to see me, Tony."

Tony felt leaden. "What did they want?"

"It was mostly about what happened that night, whose idea it was for us to split up." Sam fixed Tony with his clear blue eyes. "That prick Dana asked me if you two ever fought. I told him never."

Tony exhaled. "They know better, Sam."

Slowly, Sue nodded. "They talked to me too. They wanted to know if Alison ever confided in me about your problems."

Tony reddened. "Did she?"

"Yes."

Shame made Tony silent: Sue must know how much of that was about whether Alison would sleep with him. He could not bring himself to ask what Alison had said about him, or what Sue had told the police. Then Sue said quietly, "It's okay, Tony. It's confusing for women, that's all. She said you were never mean about it."

Tony could think of nothing to say. "Is there any way *you* can help things?" Sam asked. "Like, did you see anyone?"

Tony touched the bridge of his nose. "I *heard* someone in the park, I think running away from Alison's body. It was too dark to see him."

"That's all?"

"Pretty much." Tony drew a breath. "After that, I found her."

Sam leaned forward. "Look, Tony, maybe *we* can help you. It could be rough for you around school for a while. If Sue and I know what you told the cops, we can explain things, tell everyone your side of it. This can't be as bad as the papers made it out."

There had been much more talk, Tony realized, than Sue had wished to say. But he should have expected this in Lake City: there was never an unwed girl whose pregnancy was not followed avidly, to the moment of delivery, or whose prior "affairs"—swollen in numbers by her supposed teenage lovers—were not recounted by her peers. How much more, then, for a murder. All at once, Tony saw that his weakness was that the folk opinion of the town had rewarded him until now; aware of his own innocence, he had imagined that this good-will was his by right. Belatedly, he recalled Saul Ravin's warning.

"I'm not sure you guys can help me." Tony paused, reluctant to finish. "At least my lawyer thinks you can't."

Sam's eyes narrowed. "Why not?"

"He says I shouldn't talk to anyone. Even though I'm innocent, he thinks the cops will keep coming back to you, looking for stuff to hang me with. . . ."

"So what?" Sam looked and sounded defiant. "Who is this guy?"

"Saul Ravin." Suddenly Tony felt the need to defend his lawyer. "He's the best in Steelton."

"Some downtown lawyer who doesn't even live here? Christ, Tony, we're your friends. People will listen to us." Sam's voice rose in bewilderment. "What will they believe if you shut *us* out?"

Beneath Sam's concern, Tony thought, lay something prideful and proprietary—Tony was *his* friend; *his* relationship to Tony was shared by no one else. The knowledge that this was personal to Sam burdened Tony, and saddened him. Quietly, he said, "I don't need you to be my lawyer, Sam. I need you to be my friend." To soften this, Tony turned to Sue. "Saul thinks the best thing I can do is tell the cops what I know, and not spread it around to anyone else. The better the cops can do their job, he says, the better it is for me." Pausing, he saw Sam's look of frustration and doubt. "More than anything, I want them to find the bastard who killed Alison."

Glancing at Sam, Sue put her hand on his knee. Sam looked down at it, then at Tony, and slowly nodded. "We'll do whatever you want us to, pal. Or whatever this lawyer wants."

For an awkward moment, they were silent. Then Sue rose and came to Tony, taking his hand in hers. "We all miss Alison, Tony. But we still have you." Turning, she gave Sam an uncertain smile.

Sam stood, and then draped his arms around Sue and Tony, pulling them close. "Sure," he said. "Just like before."

TEN

"I slept with her," Tony said.

He sat with McCain and Dana in the same cubicle. But this time Saul Ravin was with him, the door was ajar, and Saul had asked McCain to quit smoking. Looking irritable, the detective fidgeted with a manila envelope.

"Why didn't you tell us that?" Dana asked.

Tony made himself consider his answer, carefully rehearsed with Ravin. As his lawyer had instructed, he looked straight at the detective. "Because I couldn't take in what was happening. All I could think about was that this was Alison's first time, and that it was nobody's business but ours." He paused, finishing quietly. "What happened to Alison wasn't real yet."

McCain scowled. "You seemed coherent to *me*—"

"If I were you," Saul broke in coolly, "I'd forget about using Tony's prior statement. Just like you forgot to call his parents, or his priest, or give him a Miranda warning, or even tell him where the bathroom was—"

"He wasn't in custody," McCain snapped.

"He's *seventeen*, Lieutenant." Saul gave the cop an amiable smile. "Let's not quarrel about this. If you want to base a murder prosecution on browbeating a teenager in shock, and then look like a jackass in front of God and the daily papers when some common pleas judge throws it out, that's up to you. I don't want to ruin your shot at fame."

McCain's scalded-looking skin grew redder than before, and he began playing with the flap on the envelope. But Dana never took his eyes off Tony. "When you say you slept with her, what does that cover?"

"What do you mean?"

"I mean, how did you do it?"

Tony glanced at Saul. His lawyer was studying the wall with a slightly bored expression. "In the back seat of the car," Tony answered.

"I mean *how*. Like, did she go down on you?"

Tony flushed. "No."

"Now we're getting somewhere. Did you come?"

"Yes."

"Where?"

"Inside her."

"Inside her?" Dana's voice was slightly derisive. "Is there some technical name for that?"

Once more, Tony thought of Alison, the way she had looked and felt. In a flat voice, he said, "Vagina."

"And she wanted that?"

"Yes." Tony's voice was tight. "Why don't you just ask me if I raped her. We didn't do it to give you thrills. . . ."

Beneath the table, Tony felt Saul's hand on his wrist. Leaning forward, Dana said softly, "There aren't many thrills in this one, Tony. At least not for me. So tell me, you do anything else with her?"

"No."

Slowly, McCain reached into the envelope. He drew forth three color photographs and laid them next to each other on the table, one by one.

"Not even this?" McCain asked casually.

In the photographs, Alison was lying on a table. Death had frozen her expression in the grimace Tony wished to forget, and now never would: mouth open in a silent cry of agony; tongue protruding slightly; flushed face;

burst blood vessels on her cheeks and eyeballs. What Tony had not seen in the yellow beam of John Taylor's flashlight was the irregular necklace of bruises on her throat, the imprints of a hand.

Tony's eyes shut.

When he opened them, Saul Ravin was studying the pictures with heavy-lidded impassivity. "I'm glad your job has *some* thrills," he murmured to McCain. "This must be a moment to remember. I know Tony will. But now you've had it, so you can put these away. What I'd appreciate is a copy of the autopsy report."

Dana stared at him. "When we bring charges, you can see it. Not before."

Saul turned to Tony with a look of deep compassion. "Do you have anything else to say to these . . . gentlemen?"

Tony fought for self-control. Then he gazed at the two detectives across the pictures that would become his enduring image of Alison Taylor, and said, "Just find the animal who did this—"

"Now *there's* an idea," Saul interjected. Rearranging the photographs, he slid them back in the envelope. "For example, a perusal of your police blotter in the *Lake City Weekly* shows that there are transients in Taylor Park at night. You file reports on the ones you stop. I'd pull those out, if I were you. Then I'd put out a teletype to every police force in the area, asking for reports on rapes and assaults. Not to mention strangulations." He stood abruptly and pinned the envelope to McCain's chest with the palm of his hand. "Tony's right," he told the red-faced detective. "You should find this guy. Unless you want more pictures to look at."

Saul and Tony sat on a park bench in front of City Hall.

The day had the clear bleached look of sunshine on a chill morning; there was a sheen of early frost, and the grass, no longer growing, was flat to the ground. When

Saul turned to Tony, giving a heavy sigh, it turned to mist between them.

"They wanted to see how you'd react," he said. "Maybe hoped you'd blurt something out."

Tony still felt numb. "I wanted to punch the fucker. But I couldn't even move."

"You did fine the way you were. Actually, you've got a lot of self-possession. Maybe they don't believe you, but now they know you'd be a problem for them as a witness. And that your prior statement is a problem too." Saul pulled up the collar of his black wool overcoat. "Anyhow, we're through with them. From now on, I deal with the county prosecutor's office. They're the ones who'll decide whether to charge you—Johnny Morelli, the head of Criminal, and, in a case like this, the CP himself."

Tony rubbed his eyes. "What were all the questions about? What we did, how we did it . . ."

Saul stared off into the distance, as if deciding how much to say. "It's a sex crime," he said at length. "We know that much for sure."

"Why for sure?"

For a moment, Saul frowned, and then he spoke quietly. "They're not mistaking first-time sex for rape, Tony. This creep did something to her. I don't know what—maybe he made her suck him first, maybe penetration was pretty brutal. That's what they're not telling us *or* the press. It's why I asked for the autopsy report and why they wouldn't give it up."

Mind reeling, Tony folded his hands in front of him, sickened. In that moment, all that he could think of was how much he hated the man who had done this to Alison—the things he knew too well, the things he could only imagine. Tonelessly, he asked, "Why not just say what happened to her?"

"Because whatever her body told them, only they and the murderer know. They want to keep it that way. Morelli's hoping the case will get better, making damn sure he doesn't step on it somehow." Saul ran his fingers through his hair. "I'll try to open his mind a little. Especially about the kind of person who strangled Alison and did whatever else to her that the police, and maybe the Taylors, are keeping to themselves. He could be a repeater, Tony. I should know—I've defended three of them. One of mine's out and running around, God help the world. And so may *this* one be.

"I'm going to ask my friend Morelli to access any sex-crime file he can, looking for anyone like that who was anywhere close to here this fall." Saul paused, eyes narrowing. "This morning Morelli wouldn't tell me a goddam thing. So we'll just have to wait them out."

"How long will that be?"

"As long as he wants. There's no statute of limitations on murder." Saul turned to him again. "I guess you know things won't be the same for a while. A lot of people live in a town like this because they want to feel safe, to keep their kids away from people they're afraid of for some reason—blacks, Jews, whatever. When a girl like Alison Taylor dies, it tells them they're not safe after all. That makes them fearful, and angry. Somehow you're going to have to ride that out. Are you prepared for that?"

"I'm not sure." In his despair, Tony thought of his mother: fearful as *she* was, the one person she always had believed in was Tony himself. Tony would be like Bill Bradley, she told him, the Princeton basketball player and Rhodes scholar she had read about in *Look* magazine—the one they already mentioned for President. Abruptly, Tony realized he had come to believe that he was special; that if he worked hard and lived right, the world would reward him. "Do you know," he asked Ravin, "what my mom used to tell me every night when I was a kid? 'Every day, with God's help, you can make your life better and better.'"

Ravin gave him a look of irony and understanding.

Not unkindly, he said, "Your mother probably didn't dwell on this small piece of history, but as late as this century, some of your Polish Catholic ancestors used to make their lives a little better by bludgeoning my Jewish ancestors to death. Many of those who led pogroms were frightened, of course—they thought that Jews were devils. But that's what inspired Grandfather Ravinsky to emigrate. In Poland, being an outsider could mean death.

"Suddenly you're not just Catholic, Tony, but a real outsider—someone people are afraid of. And yet *you* know that *you're* no different—only their perception is. Learn from that, if you can." Another faint smile. "Knowing that Sol Ravinsky's grandson will not let them make you the centerpiece of their personal pogrom."

Tony tried to picture his next weeks and months at school—perhaps charged with murder, perhaps just waiting. With real bitterness, he said, "Easy for you to call this a learning experience. What's to learn from those pictures, Saul? What's to learn from people thinking I did *that*?"

Saul drew a breath. "Maybe that the world is unfair, and not only to you. Maybe just to rely on yourself and not on a round of applause." He put a hand on Tony's shoulder. "What is it you want, Tony?"

"Now? For this to go away. For Alison to be waiting by my locker when I go back to school tomorrow."

"I mean before this. When Alison was alive."

It seemed like years ago, Tony thought. Finally, he said, "To go to Harvard. To get a scholarship—God knows I'll need it now. To live in a bigger place than this one."

Saul looked at him keenly. "What else?"

Tony's mind went blank; when the answer came to him, he was too embarrassed to say it aloud. "What is it?" Ravin asked.

Tony faced him. "I wanted to beat Sam Robb. To be Athlete of the Year."

Saul grasped Tony's shoulders, gazing intently into his eyes. "Then make sure that you do those things. Make *sure*." His voice softened. "Don't let this murderer—these cops, these people—take that from you too."

ELEVEN

"Killer . . ."

There were six seconds to play, and Lake City was tied with Riverwood at forty-two all. Both basketball teams were mediocre; by now, late January, the only thing at stake was pride. But the Lake City gym was packed: the home side because it was Riverwood, the Riverwood side because they wanted revenge. And now they had something to shout about.

"Killer . . ."

Tony Lord was about to shoot two free throws.

He stood at the foul line, the players in blue and red lining both sides of the basket, ready to fight for the ball if Tony missed the second shot.

Bending forward, Tony took a deep breath. The Riverwood chant grew rhythmic.

"Killer, killer, killer . . ."

Wiping the sweat from his eyes, Tony took the ball from the referee. He gazed at the basket, trying to ignore the crowd.

"Killer, killer, killer . . ."

After all, Tony told himself, he should be used to this.

For many at Saint Raphael, Tony had admitted his guilt; it was widely noted that he no longer took Communion, and his fellow parishioners assumed—correctly—that he had refused to make an act of contrition. His father was ashamed, his mother frightened for his soul. One Sunday after Tony had refused to go to Mass, Father Quinn came to see him.

He sat on the foot of Tony's bed; Tony stretched out, back to the wall, arms behind his head, gazing at his longtime priest with an indifference he did not feel. "You didn't give me much choice," Tony said. "If I believe what you told me that day, Alison may be burning in Hell this minute, for the terrible sin of *not* believing. So I've decided not to, either."

"Anthony," the priest said softly, "I advised you to pray for her soul—"

"And I do, Father. All the time."

Father Quinn blinked; beneath the red-gray crew cut, the seamed face for once looked, instead of severe, stricken by his failure to reach this boy who was his charge. For a moment, Tony felt sorry for him.

"Your parents," the priest ventured, "are worried for you."

"So am I. I may be charged with murder."

"For your *soul*, Tony. And because people who wish to believe in you are puzzled by your actions."

Tony felt the burden of this; he wanted to respond with ridicule, and found that he could not. Finally, he said, "But I can't please other people by returning to a church whose answers I won't accept. Even for my parents' sake."

The priest drew in a sharp breath, hollowing his gaunt cheeks. "Who are you to decide when the Church pleases *you*?"

That was right, the believing part of Tony felt: compared to his faith, he was insignificant, driven by the sin of pride.

"This defiance, Anthony, is in itself a sin."

Tony stood abruptly, opening his bedroom door, as much to protect himself as to dismiss the priest.

"Killer, killer, killer . . ."

Much of the school thought he was.

His return was eerie. Someone had painted flowers on Alison's locker; on his own locker, before he took it down, was Alison's yearbook picture, with "How could you?" printed across it. Timidly, some people offered sympathy; except for Sam, the basketball team simply tried to act like nothing had happened, as if the coaches had lectured them on how to handle this. Others avoided him, the more so as weeks passed with no other suspect, and Tony could not talk about the murder. He had been a leader, Tony realized, in part because he had never looked to see who was following—he had no gift for seeking sympathy, or explaining how much the death of Alison, devastating beyond anything he could express, had driven him deep within himself. Few could see how much pain he felt, or that it never left him.

"A lot of people think you're guilty," Mary Jane Kulas informed him. "Why are you being such a snob?"

She had chosen to confront him as he walked into the lunchroom. The attitude she took was of a friend expressing hard truths; her intensity and manner reminded Tony of a stage actress playing to the balcony. Her aquiline face was chiding, and her blond shag haircut bobbed as she spoke. "No matter what happened between us," she went on, "I'm telling you what the people who still care about you are afraid to say. Maybe they'll forgive you if you show you're sorry about how you've acted."

In his dismay, Tony saw this was her revenge. "How have I acted?" he managed to say. "All I've been doing is trying to keep my grades up, get the scholarship I need—"

"That's just it." Her voice became officious. "You're thinking about yourself, like you don't care what people think. To be honest, it makes them wonder."

All around them, Tony saw other students looking up from their lunch tables. Filled with humiliation and despair, Tony wanted to shout his innocence. Then he saw

Sue Cash, sitting with her girlfriends across the room, a silent message of encouragement in her eyes.

He turned back to Mary Jane. "Could you tell these people something for me?"

Mary Jane gave a nod. "All right."

He raised his voice just loud enough for the nearest table to hear. "Tell them that Alison was the best thing that ever happened to *me*, and that what happened to *her* was the worst. Ask them to be as understanding as you've just been."

It took a moment for the outraged hurt to register in Mary Jane's cornflower-blue eyes, and then Tony saw the deeper hurt he had caused her.

"Tony?" someone asked.

When he turned, Sue touched his elbow. "Can you have lunch with us?" Her smile, like her question, ignored Mary Jane.

Tony faced Mary Jane. "I'm sorry," he said softly, and turned away.

As they walked to Sue's table, she whispered to Tony, "That wasn't very nice."

"Mary Jane, or me?"

Sue glanced up at him. "You," she said with some asperity. "Mary Jane's a very caring person. From now on, you should try to be more like her."

Sue's unexpected sarcasm so relieved his tension that Tony laughed aloud. People turned again, perhaps wondering how Tony Lord could laugh. . . .

"Killer, killer, killer . . ."

He could not escape it. Dana would come to school to question someone about Alison or Tony, then silently appear at basketball practice, watching Tony from the stands. When Sam remarked on this, Tony did not say much; he felt Sam waiting for him to open up to him. But Tony did not wish to talk about how he felt—not just on Saul's advice but because it made him feel worse, even hopeless. This shadowed his time with Sam and

Sue. When they went to see *The Graduate*—which, as far as Tony could see, was about a girl who dumped her dorky boyfriend to run off with a lesser dork who'd been fucking her mother—Alison was as palpable as the empty space next to Tony, the void they never talked about but always felt. Tony had no heart for dating: even if he had felt like it, many parents would not have let their daughters go out with him, and any girl who did might have been chastised for sharing in Tony's callousness. He could not have borne this—the Taylors had done enough.

The *Lake City Weekly*, of which they were principal owners, demanded to know why Tony had not been charged with Alison's murder. The Taylors started the "Alison Foundation" to support public safety for girls; its meetings became a thinly veiled excuse to pressure the police and the county prosecutor to indict Tony Lord. Mrs. Taylor had once served on the school board; the day after Tony saw the Taylors slipping in to see the principal, he was summoned to his office.

"I know how hard this has been," Mr. Marks began, and adjusted his glasses. "All the more because you're playing basketball—as long as you do that, you're always on display."

"It helps keep me sane." Tony hesitated, wondering how to explain. "For a couple of hours, I can almost forget . . ."

"I understand." Mr. Marks shifted in his chair. "But aside from whatever problem you have with students, I'm sure you realize that some parents are worried about their daughters' safety. Unnecessarily, I'm sure, but you understand how these things get started. I wanted to counsel you about this."

Suddenly Tony saw where this was headed. "I'm innocent, Mr. Marks. Maybe you should counsel them."

Mr. Marks pursed his mouth. "You've been a topflight student—and citizen. But I wonder if what's best is for you to spend these last few months in another school. I can't help human nature, Tony, and I worry for you."

Silent, Tony stared at the principal, feeling the anger of this betrayal overtake him. "Aren't you worried that the scholarship committee at Harvard might think I'd done something wrong?" He reached across the desk, wrote Saul Ravin's telephone number on a piece of paper, and looked into the principal's face. "That's my lawyer's number, Mr. Marks. Give it to anyone who has a problem with me being here."

The principal had nothing more to say.

The next afternoon, his English teacher, Jack Burton, returned Tony's recommendation for the scholarship committee. Nothing had been written on it.

Tony stared at it, then at Mr. Burton. The bearded young teacher was apologetic, yet adamant. "I've struggled with my conscience, Tony. I believe in the presumption of innocence. But with this tragedy of Alison's death hanging over you, what can I say in good faith—or not say—about your character . . . ?"

For a moment, Tony was speechless; until Alison's death, Jack Burton had encouraged him, and Tony's grades had remained strong. "I'm not a murderer, Mr. Burton. I need this for college."

"For *Harvard*. There are other, cheaper colleges." Mr. Burton's manner softened. "Should the police clear this up for you, I'd be happy to give you a fine reference."

Jack Burton was considered a rising young teacher, Tony knew; he recalled that Burton had been recruited from John Taylor's alma mater, at the Taylors' request. Tony felt his voice tremble. "You promised me a reference, and the deadline's next week. You *know* that."

Burton flushed. "You caught me unprepared, Tony. Since then I've had time to reflect—"

"About what? Alison died four months ago."

When Burton did not answer, Tony felt the Taylors'

unspoken presence. "That's all I have to say," Burton said stiffly. "Perhaps others feel less strongly."

Coach Jackson, who taught Tony geography, filled out the form.

He handed it to Tony impassively. "I told them you knew where Hanoi is," he said. "They like that in the Ivy League. . . ."

But the lighter moments, like this one, grew farther apart. Each new day without relief from suspicion, Tony found that going to school was more of a battle, his studies a greater struggle. Christmas vacation had felt like a reprieve.

"Killer, killer, killer . . ."

As he always did, Tony bounced the ball three times. His mouth was dry, his palms were damp. His fingers felt like stubs.

"Killer, killer, killer . . ."

Somewhere in the stands, Tony knew, his parents watched in silent agony. Staring at the basket, he took one deep breath and launched the ball. Even before he saw its arc, he knew.

It missed the rim entirely.

The sigh from the Lake City stands was like air leaking from a tire. It was drowned by jeers, catcalls, raucous laughter. "Pretend the ball is Alison's neck," a Riverwood fan called out.

Tony bent, hands on knees. One more shot: whether Tony missed or made it, Riverwood would have six seconds to score the winning basket. Then—win or lose—Tony could leave the gym.

"Killer, killer, killer . . ."

He looked around him at everything but the crowd: the scoreboard, the pennant, the blue banner hanging from the wall, recording in white letters the names of those chosen as Athlete of the Year. Then he gazed at the basket. He made himself see nothing, hear nothing, until this was like practice, and he did not feel his sweat, his pulse, his heartbeat. But when he raised the ball to shoot, he could feel the stiffness in his fingers.

"Killer, killer, killer . . ."

Tony arched the ball.

Time seemed to stop. Then the ball hit the metal rim, caromed within, and softly settled in the net.

Forty-three to forty-two.

And then Riverwood had the ball, and Tony's man was by him, driving down the court for a last desperate shot. Sam Robb swooped from nowhere, stealing the ball. . . .

The buzzer sounded.

Sam rushed to Tony. Facing the Riverwood stands, he raised Tony's arm in triumph. Then, just as with that winning catch, Sam thrust the basketball aloft in one large palm as if it were a football. The beatific grin he gave the Riverwood crowd was to ensure that they could not miss it.

"Losers . . . ," he called out to them, and then the Lake City stands took it up.

"Losers, losers, losers . . ."

Feeling sick, Tony bowed his head, oblivious to the rising chant, the congratulations of teammates. Then he walked slowly to the locker room.

As he showered, a jubilant Sam burst in. "Unbelievable," he said in exultation. "Man, they love you."

Tony washed the soap from his eyes. "No. They don't. They just hate losing worse. God help me if that crappy shot hadn't fallen." When Sam looked deflated, Tony added, "Actually, you saved my ass. When that guy went past me, I was on Mars."

Sam put his hand on his shoulder. "Tony, you've got to enjoy what you can enjoy. Believe me, I *know* how you feel, but you can't let what happened to Alison ruin your whole life. I hate seeing you like this." Sam's eyes clouded. "I mean, someday they'll find the guy who did this, right? Then people won't suspect you anymore."

Was it that *Sam* had begun suspecting him? Tony wondered. "Maybe so," Tony answered. "Maybe not. But Alison will still be dead, and I'll still be different." He paused, trying to explain. "It does something to you. . . ."

Perhaps in acquiescence, perhaps in defeat, Sam nodded, dropping his hand. Tony dressed and walked to his car alone.

The parking lot was dark. Near his car, two figures waited; Tony thought of Sue and Alison, waiting on the night that Alison had died. Then one of the shadows stepped forward and became John Taylor.

Tony flinched. "You're a hero," Alison's father said. His face looked sunken, older. His breath was mist in the air.

"No." Tony felt his own voice shake. "I'll never be a hero."

John Taylor gripped his arm. The second figure, as slim as Alison, moved next to him. Her mother.

"I'm not going to hurt you," John Taylor said softly. "We just need to know what happened. For our own peace of mind."

Alison's mother was a taut line. "Tell us the truth," she urged. "Please. We won't go to the police."

Through his fear, Tony felt a strange bond between them that the Taylors could not know existed, this terrible sadness that had changed all three of them. More than Sue and Sam, far more than the other students whose pleasures and anxieties he no longer shared, these people understood him. Yet only he could see it.

"I want to know too," Tony said. "I want to know who killed her."

John Taylor's eyes narrowed in hatred. Stay clear of them, Saul had warned. Gently, Tony reached out and took the man's hand from his sleeve. "I'm sorry," he said to Katherine Taylor.

Turning, Tony made himself walk the few feet to his car. He wondered if John Taylor had his revolver; back tensed, he waited for a gunshot.

Nothing happened. As he drove away, trembling now, Tony saw John Taylor stiffly embrace his wife. They looked as devastated as they had in the first moments after Alison's death.

A week later, one of the Taylors' neighbors presented a petition to the school board, asking it to expel Tony Lord.

The meeting was jammed. As Tony watched, flanked by his parents and Saul Ravin, John Taylor spoke for his expulsion.

"I came here," John Taylor told the board, "not to share our grief. I am here because Alison would be here, if she had breath to speak for other Alisons."

Tony did not need to guess at the effect of her father's appropriation of Alison's voice against him; he could see it in the somber faces of the board. John Taylor paused to master his emotions. "Tonight you may hear much about the presumption of innocence. But it is *Alison* who was innocent, right to the moment I found the boy who she thought loved her bent over her dead body.

"*All* of our daughters are innocent. And what Alison would ask for them, what I ask, is that their parents never look into the face of a daughter who has had the last breath strangled from her."

Tony saw the school board president take off her reading glasses and close her eyes. Next to him, his own father and mother looked anguished.

"In the sleepless nights that have followed, and seem never to end, I keep returning to a single question: What kind of a boy would murder a young girl for the simple crime of trusting him?"

Voice breaking, John Taylor briefly stopped, then went on. "I needed to make sense of what was senseless. In desperation, I went to three psychologists and asked them the same question: What kind of boy would do this terrible thing? It is their answer which has brought me here."

In the stifling hush, the board was very still. "Because *that* kind of boy," John Taylor said, "will do *this* kind of thing again.

"I can't give you technical terms. But I can tell you what the experts say. That this kind of boy despises not one woman but *all* women. That this kind of boy is the slave of his own twisted impulses." For the first time, John Taylor turned to Tony Lord. "That this kind of boy considers inflicting torment like Alison's his right and pleasure or, as frightening, believes that his brutal murder of a young girl is just a momentary, uncharacteristic lapse of self-control. A 'lapse' which should not deprive him of whatever else he wants in life.

"This"—John Taylor still stared at Tony—"is a monster whose worst acts may lie ahead of him, and all of *us*."

Abruptly, Alison's father faced the board, his tone oddly informational. "If these monsters looked like monsters, we'd know to avoid them. But often they are plausible, even charismatic. That's how they get as close as this murderer got to Alison.

"I did not start this petition. I did not even sign it." Pausing, he touched the shoulder of his pale, stoic wife. "But our daughter's brutal death will have no meaning unless we learn that monsters must be labeled.

"We found Tony Lord with our daughter's body at one o'clock in the morning. We learned what kind of boy would do this." John Taylor raised his ravaged face to the board. "We did not learn in time to prevent our daughter's murder. You have."

Abruptly, John Taylor turned to his wife, who was weeping now, and sat with her.

The soundless void that followed, barely punctuated by nervous coughs, felt like death to Tony. Only the knowledge of his innocence kept him where he was.

For two more hours, Tony stayed there. Coach Jackson spoke for him, and then Saul. At the end, the matter was tabled; the police had brought no charges, Saul argued, and the board should not prejudge Tony Lord. But only the threat of a lawsuit, Tony knew, had saved him.

Afterward, Saul took Tony to Lake City's only bar. They sat in a dark corner, half listening to the jukebox, half watching two retired truckers shoot pool. The stocky owner, George Corby, gave Tony a Coke without asking what he wanted; George let the high school boys shoot pool here but, respecting their parents, did not serve beer to minors. The police knew not to worry about George Corby, just as George Corby knew to stifle his surprise at seeing Tony Lord tonight.

To Tony, the trip from near expulsion to the Alibi Room was surreal. "You saved my ass," he said to Saul.

Saul sipped his double whiskey slowly, like a man conserving his last glass of water. Finally, he said, "True. But I may not have done you any favor."

"I wasn't expelled—"

"I didn't expect you to be. But stripped of hearts and flowers, our argument was, 'Wait for the prosecutor to indict him.'" Pausing, Saul locked his eyes on Tony's. "That was all I had. But it's like a road map for John Taylor. Tonight he asked the board to give him a reason to believe that you're paying some sort of price. They didn't. Pressing the CP to indict you is the one thing he's got left. And you're all the *CP* seems to have."

When another Coke arrived, Tony did not touch it.

"Sorry," Saul finished softly. "You've had too few good nights for me to ruin this one. But I want you to be every bit as careful as you have been. Because my guess is this is nowhere close to over. And, in some ways, it may never be."

That night, Tony's nightmare began—the moment he found Alison dead, in terrible slow motion. In the dream, as in his life, Tony could do nothing.

TWELVE

By a seven-year tradition—its entire history—the annual membership meeting of the secret Lake City High School fraternity, the Lancers, took place in late March. It was held in Dave Suggs's basement: Dave's dad, Jack, as a thirty-second-degree Mason, had such a great respect for secret societies that he had helped Dave's older brother draw up the rules. At first, it had occurred to Tony that if the Masons were all that secret, no one would know what degree Jack Suggs was, or even that he was a Mason at all. But then he realized that, just as keeping Catholics out of the country club was a means of defining status for the Taylors and their friends, a secret society was no good unless those who were excluded were allowed to envy those selected. That the Lancers were discouraged by the school administration only made the honor of the thing more exciting, the pleasure of breaching secrecy a little greater. There was little the school could do.

The greatest honor was to be tapped as a sophomore. This had happened to both Sam and Tony. Distinction in sports and the consumption of alcohol were the Lancers' highest values: Tony excelled in one, and Sam was already a standout at both. At fifteen, Tony was pleased: it meant that the older boys thought he would be a star athlete and, as wise stewards, were securing the future prestige of the Lancers. But Sam was elated. It was another sign of the recognition he craved, and that he was worthy of his older brother, who had helped found the Lancers and whose memory now, as a dead war hero, was revered.

The induction ceremony consisted of reciting a secret oath and then igniting shots of whiskey with a Zippo lighter and drinking them until you barfed. Someone purported to know that Joe Robb had consumed eight shots; Sam drank nine, counting each one aloud, and then passed out from near alcohol poisoning. The fact that he had never vomited was still the subject of admiration.

Now, as seniors, Tony and Sam sat cross-legged on the basement rug with fourteen other members, eight seniors and eight juniors, the seniors nearest the ceremonial white porcelain bowl, which Dave's mother sometimes used for salads and which now was set amidst them. Each boy held a bag of marbles, ten white, ten black, of the type used for Chinese checkers. But here each marble had a talismanic power: with every candidate brought up for a vote, each Lancer went to the bowl with a marble in one closed fist, reached beneath the cloth, and dropped a marble in the bowl with a fateful plunk. This helped secure the sanctity of a process whereby a single black marble meant rejection—no Lancer could be pressured to approve someone whom he, after thinking on his obligations, deemed unworthy. Though the members were drinking, the dropping of marbles had such gravity that it proceeded in relative silence. That it was a Friday night, and thus the members' absence from the high school social scene would be duly noted by the envious and the hopeful, added to the sense of moment. The Suggses' basement lights were turned down low.

The first hour of the meeting was cordial. Though the *Lake City Weekly* had renewed its call for his indictment, the fact that Tony Lord was believed by many to have strangled Alison Taylor, while it made some boys uncomfortable, went unremarked: he was a Lancer, after all, and they had taken an oath of loyalty. Tony found this comforting—it was the closest he had come to understanding why adult males gather in clubs. And then Johnny D'Abruzzi brought Ernie Nixon up for membership.

Johnny was no politician. It was Tony who watched

the guys in back—Bobby Strob; Charlie Moore; Larry Saddler; Steve Sawback—and noticed brows furrowing in consternation, faces seeming to close. Glancing at Sam, Tony saw that he read this too.

Toward the end of his speech, Johnny seemed to feel it. He looked around him, his guileless brown eyes filling with resentment. Tony knew from playing football with him that Johnny was a simple mechanism; his emotional range included good cheer and great anger, but not subtlety. His voice gained timbre.

"All right," he said. "Ernie's a Negro. But I don't look at him that way. To me, he's a guy I play with, the one who cut down that linebacker in the Riverwood game. He plays hard, he's a nice guy, and this would mean the world to him. Besides, next year he may be the best jock Lake City has. Just like Tony Lord is now—or Sam."

"Doesn't look much like Tony," Charlie Moore retorted, and pretended to scrutinize Sam. "Doesn't even look like Sam. Well, the lips, maybe."

There were a few chuckles; Sam, whose full mouth girls remarked on favorably, gave a rueful smile. For Tony, this confirmed two things he had already guessed: that Ernie Nixon was in trouble, and that even the other Lancers were afraid to joke with Tony himself.

Johnny D'Abruzzi flushed. "That's why Ernie keeps to himself so much—he knows what people think." Around the circle, some looked receptive, and a few even nodded. "That's another reason to take him. To prove we're better than that."

In front, Terry Clark spoke up. "Ernie's got a good sense of humor, you get to know him. I don't know whether it's good enough to want to spend time with this pack of assholes. But if he's that crazy, it's okay with me—"

"*You* won't be here," Steve Sawback shot back. "But eight of us will. It should be up to the juniors if we want to take a Negro. . . ."

"So what's the problem with Ernie?" Johnny D'Abruzzi demanded.

Steve Sawback looked defensive. "I just don't believe in it, that's all."

For the first time, Sam spoke up. "No one's asking your sister to marry him, Steve. At least not until the initiation ceremony."

There were widespread chuckles; the effect of Sam's wisecrack, Tony saw, was to bring the guys closer by holding Steve's stubbornness up to mild ridicule. It struck Tony that Sam was becoming cleverer than Tony had noticed.

"Look, Steve," Sam went on, shooting a look at Charlie Moore, "just send your sister to Sue. She can explain everything."

Now Charlie Moore joined the laughter; without speaking on Ernie's behalf, Sam seemed to be defusing things. But the way Sam went about it made Tony think about what it must be like for Ernie just to walk into the cafeteria.

He had never considered this much and, now, pondered his position. It was, he decided, fairly simple: Ernie was no worse than the rest of them, and perhaps better than many. Helen and Stanley Lord considered Negroes en masse a pernicious nuisance—he recalled his mother viewing Martin Luther King's March on Washington primarily as a littering problem caused by people too lazy to pick up after themselves. But that had nothing to do with Ernie Nixon, the only black kid in Lake City High School. As Tony wondered whether it would do Ernie more good if he spoke or remained quiet, the unwelcome thought struck him that they had more in common than before.

The debate went on around him. "This is a free country," Dave Suggs was saying. He took a quick shot of whiskey. "What that means is we can associate with anyone we want to and keep out groups we don't want to. Like at the country club."

Like Catholics, Tony said to himself. He had considered himself fortunate that the Lancers overlooked religion; now, on the inside, he found himself uncomfortable. "What if some of us want to associate with Ernie Nixon?" he asked mildly. "Should people keep him out because he's a member of a group?"

Dave Suggs frowned. "I don't like Negroes."

"But did *Ernie* ever do anything to you?"

"No." From his scowl, Dave did not appreciate being questioned about articles of faith. "This isn't personal with Ernie. It's about Negroes."

"How many other Negroes do you know?"

Dave Suggs looked nettled now. "That's none of your business."

Tony shrugged. "I just hadn't seen any others around here lately. I'm sort of surprised I missed them."

Dave Suggs looked angry now; to Tony's left, Sam shot him a look of warning. Tony backed off.

There was a momentary silence. Tony found himself thinking not of Ernie but of himself. His life remained a no-man's-land—waiting for the police to indict him, hoping for Harvard to accept him, trying to get through each day, thinking of Alison at night. He did not know where he would be next year, in college or on trial, and the town did not know, either. The company of the Lancers meant more to him than he had known.

"Nigger," Steve Sawback said *sotto voce.*

When heads turned, Steve looked both spiteful and confused. "There," he snapped. "Somebody finally fucking said it: 'Nigger.' I want to be able to call them that anytime I want to. Why are we being such pussies about it—"

"Because I don't want you saying that around me." Johnny D'Abruzzi rose to his knees. "I think you oughta *stay* a pussy, man. I might get pissed off."

"All right." For the first time, Doug Barker spoke up. "Let's settle down here and talk like Lancer brothers."

Still staring at each other, Johnny D'Abruzzi and Steve Sawback fell silent. The others turned to Doug Barker, some taking the time to bolt a shot of whiskey, and the room calmed a little.

Doug Barker was their president. He was self-confident and serious, and knew his role. Owner of the town's insurance agency, his father was past president of the junior chamber of commerce, and it was the town consensus that Doug himself was marked for leadership in Lake City, perhaps even in the state. Among the Lancers he was an anomaly, selected for his soundness: Doug seldom joked, but he listened well and spoke with a measured gravity unusual in one so young. Each word carried its own weight; even Doug Barker's appearance—blondish crew cut, square face, sincere blue eyes—inspired trust. He leaned forward, ready to share his thoughts.

"I've been reading a book," he said. "About Branch Rickey. You know, the guy who integrated baseball by signing Jackie Robinson. I think it's something we can learn from."

As Doug Barker had grown to expect, the others listened. Tony felt hopeful: as he had always understood it, the lesson of Jackie Robinson was that baseball got over it, so perhaps Doug Barker would throw Ernie Nixon a life raft. "I don't think we're that far apart," Doug went on. "What we're talking about is whether we want to associate with Ernie Nixon as a person, and some of our brothers also aren't comfortable about a Negro member.

"*Here's* what Branch Rickey did. *Before* he ever signed Jackie Robinson, he had a detective follow him around for six months. *After* the detective came back and gave Jackie a clean report, Branch Rickey signed him up.

"Just like the Dodgers, this is a first for us. So what we can do is take turns keeping an eye on Ernie Nixon, see how he acts when he knows we're watching him. If he measures up, then we can bring him up for a special vote next January."

There was silence; taking in the proposal, people drank a little more. After a while, Dave Suggs nodded sagely. "That's good, Doug. It gives the brotherhood time to think."

Tony turned to Doug Barker. "I don't know how I'd feel," he said, "having people follow me around."

Doug looked vaguely displeased. "Maybe we *should* have," Dave Suggs snapped at Tony.

It took Tony a moment to catch the meaning of this. In the stricken silence, he turned to Dave Suggs. Softly, Tony answered, "Maybe you were, Dave."

"Jesus . . . ," someone murmured.

Tony and Dave Suggs stared at each other until Dave looked away. Still watching Dave, Tony said, "This lets people who don't like Negroes say they're just being careful. But whenever Ernie comes up for his four long months of Lancer brotherhood, he'll still be a Negro. We ought to face that now."

"I think that's right," Johnny D'Abruzzi said quickly. "What good does Ernie get out of four months? Why treat him different than anyone else . . . ?"

"Because he *is*," Steve Sawback snapped.

"That's just it," Doug Barker said to Tony in a tone of great patience. "There's a real division in the brotherhood. This lets us look Ernie Nixon over and keep ourselves together."

He said this with such calm assurance that it deadened the room. To no one in particular, Sam Robb murmured, "Too bad Jackie Robinson isn't with us. *He* could tell us what to do."

Watching Doug Barker try to ignore this, Tony smiled a little. Then Dave Suggs said, "I move to adopt Brother Barker's motion," and Doug Barker looked pleased again.

"Second," Charlie Moore put in.

The motion would carry, Tony knew. The quickest way to put this behind him was to vote yes. But, he supposed, the way to serve his conscience was to vote no and let consensus take its course.

"All in favor?" Doug Barker asked, and eleven hands followed, including all of those who had spoken against Ernie Nixon.

"All opposed?"

Five hands came up, including Sam, Tony, and Johnny D'Abruzzi. Ernie Nixon's friend Johnny gazed at the floor; Johnny was learning a lesson, Tony supposed, in Lancer brotherhood.

"Carried," Doug Barker said.

There was a stirring, a little disappointment, mostly relief. Tony still watched Johnny D'Abruzzi, who could not seem to look at anyone. Johnny seemed like a second victim; suddenly Tony felt dirty, complicit.

"The important thing," Doug Barker told them, "is to preserve the unity of the brotherhood when times aren't easy. Regardless of how we feel as individuals, I think as brothers we can all be proud of what we've done."

There were a few nods, a token nod from Johnny D'Abruzzi, still staring at the floor.

Perhaps that was it. Perhaps it was Ernie Nixon, or what had happened to Tony himself. All Tony knew, to his surprise, was that he did not belong here anymore.

He pulled the cloth off the salad bowl, stood, and emptied his bag of marbles. They rattled, bouncing around the bowl and out onto the floor. "I'd better start watching Ernie," he said. "Expect to hear from me next year."

Ignoring their astonishment, he headed for the basement steps, then thought of Dave Suggs. Turning, he said, "I'll walk real slow, Dave. In case you want to follow me."

Even as he reached the steps, a part of Tony wondered

at his anger. But a second part told him he had not quite said enough. When he turned again, it was to Doug Barker.

"By the way," he said to Doug, "you're the biggest asshole in this room. I thought I ought to let you know, as one Lancer brother to another. 'Cause nobody here is even close."

With that, Tony realized that he could never say enough, and left.

THIRTEEN

"Tony!"

It was Sam, following him out of the Suggses' house. Tony stopped by his car.

Sam's face was filled with worry and surprise. "Come on, man. Ernie Nixon's not worth it. You're walking out on friends."

Tony felt the energy seep out of him. His solitude was more than a matter of anger, or even of Alison; at some point he could not identify, Tony had stopped being like the others, and now he did not wish to try. He leaned against the lamppost, arms crossed. "What am I supposed to do?" he asked. "Go back and apologize? Would you?"

Sam stared at the ground. "No," he said finally. "Not me."

"Not me, either." Tony dug in his pocket for his car keys. "Look, get back in there. This isn't about you—"

"It's about *you*." Sam put his hands on his hips. "You're my best friend, and I've stopped even trying to figure out what the fuck you're doing."

Tony sat on the hood of his car, not looking at Sam. "I'm not *doing* anything," he said at last. "One night I found my girlfriend strangled to death, the next day most people think I killed her, and now my whole god-damned life is blown apart. Don't try to understand what that's doing to me, because *I* can't. All I know is that even when I'm with you and Sue, I'm alone."

"That's *your* fault, Tony."

Tony turned to him. Softly, he said, "Go back there, all right?"

Sam was silent for a while. "No," he answered with quiet stubbornness. "I'm coming with you. You're still my best friend, and I've got some whiskey in the car."

Through the fog of his emotions, Tony realized that he felt grateful. "Okay," he said. "If I'm going to be alone, it'll be better if you're there too."

They sat on the edge of the Lake City pier, passing the bottle between them. Tony caught himself imagining what this would be like if their lives, from the moment of the winning touchdown until now, were the same as before. Then Sam said, "It's been a long time, pal," and Tony knew he was thinking this too.

The night was a riot of stars. Tony leaned back on his elbows, looking up, feeling the lake breeze on his face. The more he drank and watched the stars, the more the world seemed as it had been. He would have been happy to stay here, suspended in this moment, and have the morning never come.

"After we get out," Tony asked, "what are you going to do?"

Sam considered this. "Go to college around here. Stick with Sue." He paused for a moment. "Know something? What happened to Alison changed me too. I just want normal. I want to be where people know who I am. Where they already know what to think about me."

Never had Tony heard Sam express his insecurity this openly, and the wish for convention conflicted with his wilder side. But somehow this seemed more than whiskey-soaked musings on a warm spring night. For a long time, lying stretched out on the pier with the bottle between them, they said nothing else. Then Sam asked quietly, "Are you ever getting over her?"

There was something tentative in the question, as if Sam feared the answer. In a flat voice, Tony answered, "Not if I go to jail."

"I mean *inside*, Tony."

For Tony, the stars vanished. He saw Alison lying beneath him, then Alison as he had found her, the Alison of the photographs. "No," he answered. "I'm not getting over her."

Sam rose to his elbows. "*I* could, Tony. I mean, I'd have to treat it like something that happened to somebody else." He turned to Tony, as if to reach him. "*You're* not any different now—you're still the same guy, you can have the same life. What's different is how you *feel*. For your own good, you've got to find some way to change that. Or all you'll be is the guy that some people think killed Alison Taylor."

Tony put down the bottle. "You weren't there, Sam. Don't talk about what you'll never get on the smartest day of your life."

Sam lay back. "You don't think I even miss her, do you? Sure I gave her shit sometimes, because she thought she was special. But she was. I knew it, and so did everyone else. I still think about her. . . ."

"When *you* think about her," Tony snapped, "you're a fucking volunteer. She was *my* girlfriend, not yours. . . ."

"She *was* your girlfriend." There was a new tone in Sam's voice, somewhere between regret and bitterness. "Because of that, you and I aren't the same. I don't want it that way."

Tony still felt taut. "I don't, either. . . ."

"So why has it made *us* different? If it happened to

me, whatever else, I'd be damn sure it didn't change us. Because you're important to me, all right? No matter what happens, or what you do, you're *important*."

Tony felt the whiskey in him; the conversation had taken on too many shades and tones. He righted himself, sitting cross-legged as Sam stretched on his elbow. "Sam," he said, "you're the closest friend I've got. But I'm not sure I know what the fuck you're talking about."

Sam gazed at the railroad ties beneath them. "Don't you?"

"I don't think so."

Tony watched Sam search for words. "It's like those other guys back there—the Lancers. They know you, you know them. But not really. I mean, one of them could die, or you could die, and everyone's sad and then gets over it." Stopping, he glanced at Tony, hoping to see comprehension.

Coolly, Tony asked, "Are you talking about Alison?"

Sam sat up. "For once can you get off Alison? This is about our friendship and what it means—"

Cutting himself off, Sam stood abruptly and walked to the end of the dock, watching the black lake swirl below as it smacked against the iron legs of the pier. Tony still sat cross-legged, sorting through his emotions—confusion, anger, the fierce desire not to lose this friend, so much a part of him. The next swig of whiskey felt raw in his throat; watching Sam, a solitary figure on a pier projecting into dark water, he felt they were alone at the end of the world.

Sam turned to him. "This is wrong, Tony. Because it doesn't matter."

"What doesn't matter?"

Sam walked slowly back to where Tony sat and lay next to him, looking up at the stars with his hands behind his head; something about this made Sam seem open, vulnerable. "Nothing matters," Sam repeated softly. "It wouldn't matter to me if you'd killed her."

Suddenly Tony felt cold. " 'Wouldn't'? Or 'doesn't'?"

For a moment, Sam was quiet. "Wouldn't. Doesn't. It's all the same to me."

"Are you asking if I killed her, Sam?"

Sam turned to him now. "Did you?"

Tony stared at him. It took all his effort just to say, "What do *you* think?"

Sam's gaze was silent, fearless. "I've stopped thinking about it."

All at once, Tony felt the months of pain and anger cut loose. He grabbed the neck of Sam's T-shirt and jerked him upright, his right fist cocked in the air. He could feel Sam's breath on his face. "What do you fucking *think*, Sam?"

Sam made no move to defend himself. His eyes looked into Tony's with an odd calm. "That they don't have anyone else yet. And that it doesn't matter to me."

Blood pounded in Tony's head. Hoarsely, he said, "It matters to *me*," and let go of Sam's T-shirt.

The back of Sam's head struck the wooden pier. He lay there, squinting from the pain, still looking up at Tony.

Tony almost whispered, "You should have stayed with the people you're going through your fucking life with."

Standing, he walked quickly down the long, narrow pier. The echo of his own footsteps followed him.

The next afternoon was unseasonably warm. Tony sprawled on the chaise longue in back, wearing gym shorts and no shirt. He had no desire to go anywhere, to do anything, to see anyone. The one phone call he had made was to leave a message with Saul Ravin's answering service, to ask Saul where things stood. He did not go to the mailbox because, today, he could not stand to lose the hope of Harvard; for the last five months, he had lived in fear that nothing—his grades, athletics, references, last summer's strong interview—would matter if the admissions committee in Cambridge learned of a murder in a small Ohio town. If he could have stayed in this house until the next change happened to him—going to some college, or through a murder trial—he would have. On waking that morning, he had discovered what it meant to be truly alone.

"Tony?"

Startled, he realized that he had not heard Sue walk across the lawn. He moved his feet, and she sat on the corner of the chaise longue. She did not say anything; at first, it seemed that she had merely come to sit with him.

"I guess you heard," Tony said.

Sue turned to him, eyes filled with questions. "Just that you were drinking and fought—sometimes it's hard for Sam to explain himself. But I know he was embarrassed by whatever happened."

Tony felt his anger return. "I don't see why. All he did was ask me what everyone else wants to know."

Sue's pretty face was unusually grave. "If Sam asked you that, it was stupid. He knows you better."

Tony lay back on the chaise; though the person he saw was Sue Cash, the girl he had always liked, some perverse desire to break all ties pushed him on. "So you came to clean up his mess."

The first trace of resentment crossed Sue's face; he watched as she recaptured her patience. "If you give Sam time, he'll apologize. I don't think he wants to be without you."

"Fine," Tony said caustically. "Then tell him I didn't kill Alison, and that if he tells me where *he* was that night, we can just go right on like the whole thing never happened."

Sue flushed and then gazed at him. "Sam was with *me* that night, remember? We wish you had been too, not just for Alison. Maybe Sam more than anyone."

"Sorry, I forgot. It's just that Sam's missed out on so much already, like wondering which person is worrying about who he'll murder next. At least having his 'best friend' ask if he strangled Alison would give him the flavor of the thing." Tony paused, then finished in a tone more indifferent than he felt: "I'll even tell him that the answer doesn't matter."

Sue regarded him for a moment, quiet. "Sam has a lot of feelings, Tony—for you more than almost anyone. But he gets confused about how to say that."

Tony felt his surge of temper become something that, as far as Sam was concerned, felt colder and more certain. "It's no good," he said at last. "I can't help how I feel about what Sam asked me, or what it means that he did."

"Then who will you talk to?"

Tony shrugged. "Who cares?"

"I do."

She said this simply. As if it were obvious, a commonplace.

"You're Sam's girlfriend," Tony said.

Sue looked disconcerted, then annoyed. "That was stupid too. How about 'You're my friend, Sue.' How about 'I know you miss Alison too.' Or maybe just 'I don't blame you for whatever dumb thing your boyfriend says. . . .'" She stopped herself, "*I* know you didn't kill Alison. You never could have."

Tony looked at her. She had never said this to him directly: to Tony, the way she said it now bespoke a deep feminine conviction that was neither about fact nor about raising his morale—that he was innocent was simply something Sue Cash *knew.*

For the first time, she was smiling a little. "You don't have to fight with me too, all right? I'm just me."

Tony studied her face, so familiar and suddenly so welcome. "How long have I known you?" he asked after a time.

Sue looked skyward. "Three years, anyhow. Since sometime in ninth grade . . ."

"Actually, I remember seeing you my first day at high school. You were wearing a pink-striped dress."

Sue nodded. "It was my favorite. The night before, I made my mom iron it." She smiled at him, dimples showing. "I was waiting for someone to say how pretty I looked."

Tony imagined the fourteen-year-old Sue, filled with anxiety and anticipation, watching her mother iron a pink-striped dress. "You *were* pretty," he said.

Sue looked down—still half smiling, eyes serious now—and then gave Tony's hand a squeeze. It was an impulsive, affectionate gesture, Tony thought, so typical of Sue. Sam was luckier than he deserved.

"You're a good person, Sue."

"Why do people always tell me that?" she said in mock complaint. "What if I wanted to be really, really wicked?"

"If I were you, I'd start by leaving town."

This seemed to make her thoughtful, though the smile lingered. They sat together in silence.

"Tony!"

This time it was his mother, hurrying across the yard with an envelope. "Mail for you," she said. "From *Harvard*."

Tony could see the anxiety on her face; for all that she could annoy him, he knew that what she was feeling was not much different from the sudden, clenched-fist tightness in his stomach. As Helen Lord slipped the envelope into his hand, waiting expectantly for him to open it, Sue looked from Tony to his mother. "I should go," she said.

Tony shook his head, mute, already fumbling with the cream-colored envelope. He barely felt his mother and Sue watching as he read the first line.

We are pleased to inform you . . .

Tony kept reading until he reached the word "scholarship."

"God . . ."

"What is it?" his mother asked.

"I'm *in*." He looked up at her in wonder. "They gave me a *scholarship*, Mom. I can go. . . ."

It was the thought of the county prosecutor, not Helen Lord's hug, that cut off his elation. But he let her enjoy this; he could feel all her hope, all her fears, in the fierceness of the way she held him.

"Okay, Mom," he said in a husky voice. "Please, I can't breathe. . . ."

His mother backed away, giving a shaky laugh. She still looked as if she did not believe it. "It's so wonderful. Sue, isn't this *wonderful*?"

Sue smiled. "Yes. It is."

Helen Lord took the letter from Tony's hand. "I'll go tell your father . . . ," she began, and then hurried to the house, calling for him. Tony was far too moved to smile at this.

"Well," Sue Cash said softly. "You made it."

"Yeah. I made it. At least so far."

Smiling, Sue shook her head, as if refusing to believe that anything would stop him now. Half facetiously, she looked to see if Helen Lord was there, and then kissed Tony softly, warmly, on the mouth. When she leaned back, her eyes were filled with pleasure for him.

"There," she said. "Now I've kissed a Harvard man."

That evening, Saul Ravin returned Tony's call.

"I got into Harvard," Tony told him.

"Hey, Tony, that's great." For that moment Saul sounded genuinely pleased, and then the good humor faded from his voice. "I guess you called for a status report."

"Yeah. Can you tell me anything?"

"Not much. 'No change I know of' is about the best I can do."

There was a reserve in Saul's tone. Since Alison's death, Tony had become more sensitive to nuance, particularly when that left unsaid was bad. "What is it?" he asked.

There was a long silence. "They've still got the coroner's report under lock and key. But what's more unusual is they won't even tell me anything about it. It's been nearly five months now."

Tony felt his apprehension grow. "What does that mean?"

"I'm not sure." In the silence, Tony imagined Saul exhaling. "Maybe that there's something unusual in the report itself. I'm afraid they're still thinking about how to trap you, not clear you."

"Is that the only reason you think so?"

There was another silence. "All right, Tony . . . I don't want to worry you, but I guess you've earned the right to be treated like an adult.

"There's a meeting on Thursday. Morelli, the county prosecutor, *and* the Taylors. The pressure's on—you've seen the local paper. Morelli won't tell me what, but they seem to think they have more on you."

Tony felt the excitement of his letter from Harvard come crashing down around him. "Isn't there something we can do? At least find out what it is?"

"Not really . . . at this meeting, we don't get a vote. But I'll take a last run at Morelli." Saul's voice was softer now. "All you can do, Tony, is what you've done too damn much of: wait."

FOURTEEN

With his acceptance to Harvard, all that remained for Tony—were it not for Alison's murder—would have been the hope of winning Athlete of the Year. But for the five days between his conversation with Saul and Thursday evening, when Saul would report back, the specter of prosecution became Tony's sole obsession.

He could not shut it off. In the middle of physics class, he imagined calling the Taylors, begging them to believe him innocent. Reviewing that night—as he had every day since Alison's death—Tony again tried to imagine who could have done this. He could not think of anyone in town: the fact that Alison and he had walked through the park was a fluke, caused by the frosted windows of his car, and someone watching her home would have waited by the driveway, not the back porch. Tony had seen her in the porch light; no one else could have known she would come out again. This left a murder of haunting randomness—a transient, near the grove of trees by happenstance. But the night had been cold, and the scene of Tony's imagining required three people in the dark: two lovers unaware, a stranger so malevolent that, overhearing Alison and Tony, he had decided to lie in wait for her. None of this was plausible; nor, Tony was quite certain, could anyone have followed them to the park. Which brought Tony face-to-face with the conclusion he long ago had reached, all the more terrible because of Thursday's meeting: that if he were the police, or the Taylors, he would believe that Tony Lord had strangled his girlfriend.

On Thursday afternoon, Tony was scheduled to pitch against Stratford. The game crept up on him, almost unnoticed; when Tony walked on to the field, tired from a night without sleep, the cop Dana was watching from the bleachers.

From the first warm-up pitch, Tony wondered if Dana would arrest him.

Johnny D'Abruzzi was the catcher. Tony entered a twilight state of consciousness; he threw the ball to Johnny, caught it, threw again. It was as though he and Johnny were in a tunnel; Sam was playing first, as always, but Tony barely saw him. Some superstitious part of Tony felt that if he pretended Dana was not there, the detective would not come for him.

For the first six innings, Tony did not talk to anyone, and Dana did not move.

The game was nothing to nothing. Tony was not an overpowering pitcher; his success depended on throwing where Johnny held the catcher's mitt, low and at the edges of the plate. Doing this again and again was all that kept Tony from going crazy; his focus was so complete, so desperate, that he had seldom pitched so well. He ignored the chatter of his teammates, their encouragement between innings; like Dana, they were part of a larger reality he needed to ignore. He did not give a damn about the team.

When Sam hit a home run in the last half of the sixth, crossing the plate with the nonchalance that comes from deep self-pleasure, all that Tony thought of was that in one more inning the game—his last protection—would end, and Doug Dana would still be waiting.

"Are you all right?"

Johnny D'Abruzzi was standing over him. Only then did Tony realize that everyone else had rushed from the bench and begun to pummel Sam. The catcher gave him a puzzled look, then glanced at Ernie Nixon, their right fielder, standing at the edge of the celebration.

"Sorry about the Lancers thing, Tony. I guess I started a lot of trouble."

"Not for me."

His tone was so indifferent that Johnny looked troubled. "One more inning," he said awkwardly, and went to join the others.

In the seventh inning, Tony took the mound again.

He was aware of his surroundings—the bleachers filled with spectators; the factory-like high school to one side; the backstop and foul screen behind Johnny D'Abruzzi; the green wire fence behind the outfield—in the same way an actor might be aware of the artificial backdrop of a play. Then, at the edge of his vision, he saw someone move. He did not need to look to know it was Doug Dana.

As the first hitter stepped into the batter's box, Dana appeared behind Johnny D'Abruzzi on the other side of the foul screen. For Tony, it was like double vision—Johnny, the means of his escape; Dana, the symbol of his fears. And then Alison's father was standing next to Dana.

Together, they watched Tony through the screen. They must already know the county prosecutor's decision, Tony was certain. Only Tony, unable to reach his lawyer, did not.

The home plate umpire crouched behind Johnny D'Abruzzi, ready to call balls and strikes. Like an automaton, Tony focused again, threw his first pitch.

"Ball one," the umpire called. Turning, Dana said something to John Taylor.

Tony walked the batter on four pitches, then walked the next.

"Come on, Tony. Just get it over."

Sam's voice.

Fuck them. Fuck them all.

Tony's third pitch, a slow curve, fooled the batter so completely that he did not swing until the pitch was by him.

"Strike three."

Tony kept staring at Johnny D'Abruzzi's mitt, his salvation. The next batter swung at the first pitch, a low fastball.

The ground ball bounced toward Tony. It surprised him; so total was his focus on pitching that he had forgotten to crouch for grounders. He snagged the ball off balance, looked back at the runners, and threw the batter out at first.

One more out.

"Killer . . ."

The Stratford crowd was small, the catcall ragged, with no gym to echo it. But Tony flinched; against his will, he looked through the foul screen at John Taylor.

Silent, Alison's father nodded. Not at Tony, but at the word, repeating now.

"Killer . . ."

Her father must be here to watch Dana take him in.

Clayton Pell, the Stratford clean-up hitter, stepped up to the plate.

"Tony!" Sam shouted.

Startled, he turned and saw that the Stratford runners were stealing second and third. Tony started to throw toward second. Years of practice stopped him; all that he could do was risk a wild throw—the runners were almost there. Tony had forgotten them.

From the Stratford stands came jeers and laughter.

"Time out," Tony heard Sam call.

Sam came running up to him, his eyes filled with disbelief. "What the fuck are you doing, man? We've got a one-run lead."

Tony put his hand on Sam's shoulder, trying to control his voice. "Just tell me it doesn't matter to you. That would help a lot."

Sam's face became suffused with blood. His voice was tight when he spoke. "This *does* matter. I'd still like to have some respect for you."

He turned his back abruptly and trotted back to first.

"Play ball," the umpire shouted. Across the diamond, Tony stared at Sam; when he willed himself to face the plate, Dana and Alison's father were studying him, with their arms folded, as if watching his conscience reveal itself at last.

"Killer . . ."

At the plate, Clayton Pell waggled his bat in a left-handed stance, a study in controlled impatience. Tony's head pounded with fury.

When Johnny called for a curve ball, his mitt held low and inside, Tony shook his head in defiance.

Through the catcher's mask, Johnny gave a look of bewilderment. Then he signaled for a fastball, away from Pell's strength.

Tony reached back and threw the ball as hard as he could down the middle of the plate.

Clayton Pell's swing had a strange beauty. Uncoiling smoothly, his arms extended, it caught the ball on the fat part of the bat. Tony did not have to watch it. Only at the last minute did he turn, see Ernie Nixon in right field sprinting to the fence, then watching as the ball bounced twenty feet beyond his reach. A full-throated cry rose from the Stratford stands.

The rest was fragments: the last Stratford batter, out on a streaking liner that Sam Robb speared as it headed for right field; the silence on the bench during the last half inning no one had wanted, Tony Lord's unwelcome gift; the desperate two-out rally, when Ernie Nixon and Johnny D'Abruzzi scratched out hits. Then, in a haze, Tony struck out on four pitches.

It was over. Tony sat hunched on the bench, waiting for Dana. A few teammates came by; Tony was faintly aware of Sam, looking back at him as the rest of their team left the field.

When Tony turned at last, Dana and John Taylor were gone.

* * *

Tony was still there, a half hour later, when Ernie Nixon wandered out in street clothes.

Ernie sat down next to him. "Tough luck," he said.

Tony turned to him. He could not remember ever talking to Ernie alone, or even studying him for the simple purpose of doing that. Now it struck him that Ernie had a somewhat pensive, philosophical appearance: his one remarkable feature—startling green eyes—suggested genetic ironies that Tony had never contemplated. "I tried to do something I can't," he answered at length. "Blow the ball by the other team's best hitter. No luck about that."

Ernie did not answer. Together, they watched the baseball field; without players, it had the stillness of a photograph. After a time, Ernie said, "I heard about the fraternity. You didn't need to do that."

Tony felt surprised, then uncomfortable. "It was more about me than you. I just couldn't stand how stupid it was."

"It's how they are, man. It's just how they are."

The sentence held a certain bitter fatalism. For reasons that Tony did not fully understand, it made him want to talk. "You know what really happened today?" he said. "I thought Dana had come to arrest me."

Ernie turned to him, watching his face.

"I didn't do it, Ernie. Someone else was there that night."

Ernie cocked his head, green eyes narrowing. "Did you see anyone?"

"No. But I *heard* him."

Ernie propped his chin on folded hands, gazing at the field. "Lots of people in that park. Lots of places to hide. I probably know most of them."

The offhand comment surprised Tony, then disturbed him. He had never explored the park; since Alison's murder, he had not gone near it.

"Can you show me?" he asked.

* * *

The two of them stood in the park, looking through the grove of trees at the Taylors' Gothic roofline. It was late afternoon; for a moment, he imagined Alison's mother, preparing to serve dinner to three people and an empty chair. A dull sickness settled on him.

By unspoken consent, they turned and walked from the grove.

For the first time in Tony's memory, the park seemed exotic, haunted—clusters of oak trees crowding each other where their seeds once had fallen close together; a hedge of vines and thistles, taller than both of them, extending from the grove that marked the Taylors' lot to circle the front of the park. As they approached, Tony saw that the hedges were thickets—twisted, tangled, green with new spring growth.

Silent, Ernie reached out and pulled back a clump of vines.

Behind it was a hollow space hidden amongst the vines and branches—a matted patch of grass, sunless and dark, like a cave. On the grass were an empty cigarette pack, cigarette butts stained by dampness, the torn foil from a condom. Ernie gave a soft laugh.

The furtive traces of a human presence unsettled Tony. "How did you know to find this?"

"My brother showed me, when I was fourteen. Summers, we'd sneak out of the house at night, pretend to be commandos, and go different places. Some nights we'd sleep in the old graveyard, other nights we'd come here." He paused, remembering. "Pretty soon, we figured out we weren't the only people out here late at night. There were bums, people fucking—lately even a few guys selling marijuana. Lot more folks hitching through town these days, it seems like, college-age kids a lot of them. The cops know all that—they come through in patrol cars at two, three in the morning, sometimes sniffing around with flashlights. Ducking the cops was the best part of it. That, and wondering who else was out there."

Tony found himself staring at the crushed cigarette pack; though Saul had mentioned transients, this evidence of a second, nocturnal park, which had once surrounded him and Alison, disturbed him deeply. "There are a lot of places like this," Ernie said. "But people don't know to find them."

Tony turned to him. "Ever come out here alone?"

"Now and then. Until she died." Ernie let go of the vines in his hand, covering the hiding place. "It was lonelier when my brother left. But some nights it was like being the secret king of Lake City. For a few hours, no one could see me, and I could do any damn thing I wanted." He gave a final ironic smile. "Midnight to five, it was the one country club in town that let in blacks. But it wasn't exclusive—there are a lot of people in this park who could've killed her. The cops know *that* part too. *She* must have known it."

"Alison?"

"Sure. Even when I was a kid, and my folks would bring Gerald and me here for picnics, I'd see her playing here all the time." Ernie's voice grew softer. "You know, with her friends."

The last phrase, Tony felt certain, carried a secret, perhaps unconscious meaning—that it had not then been in the order of things, social or racial, that Alison Taylor and a black boy be friends.

"I miss her a lot," Tony said simply.

After a time, Ernie nodded; the gesture was oddly reluctant. "She seemed nice. But if you're me, you never really know what that means. I mean, are you supposed to think she wants to go out with you?"

Tony knew the answer. He had seldom imagined Ernie Nixon other than as a teammate or a social curiosity; now he sensed what lay behind Ernie's reserve—some people were nice, others weren't, but all of them saw you for what, in their minds, you were and would always be.

Against his will, Tony once more gazed at the Taylors' backyard, thought of what he had found there, and turned away.

Silent, they walked across the grass to Tony's car. The park was unpeopled, quieter than Tony had remembered. Only when they got to the car did Tony speak again. "I'm sorry about the Lancers. But it really *is* stupid."

Ernie did not answer for a while. "Maybe. But 'stupid' is something other people get to decide."

Tony turned to look at him, and then curiosity overcame self-consciousness. "Why did your parents ever come here?"

Ernie's green-eyed gaze combined irony with a certain tolerance. "Probably for the same reason your parents did," he answered. "Lake City's a great place to raise kids."

"What happened?" Tony asked. He held the telephone tightly, wishing that he could see Saul Ravin's face.

"I'll put it this way, Tony. From what Morelli tells me, John Taylor went away mad. So did the police."

"They're not charging me?"

"Not yet. Morelli's still against it. He's a smart and principled man, educated by your friends the Jesuits, and capable of placing justice above politics."

"Then what was this 'new' evidence?"

"I'm not sure, except that it's something they found on the body which squares with your blood type—whether it's blood different from Alison's type, or hair, or something else altogether, they won't say. But I did point out to Morelli that sixty percent of the populace has the same blood type as yours, so that all he could say is that you weren't ruled out."

"Did you talk about anything else?"

"I told him I thought you were innocent. It seemed to leave him speechless."

"Why?"

"I don't know." Tony heard the first trace of humor in Saul's voice. "I guess because I've never said that to him before."

For a moment, Tony himself did not know what to say. "Thanks, Saul . . ."

"Don't thank me. Morelli knows what a prosecution would do to you. He's got the rest of your life to put together a case."

Tony felt himself slump, torn between relief and this seemingly endless shadow. "At the baseball game," he said, "Dana and Alison's father were there, watching me. I spent the whole game thinking Dana would arrest me once it was over."

For a moment, Saul was quiet. "Then I'm sure that's why they did it—to make you stew in your own guilt. As I say, they're frustrated." His voice turned apologetic. "I should have told you, Tony. What would happen is Morelli would call me, and I'd take you in myself. This is bad enough without your having to see ghosts."

"Jesus . . ."

"So that's it. You're not going to be busted tomorrow, or the next day." Saul sounded tired now. "We can all go back to watching television."

Tony gave a short laugh. "Not me. I'm catching up on my sleep. . . ."

"Haven't you heard?"

"What?"

"Martin Luther King's been shot, Tony. He's dead."

Tony was stunned. "God, I'm sorry. . . ."

"So am I. There'll be hell to pay for this, and for years. It's a loss for every decent person in this country." With that, Saul got off.

Tony went to the basement, turning on the television. He did not tell his parents what had happened.

On the screen, Robert Kennedy, campaigning for President in Indianapolis, stood before a silent crowd in a black neighborhood. Many in the crowd seemed to be weeping; Kennedy spoke spontaneously, near tears himself:

"Martin Luther King dedicated his life to love and to justice for his fellow human beings, and he died because of that effort. . . .

"What we need in the United States is not division; what we need in the United States is not hatred; what we need in the United States is not violence or lawlessness, but love and wisdom, and compassion toward one another, and a feeling of justice toward those who still suffer in our country, whether they be white or they be black. . . .

"So I ask you to return home, to say a prayer for the family of Martin Luther King, Jr., that's true, but also to say a prayer for our own country, which all of us love, a prayer for understanding and compassion. . . ."

Listening, Tony discovered that he, like Robert Kennedy, was deeply shaken. For a moment, he thought to call Ernie Nixon, to say that he was sorry for what happened. But that would have been presumptuous, Tony thought, even foolish. Ernie Nixon lived in Lake City; his life tomorrow would be much like his life yesterday. Martin Luther King had little to do with Ernie Nixon.

FIFTEEN

Fumbling with the studs to his rented tuxedo, Tony had steeled himself for a senior prom that, a week before, he had sworn not to attend.

"At least think about it." Sue's brown eyes were serious. "It's like you're running away. . . ."

"As fast as I can. From all the extra chaperons they'd need to make sure the girls make it home alive." His voice rose in irritation. "Sue, you're the homecoming queen. I'm a murderer."

Sue looked down. Quietly, she said, "Only if you act like one. If you go, people will respect that." She gazed up at him again. "How are you going to feel that night, watching TV by yourself? Any better?"

Despite himself, Tony was suddenly touched by her hope, forlorn as it was, that at least this moment of his senior year would be a little like the yearbook picture she might once have imagined for the four of them. More gently, he said, "I can't bring a date, Sue. While you're with Sam, getting your prom picture taken, I'll be alone in a corner—"

"*I'll* dance with you, Tony."

For the first time, Tony smiled. "Do you plan on sedating Sam? He hasn't dropped by to encourage me to go—"

"But he'll support you." Sue's voice took on an unwonted firmness. "We've all been friends too long. It's time for both of you to grow up."

Tony felt this strike his deep vein of resentment toward Sam: he sensed that neither the prom, nor watching Tony dance with Sue, was a likely occasion for Sam to bury his own grievances. Then, perversely, Tony decided to put Sam to the test. "Maybe," he said, "for a little while . . ."

Which is how it was that, after suffering through his parents' picture-taking session, Tony found himself holding Sue Cash as the band played "The Way You Look Tonight."

The Lake City Country Club was theirs for this one occasion, the first time Tony had set foot inside, and swirls of paper and makeshift balls of glass hung from the ceiling. Tony found the effort somewhat short of magical: the band was a compromise with faculty and parents—its singer was much better at "Smoke Gets in Your Eyes" than "A Hard Day's Night," and Aretha Franklin's "Respect" was entirely beyond him—and the Casino Night theme, featuring roulette wheels and blackjack tables where one could gamble for stuffed dolls and drink pink lemonade from champagne glasses, was the parents' wan attempt to prevent satellite drinking parties on the golf course. Nor, Tony thought, could the alchemy of black tie and evening dresses turn a bunch of teenagers into Cary Grant and Grace Kelly in *To Catch a Thief*: too many guys wore their ties askew, and others looked so stiff that they resembled the protagonist of an open-casket funeral. There was the usual prom-night complement of awful pairings, social noncombatants fixed up by a committee of teachers so that everyone would have a partner. Spotting Ernie Nixon trying to extract conversation from his date, an unattractive blonde who occupied a folding chair in a state of mortification that seemed almost otherworldly, Tony regretted that he had hardly spoken to Ernie since the night Martin Luther King was shot. But a look at Sue Cash tonight, Tony admitted to himself, was nothing to regret.

She had a light tan—by May the first sunny days had come—and that and her makeup went so well with her pink satin gown that the effect was one of great naturalness. The gown itself had been sewn by her mother, and it fit Sue's round curves without seeming to make a point of them. For Tony, the effect was both touching and a little awesome: it was as though Sue Cash, his friend, had graduated to womanhood with such ease and assurance that the Sue in his arms was someone new to him. Yet she felt warm, relaxed; though they had never before danced together, from the first few notes it seemed quite effortless. The touch of her hair against his face carried the scent of perfume.

"You," he murmured, "are absolutely beautiful."

He felt her smile against his shoulder, and then the music ended. As she leaned back, the grin she gave him was the old Sue with a little mischief thrown in. "Better than in the pink-striped dress?"

Tony eyed her critically, pretending to consider this. "I really don't think it would fit now, Sue."

For a moment more, they smiled at each other, and then she went to find Sam.

Curious, Tony let his gaze follow her. It was clear that with respect to Tony, Sue was on her own. Sam had turned from the dance floor and was laughing with Charlie Moore; Tony sensed something a little stagy about his indifference to Sue's return, and he and Charlie looked as if they were united in the superiority of a secret shared. Then Sam took a quick, emphatic swallow from his paper cup, and Tony guessed the secret— whiskey, hidden in Sam's locker in the men's shower room. Perhaps, Tony thought, it was time to test Sam's feelings.

As Tony joined them, Sue turned, saw him, and made room in the circle. Charlie, the Lancer, gave a curt nod; taking her cue, Jane Jeffords flashed a perfunctory smile. Sam seemed to take Tony in slowly, with mild surprise, as if his presence required time to register.

Tony nodded. "Hi, Sam."

"Hi, Tony." Sam's face was flushed, Tony saw. "No date?"

The words had an edge; Sam well knew Tony had no

date, and the remark seemed directed at Sue. Glancing at Sue, Tony saw her hurt expression.

"No date," Tony answered. "It's going to be an early night for me."

Sam raised his eyebrows. "Too bad," he said carelessly. Taking another swallow of whiskey, he turned back to Charlie Moore.

Next to him, Tony felt Sue tense. Leaning closer to her, he whispered, "Thanks for the dance, Sue. It's time for me to become a pumpkin."

Sam turned abruptly, as if he had caught them. Then he smiled, his too-bright eyes meeting Tony's. "Am I missing something, guys?"

For Sue's sake, Tony held his tongue. But the look she gave Sam was less hurt than angry. "I just asked Tony for another dance," she said. "You don't mind, do you?"

The undertone in her voice warned Sam not to mind. Someone who knew Sue less well, even Charlie Moore and his date, might not have heard it.

Sam flushed. "Why should I?" he answered blithely, and turned to Charlie. "Quick trip to the boys' room?" They were gone before Sue and Tony had moved.

Tony walked her just far enough so that no one could overhear. "It really is time to leave—"

"Dance with me, Tony. Please."

He took her in his arms, moving slowly to "A Thousand Stars." "What have I missed in the last few minutes?"

She leaned against his shoulder. Softly, she said, "That it's not enough that I love him."

"Why?"

"Because *you* haven't apologized, so he thinks I'm taking sides with you. He stops making sense when he drinks."

Tony held her closer. "It's not just him, Sue. From the moment you asked me to come, I knew he'd be like this. I forgot about you too."

She leaned back, looking into his face. "Are you jealous of him?"

"No. But I compete with him. And I'm still angry."

Sue shook her head, as if to herself. "Then it's different," she said at last. "Because Sam's jealous of you."

Tony wanted to deny this. "You never gave him reason—"

"It's not about me." Her voice was sad and very clear. "It's about you. Whatever he thinks you have, he's afraid he doesn't."

Listening, Tony felt leaden. "Why do you say that?"

"When I came back from our dance, I saw the way he looked at you." Her gaze was troubled but direct. "But it's more than that. I think part of him wants to *be* you—"

Tony felt a tap on his shoulder. "Cut in?" Sam asked amiably. His breath was raw with whiskey.

Tony studied him. Sam's face had an odd defiance; Tony wondered what he might have heard. Still in his arms, Sue looked from Tony to Sam.

Stepping back from her, Tony spoke as if nothing were wrong. "You guys enjoy the rest of your night."

Sue mustered a smile, joining the pretense of normality. "We're glad you came, Tony." Sam said nothing.

Tony left them there.

All around him, more couples were dancing. Tony took in the scene: the swaying couples, the clumps of parents to the side, the muffled sound of chatter beneath the music. It was beginning to seem like a party; for the first time, he permitted himself to imagine this night if Alison were with him—how she would look, how funny or pointed her observations might be. Suddenly he felt a new anguish for her and, for himself, a shock as fresh as the first days after her death, discovering once more how irretrievable his loss had been, how unfathomable it would always be. The sight of Sue, eyes shut as she leaned against Sam's shoulder, filled him with loneliness. This was a night for couples.

He drifted off the dance floor, killed a few more minutes with Ernie Nixon and his listless date. One of the chaperons, a mother with a pink corsage, began eyeing him suspiciously.

"Tony!"

It was Jane, Charlie Moore's date. She was alone and, it seemed clear, emboldened by whiskey. Her round face looked a little slack, and the movement of her lips was exaggerated, as if mouthing words for a grandmother who was hard of hearing. "Why don't you dance with someone else?" she demanded.

Tony managed a smile. "Everyone else has a date."

She nodded solemnly. "It's still so terrible about Alison."

Tony stared at her. Sighing, she gathered herself with the presumptuous emotion of a woman just drunk enough to mistake tactlessness for feeling, and then to impose it on someone else. She peered up at him, demanding attention. "I mean, I see you dancing with Sue, and I just keep thinking that Alison should be here."

For his own sake, Tony decided, it was better not to respond. In an even tone, he asked, "Where's Charlie?"

"In the locker room, getting a little more you-know-what." She smiled brightly. "Sam's got his own locker here. They're members, you know." The thought stopped her abruptly. "Alison was a member too. . . ."

"I know." He still spoke quietly. "Maybe you should wait here for Charlie, Jane. Someone might think you're drunk—"

"Hey, man—you trying to snake me?" It was Charlie Moore, as drunk as his date, teetering that fine line between bluff humor and inebriated menace. "Isn't Sue Cash enough?"

"More than enough," Tony said, and then Charlie turned to Jane, forgetting him, and emitted a wet-sounding screech of laughter.

"That sonofabitch!" Charlie said.

Her eyes widened. "Tony didn't—"

"*Sam.*" Haphazardly searching the dance floor, Charlie hovered between mirth and indignation. "There were two bottles, and now I can't even find one. Sonofabitch must've taken it."

Tony turned, looking for Sam and Sue. But he could not spot them in the crowd of couples. He did not think that Jane or Charlie rated a goodbye.

Outside, he leaned against the door of his car.

The night was warm, starry. Except for the sound of the band, faint now, the parking lot was quiet. It was nearly midnight; soon, Tony supposed, couples would begin sneaking past the chaperons and head for the golf course to drink or make out. That this dance was a time of passion was part of high school lore: how many girls, Tony wondered, had lost it near the eighteenth green on prom night? Part of him still ached for Alison.

Over the sea of car hoods, two voices drifted to Tony. Lost in thought, he did not try to listen. That one voice was male, the other female, was no surprise to him. Someone had to be the first.

"*No,*" the girl said.

Tony stood straighter. Across several rows of cars, he saw the profile of a woman—much shorter than the man she spoke to—looking up in apparent anger.

Even in the dark, Tony thought, he could recognize Sam Robb anywhere. "I don't want to," the woman said again, and now her voice was Sue's.

Moving quietly, Tony began to slide between the cars.

Sam had opened the trunk of his car. He stood with his back to Tony, a bottle of whiskey in one hand, a picnic basket in another. Sue had backed away from him.

"Come on," Sam said. "No one's going to miss us. And who cares if they do."

Sue shook her head. "I care. Especially when you're like this."

"Like what?"

Three rows from them, Tony stopped. "Drunk," he heard Sue answer.

Sam dropped the blanket to the asphalt. "Not like him, you mean."

"You *are* drunk, Sam. You wouldn't say that if you weren't." She paused, her exasperation becoming a plea. "Please, let's not ruin our night over Tony."

The sound of his own name stopped Tony where he was. For a moment, Sam was silent. Frozen there, Tony thought that the worst had passed.

Softly, Sam said, "You embarrassed me, in front of our friends. They saw the way you were with him."

"How was I?" Sue asked in tones of weariness.

"Like you wanted him." Drunkenly, Sam nodded for emphasis. "Like Tony Lord's the one you want tonight."

"No. I feel bad for Tony. That's not the same thing."

Sam took a lurching step. It was this loss of coordination, more than Sam's voice, that showed Tony how truly drunk he was. He felt himself tense, watched Sam put both hands on her shoulders as he asked, "Then who *do* you want, Sue?"

Looking up at Sam, Sue seemed to draw breath. "No one. Not right now . . ."

"But I want *you*." Sam's voice seemed to move between anger and panic. "I need you to prove whose girl you are—"

"*Mine*. I belong to me, Sam." Sue turned, starting for the country club.

Sam grabbed her by the wrist. "Get in the car with me. Please, I need to know—"

"You're *hurting* me," Sue said, and Tony moved without thinking.

Sue saw him first. She froze, eyes wide, mouth forming a silent "No." Sam, hand still on her wrist, followed her gaze to Tony.

Sam straightened, dropping her arm, eyes filling with feelings he could not seem to control—shame, jealousy, anger. "You're sloppy drunk," Tony told him. "And you're hurting your own girlfriend."

Sam looked astonished. "I'm not hurting her. . . ." Then his voice trailed off and his hand fell to his side.

Tony put his own hands in his pockets. "My mistake," he said softly.

For an instant, Sam seemed mollified, and then the alcohol seemed to hit him again. "It was none of your business, Tony. *Your* girlfriend is dead. Sue's mine."

Tony felt his self-control slipping. From behind Sam, Sue gazed at Tony, conveying a silent prayer for reason. Teetering, Sam stepped forward, looking Tony in the face. "What do you have against me, Tony? Why were you trying to take Sue?"

"I'm not."

"Don't *lie* to me." Sam straightened. "You're a liar—"

"Stop it," Sue cried out. She grasped the sleeve of Sam's tuxedo. "Tony hasn't done anything—"

Shoving her aside, Sam grabbed the front of Tony's lapels. "Why is she watching out for you?"

Tony looked him in the face. Still quiet, he said, "Because she may need someone sober enough to drive her home."

Face contorted, Sam raised his fist. Tony pushed him off balance. "Don't be an ass," he snapped, and then Sam swung at him.

As Sue screamed, Tony moved his head back. Sam's fist, missing his chin by inches, freed seven months of anger.

Stepping to the side, Tony hit Sam in the stomach with all the force he had.

The shock ran through Tony's arm. Sam grunted, air gasping from his lungs. He fell, sitting on the asphalt. His head bent forward.

Sam twitched, and then the sound of his retching echoed in the parking lot. Tears in her eyes, Sue looked from Sam to Tony.

Tony felt his anger die. "I'm sorry," he said.

Sitting between them, Sam began coughing, the first wave of dry heaves. Head still bent, he stared into the pool of his own vomit. Sue bent over him. "Can you help me?" she asked Tony.

He took one arm, Sue another. When they pulled Sam into an upright position, his eyes were empty with shock, and the front of his tuxedo was stained.

"He can't go back in," Sue said.

It was as if Sam were not there, Tony thought. "What should we do?"

"Take him home." Sue was somewhere between anger and defeat. "He can't drive like this."

Tony looked in Sam's pockets for his car keys, opened the back door of the car. Together, he and Sue lifted Sam. As they dragged him the few feet to the open door, he groaned in feeble protest. But by the time Tony pulled him across the back seat, and Sue had laid his head down, Sam was asleep.

Tony stared at her. "Who gets to wake up his parents?"

Sue shook her head. "Not me. And I can't sit up with him until he gets better. I hate him too much right now."

Tony puffed his cheeks. "There's a hammock in his backyard. We can let him sleep it off there. You drive him. I'll follow."

Sue nodded slowly. "All right."

Twenty minutes later, they carried Sam across his backyard, Sue by the arms, Tony holding his feet.

The hammock was bound to two apple trees. As they laid Sam inside it, he sighed, stirred slightly, and was still again. In the thin light, he was pale, his mouth slightly open.

Sue put two fingers to his lips, to make sure he was breathing.

"Is he all right?" Tony asked.

"Yes."

Together, they watched Sam's face, now serene as a baby's. "Look at him," Tony said softly. "He'll probably die in his sleep, from old age. You wouldn't think anything had happened, would you?"

For a time, Sue gazed at Sam, silent, as though trying to read what lay beneath. Then, walking away from the hammock, she stood alone in the middle of Sam's yard, looking up at the stars. After a moment, Tony joined her.

"Well," she said. "I certainly screwed up your night."

"And I certainly screwed up yours."

She was quiet for a moment. "No, you didn't."

He shifted his weight, listening to the chirp of crickets in Sam's backyard. "I guess I should drive you home now."

Turning, she looked back at Sam. "Do you really want to go home?"

He shrugged. "For me, the party was pretty much over. By now a bunch of them have headed for the golf course, or the beach. Waiting for the sun to come up."

Sue looked down. "Do you want to do that, with me? Wait for the sun to come up, I mean."

Tony hesitated, glancing over at the silent hammock. "Are you okay with that?"

"Uh-huh." Looking up, she smiled a little. "We're supposed to stay up late, remember? I don't want to miss out on everything."

SIXTEEN

Tony would not drive to the beach until dawn, he told Sue—he could not imagine being near Taylor Park at night. The only other place Sue knew was a grove of abandoned maple trees; all that she wanted from the next few hours, she told him, was to be where she did not have to explain Sam to anyone, or even think of him very much.

Tony knew this was not possible. The maple grove was where she had gone with Sam the night that Alison died; the blanket they spread before them was his; the picnic basket—orange juice, fruit, breakfast rolls, a bottle of cheap champagne—was what Sue had prepared for them; the dress she still wore as she walked in the dewy grass, barefoot now, was the one she had wanted Sam to admire. Tony was quite certain that even he was a reminder of Sam, just as Sue had made him think of Alison.

She sat next to him on the blanket, pensive. The dark was streaked with moonlight, the night warm and clear and windless, the only noise the rise and fall of crickets chirring. "Last year," Tony told her, "if we'd tried to imagine this, Sam would be with you, Alison with me. Since the night she died, everything changed. Including Sam."

Sue was quiet. "You've changed too," she said at last.

Tony shrugged. "I guess I've never really been sad before. Now I'm sad most of the time."

She turned to him. "Not just sad, Tony. It's as if you've already left here—Lake City, Sam, me. Like you've started thinking a lot of things you don't say and we don't have any idea about."

This seemed right to him, although Tony could not define the changes. "You sound like Sam," he told her.

"I don't mean to." Rearranging her dress, Sue seemed to sort through her thoughts. "I can deal with whoever you are, Tony. But I think it's harder for Sam."

"How do you mean?"

"That you're moving away from him." Sue paused, voice filling with doubt. "I'm not sure, exactly. Maybe as long as Sam thinks you both want the same things, like Athlete of the Year or to be the hometown hero, he doesn't have to be jealous. In Lake City he can beat you. But if what he wants more than anything doesn't mean that much to you, maybe *he* doesn't mean that much. . . ." Abruptly, she stopped, as though her thoughts embarrassed her.

"Go on," Tony said.

She faced him. "This may sound funny, but he hates himself for feeling that. Because Sam really loves you, Tony. I think that's what the fight was all about—he was trying to say he was your friend no matter what, and he didn't feel it coming back to him." She turned away. "Does any of this make sense to you?"

It was the first speech Tony had ever heard from Sue; it seemed to him that she was trying to explain Sam to herself. "Maybe," Tony answered. "But what about tonight?"

Sue exhaled. "That's simple. He's always thought I liked you, more than I should. Now that Alison's gone, he thinks I'm closer to you than he is."

"Trying to put yourself in my place, Sue, was a nice thing to do. God knows Sam didn't."

Sue fell quiet. "That's me," she said. "Nice."

He could not identify the note in her voice. Suddenly Tony felt selfish—so much of this had been about Sam, or Tony, so little about Sue herself. It struck him that he, like others, took the sunny, sensible girl they saw for the whole of her. "Is that why you put up with Sam when he drinks like that? Because you're too 'nice'?"

"I don't think anyone's that 'nice'—not Sam, or you,

and certainly not me." Turning, Sue looked up at the stars. "I stay with Sam because he feels more than he can always say. And because I need other people to need me, and Sam always will."

"But is that what you want?"

Idly, she brushed back her hair. "I don't have a clear picture yet. Sometimes all I want is to be part of someone's life and help make our life a good one—I think that I could be happy, or miserable, anywhere. Other times, I wonder what it might be like to be more like you." She turned to him. "Do you understand how I mean that?"

"I think so. . . ."

"I mean, Sam will talk about marriage, or Lake City, and that will sound just right to me. And then I'll lie in my bed and not think of him at all. Instead I start imagining all the places I've never been, and maybe never will be." She shook her head. "I've never really *been* anywhere."

"Neither have I."

"But you think about it, don't you? You always have."

"Yes."

She tilted her head. "Where would you go?"

"Other than jail?"

"Other than jail." Her voice was softer now. "You're going to have the life you want, Tony. They don't put people in jail for things they didn't do."

As before, this touched him. "Then let's drink your champagne, and I'll consider it." He smiled again. "After all, it's our prom night."

Reaching into the basket, Sue pulled out the bottle of champagne. Tony twisted the plastic cork; it rose into the night, vanishing with a soft pop, and then he poured champagne in two paper cups.

"To Italy," he said.

Smiling, Sue took a swallow of champagne. Only then did she ask, "Why Italy?"

"For one thing, Sophia Loren lives there."

Sue looked dubious. "We're drinking to Sophia Loren?"

Tony shook his head. "I saw this article. In *National Geographic*, just last summer." In truth, Tony had forgotten this; now, as he talked to Sue, the photographs came back to him. "There was an island called Capri, with grottoes and fishing boats and beaches, and water so blue but so clear it looked like you could see your hand in it. . . ."

Sue seemed to consider this. "That sounds nice," she allowed. "Where else?"

"Well, there's Venice. Imagine being in a city built entirely on canals, with churches and spires and no cars anywhere. It has all these boats, and sidewalk cafés by the water. I'm going *there* for sure."

Sue tilted her head. "I've seen pictures. But I think I want more choices."

This made Tony smile. He took off his tuxedo coat, poured more champagne. "There's always Tuscany. It's one of their wine regions, the article said. Very sunny, with a lot of hills with villas or old castles on them." He grinned. "A lot of full-breasted women on them too, from the pictures. The good old *National Geographic* never misses a chance. . . ."

Sue gave him a skeptical look. "Are you sure this isn't still about Sophia Loren?"

"Of course not." Tony tried to appear wounded and then realized that, in truth, he had begun to imagine a future which, for months, had extended no further than Harvard or, in his fears, the call he dreaded from Saul Ravin. "No," he said softly. "It's about freedom. And choosing."

Sue fell silent again. "Then maybe I can go too. If I won't be in the way."

"I'll break it to Sophia gently." Tony poured champagne again. "So does any place sound good to you?"

Sue watched his face; Tony sensed that she saw that his worries had returned, and wished, for his own sake, to keep him in Italy. "Capri," she said.

"Why?"

"Because I like beaches, and warm water." She hesitated. "If that's all right with you."

Tony looked at her face, suddenly serious. Softly, he answered, "Capri would be fine with me."

For a time, they were quiet. They sat closer in the dark now, immersed in their separate thoughts, neither wanting to talk. Then it came to Tony, swift and quiet as a heartbeat, that he no longer felt alone.

It took him by such surprise that all he could do was stare at her.

For an instant, this was safe; she was gazing down at the paper cup in her hand, seemingly far away. That she was aware of him showed first in her new stillness. But Tony could not look away. It was as if, he suddenly realized, he had just discovered her.

Her eyes rose to his, filling with questions. At first, the questions were for Tony, he sensed, and then, as she watched him, for herself.

Tony put down his paper cup.

She gazed at it a moment and then, still silent, placed her cup beside his.

As she looked into his face, Tony reached for her. Her eyes were still open.

Her mouth was soft and warm. Tony did not wish to stop; he felt Sue move closer, so that he would not have to stop. When he cupped her breasts, she did not move. And then, gently, she pulled back, looking into his face again.

"We're not in Italy, Tony."

"I know."

Tony found that he could not ask her. Time seemed in suspension. A few seconds earlier, Tony had not known he wanted her; now, silent, he ached to have her close.

A moment passed.

Still watching his face, Sue reached behind her, unzipping the back of her dress. Her shoulders were bare in the moonlight.

"Yes," Tony whispered. "Please."

Gracefully, she stood. As her dress fell, rustling softly on the blanket, her eyes did not leave his. They did not leave as she unhooked her stockings; it was as though, with each new step, she asked the same question of Tony, of herself.

In silent response, Tony stood and took off his shirt and slacks. Still watching him, Sue unfastened her bra.

Her breasts were round and full. Just as, Tony realized to his surprise, he had imagined them. As she did the rest, his throat caught.

Sue Cash, his friend, was beautiful.

They went to each other. Her breasts were warm against his chest. She leaned her face on his shoulder.

He held her close to him, torn between sheltering Sue and wanting her. Then her mouth found his, and their second kiss was deep and long and sure. He felt her quiver with her own desire.

Slowly, mouth grazing her breasts and stomach, Tony slipped to his knees and, by instinct, did for Sue what he had never done. Her soft cries seemed to come from far away. He could feel his own readiness, and yet, what was also new, this lack of haste.

All at once, Sue knelt and put her mouth to his. The rest, somehow, they knew without speaking—that Tony should lie on his back, that she would bend her face to him and then, raising her head, move her hips to take him inside her.

For Tony, the night became the warmth of her, the look on Sue's face.

She was with him, but not with him; first smiling down at him, then with her head back, her eyes half shut, cries caught in her throat. Tony felt his own surge begin.

He caught himself, straining to hold out. Then, quite suddenly, Sue's eyes flew open and the cry, long and thin and very soft, was freed from her throat at last.

In the instant before he felt his own shudder, Tony knew what had happened to her, and that it was new for them both.

Sue bent forward and kissed him.

"Don't move," he said softly.

"I don't want to."

When she did, finally, they lay together, each touching the other, not needing to talk.

Gently, Tony broke the silence. "We did that all right, didn't we."

Sue gazed back at him. "Yes," she said softly. "We did that all right."

Leaning his face to hers, Tony kissed Sue again.

She looked at him, eyes full of wonder. And then, to his surprise, she rolled over on her back and spoke to the stars with a hushed vehemence.

"God, Sue Cash, you are such a *liar. . . .*"

Tony propped himself on his elbow, placing a hand on her stomach. "Why a liar?"

She rolled her head to see him. "Isn't it sort of obvious? I told Sam I didn't care for you, except as a friend. I even tried telling myself that. So here I am, the American Red Cross in action." She gave him a rueful smile. "If this is what friends do, Tony, what do we get to do next?"

Even as he smiled back, Tony felt the world, kept at bay for these few moments, intruding on their deep pleasure in each other. "I don't know, Sue. Do we have to know right now?"

Lying against the blanket, Sue moved her head from side to side. "No," she said. "I don't even want to."

After a moment, Tony took her hand and lay next to her, gazing up at the stars. Between them, he felt something proprietary growing—this night was theirs, and whatever happened in its protection belonged to them, forever. Her next question, though unexpected, did not really surprise him.

"Do you think you'll win Athlete of the Year?" Her voice seemed almost casual. "Does it still matter to you who wins?"

The question was not an idle one, he sensed it—it carried shades of Sam, and of Alison, and the knowledge that, in their new closeness, Sue Cash and Tony Lord could avoid neither.

"It doesn't matter," he answered. "Because I won't win."

Sue was quiet. "I think you deserve to," she said at last.

"I used to think so. But I lost that Stratford game single-handed, after Sam had almost won it." His fingers tightened around hers. "Anyhow, they don't award Athlete of the Year for murdering the senior class president. I'd say that gives Sam the edge."

Sue turned to him. Softly, she asked, "Do you feel guilty? I mean, about us."

Silent, Tony parsed his thoughts. "I guess I feel confused. Last night, at the dance, I was missing Alison so much it hurt."

Sue watched his face. "Maybe you still do, Tony. Maybe you kept on missing her, and I was here."

"No," he said reflexively, and then, looking at Sue, realized that he meant this. "Nothing can stop me from missing her. But this doesn't feel like we're all about Alison. I don't think we ever were."

There was something new in her eyes, he thought: the wish to believe this, yet the refusal to ask him what, in her heart, she thought unfair to ask. He touched her hair. "Tonight was different, Sue, than how I was with Alison."

"How?"

Tony breathed in. "The night she died," he told her, "I was ashamed of wanting her. Even before I found her that night, I believed what we did was a sin, something to confess." He paused, finishing softly: "Maybe I *have* changed. But you don't feel like a sin to me. Except maybe against Sam."

For a moment, she touched his face. "At least you don't have to live with it alone."

Tony pondered her meaning. "Do you plan to tell him?" he asked.

She slid next to Tony, holding him tight. "I don't want to think about it. I don't want to think about anything but this."

Tony held her, stroking her hair and back. After a time, her body relaxed, her breathing eased, and then she was still; to Tony, it was as if her desire to escape their shared betrayal had resolved itself in sleep. He drew the blanket over them. The tenderness he felt, growing with each breath she drew, was a secret only from her.

Tony could not sleep. At first, he thought of Alison, with deep sadness but not guilt. And then, for a long time, he wondered what would happen to the three who remained—to him, to Sam, to this lovely girl, his friend, suddenly Tony's for a night. But the night was already fading; with the first streaks of light, erasing the stars and graying the darkness, Sue Cash stirred in his arms.

Waking, her face was fresh, untroubled. For an instant, she looked up at him in surprise, and then, remembering, she smiled.

"How long was I asleep?"

He kissed her. "A long time."

"Too long." When she looked at him again, her face was sad. Softly, she said, "We've got to go."

Tony was silent. After a moment, Sue began to dress. "No," he said. "Not for a minute."

Sue stood there for him, naked, looking into his eyes. Then she came forward and put her arms around him, as if kissing Tony goodbye, and picked up her gown again. They watched each other as she dressed.

Turning her back, she asked, "Get my zipper?"

He did that. "I don't like this part," he said. It was meant to sound joking, but did not, quite. Nor did Sue look at him when she answered.

"I know."

She helped him with his studs. As they picked among the wreckage of their picnic, Tony felt like a scavenger at the end of the world. When everything was in his trunk, they stood next to each other, looking at the bare matted grass.

"In an hour," Sue said, "no one could ever guess."

Quiet, they drove to Sue's. In the first light of day, the town was still silent, street upon street. He had not been up this early, Tony remembered, since driving home from the police station, dull and heartsick, on the morning after Alison's murder.

He felt Sue's hand on his knee and covered it with his own.

"Can we talk?" he asked. "In a couple of days, after this has sunk in a little."

She turned to him. "I'd like that, Tony."

He felt a kind of peace settle in. They were quiet the rest of the way; as they turned into Sue's driveway, her hand was curled in his.

Sam was sitting on her front steps.

Tony felt Sue tense. Neither spoke; only when they parked did Sue withdraw her hand.

By unspoken consent, they got out of the car together, to face whatever happened.

Sam still wore his tuxedo pants and ruffled shirt. He was pale, his hair disheveled. Sue had kept his car keys; Tony guessed that Sam had walked the mile to Sue's house from his own. His eyes seemed bruised, rimmed with red.

As Tony and Sue stopped, a few feet from him, Sam looked from one face to the other. He stood, walking toward Tony.

Tony braced himself. Their eyes met, and then Sam rested his hand on Tony's shoulder and slowly shook his head.

"I'm sorry, pal. I'm really, really sorry. For all of us."

It took Tony by surprise. After a moment, he said, "So am I."

"Not your fault." Pausing, Sam tried to smile. "Thanks for looking after Sue."

This was, Tony knew, meant as both thanks and dismissal. Tony turned to Sue, hesitant. The time that he spent looking into her eyes, suddenly moist, seemed longer than it must have been.

"Bye, Sue," he said softly, and felt Sam turn to watch her. The smile she gave Tony changed nothing on her face.

"Thanks, Tony. For everything."

Tony walked to the car. He switched on the motor, trying not to look back at them. When he finally did, in the rearview mirror, Sam was leaning his forehead against the crown of Sue's head, mutely asking her forgiveness.

SEVENTEEN

Two days after making love with Sue, Tony sat in the high school gym for what would be the last time, watching the coaches pass out the final sports awards.

Tony had begun here as a freshman and become the quarterback; the three sports assemblies held each year, fall, winter, and spring, had punctuated his life as he passed through Lake City High School. Each marked another season of striving; of teammates and new memories; and, at the end, a token block-shaped L. Now his drawer contained eleven letters. This assembly, his twelfth, was the culmination he once had imagined, as early as his freshman year, when Tony knew that either he or Sam Robb would become Athlete of the Year.

Sam sat across the gym, with Sue. She was quiet, Tony saw. This afternoon they would meet; perhaps, like Tony, she was not sure what would happen. He knew only that, with an intensity that surprised him, he wished Sue Cash were with him now.

Next to him, Ernie Nixon whispered, "Taking bets on your chances?"

Tony did not take his eyes off Sue. "Slim," he finally answered, "and none."

Below them, the awards went on. Tony already held his baseball letter; for him, the coach passing out the track team letters was background noise. Restless, he saw Sam watching the letters dwindle, his mind clearly elsewhere. Tony waited until Sue spotted him; she tilted her head, one corner of her mouth forming a slightly querying smile. To Tony, the current between them was so strong that it seemed as though Sam could not help but feel it, and then Sue looked away.

The last few letters passed as slowly as a minuet. At the corner of his eye, he saw Sam stare at the speaker's podium. Tony had never seen him sit so still.

At last, the track coach sat, and Principal Marks came to the podium.

It had become the principal's privilege—because George Marks enjoyed the drama—to award the trophy for Athlete of the Year. The coaches who sat in folding chairs behind him—football, basketball, baseball, and track—had already made their choice. Tony tried to read Coach Jackson's face; that it was grim, as usual, gave away nothing. The award was Sam's, Tony told himself again.

On the floor of the gym, George Marks gazed admiringly at the bronze figure of a Greek marathon runner.

Tony sensed some kids glancing at him, others gazing at Sam.

"This highest award," George Marks began, "is given to that senior whose talent, determination, and sheer hard work best epitomize the spirit of Lake City High School. . . ."

In other years, this peroration had made Tony smile. "You'd think it was the Medal of Honor," he'd once joked to Sam. "I keep expecting him to say, 'tested on foreign soil.'"

"This year's winner," Marks went on, "is more exemplary than most.

"True, he has been a star in three sports—football, basketball, and baseball. But much more than that, he has shown those traits that we all need in life: character, leadership, grace under pressure, strength in adversity, and, no matter what, the refusal to be distracted by anything but the task at hand. . . ."

For the first time, despite everything, Tony felt a sudden stirring hope. "And yet there is more," George Marks said solemnly. "For this young man has also endured a tragic loss. Something which, in a lesser person, might have distracted and even damaged him. . . ."

Tony froze; people were turning to stare. Across from him, Sam looked stricken.

"And so," George Marks concluded, "the winner of the coveted Athlete of the Year award, like his late brother Joe before him, is *Sam Robb*."

Tony shut his eyes.

When he opened them, Sam sat motionless. Then Sam stood abruptly, as if pulled from his seat, face filling with amazement and, then, something close to rapture. Sue turned from him, to Tony. And then Sam was hugging her; for an instant, she looked startled, then she hugged him back.

Breaking away, Sam headed for the floor, two stands

at a time. The cheers rose; as he walked toward George Marks, Sam's face shone with an astonished, innocent joy. He looked, Tony thought, like a man delivered to himself.

On another day, Tony might have been happy for him: the way Sam cried out for generosity. Even as, on some other day, this might have moved Tony to wonder about the transcendence of a single moment, the illusion—which the years would surely betray—that such a moment can change a lifetime. But what Tony felt, to his surprise and even shame, was jealousy. He could only hope that Sam Robb's feelings lasted longer than his own.

"Sorry," Ernie Nixon murmured.

"It's okay. I wasn't expecting it."

Sue, he thought, would understand. But she was smiling at Sam now, knowing what this meant to him.

For once, there was no exultation in Sam's posture, no showiness. He took the trophy from George Marks and gazed at it, shaking his head in wonder. Perhaps, Tony thought, this trophy had brought Sam closer to the best in him—there was something attractive, even humbled, about Sam in his moment.

Sam turned to the stands. For a moment, Tony did not realize that Sam was coming to him, trophy in hand.

Tony sat there, watching with a kind of fascination as Sam stopped two steps below him. As the others moved aside, Sam took the trophy and tossed it underhand, to Tony.

"Nice catch," Sam said.

Tony looked up from the trophy. Taking the last two steps, Sam pulled Tony to his feet and hugged him.

The first applause was scattered. Then the gym filled with it, as though Sam had bestowed forgiveness on Tony Lord. Tony could feel Sam's emotions in the tightness of his embrace.

As he leaned back to see Tony's face, Sam's eyes shone

with tears. In a husky voice, he said beneath the white noise of the gym, "You'd have won . . ."

"No. You were always going to win."

Sam slowly shook his head. "If we're not friends," he said softly, "I'd sooner have lost it."

Tony tried to smile. "Then we're friends," he said, and handed Sam the trophy. "Congratulations."

Their moment was over.

Gratefully, Sam gripped Tony's shoulder. Then he turned and walked across the gym, to Sue. Amidst the cheers, Tony was left with the sudden reversal of their roles, the sour aftertaste of Sam's blessing, the sudden bitter knowledge that, in his pride, Tony had taken as his right that he would always be the leader and that Sam, the led, would envy him.

When Tony looked up again, Sam was holding Sue.

Waiting where they had made love, Tony saw Sue appear in the grove of maples. A few feet from him, Sue stopped, and then she ran forward to kiss him.

"I've missed you," Tony said.

"I've missed you too." She took both of his hands in hers. "I'm sorry, Tony."

He looked at her, trying to see what she meant. Softly, he answered, "It mattered to me, after all. But maybe Sam needed something to win."

She tilted her head, brown eyes probing. "Am I something to win?"

"Is that what you think?" Tony's voice filled with feeling. "Two nights ago, we were right here. If I can't think of you with him, it's because of that."

Suddenly there were tears in her eyes. "Tony, this is about a lot more than who I sleep with. It's more about if I can sleep at all. . . ."

Tony pulled her close. Resting against his shoulder, Sue murmured, "Try to understand what's happening to me."

"Tell me, all right?"

"I think I'm falling in love with you." She leaned back, touching his face. "We've always been friends, Tony. Talk to me like your friend Sue, who's in love with a boy she isn't sure she should love, and doesn't know what to do."

Tony knelt to the grass, taking her with him. "Today, in the gym, I wanted you with me."

Sue closed her eyes. "I know. . . . I could tell. But that's not an answer." She looked at him again, hands resting on his shoulders. "Sam needs me too, more than you ever will. Can you understand that part?"

Tony's throat constricted. "I think so. But that's not all there is."

Sue looked down. "You say that so easily. You must know what this would do to him, how bad it would be that it's *you*. . . ."

The truth of this made Tony quiet for a moment. "But what about *you*?"

"Me?" Sue slowly shook her head. "I feel like I'm falling, in a dream. . . . I don't know where I am, or how the dream will end."

"I'm not a dream, Sue."

"I know." Once more, she leaned against him. "But maybe *we're* one."

Tony held her, kissing the top of her head. Sue's voice was a murmur. "When did I start loving you? I keep asking myself. How could I want you like that, when there's Sam, and *we'd* always just been friends? What does it say about me?"

"That you're not in love with him."

Sue turned her face to his. "I can't say that, Tony. I wish I could." She paused again, as though struggling to find words. "All I know is that what I feel for you is so different, it could turn my life upside down. . . ."

"God, Sue, I could never hurt you. . . ."

"You'd never mean to, Tony." She leaned away from him, as if to see him better. Softly, she asked, "If Alison were still here, would you have made love to me? Could you have done to her what I've done to Sam?"

Tony found that he could not answer this. "Does it matter that much?"

Tears glistened in her eyes. "That wasn't fair, Tony. I already knew you couldn't answer."

The way she said this pierced Tony's heart. "Sue, what matters is how we feel now. . . ."

"No." The quiet firmness in her voice seemed directed at Sue herself. "How we feel isn't the same. We're not the same."

He spread his palms in entreaty. "Why not? Just tell me why."

"Oh, Tony . . ." Briefly, Sue could not speak, and then she shook her head. "Don't you see it at all?"

He reached out to her again, hands beneath her wrists. She looked at him with a new resolve, as though to say what must be said. "If you asked me to, I think the deepest part of me would follow you . . . throw away anything I've ever known, all the security. No matter how I felt about Sam, or felt about myself for hurting him, I'd give myself to you in a way that I never imagined giving myself to anyone. Just so I could feel the way I did two nights ago." She paused, unable to finish, and then her voice was quiet again. "That's why I need you to be my friend. Because I know it's not like that for you."

Tony exhaled. "How can you know that?"

"Because we *are* friends," she answered softly. "And I know that my friend Tony, who I care for *so* much, is still in love with Alison Taylor. Because she was right for him."

Tony looked at her steadily. "Part of you is still in love with Sam. It doesn't keep me from wanting you."

Sue's faint smile did not change her eyes. "If it were just Sam and Alison . . ." She shrugged, helpless. "But it's not."

"What else is there?"

"You. And me." Her voice was sad and very clear. "Alison was poised and sophisticated and very smart. I'm just *me*. . . ."

"Just *you*? Don't you know what that is to me?"

Sue shook her head. "I know what I am to you now, when you've lost a girl you loved, when half the town has turned against you, and when all your energy has gone into just getting through the year. And now you almost have." As she paused, looking at Tony again, her eyes held affection and candor. "You're not like me. . . . You always needed to leave here, and now you need it more. Next fall you'll be at Harvard, meeting more girls like Alison. How can I ask you not to love one? Can you ask me to believe that you won't?"

Tony felt his stomach knot, and pulled Sue close to him. Silent, he stroked her hair, kissed her face. She did not resist or respond. "Please, Tony," she murmured, "be my friend."

As he held her, Sue's body shivered with silent tears. "Sue, I just can't lose you. . . ."

She hugged him fiercely. "And I don't want to lose you, Tony. It would tear me up inside."

Tony's eyes were damp. Miserably, he told her, "I don't know what to say to you."

She burrowed closer to him. "Then you've said it, Tony. You've already said it. Just hold me for a while."

He did that. Silent, they wept for each other.

When she was done, Sue took his face in her hands. "We'll write, okay? I want to know all about Harvard, once you get there."

Tony fought back disbelief. "Of course I'll write. . . ."

"After a while, you can even tell me about the girls you meet." She smiled a little. "Last night, I made a bet with myself. That after you graduate from Harvard, you'll marry an heiress or a movie star."

He could not smile. "After you," he said softly, "how could I marry anyone?"

A shadow crossed her face. "That's the question I've been asking—about me. But I think you will. Once you put Lake City behind you, you've got so many good things to do. Things you don't even know you want yet."

Looking into Sue's face, Tony could not imagine his life without her. It took all his willpower to ask, "Then what will you do?"

The smile she gave him, pensive and sad, was one he had not seen before they had made love. "I thought I knew. Now I really don't. I guess I'm more like you than I thought."

All at once, Tony felt his throat constrict. "I don't want this, Sue. I didn't come here to do this. . . ."

There were fresh tears in her eyes. "But I knew you would. Because you're my friend."

Gently, she placed her mouth to his. Her kiss was long and slow and passionate. "I love you," she said. And then she stood, turning suddenly, and ran across the field.

Tony did not go to his graduation or to the party afterward. It was nothing he owed himself, and seeing Sue with Sam would have been too hard on both of them. Tomorrow he was leaving for the summer.

In three months on an ore boat, hauling iron ore to Steelton from the Mesabi Range on Lake Superior, Tony would make enough to replace what his father had spent in legal fees. He was lucky to have the job; his uncle Joe had gotten it through the steelworkers union, and when Joe had suggested this weeks before, all that Tony could think of, besides the money, was getting out of Lake City. Now what he felt for Sue made this both a torment and a mercy.

Tony could not sleep. The California presidential primary election was today, he remembered—Kennedy and McCarthy, with the survivor facing Humphrey for the Democratic nomination and the chance to run against Richard Nixon in the fall. At one in the morning, restless, Tony went to the basement and switched on the television.

When Robert Kennedy came on, grinning at a crowd of well-wishers, Tony knew that Kennedy had won.

Tony listened for a while. He did not follow politics that much, and so was not sure why he liked Bobby Kennedy—except that he was Catholic and, unlike his older brother, gave Tony the sense of being a plugger, for whom public speaking did not come easily. But now Kennedy bantered with the crowd.

"I want to thank my brother-in-law, Steve Smith, who's been ruthless but effective. . . ."

Laughter.

"I want to express my gratitude to my dog, Freckles. . . ." There were a few more thank-yous, and then Kennedy became serious:

"I also want to thank my friends in the black community, who made such an effort in this campaign. . . ."

Once more, Tony thought of Ernie Nixon. Perhaps the reason he liked Robert Kennedy lay somewhere in the last seven months—his own struggle and, through that, the things he had seen in others. On the ore boat, he would have plenty of time to think about this, and who Tony Lord might become.

"So my thanks to all of you," Robert Kennedy finished, *"and now it's on to Chicago, and let's win there."*

Blankly, Tony watched the picture become a test pattern. Before he fell asleep, still lying on the basement couch, his last thoughts were of Alison, and of Sue.

He awoke to the sound of a newsman's voice.

"Senator Robert Kennedy is in critical condition after being shot in the head. . . ."

Tony stared at the television, not comprehending. Only gradually did it come to him, from the newsman's guarded comments, that Kennedy would die. The ache in his heart confused him; somehow this felt like the end of something, for others and perhaps for him. He wished that Sue were here.

He could not bring himself to switch off the television. Numbly, he went upstairs and began to pack.

EIGHTEEN

For two and a half months, Tony worked as a deck watch on the *Robert Milland*. The monotony of the end-less runs from the Mesabi to Steelton—four hours off, eight hours on, around the clock—was relieved only by bad weather, a few hours a week in some waterfront bar.

The *Robert Milland* was a six-hundred-foot solid-steel tanker, built at the turn of the century to last until the boiler cracked or the boat sank in a storm. Tony lived in a four-man cabin, two bunk beds jammed in a small space, with a college kid, a Mackinaw Indian who had been cashiered from the navy for assaulting an of-ficer, and a wizened recovering alcoholic who had been on the Great Lakes for twenty years. The captain, a fearsome Hungarian with a foul temper, would sit drink-ing in his cabin for three-day stretches. As the weeks passed, Tony's life narrowed to avoiding the captain, scraping and painting the steel hull, shoveling iron ore in the holds when its weight shifted, reading any paper-backs and magazines he could find. One magazine had an article on San Francisco; looking at photographs of this city on hills, exotic and somehow Mediterranean, Tony wondered what it would be like to live in such a place. Amidst the blank nothingness of the Great Lakes, his own life in suspension, this seemed as real to Tony as anything else. He felt like a fugitive.

The fear never left him that, at the end of his next run, a warrant would be waiting. When he thought of Alison, her image was not that of a living person; over and over, he wondered who could have killed her. With school behind him, Tony's hatred for her murderer was unrelieved by any sense of purpose; its companion, the thought of Sam with Sue, gave him no relief. Her letters told him little.

In the middle of August, an hour out of Steelton, the *Robert Milland* hit the tail end of a water spout. The sky was black, the rain drove sideways; as the boat pitched and yawed, waves covered it completely, and the steel hull bent and creaked in the storm. On the deck, Tony was linked to a web belt with five other hands, securing the hatches so that the *Milland* did not take on water. In the savage pounding, all that Tony could do was cling to the steel rope. Near him, he heard the college kid retching into the blackness.

Tony had never before feared for his life. In the rain and storm and howling wind, as awesome as creation, his mind went dark. And then the storm passed suddenly, replaced by utter stillness, more eerie for what had gone before.

When they saw Steelton, it was a little past eleven in the morning, and Tony's watch was over.

He went to his cabin, stripped off the yellow slicker, fell exhausted on his bunk. All that he could muster was a dull acceptance of what he had just passed through; it was as if he had lost his capacity to feel. Then the third mate came to tell him that a Saul Ravin was waiting for him at dockside, and Tony knew that he had not lost his capacity for dread.

The dingy waterfront—steel piers, giant cranes, corrugated warehouses—reflected the strange airlessness of a storm that had passed, the electric sky, the slick sheen of water on steel. Numb, Tony went to the Waterfront Bar and found Saul Ravin at a table, with two shot glasses of whiskey in front of him. In between the shot glasses was the police photograph of a black man.

"Here he is," Saul said without preface. "Your deliverance. Donald White, deceased."

Tony sat down. With a small smile, Saul said, "How are you, Tony?"

Tony did not reach for the shot glass. "Who is this guy?"

"The one they think killed Alison. Maybe."

Tony stared at the picture. Donald White had close-cropped hair, a thin face, and a look of hard abstraction, which could be fear or hatred or indifference. Tony found that he could muster no feeling.

"Who is he, Saul?"

"A convicted rapist. I found him through Johnny Morelli. Seven years in the Ohio pen, released in May 1967." Saul looked up from the picture. "He's also a suspect in two rapes last fall—October fourth in Columbus, October twenty-first in Akron. Both in parks, at night."

"Are there witnesses?"

"Just the victims, both teenage girls who described a generic black man. But we know he was there; on the day of each rape, he made collect calls to a sister in Detroit." Saul drew a breath. "On November fourth, the day after Alison was murdered, he called his sister from a pay phone outside your favorite Lake City bar. I've spoken to her—she remembers White saying he was in some unspecified trouble, that he was coming home. I've suggested to Morelli that it's more than a coincidence."

Staring at the photograph, Tony felt relief, then nausea as he imagined this man strangling Alison. Quietly, Saul continued, "It turns out the police have a statement from a woman, a mother who was in Taylor Park with her two kids that evening, around twilight. From a distance, the mom said, she saw a black man about this guy's size, hanging out near the bushes by the Taylor property. Donald White could be the one."

Tony could not take his eyes off the picture. Staring back at him, Donald White's frozen eyes seemed empty, soulless. "Have they said what he did to her?"

Saul touched his arm. "Alison was raped, Tony. That's all they've told me—and that, like you, White's blood type matches whatever physical evidence they have. They can't rule *him* out, either." The lawyer's gaze was level, sad. "If I knew what all he did to her, I'd tell you. But I don't."

After a time, Tony looked up. "How did he die?"

"Tried a holdup in Toledo—one of those convenience stores with a gas pump in front. The owner blew White's head off with a shotgun. A squalid end to a bad life. Which, if he killed Alison, is also too bad for you."

Tony sat back. The bar smelled of fried food, stale beer, the grimy Steelton waterfront; part of him could not accept that it was here, so far from Alison Taylor's world, that he was learning the answer to her death.

"Do *you* think he did it?" Tony asked.

Saul shrugged. "Maybe. Probably. It's not a prosecutable case, but the man's dead, so they can blame him if they want to without the inconvenience of a trial. He suits *their* purposes for the same reason he suits ours."

Tony watched his face. "But you wonder."

"It's not my job to wonder." Saul finished his shot and signaled for another. "If it were, I suppose I'd ask why White killed Alison, when the one thing he seemed very careful to do was not hurt his other victims." Saul grimaced. "Beyond raping them, that is. So I suppose that's a quibble not worth wondering about, especially when White never used a weapon to force submission, and it looks like this guy didn't, either. And I doubt the Lake City cops will quibble much."

"What are *they* going to do? Apologize?"

Saul gave a faint smile. "Not exactly. But, at my urging, Johnny Morelli is making a statement to the press this afternoon, disclosing the possibility that Alison Taylor was murdered by Donald White." His face grew serious. "It's an out for them, Tony. Their case against you is no better, and I think they now believe it will never be. And it will take some pressure off the cops. I mean, who do you think your fellow citizens would rather believe murdered Alison—Tony Lord, Harvard freshman and former high school hero, or Donald White, black serial rapist?"

It was true, Tony knew. "Donald White," he said slowly.

Saul nodded. "For some people, the idea that it's a black will be positively congenial. A lot of others will be relieved that it's a stranger, and a dead one at that, and not this boy who lived among them. It means Lake City is the kind of place they thought it was, and that they're safe again."

He should feel relieved, Tony knew. But what he felt was more bitterness. "It's a little late, Saul. Maybe not for them, but for me. What's so great about being forgiven for something I didn't do, to a girl I cared about a whole lot more than those assholes ever will? Except for her parents."

Saul studied his drink, frowning. "Yes, I suppose I should mention the Taylors. They're not willing to accept this—especially the father."

It interrupted Tony's anger. Quietly, he asked, "Why not?"

"Because John Taylor still believes what he thinks he saw that night. Maybe he always will." Saul looked up at Tony. "Leave them be, is my advice. Let them give this up on their own."

Tony shook his head. "So where am I, Saul?"

Saul folded his hands. "It depends on how you view it," he said finally. "In a way, you've entered legal purgatory—you'll never be charged, and I doubt you'll ever be cleared. For some people, you'll always be the boy who may have gotten away with murder." Saul's voice softened. "But you're free, Tony. You have your life back. You've damned well earned it."

For a moment, Tony did not know what to think, or feel. "For what it's worth to you," Saul added gently, "I've never had a client I respected more. Whatever you do with your life from here, it'll be something good."

Tony gazed at him, this rumpled, ironic man who, when no one else could, had saved his future. Suddenly there were tears in his eyes; it was not Saul Ravin's fault that some things could not be fixed. "Do you think I'd make a lawyer, Saul?"

Seeing his face, Saul took away the photograph of Donald White and placed the shot glass in Tony's hand. Softly, he said, "Let me buy you a drink, Tony. We can talk it over."

NINETEEN

Tony found Sam Robb in the hammock in his backyard, listening to a ball game on a transistor radio. Sam looked up at him, hands behind his head, quiet for a time.

"So," he said, "you're off to Harvard tomorrow."

"Yeah. I thought I'd say goodbye."

Sam sat up, watching Tony's face. "You make that sound pretty final."

Tony shrugged. "My folks are moving to Chicago— Dad asked the company for a transfer. So they won't be living here anymore."

Sam stared at the grass, hands in his pockets. He emitted a low silent breath. "I let you down," he said at last. "I could never say it right, how I felt. Instead I fucked up and lost the best friend I ever had."

Tony shook his head. "It's not you, Sam. It's everything else."

Sam's eyes met his. "But you've been cleared, man. It's over."

"Not for me."

Sam turned to the yard, silent, alone in his thoughts. Tony followed his eyes; together, they gazed at the apple trees that had once served as their goalposts, on the day when they had first become friends. "Remember making up that play?" Sam asked.

"Sure."

"I'll always remember that. And all the rest of it too." Sam turned to him again, his face puzzled, as though wondering how that time, and that feeling, had slipped through his hands. "I used to think we'd be friends all our lives, Tony. Maybe even watch our kids play football together."

For a moment, Tony was quiet. "Not here," he answered. "Not ever."

In the background, the southern-tinged voice of a broadcaster was calling out balls and strikes. Sam turned to the sound. "You know this guy Nolan Ryan," he said, "rookie pitcher for the Mets? They say he's got a real fastball."

This did not call for an answer, Tony knew. He felt Sam stretching out the moments, unable to face what had changed. But the deepest sadness for Tony was that, now, he could not feel what Sam did.

There were tears, he saw, in Sam's eyes.

His friend shrugged at his own weakness, and then stepped forward, as though to hug him. Then he stopped himself and stuck out his hand. "Good luck," he said softly. "I'll always think about you."

Shaking his friend's hand, Tony felt the passing of a time in his life—sweet and tragic and confusing—of which Sam Robb would forever be a part. "So will I," he answered softly, and left without another word. Only then did he realize that neither of them had mentioned Sue.

"Does he know?" Tony asked.

They sat at the end of the Lake City pier, at sunset. From the west, a last failing light cast shadows on the lake, turning the water gray blue.

"No," Sue answered. "At least not from anything I've said." She paused, not looking at him. "Sometimes I think he maybe guesses, from how I've been. But he's already talking about marriage."

Tony found that he, too, could not look at Sue. "And you?"

"I don't know. I have a lot to think about."

Quiet, Tony touched her hand.

"I know you have to leave," she said after a time. "It's just that I can't imagine it. You were so real to me that night, and now you'll be like this dream I had."

At first, there was nothing he could say. Gently, he turned her face to his. "You'll always be real to me, Sue. If you ever needed me for anything, I'd come."

Silent, she rested her face against his chest. "I know," she said softly. "I know."

When he dropped Sue at her house and drove away, Tony could see her in the rearview mirror, a shadow in the driveway, watching him leave. All at once, he knew that this was his true goodbye to Lake City.

Tony immersed himself in Harvard, went out for crew, visited his roommate at Thanksgiving. By Christmas, his parents had moved; he never returned to Lake City. When Sam called, and then Sue, he did not know what to say.

The nightmare, haunting in its sameness, never left him.

His senior year had everything to do with who Tony Lord became. But in the years that followed, he rarely spoke of it at all, until he told everything to Stacey Tarrant, the singer and actress, his second wife, a few months before they were married.

PART TWO
MARCIE CALDER

THE PRESENT

ONE

Two days before her seventeenth birthday, Marcie Calder killed herself; died in a fall; or was murdered.

A half hour from landing in Steelton, Anthony Lord reviewed what little he knew. From the pictures in the newspaper, Marcie appeared dark and slight and pretty. She was the oldest daughter of a family with three girls; a solid B student at Lake City High School; an observant Catholic who was a member of Tony's old parish, Saint Raphael's. The *Steelton Press* described her as shy; her best friend, Janice D'Abruzzi, interviewed after the funeral, said that she had not dated anyone special. The newspaper accounts of the grief counseling that followed, a chance for her fellow students to face what had happened, told Tony less about Marcie than about the feverish contagion of teenage sadness, the grim resolve of the town to cope with the inexplicable. Not since the murder of Alison Taylor, Principal Burton said, had Lake City suffered such a tragedy. The thing he most remembered about Marcie struck Tony Lord as rather sad: that she was the fastest girl on the track team and, when competing, ran with a joy and abandon that was beautiful to watch.

Four days prior to her death, in her last competition as a runner, Marcie had done poorly. Afterward, her teammates recalled, she was listless, unresponsive. On the following morning, the police had found her on the beach below Taylor Park, a ribbon of blood on her head and cheek. From the condition of the body, it was plain that she had died sometime during the night. No one knew how.

There were several theories. The drop to the beach from the cliff above was more than ninety feet; from the mud on her blue jeans, and the marks on the cliff itself, it appeared that Marcie had fallen. But a rock on the beach yielded samples of Marcie's blood and hair. The man who had taken her to the park that night—the last person to admit seeing her alive—was not available for comment. Her track coach, Sam Robb, the assistant principal of Lake City High School.

For a final moment, Tony studied the newspaper photograph of Marcie Calder and, next to it, that of Alison Taylor. He could never look at Alison's picture, Tony realized, without feeling the same rush of grief and loss, as fresh as yesterday.

He put the paper in his leather briefcase and wondered how, after twenty-eight years, Sam Robb's wife would seem to him.

He would have recognized her, Tony thought, even on a beach in Capri.

He was first off the plane. She seemed not quite ready for him; after a moment, she mustered a tentative smile, the shadow of her old dimples. When he put down his briefcase and opened his arms, she ran forward to meet him.

For a time, Tony simply held her, close and tight, senses filling despite everything with the surprise and wonder of Sue Cash in his arms again—the fresh, clean smell of her, the strange familiarity of how she felt to him. "Oh, Tony," she murmured. "It really is you."

"Yes. I decided not to send someone."

She leaned back, looking at him, her expression a complex mix of sadness, emotion at seeing him, relief that he was here. Even with lines in her face, her skin was smooth and fresh; the vibrant dark eyes were the same, the dark curls shorter now but still much as before. She was, if anything, more slender.

Tony backed up a foot, inspecting her. The tightness in his throat was yet another surprise. "This is probably the wrong thing to say," he told her at last. "But you look like you to me."

Once more, she tried to smile. "It's never the wrong thing to say. Just a little bit of Clairol and a lot of time at the gym. A few years ago, I'd look back and see my bottom, and wonder who was following me around." Suddenly her eyes shone with tears. "I'm surprised I look like anything at all. . . ."

Tony drew her close again. When she raised her face, the tears were gone, though her voice was tremulous. "You look good too, Tony. Better than you can ever know."

They did not, at first, talk about Marcie Calder.

Sue drove the Ford Taurus away from the airport toward Lake City, through housing developments and shopping malls that Tony, squinting in the sun of a bright spring morning, recalled as flat green fields. What Tony wanted most to know—how she was, what her life with Sam had been until now—were things he did not ask. But eliciting more routine facts seemed to help them both. Their two kids, Sam junior and Jennifer, were both out of college. Young Sam, never the athlete his father had hoped for, was studying for an MBA at Kansas University; Jenny taught preschool in Florida. Sue had finished her degree in library science; she worked part time at the Lake City Public Library, helping with the children's section. Sue's tone seemed almost normal; it was as though, if she kept talking, her humiliation would not surface. She did not mention Sam.

"How's the town?" Tony asked. "Still the same?"

"To look at it, except the empty lots are filled with houses now. But things have changed beneath the surface—we have drugs at high school; Protestants don't hate Catholics anymore; and about every other family is divorced or has both parents working. The kids don't have to go parking now; they can make love after school, in the privacy of their parents' home. . . ." She stopped abruptly; Tony did not have to guess at her thoughts. Softly, she added, "It's still small, Tony. At a time like this, you feel how small it is."

For a moment, the present slipped away, and Tony was back in a crowded high school gym.

"Killer, killer . . ."

"The Taylors," he asked. "Are they still alive?"

"Yes." Sue gazed fixedly at the road. "I don't know how you remember them. But to me they look like bitter old people, serving out their lives." She paused for a moment. "Katherine Taylor told my mother, only four or five years ago, that there has never been a day since Alison died that they don't remember. When I think of Marcie Calder's parents, I think of that."

Tony felt his heart go out to her. At length, he asked, "How is he, Sue?"

Her fingers seemed to tighten on the steering wheel. "Scared," she said. "You know what that's like."

Something in Tony resisted the comparison. "All I know is what it was like for me."

Sue was quiet for a moment. "He could be charged with murder," she said in flat voice. "Or, if he's lucky, all that we'll have to worry about is the end of his career as a teacher. Unless he can explain to the school board what he was doing in Taylor Park, at night, with a girl on his track team."

What had Sam told her? Tony wondered. "If he takes my advice as a lawyer," he answered, "Sam won't say anything to the school board. Not until we see what the county prosecutor does about her death."

Sue did not answer. The roads became narrow; at the edge of a field, Tony saw the first familiar landmark—the white spire of Saint Barnabas Episcopal, where Alison's funeral had been held. Then they passed a white wooden sign, not unlike the one Tony remembered: "Welcome to Lake City, Home of the Lakers. Population 15,537."

The next few miles were strange. It had been so long that, for an instant, this seemed like entering a place Tony had seen only in pictures. What hit him first was nostalgia and then remembered trauma—feelings from before and after Alison's death—followed by the sudden superstitious certainty that he should not have returned. Quietly, he said, "I never thought I'd come back here."

"I know."

They took a curve in the narrow road, past an elementary school and some wood-frame houses, and then Tony saw something that had not been there before—a large wrought-iron gate to the entrance of a development of brick ranch houses. The contractor had left just enough maple trees to justify the iron lettering above the gate: "Maple Park Estates."

In spite of himself, Tony turned. And then he felt Sue watching him.

"Remember?" she asked.

What he felt, Tony realized, was a rush of pain and sweetness, surprise at the power of memory, the immediacy of his youth. "Remember?" he said softly. "It was the sweetest thing that had ever happened to me."

Sue smiled a little. "If I'd known that, Tony, I'd have made you do it twice."

As they drove on, silent, Tony felt his unease return, the moment slip away. More than being in Lake City, this came from thinking of Sam Robb again—whoever he might have become.

Reaching the town square, Tony saw the police station. "I have a favor to ask you," he said after a time. "As a lawyer, I suppose. Before I see Sam."

"What is it?"

Tony turned to her. "Could you take me to Taylor Park?"

When they turned into the park, Tony tried to see it with detachment, as a crime scene. But for a moment, he could not move.

Quietly, Sue asked, "What is it you wanted to see?"

"Where this girl went over the cliff, I thought."

Near the cliff were metal stakes driven into the ground, bound with yellow tape to mark off where Marcie Calder might have fallen. But Tony did not go there; leaving the car, he saw the grove of trees where he had parked with Alison Taylor.

"Do you mind?" he asked Sue.

"No." She paused. "Do you want me to come with you?"

"If you like."

When he began walking toward the grove, Sue was with him, a few steps behind. They were quiet.

The park was sunny, the breeze from Lake Erie fresh. But beneath the bower of trees where he and Alison had made love, there was little sun, and the ground was dark and mossy. It struck him that the park was almost empty.

Tony stood there for a moment, recovering that part of him that was a professional. "Who uses this?" he asked.

Sue stood behind him. "Kids, families. We used to bring ours here."

"What about at night?"

"Kids still, parking." She paused; Tony could feel her imagining her husband, parked with a teenage girl younger than their own daughter. In a thin voice, she added, "For a while, after Alison, high school kids found other places. Then people forgot."

"Anyone else?"

"From the local paper, other kids dealing drugs, sometimes a few homeless people." Her tone was flat again. "Sam always told Jenny not to come here."

It would be wrong, Tony thought, to avoid looking at her. When he did, Sue simply shrugged. Her eyes were abstracted, almost lifeless; somehow she looked smaller than before. He did not ask about Sam.

Together, they left the grove.

Just as he had twenty-eight years before, hurrying home with Alison in the last hour of her life, Tony walked across the grassy park. As he moved from the trees that marked the Taylors' property, he stopped, overtaken by emotion. He felt the beating of his own heart.

The Taylor house needed repainting, he saw; the wooden shingles of the roof were warped and cracking, and the Gothic turrets looked dingy. His eyes followed a line from the back porch to their rear yard. He did not simply remember her face in the beam of the flashlight; for almost thirty years, this had been a recurring nightmare, awakening him at the moment that the light revealed her face.

Behind him, Sue said, "You almost never see them outside."

Tony made himself turn to the house again. "Not exactly the House of Usher. But not what it was."

The thickets where Ernie Nixon had shown him the hiding places were, if anything, more overgrown. He did not bother to inspect them.

"Someone was here that night, Sue. Someone could

have been here four nights ago." He turned to her. "Marcie Calder left his car, Sam says?"

Sue's face lost all expression. "Yes."

After a moment, Tony nodded. "I'd better take a look."

There were two sections to the crime scene, Tony saw. The first, an area roughly forty feet square, was a section of the grassy bank extending to the edge of the cliff. Erosion made the cliff quite sheer; beneath its face—sixty feet of rock and clay and the occasional windswept bush—an area of beach had been cordoned by more stakes and yellow tape. Near the foot of the cliff, this time in white tape, the outline of Marcie Calder's body resembled a child's drawing.

"In the dark," Tony said, "she could have fallen easily."

"Wouldn't she hear the lake?" Sue asked, and turned away. In the deep susurrus of the water, Tony wondered if Sue believed that her husband—a man Tony no longer knew—was capable of murder. He went to where she stood, arms folded, staring at the ground.

"Have the police talked to you?" he asked.

Sue did not look up. "They tried. Just before I called you, when they searched the house and impounded my car. The one he drove that night."

Tony shoved his hands in the pockets of his khakis. "Did *he* want me to come here, Sue? Or was it you?"

"It was my idea, at first." Her eyes met his. "Sam's very proud, Tony. Still. He let you down about Alison, he said—how could he ask you to help him now? But after a while he knew how much he needed you." She paused for a moment. "We both saw you on TV, defending the man who shot Senator Kilcannon. Sam couldn't believe how good you were. But I could."

Tony watched her. There had been a change in her; at some time between then and now, as time and perhaps disappointment had done its work, her face had become hard to read.

"What is he like, Sue?"

"Before now?" Looking at Tony, she smiled without humor. "Not like you, Tony. Sam achieved his goals too soon."

"How do you mean?"

"Oh, I think you understand. He stayed in Lake City; he married me—it was like he could preserve Sam Robb at seventeen, the way he felt then. But he couldn't." The smile became a frown without changing very much. "Sam's a vice principal, not the principal. He needs someone to help him make good judgments—he knows that, and he hates it. In his eyes, he's become a small man in a small town: good old Sam, quick with a joke, the vice principal for life. So there's this terrible restlessness."

"And you?"

"I'm different. We have two good kids, some friends we like, and what I do seems worthwhile to me. If Sam were happy, I could be happy." She shook her head. "It's so funny to me—I remember seeing you with Stacey, on some awards show I think it was, and smiling to myself because you *had* married a movie star, and she was gorgeous. But it wasn't until my own husband turned to me and said, 'Look at who Tony's with now,' that, just for a moment, I wished *I* could be her. Because I saw Sam jealous of you, and not happy with his life."

"But what do *I* have to do with anything?"

"For Sam? A lot, I think, sometimes." Pausing, Sue seemed to muse aloud. "This may sound funny, as far away from here as you've been, and for so long now. But if you'd stayed, and been the basketball coach or something, I wonder if Sam would be a little less disappointed with himself."

Sue, he was certain, already knew how pointless this was. Softly, he answered, "He was never going to be like me, Sue. After Alison, the only question was who *I* was going to be."

Sue tilted her head. "Are *you* happy with who you are?"

"Mostly. There are still parts of me—because of Alison's murder, I'm sure—that I wish I could tear out by the roots. Sometimes I find myself waiting for the other shoe to drop, some terrible thing to happen to Stacey or to Christopher, or even to me." For a moment, he paused. "But it hasn't, yet. And the rest of me, more days than not, is happier than I ever believed I could be."

Sue was quiet. And then she touched his face, the gesture of a friend, gladdened that the life of *her* friend was as he wished. In that moment, Tony realized that being with Sue was still, despite everything, mercifully easy— that, even now, she understood things about him that the two people he loved most never could. What he wanted, for both their sakes, was to hold her one more time.

Perhaps Sue wanted this too, Tony thought. But he was here as a lawyer, and must start to find his way. "I hope I can help you," he said. "And Sam."

"You already have," she answered softly. As she removed her hand, Sue's fingers grazed his cheek. "We'd better go, Tony. Sam's waiting. The last four days, it's all he's had to do."

TWO

From the basement couch, Sam Robb gazed up.

His quick glance at Sue, his look away, struck Tony as instinctive shame. But his rueful smile at Tony was like that of a man caught cheating at golf. Perhaps, Tony thought, Sam was still working out what had happened to him. He appeared no more ready for Tony than Tony was for him: Tony's first thought, sickening and inevitable, was to wonder if he was gazing at a murderer.

"Hello, Sam."

Awkwardly, Sam stood, and the two men embraced. "Tony Lord," Sam murmured. "Sweet Jesus Christ."

"Oh," Tony found himself saying, "I'm not quite that good."

Sam gave a short laugh, harsh in its suddenness. He leaned back, clasping Tony by the shoulders. His face was puffy, Tony saw, the white-blond hair streaked with silver. But his eyes had a sudden bright glitter; it was like seeing the seventeen-year-old Sam peering at him from behind a mask. "Sue thinks you're that good," he answered, and then his voice softened. "I sure need you to be."

Sue had turned from her husband. "I'll be upstairs," she said to Tony. "If you need a sandwich or something . . ."

"Thanks, babe," Sam told her.

Her eyes flickered; in a room with Sam, Tony thought, there was something stricken about her. She went upstairs without acknowledging her husband.

Sam exhaled, running a hand through his hair. Above the top of his sweatpants, Tony saw a small, but noticeable, belly; his chin was soft, his face creased. The effect was somewhat raffish, but not unattractive. He looked like a once youthful actor who, ten years past his prime, had not so much aged as dissipated; the boyishness kept showing through. For an instant, Tony could imagine him with a teenage girl, and felt an instinctive flash of revulsion.

But what stayed with Tony was sadness, the sense of promise lost. The room around them was dark, cramped; a sliver of daylight came through a small window at ground level. On the mantel of a brick-veneer fireplace Tony saw a couple of gold trophies from the Lake City

Country Club; a picture of Sam and a slim, dark-haired boy who looked more like Sue; and another trophy Tony recognized at once. SAM ROBB, the brass lettering said, ATHLETE OF THE YEAR—1968. Suddenly Tony felt claustrophobic.

Sam was watching him, Tony realized. "I told Sue you'd never come back," he said softly. "But then she always had a better sense of you, I guess."

"You're in trouble, Sam."

"So were *you*, once." Sam's gaze was steady, penetrating. "You're still not over it, are you?"

"That never quite happens, I'm afraid."

Suddenly Sam looked down. Softly, he said, "I didn't kill her, Tony. That's why I went to the cops."

The fierceness of Tony's desire to believe this took him by surprise. With equal quiet, he asked, "What happened to you, Sam?"

Sam turned to the window. For a moment, he was quiet. "We were all right, Sue and I. Not great, maybe, but all right. We were good parents. We did the right things—went to their activities, saved our money, sent them to college. They were the center of our lives. Then they were gone, and here I still was, not going anywhere. . . ." Pausing, Sam faced Tony again. "That's why I didn't want you here. To see that."

In its raw simplicity, the statement startled Tony— that Sam had come to know this and could say it to him so soon. Almost gently, Tony said, "Tell me about Marcie Calder."

Sam glanced upstairs; to Tony, the presence of Sue, the delicate balance between wife and husband, was suddenly, palpable.

"Let's go for a walk," Sam murmured.

The house, which once had been Sam's parents', was a few blocks from the high school. For most of the walk they were quiet; remembering each street, the wood-frame houses or brick bungalows of kids he once had known, Tony felt connected with a time, long before Alison had died, when this place and its sameness were comforting, the only world he cared about. He stopped in front of the white house, now covered with aluminum siding, where Mary Jane Kulas had lived.

"Know what happened to *her*?" Sam asked. "She's a nurse. And a grandmother."

"Jesus."

"That's not the half of it. She must weigh three hundred pounds. . . ."

It was odd, Tony thought; listening, he felt like a ghost. *I swear I saw Tony Lord,* he imagined someone saying, *the kid who killed Alison Taylor, big as life, hanging out with Sam Robb. Probably comparing notes . . .*

Sam had stopped talking. "This is weird for you," he finally asked, "isn't it?"

"Yeah."

They stood face-to-face on the sidewalk. Softly, Sam said, "I haven't left the house since Monday. Couldn't face anyone." He paused, tears in his eyes. "That's when I knew how big an apology I owed you, Tony, all those years ago."

They sat in the wooden stands, gazing at an empty football field. There was no one around.

"What about Coach Jackson?" Tony asked.

"Oh, he died, man. Popped an aorta, about five years after you left." Sam propped his chin in his hands, looking straight ahead. "You knew he was fucking my mother, I guess. Everyone knew."

Silence, Tony thought, was answer enough.

"Well," Sam said after a time, "at least she wasn't in high school."

The naked self-contempt jarred Tony; perhaps he had been hoping for Sam's expression of sadness, some regret that a girl he had known was dead. But it was not the first time that Tony had seen this; the self-absorption of those facing murder charges was so total, their fear so complete, that they often forgot the victim. And seldom more so, Tony reminded himself, than when they were guilty.

Sam was watching him again. "There was something I've always wondered, though. About Sue. You were fucking her, weren't you?"

Surprised, Tony made his face blank, a lawyer's reflex. "You give me too much credit. And Sue too little."

Slowly, Sam nodded. "Yeah. She'd never do that to me, would she."

Once more, the words had a self-lacerating quality. "I guess you were 'fucking' Marcie Calder, then."

Sam sat straighter, inhaling. He did not answer.

"Let's get something straight," Tony said evenly. "I'm your lawyer now—not an old friend, someone you've met again at a high school reunion and want to impress. As a lawyer, my role is not to judge you but to give you the best advice and, if necessary, the best defense.

"For those purposes, it doesn't matter if you slept with her—it shouldn't to me, and it can't to you, however we might feel as friends. But this is one time I'll fire a client for lying to me. Because it damn well matters if you try to use me, and if you do, all you'll get is the stupid advice you'll deserve."

Sam turned to him, flushed. "Look . . ."

"Screw around with me now," Tony said in his most unimpressed voice, "and you'll lose your career, and maybe the rest of your life. The only way I can help you is to get the truth. Whatever that is."

Sam drew a deep breath. "Oh, you'll get the truth, Tony. Just like you've always given it to me. So don't *you* lie to me now. You *care*. Your own girlfriend was murdered when you were seventeen, and you care a lot. Not about sex, maybe. But about whether your old friend Sam is a murderer."

Tony felt himself tense. "All right, Sam . . . I want you to be innocent. Not just because of Alison, but because of Sue. *And* you." He paused a moment, and muted his tone. "If you're guilty, tell me now and I'll find you another lawyer. Because I won't be the one you need. I know that, going in."

Leaning forward, Sam's eyes locked Tony's. "I've done a lot of things, pal. Things you won't respect. But I am *not* a murderer." He paused, finishing softly: "Please, I need you to believe that."

Sam's voice was husky with suppressed emotion, the sound of truth. Through his own desire to believe, Tony found himself wondering which part of the statement was true—all of it, or only the last. Finally, he answered, "Then I do."

Sam's bulky frame seemed to relax. After a time, he asked, "So what do you want to know, Tony?"

"Everything. To start, what Marcie Calder was like."

Sam gave him a long look before answering. "To tell you the truth, Tony, she reminded me of Alison."

It was the way she carried herself, Sam explained— graceful, a little aloof, as if living in a secret. Marcie was not as smart, and surely not as privileged; yet there was this sense of privacy, of a girl who held herself back. Her greatest freedom seemed to be in motion.

She was tall and slender, Sam said; she had pale skin, straight black hair, which fell across her cheekbones. But her reticence seemed more like shyness than some deeper commitment to privacy; where Alison was practical—a realist, as Sam remembered her—this girl struck him as a romantic. It fell to Sam, her coach, to impose some discipline on her talent.

But she *had* talent and, Sam admitted, he liked to watch her, the careful way she listened to him, how she believed in him with her eyes. Next to those eyes, Marcie's legs were the best part of her; she was almost flat-chested, but she had the legs of a ballerina, strong enough to run not just the hundred-yard dash but also the two-twenty. Sam's assignment to the girls' track team had been an afterthought of the principal—an insult, Sam believed, because it suggested that he considered Sam's time unimportant—and Sam saw himself as the faded athlete, shepherding young girls on the field where once he had excelled, which now had become the treadmill of a stalled life. But Marcie had transformed this: not only did she admire him, but he could make her special. When she first asked to stay after practice, to work with him in that vital burst from the starter's block, he had been happy to do so. An hour later, she was much better; for the first time, watching from behind as she bent over the cinder track, Sam admired the sinew of her thighs, the tightness of her bottom. There was something sensual about the way she froze there, waiting for his command to start.

The first meet of the new season, Marcie won both races.

Even then, she was not talkative. But Sam could see it in her eyes. They *shone*, he said to Tony; he had helped her discover something even more important than the love of running—she, Marcie Calder, was the best. When she ran up to hug him, the pressure of her body, closer than Sam expected, made him feel aroused.

The girls went to their locker room; Sam to his office, next to the principal's. The secretaries were gone; the principal was attending a convention. Sam began reviewing the attendance report.

He heard footsteps in the front office, quiet and soft. There had been a problem with student theft; as he started to get up, Marcie Calder appeared in his doorway. She was still in her track suit; the surprise of this made Sam's heart skip. He took in her long legs and then her eyes, grave and very still, the light sprinkling of freckles on the bridge of her nose. Even before she said anything, he felt that strange electricity that any man knows—the sense that something never spoken no longer needs to be.

He tried to smile. "Hi, Marcie. What's up?"

She gave the smallest shrug of her shoulders, eyes not moving from his. "I wanted to say thank you."

"For what? *You* won the races."

Slowly, Marcie shook her head. "You made me win." Her voice was soft. "Please, can I close the door?"

Sam felt a constriction in his throat. How many times, he wondered, had he told his teachers never to meet with students behind closed doors—with how paranoid parents were these days, the dangers of sexual harassment charges, the risks of privacy were too great. "All right," he heard himself say. "If you think you need to."

Head bowed, she closed the door behind her. When she faced him, Marcie hesitated for a minute.

"I'm in love with you," she said.

Blood pounding in his head, Sam ventured another smile. "Just like Jennifer, my daughter. Until she saw through me."

Her eyes did not accept this; where had she learned so much, Sam wondered, and how had he given himself away? Calmly, she answered, "Like a woman, Mr. Robb."

He should have smiled at that last. But all he said was, "Oh. Like that."

She was by his chair now. He could see the crucifix around her neck, the delicacy of her collarbone. "I've never slept with a man," she said quietly. "I don't think I'm ready."

"Neither am I. And when you are, Marcie, it'll be someone more age-appropriate, like they say at teachers meetings."

"No," she said. "I want it to be you. Just not now."

The blinds beside him were open, he realized. From the inner yard, some janitor might see them. "Then what is it you want?" he asked.

She had followed his eyes. When she lowered the blinds, he did not stop her.

Kneeling, she unbuckled his belt.

"Marcie, for God's sake . . ."

She looked up at him. "I know how," she said. "Not from experience. But people talk, you know. . . ." Then she paused, and the crown of her head bent forward.

Sam stopped thinking.

He raised himself slightly. When he looked down, he saw what he had already felt. Her black hair grazed his thighs.

For a time, he did not move, or make a sound.

To Tony, it sounded wrong: the seductive student, the aging man.

"Have you just finished *Lolita*?" he asked. "It's classic male fantasy."

Sam shrugged, staring straight ahead. "I guess that's why it happened."

Pausing, Tony reviewed his incredulity. "This sixteen-year-old just came to you like that? No come-on from you, no double entendres, nothing to tell you that *she* was a little off? Just out of the blue?"

"You wanted the truth, dammit." Sam turned on him. "This wouldn't only get me run out of Lake City, or even just cost me my license to teach anywhere. If a teacher told *me* that story tomorrow, I'd be obliged by law to take this to the county prosecutor. I don't know about San Francisco, but in this state, statutory rape and oral copulation with a minor are good for time in prison." His voice was soft with bitterness. "As an assistant principal, I'm a perfect object lesson for some judge. I'm already on administrative leave because I *might* have had sex with her. So my 'classic male fantasy' is way too dumb to be a lie, Tony. Even before the part where Sue walks out and my kids can't stand to look at me."

Tony sat back, gazing at the football field where, twenty-eight years before, with Sue and Alison watching, he and Sam had achieved together the moment they had always imagined. "All right," he said softly. "Tell me about the night she died."

THREE

They met at twilight, around eight-thirty, in the parking lot of a defunct gas station. It was the second time they had done this; as before, Marcie left her car and slipped into the passenger seat next to Sam. On the first night, six weeks before, the risk had lent a sense of danger to a novelty that, Sam confessed to Tony, aroused him—a willing girl for whom everything they did was new. They had gone to Taylor Park; hidden by bushes, Marcie had undressed. As Sam had slipped on the condom, she lay back on the sleeping bag, legs open for him, waiting. He was careful not to hurt her; when he entered, Sam could feel the light skipping of her heart, her soft breath against his face. Then she had whispered, "I love you," and her voice had been so wispy, so young, that his own climax had filled him with shame.

As Sam told it, the night she had vanished was to be the end. The lawyer in Tony could not assume that Sam's story was true. But Sam had the storyteller's gift: from the beginning, Tony could imagine the silence in the car—a man hoping to pull back from self-destruction, a girl lost in fantasy, oblivious to the gulf between them.

Tony sat back and allowed himself to envision the

night as Sam described it and even, at some moments, to believe him.

The evening was cool, clear. It was a school night, and the lot at Taylor Park was empty. When the car stopped, Marcie moved close. Softly, she asked, "What do you want tonight?"

Sam glanced at his watch, already anxious. He had forgotten some papers, he had told Sue, and so would work at school. That gave him roughly an hour to leave Marcie still adoring, still committed to secrecy.

"No one knows you're here?" he asked.

A quick bob of the head, a kiss on his cheek. "Right now, people wouldn't understand."

The sad thought struck Sam that this girl, who had given him her innocence, did not know what name to call him. Then her meaning hit him hard: in some illusory future, Marcie Calder imagined that Lake City *would* understand.

"Let's just talk for a while," he said.

With a trust that touched him, Marcie slid into his lap, nuzzling her head against his face. She felt more slight than ever; Sam had the jarring memory of Jennifer, wearing a cotton nightgown on Christmas Eve, nestled in his arms as Sue read aloud from "'Twas the Night Before Christmas."

"I think we should get married," Marcie murmured.

Holding her in the dark, Sam was speechless with surprise. How could he have missed that this girl was so young, even for sixteen; that her feelings were so like an adolescent's fixation on a movie star—or, as bad, a father substitute.

At last, Sam answered, "I don't think we ever could."

She leaned back, gazing into his face. "Why not?"

Where to start? he wondered. "There's my wife," he said simply.

As he watched her absorb this, Sam's sense of the

grotesque overwhelmed him—he was discussing Sue,
his wife of twenty-four years, with a teenage girl who
imagined replacing her. "There are a lot of things," he
went on. "Your parents, my job, the way people would
look at me. The way they *should* look at me—a middle-
aged guy who betrayed his student's family, her school,
her natural affection for him—"

"*No.*" Sam heard sudden tears in her voice. "My feelings for you are so much more. . . ."

"Then I'm lucky." Desperate, Sam called on his gifts
of flattery. "I'm lucky even to have been a part of your
life—"

He stopped abruptly. Headlights had appeared in his
rearview mirror; turning, Sam prayed that it was not a
cop. Then he saw the car park some distance away, ex-
tinguishing its lights. When he held Marcie close again,
heart racing, her body felt wiry, resistant.

"I want you to *be* my life." Her voice became strong,
eerily certain. "Once we get married, people will accept
it. I can finish high school and go to college, just like my
parents want—"

"Marcie," Sam cut in, voice rising. "I've *met* your
parents. Can you imagine your father with a son-in-law
older than he is—your track coach?" He caught himself,
fearful of angering her. "It's possible for us to love each
other, Marcie. But I'm too far along to ever become your
life. You'd have ten years with a guy way too old for
you, and then throw away the next twenty taking care
of an old man."

She was very still now. In a different voice, cooler and
older, she said, "You can't leave your wife, then."

The undertone in her words worried him, but he seized
on their bracing realism. "No," he answered. "I never
could."

Tense, he hung on Marcie's silence. "All right, Sam."
The name, used for the first time, held a note of youthful
contempt. "I won't tell anyone. Is that what you want?"

Sam's next breath was almost a sigh. "Yes. It would be the best thing for *you*, Marcie. And it would help me too."

"I'll help you," she said coldly. Then her face appeared in a sliver of light; her skin was pale, her tears like streaks on marble. Abruptly, she pulled away, jerking open the car door. "I'll start helping you right now—"

Sam grabbed her sleeve. *"Wait—"*

Marcie jerked it away. "For what?" she asked with vehemence. "For you to give me more precious memories . . . ?"

Her voice caught, suddenly she was out the door, running away.

Sam opened his door without thinking. As the cool air hit his face, he squinted to spot her, a swiftly moving shadow, outlined by the moon above the lake. He started after her; as he stopped, remembering the other car, Marcie vanished in the darkness.

He froze, irresolute. And then he felt his real life pull him from this precipice—he had to leave, put himself somewhere where he could be, once again, the Sam Robb whom people expected. Marcie's car was parked less than a quarter mile away: when her emotions had subsided, she could find her way back, become a sixteen-year-old girl with a curfew. By tomorrow, at school, Sam could begin the edgy work of pretending she had never been anything else.

Glancing over his shoulder, he got back into the car.

The seat next to his seemed too empty. Leaning over, he shut the passenger door, turned on the radio for reassurance. He was still shaken; driving from the park, the last thing he saw in his headlights was a shadow of the parked car, a single head, barely visible above the dashboard, which seemed to watch him leave.

He could not go home. Instinctively, he drove to school, where he had told Sue he would be working—the easiest lies to tell, Sam knew, contained an element of truth. He needed time to think.

Beneath the bleak fluorescent light, Sam slumped in his chair.

His thoughts were jumbled, fretful. All that he could do was try to reenter his life, step by step.

The first step, he decided, was to call Sue.

He dialed, bracing for the sound of her voice. When, instead, he heard his own voice on the answering machine, he had the sudden fear, as piercing as superstition, that Sue had somehow followed him—that it was *her* head in the shadowy car, that *she*, even now, was confronting Marcie Calder in Taylor Park.

On the telephone, his last taped words were followed by a beep.

"Hi, honey." He tried to make his voice sound normal, perhaps a little tired. "This stuff took longer than I thought—staff evaluations. Another few minutes, and I'll be home. . . ."

Putting down the telephone, he felt a moment's peace—this would be his last lie. And then, riding the roller coaster of anxiety, he wondered again why Sue had not answered.

The drive home, perhaps two minutes, was shadowed by his imaginings of Marcie. Perhaps she was still in the park. Sam wondered if he should go back. Then, more vividly, he envisioned Marcie with her parents, telling them—in a sudden, hormonal outburst—everything Sam Robb had done with her. He found himself opening his own front door, a coward.

Downstairs was dark and quiet. In this mood, the silence made him nervous.

Slowly, he walked upstairs.

Voices came from the bedroom. Softly, he walked down the hallway, pausing with his head to the bedroom door. And then, heart pounding, he entered it.

Sue was in bed, filing her nails, half listening to the eleven o'clock news.

"I tried to call you," he said.

She looked up at him, incurious. "I must have been in the shower," she said, and then frowned. "Broke another nail—my hands look like a washerwoman's."

Sam stood there a moment. "You've got beautiful hands, babe. Long fingers."

Sue smiled a little. "Well," she said, "they're not as beautiful as Jenny's."

Somehow this made Sam want to kiss her. But he stopped himself; he did not know what behavior might seem odd, or repentant. He changed into his boxer shorts and crawled into bed.

"I'm tired," he said, content to tell the truth.

Sue reached for the remote. "Go to sleep, then," she answered, and turned off the TV.

Another step taken, Sam thought. Reflecting on Marcie, dreading their first meeting tomorrow, he lay awake in the darkness of their bedroom, very still, so as not to draw attention to his restlessness.

The next morning, three cups of coffee feeling like acid in an empty stomach, Sam Robb, the assistant principal of Lake City High School, sat waiting in his office for the homeroom attendance sheets.

Jane Moore, his old classmate's wife, was the front-office secretary. He poked his head out the door.

"Have the attendance sheets come in yet?"

She turned to look at him, brow furrowed. "No," she said. "But we just had a call from Nancy Calder, Marcie's mother. . . ."

"What's wrong?"

"Nothing, I hope. But they don't know where she is."

Sam cocked his head; at this worst moment of his life, with the ground slipping out from under him, he was proud of how professional he sounded—concerned, not panicked, just the right note of worry. "When was the last time Nancy saw her?"

"At about eight o'clock last night. Marcie said she was going to a friend's, but she never came back. Nancy's called the police."

Watching her, Sam felt the weight of his own silence. "Keep me posted, all right?"

At nine-thirty, no one had seen Marcie.

Leaving the office, Sam sat in the parking lot, alone. In the worn felt of the passenger seat he imagined seeing the smallest indentation, the imprint of her body.

Moments of calculation passed. With every minute, Sam saw his cowardice more clearly. Desperate to reclaim himself, reckless of consequence, he drove to the police station.

Two detectives, Jack Seed and Carl Talley, stood holding cups of coffee. Somehow this was a relief: both had sons in high school, knew Sam as someone who liked their boys. Jack Seed raised his eyebrows. "Hi, Sam. What can we do for you?"

"I'm here about Marcie Calder. I saw her last night, after her parents did. From around eight-thirty to maybe ten."

"Ten?" Jack Seed sounded relieved. "Where?"

"Taylor Park."

For the first time, Sam noticed how keen Seed's eyes were. "Taylor Park," the detective repeated. "Think you can go there with us?"

The squad car stopped in the parking lot, Sam in the back seat. Sometime in the night, it had rained; the park looked slick, and a chill mist hung over the lake.

Sam leaned over the front seat, pointing. "There," he said. "That's where I last saw her, running."

Jack Seed turned to him, his thin face reflecting only mild curiosity. "At night? Know why she was running here?"

"We'd been talking. She was . . . upset."

Seed pursed his lips. "Oh," he said, and turned to Talley. "We'd better take a look."

It was a moment before Talley stopped watching Sam's face. They got out of the car; when Sam followed, neither protested.

Crossing the grass, Seed looked around him. "Shitty day," he said.

"Shitty night," Talley answered. It was as if Sam were no longer there.

A few feet from the cliff, Seed stopped, staring down at the ground. Turning, he murmured, "Can you stay back, Sam." Stopping, Sam saw the two detectives change direction slightly, as if not wishing to step in something.

The two walked to the edge of the cliff, peering downward.

It was Talley, Sam saw, who slumped a little; Seed became quite still. "Damn," Seed said softly.

Sam walked over. When he stood between them, gazing down at Marcie, no one spoke.

She lay near the foot of the cliff, face turned up, still wearing the track team sweatshirt she had worn the night before. It hid her secret, she had said flirtatiously, sliding into Sam's car—no bra. From here, she looked tiny, a rag doll.

Sam sat at the edge of the cliff, numb. Above him, he heard Seed murmur, "Better call the EMTs."

Only then did it strike Sam that his life, as he had known it until now, was over.

For a long time, Tony did not speak; the narrative, he realized, had taken him deep into the past, to Alison. He could imagine Sam as himself—innocent, horrified, trapped by circumstances. And yet Tony was more touched by Marcie's tragedy: he could remember too well the operatic emotions of a teenager, felt without warning. Even taken as true, much of Sam's story—the self-indulgence, the betrayal of trust—was selfish and despicable.

Tony stood, feeling the stiffness of sitting too long on hard wooden bleachers. Next to him, Sam remained sitting, his gaze abstracted. "I was responsible for her," he murmured. "I knew it, and now there was nothing I could do."

It was clear to Tony that Sam could not look at him. "What did you tell the police?"

Sam seemed to gather himself. Softly, he said, "I told them bullshit."

"My question was what kind of bullshit."

It came out harsher than Tony had intended. Sam sat straighter. "About what you'd expect. That she'd had a crush on me and that I'd rejected her. That it was stupid to be alone with her, especially there, but she'd been so damned irrational that I thought she must be in terrible trouble—drugs or something. All I could think of, I told them, was to help her. But all I could *really* think of was to somehow save myself."

"What made you think that story would fly?"

Sam turned to him, eyes glinting with an old defiance. "She was dead, Tony."

The baldness of this made Tony pause: the remark, ruthless in its practicality, was as true of the story Sam had just told to Tony as of the one he had told to the police. Unsettled, Tony wondered what part might be manipulation, what part true. And then Tony remembered, as clear as yesterday, lying to the police about Alison.

"And Sue?" he finally asked.

The look of defensiveness vanished. "I told her the same thing." Sam paused, standing. "Was I supposed to confess sleeping with Marcie and then ask my wife to lie if someone asked her? I did Sue a kindness, really. Even if she doesn't believe a word."

Once more, Tony was struck by the keenness of Sam's instinct for survival; knowing that it was safe,

Sam had told Tony a more credible version, admitting his shame while appealing to Tony's sympathy for the innocent man made by random chance to appear guilty of murder. Quietly, Sam said, "I never wanted to admit this to anyone, Tony. When Sue wanted to call *you*, all I could think of was how pathetic I would look to you. But I didn't know until now just how much I'd hate that."

Tony shoved his hands into his pockets, silent.

"So," Sam continued, "what do we do about Sue?"

The delphic question unsettled Tony. When he looked over, Sam regarded him with a thin, ironic smile. "You can't tell *her*, of course—you're my lawyer. How will that feel for you: stuck in the middle between your oldest friend and his wife? Or, looked at another way, your oldest friend and her husband."

For an instant, Tony had the sense of being taunted, of Sam's subtle reprisal for his own humiliation. Quietly, Tony answered, "I'll explain it to Sue, pal. I wouldn't care to add to your troubles."

Sam blinked, and the irony vanished from his face. "I'm sorry, Tony. I really am. For that, and for everything I've had to tell you. But I never, ever have been capable of murder."

When they returned, Sam drifted upstairs to the bedroom, leaving Sue and Tony alone. The mirthless smile with which she regarded him reminded Tony of Sam, save that Sue's was sadder and without any malice.

"You have something to tell me," she said.

He sat close to her on the couch. "Only that, as his lawyer, I can't tell you anything. And neither can he."

Sue watched his eyes. "I thought a wife could never testify against her husband."

"That's somewhat complicated. But the short of it is that, in some instances, it might be up to you, not Sam." Touching her hand, Tony felt again the strange duality of his role. "For now, Sue, not being part of this is a mercy. Later, when it's about your marriage, and not law, you can talk this through with him."

Still Sue studied him. "Oh, Tony," she murmured, "he was sleeping with that girl, wasn't he?"

He did not answer; her question did not ask this of him. "I only hope," she said at last, "this doesn't get any worse."

"He says he didn't kill her, Sue. I think people will accept that." Pausing, he tried to give her some encouragement. "I'm going to see the county prosecutor tomorrow. Maybe that part will go away."

Sue smiled faintly. "Go away? Things like this don't 'go away.' You know that better than anyone."

All at once, Tony remembered something else. He spoke more quietly yet. "There's at least one thing I should tell you, Sue. Today, more or less in the middle of everything, he asked if we'd ever slept together."

Her face registered no surprise. Slowly, she nodded. "It's come up before. What did you tell him?"

"The same thing you must have."

Sue was quiet for a moment, and then she shook her head. "Poor Tony," she said. "So many secrets to keep. Even ours."

FOUR

The passage of time had done little, Tony saw, to change the face of Steelton. Nothing could reverse the way soot and harsh weather had seeped into the pores of gray concrete buildings; or the indifference of heavy industry, a century before, to preserving green space on the riverbank; or the absence of trees anywhere; or the fact that its stolid architecture, with a few faceless glass exceptions, was frozen in the last great period of rust-belt vitality, the forties and fifties. The pigeon still seemed to be the municipal bird; flocks strutted up and down the barren cement of Steelton Square, fouling the base of its presiding statue, a cast-iron Marshal Pilsudski. Tony had always imagined Eastern Europe as gray and feudal; in his mind, the Poles and Czechs and Lithuanians and Slovaks who had settled in Steelton were predisposed to the bleakness that the Calvinist barons who had built the mills and factories had done so much to provide. Approaching the office of the county prosecutor, a forties-style concrete bunker next to the courthouse, Tony recalled uncomfortably that his fate once had been decided here; he wondered if some file with his name on it, or Alison's, was still stored in its bowels.

On the fourth floor, Tony presented himself to the male receptionist who eyed him through a bulletproof glass partition. He asked for Stella Marz.

The woman burst through an unmarked wooden door, all energy and movement. Extending her hand, she inspected him with interest and the faintest glint of humor, as though the presence of Anthony Lord in the life of an assistant county prosecutor might prove to be a challenge or, at least, a stimulating novelty.

"Stella Marz," she said and, without much more, steered him through a linoleum maze of hallways to an office with a view of Lake Erie over the cement breakwater—gray on gray. She nodded toward the window. "I hope you enjoy the scenery," she said. "Until last week, I had an office overlooking the parking lot." Her tone suggested that she had been too busy to consider the view herself; at once, Tony pegged her as a true believer beneath the brisk, professional manner.

She was mid-to-late thirties. If Tony's experience was any guide, her assignment to a major potential homicide meant that she was a rising star who, as they were meeting alone, did not require baby-sitting by the head of the Criminal Division. She was sturdily built, and her broad face was quite attractive, with a cleft chin and somewhat exotic brown eyes, a hint of Eurasia that Tony had learned to associate with certain Slavic women. Her hair was brown and her skin pale and, judging from her makeup and well-tailored gray suit, she took care with her appearance. The gym bag in the corner of her office reinforced another guess: that she worked out, and did not fool around about it.

"You're a long way from home," she said.

"Not so long. I was born here."

"I know. Your uncle Joe, I think it was, helped my father join the steelworkers union."

Tony smiled. "Joe Stanicek. My mother's brother."

"That's right. But by the time I was born, your family had moved out of the neighborhood."

Another guess had been correct, Tony knew: she was a working-class Polish girl who had struggled hard to get ahead. He wondered how much, if anything, she knew about what had happened to him after his parents left. "My family moved to Lake City," he said. "That's how I know Sam Robb."

She tilted her head, considering him. Tony sensed that she knew that he had not visited his parents' old neighborhood in decades and, as to his relatives, maintained only Christmas card relations; he sensed, further, that such loyalties were important to Stella Marz. "Lucky for Sam Robb," she said finally. "How much do you know about this?"

Tony shrugged. "I know what he told the police. But, from your side of it, nothing. Is there anything I should know?"

She frowned. "I don't believe in hiding the ball, Mr. Lord—"

"Tony, please . . ."

"If we bring a case, Tony, I have to disclose my evidence, and I'd rather know in advance if a case has problems." She folded her hands. "That's just how I work."

There was something defensive about this, Tony thought; she wanted him to know she was not going to roll over because he had a reputation or appeared with his wife in the pages of glossy magazines. Respectfully, he said, "I appreciate that, and prefer it. On both sides."

Stella smiled a little. *Okay,* the look said to him, *we've both announced what nice people we are—let's see how it works.*

"For openers," she said, "I'm pretty sure this girl was murdered."

It was blunt enough to unsettle Tony. "Not an accident or suicide? I know next to nothing about Marcie Calder. But she *was* upset, Sam tells me, and teenage kids have scary highs and lows—every bad experience is a first. And some don't have the resources to cushion the fall."

"As it were." Stella's tone was dry, but her eyes were not laughing. "Or, as we believe, the push."

"How so?"

"The Lake City cops, who are pretty good these days, did some careful work at the crime scene. So did the criminalist from our coroner's office.

"To start, the last few feet of the cliff above where we found the body are dirt, not grass. There were no footprints the size of Marcie Calder's. But there *were* footprints—size eleven running shoes." Stella raised her eyebrows. "Sam Robb's shoe size."

Tony smiled. "And mine. I assume you searched his house for running shoes to match, and found . . ."

"Other size eleven shoes. Which means either that the footprints weren't his or that he got rid of the shoes." Pausing, she steepled her fingers in front of her. "What's more troublesome are the skid marks on the cliff, running parallel to the size eleven shoeprints—the kind made by someone's feet when someone *else* is dragging them. There's the same mud on the toes of Marcie's tennis shoes. So it's a pretty good guess that Marcie was dragged, then thrown over the cliff."

Stella's face was grim now; watching her imagine this girl's last minutes, Tony sensed the passion that had made her a prosecutor. "For that," he responded, "she'd have to be dead, or unconscious."

"Dead, I think. From three blows to the head with a rock the size of a football, taken from above the beach. Or so the coroner believes."

"Couldn't she have hit her head going down the cliff?"

Stella nodded. "Could have—maybe. But we found a rock on the beach with Marcie's hair and blood type, AB, all over it. It was several feet from the body, like it'd been thrown there. Otherwise"—here, Stella compressed her lips—"Marcie's head would have had to knock it sideways, like a cue ball. Pretty strange physics. And there's an awful lot of hair and blood on the rock for that."

He had been doing this, Tony reflected, for roughly twenty years. But in every homicide, there was always some moment when he imagined the death itself. Now, involuntarily, he saw and heard the crunch of a stone on the skull of a black-haired girl.

"Even if you're right that this was murder," he said, "I've known Sam Robb for a long time."

She nodded. "And he's not talking to police anymore, right?"

"Right. It's all going through me."

She watched his face. "Then ask your old friend something for me, okay? Ask why we found specks of blood on his steering wheel."

Tony made himself go blank. "What type?"

"AB." Stella's voice was flat. "Maybe there's some simple explanation he'd like to share with us. . . ."

This hit him much harder than it should have. All at once, Tony felt his weakness: he needed Sam to be innocent. In his best conversational voice, he said, "I assume you're running DNA on the samples."

"Sure. But the results won't be in for a while."

"What about the coroner's report?"

"Not yet." She paused. "That's something I give you only when I have to—when, and if, charges are filed."

Tony reflected. "Let's assume for a moment you're right—someone bludgeoned her to death with a stone. You're not only going to get blood all over the murderer—you'll get it on her body *and* on the ground near where it happened. . . ."

Slowly, Stella nodded, eyes locked on his. "You'd think so."

"Find any blood at his house, or on his clothes?"

"No. Of course, any sane killer would get rid of the clothes."

"But what about blood near the cliff?"

"It rained that night, remember?"

"No witnesses, either, I assume."

"Not yet." For the first time Stella looked impatient. "If this were indictable right now, we'd indict him."

Tony decided to back off a little. "I appreciate that, Stella. But I can't help but wonder what his motive is supposed to be."

Stella raised her eyebrows. "How about shtupping a sixteen-year-old girl? If she exposes him, Sam Robb is toast."

Tony kept his voice neutral. "He told the police he wasn't, as I recall. Anyhow, murder isn't a cookie-cutter solution to a crisis—*lying* is. To murder someone, you've got to be capable of murder, and there's nothing whatsoever in Sam Robb's life to suggest that he is." Tony paused, leaning forward. "If he were so afraid of exposure, why in the world would he go to the police? The only reason you and I are sitting here, with Sam at risk of losing his job and maybe worse, is because he *did*."

Stella looked unimpressed. "Maybe he was afraid some witness would put him there—he did tell the police about seeing another car. And he wasn't in a great position to ask his wife to lie for him, was he?"

It was a standoff. "About Sue Robb," Tony said. "This hasn't been great for her. Please tell the cops to leave her alone."

"Spousal privilege?"

"Uh-huh."

Stella nodded: this was nothing more than she expected, her expression said, and she was too professional to let it bother her. "Anything else I can do for you?" she asked.

"Just keep an open mind." He paused. "Even if you think this may be murder, there are a lot of people in that park at night."

Stella was quiet for a time; for once, she did not look at him. "I know what happened to you," she said at last. When she looked at him, and her face softened at what she saw, Tony knew that his own impassivity had deserted him. "A reporter called this morning," she went on. "Someone saw you at the airport with Sue Robb. I may be too young to remember the Alison Taylor case, but it was the last murder in Lake City. This guy reminded me that you were a suspect."

Once more, Tony felt the depression of his return descend on him. "Then you know I've got some feeling about this."

Stella studied him, as if waiting for Tony to protest his own innocence. When he did not, she said, "I don't like the feel of your friend Sam—I know why he was there with Marcie Calder, and so do you." She sounded certain; Tony wondered whether, in this instance, she knew more than she was saying. "I also happen," Stella went on, "to believe in the value of every human life—it's a religious and moral principle with me, from abortion to the death penalty. So I can't go along with my friends in this office who see some murders as public service killings and executions as God's will. But the murder of a teenage girl, if that's what this was, hits me harder than most. This girl should *never* have died, and her parents *never* should have had to feel what they're feeling."

"That's what I felt about Alison, and Alison's parents."

Stella nodded. "What I'm telling you is this—if I think your friend killed Marcie Calder, and I've got a prosecutable case, I'm going to try my damnedest to nail Sam Robb to the wall. But I'll be careful, very careful, about deciding that. And you'll always get a hearing from me."

"That's all I could ask." Tony paused, curious. "Do you still go to Mass, then?"

"Every Sunday." A small smile of her own. "The Church helped free Poland, after all."

"Poland," Tony could not resist answering, "but not women."

"That'll come," she responded crisply. "Sometimes I wonder why men and lapsed Catholics want to do my worrying for me." She paused a moment. "Especially ones who may have forgotten where they're from."

Tony considered his answer. "You're right," he said at last. "It's hard to judge someone else's faith—or life. As for my own disaffection with the Church, it's more complex than you could know, and rooted in a particular time and circumstance." His voice took on a slight edge. "Believe me, Stella, I haven't 'forgotten' anything."

Stella gave him a somewhat rueful smile. "Sorry. I shouldn't have said that. Actually, you were a little bit of a hero to me—especially knowing where you were from. During law school, when the Carson murder trial was on TV, I watched you whenever I could. I was torn between wanting to grow up to be like you or to be the kind of prosecutor who kept lawyers like you from walking people like Harry Carson. Either way, I admired you for having come so far. So this has been interesting."

Tony smiled. "I'm glad you added that last."

Stella stood, extending her hand. "Anyhow," she said, "welcome back. I hope you're prepared for the media."

"Do I have a choice?"

Stella shook her head, not smiling. "No," she said. "Not anymore."

FIVE

"Well," Saul Ravin said, "if it isn't Hollywood Tony Lord."

Tony laughed. "Hello, Saul."

They shook hands, and then Saul stepped back and gave him a mock once-over. "Better clothes too, I'd say. Not bad for a Polish boy."

"You created a monster, Saul. No question."

"A monster I could live with—I've represented several. But a *criminal defense lawyer . . .*" Saul paused, shaking his head. "Oh, well, Tony, it's too late now. So have a seat."

Saul's office was much the same. Saul was not: his hair was a curly white nimbus, and his paunch had become a belly worthy of a sumo wrestler or a Mafia don. His eyes were still bright, but the red flush to his skin was worrisome and, at a little past two, there was an open bottle of Scotch on his desk. Tony had seen the signs before—the aging criminal lawyer, perhaps still sharp but too mired in drink and cynicism and the fatigue of too many trials for too many years to function in more than short bursts. Tony realized that he had preserved Saul in his memory as the savior, a lawyer at his best, and that part of him still wished this to be so. Instead Tony found himself pondering once more the hidden cost of the criminal lawyer's life—the need to submerge personal feelings to serve abstract principles: the burden of proof, the presumption of innocence . . .

"Drink, Tony?"

"No. Thanks."

Saul eyed the bottle, shrugged, and did not touch it. "Slow day," he said. "Ever find this work wears on you?"

So his guess was right, Tony thought. "Sometimes," he allowed, "it's stressful."

"Suppose that's what it is? Maybe it's more the energy you spend trying not to think about stuff that any normal person would think about—like what your client did, or may do next—while you're keeping the system honest." Saul frowned. "The other day, I found myself thinking about this child abuser I got off because the kid was scared to testify. Two years later, Dad killed the kid with his favorite set of fireplace implements. To my conscious mind, I hadn't thought of him in years. But I must have been, all along. . . ." Slowly, Saul shook his head. "I'm getting sentimental, Tony. The older I've gotten, the more important clients like you are to me. You're one of that elite group I was damned sure either didn't do it or deserved a better shake than the system would have given him, and then made something of what *I* helped give him. I hope to God *you're* not such a sensitive soul."

Tony shrugged. "I try not to be, Saul—for the sake of my clients and my own sanity. Sometimes my wife thinks I've succeeded."

Saul waved a hand. "Civilians," he said with irony. "They just don't understand the higher morality of what we do. I suppose it's enough for you that she's talented and beautiful."

"It'll have to do." Tony smiled. "Although, unlike my *first* wife, Stacey tries to distinguish between my clients and me."

Saul propped his head on one palm, leaning on the desk, and contemplated Tony with silent bemusement. "So," he said at last, "here we are, brothers at the bar. And now it's your old friend Sam who's supposed to have killed a teenage girl."

"Stella Marz seems to think so."

"Stella—not a woman who's afraid to try a case." Saul's eyes narrowed. "I won't carry your bags, Tony. I don't need the money."

There was a new hardness to Saul's voice. Tony's image of a warm reunion receded a little more; like any trial lawyer, Saul Ravin had a space-taking ego, and the role of avuncular counselor to a teenage boy was clearly more congenial than being overshadowed in his own town by a visiting defense lawyer with a bigger reputation. The fact that Saul might be slipping, and knew it, would only make this worse.

"There *is* no money, Saul—at least not enough for a state-of-the-art defense. As you say, they're friends, and thanks to Stacey's success, every now and again I can take on a client I believe in, for free."

"That's a nice luxury." Saul raised his eyebrows. "You feel that strongly about him?"

"It's just something I have to do." Seeing Saul's quizzical smile, Tony shrugged. "All right, I don't want Sam to have done it. Maybe for that reason, I can't believe he did. That's why I'm here—for spiritual counseling. Just send me a bill for your time."

Still smiling, Saul narrowed his eyes and cocked his head, as if weighing this. "I'll take the bill under advisement," he said, and then his tone became practical. "Your buddy was fucking her, you say."

"Afraid so."

Saul shook his head, a man confronted with the in-calculable depth of human folly. "Think he fucked her the night she died?"

"He says not."

"Better hope *that's* the truth—seeing how he told the cops they were in the park for a little private counseling. Or at worst, pray that he used a rubber."

Tony considered that. "Even with a rubber, he might have left pubic hairs, maybe traces of a petroleum-based lubricant. But at least they couldn't DNA the semen."

Saul gave him a sour smile. "Don't you find it a little funny that *we're* the ones having this conversation?"

"I stopped laughing about an hour ago, Saul. When Stella Marz told me about the blood on Sam's steering wheel."

Saul's smile vanished. "There are a thousand possible explanations, my son. Even if it's hers. They can't con-vict on that."

"I know. But that's not enough to make me feel better."

Saul reached for the bottle, pacing himself a precise two inches, neat, in a tumbler. He sipped it slowly, al-most too carefully; all at once, Tony remembered this from before and realized that, even then, the drinking must have begun. "Maybe you should go home to your wife and son, Tony. Hope Stella's case doesn't get better. Avoid stirring things up."

Tony imagined Sam's daily agony, and Sue's—their life a marriage on hold, murder charges looming—then slowly shook his head. "I remember what that's like— the waiting eats you alive. I was hoping to give Marz an affirmative reason not to indict, somewhat like you did for me."

Saul took a long sip of Scotch. "Suppose Marcie was seeing a psychiatrist? Her shrink would know whether she had another boyfriend. Or if she was self-destructive."

"*Or* that she was sleeping with Sam."

Saul nodded. *"That,"* he answered, "is part of what I meant by not stirring things up."

Tony stood, walking to the window; suddenly he remembered doing this on his first visit to Saul's office, gazing at the smokestacks, which now had vanished with the jobs they once symbolized.

"What a place," he murmured.

"Unimpressed by Steelton's renaissance, are you? The *Ice Capades* comes every year now. Or were you referring to your old hometown, the Disney World of decency?"

Tony did not turn. "I need a picture of Marcie Calder—from her parents, her friends, or whoever else. I don't want to leave Sam Robb to fate, in the person of the Lake City police."

Tony heard the splash of whiskey pouring, and then Saul drifted to the window, standing next to him with a fresh drink in his hand. Tony could see his ruined profile; the crepe of his chin, burst vessels on his cheeks, the chafed-looking skin. In the midst of this deterioration, his eyes seemed terribly sad, painfully lucid.

"Can I give you some advice?" Saul murmured.

"That's what I came for."

Saul seemed to gather himself. "Don't treat your case as the paradigm for this one. You knew that you were innocent. You don't know that about Sam Robb, and you can't. And for what it's worth, my gut tells me you shouldn't." Pausing, he turned to Tony. "He may be guilty, Tony. I don't envy you the moment, if it comes, when you realize that's so. The only thing that could make that any worse for you is if you've blown his defense, and lost your identity as a lawyer, because you'd forgotten to distinguish between Sam Robb and Tony Lord." Saul's voice softened. "Unless they're completely amoral, most good defense lawyers are two people, Tony—they have to be. This case could hurt both of you."

Tony was quiet; what Saul said was unanswerable. Saul looked at him and put his drink on the windowsill. "All right," he asked, "what about the wife?"

"Sue?"

"She wasn't home, didn't you say? At least she didn't answer the phone when Sam called her."

"He says not." Like a delayed reaction, Tony felt his own incredulity hit him. "And you're not serious."

"Why not?"

"Because I *know* her, for Christ sake."

Saul's face changed; for an instant, his eyes held the merciless dispassion of a recording angel. "You really don't have to try so hard," he said softly, "just to make my point."

Tony felt stung. "Look, Saul—the last thing that marriage, *or* Sam's defense, needs is for him to point a finger at Sue. What Sam needs more than anything is a very loyal, very quiet, wife."

Saul looked unimpressed. "I didn't say you couldn't rationalize your biases. Only that you have them." He seemed to have forgotten about his drink. "How much does Sue know?"

"Very little, I think."

"That'll take some handling. Especially if there's a trial."

"I know that. But you don't know Sue."

"Do you, still? After twenty-eight years?"

Tony nodded. "I think so. It feels like that, anyhow."

Slowly, Saul turned to the window, hands in his pockets now. "You seem surer of her than of him."

Silent, Tony took inventory of his emotions: Saul's questions, he realized, had served the purpose of reminding him how far away he was from who he tried to be, the lawyer as surgeon. "At times I think I know her better," Tony said at last. "Maybe that was always so, but I never really saw it before. Or maybe it's just that, in certain ways, there's less complexity than with Sam. There's certainly a lot less that's disturbing."

Saul surveyed the city—glass towers, empty lots, abandoned factories—the wreckage of an economy in decline. "You're right," he said. "Some days this place looks like fucking Beirut." He paused a moment. "All I was saying is to watch yourself. Too much of this case is too much about you."

Tony no longer felt like arguing. "Stella Marz knew who I was. From before."

"Of course she did. You may have left all this behind, but you didn't become a different person." Saul faced Tony again. "You're bringing some publicity that may not be so helpful to your client, or pleasant for you— 'Killer defends killer.' "

"Maybe. But I'm old enough to deal with that, and they need me. Besides, the price is right."

Saul picked up his drink. "Maybe for them," he said.

SIX

There were fresh flowers on her grave.

Nearly thirty years had passed; this corner of the Lake City cemetery, preserved for John Taylor and his family, was now circled by newer, fresher graves. From a distance, only the empty space surrounding her granite marker denoted that she had died far too young.

"Alison Wood Taylor," the marker read. "May 4, 1950—November 3, 1967." It was strange to have forgotten her middle name.

The flowers haunted him. They bespoke the living presence of the Taylors; their ineradicable loss of Alison.

However imperfectly, Tony had been able to leave her here. Her parents would be with her to the end.

He stood with her now, beneath the shade of an oak tree, watching the shadows encroach on the gentle light of a spring afternoon.

The press had found him. There were two messages at the Arbor Motel, the only one in Lake City; both requested interviews. He could expect the first stories tomorrow.

Knowing that, he knew there was one thing left to do.

Standing on the Taylors' porch, Tony found himself wishing that no one would answer.

The door cracked open. An old woman stared at him, mouth parting; as he watched her realize who he was, he saw in her face, white as chalk, the woman who had been Alison's mother.

"I'm sorry to come here," he said. "But I felt I should."

Her silence pained him. She looked like a stroke victim, he thought, who could think, or speak, only with great effort. The one sign of comprehension was in her eyes.

"May I speak with you a moment?" he asked.

"Let him in," a harsh voice said. The door opened behind Katherine Taylor, and Tony saw the true cost of his return.

John Taylor's face was gaunt, desiccated, cross-hatched with lines and wrinkles; his gaze at Tony was like that of a bird—unblinking, cold. The room behind him had not changed much; the antiques were the same, the silence museum-like. On the mantel were new swatches of color—photographs of Alison's sister as a bride, then a mother. Between them, forever caught in the year 1967, was Alison. Tony felt himself wince at the contrast.

John Taylor remained as still as Alison's photograph. Katherine Taylor retreated to her husband's side, silent.

"I've come to help Sam Robb," Tony said softly. "I'm afraid the press will dredge up what happened, all over again."

"They've already called us." John Taylor's lips seemed barely to move. "We thought it ironic."

"That occurred to me." Tony paused, and then forced himself to go on. "But I was innocent, and I assume no less about Sam—"

"Innocent." John Taylor's voice rose. "Do you know who you remind me of? O. J. Simpson, offering a reward to whoever finds the person who killed his wife. Perhaps, as with Alison, it will be a man who can answer no questions—"

"John." It was his wife's first word, barely above a whisper. Yet it made John Taylor flinch.

Tony felt his stomach knot; perhaps he would never face these people without feeling what he had felt at seventeen, the fear of either speech or silence. "I loved her," he said at last. "More than you ever knew. But I could never truly understand all you lost, and what you've gone through, until I had a child of my own."

John Taylor nodded, the fierceness of his eyes undiminished. "Then you know how we feel about you, Anthony Lord. And always will." His voice was soft with anger. "One way or the other, you caused my daughter's death."

Silent, Tony made himself imagine what Christopher's death might do to him. He could not quite: his only certainty was that, could Alison but see it, she would hate what her death had done to *them*. But this was not his to say.

"I'm sorry to have disturbed you," Tony said, and left.

SEVEN

The Calder family lived in a brick bungalow not un-like the home of Tony's youth—a one-story rectangle on a postage-stamp lawn, in a neighborhood so neat and uniform that it was hard to distinguish one house from another. Coming from the Taylors, Tony had sat in his rented car in front of the Calders' house, reluc-tant to intrude on parents whose grief was so fresh. But Nancy Calder had agreed to see him; waiting for tomorrow—with its inevitable headlines—would be foolish. At a little past eight o'clock, Tony rang the doorbell.

The first few moments had an unnerving veneer of normality. Nancy Calder answered the door; except for the shadows beneath her eyes, the drawn look to her face, she could have been greeting an insurance agent, whose presence in her home was one of life's require-ments. She offered Tony coffee and sat on the couch in the tiny living room, tightly holding a cup of her own. The room was orderly, and so was she—in slacks and a sweater, she seemed a fortyish version of the pretty, dark-haired daughter in the photographs. And then her husband entered the room, and without looking at him, Nancy Calder began silently to cry.

Tony stood. Everything about Frank Calder, he thought, seemed spare and grudging: the crew-cut brown hair; narrow blue eyes; a hard Irish face—thin lips, high cheekbones, skin so close to the bone that it seemed to have been stretched. But it was Calder's wife, Tony found, who made him regret the need to be here.

"Nancy wanted to see you," Calder said abruptly. "I didn't. Why in God's name should we talk to his lawyer?"

Tony steeled himself. "I'm just trying to understand

this," he answered. "Sam Robb is an old friend, and he seems devastated by what's happened. But if I ever became certain that Sam Robb harmed your daughter, I'd leave Lake City in a heartbeat." That much was true; Tony had defended guilty clients before but could not do so if this man, his friend, had murdered a teenage girl. His last moments with the Taylors, his time at Alison's grave, had settled that for him.

" 'Harm,' " Frank Calder repeated. "Is that what you call it?"

Calder seemed to have forgotten his wife, Tony saw; it was as though hostility were a permanent part of him, their grief an overlay. She fingered the crucifix she held, as though striving to withdraw from her husband's rage. Facing her, Tony murmured, "If there's some better time . . ."

Slowly, Nancy Calder shook her head. "There will *never* be a better time," she said, and Tony saw that her tears had stopped.

Without looking at Frank Calder, Tony sat across from her again. Softly, he said, "I'm sorry I didn't know her, Mrs. Calder."

Nancy Calder grimaced. "The last two years, I was working, Mr. Lord. So maybe I didn't, either."

It was better just to listen. "Tony," he said gently. "I go by Tony."

Blank-faced, Nancy Calder nodded. "I was never home after school," she said after a time. "That's when the girls are fresh, when they tell you about their day. . . ."

"We were saving for college." Sitting next to his wife, Frank Calder spoke in a harsh voice. "You know what college costs these days."

Again, Tony heard a strange defensiveness; he guessed that to Frank Calder, the failure to provide for their family by himself was galling. Calder was an accountant, Tony recalled from the newspaper clippings he had read, for a large trucking concern; though Stanley Lord had been far gentler, Tony sensed the same trapped grievances, the frustration of feeling like a rat in the corporate Skinner box, of a man serving out his time.

"Well," Frank Calder said to his wife, "we won't have to save for her now."

It could have been cruel; but to Tony, it was his first acknowledgment of their shared loss, and the edge to his voice was submerged in weariness. His eyes were bloodshot.

Quietly, Tony asked, "Was there any sense in which she worried you? In the last few weeks, I mean."

Silent, Frank Calder turned to his wife. "She seemed more distant," Nancy Calder said at last. "Like she was somewhere else."

"Nothing more specific?"

Nancy Calder shook her head. "Her grades were down a little. But she still went with us to Mass—there wasn't the kind of rebelliousness or questioning Father Carney, our priest, sees in so many young people. She was so good to her younger sisters—" Nancy Calder stopped abruptly, and then finished in a different voice, flat with repressed anger. "And she still loved track, of course. The last time I saw Sam Robb, he made a point of telling me how hard she was working."

Tony felt the moral ambiguity of his position; he knew from Sam himself that his friend had slept with Marcie—or, in Sam's telling, that Marcie had tried to seduce him. Cautiously, he asked, "Did Marcie seem attracted to him?"

Nancy Calder's eyes clouded with bitterness. "From what *he* told the police," she said, "Marcie had a crush on him. But I never saw any sign of that." She turned to her husband. "Did she talk about *him* any more than about Mr. Nixon?"

Frank Calder's gaze focused on the carpet. "No," he said.

Nancy Calder nodded in affirmation. "She may have been looking for a parent figure—someone who wasn't us. But she wasn't looking for an affair."

Her husband would not look at her. Replaying the phrase "parent figure," Tony heard the word "father"; he sensed that Marcie and her parents had been more divided than the Calders said. "Were there *any* difficulties?" he asked. "Disagreements?"

Nancy Calder glanced at her husband. "One," he said tersely. "I wanted her to go to a Catholic women's school. With all the drugs and sex—" He cut himself off. "She didn't want to, and Nancy didn't want to push it. So that was *my* fault, I suppose."

This sounded closer to the mark; Frank Calder seemed like a man with rules, better at proscribing than at listening. Gently, Nancy Calder said, "You wouldn't have made her go, Frank. Marcie knew that."

The sadness of this struck Tony hard: a limited man, regretting what he had said to a daughter to whom, suddenly, inexplicably, he could now say nothing; his wife offering him consolation that perhaps she did not believe. "Were you worried about emotional problems?" Tony asked.

"No." Frank Calder stared at him now. "There was nothing like that. Our daughter certainly didn't need a psychiatrist."

Nancy Calder compressed her lips. "There's no question of suicide here, if *that's* what you're asking. Marcie was much too stable—a little quiet, that was all. *And* a believing Catholic, too devout to ever think of taking her own life." Her voice hardened. "Over her track coach, or anyone else."

Tony decided to shift ground. "You mentioned a Mr. Nixon."

Still lost within her anger, Nancy Calder gave a brief nod. "Ernie Nixon," she said. "He's the town recreation director here. A black man."

Tony covered his surprise. "Yes. I know him. Or did, once."

"He was the first person to encourage Marcie about her running. Before his divorce, Marcie would watch his kids from time to time." Her eyes misted abruptly. "Marcie loved children, and children loved her. Starting with her own sisters . . ."

Suddenly Tony sensed something beneath the surface of this meeting, more volatile than grief. Softly, he asked, "What do you think happened to her?"

Nancy Calder raised her head. "Sam Robb murdered her," she said quietly. "To keep from being found out. Sooner or later, *you'll* have to face that too."

All at once, Tony felt certain that the Calders knew that Sam and their daughter had been having sex. But there was no way to confront this. With equal quiet, he said, "It could have been an accident, Mrs. Calder. Or someone else."

Nancy Calder flushed. "There *wasn't* anyone else," her husband said tightly. "Marcie wasn't a slut. . . ."

"Please, I wasn't suggesting that. My 'someone else' could be a stranger."

They both fell silent; from their fixed expressions, they were mollified—if at all—not by the possibility of a stranger but by Tony's concession. The sense of something left unsaid bedeviled him.

"Who was Marcie close to?" he asked.

Nancy Calder's eyes flew open, as if the question were an accusation that she had failed her daughter. Then she answered tersely. "Janice D'Abruzzi. Her best friend."

She spoke the words like a curse. Frank Calder stood abruptly. "Go home," he said to Tony. "Leave us with our daughter's memory, and at least some hope of justice. For *him*, if not for her." He left the room.

Nancy Calder gazed after him. "We're very tired," she said simply, and Tony knew that his time was up.

She saw him to the doorway, composed again. Her eyes met his. "Please," she said with hushed urgency, "don't defend Sam Robb. Not if you're a decent man . . ."

EIGHT

The article was on page three of the *Steelton Press*. Next to a photograph of Tony and Stacey, the headline read: "Robb Lawyer Linked to Prior Slaying." In the photograph, Tony was grinning broadly.

"Nice picture," Sam Robb remarked. "Your very best killer smile."

Tony stared at him across Sam's breakfast table, annoyed by his friend's insouciance, troubled by Stella Marz, the Taylors, Marcie's parents. "If I were you," he said, "I wouldn't be that happy, either."

Sam looked up. "I'm not, Tony. I still remember how much you wanted to leave all this behind." He paused and then placed his hand on Tony's forearm. "What I'm trying to say is that I'm grateful for your help, that I'm proud you're still my friend, and that I'm bothered by this bullshit because it bothers *you*. Maybe this time out I'll learn to tell you what I mean."

To his surprise, Tony felt touched. "It's not the press, Sam. It's that I can't seem to go an hour without my own feelings about Alison bubbling to the top. That's not what you want in a lawyer."

Sam nodded. "Seeing the Calders was hard, I guess."

"Yes. And the Taylors."

"You *saw* them?"

"I felt as if I had to."

"Jesus." Sam's eyes met Tony's again. "Look, I brought this mess on myself, because my judgment took a hike. You never deserved any of it—then or now."

Tony shrugged. "Life is unfair, Saul once told me."

Sam got up abruptly. Without asking, he poured Tony more coffee, then some for himself. "I think I was wrong, Tony. Letting you come here."

The remark unsettled Tony. "Why 'wrong'?"

"Not wrong, maybe. Selfish." Sitting, Sam looked at Tony over the rim of his cup. "If you stay here, this article won't be the last. You'll make the fucking cover of *Vanity Fair*—we even get that in Lake City, you know." Sam turned, staring out the window. "I've spent one week living in a town where a lot of people probably think I killed her, and I already know my life here will never be the same, unless I can somehow prove I didn't do it. *You're* famous, Tony—Alison's murder will follow you everywhere. And from the way you look this morning, you'll be taking it with you anyhow." He turned to Tony, finishing softly. "Go back to San Francisco, pal. I didn't kill her, so at least they can't prove I did. And there's nothing I can do to save my job but lie."

Somewhere in the last two days, Sam seemed to have achieved a certain calm. "Have you just found God?" Tony inquired.

Sam smiled a little. "Actually, I was remembering when we were seventeen. You were able to go on because you had a core—you knew the 'murderer' people hated wasn't you." His smiled faded. "Well, it's not me, either. It's just not me."

Tony waited for a moment, torn between the role of lawyer and that of friend. Quietly, he asked, "Sue's not here, I guess."

"She's at the gym." Sam's eyes grew keener. "Why? Is something wrong?"

"The cops lifted some blood off your steering wheel. You don't happen to be type AB, do you?"

Sam sat down. "No," he said slowly. "Sue is."

"So was Marcie Calder."

Sam sat back; his face went slack with surprise, and then his eyelids lowered. "They can tell the difference, can't they? DNA."

Tony nodded. "Is there a reason why Marcie's blood would be in your car, if that's whose it is? One I can take to Stella Marz?"

Sam shook his head. "Not unless someone else put it there," he said at last.

Tony's voice was soft. "The 'real killer,' Sam? Or the cops, like with O. J. Simpson?"

Sam looked pale now. "I'll have to think, Tony. I'll have to think real hard."

Tony watched his face. "While you're thinking, maybe you can come up with a reason that Marcie's parents seem certain—not just guessing, but *sure*—that you and Marcie had sex."

Sam bit his lip. "Not unless someone told them," he said at last. "What did they say?"

"Nothing much. It's more what I divined."

Sam was quiet for a moment. "They hate me, I guess."

"It's a little more specific. They think you killed her. To cover up your seduction of their very shy oldest daughter—who, at most, was looking for a father figure."

Sam looked up sharply. "What exactly are you driving at?"

"Whether the Calders know something I should know. Something you don't have to think real hard about."

Sam folded his arms. "Go home, pal. This is bad enough without watching you wrestle with your own doubts."

"Just answer my question, dammit."

Sam took a moment, a man who would not be pushed. Quietly, he said, "I'm no more guilty than you were, Tony. And I hope you can believe that more than I did. By now I've said it enough."

* * *

The group of girls milled at the fifty-yard line, practicing cheers. Standing near the fence, Tony guessed at which might be Janice D'Abruzzi—the captain, he decided, a dark-haired girl who, in her athleticism, reminded Tony of Sue. When the practice broke up, and the girl was first off the field, Tony took a chance.

"Janice?" he asked.

She stopped, looking at him warily. She was dark and quite pretty and, to Tony, there was something Florentine about her: olive skin, full figure, a certain vibrancy that, even in her stillness, suggested movement and a sense of life. It reminded him, uncomfortably, of how attractive a girl of seventeen can be.

"Are you Johnny's daughter?" he asked.

She nodded, silent, not moving.

"I'm not a reporter," Tony told her. "Your dad and I played football together, a thousand years ago. I'm a lawyer now—Tony Lord."

Janice pulled her cheerleader jacket close around her. "I know who you are."

She had a low, husky voice; there was something sexual about it, a womanly quality. "How *is* your dad?" Tony asked.

She was quiet for a moment. "He died, six months ago. Of a heart attack."

It startled Tony; it was, he supposed, a harbinger of more such surprises, the first tragedies of middle age. "God," he said. "I'm really sorry."

She cocked her head slightly, her only acknowledgment. Quietly, she asked, "What do you want?"

Tony paused a moment. "I was hoping to talk about Marcie. You were her closest friend, I know."

Her dark eyes became quite still. "Who told you that?"

Again, Tony hesitated. "Her mother."

Janice flushed, then looked down. Watching her, Tony thought of Christopher and his friends. It was often better, he reflected, to talk to them like the adults they wished to be and, on good days, almost were—the way Saul Ravin had talked to another seventeen-year-old, all those years ago. "Janice, I know there's some problem between you and Marcie's parents. But I don't have a clue what it is. I'm not trying to make this worse for you."

She looked up at him again. "Then what *are* you trying to do?"

The tremulous note in her voice surprised him. "To understand what happened to Marcie. And why."

She glanced over her shoulder, watching the other girls as they headed for the locker room, and then she turned to face him. "This has been really bad, okay? I've already told the police about that."

"About what?"

"About Marcie," she said bluntly. "How I helped get her killed."

Tony tilted his head. "How could you have done that?"

There was something new in her eyes—intense, emotional. "Marcie's mother called that night, looking for her. I told her we'd been working on a paper and that she'd gone to the library." Her voice grew husky. "You know, to look something up."

Tony remembered the small acts of defiance, often ill-advised, through which he and Sam had defined themselves as different from their parents. And then, like a delayed shock, he remembered planning with Alison that she leave her parents' house that night. "I guess Marcie asked you to say that."

"Yeah." Her voice was bitter now. "I was her best friend, remember?"

"Then she must have told you why."

Janice watched him a moment, as if deciding whether to stay or go. Then she walked to the fence surrounding the football field and leaned back against it, the sun on her face. "Some of it," she said finally. "There was a guy. But she wouldn't say who he was."

Tony forced himself to hold back, ask just enough to serve as a mirror for her thoughts. "Do you know *why* she wouldn't?"

"Because he'd get in trouble, Marcie said. He'd made her promise him."

This was said in the literal tone of a girl immersed in the drama of another teenage life. But what Tony heard was how lethal this would sound at a murder trial. "Did she give any reason for protecting him?"

Janice looked at him directly. "Only that he was older. And married."

Tony held her gaze. Softly, he asked, "Why did Marcie get involved with him, then?"

Janice frowned. "Marcie was a great friend—smart and loyal, easy to talk to. But about guys she was the most naive girl in Lake City, especially when it came to sex. I'm sure this guy was her only one." She folded her arms. "Her dad yelled at her all the time, like he wanted her to be some kind of nun. This guy believed in her, she said. So, yeah, I could see her falling in love with an older man who didn't yell at her."

The combination of adult acuity and identification with Marcie's resentments interested Tony—Janice D'Abruzzi was not a stupid girl, or a simple one. "Weren't you a little hurt?" he asked. "I mean, that Marcie wouldn't confide in you."

Janice shook her head. "You didn't know her," she said. "Marcie had promised him, and Marcie kept her promises. I mean, if I ever asked Marcie to keep a secret for me, I knew she would—absolutely." She stopped, and then her eyes filled with tears. "That's a nice thing to know about a best friend. It's what I was thinking when I lied to Marcie's mother."

Tony watched her, silent; Janice bent forward, and she seemed to compose herself. Suddenly he felt real warmth for Janice D'Abruzzi, and greater sorrow; she seemed a more complex version of the openhearted boy who had become her father. Finally, he ventured, "You must have wondered who it was."

She gave a weary shrug. "Oh, yeah."

"Did you think it was Sam Robb?"

Her look was sideways, guarded. "No. I never thought that."

Tony nodded. "You thought it was Ernie Nixon, didn't you? Your dad's friend."

Janice's guarded look became a stare. She would not answer.

"You don't have to say anything," Tony said. "I know that she was fond of Mr. Nixon."

After a moment, Janice's expression softened. "Marcie was very idealistic," she said simply.

To Tony, the phrase said more than Janice perhaps had meant—about Janice, about Marcie, about one friend's feeling for another. "Did Marcie have any boyfriends?" Tony asked. "I mean, guys in high school."

Janice shook her head. "Not really. There's a bunch of us, boys and girls, who sometimes do stuff as friends— I'm not sure her dad ever quite got that. But the guy she usually went to dances with, Greg Marsh, is gay." She stopped herself. "Hardly anyone knows that, *especially* the Taylors—his rich grandparents. But Marcie liked Greg, and she helped cover for him. She was sort of shy with boys, so it worked out okay for both of them." Pausing, Janice gave a fleeting smile. "But she always made him kiss her good night, she told me, in case he ever had to get married."

It was the first suggestion that Marcie had a sense of humor, and it added a line to his sketch of Marcie— kind and, in her teenage way, principled: Tony could imagine life was not easy for Alison's nephew, if that's who this boy was. Then it struck him that Janice D'Abruzzi seemed too earthbound for Marcie, her closest friend, to have been an ethereal dreamer, divorced from reality.

"Marcie sounds like a good person," he said at last.

Janice gazed into some middle distance. "Marcie," she answered, "was a great person."

He put his hands in his pockets, giving her some time with the thought: "Do you think she wanted to marry him?"

The question disarranged Janice's features—they showed distraction, then surprise. "The older guy? No way."

"Why do you say that?"

"Because Marcie loved him—she told me that. She wasn't crazy, and she didn't want to ruin his life. They had their own world, she said, and it needed to stay that way." Pausing, Janice shook her head. "I remember her saying she had to keep her dad believing in the Virgin Marcie. No way she'd ruin *that* make-believe."

The remembered gibe—so perfect in its teenage subversiveness—jarred Tony as much as anything he had heard: it was too much at odds with the girl Sam had described to him, intent on her fantasy of marriage. "That night," he said carefully, "when Marcie asked you to cover for her, what did she say?"

Janice leaned back, gazing at the sky. For a time, Tony thought he had lost her, and then she began to speak.

As Janice described her, Marcie seemed scared.

It was almost five-thirty, and the first shadows of late afternoon crept into Janice's bedroom. They sat cross-legged on Janice's pink quilt; Marcie was pale, and for once she could not look at her closest friend.

"I have to see him," Marcie said. "I *have* to."

"Why tonight?"

"We need to talk." Marcie's throat worked. "As soon as I can, I'll tell you everything. But I can't yet."

Janice gazed at her friend. She had known Marcie

Calder for so long, day after day for years, that Janice could not clearly remember what Marcie had looked like at ten, or twelve, or even fourteen. But tonight Marcie seemed so young that Janice was frightened for her—muted, lost, overwhelmed.

"Are you in trouble?" Janice asked.

Marcie gave a quick shake of the head. "No," she said, and looked up for the first time. "Please, Jan. Please do this for me."

The desperation in her friend's voice frightened Janice. She looked at the glistening brown eyes, the delicate freckles that, more than ever, made her look like Janice's younger sister. "If she calls," Janice asked, "and you're not here, what do I tell her?"

"I don't know. Anything." Marcie took both of Janice's hands in hers. "Tell her I was here, working on our paper. But then I went to the library for extra articles. That'll make my dad happy—he's always bugging me about 'effort.' "

Janice paused. Her objections were practical, not moral; she did not want them to be caught in a lie.

"*Please,*" Marcie said again.

Janice saw the look on her face and, in spite of herself, nodded.

When Marcie hugged her, Janice remembered, there were tears in her eyes. As there were in Janice's, turning to Tony Lord.

"At the funeral," Janice said softly, "I couldn't look at her mom. At either of them. I never will again."

Tony saw the tears running down Janice's face and thought of his own, finding Alison. "You were true to your friend."

Silent, Janice turned away from him.

NINE

The Lake City Recreation Center was the former Taylor Library, a rambling nineteenth-century house on a grassy rise overlooking Taylor Park. On the lawn was a bandstand and a carousel; to Tony, the scene recalled the set of a Frank Capra movie, as though the artifacts of wholesomeness could provide the real thing. Nearby, on a dirt field, Ernie Nixon was holding softball practice for a group of seven-year-olds.

Tony watched them for a while. He was too far away to hear Ernie or the kids; what he saw was a silent film of a patient coach, pausing to give instruction, lobbing an extra pitch or two until the batter hit the ball. At the end, a couple of kids ran up to Ernie, seemingly reluctant for their practice to end. He showed one kid how to wear his cap, bill pulled down over his eyes at a jaunty angle. Then Ernie gathered up the balls and bats in a canvas bag, and the kids went off with whoever had brought them.

Tony walked across the field. Spotting him, Ernie put down the bag. From his posture, unsurprised and a bit resigned, Tony sensed he was expected.

"Hello, Tony."

"Hello, Ernie." They shook hands formally, almost ceremonially. "It's been a while."

"Well," Ernie said, "you still look like you. Could have picked you out of a lineup, if that's an appropriate thing to say."

Tony smiled. "From this morning's paper, I'm not so sure. Anyhow, you look good too. No fat."

"No fat, and less hair." Ernie drew a hand over his high, narrow forehead, his close-cropped salt-and-pepper hair. "Middle age—there's no beating it, is there? Though it looks like you're giving Father Time a run for his money."

"Trying. So how's your life these days?"

Ernie shrugged. "Two kids—a daughter nine, a boy seven. I miss 'em both. Their mother left with them, went back to Chicago." His gaze turned to Taylor Park, and his voice softened. "Other than that, Mrs. Lincoln, a very nice girl got murdered here last week. I guess you remember what that feels like."

There was more to this, Tony knew at once, than the flat statement "murdered"; a tacit accusation—perhaps against lawyers, or Sam Robb, or Tony for helping him. But Tony pretended to notice only what was explicit.

"Why do you say murdered?"

"Because I knew her." His face hardened. "Marcie's what you came to ask me about, right? Maybe figure out a way she just stepped over the cliff, or threw herself off one?"

Tony was quiet for a moment. "When *we* were kids, Ernie, you gave me the benefit of the doubt."

Ernie put his hands on his hips. "That was *then*, man, and it was you. You were a pretty good guy then—I knew what you were going through about Alison, and you carried yourself like a man. Now it seems like you've done just fine—money, married to Stacey Tarrant, the whole nine yards." He paused, and his voice was quiet again. "Now you're somebody else's lawyer, looking to get him off. No, not *somebody's* lawyer. Sam Robb's lawyer."

With the training of years, Tony kept his own demeanor mild. "What have you got against Sam?"

Ernie scowled, gazing at the park. "You and Sam Robb had this thing going, the two biggest stars, fit company only for each other. I'm sure that was more him than you. But I'm not going to help you paint a fine young girl different than she was just to save his sorry, overconfident ass."

Quickly, Tony sorted his thoughts—interest in how his friendship with Sam had looked to Ernie; an awareness that Ernie had taken the offensive to deflect Tony's question; a disturbing undertone of certainty regarding Sam similar to the Calders'; the sense that Ernie reserved his strongest feelings for Marcie herself. He chose to address only the last, and only by indirection.

"What was Marcie like?" he asked.

For a long time, Ernie did not answer. Then he turned his startling green gaze to Tony and softly said, "An innocent, man. A total innocent."

"You seem to have been fond of her."

"You could say that." He nodded toward the recreation center. "In this job, sometimes you can touch kids' lives. But you don't know how long, or how permanent, it'll be. With Marcie, I thought maybe I could do some good. She was just so damn *sweet*, and open. That is, if some grown-up took the time to *listen*, not just talk at her." His voice went cold. "I guess Sam Robb figured that one out too. In his own way."

"Why do you say that?"

Ernie turned away. "You've met the parents?" he inquired after a time.

Once more, Tony had the sense of deliberate evasion, of a man determined to control where the conversation went. "Yeah. I've met them."

"Well, Marcie needed *listening*, and the old man's not a listener—or a major feminist, either. Meet him a few times, and you get the picture: women don't work out in the business world, 'cause they just want to get pregnant and then get paid for it." He gave a brief sardonic smile. "You know, they want 'special privileges,' like some other 'groups' out there. Her father had her figured for a 'woman's job,' like teaching or counseling— one of those 'nonserious-type' jobs that women can just fall back on if their husbands die, still get their summers with the kids. The world scares him, and so did the idea that his quiet little girl had any thoughts of her own. So he raised his voice, I guess, so he wouldn't have to hear them. It worked too. He didn't."

Tony stood next to Ernie, gazing out toward Taylor Park. From where they stood, he could see to the edge of the park, the two bands of blue beyond—water, then sky.

"So she came to you?" Tony asked.

He nodded. "Sometimes she'd drop by the office. A few times she baby-sat the kids, and after we'd come home Dee would go to bed, and we'd just sit up talking for a while."

"About what?"

"Whatever was in her mind. A few times, it was that she wanted to write stories—not for adults, but for kids—maybe illustrate them herself, 'cause she was always good at drawing. Even drew a picture of me once. Other times, it was what college she could go to that was big and away from here and not run by the Church. Maybe in a city, even." His voice became sardonic. "Her old man said she was so quiet. With me, she could talk for hours. All you had to do was listen, maybe ask a question or two. I guess Sam Robb figured *that* out too."

For the first time, Tony sensed more than simple anger. "Did she ever talk about Sam?"

"Not by name." Ernie paused, then added grudgingly, "Toward the end, she said she'd gotten 'close' to someone. I knew what she meant."

"Sex?"

"Yeah."

"She talked with you about that?"

In profile, Ernie gave a thin smile. "*You* got a kid, Tony?"

"A son. Seventeen."

"Well, if you're around them enough, like I am, you'll notice that kids these days will talk about damn near anything, even on *Geraldo*—unless maybe their parents are listening." Ernie shook his head. "Sometimes I think we give these kids so much sex education, it's like handing them the keys to your sports car and begging them to try it out. Besides, they see it all the time on *Beverly Hills 90210*."

Tony felt his patience slipping. "I'm a little lost," he said. "What does this have to do with Sam?"

Ernie turned to him. "She came to me about a month before she died. Just walked into my office, closed the door behind her, and said she needed to talk."

For a fleeting instant, Tony thought of Sam's account of Marcie shyly closing the door behind her, needing to tell him something.

"What happened?" Tony asked.

The door clicked softly behind her. The first thing Ernie thought of, he said to Tony now, was how this might look to someone else. And then Marcie said, "I need your help," and, as Ernie described it, something in her voice made him stop worrying about himself.

"What is it?" Ernie asked.

She sat in a chair, looking at him intently. A girl who could tell her friend Ernie Nixon anything.

"I've started having sex," she said.

Her voice was soft, determined. But to Ernie, there was something heartbreaking in the words—a sense of lost innocence and, in a way, enormous loneliness, that she should need to tell him this. Almost against his will, he asked, "Is that a good idea?"

Marcie nodded slowly. "I love him, Ernie. I wanted to give myself to him."

For a moment, Ernie felt himself not wishing to hear anymore. "I guess it's a boy at school."

"No. He's older." She paused at the expression on his face, and then said quickly, "It's better that way, really. I don't know anything, and he can teach me."

Inwardly, Ernie winced. "I guess I was hoping you might wait a little while. When it happens, there's a lot of emotion, and a whole lot of confusion. It's a bunch to take in if you're not ready."

To his surprise, Marcie did not take offense. "I wasn't sure I was," she said. "Then he said he wanted me, and I knew it was time."

Watching her face, Ernie felt defeated. All that he could do was listen. "How can I help you?"

"Talk to me." She looked down. "You know what it's like. I mean, to be him."

Ernie felt this like a slap. "If I were him," he answered gently, "we'd stop this right away."

Her eyes opened wider, and then he saw a first film of tears. "His condom broke," she said.

"What?"

"His condom broke." Ernie watched Marcie force herself to go on. "I was wondering what else might be best for him, and for me."

Ernie drew a breath. "This is hard for me, Marcie. I guess your parents don't know."

"No." She looked alarmed. "They *can't* know, ever."

"Then you should talk to your doctor." Ernie paused. "Do you know where else this guy's been? And with who?"

Marcie flushed. "He's all right that way. I know it."

Ernie sat back. "I don't much care what's best for him," he said at last. "But I know what's best for *you*. Not catching something. Not getting pregnant. Laying off."

Her eyes filled with tears. "I can't."

Ernie watched her for a while. Absently, she brushed her long black hair from her face, trying not to cry. "About what *you* use," he told her quietly, "your doctor knows more than I do. But promise me this, for your own sake, and for my own peace of mind. Promise you'll make him use a rubber, always."

Her eyes, still moist, shone with gratitude: she could talk to him, and he still cared for her. It was more poignant than he could ever describe.

Perhaps Marcie saw this. Suddenly she stood, circling his desk, and fleetingly kissed the top of his head.

"I really love you," she said, and was gone.

For some moments, Tony was silent. "I guess you never told her parents," he said.

"Wish to God I had." Ernie gazed out at the park. "But that would have betrayed her, and if you want the truth, me having that kind of talk with a teenage girl would make some folks pretty nervous. And not just *her* folks."

"Did you think she had a crush on you?"

"Maybe." His voice was bitter now. "Maybe, in that sense, I was the first. But *being* the first takes a different kind of man." He turned to Tony. "She was a sweet kid," he said more softly. "The kind who makes you wish you could be sixteen again, to see things the way they see it. But if you're sane, you *know* you're not sixteen. Especially if you're me."

This was said with dispassion, the hint of resignation. "Why did you come back here?" Tony asked.

Ernie gave another faint smile. "Why does *anyone* come to a place like this? Because it's safe—the schools are pretty good, the drug situation a lot better than most, and your kids can chase around and ride their bikes without getting run over or snatched off the streets." He paused, shrugging. "Johnny D'Abruzzi called me, maybe five years ago. I was in Chicago, not liking my job, my neighborhood, or all the money I wasn't making, and we'd kept in touch. Next thing I know, he's persuaded Doug Barker—the mayor—I'm not a threat to property values, and I'm down here interviewing for a job—"

"Doug Barker was the *mayor*? The same jerk who helped keep you out of the Lancers?"

"Uh-huh. Now he's school board president. Doug's finally gotten to be what he was practicing for all those years—a pompous middle-aged man without a thought in his head that someone else didn't have first. In this case, Johnny." He shook his head. "Maybe it would be different now, I thought, better for the kids than where we were. And it's some better, but not great. No place to raise black kids, Dee finally told me, especially with a man who doesn't know he's black, and a town full of folks who can't find some normal way to *talk* to blacks." His voice grew bitter again. "So she went back to Chicago, to our old neighborhood. Schools are shitty, but there's a truckload of black folks. Can't fault her math at all—with my family gone, I'm back to being the only black in town."

Tony nodded, silent. He remembered the sense of solitude he had perceived in Ernie Nixon. He could feel it now. Yet he wondered, too, whether the end of Ernie's marriage was nearly that simple. And then he had another thought—that Marcie Calder, in her openness, would in some ways be better company for a guarded black man than Marcie's parents ever would. Or, perhaps, the man's own wife.

"About Marcie," he said, "I'm really sorry."

Ernie faced him again. "Tony," he said, "you've forgotten what sorry is. You want to come around here, fine—we can talk about old times. But we're not talking about Marcie Calder ever again."

Picking up the telephone in his motel room, Tony saw that it was well past six o'clock.

"Stella Marz," she answered briskly.

"It's Tony Lord, Stella. Working late?"

"Not for me." She had the crisp tone of someone who did not welcome this distraction. "What can I do for you?"

"I just was wondering whether you got the autopsy report back."

There was a pause. "Actually, I'm reading it."

This made him edgy; something in her voice was close to hostile. "Is there anything new?" he asked.

"At least one thing. Marcie Calder had sex that night."

This gave him pause; either Sam had lied to him or there was someone else. "You can DNA the semen, I suppose."

"There is none. The coroner found traces of a lubricant used on a common brand of condom." Her voice was flat. "It's called Adam's Rib. Because of the ridges."

Tony was quiet for a moment. "Guess I've missed that one."

"I wouldn't know." Stella paused. "It was in the anus, Tony."

Tony sat back. "As in sodomy."

"Yes."

"Was it forced?"

Stella was silent. "There were abrasions," she said coolly. "But maybe it was just her first time. I suppose you can ask Mr. Robb."

What he had heard, Tony realized, was anger. "It could have been anyone, Stella. It could have been rape. Without sperm, you're not going to know. Unless you get a match on a pubic hair."

She went quiet again. Tony guessed that there had been no hair; in this, whoever had anal intercourse with Marcie Calder had been lucky. Especially if it was Sam.

Cautiously, Tony broke the silence. "Is there anything else?"

"Not until we get the DNA results. Any explanation for that spot of blood, by the way?"

"Not yet."

"Too bad," Stella said, and hung up.

TEN

"Sam's gone running," Sue told him. "He took a look at you and decided he was out of shape."

On the telephone, her voice had an edge; Tony wished that he could see her face. "I'd like to talk with him."

There was brief silence—worry, Tony guessed. "I can have him call you," Sue answered. "Or you can just come over."

Tony thought for a moment. "I'll come over."

When he pulled up to the house, it was twilight. Down the street, a shadowy runner passed beneath the trees; even now, thirty years later, Tony recognized the loose-jointed grace of the boy he had once played catch with, laboring to carry the thicker, older body that now contained him. The shadow became Sam, stopping beneath a streetlight. Rivulets of sweat ran down his reddened face. His chest rose and fell as his lungs sucked air.

"You'll have a frigging heart attack," Tony said. "I guess Johnny D'Abruzzi already did."

Sam's eyes narrowed, "Johnny," he answered, "let himself become a fat piece of shit, then died like one. If I've got all this time off, I'm going to do something with it." He paused, wiping the sweat out of his eyes. "What do *you* do?"

"A lot of cardiovascular, mostly. Some weights."

Sam inspected him. "Haven't gained much, have you. Play any sports?"

Shrugging, Tony tried to cover his impatience, born of anxiety. "Pickup basketball, every now and then . . ."

"Then we'll play. As long as you're here, you can start working out with me. Six-thirty a.m., at our gym? I can pick you up."

You're still throwing off your back foot, Tony remembered Sam saying. "I'll consider it, Sam. But right now, we need to talk."

Leaning over, hands on knees, Sam took several slow, deep breaths, the act of an athlete renewing himself. "Let's sit down somewhere," Tony said.

Silent, they walked to the backyard. There was still a hammock in the place where Sue and Tony had once laid out Sam. As they sat, it occurred to Tony that he had not seen Sam drinking. "You give up liquor?"

"No. But since Marcie died, I haven't felt like a drink. But then I haven't felt much like eating. Or sleeping." He turned to Tony. "Was that what it was like for you? Like your life before Alison was killed happened to someone else?"

"A lot like that, yes."

Sam inhaled. "Poor Sue," he said. "In one week, she finds out about Marcie—at least, enough to guess. And all the help she's got is a husband who's lying or isn't really there at all." His tone sharpened. "She doesn't even have you, does she, Tony?"

Tony tried to read his meaning. "I'm your lawyer, as you've already pointed out to me. Anyhow, I suspect she was used to you being off somewhere. Isn't that what happens when you have an affair? Or were you able to separate Marcie from Sue, and live in both worlds like nothing was wrong?"

Sam gazed at him. Night was falling, and Tony could not read his expression; he felt the weight of Sam's scrutiny in the length of his silence. "You have to try," Sam answered coolly. "Unless you want to go crazy. But then you find out, like I did, that you've lost control." He sat back in the hammock, putting his arms behind his head in a pantomime of boredom. "So what's new, pal? I already know that Johnny had a heart attack. So this must be something else."

"It is," Tony said. "Someone sodomized Marcie Calder."

Sam raised his head a fraction. "Meaning . . . ?"

"That the night she died, some guy fucked her in the ass. Could have been consensual, could have been rape. Could have happened after you saw her. Or while."

Sam became quite still. "What does your lady prosecutor think?"

"She's got an open mind. The guy used a condom, called Adam's Rib. So there's no semen sample to DNA."

For a long time, Sam was quiet. "How do they know about the condom?"

"Why?" Tony asked softly. "Did they get the brand wrong?"

Sam sat up. Head propped in his hands, he stared ahead, as if Tony were not there. In the kitchen, a light went on. Sue's face was framed in the window, bent over the sink, rinsing dishes. Every so often she gazed at them; Tony was not sure that Sam had noticed her.

Silent, Tony tried to sort out his emotions. "You'd better tell me," he said at last. "Unless you bought the rubbers in another state."

"Does *she* do this?" Marcie asked.

Sam's mouth felt dry. "No."

She lay on her stomach, naked, in the back seat of his car. "Go ahead," she whispered. "I want you to. I want us to do everything."

He should not do this, Sam knew. He should say what he had come to say.

In the moonlight, her slender back was like marble. There would never be, for the rest of his life, another moment like this. His heart raced.

Slowly, she presented herself to him; for an instant, he remembered her, bent over in the starting blocks, the first pulse of his desire for her . . .

The next few moments were vivid, fleeting. Her small

cry. The painful slowness of it and then, finally, the ecstasy of having her. It's all right, she kept saying in a
muffled voice, it's all right.

Afterward, she lay beneath him. He shuddered in his
solitude and shame.

"I want us to get married," she said.

Listening to Sam's story, Tony watched Sue in the window. It made the moment that much more painful.

"I couldn't tell you," Sam said.

"Couldn't?"

"I was ashamed, all right?" Sam stood, not facing
him. "Here I was, wanting to break it off, and this beautiful sixteen-year-old wants to do something I've never
done."

"That's pretty advanced for the girl everyone else
describes to me."

"We'd talked about it, all right? Before. She asked me
what I wanted—" Sam stopped abruptly, gazing at Sue.
Quietly, he finished, "With a rubber, Tony, how would
they know?"

"Oh, the locals are quite sophisticated these days.
And so is the coroner. The march of science and all
that . . ."

"Next time," Sam murmured. "Next time, I said to
myself, you can tell her somehow. Then she said we
should get married, and it all snapped." He turned back
to Tony. "The rest was just like I told you, Tony. I didn't
kill her, and I didn't think this part mattered—to you.
Only to me and the school board."

Tony stood. "According to Janice D'Abruzzi, Marcie
begged Janice to cover for her. That there was something important she had to tell you."

Sam shook his head. "It was about getting married, is
all I can think." His voice fell. "Or maybe she just
wanted to please me. . . ."

In the window, Sue turned out the lights.

Tony's voice went quiet again. "I asked you not to lie to me. Perhaps you didn't hear me. But this is the last time I ask."

Sam folded his arms. "I didn't kill her, Tony. This is the last time I tell you that."

For a time, Tony was silent. Because of who Sam was, Tony knew, his friend paid a price in Tony's disillusionment and anger that no other client would. But that did not make Sam Robb a murderer. "What are the chances," Tony inquired at last, "that Marcie was involved with someone else?"

Sam looked at him sharply. "Someone else?"

Tony hesitated. "Like Ernie Nixon, perhaps. She seems to have been attached to him."

Sam shook his head. "No way, Tony. No way."

"Why not?"

Sam stood straight again. "Because she wasn't like that. For better or worse, *I* was the one that Marcie wanted."

Tony watched him. Under his breath, he murmured, "Jesus, Sam."

At nine-thirty, Tony lay on the bed in blue jeans, shirtless, gazing up at the ceiling.

There was a knock on the door. Rising to answer, Tony wondered whether it was a reporter, or Sam, or maybe even Ernie Nixon. But, opening the door, he realized that he had expected her.

Sue wore jeans, a sweater, and a denim jacket; in the dim light outside his motel room, she looked smaller, younger. It was like a sudden glimpse of the girl he had loved, which left him quiet for a moment.

"I'm sorry," she said. "I can come back."

"No," Tony answered. "You just caught me by surprise. Come on in, and I'll throw something on."

As he buttoned his work shirt, she sat in a corner, looking over the room. "Not much, is it?"

Tony smiled. "Kind of stark. Like my room when I was a kid."

Sue looked up at him. "Well," she said, "things have gotten better. At least for you."

Tony nodded. "Lately. In more ways than one, I've been luckier than I deserve to be."

Sue stood, hands in the pockets of her jacket. "After that night," she said at last, "the one that you and I had, Sam tried so hard. He watched his drinking, was much more thoughtful of me. It was like you and I—just the thought of us together—had scared Sam into seeing how awful he could be. When we got married . . ." Pausing, she shrugged. "Eventually, he started drinking again. Mostly at home, where people didn't see him. But the children didn't like it—liquor throws his emotional balance off. I guess, for him, it dulls his disappointment."

Tony watched her. It was as though, in her loneliness, she were resuming a conversation with an old friend, one that had been interrupted only yesterday, or the day before that. "He tells me that since last week, he hasn't drunk a drop."

Sue nodded. "Something happens that scares him, and he stops. Maybe this time it'll be for good." She looked at him. "Did he tell you he'd been drinking that night?"

Surprised, Tony tilted his head. "How much?"

"Enough to make his eyes bright. You know that one."

"Yes."

"I keep thinking about that night. Whether I *knew*, deep down. Whether I could have stopped him. The way he was when he came home . . ." Her voice fell off.

Tony felt his own discomfort. "How was that?" he said at last.

She looked away. "Contrite, careful. Like someone who'd been scared sober. He wasn't the same person who'd left the house."

She did not wish to look at him, he saw. Just as he did not wish to question her. Finally, she faced him. "Where is this going, Tony? Sam won't say."

"He can't say. And neither of us knows." His voice softened. "I hate this, Sue. For me, who's still your friend, but most of all for you. I wish there was some other way to help you than being a lawyer."

"A lawyer is what I asked for. Because that's what Sam needs. For me, you can't make this any better, except by helping him. Sam's still our kids' father, the man I chose. I just wish I could see the end of it." Pausing, Sue touched his arm. "And that there was something I could do for *you*. Instead of being someone else for you to worry about."

"You're not. The problem is with me. Part of representing a client is to put your personal feelings aside." Tony paused, speaking more softly. "But this is harder for me—because of Alison, of Sam, and, most of all, because of you. Tony and Sue, I sometimes think, still looking out for Sam. Except, this time, you and I will never get the night off, and I don't even get to be your friend." He tried to smile. "Which makes me just another guy asking you for understanding."

"Understanding?" Sue's own smile was fleeting. "Yes, I'm good at that. Anyhow, I never thought that understanding *you* was anything big to ask."

Gently, she kissed his cheek, and said goodbye.

When she left, Tony tried to fathom why he felt so sad, and who the sadness was for.

ELEVEN

"Why," Tony said, "do I get the feeling that you know something I don't."

"I probably do," Stella Marz answered, and took a bite of her hot dog.

They were standing in Steelton Square, near the statue of Marshal Pilsudski. It was a fresh spring day; around them, office workers, released from their air-conditioned tombs, patronized the hot dog and pretzel vendors, some feeding crumbs to the pigeons who straggled behind them. Fresh from court, Stella had only an hour; she had given Tony ten minutes between mouthfuls. "Do I have to guess?" he asked.

"Look, Tony. I've got no obligation to tell you everything I may know, or suspect, about Sam Robb. Just like I'm not obliged to file charges because the Lake City cops—or the media—want me to." She paused. "Or to give the *Steelton Press* a copy of the Alison Taylor autopsy report."

"They wanted it?"

"Uh-huh. I told them it was still an open file, so no dice."

Tony shoved both hands in his pockets. "I appreciate that."

Stella shrugged. "The Taylors still have feelings too."

Tony waited for a while. "About Sam," he said, "I can't speak to things I don't know about."

Stella turned to him. "Again, there are other people whose feelings are involved here. It isn't just me and you."

"Marcie's parents, you mean."

Stella wiped her lips with a napkin. "My telephone's been ringing off the hook—you've seen the Calders, Ernie Nixon, Marcie's friend Janice, even Alison Taylor's parents. So you've begun to get the drift: Marcie

Calder wasn't suicidal; she *was* sexually involved with an older man; she needed to tell him something the night she died; and she was sodomized before, during, or after her death." She turned to him again. "And, because I'm certain of it now, I'll tell you one new fact. The blood on Sam Robb's steering wheel was Marcie's."

Though he was prepared for this, Tony felt shaken. "The DNA came back."

"On her blood. Yes."

Tony loosened his tie. "I've got the clear impression, Stella, that Marcie's parents take it as fact that Sam was having sex with her. Is it the sodomy? Because they're not the kind of people who would easily believe their teenage daughter was sleeping with a married man. Unless they had no choice."

Stella looked at him steadily. "Then you should feel sorry for them. Just last week, they had an innocent, living daughter."

Whatever else there was, Tony knew, Stella would not tell him. Perhaps she was not yet sure of it.

"Are you indicting?" he asked bluntly.

"Not yet." Her face betrayed nothing. "Before I do, I'll tell you that. And why."

There was still a piece missing, he guessed. Just as they once had with Tony himself, the prosecutor's office was waiting for the case to get better. He wondered how much of the queasiness he felt was for Sam, how much from the memory of feeling stalked.

"How much time do I have, Stella?"

She turned from him, eyeing the pigeons. "If you can find anything to help him," she said finally, "I'd do it soon."

The young woman looked up from her notepad, pushing the wire-rim glasses up the bridge of her nose. "Is it strange for you," she asked, "returning to Lake City in a case so similar?"

Tony's eyes gave her nothing—no resentment, no surprise, no relief from his own scrutiny. "Alison Taylor was strangled. I know, because I found her. But the chances are considerable that Marcie Calder died in a fall."

It seemed to fluster her. She sat back, gaze flicking around the bleak cafeteria of the *Steelton Press*. "All right. But both Alison and Marcie died under suspicious circumstances, and you—then—and Sam Robb were both placed at the scene."

"*I* was found at the scene. Sam Robb put himself there." Tony kept his voice level. "Before you write this article, comparing Sam and me to the Menendez brothers, remember that Sam Robb went to the police voluntarily. I'm really a much better target for the kind of article you seem bent on writing now. Because I was a far better suspect."

She flushed; Tony watched her wonder if she was drinking coffee with a murderer. He had no interest in making this any easier.

"Do you *believe* him?" she asked.

Tony permitted his eyes to widen. "Twenty-eight years ago," he said succinctly, "Alison Taylor's father found me by her body. People from this paper, with inquiring minds like yours, printed that we'd had a stormy relationship and implied that I might have killed her in the process of a sexual assault. They nearly ruined my life, and they did it without conscience, for a story." He made his voice soften. "If I told you I was innocent, and that I never quite got over what people like you did to me, would *you* believe *me*? Because you seem ready to do it all over again, and this time take Sam Robb with me."

She began fidgeting with her hair. "You're saying that he's innocent, like you were."

"I'm saying something more important: that Sam Robb is innocent under the law. Blemish me if you like— I'm almost past caring. But don't make Sam Robb's reputation the price we pay for the First Amendment." For the first time, Tony permitted himself a smile. "Please tell me if I owe you an apology. I'm afraid I bring my own experience to what Sam Robb *and* his family are suffering now. And, like me, Sam Robb hasn't been charged with anything."

She sat back, relieved that Tony had lowered the tension a little. "I understand," she said. "Believe me, I want to be fair."

"That's all I can ask." Tony paused a moment. "If Donald White had never come to Lake City, Alison might still be alive. And if Saul Ravin hadn't uncovered him, I might not be free to speak for someone else's innocence."

When she began scribbling furiously, Tony knew that he had just written her closing paragraph—that his coldness, followed by a thaw, had worked as he intended. It was just as well that she did not know that only the coldness was real and that, try as he might, Tony Lord could not separate her from what other reporters had done to him before she was ever born.

Saul cast an ironic glance around him. "To Donald," he said, and took a swallow of whiskey.

They sat in the same waterfront bar where, twenty-eight years before, Saul had freed Tony to go on with his life. To his surprise, Tony remembered it well and saw that little was new—a couple of placards for lite beers that had not existed then, some video games. The food smell, the darkness, the dull sheen of varnish on the bar and tables, were as before.

"I'd have given a lot," Tony said softly, "to look Donald White in the eyes. To know what he did to her, and whether she suffered."

"It's done, Tony. Except for the press, it's done."

Tony shook his head. "For some people, you once told me, it'll never be done. You just forgot to mention that I was one." Pausing, he took a sip of his Scotch.

"It's like a time warp—Alison, Sue, Sam . . . Even now, he can't resist competing with me. It's instinctive."

"It probably doesn't help that you slept with her and then went on to Stacey Tarrant. It's just another reminder that you left him in the dust."

Tony looked up. "He doesn't *know* that, Saul. And neither do you."

"Oh, he *knows*." Saul gave him a small smile. "People like the Sam *I* imagine would know you screwed her even if you hadn't. By the way, what do *you* make of your old friend these days?"

Idly, Tony traced the rim of his glass with the tip of a finger. "I'm not sure," he said at last. "Sometimes Sam seems sensitive, even brave—he did go to the cops, after all. At other times he seems callous and self-interested to the point of narcissism: the Marcie Calder he describes to me, the compliant sexual adventurer, doesn't jibe with what I'm getting from other people. I don't know whether it's a lie; an excuse; Sam's distorted vision of reality; or my own unwillingness to believe him even though I want to. But anytime I find myself appalled by his affair with Marcie, part of me can almost get how it happened, and the shame he feels now. Then I'll remember myself in the confessional, praying for expiation, and I don't know whether my compassion—if that's what it is—is for Sam or for myself. And now that he seems cornered, with the facts getting worse, it's my instinct to defend him."

"Even if Sam killed her."

"No. Not then. But I don't *know* that."

"But you think he might have."

Tony folded his hands. "He'd been drinking that night, Sue tells me. A kind of impulsiveness goes with that, a lack of self-control."

"To the point of murder?"

Sitting back, Tony tried to imagine his friend with a

rock in his hand, bludgeoning the pretty girl in her parents' photograph until she crumpled to the grass. Finally, he shook his head. "My memory is from when we were kids, Saul. I can't know what might have happened to him since."

Saul considered him. "Drunkenness *is* a defense."

"Only if Sam admits to killing her. He hasn't, and I don't think he will."

Saul looked around them. A couple of crew from an ore boat were drinking beer and playing video games; otherwise, the place was quiet. Finally, he asked, "Any guess what Stella's waiting on?"

"I'm not sure. The coroner has already opined that the skull fractures were no accident. So maybe it's something else from the lab, like some high-tech effort to lift Sam's prints off the rock. That would be no help."

Saul shrugged. "You can always find an expert of your own. There are a million ways to attack theirs."

Tony drained his Scotch and ordered another. "What I could use," he said at last, "is another Donald White."

Saul gave him a skeptical smile. "They don't grow them on trees, thank God." Abruptly, he stopped, looking into Tony's face.

Tony met his gaze. "Ernie's possible, Saul. How many men invest hours in the company of a single teenage girl, unless there's at least *some* element of desire. If Sam crossed the line, he could have too. I mean, count the college professors you must have known who went off the deep end."

Saul's smile became a look of bleak amusement. "They fucked them, Tony. They didn't kill them. For all you know, he was out with friends that night."

"For all I know, he was the one Sam saw in the other car."

Saul's smile vanished. "You know what you're doing here, don't you?"

Tony felt stung; in the case of Ernie Nixon, he found, the defense lawyer's carapace did not numb his feelings. "Of course I know. That's also an odd remark, coming from you."

Slowly, Saul placed the drink down. "I'm beyond cynical, Tony. I don't need it anymore."

"So you drink instead?"

Saul's eyes grew hard. "There are a thousand reasons why I drink. You'll never know me well enough to know them all."

Tony drew a breath. "Sorry," he said at last.

Saul regarded him for a time. "Don't mention it. I know how guilty you can feel, and you've only just begun. . . ."

"Dammit, you know as well as I do what my obligations are, and my *feelings* can't get in the way. As long as I'm Sam Robb's lawyer, my only loyalty is to him. It's incompetence of counsel not to check out a defense."

Saul smiled with the side of his mouth. "A black man in Lake fucking City, the only black in town. Beautiful, Tony. Truly."

Tony's head had begun throbbing. "I know," he said softly. "Just find me a detective, all right?"

Saul looked at him hard, shaking his head, and then he glanced toward the pay phone. "Got a quarter?" he asked. "Maybe we can ruin Ernie before I get too drunk to care."

TWELVE

In profile, Sam's face was set. "Jack Burton called me late last night. My principal."

They were driving to the gym. It was roughly six-thirty in the morning; the sky was cloud-streaked, and dim yellow light seeped through the gray. To their right, its shapes emerging from the darkness, Taylor Park went unremarked.

"I remember him," Tony answered. "He refused to give me a recommendation for Harvard. I always thought John Taylor had gotten to him."

"Well, he probably has again."

"How so?"

"They're petitioning the school board—Marcie's parents *and* the Taylors. To have me fired outright."

Tony turned to him in surprise. "The Taylors? I thought they pretty much kept to themselves now."

"Not entirely." Sam's voice was muted. "I guess I'm a cause worth coming out for."

"Did Burton say what his position will be?"

Sam was quiet for a moment. "He won't support me, Tony. 'Sometimes appearances are the reality,' he said."

Gazing out the windshield, Tony recalled the last spring morning he had seen Lake City this early; driving Sue to her parents' house, her hand resting lightly on his leg, to find Sam Robb waiting on her front steps. "What do you want to do?" he asked.

"We need the money." Sam did not wish to look at him, Tony realized, and his voice bled self-disgust. "My folks left me the house, but not much else, and we've borrowed against it to pay for the kids' college—both of them went to Denison, and it's not cheap. There's not a lot left for Sue and me if I don't have a paycheck."

Tony tried to imagine how Sam felt this morning,

facing the chain of consequences his own actions had caused. "Sooner or later, Sam, you'll have to deal with the job problem."

Sam drew a breath. "Can we at least buy time? I don't want to put Sue through this now. I know how that sounds, but . . ."

He did not have to finish; Tony could hear his shame and desperation. Gazing out at the passing houses, Tony saw that many of the old lakefront houses—rambling wooden structures or vacation cottages once built by the wealth of Steelton—had been torn down; in their place were larger structures, quasi-Tudors or mock-Colonials, someone's derivative notion of the good life. For some reason it made Tony think of how long it had been since that game against Riverwood.

"It's not my area of the law, Sam. But I don't think they can fire you without a hearing."

Sam bit his lips. "I can't testify at a hearing. Not about Marcie."

"I can try to stall it. In time, maybe we could work out some sort of deal—a voluntary resignation, severance pay, keeping your benefits." Pausing, Tony added quietly, "As you once pointed out to me, Marcie's dead. As long as you're not talking, they don't have an admission of a sexual relationship."

Sam stared straight ahead. "People tell you the worst," he said at last, "and then you try to help them. Does it make you feel like God, or a creep?"

The question went to some truths of a lawyer's life: the client's helplessness; the lawyer's sense of power; the uneasy mix of sympathy and contempt Tony so often felt; the way that the duties of advocate must take precedence over the private conscience of the human being. "Sometimes I feel like God," Tony answered, "and sometimes like a sleazebag. At most times I feel like neither one. And when I find myself questioning what I do, I remind myself what happened to me. Not to mention a lot of other people who, one way or the other, don't deserve what happens to them."

"And now? Defending me?"

Tony turned to him. "You don't get the benefit of my professional detachment, I'm afraid. But for what it's worth to you, I don't believe that your involvement with a sixteen-year-old girl, however wrong, makes you irredeemable. That would be a very inconvenient belief for a lawyer, especially one who has regrets of his own." Tony tried to lighten this. "To start, I'm twenty-eight years overdue on my last act of contrition. I think it's like a library fine—after a while, you don't even want to know what the tab is."

Sam watched his face. "What *do* you regret, Tony?"

"Beyond wanting Alison to come out that night?" Pausing, Tony wondered whether to treat Sam as the friend he once had been, and then decided that it would be a kindness. "I cheated on my first wife, for one. There were the usual extenuating circumstances—our marriage was rocky, I was in the middle of the Carson case, and it seemed this woman was always there. But I made a choice, and it cost me the marriage and, for a good while, Christopher. It's been twelve years now, and I still cringe whenever I think about it. But an attack of conscience after the fact never undoes the harm you've already done. At most it's a warning against the next time."

"That sounds like you." Sam's voice was strangely gentle. "Especially the conscience part."

For a moment, Tony wondered if his friend's thoughts included Sue. Then they arrived at the gym, a modern building with a corrugated roof, resembling an airplane hangar, which sat where an old farmhouse once had been. Sam made no move to get out.

"This school board meeting, Tony. Do you think you can handle it?"

"I can try. But Jack Burton could be critical." Tony

paused a moment. "Do you have *any* other problems that Burton could hang his hat on? Anything that could be construed as sexual harassment, mistreatment, or intimidation of a student?"

Sam's eyes went cold. "There's nothing. I don't even have to think about that one."

Tony examined his face. "Then tell me about the school board," he said finally.

A certain bleak amusement flashed in Sam's eyes. "For openers, your old friend Doug Barker is president of the board now. Remember the night you told him he was the biggest asshole in the room?"

It was the night that he and Sam had fought. "That was just before," Tony answered, "you asked me if I'd murdered Alison."

Sam's eyes glinted. "I just didn't know how it would feel, Tony. Now I do. But Doug Barker's *still* an asshole."

Tony smiled a little. "Why do you think I moved away?"

Quiet, they walked to the gym together.

At two o'clock, Tony appeared unannounced at Lake City High School. For a few minutes, he wandered the halls, once more feeling like a ghost. He passed his old locker, then paused at Alison's. Time had not been kind to the school, and twenty-eight years—two rows of names beneath Sam Robb's on the banner in the gym— had intensified the institutional grimness of the place. But it did not account for Tony's sense of being trapped in the past; all at once, he wanted to do his business as quickly as he could.

From her desk in front of the principal's office, Jane Moore looked up in surprise.

"Tony Lord," she managed.

"Hello, Jane." Tony walked past her and opened up Jack Burton's door.

Burton started. Tony watched the first signs of recognition, a widening of the eyes, then a stillness. Burton's hair was thin and white now, and his face more gaunt, but the liquid brown eyes contained the same untrustworthy caution that Tony had learned to read there.

"What can I do for you, Tony?"

"I was kind of hoping you'd filled out that recommendation form."

Burton blinked. "Those were difficult circumstances. I've always regretted them."

"Then you should start trying to do better." Pausing, Tony looked around him. "You know, Jack, the last time I was in this office, George Marks tried to get me to leave school."

Burton sat back. "You're here for Sam Robb, of course."

"Uh-huh."

Burton folded his hands. "Sam," he said, "admits to being with a female student, at night, under circumstances which led to her death—"

"And 'sometimes appearances *are* the reality,' right?"

Burton's back stiffened. "Precisely. Certainly for a responsible adult—a teacher and administrator—who knows that his behavior is improper."

As a parent, Tony knew, he would not quarrel with this man. Evenly, he said, "But is being alone with a student automatic grounds for suspension? I wouldn't think so."

"You know perfectly well he shouldn't have been there—"

"And *you* don't know a thing about what really happened. Just like you didn't know with me."

There was something cornered in Jack Burton's eyes. "What do you want, Tony?"

"To talk about what you *do* know. Sam's been assistant principal for nine years now, right?"

"Roughly."

"Ever had any student complain about his conduct?"

Burton frowned. "Not until now. But *this* is something an assistant principal doesn't have to do twice."

"You don't know Sam did it once. Tell me, did you evaluate him over that time?"

"Yes."

"And what kind of reports did you give him?"

Burton's pale skin betrayed a first, faint reddening. "Sam Robb has been a decent assistant principal. Sometimes he scares students, sometimes he charms them— generally, he keeps them in line. But he can drink too much, and he has a temper."

"Ever mention *that* in your reports?"

Burton hesitated. "No."

"How did Sam come to be your assistant? Surely not over your objections."

"No, but I didn't recommend him, either. He has friends on the school board."

For the first time, Tony smiled. "And how did *you* come to be the assistant principal, before Sam?"

Turning, Burton stared out the window. "There was a search committee. Several candidates were considered, including four outside the school district. The board committee recommended me to the board, and I was hired."

Tony let that hang there for a moment. "Which Taylor was on the search committee?" he asked. "John or Katherine?"

Burton turned to face him. "Katherine was, as I recall. But that was twenty years ago, and it's hard to remember—"

"It was only eight years after you shafted me—I'm sure the Taylors remembered *that* quite well." Tony's voice turned cold. "Please, don't even *try* to tell me you didn't discuss that with them. *Or* that you haven't discussed Sam Robb with the Taylors now."

With a certain detachment, Tony watched Burton absorb the fear that Tony had intended to implant: that he

had given Burton's vulnerabilities great thought and disliked him enough to act on them with pleasure. "If it's
filed," Tony went on, "Sam has a lawsuit against you for
conspiring with the Taylors, *and* the school board, to
violate various of his rights without due process. I've
read the insurance policy that covers you as principal,
and it excludes deliberately unlawful acts. That should
entitle Sam Robb to go after your house, savings,
pension—the exact assets Sam and Sue would be forced
to exhaust once he's terminated. Which has a certain
symmetry, I thought."

Burton opened his palms; the gesture seemed puzzled, precatory. "What would you have me do?"

"I want you to say in public exactly what you've told
me here: that Sam Robb's evaluations have been excellent, that in all his years as teacher or administrator there
have been no complaints of misconduct, and that nothing
in your association suggests that—in fact, as opposed to
appearance—his relationship with Marcie Calder was
improper." Tony paused. "*And* that you believe Sam Robb
should stay on paid administrative leave until the legal
process determines whether he has committed any
crime."

"And if I sincerely feel that's not the right thing to
do?"

"Then I'll be obliged to advance my client's interests,
by whatever legitimate means occur to me. Just like you
once tried to ruin *me* to advance yours." Tony's voice
became soft, ironic. "Whatever your motives, Jack, it's
not too late to learn the true value of loyalty."

Burton looked down. "There are others, you know,
who feel even more strongly than I do."

Tony smiled again. "It's *your* salvation we're concerned with now. So when you call the school's lawyers
for advice, ask whether they'll issue you a guarantee."

"I'll call them, of course."

"Good." Abruptly, Tony stood. "Because if you help

take down Sam Robb, you're going with him. Which would provide me with at least *some* sense that justice has been served."

But it would not, Tony thought as he left. Except for sparing Sue, there could be little satisfaction in frightening this sanctimonious and self-serving man to protect Sam Robb. Especially when Tony knew that—whatever his motives and however arbitrary his actions—this time Jack Burton was acting on the truth.

THIRTEEN

Despite their rasp, John Taylor's first words echoed through the meeting room. "Nearly thirty years ago, in this same room, I spoke to the murder of our daughter Alison. Now, to my sorrow, I speak to the death of another."

The school board sat above him on the stage, three men and two women, facing a cramped room crowded to capacity by townspeople, reporters, cameras. Outside, a large crowd kept vigil, carrying placards, with photographs of Marcie Calder, which implored the board to "Remember Our Children." For Tony, the night was as surreal as it must be for John Taylor.

But the town had changed, and so had the political calculus. Three members were up for reelection in November, Sam had informed him—the bare majority that protected a superintendent whose message was that the Lake City schools, like the town, required no improvement. The two remaining members had moved to Lake City in the last ten years, as it became more of a bedroom community for Steelton, and represented a growing belief that its schools were smug and ossified. For

Tony, the leaders of the warring factions personified the divide: Doug Barker, jowly now, wore tortoiseshell glasses, a Kiwanis pin, and the weighty gravitas of a provincial worthy; the leader of the insurgents, Kay Marston, had artificially bright blond hair, dangling gold earrings, and a sharp expression that suggested that her cross to bear in the service of progress was listening to the unctuous drivel that issued from the mouth, if not the mind, of Doug Barker. Tonight all that both factions shared, Tony suspected, was the fear that not terminating Sam Robb would jeopardize their agenda. Tony's job was to make them fear him more.

He sat in the front row with Sam, Sue, and a few friends who had come, it seemed, with mixed loyalty and puzzlement. Sam wore a sober gray suit and a look of deep shame. Watching Sue in the role of loyal wife, her own humiliation plain, Tony hoped she would not have to suffer through a murder trial.

Standing behind a podium in the center aisle, John Taylor spoke to the board.

"But this is a different case. And I recognize it as such.

"True, Sam Robb was alone with a teenage girl at night. But he himself is *not* a teenager.

"He is a forty-six-year-old man, entrusted with the safety and welfare of the students at Lake City High School. Instead he took a lovely sixteen-year-old girl to the park at night, alone."

Sam gazed at Alison's father, too ashamed to look away. Glancing at Sue, Tony saw her eyes close.

"Oh, I know all the arguments," John Taylor went on. "That it's not *proven* that Marcie Calder was murdered, or that Sam Robb is guilty of anything 'beyond a reasonable doubt.' It's painfully familiar to me, and has been for too many years.

"But what on earth does *that* have to do with whether Sam Robb is fit to continue as vice principal?

"*Nothing.* Because Sam Robb has condemned himself out of his own mouth."

As John Taylor turned his haggard face to Sam, Tony saw, more clearly than ever, what the worm of hatred had done to him. Slowly, John Taylor raised an accusing finger, his voice trembling. "Why don't you explain yourself? Why do you sit there, silent, hiding behind your lawyer?" Now his voice was laced with contempt. "*Anthony Lord.*"

Sam flushed with anger; staring at John Taylor, Tony concealed his own. The board sat in veiled silence, their attentiveness not masking the difficulty of the moment.

Abruptly, John Taylor faced them again. "Let Sam Robb speak for himself, *tonight.* Otherwise, he has no right to our money, or our trust."

Without more, John Taylor turned and took his seat next to the Calders. Awkwardly, Frank Calder touched his shoulder; Tony considered what odd allies they were, the thwarted striver and the wealthy man who once had disliked Catholics, united by their loss and sorrow, tormented by a hatred against which, had John Taylor more compassion, the older man might have warned the younger.

Behind his glasses, Doug Barker seemed to squint, like a man with a headache. "The board appreciates," he said, "the concern for others which John Taylor has shown us. It will not soon be forgotten."

"Hang in there," Tony whispered to Sam. "It's better if I go last."

After consulting *Robert's Rules of Order,* Doug Barker invited a gaunt, birdlike woman to the podium: Jane Whitman, former head of the PTA, designated to speak for a coalition of concerned citizens—including the Alison Foundation.

"People are afraid," she said flatly. "And who can blame them? The vice principal of our high school is the only suspect in the suspicious death of Marcie Calder.

"I don't know why Sam Robb hasn't been charged. Perhaps the police and county prosecutor have the luxury of building an airtight case on a death that's too late to stop. But that's no excuse for retaining a vice principal who, if he had any sense of decency at all, should have resigned his job in shame.

"If he stays in this job, the shame is ours."

Suddenly she snapped her head toward Sue and Sam. "We can't make this man leave Lake City. All we can do is make sure he's not in charge of our daughters, ever again."

Instinctively, Sue reached to cover Sam's hand with her own. As if startled, Jane Whitman turned to the Calders for support, saw the tears on Nancy Calder's face. "We're sorry, dear." For a moment, her voice was gentler, that of the schoolteacher she once had been. "We're all so sorry. I only wish we'd known."

Pausing, Jane Whitman turned to the board again, fixing each with an accusing gaze. "What should we value more—the 'rights' of this man, or the safety of our children? If you were Frank and Nancy Calder, you'd already know the answer.

"The standard here is not reasonable doubt, but the moral fitness of our teachers and administrators. And by that standard, there is *no* doubt that Sam Robb should never guide our children again." Here, she paused. "To the park at night, or otherwise."

When she sat, there was ragged applause. Three speakers followed—a pharmacist, a gas station owner, and the head of Rotary—all calling for Sam's termination. And then Frank Calder stood, wiping the sweat from his forehead with a handkerchief. His voice was flat and unresonant, the twang of the Midwest; it seemed to give the unadorned words a certain dignity.

"I'm Frank Calder," he said. "Marcie's father."

Doug Barker's face showed genuine anguish. "We know, Frank. On behalf of the board, we want to tell you how bad we all feel."

Nodding, Frank Calder bowed his head. "We come here for the schools, you know. So that our three girls could have the best public education and the safest place to be. That's what we wanted for them, Nancy and I."

"Jesus," Sam murmured. He was right to worry, Tony knew: no matter what he said, or how he said it, Frank Calder personified the hopes and fears of Sam's hometown. Tony found it painful to watch this repetition of a nightmare.

"We never expected to have our innocent daughter tell us lies," Frank Calder said baldly, "so that she could meet Sam Robb on lovers' lane.

"*He* says Marcie wanted to have a talk with him. His office isn't good enough? He has to meet her at Taylor Park, at night?" He paused, swallowing. "We *know* what he had in mind. And we all know what happened to Marcie, don't we?

"This is the kind of thing we expect our schools to prevent, *not* promote. We *trusted* him. . . ." His throat caught, and he started again. "We trusted *him*, and we trusted you. And look where it got us.

"Well, now we know. *All* of us know. Nancy and I agree with Mr. Taylor—let him talk. Or, in the name of all that's decent, fire him outright . . ."

His hands were trembling, Tony saw. Frank Calder opened his mouth to speak again and then could not, as if his own thoughts had stricken him. He began backing to his seat, still staring at the board. When Nancy Calder stood, taking her husband's arm, Tony felt this suck all noise from the room.

Doug Barker glanced toward Sam. "Is there someone," he asked, "designated to speak for Mr. Robb?"

Their opponents' strategy, Tony had warned Sam, would be to shame Sam into resigning, or—at the least— into speaking. Watching Sam restrain himself, Tony felt the weight of his responsibility to speak for him. As he stepped to the podium, holding a manila envelope, Tony's palms were damp.

"Hello, Doug," he said quietly.

Doug Barker looked surprised. "Hello, Tony," he answered.

Laying the envelope in front of him, Tony felt Kay Marston watch him, curious. "For those of you who don't know me, I'm Anthony Lord—Sam Robb's lawyer, and his friend. I used to live here, once. And, for many reasons, I deeply regret the tragedy which has brought me here again."

As Tony expected, the effect of understatement, combined with the known facts of his life, purchased their attention. The room felt as still as before.

"Twenty-eight years ago," he went on, "Alison Taylor was murdered in that same park.

"I had been waiting there, for her to sneak out of the Taylors' house, as kids in this town had done before, and no doubt have done since. And when Alison did not appear, I went to look for her.

"There were others in the park that night, just as there are now. I heard footsteps, someone coming from the Taylors' backyard. And then I found Alison lying there, a moment before John Taylor found us both." Tony paused, watching the stunned faces of the board. "That moment has haunted me ever since. It will haunt me for the rest of my life. Not only because of Alison, whom I loved, but because so many people in this town found me guilty without proof.

"First among them, for reasons I understand, was John Taylor. But we share another common memory, one which he alluded to. Twenty-eight years ago, he asked the school board to expel me. My lawyer came here to speak for me, as I speak for Sam tonight. And by a one-vote majority, the board permitted me to graduate.

"Because of that, I am a graduate of Harvard College

and its law school. Because of that, I live a happy and successful life, in which *no* one—except perhaps in this same town—believes me capable of murder.

"My task, all these years later, is to ask this board to act with that same caution. And to remember all of the years that Sam Robb has given to this school.

"For that, a single letter will do. It is the letter of Jack Burton, principal of Lake City High." Pausing, Tony handed up the envelope to Doug Barker. "I have copies of the letter for each of you. What it says is beyond dispute—that Sam Robb has been at Lake City High for twenty years without a student complaint of any kind, or any prior reason to believe that Sam Robb had indulged in *any* improper conduct toward *any* student. In its own way, it is an eloquent document."

It should be, Tony thought—he had written it himself, not trusting Jack Burton to speak in public or even compose the words. And no words could do justice to Burton's expression as he signed it, as complex as Tony's feelings now.

"Regrettably, Principal Burton is ill this evening. But what his letter tells you is that Sam Robb has an unblemished record of excellence. And what Principal Burton recommends you do, in simple fairness, is retain Mr. Robb on administrative leave until the facts are adjudicated."

Tony paused, waiting until Doug Barker looked up from the letter. "The proponents of termination, on the other hand, assume despite this record that Sam Robb is a danger, perhaps a murderer, because of what has befallen Marcie Calder. But as Principal Burton confirms, if you'd given this description to Sam Robb's friends, his colleagues, his students, or to anyone else who knew him, they never would have imagined it applied to Sam." Glancing at Marcie's parents, Tony added softly, "And that, I'm sure, includes the Calders.

"Now they search for answers to a tragedy. But with

the deepest respect for all that they have suffered, and will always suffer, there are no answers here." Pausing, Tony spoke directly to Doug Barker. "This board cannot decide either *how* she died or *who* is responsible—you know only that, as soon as Marcie went missing, *Sam Robb* acted responsibly. So it is beyond your knowledge, or your authority, to decide what the courts have not decided. Mindful of your responsibility to Sam Robb *and* for the sound governance of Lake City's schools—moral, legal, and financial—you should not try."

The veiled threat, Tony saw, made Kay Marston sit straighter. "This board," Tony went on, "has already reported the appearance of potentially improper conduct to the criminal authorities, as is its obligation by law. Until the legal system has spoken, this specter of a dangerous man, so different from the Sam Robb that all of you know well, should not become the pretext for a witch hunt.

"As for the presumption that Sam Robb's relationship to Marcie Calder was improper, my response is simple—wait your turn.

"We've abolished burning at the stake or—as one of the speakers apparently regrets—banishment." Once more, Tony's voice was quiet. "Your obligation to the Calders is to honor Marcie's memory. Do not try to comfort them with the gift of a second ruined life, which does nothing to mend their tragic loss and which later, as time passes, they may regret having asked for in their daughter's name. As, long before, may you."

Without more, Tony sat. Slumped, Sam clasped his shoulder with one hand, looked as exhausted as Tony, quite suddenly, felt.

The board looked tense, irresolute. As Doug Barker turned to the others, Tony saw the doubt in his eyes. "Before we entertain motions, does any member have a statement for the record?"

After a moment, one of Barker's allies, Allan Proctor,

the smooth-faced owner of the local Dale Carnegie franchise, leaned toward his microphone.

"In my job," he said, "I hear a lot of rhetoric. I think what we've just heard, however cleverly put, is diversionary rhetoric and empty threats. What Mr. Lord is implying is that we should wait—give Sam Robb a full hearing *after* the courts have made some determination of criminal conduct." Turning, he gave Sam a look of contempt. "But I don't believe Sam Robb would ever go through a hearing—he'd have to say what he was doing with Marcie, or *refuse* to say, and either way it's an admission of guilt. So I don't think there's a whole lot of danger in firing the man ASAP."

It was shrewd, Tony knew—if all he could do was to get Sam a hearing, too soon, the string was almost played out, for Sam would have to invoke the Fifth Amendment. But Kay Marston's sharp look at Proctor telegraphed her skepticism. "Did you discuss this notion with Mr. Lord? Or our lawyer?"

Proctor pursed his mouth. "No."

"Were you going to?" Marston snapped. "I mean, before we fired him?"

"It's just common sense, Kay. . . ."

"So your 'thought' is that *after* we fire Sam Robb, instead of suing the school system, he'll be grateful we spared him the trouble of a hearing." Kay Marston turned to Tony. "Any thoughts about *that*, Mr. Lord?"

Tony stood. "Two. First, as your lawyer no doubt agrees, Sam is entitled to a formal hearing. Second, firing Sam Robb now would shatter his reputation without cause, and lead to substantial damages."

Kay Marston nodded briskly. "Translated," she said to Proctor, "that falls a little short of 'thank you.' "

For a moment, their tension silenced the board. Then Proctor turned to Sam and asked, "Why don't you just leave? How, in God's name, could you take this girl to the park and then put her parents and all of us through an ordeal like we've had tonight?"

Instinctively, Sam began to stand. Putting one hand on his chest, Tony turned to him and whispered, *"No."* Sam flushed, chest pressing Tony's hand, and then sat back again.

Belatedly, Doug Barker resumed control, trying to preserve the form of an orderly meeting. "Are there any motions," he asked, "as to how we should proceed from here?"

Both Kay Marston and Allan Proctor raised their hands. With the shrewdness of a small-town politician, Doug Barker let his nemesis take a position first. "All right, Kay."

Tony watched Marston, his mouth dry. "Believe me," Kay Marston began, "I share the deep concern and sorrow many have voiced tonight. No one feels more strongly than I about *any* misconduct toward women, let alone the girls in our schools. But we don't have the legal authority to fire without a hearing." She gazed out at the spectators. "Our lawyer suggests that we wait."

"In other words," Allan Proctor broke in, "do nothing."

Taut, Tony watched their rivalry, knowing that Sam and Sue's immediate future hung in the balance. "No," Kay Marston retorted. "Do nothing stupid. We'll reconvene if charges are brought, and have our hearing then. Right now, you're inviting a lawsuit you know we'll never win but which allows this board to pass the buck to some judge in Steelton, who will then pass our bucks to Sam Robb and his lawyer. I don't believe in hiding the facts from voters."

Allan Proctor stiffened with offense. Unhappily, Doug Barker looked at the others. "Votes?"

Tony saw John Taylor lean forward in his seat, the

Calders holding hands. "All in favor of Mrs. Marston's motion," Barker said, "please raise your hands."

Kay Marston did so and then, reluctantly, her ally, a chemical engineer who commuted to Steelton and now stared at the table.

"Two," Doug Barker said in a quiet voice. "Opposed?"

Allan Proctor thrust his hand up first, then Doug Barker's second ally, a retired schoolteacher with tight gray curls. Numb, Tony waited for Doug to cast the final vote for termination.

"Two," the board president announced grimly. Tony saw Sam grasping the armrests of his chair, Sue closing her eyes again.

Doug Barker massaged the bridge of his nose. "Tonight I wish I weren't on the board," he said at last. "I deplore the death of Marcie Calder more than I can say. But I have to agree with Tony Lord—we've known Sam Robb too long to rush to judgment, and prudence suggests that the law should do its work." Facing Sam, he finished: "I hope to God I never regret this, Sam. Mrs. Marston's motion carries, three to two. . . ."

There was a sharp intake of breath. Doug Barker looked up, as if astonished at what he had done, then mumbled into the cacophony: "That concludes our business."

Sullen, confused, the crowd was slow to rise. Torn between relief and instinctive sympathy, Tony watched the Calders staring at the empty stage.

Sam Robb bent forward in his chair, and wept.

FOURTEEN

Sam's hands covered his face; the image—a man mired in relief and shame—was so riveting in close-up that, for a few seconds, a startled Tony Lord forgot what he was doing.

"Hang on, lover," he said to Stacey, and put down the telephone.

As Tony walked to the television and turned up the volume, Sam was replaced by a slender woman in her early twenties, sitting alone on a couch. "When I saw that school board meeting on the news," she told the camera, "I had to come forward. No matter how hard it was."

On the screen, her strong features, unadorned by makeup, gave the impression of sincerity and terrible anguish. "I don't know if there were other girls. But I know that Marcie Calder wasn't the first." Briefly, her voice caught. "Maybe *I* was. . . ."

Stunned, Tony murmured, "*No,* goddammit. . . ."

Off-camera, a woman asked, "Can you tell us how it happened, Jenny?"

She bobbed her head, struggling for self-control. "I was seventeen and on the track team, like Marcie was. He told me I was special. . . ."

"And you had sexual relations?"

"Yes." She paused. "Once in his office, the other time in a motel."

"Why are you coming forward now, after six years?"

The woman seemed to gather herself. "If I'd had the courage to do this *then*, Marcie Calder would still be alive. Sam Robb should *never* be allowed to touch another girl. . . ."

As the camera closed in, the woman bit her lip, fighting for composure. Tony felt an emptiness in the pit of his stomach.

"This is Tamara Lee," the newswoman's voice said, "for *Headline News*."

Numb, Tony walked to the telephone. "Sorry, Stace. I need to call Sam right away."

As he stared out at Lake Erie from the pier, Sam's face looked haunted. "She's lying, Tony. She wants to ruin me."

How many times, Tony wondered, had he heard this from a client. "Now it's *two* girls," he shot back. "And what reason does *this* one have to lie?"

Sam drew a breath. The response seemed heavy and burdened, as though Sam's persona had been stripped away by this last, public humiliation, and all that remained was some primal self who resisted his fate by instinct. "Six years ago," he said wearily, "I threw her off the track team. For having marijuana in her locker."

Pensive, Tony watched the evening sun slip toward the water, spreading faint light in the deep blue-gray. "Then someone else must know that, right?"

Sam slowly shook his head. "I let her say she would quit. It was one thing not to want her on the team, spreading this shit around, and another to screw up her life with an expulsion." He gave Tony a sour smile. "I should have tossed her out. But I remember thinking that at her age I kept a fifth of whiskey in my trunk."

The answer gave Tony pause: this was either an inspired lie, invented within an hour, or Sam had acted with more compassion than Jack Burton, in his bogus piety, had granted the seventeen-year-old Tony Lord. "This charge could devastate you," Tony said at last. "It'll give the school board a pattern of 'moral irresponsibility,' if not a reason to say that you're emotionally unbalanced. And Stella Marz may try to use Jenny to show that you lied to the cops *and* that you're obsessed with teenage girls. The question is why, after six years, she'd still hate you enough to make this up."

Sam turned on him abruptly. "Jenny Travis isn't stable. Push her hard enough and she'll fold."

The change startled Tony; Sam's eyes flared with anger, and there was a cruel practicality in his tone. "I didn't ask if I could break her, dammit. I asked you why she'd lie. . . ."

"Look, Tony—Jenny Travis had a reputation for fucking a lot of guys, even then. Later, there were stories about her and another girl on the track team." Sam's lips tightened. "When someone doesn't know which end is up, who knows why they do things."

Watching the desperation in Sam's eyes, Tony thought of Sue, suffering in stoic anguish through the school board meeting. "How's Sue taking this?" he finally asked.

"How do you think?" The mention of Sue changed Sam's vehemence to despair. "I told her what I'm telling you—that Jenny Travis is a liar. If I can't make Sue believe me somehow, I've lost her." He paused, shaking his head. "I can't imagine that, pal. Just can't imagine it . . ."

"All right." Tony's voice was as reluctant as he felt. "I'll try to talk to Jenny Travis. But understand that it's a risk. If the conversation goes south, she can testify to that as well: the bullying lawyer, trying to intimidate her for the sake of his guilty client. And then I'll have made things that much worse for both of us."

The private investigator Saul had located, Sal Russo, was efficient. Within twenty-four hours, Tony knew that Jenny Travis was an aerobics instructor in Riverwood; had shared an apartment with a woman named Ellen Fox for the past two years; had no criminal record or involvement in civil suits since graduating from Lake City High School; was twenty-three; had never been married; and had a clean credit record. As far as Sal could tell, neither she nor Ellen Fox, a day-care staffer, had a boyfriend.

As he sat in the small office cubicle, waiting for Jenny

Travis, Tony watched the last five minutes of Jenny's aerobics class. She called out orders like a drill sergeant, upbeat but no-nonsense, to the militant beat of rap music; her sweaty and determined charges, various in their shapes and capacities, mimed her calisthenics on a sliding scale running from the sensual to the foolish. On some better day, Tony might have reflected on his own faltering efforts at basketball—the aging ex–high school star outrun by younger lawyers, all of them pale from overwork and as self-serious as he about their competition—and smiled at the human comedy. But these thoughts were too benign to suit his duties to Sam.

The class ended. The students chatted among themselves like kids released from school. Jenny spoke to most of them, squeezing shoulders and offering encouragement; her manner was almost too intense, as if she were preparing her troops for some future assault on life. When a few hugged her back, Tony wondered if they were offering support in her newfound notoriety. Then Jenny Travis came through the door, wiping sweat from her forehead with the back of her wrist. Then she saw him, and her eyes widened in alarm.

"You're Tony Lord," she said. "I've seen you on television."

Her voice had an astringent quality, brittle and a little afraid, and she did not try to feign goodwill. This seemed to fit the rest of her: the short pageboy haircut, the clear blue eyes, the complete absence of makeup to embellish skin so pale that, combined with her drab brown hair, it made her look drained of color. She was almost too slender, and beneath her brisk movements and challenging gaze, Tony felt something defensive.

He met her stare. "I thought it would make sense to look at where this thing might go. Before it goes there."

It came out as more threatening than he wished, less

reluctant than he felt. "Marcie Calder's dead," Jenny retorted. "So she's already gone there."

"True. So this won't go away—you've already been overrun by the media, and now they're talking about another school board hearing."

Jenny's narrow-eyed look conveyed worry, distaste for who she conceived Tony to be, contempt for his moral opacity. "And *you* already know that Sam Robb had sex with another student. Maybe you knew that *before* the school board meeting."

She spoke as though her truthfulness should be as clear to him as it was to her. "I only know what you told Channel Seven," Tony answered, "and I didn't hear that much. . . ."

"Well, what does *he* say?"

"That it isn't true, and that he's willing to face a hearing."

Jenny grimaced. "He really *is* a liar. *And* a murderer." She leaned forward. "Do you know *why* I know that Sam Robb murdered Marcie Calder?"

It startled Tony. "No."

"Because he blackmailed me, for sex. A man who likes to force a woman is capable of taking it all the way."

Pausing, Tony reined in his emotions; to frighten her could be fatal. In a different voice, lower and softer, he said, "I'd like to know what happened."

She gave him a look of doubt, followed by a what-the-hell shrug. "If I'm going to have to tell it over and over again, I might as well tell it to you. After all, I've been living with it for the last six years."

That would make Sam barely forty, Tony realized, and Sam's own Jenny, his daughter, roughly the same age as this woman. "Was Jenny Robb in school with you?"

Jenny Travis stared at him. "Classmates," she said.

"Did you know her at all?"

"Everyone knew her—she was senior class president. But we were in a different group."

Tony caught a hint of dislike, perhaps hostility. But there was no way to probe this without talking to Jenny Robb. Tony found it hard to imagine the recklessness, if this woman's accusations were true, of a school administrator who would have sex with a daughter's classmate.

"When you say that Sam 'forced' you . . ."

Jenny crossed her legs. Behind her, another class was forming, a handful of women in tights. Tony became acutely aware of silence: the silence of the women on the other side of the glass, the silence of the woman in front of him.

"He caught me with drugs in my locker," she said at last.

Jenny Travis closed the door behind her.

Coach Robb sat at his desk, studying her with a heavy-lidded gaze. Then he took two joints from his drawer and put them on the desk.

Jenny felt her heart race. It was better not to speak.

"You could be expelled," he said. "It's my duty to report you."

Mute, she nodded.

Sam grimaced in dismay, a man faced with a distasteful task. Softly, he said, "Sit down, Jenny."

She did that, miserable, staring at the joints.

He leaned forward, looking at her across the desk with those clear blue eyes that were the youngest part of a still young but softening face. "You have such potential," he said. "As an athlete and as a person. Why are you throwing it away?"

Jenny shrugged, struggling for an answer, trying to determine from his manner if her fate was still open. All that she could manage to say was, "I don't know."

"Well, you're going to have to figure it out, all across the board." He paused, folding his hands. "You test well, Jenny, but your grades are average. In track you don't run to your potential. And now this . . ." He paused, staring at his desk. "Maybe I should talk to your parents. That's what I'd want if you were *my* Jenny."

It was the first hint that he might do something short of expulsion. But the idea dismayed Jenny—she could see her tight-lipped mother, her choleric father bellowing with rage. The point of smoking dope was to get her away from all that, into the world of fantasy and sinuous music she concealed in her head. "Please," she said. "They'd just yell at me. They wouldn't understand."

He looked up at her. "*I* don't understand, Jenny Travis."

There was a new intimacy to this, Jenny felt: Coach Robb talking to her like a person. She had always thought there was something attractive about him, but beneath the easy jokes, the cocksure manner of the once great Lake City athlete, he seemed remote. She had no sense of knowing him, and now would have to try. "Sometimes I want to escape," she said. "It's like I don't fit, and I don't know why."

He seemed to consider this, gazing at his desk with veiled eyes. As she watched him, part of Jenny was grateful; the other part, whose existence was a surprise to her, thought suddenly that his interest was a pose, beneath which he had no respect for her at all. And then he looked up with those clear blue eyes, seeming to see through her. "You *could* be somebody wonderful, Jenny. But you won't find that someone by smoking joints."

They were still talking, Jenny thought. Hope and fear and confusion brought tears to her eyes. *"Please,"* she said. "You don't know what they'd be like. . . ."

Coach Robb gave a shrug of helplessness. In a reluctant voice, he said, "Maybe I can counsel with you." Pausing, he placed his hand over his eyes. "I'm going to need to think about it. . . ."

She kept herself still, silent, afraid to do anything that might affect the balance, apprehensive that, even at six o'clock, someone else could walk in the office and see the joints on his desk. He seemed to struggle with himself. "I shouldn't say this," he said softly, "but the fact that it's you makes it that much harder. People can't think I have favorites. But you've always been a favorite of mine."

Something had changed between them, Jenny suddenly knew. She felt herself swallow. "You can't keep running away," he told her. "Boys and drugs and all the rest. You know that, don't you?"

Jenny nodded. She would have nodded at anything he said.

Silent, he put the two joints back in the drawer. "All right," he said slowly. "I'll help you."

Jenny felt her own tremulous smile. "Thank you . . ."

As she stood, so did Coach Robb.

They looked at each other, Jenny in confusion, and then he opened up his arms. Hesitant, she went to him.

He felt strong, not slight like the boys who had made her feel nothing. "It's all right." He held her tight now. "We'll get through it. . . ."

When she drew back, looking at his face with gratitude, he shook his head with a funny half-smile. "Ah, Jenny . . ."

There was no mistaking the thickness in his voice. She felt the pit of her stomach clutch, and then he kissed her.

She did not resist this, or encourage it, but seemed to exist outside herself, caught in disbelief, fear, wonder. His tongue slipped into her mouth.

Jenny let him do this, imagining her parents' faces, afraid of pulling back from him, frozen by the two joints in his drawer. Then he leaned his forehead against hers. "Is this all right?" he asked.

She did not say yes or no. Kissing her forehead, Sam released her, walking to his door. As he did so, she realized that he had asked her to come to his office after practice, at a time when no one was here.

Still facing the desk, Jenny heard the click of his door lock.

Even before he leaned his body against the back of her, hands circling her waist, Jenny knew that he would touch her breasts.

Her eyes shut. He found her nipples through the thin cotton of her T-shirt, sending warnings to her brain, shivers to the core of her. His breath warmed the back of her neck.

The rest evolved from moment to moment, a dance she already knew, yet somehow stood outside of. The confident hands unsnapping the top of her jeans, fingers finding her wetness, his lack of hurry, the fact that she could have stopped him and yet dared not, even when he bent her over. As he entered her from behind, her hair, falling across her face, grazed his desk. She felt his thrusts, then his shudder, and wondered if the risk was part of his excitement.

Softly, calmly, Sam Robb murmured, "This can't be the last time, Jenny," and she realized that he owned her.

Wondering if the account was true, Tony was shaken by its similarity, at least in certain particulars, to Sam's own story of his "seduction" by Marcie Calder. So that it was a moment before he asked, "Back then, did you ever tell *anyone* about this?"

Jenny folded her arms. "No."

Tony hesitated. Even were he to discourage Jenny Travis, Stella could subpoena her, perhaps compel her to testify against her will. But unless he tried, her testimony—if allowed—could be lethal. And despite himself, Tony needed to hear everything. "There was one more time with him?" he asked.

"Yes. At the Motel 6, about a mile from here."

At least it wasn't in a car, Tony thought with bleak irony. "What happened?"

"I went down on him. He held my head there until he was finished."

Her body was rigid, and her uninflected voice spoke of hatred under tight control. "What you're telling me," Tony said with care, "isn't pretty. But there's some distance between exploitation—even abuse—and murder."

The first color showed in her cheeks. "I gave him what he asked for. What if I hadn't?"

"I don't know."

She stood, turning to the glass windows, watching the forms of other women. At length, she stood straighter, turning to face him again. "He wanted me twice," she said. "The second time, he rolled me on my stomach across the bed. When I tried to get out from under him, he just went ahead and did it. He *hurt* me." Her voice filled with contempt. "And then, when it was over, he *apologized*. 'I'm not like that,' I remember him saying."

Her eyes bored into Tony's now, demanding to know how he could represent this man. Evenly, Tony asked, "Did *what*, Jenny?"

She gave him a quick querying look, then angrily shook her head. "Not *that*," she said. "He just made me feel cheap and dirty and exploited. Maybe, in *your* life, that's nothing."

Tony was aware of his own jumbled emotions—fear of who Sam might truly be; the unwelcome question of what married life had been for Sue; the intuition that, in Jenny Travis, the unwillingness to differentiate between Tony and his client went deeper than anger at Sam, or dislike for lawyers. There was something as yet unspoken, and now Tony could guess what it was: in that moment, he felt deep compassion for Jenny Travis, anger that he, as Sam Robb's lawyer, must risk telling her what Stella had not—that the legal process, once entered, would slip beyond her control.

"In *my* life," he answered, "it's hardly nothing. But I'm representing a client. And in fairness to him, I have to point out how damaging your account can be, let alone how serious it is to suggest that you believe him capable of murder. Even on the basis of sexual coercion." Tony kept his voice level; perhaps she could be made to see that coming forward was of limited value. "Because of that, I'm very sure that I could keep your testimony out of any murder trial—it's far more prejudicial to Sam than it is probative of murder.

"That only leaves a school board hearing. But Sam's already under suspension. If it helps, I think I can assure you that he's never coming back to Lake City High School."

Stubbornly, Jenny Travis shook her head. "You're sounding like a lawyer. But I was a victim, and so was Marcie Calder. I was quiet for six long years, and all it did was hurt me. I'm doing this for girls like Marcie, and I'm also doing it for *me*."

There was no stopping her, Tony knew, without explaining the rest. Stifling his reluctance, Tony went on. "Then in fairness to Sam, *and* to you, I should tell you what any lawyer will be forced to ask. You *did* quit the track team, right?"

She gave a curt nod. "After the motel, sure. I couldn't even look at him."

"There are no witnesses to confirm your story, or to persuade me—as Sam's lawyer—that it's so. Granted that's always the problem with what you say Sam Robb did to you. But there's no one else to say, Jenny, that Sam didn't let you quit out of kindness, as he claims, instead of expelling you for drugs. Or that anything else you just told me is true. It's a classic 'he said/she said' conflict, and those aren't easy to resolve."

Jenny stared at him. "I knew that six years ago. That's why I kept my mouth shut, so that Marcie Calder could step into the same trap I did. Now I'm ready to put my word up against Sam Robb's."

Part of Tony wished, for her sake, that this were as simple as she felt. But it was not. "Where that takes you," he said finally, "is a battle of credibility—"

"And Sam Robb's *credible*? After this?"

It was the crux of the matter, Tony knew. "It's a real problem," he conceded. "In the end, Sam's lawyer will be forced to go after you. To try to suggest that because of who *you* are, there may be reason to doubt your word."

Jenny's jaw tightened; for the first time, Tony was sure that the defensiveness he had seen was visceral, and very deep. "On what grounds?" she demanded.

"Anything that reflects on your veracity, or objectivity." Watching her face, Tony made his own voice as gentle as he could. "That's not just drug use, or promiscuity. It's everything about you." He stopped abruptly, staring into her frozen eyes. Softly, he asked, "Do Ellen's parents know?"

Her skin seemed paler than before. With equal quiet, she answered, "You bastard."

"So," Saul asked, "she's going away?"

"I think so," Tony answered wearily. "If Stella lets her. Jenny clearly cares for this Ellen, and she hadn't realized what testifying might mean to her."

On the other end of the line, Saul was quiet for a moment. "Think she's telling the truth?"

"It's surely possible—God knows she hates him. But there's an intensity to her that's not about injustice but personal psychology. Or so I keep telling myself." Tony paused, reaching for the martini on his nightstand. "Frankly, Saul, I feel like I've contracted leprosy. Only a decent sense of shame kept me from telling her about all the gay and lesbian friends Stacey and I invite for dinner back in liberal San Francisco."

Saul snorted at this. "All you did was tell this girl the truth. And doing to her in public what you did in private would have felt a whole lot worse. Or knowing someone else would do it."

It was true enough, Tony knew. "I guess what bothers me most is the idea that I don't know who Sam Robb has turned out to be." He paused for a moment. "My old friend is either the victim of bad luck, worse judgment, and truly substandard morals, or he's pathological enough to have murdered Marcie Calder."

The bald admission deepened Tony's depression. "Under the circumstances," Saul said at length, "I don't know whether this will cheer you up. But your guess about Ernie Nixon may have been right, after all. At least right enough to make him look bad."

It did not surprise Tony that he felt no better. "Tony Lord," he said, "the scourge of blacks and lesbians. For years it's been my highest aspiration." Draining his martini, he finished, "So tell me about Ernie."

FIFTEEN

Through Sarah Croff's window, Tony could see Ernie Nixon's home quite clearly, a modest white wooden house from about the 1920s, with a front porch, shade trees, a flower bed that seemed to have fallen into neglect, an unmowed lawn. Following Tony's gaze, Sarah Croff said with disapproval, "He's letting things go."

It was the wages of divorce, Tony guessed. Even in the generous light of morning, Ernie Nixon's home bespoke abandonment. To Sarah Croff, he said, "You can certainly see who comes to the house, can't you."

"Oh, yes. Just like I told your Mr. Russo."

There was a note of querulous superiority in her voice,

as if Tony were an annoyance and not very bright. Tony guessed this was habitual, and not just a matter of being seventy or so: beneath her thinning white hair, her face seemed pinched with uncharity—hollow cheeks, a down-turned mouth, sharp eyes that Tony could not imagine crinkling in a smile. Turning to look at her again, he tried to remember why she seemed so familiar.

From behind her, sitting on the couch, Saul Ravin gave him a look that was faintly droll. *She's all yours*, the look informed Tony. *I'm just here to satisfy my curiosity.*

Mildly, Tony said to Sarah Croff, "What you told Sal could be very important. That's why I wanted to meet you myself."

Mollified, Sarah Croff nodded toward the couch, indicating that he should sit beside Saul. "Sam Robb is a fine man, has always been my impression. I can remember him at sixteen or so, giving a wonderful sermon at a sunrise service here. My late husband and I were quite impressed."

That was it, Tony realized. Only his client's need for this woman kept Tony from laughing aloud: she was the anti-Catholic crone-in-waiting who had looked at Tony with such disapproval when he dragged Sam off at the conclusion of the sermon, announcing that it was time for them to go to Mass. He sensed that she had looked with disapproval at so many people that she no longer remembered this. But it was clear from her expression now that she remembered the murder of Alison Taylor.

"I know Sam very well," Tony said. "In high school, I was his best friend."

"You were also suspected of murder. Until they found the black man who killed that lovely girl."

Her voice had filled with distaste. Tony caught the implication at once—for Sarah Croff, his redemption through the exposure of a black man had resonance for Sam Robb. "Yes," he answered, "I was lucky."

"You were *blessed*. But then the press always sensationalizes things, doesn't it. That's why I feel so sorry for Sam Robb and his family."

Much sorrier, Tony felt quite certain, than she had ever been for Tony Lord, the Catholic from a Polish neighborhood in Steelton. Silent, Tony took his seat next to Saul, gazing around her living room, scarcely bigger than a railroad car, yet filled with lithographs of what she must imagine to be the natural order of things, all derived from the nineteenth century: pastorals, hunting pictures of horses ridden by men in breeches, a full-masted schooner. A Valhalla for white folks, Tony thought mordantly—Sarah Croff seemed like the kind of woman who had traced her lineage through generations of Methodists and Presbyterians, confident that her family tree contained no ethnic horrors. The strength of his renewed dislike for her impressed him; more than he would have liked, Lake City lived within him still.

"Can you tell me about Ernie Nixon?" he asked.

Nodding briskly, she sat across from him on a cane-back chair. "What struck me was that poor girl, Marcie Calder, though I didn't know her name until I saw her picture in the *Steelton Press*. As soon as Mr. Nixon's wife moved out, she began coming over to see him." Her mouth pursed. "The first few times, they sat on the front porch and talked. Later, they stayed inside."

Her tone was chaste, as if to convey that she preferred not to consider the implications of this but could not avoid it. "How often did she come?" Tony asked.

"Four or five times, I saw her—usually on weekends. After a while, all I'd see was her car, a red compact of some kind." She folded her arms, adding in a defensive stare, "I'm not an eavesdropper, Mr. Lord. But it stuck in my mind—a pretty girl that age, coming to see a man whose wife has gone off, so that he's living as single. I couldn't help but wonder."

You surely couldn't, Tony thought. As if reading his

mind, Sarah Croff added, "But it was none of *my* business, after all."

She was not a fool. "I understand," Tony said carefully. "And no one *wants* to think poorly of their neighbors. Unless it's unavoidable."

Sarah Croff hunched in her chair, giving her thin frame an air as doleful as her expression. "It wasn't," she said, "until that evening."

Feeling Saul stir with interest, Tony permitted her a decent interval of silence. "Tell me about it," he said.

For the next few moments, listening to her parched voice, Tony imagined the scene as she described it.

It was dusk. Preparing to close the curtains to her living room, Sarah Croff saw that Marcie Calder's car was in his driveway.

It stopped her for a moment: this was the first time she had seen the red car at night. Where were the girl's parents? she wondered. Then the front door opened, and Marcie Calder came out.

Ernie Nixon was right behind her. She was in a hurry, not looking back at him, long hair swirling around her face. Then he caught up to her on the stone path to his driveway.

Marcie stopped abruptly, facing him. Soundless, they were like two quarreling figures in a pantomime. His body seemed taut with anguish. From a distance, her pretty face was a mask of distress and indecision, and she seemed to be fighting tears.

Suddenly she turned from him, walking quickly toward the car.

When Ernie Nixon grabbed her arm, Sarah stiffened.

Marcie herself froze, staring at the black fingers on her arm, then at Ernie's face. Her lips moved briefly, and his hand dropped to his side.

Almost gently, Marcie touched his shoulder, and walked slowly to the car.

He stood there, defeated, as she backed the red car from his driveway.

When she disappeared, something seemed to snap in him. Hurriedly, he opened his garage, got into his station wagon, and backed out the car so quickly that his tires crossed the lawn. The last thing Sarah Croff saw were his red taillights in the dusk, pursuing Marcie Calder.

"I closed the curtains," Sarah Croff said now. "You don't want people peering into your living room at night. But it wasn't right. Frankly, it reminded me of that terrible Simpson thing."

Her eyes reflected genuine fear, as if, in retrospect, she had seen the prelude to a tragedy. Even Tony felt his own frisson.

"This was the night she died?" he asked.

"Yes." Sarah Croff shut her eyes. "The next day was when I saw her picture."

Shifting his weight, Saul leaned forward. "Why didn't you call the police, Mrs. Croff?"

She stiffened. "I'm not a busybody," she answered in a brittle voice. "I thought the police could handle it themselves."

So she *knows*, Tony thought: the woman's a racist and does not wish to be exposed as one, obsessively watching her black neighbor's house. The fear had distorted her conduct, and, for a time, Ernie Nixon had benefited. But no more.

Fearful, she looked from Saul to Tony. "Will I have to testify?" she asked.

For a moment, Tony felt almost sorry for her. Gently, he answered, "I hope not."

Outside, Tony stood by his car, letting the bright sun dissipate the mustiness of Sarah Croff's living room. "Oh, Marcie," he murmured, "what a busy girl you were."

"What do you think *that* was all about?" Saul asked.

"Other than this woman's Othello complex? Nothing good for Ernie Nixon. Maybe there's an innocent explanation, but it surely isn't covered by anything that Ernie chose to tell me."

Saul glanced back at the house. "Put her on the stand, Tony, and she'll make it sound like a lovers' quarrel. If he doesn't have an alibi that night, she's truly a gift from God."

Tony nodded. "I'm going to see him now. It's the least I can do."

"Very decent of you," Saul said dryly. "You also want Sal Russo to find Ernie's wife, I assume."

Tony fished out his car keys. "I'm afraid so," he answered, and drove away.

SIXTEEN

Tony found Ernie on a bench by the baseball field, eating his lunch from a brown paper bag. Sitting beside him, Tony recalled the afternoon of the Stratford game, when Ernie had sat on the empty bench with Tony. But Ernie had come to console him; for Tony, this underscored the conflict between his duties to Sam Robb and what those duties had come to involve.

Turning, Ernie regarded him with a silent impassivity that suggested that he had expected Tony, and that the visit was not welcome. "Shall we start all over again?" Tony asked.

At once, Ernie's sensitive face took on the defensive opacity Tony recognized from all those years ago. "What do you mean?"

That Tony was Sam's lawyer, he now knew, had made them enemies from the start: then, Ernie had misled him; now, Ernie was probing to see how much Tony knew. Instead of obliging him, Tony asked simply, "Did *you* kill her, Ernie?"

Ernie's face twisted; for a moment, he lost control, staring at Tony with a fear that seemed years deep. When he stood, walking away, his pained expression reminded Tony of someone forced to look at the sun until he no longer could. He stood by the pitcher's mound, staring at the ground with his arms folded.

"I'll have to take this to the prosecutor," Tony said. "You know that."

Slowly, Ernie looked at him, bitterness in his eyes. "You think I didn't tell them, just like I didn't tell you, because I've got some terrible thing to hide. That'll make a nice story come trial time, won't it? Sure worked for *you* well enough, with Alison Taylor. No reason not to try it out for Sam—"

"Quit playing the martyr," Tony snapped. "You lied about Marcie Calder, and now I've caught you at it."

Ernie stood straighter. "Lied to *you*? Who are *you* that I owe you 'the truth' about anything, all so you can set me up. What kind of truth are you after here? Because if Sam Robb has told you the *real* truth, and you're still in Lake City, you've become a lot worse human being than you've got any excuse for."

Tony faced him. Softly, he said, "I've been here two minutes now. So far you've accused me of racism, amorality, and a conscious attempt to spring the killer of a teenage girl. If I'd known you'd be this pathetic, I'd have gone straight to Stella Marz."

Ernie's mouth formed a smile of derisive anger. "To do what, Tony? Accuse me of fucking a sixteen-year-old white girl I cared for because some old biddy used to watch us from across the street? Got so we couldn't sit on the front porch anymore, what with her peeking at us all the time. That's what you've got, and it's *all* you've got, because there isn't any more *to* get. So go right ahead and see the prosecutor—don't let *me* get in your way."

In his secret doubt, Tony hesitated. "Not quite all," he said. "For example, where were you the night that Marcie Calder died?"

Ernie's smile vanished. "At home, in bed. Not an alibi in the world." He tilted his head, asking softly, "So the old lady was peeping that night too?"

"Don't blame it on her, Ernie. Or me. You saw Marcie Calder the night she died, and didn't bother to mention it to me. When I do with that whatever I decide a good defense lawyer should do, remind yourself that I came to you first."

The anger died in Ernie's eyes. "Good luck," Tony said, and turned to leave.

"All right, Tony. You want to know what really happened?"

Tony faced him again, hands in his pockets, silent. In the sunlight, Ernie's gaze seemed hooded.

"I knew it was trouble," Ernie began, "from the moment I saw her face."

Marcie stood in the doorway. She looked pale, lost. In her seeming disorientation, there was something waiflike about her—thin, lacking energy. The difference in her struck Ernie like a slap in the face.

"Can I come in?" she asked.

Even the request was strange, like she was dragging trouble behind her. So that he hesitated a moment before saying, "Sure." But her eagerness to come inside, her need for him, were touching—he was concerned for her, after all, and in some strange way, her company had consoled him once his wife and kids were gone. When she sat on the couch across from him, as she always did, he chided himself for his nameless apprehension.

"What is it?" he asked.

She flicked her hair back with nervous fingers, forcing herself to look at him. Softly, she answered, "I'm pregnant."

Ernie felt his own spirit drain from him. Sitting in the bare living room, among the scraps Dee had left to him—a couch, a chair, a picture of his kids—they seemed to Ernie like the last two people on earth. After a moment, he got up from the chair; Marcie met him in the middle of the room, leaning against him.

Silent, he held her, feeling her soft hair on his face. The only sound either of them made was Marcie's muffled crying. He stroked her hair as though she were his own wounded child.

"Do your parents know?" he asked.

She shook her head, forehead still resting on his shoulder. "No one does, except my doctor. Not even Janice. Or him."

It made him feel touched, and terribly sad. "What do you want to do?"

"I don't know." She leaned back, eyes still moist. "I'm telling him tonight."

"What about your folks?"

"Not yet. I mean, I've only known for sure about the baby since this afternoon." She swallowed. "This could ruin him, and I'm afraid of what my parents might do if they found out who he is—"

"Marcie," Ernie cut in gently. "You should worry about *you*. Let's talk about Marcie Calder for a while."

He led Marcie to the couch again, holding her hand as he had never done before. She sat with her knees together, gazing at the floor. "You have choices," he said. "You know that, don't you? This doesn't have to be a trap."

She turned to him, eyes wider. "What do you mean?"

"What I guess your doctor already told you, for one thing."

Marcie bit her lower lip, to keep from crying. "I can't do that," she said. "A fetus is a life."

"So are you, Marcie. Why pay such a price for the one mistake I know you'll never make again?"

She looked at him now, so sincere it broke his heart. "But it's a baby—*my* baby. How can I kill it for being my mistake?"

Ernie felt despair seep through him. "There's so much *to* this, Marcie. Like who cares for the child once it's here."

"*I* do."

You're a child yourself, Ernie wanted to say. But that surely would not work; before his eyes, he saw Marcie Calder assume the pseudomaturity of a young girl whose biology had so outrun her experience that she was trying desperately to reconcile them. "You'd be living with your parents, Marcie. Your choice would be to drop out or ask your mom to raise the baby, and have them blame you for all the time it takes, the money it costs, the old-fashioned shame they're bound to feel." As he talked, Ernie felt himself envision how grim her life could become. "Do you really think much good would come from that for anyone? Even the child?"

Marcie looked down. "Please. Whatever happens, just keep on being my friend."

Ernie felt defeated. Softly, he asked, "Can the father help you?"

Her eyes misted again. "No. I don't think so."

This, perhaps, was another opening. "Then, for his sake, it might be better if you considered *all* your choices."

She sat straighter. In a new voice, clear and determined, she said, "I'd never ask him to come forward. Unless he decides to, I'll keep who he is a secret."

The thought seemed to burden Marcie; the spurt of life in her expired, and she looked wan and thin again.

Helpless to do more, Ernie asked, "When was the last time you ate anything?"

Marcie stared at the floor again. "Last night, I guess. In the morning, I've felt kind of sick."

"You should at least try to eat something," Ernie told her. When Marcie did not argue, he went to the kitchen.

He had left the breakfast dishes in the sink, he saw, a symbol of his own listlessness since his family had left him. When he looked in the refrigerator, all he had besides hot dogs, milk, and beer was the makings of a tuna sandwich. Suddenly it struck him that his life seemed empty as the refrigerator, and that he did not wish for Marcie's life ever to be like this.

Pensive and sad, he took her a tuna sandwich on a plate. "Here," he said. "Why don't you have some of this."

She tried to smile. "I guess I should. After all, I'm eating for two now, aren't I."

The incongruous sound of this on the lips of a teenage girl he knew and cared for filled Ernie with sudden anger—at her fate, at her parents, at the baby's father most of all. That Marcie should strive to be the adult she was not, about to live a life she could only dimly imagine, should never be: Ernie was failing his own children by his absence, and now could not stand that everyone else should fail *this* child.

Silent, he watched her eat for a time. Then, tentatively, he said, "Maybe we can talk a little more."

It seemed to startle her. She put down the sandwich, looking at her watch. "God," she said. "I have to meet him. . . ."

Already she was somewhere else, plunging toward her unhappy new life. "You *don't* have to meet him," Ernie protested. "Not yet. Before you decide anything, let me take you to Planned Parenthood. You shouldn't be talking to him before you figure out your options."

Marcie stood abruptly. "You've always listened to me—that's why I wanted to tell you. But it's *our* baby, and I have to talk to him." Her eyes filled with tears again. "I love him, Ernie, and I'll love our baby too."

Ernie watched her, feeling his frustration swell and, he realized, a jealousy he did not care to think about. Marcie came to him, kissing him on the forehead. Gently, she said, "Thanks for being a friend. . . ."

Thanks for being a friend, he thought. It was as meaningless as a yearbook inscription for someone you might never see again. As she went through the door, Ernie said, "I'm *not* just a friend, Marcie—"

The door closed behind her.

Crossing the room, Ernie opened it again, hurrying after her.

He caught her on the front walk, grasping her arm. "I'm more than a friend," he repeated. "I'm an adult, and I *care* for you."

She looked at his hand, then at Ernie. "I know," she answered softly. "Because I care for you. But you're not the father, Ernie. He is."

He dropped his hand. "I just don't want you to throw your life away."

Gently, she touched his shoulder. "But I won't," she said. "I'm just starting someone else's life."

The words were so simple, so touching in their naive faith, that they disarmed Ernie utterly. He stood there—hardly moving—and watched her drive away.

Who *was* he? Ernie wondered.

Something snapped inside him. Without thinking, he opened the garage and got in the car to follow her.

Ahead, Marcie turned, perhaps headed for Taylor Park.

He followed her, glancing in the rearview mirror, as though looking for police. But suddenly what he saw was a middle-aged black man following a teenage girl who was not his lover or his daughter, and who didn't know she needed him.

He pulled over to the curb, watching her taillights vanish in the dark.

"So I came home," Ernie said, "and spent the night alone, as always." He paused, adding with sardonic bitterness, "But I was wrong. Marcie Calder didn't throw her life away. Your friend Sam threw it away *for* her."

Tony found that the story had shaken him too badly for a quick response. Quiet, he pondered the difference between the unworldly but self-absorbed girl Sam had described and the resolute and unselfish one Ernie asked him to imagine. If this story was not true, still Ernie told it well. And if it was . . .

"I can see it in your eyes," Ernie told him softly. "You've still got quarterback eyes, Tony, and you're still wondering if you can pin this girl on me. But it won't work. Because I'm not the father." Ernie gave him a sudden, mirthless smile. "Just like I told the police and Stella Marz," he finished softly, "the day after they found her body and it hit me who the father was."

"Jesus," Saul Ravin said, and took another swallow of whiskey.

For a moment, Tony stared out Saul's window, watching Steelton vanish in the fading light of dusk. "That's what the Calders weren't saying, what Stella Marz refused to tell me. She and I have been playing cat and mouse, and Stella's been the cat.

"She's known from day two that Marcie Calder was pregnant—she had Ernie and the autopsy to tell her that much. But it takes a while for the lab to DNA fetal material and come up with a dad. That's what she's been waiting for."

Saul nodded. "She's been waiting for motive, Tony. A dad who feared exposure, if dad turns out to be Sam."

Tony could not shake the confusion he felt, the clash

between the lawyer's judgment and his own pointless wish that Sam be innocent; today, he could not bring himself to confront Sam with Ernie's story. "That's if Ernie was telling the truth," he finally answered. "If *Sam* is, maybe she didn't tell Sam because the baby wasn't his but Ernie's. No way Ernie's kid could be Sam's, or vice versa."

"I expect Stella Marz will tell you, soon enough. At least if she decides to bring murder charges." Saul pushed a packet of papers across his desk. "In the meanwhile, Sal Russo found Ernie's wife's divorce petition. Which, as you suspected, involves a little more than Ernie choosing to live in whitebread city."

"What's in there?"

"Nothing elevating, unless you're us. Although there's nothing that points to Marcie as the problem." Finishing his whiskey, Saul gave Tony a first, bleak smile. "According to Mrs. Nixon, Ernie whacked her."

SEVENTEEN

"You're Mr. Lord," Dee Nixon said.

Standing on the front porch, Tony tried to conceal his surprise, taking in the woman as he did. His first impression was of intellect and a certain haughty severity—close-cropped brown hair, a high forehead, unsmiling eyes behind wire-rim glasses, a thin, somewhat regal face, a defiant tilt to her lanky blue-jeaned frame. She struck him as a woman quick to reach a judgment and perhaps unwilling to change it once she had done so.

"Well," she said, "you've come a long way for not very much."

Tony glanced out at the street—a neighborhood of

row houses that seemed barely middle class, with a seedy corner store and a few unkempt lawns that stood out like bad teeth. "So have you," Tony answered.

To his relief, this seemed to amuse her a little, as if she placed a value on candor for its own sake. "This is only for the rest of the school year," she said, "until we get settled in our own place. But it's not Lake City, Ohio, so that's something."

She pronounced "Ohio" in three distinct and mocking syllables. She did not seem like someone who gave much quarter or was inclined to mercy in argument; for that matter, Tony realized, she had yet to ask him in. Silent, he raised his eyebrows, looking past her into the living room.

"Oh," she said dryly. "I almost forgot. Do come in." She moved aside, just enough for Tony to enter, and closed the door behind him.

The living room was small and dark, brightened only by school pictures of two girls and a boy, presumably belonging to the sister who had taken Dee Nixon in. Dee sat facing him, legs crossed and hands folded; her motions had a certain precision, almost an elegance, and Tony found it easy to imagine her as the algebra teacher she was.

"Let me save you some trouble," she said, "so you don't sit there trying to figure me out. The first thing I did after you called me was to call Ernie. So you should know right away that I don't hate him. And *I* already know what you're up to—trying to see if my kids' father is a murderer or maybe just can be made to look enough like one to keep Sam Robb from being indicted. In pursuit of which you've gone over my divorce petition and decided I just might be worth talking to."

Tony found himself smiling. "There goes my first half hour," he said.

"There goes your case," she answered, unsmiling. "But go ahead, ask away. Ernie can tell you that I never lie."

The phrase carried a certain irony, though whether directed at Ernie or herself, Tony could not tell. "Then I assume your divorce petition doesn't, either."

Her shoulders seemed to slump a little. "No," she said. "But there are all sorts of truths, including a few I wish I'd never spoken. Some to Ernie, and that one too."

Tony watched her face, betraying sadness for the first time. "With domestic violence," he said, "I've never seen that much use in pretending. In the last case I had, the husband beat the wife until the night she stopped pretending and killed him instead."

Dee Nixon was quiet for a moment. "Why don't you just listen, Mr. Lord. Then you can judge for yourself."

They had gone to dinner and a movie with Johnny and Lynn D'Abruzzi, shortly before Johnny's last and fatal heart attack. Marcie Calder had watched the kids; when Ernie had volunteered to drive her home, as always, it gave Dee Nixon time to lie in bed and come to terms with how truly bored—no, just plain alienated—she was in Lake City, Ohio. By the time Ernie entered the bedroom, all that she could think to say was, "I can't stand this anymore."

Ernie stood at the foot of the bed, well knowing what *this* was—their life in a town full of white folks Dee found to be largely polite, well-meaning, and wholly alien to her own experience. Softly, Ernie said, "I thought it was a nice night."

"It was what it was," Dee said tiredly. "And they are who they are. Look, Johnny's a nice man and all, and I know you're old friends. But he's got nothing much on his mind except for sports, and even *your* friendship is based on you not pretending to be African-American, or any different than he is. I'll never be any good at that, and I don't want our kids to be." She felt her voice rise, her exasperation breaking through. "God, Ernie, did you hear Lynn D'Abruzzi saying Pat Buchanan had some 'good ideas'? Which ones? I wanted to ask her."

"She means abortion, hon. They're Catholic."

"They're *oblivious*. Do you want our *kids* to be like this? Then I guess racism is a blessing in disguise, because they can't be." Dee Nixon softened her voice. "I don't want Drew and Tonya growing up to be everybody's one 'black friend,' like we are—so damn *tolerated* by people who, if they're lucky, will see them as 'exceptions' to all those other black folks out there they don't know and never think about, except as symbols of what they've gotten away from by living here."

Ernie sighed. " 'They' want what *we* want, Dee. A safe place, good schools, somewhere kids can still be kids." He paused, leaning on the bed. "I know what this town can be like, better than anyone. But there's no paradise on earth for us, and there won't be for Drew and Tonya. If we've got a right to be here, they'll know that they do too."

She sat up in bed. "You know what this comes down to, don't you? I grew up in a black neighborhood. You grew up in a white one. It's like having a father that beats you—part of you may hate him, but he's the only father you know, so the other part of you hates *yourself* and wants to be like *him*. Till your dying day, what you'll always need most is *his* approval. And you'll never, ever get it."

He sat down on the bed, angry now, yet trying so hard not to be that it was frustrating to watch him. Softly, he said, "There isn't a white person in this town who condescends to me as much as you do. You're so damn intent on showing what my childhood did to me that you can't step outside your own. For you, everything—and I mean *everything*—is defined by being black. You take your own ghetto wherever you go, and now you want our kids to live in it."

It stung her. "How," she said bitterly, "did we ever get married? How did I not see it long before I let you drag us here?"

"See *what*?"

"I was your *consolation* prize, Ernie. What you really wanted was to marry the Lake City prom queen and make it into the white boys' fraternity. For you, life really *is* high school, isn't it? That's why you came back here—to make the fraternity at last. . . ."

"Bullshit." She could see the vein in his temple. "You're talking bullshit."

"Bullshit?" In her own anger and frustration, Dee gave him the faint, superior smile she knew that he despised. "Isn't little Marcie your prom queen, Ernie? Isn't that why you spend all those hours talking to her? It sure can't be her *mind*. . . ." She stood abruptly. "Oh, I know—you're just *concerned* about her."

He stood with her. "You fucking bitch . . ."

She stuck her face in his. "It's all so *pathetic*, Ernie. She needs another daddy, so she plays into your white-girl fantasy. She gets an audience, and all she has to do is let you imagine fucking her—"

She could see it in his eyes, the instant before his palm crashed into her face. The world went white; as she reeled back against the wall, blinking away the tears of shock, Dee Nixon was honest enough to admit to herself that she had wanted him to do this.

Ernie collapsed back on the bed, stricken by his own shame. "I'm sorry, baby. I'm so, so sorry. . . ."

Dee Nixon shook her head. "I didn't leave because I thought he'd hit me again. I left because part of me had wanted him to do it, like my father did my mother." Her voice filled with regret and self-disgust. "It was my own ugliness that scared me half to death—drove me to counseling, in fact. When my lawyer put that in the petition, I fired him. And now there's you."

Tony tilted his head. "Did you believe that about Marcie Calder?"

Removing her glasses, Dee Nixon wiped their lenses, pensive now. "If Ernie felt that way, he didn't know it. I can't really see him sleeping with that girl, and I sure can't see him hurting her. If for no other reason than that he's so afraid of his own true feelings."

Tony was quiet for a while. "In high school," he said finally, "Ernie did me a kindness once. I never thought it was because he wanted to be like me. He just felt sorry for me, that's all."

She put on her glasses, composed again. "He said you were a friend. But I don't think he had 'friends,' really—I guess what he meant by that is you'd actually been decent to him." She paused, leaning forward. "And now you're looking to make him out the worst kind of racist cliché—the violent black man, post-O.J. The thinking part of me doesn't defend any man hitting a woman for *any* reason. But *I* was there, and I know my husband. What happened between us was a private quarrel, two people's weaknesses flaring up until they exploded like they never had before. Race may have destroyed our marriage, but I don't want it to destroy *him* any more than it has already. So don't expect me to help you, Mr. Lord. Because whatever Ernie did that night, it's not nearly enough for him to deserve *you*."

On the flight from Chicago to Steelton, Tony wrestled with his conscience.

His own instincts suggested that Dee Nixon was right: that although capable of violence, Ernie Nixon was not, by nature, a violent man; that such a portrayal could, in the end, appeal to subliminal bigotry. But she had her own share of guilt and shame; her own reasons—two children—for keeping the peace with an estranged husband; her own issues, including race, which might make Marcie Calder or Sam Robb a little less important.

"Sam Robb . . ." she'd said to Tony as he left. "I used to work with him. All charisma and a yard wide, that kind of careless cocky charm that seems to take itself for granted. Until I saw how needy he was. That way, he reminded me of Ernie—hard to see a man who craves approval like that as a murderer." But it was clear to Tony that she didn't care much.

Caring for Sam was Tony's job, unless he gave it up.

EIGHTEEN

"You probably wonder," Stella Marz said without preface, "if I've been fucking around with you. But then I've been wondering what you did to Jennifer Travis."

"You *have* been fucking around with me." Tony sat down. "About Travis, all I did was preview my cross-examination. Someone else should have been honest enough to tell her that coming forward might take her places she didn't want to go. But not to the criminal courts, I'm pretty sure—whatever its truth, her story is not one bit probative of murder."

Stella considered him, her eyes brown-green ovals of thought. "You always manage to look so innocent. I can't even tell if you're embarrassed."

"Are *you*?"

"No. And I wouldn't be too hard on the Calders, either. It's understandable that they didn't want me telling you, or anyone, that Marcie was pregnant." She paused for a moment. "Until and unless it became evidence in a criminal prosecution."

Tony sat back, edgy now. "Is that why you called me?"

"Uh-huh." She folded her hands. "We're indicting, Tony. Sam Robb's the father."

Somehow her tone, casual and off the cuff, made this even worse. Perhaps because it was so clear that she had expected this.

"You've got your motive," Tony said.

Stella nodded. "That Marcie told him she was pregnant. Your friend Sam lied to us—he'd been having sex with a sixteen-year-old girl, and now she was going to have his child." Her tone held quiet contempt. "She didn't believe in abortion, so there was no place for him to hide. His career, perhaps his marriage, would be out the window. So he took *two* lives instead."

There was no stopping this, Tony knew. It was only by reflex that he asked, "So why did Sam go to the cops when she went missing?"

"Panic, guilt—his mind was probably a jumble. But I'm sure he didn't know we could DNA a six-week-old fetus, and was afraid of getting caught."

Tony stood, hands shoved in his pockets; for once, he did not care if someone saw his own distress. "It would have been less of a risk to just let her lie there, murderer that he is. Or maybe he just forgot that she was dead the last time he saw her."

Stella regarded him impassively. "That's your argument, all right. Maybe a jury will even buy it. But they'll have to, because we're trying this unless you plead him."

Tony could no longer fight off the images—Sam's face when he told him; Sue, sitting in the courtroom. Perhaps it might be better, for everyone, if he loaned them the money to find a lawyer to whom this was less personal, whose feelings were less conflicted and complex. At length, Tony asked, "Plead him to what?"

"Murder two."

It surprised him enough to grimace. "That's not an offer, Stella—it's the most you can get. Even if you could persuade twelve people that Sam killed her, you can never prove premeditation."

"So come back with a story that supports manslaughter—like that somehow he didn't mean to kill her—and I'll consider it. Though with several apparent blows to the head, it's hard to imagine what that story would be." Her gaze grew pointed. "Drunkenness, maybe. But your client would have to give the court a statement, spelling out exactly how it happened. In this kind of case, I don't want to leave any doubts around. You, more than anyone, can appreciate that."

Tony drew a breath. He no longer had to decide whether to mention Ernie Nixon; the place for that decision, now, was at trial. Softly, he said, "I think I can beat this, Stella. I'm not sure you've got enough."

Stella gazed at him a moment. "I'm sorry," she said at last. "I know this is difficult for you. But I have to try the cases I think should be tried, even if there's a chance that I could lose." She gave a fatalistic shrug. "If we do try it, Tony, I'm sure I'll learn something."

Tony managed a smile. "Maybe I will."

Stella summoned a smile of her own, looking at him with level eyes. "Modesty," she answered, "doesn't always become you. But maybe you'll learn a little something about Sam Robb. At least if you don't already know it."

NINETEEN

At around four-thirty, in a day that already felt achingly long, Tony found Sam Robb at the Lake City baseball diamond.

Watching the Lake City team play Riverwood, Sam sat alone in the grass adjacent to deep right field, well away from the stands, where his presence would have excited comment or alarm. As Tony approached, he felt pity for Sam's isolation, for what he had lost and was about to lose. In this elegiac frame of mind, Tony imagined that his friend was seeing his youth from some great distance, now barely able to hear the cries of the players, the crack of a bat, the slap of a baseball on a leather glove. Though perhaps the fatalism in Sam's gaze as he looked up was a trick of Tony's mind.

"News?" Sam asked.

Slowly, Tony nodded. "Marcie Calder was pregnant, Sam."

If this was not a surprise, Tony thought, Sam had the talent of turning pale at will. His eyes shut. "And they think it's mine?" he said at last.

"They're sure it is." When Sam's eyes flew open, Tony added, "With DNA, they can do that too. I guess you didn't know that."

For a moment, Sam's stillness was not the stillness of thought but the paralysis Tony had seen at the moment a person heard something that he could not accept—the sudden death of a parent, the murder of a child, the betrayal of a lover, the ruin of a life. Only Sam's lips moved. "It's over for me here. . . ."

"I'm afraid so."

"Sue . . ."

The name, spoken with sudden anguish, said much more than Sam could express. Tony felt his own chest tighten. "You'll have to tell her, Sam. Before she hears it from the media."

Sam turned to him, his irises pale blue in the frozen white of his eyes. Softly, Tony said, "They're filing charges tomorrow. Murder one, unless you plead. You've got twenty-four hours to decide."

Folding his arms, Sam stared at the ground. *"Sue,"* he said again, a whisper.

It pierced Tony's self-possession. "I'm sorry," he murmured. "For both of you."

Sam did not seem to hear, nor could he seem to look at him. "You should have taken her away, Tony. After Alison died, all those years ago."

Startled, Tony wondered how much Sam knew, or guessed. Quietly, he said, "That was never a choice I had."

"Worse luck for her. Now she can look back at our life and see this at the end." He shook his head, as if in awe at the devastation he had caused. "A broken rubber . . ."

Tony waited a moment. "You didn't know?"

"She never told me. . . ." Sam's eyes seemed haunted, distant, wondering. "I guess that must have been what the marriage thing was, what she said about giving me children. If I'd known, Tony, I'd have done it different. I'm not sure what, exactly. But I wouldn't have let Marcie run off into the park at night." Thoughts seemed to come to him in increments, one puzzle piece, then another. "No wonder she was so out of her mind . . ."

Tony watched his eyes film over. The defense lawyer Tony Lord had an instinct for lies and evasions that the other Tony, friend of Sam Robb, seemed to have lost. What Tony saw now was either a man in shock, confronting for the first time a bitter, damning trick of fate, or a liar so gifted yet so troubled that he was able to convince himself. But if the latter was so, Sam's greatest gift was that—at this moment—his first concerns seemed to be his wife and a pregnant teenage girl he had last seen alive and thus still could imagine saving. In his own sadness and confusion, Tony found it better simply to remain beside his friend, silent.

From a distance, Tony heard a thin cry rising from the crowd, saw a Lake City player—all churning arms and legs—round first base as the left fielder ran toward the fence, pursuing an invisible ball. He and Sam Robb were in another world, their own.

"I know how bad you feel," Sam said at last. "But I don't think there's anything more you could have done."

The phrase combined sympathy with an odd detachment, as if Sam were consoling him for the lingering, expected death of some third person. "It's not over," Tony answered. "Maybe in Lake City, but not in court. They don't have an airtight case."

"They can't," Sam said simply. "Because I didn't kill her. For whatever that's worth now."

Tony did not answer. Softly, Sam told him, "You've done enough, Tony. You came back, whether it was for Sue or me or both of us. You went through what happened with Alison, all over again. You saved my job for a while and did some things to try and save my ass that I know you didn't like doing." He turned to Tony, touching his shoulder. "I couldn't ask more from a friend, and if I'm still any kind of friend to you, I'll send you back to Stacey and to Christopher. It's time for me to let you go."

Tony felt the same whiplash of emotion he had first felt thirty years before: whenever he concluded that Sam was selfish and insensitive, his friend would touch him with some astonishing act of grace. It was all the more touching, Tony realized, because *this* was the person that some inextinguishable boy in Tony—the optimist, the Roman Catholic, the believer in redemption—had always wished Sam Robb to be, and that boy existed still.

"What will you do?" Tony asked.

"Find a lawyer. Borrow retainer money, I guess. That's what people do, isn't it?"

That was true, Tony knew from his own practice; it was the first lesson he had learned from Saul. And there was no question—but for guilt and history and a justified belief in his defense lawyer's skill and coolness—that Tony's peace of mind would best be served by his putting as much distance as he could between himself and the death of a teenage girl. As if reading his mind, Sam said, "Besides, you still wonder if I killed her, don't you? Maybe more than ever."

There was no point in lying. "Yes," Tony answered. "But so will any lawyer, until he shuts it off."

For the first time, Sam's voice rose. "You're not *any* lawyer, Tony. I'll be better off not watching you at trial, wondering if I'm capable of murder—"

"You're right," Tony heard himself snap. "I'm not any lawyer. I'm much, much better, and you're going to need every fucking bit of that."

Sam's eyes widened, and then he smiled, perhaps in surprise at Tony's burst of ego and arrogance, surprising to Tony himself. "Still a competitor," he said softly. "Aren't you?"

Tony stared at him. "I'm not a whole different person, Sam. And neither are you."

Sam's smile faded. "That's what I've been saying, pal. Before you leave this place, I just wish you'd believe it."

Tony exhaled. "There's something else I have to tell you," he said at last. "We have an offer from Stella Marz."

Sam's eyes narrowed in suspicion. "What is it?"

"She may be willing to consider manslaughter. But only if you can persuade her that you acted out of some reflex, not meaning to kill Marcie Calder. Which requires a public confession, in open court."

"*Lie*, you mean." Sam stood abruptly, voice taut. "I won't fucking plead to this. I'm going to lose my house, my career, my kids' respect, and maybe my marriage. All I've got left is that I'm innocent. I'm not going to barter that to get a lighter sentence. I'm not going to *lie* to get it." His jaw worked. "I'm going to fight this, and I'm going to win. And then I'm going to give Sue the best life I can possibly give her, try to make up for all the damage I've done. After I'm found innocent, maybe she can believe somehow that our life is worth another try."

Sitting in the grass, Tony looked up at him. "You'd be risking life in prison, Sam."

"Take your deal, Tony, and I'd be risking more than that." His voice hardened. "We're *not* that different. You still need to win, and I still need my self-respect. But this time it's not your call."

Tony stood to face him. "It's not my deal, either. And if it were my call, I couldn't take it. No matter how bad this looks for you, there's a chance a jury would believe that someone else killed Marcie Calder, or that she wasn't murdered at all. Cases like this need defending, which is why Saul Ravin defended me. That's what I told Stella Marz."

Sam gazed at him, quiet now. There were tears in his eyes; seeing this, Tony knew how much Sam needed the slightest sign that Tony might believe him innocent. But he did not know what to say or do.

Silent, Sam extended his hand. It was an oddly formal gesture, perhaps a goodbye, and it reached a pool of feeling within Tony much deeper than the present. And then Tony remembered when they were eighteen, and had said goodbye by shaking hands.

Instead of shaking Sam's hand, Tony embraced him.

All at once, Tony felt Sam's arms envelop him, holding him tight. Softly, Sam said, "Maybe we can fix this, Tony. Maybe we can."

TWENTY

Alison Taylor froze, caught in the light from her parents' back porch, black hair swirling around her face. Her eyes widened in surprise, and then the purse dropped from her hand.

"Why?" she asked.

In this, what surely must be the last moment of her life, she seemed so vulnerable that it was heartbreaking. Tears welled in her eyes. Her bare legs could not seem to move.

"Please." Her voice was husky with knowledge of his betrayal. "Please, don't do this to me again—"

Tony bolted upright, awakening from his dream.

There was sweat on his forehead. He stared at the room around him, heart pounding. Piece by piece, the knowledge of who and where he was came back to him: forty-six, a lawyer, the husband of Stacey and father of Christopher, alone in a motel room in the hometown of his youth, returned to protect Sam Robb from the charge of murdering a girl who, from her pictures, had looked something like Alison Taylor. After telling Sam that Marcie Calder had been pregnant with his child, Tony had returned to the refuge of this room and fallen into exhausted sleep; from the edges of the curtains, pale with blocked sunlight, he saw that not too much time had passed. His watch read seven-thirty.

Alison Taylor had been dead for twenty-eight years.

Tony ran his hand across his face and realized that it was trembling.

In that twenty-eight years, his only dream of Alison had been as the dead girl he had found, her face distorted by pain and horror. Now she was alive, accusing, and yet in this dream, unlike the others, he had no sense of his own presence, except as the eye of a camera.

Throughout the dream, the camera seemed to move closer: in the last instant, her face—the pale skin, the high cheekbones, the wrenching look of fear—had seemed close enough to touch.

A shiver ran through him.

In his seventeenth year, Tony Lord had learned that to push aside his feelings, focusing on the task at hand, was the price of his survival. Later, it became the price of his survival as a lawyer. Yet he had never doubted that this left a residue in the well of his subconscious, the corners of his conscience, those places where he kept feelings so inconvenient that it had taken years for his own wife, his best friend, to realize that they existed at all. Sometimes the price he paid was dreams.

He was too honest with himself to pretend that *this* dream meant nothing. But that Marcie Calder's death was a haunting echo of Alison's, at least for him, was something so apparent that it hardly required a dream to surface his warring sympathies, his profound ambivalence about representing Sam. Especially a dream that, moments later, still coursed through him like a fever.

He got up, went to the bathroom, splashed water on his face. When he collected himself, he would call home. Christopher's baseball game would be over; their conversation, a father getting the news from his son, would reestablish contact with the normal. Then he would talk over with Stacey what he should do about Sam and, if he felt up to it, his dream. He wondered what it meant that part of him feared to mention it. . . .

The telephone rang.

Perhaps it was her, Tony thought. Right now, he needed it to be.

"Hello."

"Tony?" Sue's voice was muffled, drained. "He's told me everything. I really need to talk to you, I think." She paused a moment, and her voice became tentative, as if she were no longer sure of anything. "Is that okay?"

She sounded as lonely and confused as he, Tony thought, but with far better reason. "Of course it is," he answered. "For you, it'll always be okay."

On his way to meet her, Tony mustered the rigor to confront what her call might mean: that Sue knew, or had learned, something that pointed to Sam's guilt, and now could not withhold this in good conscience.

She wanted to have a private dinner, Sue had told him; she could not stand staying in their house, and whatever their embarrassment now, the shame that would commence tomorrow—the humiliated wife, the assistant principal who had first impregnated, then perhaps murdered, a girl who had trusted him—would make going out impossible. In some distant way, it reminded Tony of the night that Sam had gotten drunk, leaving Tony as the person Sue relied on; perhaps, for a moment, had loved the most. As he pulled into the driveway of the Lake City Country Club, the echo of that night grew stronger.

It was three hours or so since Sam had told her. Tony found it hard to imagine how Sue felt now.

Pulling up in front, Tony got out and handed his keys to the valet. For a moment, he stood there, gazing at the grounds and building, part of him dreading his meeting with Sue, another part remembering that evening twenty-eight years earlier when it had seemed possible to him, were they ever to visit this place again, that it would be as a couple.

It was strange, slipping back in time like this, viewed through the prism of Marcie Calder's death. Yet the club itself maintained the same placid facade: a rambling white wooden structure from the 1920s, the manicured grass of the eighteenth hole fading in the dusk. This illusion of security and permanence, Tony supposed, was part of the allure for the worthies of Lake City, offering them the insular sense of being where it mattered to be.

Though it had been many years since Tony had aspired to belong here, or envied those who did, the sense of being excluded came back to him, surprising in its power. Perhaps Dee Nixon was right, he thought: in some crevice of our souls, we are always seventeen. The thought of her, then Ernie, unsettled him even more.

Taking a last look around him, Tony went inside.

The hostess, a plump, friendly blonde with a run in her stocking, took Tony to the dining room. It was where Sue and he had danced that night, but with, he discovered, one unpleasant difference—the same malign fate that seemed to have designed this day had ordained that, tonight, John and Katherine Taylor would be dining here.

Dabbing his mouth with a white napkin, John Taylor saw the hostess leading Tony through the tables. He became as still as his daughter had been in Tony's first dream; only his eyes, filling with shock and resentment, betrayed his offense that now there was no refuge from the affront that was Tony Lord. Though his own heart felt like a trip-hammer, Tony merely nodded, a picture of indifference on the way to dinner with a friend. He hoped that Alison's mother would not see him.

"This way," the hostess said. "Mrs. Robb's expecting you."

Sue sat at a corner table, a double Scotch already placed in front of her. The surest sign of what the years had brought to her was in her eyes; they seemed wounded, as though she had been forced to stare too long into a harsh light. The extra makeup beneath her eyes did not conceal that she had wept when Sam told her: it was perverse, Tony thought, to feel that pain had made her beautiful. He touched her arm before either of them spoke.

She gazed at his fingertips. "Well," she said softly, "here we are."

He did not need to say how sorry he was, to say anything at all.

"What are you going to do?" she asked.

"I don't know." His eyes met hers. "And you?"

She shook her head. "It's too new. Even though I've known, really, ever since she died, I can *see* them together now." Slowly, she looked up at him. "My God, Tony—a baby . . ."

Her eyes welled with tears. The fear that she would tell him something damning dissipated. In her disbelief, he guessed, she would rather be with Tony than alone. He had been there all those years ago, when their three lives were shaped.

"I thought he'd changed," she murmured. "I told myself that once we married, the restlessness would leave him. It's the oldest hope in the world, I think, and it's always the woman's." She gazed at Tony with sad candor. "When I married him, part of me still loved you, Tony—I guess that never really stopped. Maybe he's always known that."

You should have taken her away, Sam had said. *After Alison died, all those years ago.* Softly, Tony asked, "Why did you marry him?"

"I loved him too, in a different way. I knew I wasn't right for you, that I couldn't be the person you were going to need. But I was sure I was who *Sam* needed." She gave Tony a melancholy smile. "I was half right, wasn't I? You found the woman you needed. He found more teenage girls."

Tony's hand circled her wrist. "In the end, Sue, you can't fix people. If anyone could, it's you."

She looked down. "That poor, pathetic girl," she said at length. "I imagine her foolish notion of who Sam is, then remember that she's dead. So I can't even be angry at her. It's much, much worse than that. Because I can't be sure that he . . ." Her eyes shut. "How can I be? I thought I knew what our marriage was—with whatever faults, who *he* was. But I didn't, and I'm not a fool. He lied to me too well."

It was the same doubt that haunted Tony. But hearing it from Sue was infinitely worse: if Sam could deceive her, he was capable of fooling anyone, whether Tony or a jury. And the damage Sam had done to her, an open wound, was more terrible than any damage Tony could imagine to himself. There was nothing he could do but be with her.

In their silence, a waiter came, tentative and respectful. There were no secrets in Lake City, and no further harm for Sue was possible; ordering his own martini, Tony did not bother to remove his fingers from her wrist. When he glanced around them, he saw that the Taylors were gone.

She followed his gaze. "Alison's parents were here," she said. "Did you speak?"

"That's impossible. So all I did was nod, as if it were nothing, and wish for the thousandth time this week that we'd been with you and Sam that night. Instead of going off alone."

To his surprise, tears came to her eyes again. "So do I, Tony. Not just for Alison. Sometimes I think all of our lives would have been so different."

He left his hand where it was. Softly, he answered, "But then I wouldn't be a lawyer, would I?"

Sue looked up. With equal quiet, she asked, "Do you think Sam killed Marcie Calder?"

Once more, their eyes met. "There's only so much I can say, Sue. But if I knew Sam was guilty of murder, I'd be back in San Francisco, as far from Lake City as I could get. For whatever it's worth to you, I'm still here."

Silent, Sue gazed at her Scotch; she had hardly touched it, Tony realized. "He's going to trial," she said.

"Yes."

For a moment, her throat worked. "Will I have to testify?"

He shook his head. "It's as I told you, Sue. Stella Marz can't call you, certainly not against your will. And Sam's lawyer—whoever that is—won't want to. For the precise reason you just identified: Sam lied to you too well. No sane defense lawyer would remind the jury of that."

Distractedly, she took a sip of her drink. "But how do I live with that, Tony? How does anyone live with that?"

"I don't know." His fingers curled around hers. "But you're going to have to face it. Because any lawyer would want you there in court, the supportive and forgiving wife. And so will Sam, I'm sure. Whatever you decide, the consequences won't be pleasant."

"And if I stayed away?"

"Better for you. Worse for him."

She touched her eyes. "It's not just us," she murmured. "It's the kids. They'll want to be here for him." As if steeling herself, she finished her Scotch. "That's one thing I can honestly say—Sam wasn't a perfect father, but he loves them, and they love him. It's so funny: I was the manager, but they still remember how he played with them."

It was her life with Sam in capsule, Tony sensed, and it made him sadder yet. "They're lucky to have you, Sue. Including Sam. Do you really think he'd have been a better man without you?"

To Tony, her gaze was as bleak as his thoughts. "I thought he'd be a better man *for* me, Tony." She looked down. "Sometimes I'd lie there at night, when he'd had too much to drink, and wonder what might have happened if I'd been brave enough, or selfish enough, to try and be with you."

Tony felt a knot in his stomach. Softly, he asked, "What can I do now, sweetheart?"

For a long time she was silent, staring at the table. When she looked up, her eyes had filled with tears again. "Make him innocent, Tony. Maybe I'm as selfish as Sam is, and as foolish. But I don't know what else to ask now."

Her voice broke, and then she caught it again. "Make him a weak, selfish, foolish, innocent man. Because that's all that's left for me."

And all that I can offer you, Tony thought, is innocence in court, not in life, perhaps at a price to us both. His thoughts moved to all the others whom his decision might touch—the Calders, Stacey and Christopher, Sam Robb and Ernie Nixon. But most vivid at this moment was the woman right in front of him, innocent of everything but the mistakes of her own heart.

"All right," Tony answered. "I'll try."

PART THREE
SAM ROBB

THE PRESENT

ONE

Two and a half months later, on a sticky August day, the murder trial of Sam Robb commenced.

The Erie County Courthouse was a Baroque structure from the 1920s. At that time, Anthony Lord reflected, courtroom architecture had combined an aura of sanctity with the atmosphere of the men's club that the law then was—marble steps, oaken walls, varnished benches—and that even now induced a certain reverence. This era of municipal confidence had passed, of course, buffeted first by the Depression and then—more cruelly because it was particular to the rust belt—the decline of heavy industry. The deterioration of public finances showed in the building's dinginess and disrepair, even as the decline of Steelton itself was reflected in the jury pool. It was less educated and less affluent: left behind by the flight of their economic betters, disadvantaged blacks and hard-pressed ethnic whites were overrepresented. Without Saul Ravin to help pick a jury, Tony—accustomed to San Francisco—would have worried even more.

Of course, certain biases in the jury selection were universal. As discreetly as she could, Stella Marz winnowed out unemployed black males, believing that they lacked affinity for cops or the established order; reserving the Ernie Nixon option, Tony decided not to challenge her. The result was a jury that seemed better for the prosecution than for the defense.

Saul had warned Tony that the great bulk of the jury pool, midwestern and middle class, would tend to trust authority. Despite Tony's best efforts, Stella was able to impanel three Steelton Poles—a beautician, a bookkeeper, and the burly owner of a corner store—as well as two blue-collar Irish Catholic laborers and an Italian housewife. All had followed the rules as they perceived them: in varying degrees, they reminded Tony of his own parents, and he guessed that, like Tony's parents, they would have little sympathy for an assistant principal who slept with a teenage girl.

Tony himself disqualified three women who combined long-term marriages with devoted motherhood to teenage girls, and then gambled on another: a nutritionist, who, in Saul's ironic phrase, seemed closest to those "practitioners of the human arts"—counselors, psychiatrists, and sociologists—whose careers reward compassion. But neither she nor Tony's favorite juror—a donnish English professor from Steelton State, inclined to critical thought—seemed likely to emerge as foreperson. Sam Robb's best hope, Tony bleakly admitted to Saul, was that Stella had created a pro-prosecution monster that might, to her surprise, be turned against a circumstantial case through the artful use of Ernie Nixon.

The night before opening statements, they sat in Saul's darkened office, drinking Scotch. "It's not like you're tampering with perfect justice," Saul remarked. "People hate defense lawyers because they imagine we're screwing up something purer than the screwed-up world that exists in their own workplace, their own homes, or—if they're really honest with themselves—their own psyches. *Our* consolation is knowing what a sewer a prosecutor's 'justice' can really be—the snitches, the deals they make with sleazebags who are guiltier than the ones they take to trial, the racial assumptions Stella made in getting rid of blacks." Saul sipped his whiskey. "If that last part backfires on her, it's not an injustice, just another fucking irony. Except perhaps to Ernie Nixon, who isn't our client."

Despite his misgivings, Tony smiled at the word "our." "How did I talk you into this, Saul? I must be smarter than I think."

Saul waved a hand. "Oh, it's not *that*. Any lawyer dumb enough to try this case for free needs all the help he can get." He put down his drink. "Two things, really. First, I'm low on entertainment: I hear you're good, and I wanted to see *how* good. Second, you're way too close to this, which is why you took it and why you never should have. In fact, I think you're doing this more for *her* than for Sam Robb." Saul paused a moment, voice quiet now. "I'm here to watch out for you, Tony. The last time I did that, you turned into a defense lawyer. So I figure I owe you. . . ."

Now, with Saul and Sam on either side of him, Tony awaited Stella's opening statement on the morning after another sleepless night, and thought once more of Sue.

You're doing this for her, Saul had said.

Perhaps he was. At several points in the last three months, by protecting Sam's interests, he had spared Sue the immediate consequences of her husband's acts; quietly swapping Sam's voluntary resignation for a year's severance pay, he had also spared Sue a hearing at which Jenny Travis might yet appear. With Stacey's concurrence, Tony had guaranteed Sam's million-dollar bail—set to be prohibitive—putting their own finances at risk should Sam take flight, but sparing Sue and her children trips to the county jail. Even a few days before, when Tony rejected the idea of calling character witnesses to recite Sam's years of service, he had meant to avoid exposing Sam Robb to a devastating rebuttal from Jenny Travis, and, by this decision, he had saved Sue Robb from any more humiliation than the trial made inevitable.

She was here now, as Tony had asked, her composure intended as a model for her children. In other circumstances, the Robbs would have personified what men and women hope for when they marry: a quarter century of partnership; a future of serenity within their grasp; two nice kids—the requisite boy and girl—with college degrees and futures of their own. Sam junior resembled Sue, with the neat, conservative appearance of an MBA-in-waiting; Jenny had Sam's blond, athletic good looks and the warm and equable nature that had made Tony, all those years ago, able to imagine Sue Cash as the center of a family. Seeing Jenny and Sam junior moved Tony to reflect on what this role had brought Sue now: the duty to assure her adult children that she did not believe their father killed the teenage girl he had slept with.

As Tony had required, Sam dressed in a white shirt, a sober gray suit he did not like, and one of several bland rep ties Sue had purchased for the trial. Three months of hard exercise and abstinence from liquor had made Sam appear a younger man, as fit and clear-eyed as the athlete Tony remembered, and invested his snub features with a certain innocence—an improvement, Tony thought, though he found it curious that this ordeal would arouse Sam's competitive instincts. But it had: insisting that Tony and he were a team, Sam took a keen interest in the minutiae of trial tactics. Even now, Tony saw Sam trying to gauge for himself the mind-set of the judge, the Honorable Leo F. Karoly, whose seamed face, gray-brown pompadour, and pale, somewhat uncurious eyes made him look much like what Saul assured Tony he was—a veteran Democratic functionary of cautious temper and limited intellect, a better judge for Stella than for the defense.

"I think Karoly's someone we can reach," Sam murmured.

Sam still refused to look at Frank and Nancy Calder, Tony noticed. Grief had muted them, as it once had Alison's parents: Frank Calder looked less angry than diminished; Nancy Calder had lost weight and appeared pale and haggard. Perhaps, Tony imagined, they were tormented by the knowledge that they had lost touch with their daughter, who now was lost to them.

Whatever their thoughts, it was clear to Tony that the Calders depended on Stella to sustain them. During breaks in jury selection, Stella had made it a point to speak with Marcie's parents, often touching one or the other: Tony guessed that this was both good theater and genuine kindness, reflecting Stella's empathy for a couple she saw as Sam's still-living victims. As the prosecutor rose to give her opening statement, their gaze at her was close to prayerful. In the anticipatory hush, Tony touched Sam's arm, hoping that the jurors would notice.

Stella wore a navy suit and just enough adornments—makeup and gold earrings—to efface that hint of feminist severity that this jury might find off-putting. Her first words sounded husky, and her manner was direct, angry enough to keep what Tony saw at once would be an appeal to emotion from lapsing into sentiment.

"What the People intend to show you," she began, "is the last four hours in the life of a sixteen-year-old girl."

TWO

The courtroom was still.

"Imagine Marcie Calder," Stella said. "She is frightened and alone, and her doctor has just told her that she's pregnant.

"Marcie begins crying, not knowing what to do. Dr. Nora Cox—who has known Marcie since she was four—urges Marcie to tell her parents. But Marcie is too stricken to answer. All she can do, over and over, is shake her head.

"In desperation, Dr. Cox mentions the possibility of an abortion. For the first time, this girl—barely out of childhood herself—finds her voice.

" 'No,' she answers. 'My baby is a life.' "

As if she were Marcie, Stella delivered the words with quiet certainty. Tony caught Saul Ravin's eye: Saul's faint smile was of appreciation for the prosecutor, reflecting Tony's own admiration at the skillful way that Stella Marz had slipped into the present tense, giving the jurors the moment-by-moment immediacy of each fateful step toward death. The jury looked rapt.

"That," Stella Marz went on, "is one thing Marcie Calder knows for certain. And, because she means to protect that life, Marcie Calder knows that there is one more person she also must protect—the father of her unborn child.

"No one but Marcie Calder knows who that person is.

"Now she wants his comfort, and his advice. Most of all, she wants to warn him."

Stella paused, letting this sink in. Angrily, Sam murmured, "There's nothing to support *that.* . . ."

Tony clasped his forearm. *"Easy,"* he whispered.

Stella raised her head. "So Marcie goes to Janice D'Abruzzi, her best friend.

"Janice knows that Marcie has been seeing someone older, but not who, nor even *why* it is so important that his identity be kept secret. Marcie begs Janice to cover for her that night—she needs to talk to her boyfriend, and her parents can't know.

"When Marcie begins crying, Janice agrees.

"That night, at the last dinner she will ever have with Frank and Nancy Calder, Marcie tells them she is going to Janice D'Abruzzi's to study.

"In the last few weeks, they've noticed that Marcie seems preoccupied. But Marcie has always been a loving daughter, a caring sister, a good student. And, above all, Marcie never lies to them.

"When she leaves, it is with the smallest of goodbyes. For there is only one person who could tell Marcie, and her parents, that they will never see each other again.

"Before she meets him, Marcie Calder makes one final stop.

"Besides her parents, Ernie Nixon is the adult to whom Marcie Calder seems the closest. He was her first track coach, the man whose kids she's baby-sat, someone she's come to confide in. And for the last six weeks, Ernie has been wrestling with his conscience—ever since Marcie confided that she was sleeping with her first man.

"An *older* man, whose condom broke the first time they made love."

Saul's eyebrows, Tony saw, had risen at the mention of Ernie Nixon. But only Tony read the chill amusement of one lawyer watching another make her first mistake: the jury could not take their eyes off Stella Marz.

"Ernie's fear is right," she told them. "For Marcie Calder sits down on his couch and, in that soft, clear way she has, tells him that she's pregnant.

"Ernie Nixon is heartsick.

"He begs her to tell the Calders or, at least, to let him take her to a clinic for pregnancy counseling. Once more, she refuses—this, her child, is a life.

"She looks pale, lost, overwhelmed by the burden that she carries. But all that she allows Ernie Nixon to do for her is make her a tuna sandwich. For she must tell the person she has chosen to rely on—who, she explains to Ernie, she will meet in a few minutes—that he is the father of her unborn child.

"Whatever her fears, dying is not among them. She eats the tuna sandwich, Marcie says, because she's eating for two.

"Within two hours," Stella said softly, "Marcie Calder will be dead."

Sam Robb's jaw worked. "How can Marz know *that*?" he whispered.

With equal quiet, Tony answered, "Stay calm, dammit."

"As she drives away," Stella Marz continued, "Marcie Calder does not know to be afraid. All she knows is that her lover has agreed to meet her.

"Alone, she parks at an abandoned gas station. Another car is there, a gray Volvo sedan. Marcie gets out, and then the man inside the Volvo opens the passenger door.

"Eagerly, Marcie gets inside the car and turns to him, this man she loves." Pausing, Stella Marz turned to Sam. "Sam Robb. The assistant principal of Lake City High School. Marcie's track coach, and the father of her child."

In the silence, Sam gazed back at Stella Marz. His expression was all that Tony could ask, so wounded and ashamed that, if it was not genuine, Sam Robb possessed gifts beyond his lawyer's reckoning. For a moment, Stella's eyes held the coolness of real dislike, and then she faced the jury again.

"Marcie's life is in his hands now. No one—not her parents, or Janice, or Ernie Nixon—knows where she is. Except for Sam Robb, Marcie Calder is alone.

"In the darkness, he drives her to Taylor Park.

"Marcie undresses for him. And then, in his wife's gray Volvo, Sam Robb sodomizes Marcie Calder."

At the corner of his eye, Tony saw Sue Robb blanch. She reached for her daughter's hand.

Speaking with cold distaste, Stella Marz switched abruptly to the past tense. "And when this most intimate act was done, Sam Robb had used her body—at least in any way that could be remotely described as loving—for the last time.

"I cannot tell you what Marcie Calder thought in the last moments of her life, as she lay dazed and dying in her lover's arms, this man that she had admired, his child still alive inside her. Was this girl, barely more than a child herself, thinking of her own child? We will never know.

"We know only what the medical evidence will show you—that Sam Robb, to prevent her thoughts from being spoken aloud, led her from Sue Robb's Volvo to a grassy field above Lake Erie.

"That he picked up a heavy rock.

"That he struck Marcie Calder three hard blows, shattering her skull.

"That he threw her off the cliff and watched her fall one hundred feet. For in her pain, the agony of Sam Robb's betrayal, that was the only mercy left to her."

Tony saw the tears on Nancy Calder's face, her stoic husband staring at his feet. On the other side of the courtroom, Sue Robb's eyes shut, and her children were stricken cameos. Beside him, he felt Sam shudder.

Stella Marz was relentless now. "Anthony Lord is a gifted lawyer, and he will tell you about doubt. But Mr. Lord can never change what I believe the facts will show.

"Fact: Sam Robb told the police that he and Marcie Calder were merely friends, alone at night in Taylor Park to discuss her innocent teenage crush.

"Fact: Sam Robb stood to lose his wife, his family, his reputation, and his livelihood if Marcie Calder said a word to anyone.

"Fact: Marcie Calder's blood was on the steering wheel of Sue Robb's car.

"Fact: Sam Robb is the father of Marcie Calder's child.

"There will be *no* doubt about these facts.

"There will be *no* doubt that Sam Robb lied about them.

"And—when all the evidence is in and all the lawyers' arguments are done with—I am confident that you will have no reasonable doubt that Sam Robb is the murderer of this sixteen-year-old girl with whose care he was charged, and of the life-to-be he had left inside her."

Pausing, Stella Marz looked at each juror in turn. "Thank you," she said simply, and sat.

Pale, Sam gazed at Tony with hope and desperation.

"Mr. Lord?" Judge Karoly inquired.

Tony stood, making his decision. "I have nothing at this time, Your Honor. The defense reserves its opening until the prosecution puts on its proof. Which—with all respect to Ms. Marz—an opening statement is not."

From the bench, Leo Karoly looked surprised. "Very well," he said. "The court will take its morning recess."

In the slow stirring of bodies, Sam stood, face suffused with anger and astonishment. "What the fuck are you doing?"

Tony touched his shoulder. "Not here."

They sat in a cramped witness room—Saul, Tony, and Sam—at a wooden table with hard wooden chairs. Perhaps, Tony thought, it was a mercy that they were not in the corridor with Sue instead. Next to him, Saul leaned back, a spectator.

"She fucking killed us." Sam's voice rose. "I'm not an idiot, Tony—I've been reading up on trial tactics.

Something like sixty percent of jurors make their minds up on opening statements. Without one, we may have lost already. This is *my* ass we're talking about here."

"True. Which is why I'm holding back." Sympathetic to Sam's anxiety, Tony kept himself calm. "She overplayed it, I think. But I can't tell the jury that now, and I can't be sure what our best defense is until Stella's evidence is in. For example, what if she's found some way to account for Ernie's time? And if she hasn't, why warn her about what I'm up to?"

"What does *that* matter if they already think I'm guilty?" Sam's face and voice were taut. "Dammit, you could have at least said *something.*"

Tony sipped his coffee, trying to stay calm. With his own nerves on edge, the last thing he needed was second-guessing from an amateur lawyer, his client. " 'Something' would have been what Stella already made sound so pathetic: reasonable doubt. . . ."

"Oh, I don't know." With an innocent expression, Saul turned to Sam. "What about 'he buggered her, but he didn't kill her'? That might have had some appeal."

Sam reddened, staring at Saul. "The point," Tony interjected, "is that I can do better, and will. With a little luck, I'll stick Stella's opening in her ear." Reaching out, he covered Sam's hand with his own. "Your job now is to look very calm, and very sad. You've got at least two weeks of pretty bad stuff to sit through." Pausing, Tony finished softly. "It's like the Riverwood game. Just keep your nerve, and trust me."

Looking into Sam's eyes, Tony read worry, affection, doubt, and, at the last, the same resentment of Tony's guidance, his own dependence, that Tony had first seen thirty years before. After a moment, Sam nodded brusquely. "All right, Tony. I just hope it's not that close."

THREE

When Stella Marz called Marcie's doctor as her first witness, Tony knew that she intended to follow the sequence of her opening statement, tracing the last hours of Marcie Calder's life, then using the police and medical experts to tie Sam Robb to her death. For the jury, this would fuse tragedy with the sheer interest of a forensic detective story.

"Smart," Tony murmured to Saul, and turned his attention to Dr. Nora Cox.

She was a youngish-looking woman of about Tony's age, with a full mouth, bright blue-green eyes, and unruly brown hair. To Tony, Cox had the scrubbed, healthy look of a woman who liked the outdoors, and beneath her brisk manner was an air of warmth and concern. Stella Marz stood back and to the side, drawing attention to her witness instead of herself. "How long were you Marcie Calder's doctor?" she asked.

"Twelve years, Ms. Marz. Since the beginning of my practice." Cox paused, adding softly, "When Marcie was four."

"How often did you see her?"

"Around town, pretty frequently—Lake City's not that big. As a patient, her mother scheduled her every six months or so." Cox's voice fell. "Until the last few weeks of her life, that is."

Stella tilted her head. "You saw her more frequently?"

Cox nodded slowly. "Twice. On Marcie's own initiative."

Beside him, Tony felt Sam stir. "What was the first visit about?" Stella asked.

Briefly, Cox glanced at Marcie's parents. "Marcie wanted to ask me about birth control."

Watching, Nancy Calder looked wounded; her husband's gaze was unfocused. "Did Marcie tell you why?" Stella asked.

Cox folded her hands. "Marcie had begun having sex."

"When you say 'had begun,' Dr. Cox, did she tell you how recently—?"

"Objection," Tony said without rising. "Hearsay. The doctor herself has no idea when Marcie Calder first had intercourse."

Judge Karoly turned to Stella, eyebrows raised in inquiry. Unruffled, the prosecutor answered, "I'll ask it another way," and turned to Nora Cox. "During this visit, Dr. Cox, did you examine Marcie Calder?"

"Yes. Specifically, I gave her a pelvic examination."

"And what did that examination reveal?"

The glance Nora Cox gave Sam Robb, seemingly reflexive, was filled with disapproval and dislike. "Marcie's hymen showed signs of tearing, and her labia and vaginal wall were somewhat abraded. In my experience, those are consistent with initial—and quite recent— sexual intercourse. Which is what Marcie told me when I asked her."

The harm was done, Tony knew at once. Like Stella, Nora Cox was a clever woman: Tony's only recourse, a motion to strike the last sentence of her answer, would simply underscore her point. Quickly, Stella asked, "And what did Marcie say?"

"That she'd lost her virginity the day before." The doctor's voice grew softer. "Her partner's condom had broken, and Marcie was quite anxious. She thought her last period had ended two weeks before that."

With some reluctance, Tony stood for the first time. "With respect, Your Honor, none of this seems relevant. To save everyone time and perhaps discomfort, the defense will stipulate that Marcie Calder was pregnant when she died."

Stella Marz gave him a quick, sardonic glance, then

turned a bland face to Karoly. "We appreciate Mr. Lord's offer. But we believe that Marcie Calder's sexual experience—or lack of it—is relevant to the prosecution case."

She knows, Tony thought. "I'm giving the prosecution some latitude," Karoly said. "Proceed, Ms. Marz."

Sitting, Tony saw Saul's glint of amusement. "What's going on?" Sam asked him.

Tony leaned closer. "Ernie," he murmured. "She's figured it out. . . ."

"When Marcie told you about having sex," Stella asked Cox, "what was your response?"

Once more, the doctor glanced at Marcie's parents. Quietly, she answered, "I asked Marcie if she'd told her mother."

"What did she say?"

"That she hadn't." Cox folded her hands, and her brief downward glance reflected sadness and a certain shame. "One of the dilemmas I face, as a doctor, is that I learn things about minor children that I feel someone else should know. In this case, it was Marcie's parents."

"Was there a specific reason you felt that way?"

"In general, I think teenage girls ought not to be on their own when it comes to sex. And my impression was that Nancy Calder's a concerned and conscientious mother." Pausing, Cox spoke more sharply. "But there was something more. When I asked who the boy was, Marcie's answer threw me. It wasn't a boy, she said."

Silent, Stella let that linger, inviting the jury to share in her distaste for Sam. "Keep looking at her," Tony whispered to Sam. "The jury's watching you."

The prosecutor still faced Cox. "Did you advise Marcie to confide in her mother?"

"Yes."

"And what was her answer?"

"That she couldn't."

"Did she say why?"

In silent apology, Nora Cox glanced at Nancy Calder, then at her husband. Turning back to Stella, she answered, "Marcie said her father would get it out of her mother. That her father was obsessed with controlling her and that he would be furious if he knew she wasn't a virgin."

The Calders would not look at each other. For the first time, Tony wondered if they could survive this: too often, he had seen the death of a child destroy a marriage, even when there was no one to blame. From her expression, Nora Cox knew this as well.

"There was another reason," Cox added softly. "Marcie had promised this man she would never say anything to expose him. Or so she told me."

"That's *hearsay*," Sam murmured in a strained voice.

Tony did not change expression, nor did he take his eyes off Cox and Marz. Under his breath, too quiet for anyone else to hear, Tony answered, "Shut up."

"Did Marcie tell you, Dr. Cox, *why* secrecy was so important?"

Nora Cox seemed to inhale. In a chastened voice, she answered, "Only that he was married."

Watching, Tony felt each new piece that Cox provided draw the jury in. The store owner scowled; the beautician—a blond, chatty type whom Tony had watched strike up several friendships during jury selection—gazed at the Calders with open sympathy. Across the courtroom, Sue's eyes looked dead.

"What did you do then?" Marz asked Cox.

Cox drew a breath. "I fitted her for a diaphragm and said I hoped she'd tell her mother."

"What was her reply?"

Cox studied her hands. "To ask—no, beg—*me* not to tell her parents."

"To which you said . . ."

"That I was *her* doctor, and wouldn't. And then, because she seemed so frightened, I asked what she meant to say when her parents got the bill for her deductible and asked why she'd come to me." Her voice was soft again. "Marcie was so naive, so scared, that she'd never thought of that." Cox paused a moment, looking down. "It was like she was visiting the tooth fairy."

In seeming compassion, Stella paused. "What did you do?"

"What I'd thought of doing was just to send the bill and let her parents figure it out. It was clear to me that Marcie was in a bad situation, way over her head, and needed the help of an adult. Other than the man who'd taken her virginity."

Stella stepped closer. Softly, she inquired, "Did you ask if Marcie *had* such a person?" and Tony saw how well the prosecutor had anticipated him.

"Yes." Now Cox looked at her steadily. "Marcie said she had someone else to confide in. Another adult."

"Did she tell you who?"

Slowly, Cox shook her head. "Only that he was like a counselor, someone she'd known for a long time. I made Marcie promise that she'd talk to him."

"Did you say anything else?"

For a moment, watching the Calders, Nora Cox did not answer. Then her gaze broke, and she touched her eyes. "That if Marcie promised, I wouldn't send her parents a bill."

In the jury box, the beautician's lips parted. Still watching her witness, Stella Marz asked Karoly for a ten-minute recess.

Down the corridor, Sue Robb and her children looked lost; they stood together, isolated, speaking little. Huddling with Tony and Saul, Sam Robb seemed muted. "I'm sorry," he said to Tony. "You can't be objecting all the time. It would only make this worse."

For the first time, Saul looked at their client with something like tolerance. "Nothing Tony could do about the real problem. Marcie wasn't screwing around with Ernie—she was faithfully carrying out a promise to her doctor, like the honest girl she was." He turned to Tony. "Stella's seen us coming."

Tony shrugged. "There's no wind so ill," he said for Sam's sake, "that it doesn't blow a little bit of good." But he could not help wishing that he were home in San Francisco or, even better, that he believed his friend and client innocent.

When Nora Cox resumed the stand, Tony's mood lingered.

Cox had regained composure. With Stella's help, she began to paint a picture of Marcie's last visit, on the last day of her life. So accustomed was Tony to imagining Marcie Calder that, as Cox spoke, he saw a slender, dark-haired girl, solitary and frightened, sitting on an examining table. Tears ran down her face.

"It's only a home pregnancy test," Cox said gently. "But for positives, it's close to a hundred percent."

Marcie's voice was light, less that of a woman than a girl. "But you think I'm having a baby."

Cox sat next to her. "You've thrown up the last three mornings, Marcie. And this HPT is quite reliable." She took her hand. "Your period is two weeks late. The timing works out with the broken condom."

Marcie folded her arms, as if she were cold. The examining gown she wore made the crinkling sound of crumpled gift wrap.

"Let's think together," Cox said softly. "In case you are."

Marcie blinked back her tears. "There's nothing to think about," she said. "I'm a mother, that's all."

It sounded so absolute, and so pitiful, that Nora Cox shook her head. "Teenage pregnancies are *hard*, Marcie. You may see this as the beginning of a life, but it may be the effective *end* of yours. You *do* have choices. . . ."

"No." Marcie's voice turned stubborn. "I can't do that."

"You can." In her despair for this girl, one of the first patients she had ever had, Nora Cox left behind her role as doctor. "Marcie, *listen* to me. When I was in medical school, I became pregnant. The whole thing was just impossible." Cox paused, softening her voice. "The father was a teacher I admired, a surgeon. He was married. To have his baby might have damaged his career and maybe ended mine—worse, it might have destroyed his marriage. Your situation is that much worse."

Tearless now, Marcie shook her head. "I'm Catholic, Dr. Cox."

"So was I."

For some reason, Marcie's fingers curled into Nora Cox's. "Do you ever think about it?"

Cox understood the subtext of the question: that the doctor, recently married to an older man with grown children, had no children of her own. It made her quiet for a time. "Yes," she answered. "But I still think I was right."

Marcie gazed into her eyes with a look of precocity and insight that, in Cox's mood, took her by surprise. "I'm sorry," Marcie answered. "But I don't think you were."

Gently, Nora Cox released Marcie's hand, pulling back a little. To make this child face reality, she said in her most clinical voice, "There's adoption, I suppose."

Marcie blinked. Watching the girl's lips tremble, Cox saw with pity and sadness how wholly unprepared she was. Softly, she asked, "Does *he* know how worried you've been?"

Marcie shook her head, unable to speak.

"Then maybe it's time," Cox told her, "to turn to your parents. Sometimes families are best when things look worst. I know your mother, and I know how much she loves you."

Rocking forward, Marcie looked down, writhing in apparent anguish. "I can't tell my father, ever. I just can't."

Cox was quiet for a moment. "Then there's only one way out, isn't there?" She took Marcie's hand again. "If you change your mind, I'll help you. And find you counseling afterward."

Marcie leaned against her. "I can't," she said at last.

"Then what will you do?"

Marcie shook her head. "I don't know. Only that I have to tell him, right away."

"The father?"

"Yes."

"And you think he can help you?"

"No." Suddenly Marcie's voice was cool and clear. "I have to warn him."

Once more, Nora Cox was surprised. "Because he's married?"

Tears came to Marcie's eyes again. "God," she murmured. "It's so much worse than that. . . ."

Cox put an arm around her. "What could be worse?"

Marcie did not answer. Gently, she disengaged, and began to take her blue jeans off the hook.

The paper gown dropped to the floor; Marcie looked so slim that Cox saw, or perhaps imagined, the first slight swelling of her belly.

Naked, Marcie looked at her own body. "Please . . . don't tell them."

She had nearly resolved to do so, Nora Cox realized. But all that she said was, "The lab results won't be back for a day or so."

When Marcie squared her shoulders, Nora Cox's heart went out to her.

"I'll tell him tonight," Marcie answered.

FOUR

After lunch, Tony commenced his cross-examination.

It was delicate: Cox was a sympathetic witness and, at this point, the jury would have no sympathy for Sam Robb. The challenge for Tony was to do his job without exciting more dislike.

He began casually, hands in his pockets, keeping his tone mild. "As I recall, Dr. Cox, you knew Marcie Calder for roughly twelve years. How would you describe her?"

Cox hesitated. "Polite, quiet. Thoughtful, I would say."

Tony nodded, adding a pause of his own; the trick was to make each new question seem spontaneous, creating the illusion that he and the jury were discovering things together. "Did Marcie strike you as a girl who kept things inside?"

Cox frowned. "It would only be an impression."

"But from what you saw . . ."

Cox considered him, pensive. "Well," she answered, "she was certainly guarded about this sexual experience."

Tony placed a finger to his lips. "With respect to her pregnancy, she was also very frightened, wasn't she?"

"Yes."

"And alone?"

Reluctantly, Cox nodded. "So it seemed." For the first time, the doctor sounded defensive. "That was the only reason I shared with her what I did—my own experience."

But not, Tony thought to himself, the reason you shared this conversation with the jury. That was something Tony, the lapsed Catholic, thought he understood: a public act of penance from a woman steeped in guilt—perhaps from her own past, certainly for Marcie Calder's death—in the hope that Marcie's parents would forgive her. It made his task that much more difficult.

"But she rejected even the thought of an abortion, is that correct?"

Cox gave him a brief, puzzled look, as if certain that her answer could only hurt Sam Robb. "That's right— she did."

"And she also told you that she couldn't ever imagine telling her father. In fact, she seemed afraid of him."

Cox gave the Calders a brief glance of apology. "With respect to being pregnant, yes. But that's not so surprising."

Cox seemed distracted by her own remorse, Tony thought. But, in one or two questions, she would see where he was headed. "When you mentioned adoption," he asked, "how would you describe Marcie's reaction?"

Cox looked down. "It was as I said: she seemed completely unprepared to have this baby. I don't think she'd had time to consider the reality of it."

"So when you asked her to consider taking the baby to term, she seemed frightened by that too?"

"Yes."

To his side, Tony saw Stella Marz lean forward with a new attentiveness. Softly, he said, "Let me try to summarize Marcie's state of mind as you perceived it. She was opposed to an abortion, afraid to tell her father, unprepared to have a baby, and isolated from adult guidance. Is that correct?"

Cox's eyes were cool now. "Yes. Essentially."

"Did she suggest what she thought her choices came down to?"

"No." Cox's tone hardened. "Except to tell this man."

Tony tilted his head. "What about marriage?"

Cox glanced at Sam Robb. "The man *was* married, Mr. Lord."

"Did Marcie suggest to you, one way or the other, whether she'd considered the idea of marrying this man herself?"

Cox's eyes flew open. "She said that her pregnancy could ruin him. . . ."

"But did she, in words or substance, rule out the idea that this unknown man—or *some* man—could marry her?"

"Objection," Stella said. "There's no foundation for this question. How can this witness know what Marcie Calder thought about an option that Marcie never mentioned?"

"That's precisely the point," Tony said to Karoly. "It's an open question."

Judge Karoly pursed his mouth. He had a gift, Tony was beginning to notice, for making his job look harder than it was, and he did not seem in command. Turning to Cox, Karoly said at last, "You may answer."

Cox gave a shrug of irritation. "I don't know what—if anything—Marcie was thinking about marriage. . . ."

"Or how her emotional state might be affected were that option later foreclosed to her?"

Cox folded her arms. "I have no reason to believe that Marcie thought it *was* an option."

Tony did not argue with her. "But she was frightened."

"Yes."

Tony moved a step closer. More quietly, he asked, "And lost?"

He felt the jury watch him now. Stella was up quickly. "The question is hopelessly vague, Your Honor. What does 'lost' mean?"

Tony turned to Stella. "Oh, I think Dr. Cox knows. But I can ask it another way." Turning to Cox, he asked, "Have you ever had a patient who committed suicide?"

Stella stood at once. "Objection," she snapped. "Irrelevant."

"Hardly," Tony said to Karoly. "This goes to the heart of our defense."

Slowly, Karoly nodded. "You may answer," he told Cox.

Cox's face had set. "If you're suggesting—"

"Just answer the question," Tony cut in. "Please."

Cox gave him a trapped look. "Yes. I have had. As I guess you know."

Tony nodded. "For the jury's benefit, how many patients does this involve?"

"Two."

"Two teenage girls, to be precise. Fifteen and sixteen."

Cox grimaced. "Yes."

"Do you have any idea why they killed themselves?"

"Only what I read in the papers. Unfortunately."

Tony tilted his head. "Is it true that you saw one of the girls, Beverly Snowden, roughly three weeks before her death?"

"Yes." Cox made her voice even now. "But I had no idea. In fact, she seemed quite normal."

"More normal than Marcie Calder?"

"Objection," Stella Marz called out. "Calls for speculation."

"Is it true," Tony amended, "that Marcie Calder was in a fragile mental state on the afternoon of her death?"

"It's true." Cox looked at him directly. "But in the Catholic Church, suicide is a sin. As is abortion."

Tony let the answer linger. "But *you* were Catholic," he said softly, "if I recall this morning's testimony."

Dislike flashed in Cox's eyes again. "I was, yes."

"And the reason you shared your personal experience with Marcie was that you were worried for her, correct?"

"Yes. But about Marcie ending her life in a figurative sense, *not* literally. If she believed her fetus was a life, how could she kill both the fetus and herself?"

"That's an excellent question. As a doctor, are you aware of how the incidence of suicide among teenagers compares to the rest of the population?"

Cox hesitated. "It's quite high."

"And the decision to commit suicide can seem quite sudden, can it not? As with Beverly Snowden."

"Yes."

"And that's often because when the girl sustains some trauma, she has nothing to compare it to, no experience with coping."

"So the literature suggests."

"And teenage girls also can become quite isolated, true? They keep their suffering to themselves."

"Again, I'm not an expert. But that's what the literature suggests."

"Did *you* suggest psychological counseling for Marcie Calder?"

Nora Cox looked stung now. "No."

Tony paused a moment, letting the jury absorb this. "Didn't Marcie Calder need professional help at least as much as she needed an abortion?"

Cox stared at him, torn between self-doubt and open dislike.

"Objection," Stella Marz called out, quickly approaching the bench. "Dr. Cox is a pediatrician. She has not been qualified as an expert in child psychology. Mr. Lord's attempt to blame others for this tragic death is offensive."

Tony kept his own voice mild. "So is this attempt to blame Sam Robb alone for what may be the tragic result of a chain of events in which several adults, whatever their intentions, failed Marcie Calder quite badly. The jury is entitled to consider that. . . ."

"Enough," Karoly said belatedly. "Both of you." Facing Tony with the weak man's sudden stubbornness, he said, "Dr. Cox is not a child psychologist. Your question is outside her expertise."

Of course it is, Tony thought. But all that he said, quite respectfully, was, "Thank you, Your Honor." He was, indeed, most grateful: in sound-bite form, he had just given his opening statement and suggested to the jury, several of whom were Catholic, that Dr. Cox had offered this vulnerable and lonely girl the wrong sort of help. Though Sam was mistaken about the reasons, he was right about the end result—Leo Karoly could be worked with.

Tony turned to Cox again. "As Judge Karoly has reminded us, it may be unkind to belabor what I know was a very sad experience. Given Ms. Marz's objection, is it fair to say that you can form no opinion—professionally, that is—as to whether the despair you observed in Marcie Calder might have rendered her suicidal?"

Next to him, Tony felt Stella hesitate. The twist he had just put on her objection, should Cox rise to it, was to suggest that Cox's belief that Marcie was *not* suicidal had no real basis. Then Stella did what Tony would have done: placed her trust in Cox.

The witness had composed herself. "All that I can tell you is that, as a layman, I did not consider the possibility that Marcie would take her own life. For all the reasons I suggested."

Tony nodded his understanding. "Just as, in the case of Beverly Snowden, you did not foresee it, either."

"No." Pausing, Cox fought back. "But in Marcie's case, she assured me that she had an adult to talk to."

It was the response that, sooner or later, Tony had hoped Cox would give. "This adult—did you ask who he was?"

Cox steepled her hands. "Yes."

"And what was Marcie's response?"

"I don't think she gave one."

"She avoided the question, in other words."

Cox frowned. "I can't say that she did or didn't. There was so much else to think about."

"I understand. Tell me, did she give you any information about the *nature* of her relationship with this man?"

Cox's look was cool, appraising, tinged with distaste. "No."

She was braced for some insinuation, Tony saw. But there was grace in knowing when to stop, and Tony had the jury's sensitivities to consider. Politely, he said, "Thank you, Dr. Cox. I have nothing more."

Sitting down, he saw the beautician follow him. Her gaze was not hostile but filled with puzzlement and interest; at once, Tony knew that he had stopped at the right moment. But what lingered with him was the image of Nancy Calder, regarding him with a hurt and anger so palpable that Tony could feel it himself.

In the corridor, Sam clasped his arm. "That was fucking brilliant," he said. "You really got her. *Both* 'her's.'"

To the side, Saul was quiet; he seemed to know that this was a compliment Tony did not need or want. Almost gently, Tony said, "I was glad to do it, for your sake. But there's something you should understand, pal. So that you don't take it personally.

"I just humiliated a perfectly nice woman and, in the bargain, may have helped drive a wedge in the Calders' marriage. Before this is over, I'll do far worse. There may come some defining moment when the jury decides to hate me, and if that happens, it's over for you.

"That worries me. Then there's how *I* feel. I'm doing this for you as a client, and as a friend. Most days, that satisfies me, but I don't always love it." Tony paused, putting a hand on Sam's shoulder. "Just so you know that, okay?"

Sam looked at him with embarrassment, comprehension, compassion. "I understand. If I weren't so damned scared, I'd feel it too. But when you're just hanging on . . ."

His voice trailed off. Down the corridor, Tony saw Sue watching them, her own face troubled. "Go talk to Sue and the kids," Tony said. "No matter how hard it is. The jury notices things like that."

FIVE

Uncomfortable in her tailored blue suit, Janice D'Abruzzi fidgeted on the witness stand. She could not look at the Calders.

Stella Marz took her through Marcie's account of an older, married lover, whose identity Marcie had promised to protect, and then Marcie's plea that Janice lie for her on the night of her death. Janice's responses, halting and ashamed, seemed to touch the jury, supplanting the doubts Tony had raised with Nora Cox. Then Stella began attacking Tony's defense.

Her manner was firm but gentle, that of an older sister. "Did Marcie ever suggest that she was involved— romantically or sexually—with anyone other than this man?"

The thought seemed to startle Janice. "No," she answered firmly. "And it wouldn't have been like her."

"To your knowledge, was Marcie Calder sexually experienced?"

There was an objection here, Tony knew, perhaps two or three. Janice stole a sideways glance at the Calders. "Marcie told me this guy was her first. She'd never talked about sex before and didn't really know anything."

"Why do you say that?"

Janice looked down. "She wanted to know different things—I mean, what people did, exactly."

"Did she tell you *why* she wanted to know?"

"Yes." With sudden, surprising anger, Janice looked at Sam. "Marcie wanted to please this guy. He knew so much, she told me, and she loved him. She didn't want him to lose interest."

To Tony's relief, Sam's gaze at Janice did not waver. But Tony could feel Sam's restiveness: his lawyer had not objected as Stella used Janice to firm up Nora Cox's story of a monogamous teenage girl, seduced by an adult, whose first act of intercourse had led to pregnancy and death. Tony scrawled on his notepad, "The kid was *yours*, remember? Why remind them?"

Staring at the notepad, Sam nodded slowly.

"Did she ever talk about marrying him?" Stella asked Janice.

"No way." Janice seemed to gather herself. "What Marcie said was that they had their own world, and it should stay that way."

Stella gave Janice a pensive gaze. "Why, do you suppose, Janice, did Marcie need to see this man on the night she died?"

Now Tony had no choice. "Objection," he said to Judge Karoly. "I've let the prosecutor lead this witness through hearsay and speculation—on Marcie Calder's sexual experience, on Marcie's relationship to a man whose name Ms. D'Abruzzi never even knew, on what these two people said or did or felt when they were alone. But this *last* question assumes that Janice D'Abruzzi could read Marcie Calder's mind and now can tell the jury—without any factual foundation whatsoever—*why* Marcie Calder did whatever she did while Ms. D'Abruzzi was misleading Marcie's parents. In simple fairness, Your Honor—enough."

Stella Marz appeared unruffled. "Your Honor," she said mildly, "please admonish Mr. Lord not to use objections as a pretext for speeches to the jury. His only legitimate objection is exactly three words long: 'objection—no foundation.'

"As to *that*, Janice D'Abruzzi has testified to numerous conversations about what was driving Marcie Calder: that she was afraid this affair would ruin her lover's life, that she was trying to protect him—"

"Speaking of speeches," Tony interjected.

"Yes." Karoly, as always, was too slow to assert himself. "That's enough from both of you." Pausing, he

pursed his lips. "In context, I think Ms. Marz is entitled
to Ms. D'Abruzzi's opinion."

Sitting, Tony murmured to Saul, "That's one for the
appellate court." But that did not change his concern
and irritation, aggravated when Stella Marz, with a professional sweetness, milked the moment by asking the
court reporter, "Could you read back my last question,
please? The part before Mr. Lord's objection."

The reporter, a stout, middle-aged man with thinning
brown hair, thumbed the roll of paper that hung from
his machine, squinting at the shorthand symbols. "Here
it is," he murmured, and then, in a monotone that somehow made the question sound more damning, read:
" 'Why, do you suppose, Janice, did Marcie need to see
this man on the night she died?' "

As one, the jury looked from the reporter to Janice
D'Abruzzi. "To warn him," Janice answered. "So that
he'd know he was in trouble." For the first time, Janice's
voice broke. "Marcie was such a good person. She'd
want to protect him. . . ."

The courtroom was still. "Thank you," Stella said
softly, and turned to Tony. "Your witness, Mr. Lord."

Tony stood beside the defense table. He did not want the
jury to see him crowding a teenage girl—it might seem
an unpleasant echo of his client.

"Just for the record," Tony said mildly, "am I correct
that Marcie never told you why she wanted to meet this
unknown man? So that your last answer is just a guess?"

Janice eyed him warily. "It's what I thought," she
answered. "Not what she told me."

"In fact, she didn't tell you she was pregnant, either."

Briefly, Janice fingered the collar of her suit. "No."

"But if I remember our prior conversation, didn't you
ask Marcie if she was 'in trouble'?"

Janice's face filled with distrust. "Yes."

"What did you mean by the question?"

"*I* was worried that she was pregnant."

Tony nodded. "And based on your relationship with Marcie, do you think she understood you?"

"Objection," Stella said promptly. "How can this witness know what Marcie's understanding was?"

Tony kept his voice mild, a friend reasoning with another friend. "That really is the problem, Stella, isn't it?" He turned to Leo Karoly. "We started down this road, Your Honor, when Ms. Marz asked Ms. D'Abruzzi why Marcie Calder wanted to meet this man. With your indulgence, I'd like to establish a foundation for my questions."

Karoly hesitated. "Go ahead, Mr. Lord."

Tony saw Stella Marz's look of irritation; in a moment, he had reduced her from righteous prosecutor to erring colleague, his peer in some common search for truth. Turning to Janice, Tony asked, "Did you and Marcie have some common understanding of what 'in trouble' meant when you talked about girls and guys?"

The *jury* did, Tony was quite certain. Janice paused, biting her lip. "It meant getting pregnant," she said at last. "A couple of girls in school already had."

Tony nodded. "Looking back at it," he said gently, "Marcie didn't tell you the truth, did she?"

Janice stared at him resentfully. "Marcie wasn't a liar," she retorted. "Maybe she wasn't sure."

"But if she were worried, wouldn't she confide in you?"

Trapped between two bad answers, Janice looked down. "I don't know."

"In fact, except for whatever Marcie chose to tell you, you don't know *anything* about this relationship."

Janice's full lips set in a stubborn line. "I knew Marcie, that was all."

"Did you?" Tony asked mildly. "Besides trying to protect this man, whoever he was, did Marcie give you any other reason for wanting to keep her affair a secret?"

Janice stiffened. In a tight voice, she said, "She didn't want her father to know she was having sex."

"Isn't that part of the reason you covered for her?"

Reminded of her complicity, Janice slumped a little. "Yes."

"And didn't Marcie say to you that she needed to keep her father, quote, believing in the Virgin Marcie, unquote."

It was a deadly question, Tony knew: though he could imagine the remark in its teenage context, as the resentful humor of the pseudo-oppressed, in court the phrase suggested a different Marcie Calder. But just as Tony recalled about Johnny D'Abruzzi, his daughter was an honest person and would not lie. Softly, Janice answered, "Marcie was afraid of him, all right?"

"Did Marcie seem afraid that night? Even desperate?"

Janice swallowed; Tony could see her remembering how Marcie had appeared to her. "Yes. She started crying. . . ."

Tony made his voice sound puzzled. "Had you ever seen Marcie act like that before? Desperate and afraid?"

Silent, Janice shook her head, then remembered to answer aloud. "No—not like that."

"When you told Ms. Marz you didn't think Marcie wanted to get married, you based that guess on things she had said *before* that night, correct?"

"Yes."

Tony cocked his head. Softly, he asked, "Do you think being pregnant might have changed Marcie's mind about marriage?"

Once more, Stella got up. "Objection. Calls for speculation."

Tony gave her a drawn-out look of astonishment. "Oh, Stella . . . ," he murmured, and then turned to the judge. "Counsel opened up this door on direct, Your Honor. This is well within the scope of what the court has already permitted her."

It was *all* improper, Tony knew. But only the defense could take the judge's rulings to the appellate court—a potential embarrassment, Saul had assured Tony, that Leo Karoly dreaded even more than most weak judges. With unusual promptness, Karoly said, "Objection overruled."

Tony asked the reporter to read back the question, his tacit payback to Stella. " 'Do you think,' " the reporter intoned, " 'being pregnant might have changed Marcie's mind about marriage?' "

Janice glanced at the Calders, the context for her answer. After a moment, she said, "It might have."

Tony walked forward, stopping a few feet from Janice. She looked up at him, less afraid than vulnerable. Softly, he said, "You feel guilty, don't you? About misleading Marcie's mother."

For the first time, tears came to Janice's eyes. Her voice was trembling. "Marcie was my best friend. . . ."

Now Tony's compassion was not feigned but came from his own piercing memory of Alison Taylor. "And you feel as though you're somehow responsible for Marcie's death."

Janice blinked. "Yes."

Tony no longer had to think. "So now you'd like to help punish the person you believe is directly responsible."

Janice turned away, voice low. "Yes."

"And because the county prosecutor has charged Sam Robb, you think he's that person."

"Yes." Blindly, Janice rearranged her skirt. "I do."

Tony waited for a moment. "Before he was charged, you didn't think Sam Robb was Marcie's lover, did you?"

Slowly, Janice's gaze rose to his. "No."

Tony moved closer yet. Quietly, he said, "In fact, you thought it was someone else."

Janice's eyes froze. With a kind of fascination, Tony watched her make her choice. But Janice D'Abruzzi was an honest girl.

"Yes," she conceded. "I thought it might be someone else."

Tony gave Janice a brief nod. "That's all I have," he said softly, and took some consolation in her look of relief.

After court had recessed for the day, and Sam had quietly thanked him and left with his family, Tony gathered his papers at the defense table. Stella Marz stopped on her way out.

"I'm learning, Tony," she murmured. "I'm learning. And please don't call me Stella in open court."

Tony glanced around him. "Fair enough," he answered. "By the way, think we can cut down on the hearsay a little? It's clear that your friend Karoly won't, and self-help makes me weary."

Stella's oval eyes narrowed in a faint smile. "I'll think about it," she said, and left.

That night, Tony dined with Saul in a steakhouse in an old converted warehouse on the river. Across the water, the yellow lights of Steelton flickered in the dusk.

Contrary to his habit during trials, Tony had ordered a martini. "One day," he said to Saul, "and I'm already tired."

Saul was contenting himself with a bottle of red wine and the largest porterhouse steak Tony had ever seen. "The stress of a meddling client?" he asked. "Or distaste for the crime?"

Tony sipped his martini, idly contemplating a half head of iceberg lettuce with bright-orange French dressing poured all over it. "Defending your oldest friend on a charge of murder is more than enough."

Saul's eyes were curious. "You setting up Sam's testimony? Sure looks like that."

Tony was quiet for a moment, gazing out at the lights. "I'm setting up the option, that's all. One advantage is that Stella's got no idea what Sam's story *is*. But no, I won't put him on unless I think I have to."

Saul seemed to study him, and then slowly nodded. "I'd be careful, Tony. Your oldest friend overrates himself."

SIX

On a gray Friday morning, Stella Marz called Nancy Calder as her third witness.

Nancy Calder wore a black suit, which underscored her pallor, her haggard face, the dark circles and pouches beneath her eyes. To Tony, she looked ten years older than the woman he had met a week after Marcie's death. Her voice was weary, uninflected.

For the first half hour, Stella helped Nancy Calder make Marcie live again for the jury. With an eerie pride, broken by moments of grief, Nancy recalled her daughter's sweetness, her honesty, her steady grades, her unswerving Catholic faith. Even when she spoke of Marcie's love of track, Nancy Calder would not look at Sam.

For his own part, Sam regarded her with what seemed quite genuine compassion. Sue sat behind him, her face reflecting the haunted sympathy of one mother watching another confront every parent's worst fear, the untimely death of a child. But to Tony, the sanitized near saint presented by Nancy Calder was less persuasive, and less moving, than the trapped and frightened girl described by Nora Cox and Janice D'Abruzzi.

Stella seemed to sense this. "Did there come a time," she asked, "when Marcie's behavior changed?"

Briefly, Nancy Calder glanced at her husband. Hunched, with his hands folded, Frank Calder had that peculiar gaze at nothing which, to Tony, suggested shame as much as grief or anger. Tony's sense of fracture—in the marriage and in the man—deepened.

"It changed, yes." Nancy Calder's voice sounded pained. "About two months before . . . before she died."

"How would you describe this change?"

Nancy Calder paused, as if to reexamine her daughter's life for clues. "She seemed preoccupied—dreamy, but not in a healthy way. We'd say something to her, like at the dinner table, and she wouldn't hear us. She'd only pick at her food. . . ." Recalling, Nancy struggled for words. "It was like she was withdrawing from our family, from our life. She spent more time in her room, doing homework, she said, but her grades started falling off—A's to B's, B's to C's. She hardly seemed to notice us. . . . Not just Frank and me, but her sisters, Meg and Mary. She had always taken so much interest in them— and then, nothing. I could see the hurt in their eyes. . . ."

Beside Tony, Sam took a deep breath. The jurors seemed sharply attentive, captured by the mystery of Marcie Calder's slide. Gently, Stella asked, "Did this change coincide with any difference in the way Marcie spent her time?"

"Yes." Nancy Calder's voice was newly bitter. "It began shortly after Coach Robb asked her to stay late after school. For extra track practice, she said."

She straightened in her chair, seemingly determined not to look in Sam's direction. "Did you know Sam Robb?" Stella asked.

"Oh, yes. After Marcie started running." Her tone became flat again. "He was the soul of charm, Ms. Marz.

The last time I saw him was two weeks before Marcie died. He made it a point to come up to me and say just how *hard* Marcie was working after school, and that it was really paying off. Coaching Marcie was a pleasure, he said, a real pleasure. . . ." All at once, Nancy Calder's eyes shone with loss and regret, which made her voice turn tremulous. "I'd been thinking that Marcie should quit track, that it could be hurting her grades, even affecting her physically, not eating and the like. But when Coach Robb said that to me, I thought, Why take that away from Marcie. It's the thing she's doing well, that she takes pride in—"

Nancy Calder could not go on. Face covered, she wept into her hands. She made no sound at all.

Take a recess, Tony thought. But when Karoly gazed at Stella, she shook her head. After a moment, Nancy Calder straightened in the witness stand, strained but composed. Softly, Stella asked her, "Tell me about the night Marcie disappeared."

As Nancy Calder spoke, trying not to cry, Marcie came alive again in Tony's mind.

They sat at the kitchen table under a bright light— Marcie, her parents, and her two sisters.

Marcie was not eating; she picked at her food distractedly, while Meg and Mary, who adored her, looked at her as if she were a stranger. More and more, dinners seemed dominated by the vacuum that this change in Marcie had created, and the silences that came with it.

To fill the quiet, Nancy Calder asked her twelve-year-old, "How was dancing class? Did you dance with anyone you liked?"

Meg, who despised this embarrassing waste of time, wrinkled her nose. "The boys act so weird. Jesse, the one who's supposed to like me, asked a *friend* to tell me." Her voice filled with disgust. "His friend was wearing white socks with a suit."

Marcie looked up from her plate, eyeing Meg with mild interest at most. Nancy missed the Marcie who would tease with Meg, making her an ally rather than an object of ridicule. But *this* Marcie was silent.

"What's wrong?" Frank Calder asked abruptly.

Nancy watched Meg blink, then see that her father was looking at her older sister. Marcie gazed back at him without expression. "I'm not hungry," she said.

It was so typical of the new Marcie: an answer meant to be unresponsive and annoying to her father. As if to shut him off entirely, Marcie picked up her fork and, in an ostentatious show of forced appetite, began to eat a few bites of asparagus. As Nancy Calder glanced at her husband, imploring him to let it go, she felt Meg and Mary look from one parent to the other.

In a quiet voice, Frank Calder said to Marcie, "That's not what I meant."

Marcie faced him again. "I have a report due," she said. "On women who've helped change America. I'm behind." There was a trace of sarcasm in Marcie's voice, an echo of her disagreements with Frank Calder. As though afraid to anger him, Marcie turned quickly to her mother. "I'm going to work on it at Janice's. Miss Bates says we can do the report together—"

"You know the rules," Frank Calder cut in. "No going out on school nights unless there's a special reason. Plus, young lady, your grades are slipping—"

"*Please,*" Marcie was pleading with her mother; the emotion Nancy saw in her eyes was mystifying. "This is important. . . ."

Something was wrong, Nancy sensed. But it would be better to talk with Marcie alone, after she returned. Without looking at her husband, Nancy said, "All right, Marcie. But I'll expect you home by nine-thirty—"

"Ten o'clock, okay?" Now Marcie seemed a child again, with a child's desperate lack of perspective. "*Please . . .*"

Perhaps it was nothing, Nancy thought, but the age-old quarrel with rules and deadlines. "All right," she said, and then, remembering her husband, added, "That means ten, not ten-oh-one. . . ."

Frank Calder got up from the table, silently carrying his plate to the sink, and left.

Glancing at his retreating back, Marcie said, "Thanks, Mom," and went to get her jacket before her father returned. Nancy sat alone with her two younger daughters. "White socks," she said to Meg, "aren't the worst thing in the world."

From the living room, Marcie said, "'Night, Mom. . . ."

Abruptly, Nancy got up. "Wait," she called, not knowing why.

Marcie froze by the doorway, looking frail in her jacket, jeans, and outsize Lake City Lakers sweatshirt. Nancy gazed at her. "Don't you need books? Or paper, at least?"

Marcie looked startled, as if the question were absurd, and then seemed to remember what she had said. "Oh, don't worry. Janice has all the stuff we'll need."

Nancy stared at her daughter, wondering how to reach her. Then, to her surprise, Marcie took two steps and kissed her on the forehead. "I'll be back," she said. And then she was gone, closing the door behind her before Nancy Calder could find words.

"If I'd known," Nancy finished brokenly, "we would have helped. We could have raised the baby. . . ." She stopped, neck bowed.

The beautician, Tony saw, had tears in her eyes. So did the dark-haired nutritionist, who had two daughters. Gently, Stella asked, "If you can, Mrs. Calder, tell us what happened next."

Slowly, Nancy Calder composed herself. "I couldn't wait until ten o'clock. I started wondering, watching the clock. . . ." Her tone went flat again. "Finally I called

Janice D'Abruzzi. When she told me they'd been working together and Marcie had gone to the library, I felt
better for a time. . . ."

"It wasn't until eleven, when Janice admitted lying to
me, that Frank called the police."

There was a terrible simplicity in the last sentence;
the doubt-filled mother, blaming herself, the father taking over. "We waited all night long," she said softly. "At
about eleven-thirty the next morning, the police came to
our door. Marcie had been dead for hours, lying alone in
the cold and rain. . . ."

This time Stella Marz asked for a recess.

After lunch, Tony began his cross-examination.

All that he could do was show a certain softness of
manner; it was too grotesque, perhaps incendiary, to
express sympathy on Sam Robb's behalf or, however
much Tony might feel this, for what he was about to do.

"This change in Marcie," he began. "Did you try to
talk to her about it?"

"Yes." Briefly, Nancy Calder closed her eyes. "She
said that I was imagining things."

"Did you believe her?"

"No."

"What did you think it was?"

For a long moment, Nancy Calder hesitated. "I didn't
know."

Tony paused for a moment of his own. "Did you
think it was a guy, Mrs. Calder?"

Nancy Calder gave him a silent, somewhat severe
look. "She wasn't dating anyone, Mr. Lord. I had no
reason to think it was a 'guy,' as you put it."

Not in that sense, Tony thought. "But you must have
been quite worried. From what you say, the change in
Marcie included listlessness, weight loss, declining appetite, deteriorating school performance, and disinterest
in her own family."

Nancy Calder sat back, as if shamed by this recitation. "As I said, I was very concerned."

It was as if they were connected by an invisible string, Tony thought; if he tugged too hard, he would lose her. Tony put his hands in his pockets. "Are you familiar with the symptoms of depression?"

Nancy Calder's eyes widened. "I'm not a psychologist, Mr. Lord."

"But did you consider taking Marcie to see one?"

She touched her breastbone, eyes flickering to her husband. "I considered it, yes."

Tony moved closer. Softly, he asked, "Did you discuss it with your husband?"

"Objection." Quickly, Stella Marz stepped forward. "Irrelevant. I fail to see what this intrusion on the Calders' marital privacy has to do with whether this defendant murdered their daughter."

This was right, Tony knew; as before, he was counting on the judge to let him get away with something. "The question goes to Marcie Calder's state of mind," he told Karoly. "It's quite possible, we contend, that Marcie Calder killed herself. As to which the nature of her family life, the changes in her behavior, and the presence or absence of professional counseling are all directly—perhaps tragically—relevant."

Unhappily, Judge Karoly nodded. "Objection overruled."

"Thank you, Your Honor. I'll ask the question again." Turning to Nancy Calder, Tony saw that Stella, while retreating to the counsel table, remained standing. "When you suggested to your husband that Marcie receive counseling, did he disagree?"

Once more, Nancy Calder's fingers traced her breastbone. "Frank believes that families should help themselves and that psychologists are 'a waste of money.' Our medical plan doesn't cover psychiatric counseling."

At the corner of his eye, Tony saw both the nutritionist and an older juror, an Irish warehouseman, glance toward Frank Calder. But Nancy Calder stared at Tony now, as if awakened by the echo of her own response. "But if you're suggesting that Frank, or anyone, drove our daughter to suicide, then it's an insult to Marcie's memory, to her faith, and to her strength of character."

Pausing, Tony deferred to her anger. "But is it fair to say that Marcie and her father had a difficult relationship?"

Nancy Calder frowned. "There were differences, yes."

"Marcie considered her father strict, did she not?"

"Sometimes, yes. I think that's inevitable."

"But did you ever discuss this with Marcie? Outside her father's presence, that is."

Nancy Calder looked fragile now, wearied by her own emotions. "I tried," she said at last. "I said I'd help her talk to him. . . ."

"And did Marcie tell you, in words or substance, that she didn't trust you to keep confidences?"

Once more, tears formed in her eyes. In secret sympathy, Tony recognized this, the moment that a witness stopped resisting. "Yes," she answered quietly.

"Their disagreements included the subject of premarital sex, didn't they?"

"Yes."

"And what was Mr. Calder's attitude?"

"That Marcie should remain a virgin." Her head raised. "That was *our* attitude, Mr. Lord."

"But it was your husband, not you, who wanted to send Marcie to an all-women's college."

Tony watched Nancy Calder struggle with her loyalties. "Yes," she said at last.

"Did you ever tell your husband, in words or substance, that he was driving Marcie away?"

Her face was taut now. "Yes."

"And were you also concerned that, because you yourself were working, both of you were losing touch with Marcie?"

Nancy Calder's eyes met his with a stinging look of betrayal; Tony saw her regret ever letting him into their home, and fought back regret of his own. "Yes," she said at last. "Neither of us thought my working was best for the girls." Her eyes filled with tears again. "But then we were going to have three in college. . . ."

It was a touching answer, Tony knew. "I understand," he said. "So you felt a psychologist might reach your daughter, where you could not?"

"Maybe. I didn't know."

Tony paused a moment. "Whatever your concerns, they didn't involve a relationship with Sam Robb, did they?"

"No." Nancy's voice was harsh again. "He was Marcie's track coach, always cheerful and supportive. We could never have imagined he'd been having sex with her."

Quickly, she looked down again, as if knowing that the answer, however damning she intended it, might also expose her unawareness. In a tone of understanding, Tony asked, "I gather she didn't talk about Sam Robb at home. Other than as a coach."

For a moment, she appeared almost grateful. "No. She didn't."

Tony paused, taking his time, drawing the jury's attention back to him. "Was there *any* older man, other than her father, for whom she seemed to have affection?"

The jury seemed quite still now. Nancy Calder was silent for a time. Then with a veiled upward look at Tony, she answered coolly, "Ernie Nixon, our recreation director. Marcie's first track coach."

Stella had prepared her, Tony knew. In a puzzled tone, he asked, "Why does Mr. Nixon come to mind?"

Nancy Calder's face set. "I don't know what you're

implying, Mr. Lord. Ernie Nixon gave Marcie confidence, and she was grateful to him. We both were."

"Did you know she used to visit him?"

She stiffened. "Of course. A lot of young people do."

Tony watched her for a moment. Softly, he said, "At his home, I meant. Alone."

"Objection," Stella called out. "No foundation. There's been no testimony on this at all."

It was her first real mistake, Tony thought. "I'd like an answer," he said to Karoly, adding, with deliberate understatement, "subject to proof, of course. But I believe Ms. Marz plans to call Mr. Nixon herself."

Karoly hesitated, indecisive. "Objection overruled," he said to Stella, almost in apology. "But if it turns out there's no foundation, I'll ask the jury to disregard the testimony."

Tony turned to Nancy Calder. Awakened from guilt and grief, she stared at him with fresh anger that was close to feral. "Were you aware," he asked again, "that Marcie would visit Ernie Nixon in his home, alone, when no one else was there? Not once, or twice, but repeatedly."

Nancy Calder folded her arms. "No," she said tersely. "If that's even true. But Ernie Nixon did *not* kill Marcie."

It was a better answer than Tony Lord the defense lawyer could have hoped for; a worse one than the other Tony, whom Ernie Nixon had once befriended, had ever wanted. Softly, he said, "Thank you," and left Nancy Calder sitting there, a woman out of touch with her husband and her daughter, her last few words lingering in the air.

This time Sam Robb had the wisdom not to thank him.

SEVEN

Sweat ran down Sam Robb's face.

Facing him, Tony dribbled the basketball, eyes on the basket. Suddenly Tony burst by him; with a last stretch, taking him two feet past Sam, he slid under the basket and flipped the ball over his head and into the net.

Collapsing on the cement playground, Sam Robb broke out in delighted laughter. "You've still got it," he said. "I should have hired a fatter, slower lawyer."

Tony sat next to him, breathing hard. "Wouldn't help—he'd be too smart to play with you." He caught his breath. "This really *is* nuts, you know. What are the rules here—last one to have a massive coronary wins?"

Sam grinned. "I can see the headline now: 'Hook Shot Proves Fatal to San Francisco Lawyer—Robb Forced to Defend Himself.' " He cocked his head. "What are we playing for, Tony?"

Tony wiped his forehead. "Your Athlete of the Year trophy. I still want it."

"Too late. But you gave it a run, Tony. I'll say that." Raising his face to the sun, Sam inhaled deeply, seemingly content. "You ever think about those times? You know, before Alison died, when things were still fun."

Nearly thirty years later, Tony found, the thought still made him sad. "Sometimes," he finally answered. "But from the moment I found her, the time before that was like something I saw through the wrong end of a telescope. Too far away to touch."

Quiet, they gazed across the rolling grass, then Erie Road, Taylor Park with its hedgerows, and, finally, the lake, its waters soft blue in sunshine.

Why are we doing this? Tony asked himself. *Middleaged men playing a Sunday game of basketball with all the ferocity of their youth, if not the skills.* When Sam had called to propose this, breaking into Tony's preparation for Ernie Nixon's testimony, Tony had thought it pathological—a contest between two old friends and rivals who, if they followed Sam's competitive instincts, would end their days playing checkers in a rest home, for money. But when he had said this, Sam merely laughed.

"My goals aren't that long-term," Sam had answered, and Tony knew that Sam—and perhaps he—needed some relief from the darkness of Marcie Calder's death, the stifling hermetic quality of a murder trial. So here they were, on a patch of macadam on the crest of a knoll near the recreation center, playing the games of the past. Perhaps Sam's suggestion was intended as a kindness to them both: the mindless concentration, the moments of exhilaration and release, seemed to have jarred loose other memories, reminding Tony of the resonance of their friendship. It seemed to have the same effect on Sam.

"Remember my sunrise sermon?" he asked.

Tony nodded. "Frightening. You had absolutely no sense, none at all."

Sam gave him a sideways look. "But you bailed me out," he said softly. "Just like you're doing now."

Idly, Tony spun the ball on his finger. "What *I* remember is writing you a sermon, which you didn't use a line of. Instead I seem to recall you satirizing my pitiful sex life, to great acclaim, and saying afterward, 'I really fucking fooled them.' "

Sam's smile had a reflective quality. "Sometimes you have to bet on yourself, Tony. But I'm still grateful to you. Always." Standing, he held out his hand to pull Tony upright. "The score's nine apiece, and it's my ball."

Stiffly, Tony rose, knowing that Sam meant to play this to the end.

Sam looked different than he had three months ago;

the fat was gone, his face youthful again, his eyes keener. It was strange: he had no career, perhaps no marriage, and, quite possibly, would live out his days in the rancid netherworld of the Ohio State Penitentiary. But adversity, and perhaps Tony's return, seemed to have given him a purpose—even, in some strange way, to have restored him. The Sam who faced Tony at midcourt was a different man than the shamed and dissipated Sam who, at first meeting, had filled Tony with such sadness and regret.

"No way out," Sam announced, charging for the basket.

Skittering backward, Tony blocked his path. Abruptly, Sam veered right, bumping Tony with a hard shoulder, and banked in a layup as Tony reeled, ribs hurting from the blow.

"So it's that way," Tony said.

From beneath the basket, Sam shot him a pirate's grin and flipped Tony the ball.

Tony took the ball to half-court, remembering a trick he more recently had used on Christopher, until he had used it once too often. But Sam might have forgotten it.

Tony set it up by taking two jump shots on his next two tries—one in, the other barely missing. Sam's driving layup put him ahead; they played silently, intensely, watching each other as Tony crouched at half-court. Charging to Sam's left, he stopped as if to take his jump shot, then dribbled the ball behind his back and left Sam standing there, expecting the shot, as Tony collected the bouncing ball and went to the basket for an easy layup.

"Finesse," Tony said in his best laconic manner. "And patience."

Sam's eyes glinted. "I haven't forgotten. First time you pulled that on me, I was fifteen. Your team won the scrimmage."

Taking the ball, Sam went to the spot where Tony had faked his jump shot, and sank one of his own. A few minutes later, when Sam pulled the same trick on him, Tony laughed aloud.

"Fifteen all," Sam called out. "This is getting worthwhile."

They both were breathing hard now, chests heaving with the need for air. "Five more points to twenty," Tony answered. "Let's take a break."

"Need one?" Sam asked with an air of challenge.

"No. I'm just hoping that the fun will never end."

Even as he said this, Tony admitted to himself that it was yet another trick, meant to mock their competition while depriving Sam of the adrenaline rush that might carry him to victory. Sam gave him a sour, knowing smile. "Have it your way," he said, and sat down on the court again.

They were silent for a time. Interrupted from their challenge, Sam did not find conversation easy. Nor did Tony; he was preoccupied by Sam's primal need to win, his own response.

"How're your folks?" Sam asked finally.

"Good, thanks." Tony realized that, since his return, they had never spoken of parents, save for Sam's fleeting reference to his mother. "Stacey and I helped them buy a place in Florida—it's not me, God knows, but Dad's discovered golf. It keeps him, in my mom's inimitable words, from 'driving me to the funny farm.'" He smiled a little. "After fifty years, they have their routine down cold—bickering but inseparable. When one of them dies, it'll be tough on the other, especially if my dad goes first; she'll have to complain to his wedding picture." He turned to Sam. "*There's* a generation of marriages I really don't understand. Maybe if I'd stayed married to Marcia, I might."

"So how can you regret divorcing?"

"Oh, I never said I regret it—I said that I felt guilty.

That's the Catholic way of having what you want." Briefly, Tony smiled, and then his smile faded. "No, sometimes I'll wake up and look across the pillow at Stacey, and she'll be smiling in her sleep. And I realize, in spite of everything . . ."

He did not need to finish the sentence. Sam studied him, hesitant. Quietly, he asked, "Think you'd have married Alison?"

Tony shook his head in puzzlement. "I have no idea. It's so funny to think about now." His voice softened. "But if you'd asked me a moment before I found her, I'd have answered yes."

Sam gazed out at the lake. "Maybe she'd have met someone else, Tony. Maybe you would have."

It was a curious remark, Tony thought—true, but irrelevant to the tragedy of Alison. "If she were married to someone else, and happy, that would be more than enough for me."

When Sam turned to him, as though pondering his last remark, Tony suddenly wondered if his friend had applied the words to his own wife, whom Tony had also loved. "*Did* you ever sleep with her?" Sam asked.

With whom? Tony wondered. But the only truth he could tell was the one that no longer mattered. Softly, he answered, "The night she died, for the first time. That's why she came out again."

Sam's eyes first widened, then narrowed in a kind of wince, and though his lips parted, for a moment no sound emerged. "I'm sorry, Tony. I didn't know."

Tony was not sure whether this apology was for Sam's question or for some deeper reappraisal of how wounded Tony had been. Tony supposed it did not matter.

"It stayed with me," he said at last. "I still have nightmares."

Sam turned to him. "What kind?"

For a moment, Tony wished they could have talked

like this at seventeen. But he did not care to mention his last dream. "There's only one," he answered. "The moment I found her. Quite lifelike, if you can call it that, and then I wake up."

Sam stared at him and then shook his head. "I can never remember my dreams," he murmured. "Maybe just as well."

What kind of dreams, Tony wondered, *might Sam repress?* "It depends on the dream, I suppose."

Sam propped his chin on tented fingers and, for a much longer time, was silent. "I keep remembering that night at the beach," he said at last. "You and Alison, me and Sue, and all the things we didn't know. Ever wish you could hit the rewind button?"

"I used to. Now I wish I could just erase a night."

As soon as he said it, Tony felt this was a tactless answer. But Sam did not seem to hear it that way. Almost gently, he placed a hand on Tony's shoulder. "I'll buy you a beer," he said. "We can finish the game some other time."

When Tony returned to his new quarters, in Steelton—the dreary but convenient Palace Hotel—his notes regarding Ernie Nixon were strewn across his bed. It made him think again that life was full of ironies, of choices, of unintended consequences, which, once recognized, became one's own responsibility.

Tomorrow Ernie Nixon would take the stand, and Tony Lord the lawyer would be responsible for his own acts. He put the thought aside, imagining his cross-examination.

That night, Tony slept badly. At first dawn, he awakened, sweating, from his strange new dream of Alison, his image of himself that of an invisible camera, her delphic question driving him from bed.

Restless, Tony ordered room service—toast and black

coffee—and spent an hour at the hotel gym, sweating feverishly as he punished the exercise bike. Then he showered, dressed, and presented himself at the courtroom of Judge Leo F. Karoly, a lawyer with a client to defend.

EIGHT

Taking the witness stand, Ernie Nixon wore a gray pinstriped business suit, a yellow tie with a geometric design, a crisp white shirt, and a look of cool self-possession, which, for a moment, he turned on Tony Lord. Next to Tony, Saul Ravin eyed Ernie with wary interest. "He's no Donald White," he murmured.

The sardonic remark, Tony found, touched his conscience. "He never was."

Briefly, Stella Marz glanced at Tony; today it seemed that the lawyers had a heightened awareness of each other. Even the jury seemed to feel it; waiting, they were silent and attentive, without the small smiles and whispered asides that characterize twelve people settling in with one another.

Somewhat stiffly, for her, Stella led Ernie through his first eighteen years in Lake City; his college education; his decision to come back; his five years as recreation director. Ernie's answers were precise, soft-spoken, and revealed nothing about the complexity of his feelings: listening, Tony imagined Ernie's return as the last nostalgic reel of that Frank Capra movie, the homecoming of a goodhearted man to the warmth and comfort of the place he loved most. All that was missing, Tony thought with irony, was the girl.

"Yeah," Sam said sarcastically, under his breath. "It's all been great, hasn't it. . . ."

"Could you tell us," Stella asked, "how old Marcie Calder was when you first met her?"

"Thirteen, I'd say. I coach a girls' track team, eleven to fourteen." Ernie paused. "Marcie was best friends with another girl on the team, Janice D'Abruzzi, whose dad was my best friend. I guess Janice sort of brought her around."

"What was Marcie like then, would you say?"

Ernie seemed to consider this. "Shy—never any trouble. But you could see her watching, and thinking, like there was a lot going on inside her. So I'd say thoughtful, too, and sort of private. Like it took her a while to trust people." Pausing, Ernie finished softly, "I don't think that part ever changed."

It was already starting, Tony knew; Stella's portrait of a shy, inward girl whose mistake, terrible in its consequences, was to trust the wrong adult. "Over time," Stella asked, "did you come to know her better?"

Ernie nodded. "Little by little," he answered, and permitted himself a small smile. "About a year after she came out for the team, Marcie had a growth spurt. Most kids that makes kind of awkward. But what it made Marcie Calder was fast. All the sudden, she was the fastest kid on the team."

"How did she react to that?"

"I guess you could say she was ecstatic. She couldn't get enough of running, or winning. Talked a lot more too—it was like I became a hero just for giving her the chance, even though, like I always told her, she'd provided all the talent." Abruptly, Ernie's voice softened, and for the first time, he looked at Sam Robb. "Marcie needed attention, I could see. I think she'd have been attached to any adult who gave her that. Someone who made her feel important to him."

This was getting close to the line, Tony thought, but he made no move to object. "When Marcie turned fifteen," Stella queried, "and couldn't run for you anymore, did you do anything to help her?"

Ernie folded his hands again. "I encouraged her to go out for track in high school. And then, just to make sure she did, I called the girls' track coach. Sam Robb."

Beneath these few soft words, Tony heard the bitter sense of good intentions gone wrong. The first mention of the name Sam Robb had made the jury still, attentive.

"And what did Sam Robb say?"

"That he'd 'watch out for her.'" Ernie paused, gazing at Sam again. "Yes, I think those were his words: 'I'll watch out for her.'"

Sam's returning stare seemed emotionless, Tony thought, without feeling or expression. Stella let the moment linger.

"After Marcie left *your* team," she asked, "and joined Sam Robb's, did she keep in touch with you?"

Ernie still appraised Sam; something like distaste came over his features, lending him an air of hauteur that, curiously, reminded Tony of Dee Nixon. Then Ernie turned to Stella and, with a casual smoothness that seemed rehearsed, answered. "She did, yes. Sometimes she'd come around the office, sometimes we'd ask her to watch our kids. So, one way or the other, I'd see her maybe two, three times a month."

"And from time to time, did she talk to you about how her life was going?"

"Uh-huh. Sometimes at the office, other times when I'd drive her home from baby-sitting." Briefly, Ernie paused. "Once in a while, she'd just drop by the house. To talk."

"Did she ever give the impression that her enjoyment of seeing you went beyond talking?" Stella paused, adding in a flat voice, "By that, I mean that she had romantic feelings for you, some sort of crush."

"Absolutely not." Ernie's tone reflected Stella's, a shared contempt for anyone who would smear this girl—or him—to spare a guilty man just punishment. "What she wanted was an adult who was a friend, rather than a parent. You see this kind of attachment in that age kid a lot—it's normal, even healthy, and it's part of growing up. When I was a kid, I wish I'd had more of it."

For the first time, Tony glanced at the Calders: Frank Calder raised his head, and his wife nodded with silent vehemence. But to Tony, Ernie's answer was far more subtle, suggesting the man as he wished to see himself and reminding Tony that Coach Jackson, whom Tony had admired, had seemed to take little interest in Ernie as a human being. Tony sensed that an unspoken gulf lay between the Calders and Ernie, the territory in Marcie's life that Ernie felt they had left to him, the caring adult he once had wanted and now wished to see in himself.

"What kinds of things did Marcie talk about?"

Ernie shrugged. "Everything and anything—grades, school, track, guys." He glanced at the jury. "Kids that age are remarkably candid. They haven't closed up yet, like adults."

Leaning his head to Tony's, Saul murmured, "What is this, Adolescent Development 101: all little kids tell Big Bird about busted rubbers?" But there was nothing Tony could do; objecting to Ernie's generalities, however self-serving, would make Tony look too anxious.

"Did there come a time," Stella asked, "when you became worried about where Marcie's life was going?"

Ernie nodded. "Yes," he said firmly. "Very worried."

"What were the circumstances?"

Surveying the jury, Ernie talked to them directly. "Marcie came to see me, at my office. I could tell she was pretty shaken up, even before she said she needed my help." His tone was subdued, as if the memory burdened him still. "Marcie said she'd begun having sex, and she was scared."

The beautician gazed back at him, Tony thought, with unquestioning compassion. Stella waited for a moment. Quietly, she asked, "Did you ever have sexual relations with Marcie Calder?"

Ernie sat straighter. "Absolutely not. That was never the way I saw her."

Stella, Tony saw, was asking *his* questions, blunting their impact. "Even after your wife left?" she prodded.

Ernie folded his arms. "That's not something I'd do, Ms. Marz. It's not something *anyone* should do who's got responsibility for other people's children."

Though this was meant as a jab at Sam, Ernie's face was set, and his words suddenly sounded defensive, as self-righteous as a political platform and as lacking in any acknowledgment of human weakness, of desires felt but not, in the more complex and more honorable exercise of human decency, acted upon. The true Ernie, already revealed to Tony, was hidden now—perhaps because Ernie had begun lying to himself; more likely, Tony guessed, because Ernie knew that most people told themselves convenient lies about their own motives and thus might not forgive Ernie Nixon for the tangle that was his. But something had been lost, and not just from Stella's case; Ernie was no longer himself, and knew that Tony knew it.

"When," Stella asked, "was the last time you saw Marcie Calder?"

With what seemed a conscious effort, Ernie unfolded his arms. Softly, he answered, "The night she died, when she came to the house. At roughly eight o'clock."

As one, the jury stared at him. Even Leo Karoly, stepping from behind his bland bureaucratic mask, seemed rapt.

"Was that unusual?"

"Yes." Ernie's voice remained quiet. "Except to baby-sit. As soon as I saw her, I knew something was wrong."

"Did she tell you what it was?"

Slowly, Ernie turned to Sam. "Marcie was pregnant."

"Did she tell you who the father was?"

Ernie kept watching Sam. "Only that it was the man she'd been seeing. The older one."

The jury, Tony saw, had begun to follow Ernie's gaze. "How did Marcie seem to you?" Stella asked.

"Upset, and in need of understanding. But not hysterical."

"Did she say what she meant to do?"

Now Ernie turned to Stella, his voice cool and clear. "Yes. Marcie said she was meeting the father, as soon as she left my house. To *warn* him, she said."

Stella was quiet for a moment. "Did she mention the possibility of marrying this man?"

"Not at all." Ernie's tone became soft again. "In fact, she said that the father couldn't help her, and that she'd never ask him to come forward."

It was a devastating answer and, as Tony recalled, an incomplete one. But the jury could not know this. "Did you offer to discuss her alternatives?" Stella asked.

Ernie drew himself up. "I mentioned abortion. Marcie just sat there on my couch and said, 'But it's a baby—*my* baby. How can I kill it for being my mistake?' "

As before, Tony thought, Stella had anticipated him. "Did Marcie suggest who would care for the child?" she asked.

Ernie nodded. "She would, Marcie told me."

Stella allowed herself a sad and knowing smile. In a tone of quiet skepticism, she asked, "During this entire conversation, Mr. Nixon, did Marcie Calder seem in any way suicidal?"

"Objection." Tony stood slowly, taking his time in order to break the damning rhythm of questions and answers.

"Ms. Marz has not qualified this witness as a psychologist. What Mr. Nixon is, obviously, is someone who was quite attached to Marcie Calder and now wants to place all blame for her death on this defendant. But the answer to whether Marcie Calder was suicidal is not to be found anywhere in this witness's expertise—or in his wishes."

Assuming a posture of exaggerated patience, Stella Marz waited Tony out. "We can surely understand Mr. Lord's sensitivities on this point, Your Honor, seeing how he planted the notion of suicide himself. But Mr. Nixon has spent his entire career among children and young adults. More than almost anyone in this courtroom, I suspect, he has a valid lay opinion to offer."

Karoly tented his hands in front of him. "Perhaps you could ask it another way, Ms. Marz."

Stella nodded briskly. "Gladly," she said, and turned to Ernie Nixon. "Tell me, Mr. Nixon, did Marcie Calder *do* or *say* anything to suggest to you that she was considering suicide?"

"Absolutely nothing," Ernie said quickly, his tone firm. "To the contrary, the things she said and did all suggested the firm intention of keeping this baby alive."

Stella put her hands on her hips. "And did she ever say she couldn't face her parents?"

"No. Only that she couldn't tell them who the father was."

"She also told you she hadn't eaten for a while, correct?"

"Yes. So I offered her a tuna sandwich." Ernie gave a helpless shrug. "It was all I could do."

"Did she eat it?"

"She did. She was eating for two now, she said."

Stella paused for a moment. "But she didn't quite finish it, did she?"

"No. Suddenly Marcie looked at her watch and said she had to meet him. The father."

As Stella moved closer, the jury followed her. "Did you try to stop her?" Stella asked.

"Not stop her. Talk to her. It felt as if she hadn't thought things through. That she'd come to *me* for that, and now she was running off." Ernie paused. "It didn't feel right, Ms. Marz. And it didn't feel right that this father was older, and a secret. Except for me, the girl was all alone."

"But she wouldn't stay with you, would she?"

Ernie studied his folded hands, fingers twisting, his look of pain almost physical now. "No. She wouldn't stay." His voice fell, as though he were speaking to himself. "She just got in the car and drove away."

The sense of loss was palpable now: Tony could hear it in the utter silence; see it in the faces of the jury.

"After that," Stella asked softly, "did *you* do anything?"

Ernie looked up. "I followed her."

Stella tilted her head. "And why was that?"

Ernie seemed to ask the question of himself. "I wasn't sure," he finally answered. "Just that I was worried somehow. I thought maybe if I found out who the father was . . ."

"Did you?"

Slowly, Ernie shook his head. "Not then," he answered quietly. "Not then. I followed her about three blocks. Then I realized I wasn't her father. The only way I could help her, I told myself, was to sit back and wait." He looked up again. "So I stopped the car, turned around, and came home. The last I ever saw of Marcie Calder was a pair of red taillights, one blinking like it had a short. I made a mental note to tell her that. . . ."

Pausing, Ernie bit his lip. "I meant to do right, Ms. Marz, and did exactly wrong. 'Cause if I'd only followed her, Marcie would still be alive, wouldn't she."

Stella was still for a moment. Then she turned to Tony and said simply, "Your witness, Mr. Lord."

NINE

Rising with reluctance, Tony glanced at Sue.

Sitting between her two children, she gazed at him with sadness, worry, affection. Tony gave her the briefest smile of reassurance and then, lightly touching Sam's shoulder, turned and walked toward Ernie Nixon. Ernie sat back in the witness stand.

"That night," Tony asked, "did Marcie Calder say *why* she'd come to see you?"

Ernie folded his hands, eyes riveted on Tony's face. "To tell me she was pregnant. I guess she needed a friend."

"She had one—Janice D'Abruzzi. Can you think of any reason that Marcie told you and not her?"

"I don't know. Maybe she wanted advice from an adult."

Tony paused for a moment. "Isn't it fair to say, based on what she told you, that Marcie Calder had a troubled relationship with her father?"

"Objection," Stella interjected. "Hearsay."

Tony shook his head. "This falls under the state-of-mind exception, Your Honor. It's directly relevant to whether Marcie Calder, under the circumstances presented here, might be capable of suicide."

Karoly turned to Ernie. "You may answer, Mr. Nixon."

"I don't know if I'd say 'troubled.'" Ernie hesitated, shifting in his chair. "She said that sometimes they had a difficult time communicating. . . ."

"Because he intimidated her, right?"

"She said that, yes."

"And Marcie Calder had no idea, as far as you could tell, about *what* she was going to do next?"

Ernie's eyes narrowed; as Tony watched him try to understand where this was going, the quarry trying to anticipate the hunter, he felt the terrible impersonality of his role. Softly, Ernie answered, "She had an idea, Tony. She was going to see her lover."

The use of his first name, the pointed response, were clearly meant to disarm him. What they did was to arouse Tony's anger. With equal quiet, he asked, "Did she mention any idea beyond that?"

"No."

"So if Marcie Calder imagined a future beyond that night, you don't know what it was."

Ernie Nixon sat back. "That she'd have the baby. That's what she imagined."

"Living where?"

"I don't know."

Tony moved forward. "Based on your experience with kids, Mr. Nixon, would you say that life for an un-wed teenage mother in Lake City is difficult?"

"It depends on the circumstances. . . ."

"Such as?"

Ernie shrugged. "Family support, I guess."

For the first time, Tony's voice had an edge of irony. "And even with family support, scandal is sort of hard to live down in Lake City, Ohio, isn't it?"

Ernie gave a faint smile. "I guess some would say that."

"What was Marcie's demeanor during this visit?"

"It's like I said—worried but composed."

"Did she cry?"

"Yes."

"Did she want you to hold her?"

Ernie glanced at her parents. Facing Tony, he softly answered, "Yes."

"She needed comfort and affection, didn't she? That was obvious to you."

"Yes."

"So the girl you saw wasn't some poised young woman resolved to have a baby, was she? Marcie Calder was tearful, confused, lonely, hungry, *very* much upset, and—as far as you could see—without any clear vision of her life beyond this meeting with her child's father."

Ernie considered him. "She was some of those things you say, yes. As for the rest, I just don't know what she was thinking."

Tony skipped a beat. "Just like you don't *know* whether, under certain circumstances, Marcie Calder would take her own life."

Ernie's voice turned stubborn. "I saw no sign of that."

"But you're not a psychologist, are you?"

"No."

"Nor an expert on teen suicide."

"Of course not."

"Isn't it true, Mr. Nixon, that—when I first asked you about this—you said that Marcie told you she wouldn't expose the father unless, quote, he wanted to come forward, unquote?"

Ernie folded his hands again. "I think that's right."

"So from what she said to you, Marcie considered it a possibility that he *would* come forward."

"I suppose so."

"And marry her?"

"I don't know that. . . ."

"You don't know one way or the other, do you?"

"No."

"You and I have come a fair distance in a short time, haven't we, Mr. Nixon? Now we have a scared, confused, tearful, pregnant sixteen-year-old girl who was fearful of her father, who had no idea of how to cope beyond going to the *baby's* father, quite possibly hoping he could somehow make things right, and who—if he didn't or couldn't—might have reacted in any number of ways *you* couldn't anticipate or predict. Including suicide."

Tony could feel Stella rising before he even finished. "Was that a question, Your Honor, or a speech? I have no idea. What I do know is that it's compound, argumentative, speculative, lacking in foundation, and not susceptible to an answer. . . ."

"And," Tony said with irony, "a lot closer to the truth of Marcie's life than the fictitious person you used Mr. Nixon to invent. But I'll withdraw the question and ask the witness another."

Frustrated, Stella stared at him. Tony turned and asked Ernie Nixon softly, "You weren't much help to Marcie, were you?"

Ernie spread his hands. "I couldn't be."

"And you don't know who *could* help her, did you?"

"No."

"Did she ask if *you'd* marry her, Mr. Nixon?"

Ernie looked startled for an instant, then aggrieved. "It wasn't that kind of relationship, Mr. Lord."

"What kind was it, exactly?"

"I already said. I encouraged her, so she was fond of me—"

"I meant on your part?"

Ernie sat back, watching Tony with narrowed eyes. With the force of will, Tony tried to shut off any thought but the need to damage the man in front of him, a man whose dignity, or future, Tony as a defense lawyer had no right to consider.

"I cared about her," Ernie said simply.

Shoving his hands in his pockets, Tony sensed the jury's tension as they watched him. Then he forgot them: it was as if he and Ernie Nixon faced each other in a tunnel.

"Since you returned to Lake City," Tony asked, "have any other teenage girls talked to you about the intimate details of their sex lives?"

Ernie's eyes were as flat and lifeless as his voice. "No."

"Or been with you in your home, alone?"

"No."

"When did you and your wife separate, Mr. Nixon?"

Ernie folded his arms. "Less than a year ago."

"And after that, Marcie Calder started coming to your house, correct?"

"Sometimes, yes."

"How many times?"

"I didn't count, Mr. Lord."

"More than ten?"

With a kind of fascination, Tony saw Ernie Nixon wonder how closely Sarah Croff had watched him. "It could have been, yes."

"Could it, perhaps, have been more than twenty?"

Ernie's gaze broke. To cover this, he adjusted his tie. "Like I say, I didn't keep count."

"So you can't rule out the possibility that in the last six months of her life, Marcie Calder came to see you at your home, alone, more than twenty times?"

"No." Looking up, Ernie's eyes were cold. "I can't rule it out *or* in."

"How many hours might that have been, Mr. Nixon, alone with this sixteen-year-old girl?"

"I have no idea."

Tony put one finger to his lips, as though bemused. "What did you two talk about?"

Ernie arranged his features into an expression of weary disdain. "It's just as I said. Like a lot of kids, Marcie needed to talk about all sorts of things—her grades, her track, her friends, her parents—"

"That reminds me," Tony broke in, "did her parents know she came to your home?"

"I have no idea."

"But *you* didn't tell them?"

"No."

"Didn't you think they might be concerned?"

Ernie threw up his hands. "Look," he said, "I don't know if they knew or not. It wasn't anything I thought about."

Tony assumed a puzzled air. "What did *you* talk to Marcie about?"

"I don't remember. Mostly, I listened. . . ."

"About your marriage?"

Ernie's jaw set. "I really don't remember."

"You'd gone through a marital breakup, Marcie was constantly at your house, and you don't remember if you talked about it?"

"No."

Tony gave him a fleeting smile of disbelief. "While we're on the subject of memory, Mr. Nixon, isn't it possible that your memory on the subject of whether Marcie came to your house at night is somewhat faulty?"

Ernie stared up at him, silent. It was odd, Tony thought, how many people can persuade themselves that they are invisible and, as witnesses, forget that defense lawyers hire detectives. "What do you mean?" Ernie parried.

"What immediately pops to mind is those several Saturday nights when Marcie rented a video and brought it over to your house." Tony paused a moment. "Which one was your favorite—*Sabrina*, or *Love Story*?"

"Objection," Stella said. "That's not a question but an insinuation. If Mr. Lord has a question to ask, he should ask it."

For the first time, she was clearly rattled. Before Karoly could answer, Tony said, "I'll ask several," and turned to Ernie Nixon. "Did Marcie come to your house, alone, on at least four Saturday nights?"

Briefly, Ernie's throat worked, and then he assumed a look of attempted recall that Tony knew was feigned. "I seem to remember a few times like that, where she'd just show up." Pausing, Ernie made his voice dismissive. "It comes back to me that Janice D'Abruzzi had a new boyfriend she was seeing, and sometimes Marcie wanted company. She knew I was alone, with nothing much to do, so she'd bring a movie. Yeah, I remember that now."

"Where did you watch the movie?"

Ernie's face filled with anger. "In my basement. That's where the VCR is." His voice was hard. "Back when my family was together, and Marcie would baby-sit the kids, they'd sit downstairs and watch films together. It was something she liked."

"And something you liked."

Ernie gave a grudging nod. "Yes."

"And when the two of you watched movies, where did she sit?"

Ernie glanced toward Stella. But no help would be forthcoming, Tony knew; any objection would draw a lethal speech from Tony before Karoly overruled it. Tony noted with interest that Karoly himself had begun watching Ernie with an air of puzzlement and disapproval, which several jurors seemed to share.

"Sometimes she sat on the floor," Ernie said, "and sometimes on the couch."

"And you sat next to her."

"Sometimes."

"Other than watch a movie, what did you do?"

"Normal things. Made popcorn, talked about whether we liked the film. After it was over, she didn't stay long."

"Did you ever touch her, Mr. Nixon?"

"Absolutely not."

"Not even a goodnight kiss?"

With a look of outrage, Ernie straightened in his chair. "She was *sixteen*, Mr. Lord."

"Indeed. Where did her parents think she was?"

"I have no idea."

"But according to Mrs. Calder, they didn't know she was with you. Why would Marcie hide it?"

"I don't know that she did. Or why she would."

"No? And yet, when Ms. Marz asked you, you didn't tell the jury about any of these visits."

"They were *normal*, like I said. What stuck in my mind was how different she was the night she died."

Tony paused. "During these 'normal' Saturday nights when she'd come to see you, was it your understanding that Marcie had a boyfriend?"

"My understanding was that she didn't. Marcie could be shy. I don't think she always clicked with guys her own age."

"Was it your understanding, at *that* time, that Marcie Calder had ever had sex?"

As if it were a luxury, the anger left Ernie's eyes, replaced by the taut wariness of someone forced to think hard and guess quickly, not knowing where the traps were. "I assumed she hadn't. I don't recall we talked about that."

"So that six weeks before she died, when Marcie told you she'd begun having sex with an older man, you were surprised."

"Yes. I suppose I was."

"And jealous?"

"No—not jealous." Ernie paused, his voice trembling with fresh outrage. "I was *worried* for her. This was a sixteen-year-old girl, being exploited by an older man. . . ."

The answer trailed off. "An older man," Tony said softly, "who Marcie said was teaching her things."

Ernie's eyes filled with hatred and humiliation. His answer, "Yes," was a hiss of air.

Stay calm, Tony reminded himself. "And so, on the night she died, you asked her not to go to him."

"I wanted her to stop and think."

"And when she didn't, you followed her out the door."

"Yes."

"Did you touch her *then*?"

Ernie glanced at the jury. "What I may have done," he said at last, "was grasp her arm. Just so I could say one final thing."

"Which was?"

"Not to go."

"And when she did, you followed her."

"Yes."

Tony paused. "You followed her," he repeated softly, "to find out who the father was."

Ernie twisted in the witness chair, plainly aware of how this sounded now. "Yes."

"And you did, didn't you?" Pausing, Tony kept his own voice quiet. "You followed Marcie Calder to the gas station and saw her get in Sam Robb's car. And then you followed them to the park."

Ernie Nixon's chest heaved. "No," he said in a thick voice. "I came home. Like I said."

"When was that, Mr. Nixon?"

"About eight-thirty."

"Did anyone see you?"

Wearily, Ernie shook his head. "I don't know. Depends if they were watching me."

Tony walked closer. "You know Taylor Park well, don't you?"

There was silence. For himself, Tony would have given a great deal not to see the terrible look of betrayal Ernie gave him, personal and years deep; it reflected far too clearly the day a black teenager had taken a white one to the park, to express belief in his innocence. "You know that," Ernie answered softly. "When I was a kid, I played there."

"And hid there."

"Yes."

"Sometimes even slept there overnight."

"Yes."

"And you learned all the hiding places."

Ernie folded his arms again, his eyes expressionless once more. "I was a kid," he repeated. "Kids like hiding places. Grown-ups don't."

Tony cocked his head. "Do you have any way of proving that when Marcie Calder was in Taylor Park, you weren't watching her?"

Ernie looked at him steadily. "At ten-eighteen," he said, "I called my wife. I still have the record of the call."

It was Tony's first surprise. He imagined Stella, knowing or guessing Tony's intentions, grilling Ernie on any way he might eliminate, or narrow, time he could not account for; though it did not close the door, a ten-eighteen telephone call left Ernie precious little time to commit murder. With as much unconcern as he could muster, Tony asked, "How long did you talk to her?"

"I didn't. I got her machine."

"Did you leave a message?"

"No. There was nothing I wanted to say to a machine."

This could sound like an alibi, Tony saw at once—a call made to place Ernie in the house. In a tone of skepticism, Tony asked, "Why did you call in the first place?"

Ernie considered him. "To ask Dee if she'd come back," he answered softly. "Give me another chance."

"Had you talked about that?"

"Not for months." Ernie paused, looking directly at Tony. "That night, I thought about a lot of things. Dee was where my thoughts ended up. Dee, and our kids."

If he followed Ernie's psychology, Tony thought, this was at least plausible: a man, confronting where a semiconscious fantasy had taken him, jolted back to what was real and important. "Did you ask your wife to come back?"

Slowly, Ernie shook his head. "The next morning, it seemed hopeless. Something about the difference between darkness and sunlight."

It was, perhaps, true—or an excuse for not having a conversation that Ernie Nixon had never meant to have, offered to cover his lie now. But it led Tony, at last, to where he had known he must go since the night, three months before, when he had promised Sue Robb that he would try to give her an innocent husband.

Walking back to the defense table, Tony felt the jury follow him. With a fractional smile—the slightest narrowing of his eyes—Saul Ravin handed Tony a small manila envelope.

Unsealing it, Tony reached inside and extracted a black plastic watch. "Your Honor," he said. "I have here what has been proposed as defense Exhibit 1—as you see, a plastic watch. I ask the court to receive it into evidence, so that I can ask Mr. Nixon about it."

Judge Karoly turned to Stella. "Ms. Marz?"

Stella stood. "I don't understand what we're doing, Your Honor. To my knowledge, this watch has nothing to do with this case."

Tony stepped forward. "With counsel's indulgence, I'll ask one or two brief questions. Which may well prove her right. I can state for the record that I bought this at a drugstore yesterday."

Karoly raised his eyebrows. "Go ahead, Mr. Lord."

Quickly, Tony handed the watch to Ernie Nixon. "To your memory, Mr. Nixon, is this the type of watch Marcie Calder was wearing the night she died?"

Ernie fingered the watch, brow furrowed. "I really don't remember it."

"Please, take a good look."

Ernie turned it in his hand. "It really doesn't help," he said in a weary voice. "That night, the last thing I cared about was her watch."

Tony shrugged. "All right," he said, and took the watch from Ernie's hand.

Facing Judge Karoly, Stella said, "We *have* Marcie Calder's watch, Your Honor. *This* watch proves nothing and is therefore useless as an exhibit."

"Given Mr. Nixon's testimony," Tony said to Karoly, "we won't quarrel." Putting the watch back into the envelope, he handed it to Saul, who assumed a look of boredom and disinterest.

Once more, Tony turned to Ernie. Softly, he asked, "Do you consider yourself a violent man?"

Ernie sat straight again, achieving a credible, if tenuous, dignity. "No," he said tersely. "I don't."

"Then perhaps you can tell me why your marriage broke up."

"Dee and I had disagreements. She didn't like Lake City—"

"She didn't like being *hit*, did she?"

Despite himself, Ernie flinched. "Objection," Stella said. "Irrelevant."

Gazing at Judge Karoly, Tony spread his arms. "Do I have to spell it out, Your Honor?"

With narrowed eyes, Karoly studied the witness. "No. You don't. Objection overruled."

Turning to Ernie, Tony saw the beautician turn with him, as if demanding an answer. "I'll ask you again, Mr. Nixon. Did your wife object when you struck her on the face?"

Ernie's own face was suffused with shame and anger. "It only happened once—just once, in fifteen years of marriage—and you're talking to me like—"

"Did you hurt her?" Tony snapped.

"Yes. That once."

"And—that once—her lip bled, and her mouth became swollen."

Ernie exhaled. "Yes."

"And, within days, your wife left you."

"Yes."

"So, effectively, this marked the end of your marriage."

"It was a lot of things. . . ."

"What had your wife done, in your view, to earn being struck in the face? Let alone with enough force to do that."

"No woman deserves that. We'd fought, and Dee said things that hurt me, and I hit her without thinking. Right away, I apologized—"

"But by then," Tony cut in softly, "she was bleeding."

"Yes."

"You must have been quite angry, Mr. Nixon."

"Yes. I was. But only for that moment."

"A moment's all it takes. So perhaps you can tell us, precisely, what your wife said which caused you to lose control."

Ernie gazed at him with glassy eyes. "I don't remember."

"Really. Didn't the name of Marcie Calder come up?"

"I *don't* remember—"

"Specifically, didn't your wife call Marcie Calder your fantasy white girl and accuse you of wanting to sleep with her?"

Stuck with his evasion, unable to turn back, Ernie Nixon summoned all the dignity he possessed. Arms folded, he answered softly, "People say a lot of ugly things in a marriage. It's best not to remember them."

Tony gave Ernie the long look of disbelief he had earned. "Yeah," he said with equal quiet. "I might not want to remember that one, either. Especially now."

Ernie simply stared at him, his sensitive face stripped of all defenses, save the one Tony remembered from his youth, the weary fatalism of a boy taught to expect too little, whether in loyalty or in simple friendship. Suddenly Tony could not look at him.

"No further questions," he said to Karoly, and sat down. The last face he noticed, as he had at the beginning, was Sue's, looking at Tony with compassion.

It was a two-martini night. Midway through the second one, Tony began to imagine Ernie Nixon, pacing his empty home. What might his night be like, Tony wondered, and what might he face in the morning?

"Shit," he said aloud.

Saul shrugged. "What's a ruined life or two? You did your job." He paused, speaking more softly. "I hoped you wouldn't take this one. But now you have, and Sam's your client—*our* client. So there's no help for this."

"And there's nothing more pathetic than a lawyer enjoying the luxury of ex post facto conscience, is there? Wallowing in what a sensitive soul he is."

Saul looked around the smoky bar, one of several haunts he knew that, as he put it, still had patrons willing to look death in the face while they sucked it down their lungs. "Tell me," he said, "you think there's the remotest chance Ernie did her?"

"The very remotest. My guess is that Ernie looked bad not because he's a murderer but because there're some things he doesn't want to know about himself, and others he doesn't want anyone else to know. Which makes him like the rest of us." Tony took another sip. "But it's a theoretical possibility, which is what Sam needs."

Saul grimaced. "Even *he* didn't look that happy."

"Well, it wasn't pickup basketball, was it."

Saul paused a moment. "Not hardly," he said.

TEN

The next morning, the headline in the *Steelton Press* read: "Lord Attacks Key Witness as Suspect." The photograph next to that was of Ernie Nixon leaving court, gaze averted from the camera. Tony did not buy a copy.

Arriving, he felt a different atmosphere in court. There were more reporters, including one from *60 Minutes*; another, from *Vanity Fair*, wanted to interview

Tony regarding Alison Taylor. Sue and the Robb children, careful dark-haired Sam junior and tall blond Jennifer, sat in the front row, ignoring the media. But the Calders had begun speaking to reporters; knowing that their outrage at his questioning of Ernie had driven them to this, Tony had the melancholy awareness that those who start to feed the press often find this hard to stop.

Sam himself said little, other than to ask Tony whether he thought that Ernie Nixon had killed Marcie Calder. Tony had a troubling sense of subtext—that Sam had asked the question much as Saul had, without belief or anger. Wondering if this thought issued from his suspicions of Sam or from his own divided conscience, Tony gazed across the courtroom at Stella Marz.

Stella had the grim intensity of a lawyer who had suffered through a sleepless night. She had not acknowledged Tony on arriving and did not do so now. Studying her, Saul Ravin murmured to Tony, "It's war, for sure."

It struck Tony that Saul was faring better than he: throughout their strategy sessions, some quite late, Saul had controlled his drinking, and though his jowly face still looked tired, it was less flushed, and his brown eyes were bright and clear. Much like Sam, Tony thought to his surprise, although, unlike Sam's, Saul's renewed vitality raised no troubling questions.

"It is now," Tony agreed, and then Stella called Jack Seed.

The Lake City police detective was trim and courteous, with translucent gray eyes that lent a perceptive look to his face. From the first few questions, Tony saw that Seed was the perfect policeman for this jury—capable, methodical, and white, the image of authority for those who wished to trust it. The attentiveness of the jurors suggested that they did.

Quickly, Stella and Seed covered Marcie's disappearance—the discovery of Marcie's car behind the abandoned service station; the fruitless search of the nearby woods in the first light of a gray and drizzly morning; the absence of clues to Marcie's whereabouts or to the identity of the older lover described by Janice; Seed's surprise when Sam Robb, a man he had known for years, appeared at the police station to say that he had been with Marcie Calder the night before; and then, finally, the first moments in Taylor Park. Resting his arms on the table, Sam folded his hands in front of him, as though bracing for a long ordeal.

"So we got out of the car," Seed continued, "and walked in the direction Sam said Marcie Calder had been running. It was raining, and the grass was wet. But toward the edge of the cliff, where there was mud instead of grass, I found marks."

Stella paused, resting one hand on the prosecution table. "Could you describe the marks."

"They were what appeared to be prints from an athletic shoe—a man's, judging by size and shape, leading from the grass to the edge of the cliff. Next to the footprints, running parallel in the mud, were two shallow, irregular lines. To me, they looked like marks made by something being dragged. So we stepped around the footprints and followed them to the edge."

In the jury box, the nutritionist touched her eyes.

"And when you got to the edge, what did you see?"

Seed gazed at Stella steadily. "A sixty-foot drop. Then, near the bottom of the cliff, I saw the body of a woman—lying on her back. Even from a distance, it was clear that she was young and her hair was long and straight and black, like Marcie Calder's in the picture her folks had given us." Seed's voice became soft. "She was wearing a Lake City sweatshirt, just like her mom had said."

Nancy Calder, Tony saw, wept in silence. Awkwardly, her husband put his arm around her.

"And the defendant?" Stella asked quietly.

"He took one look at the body, then sat at the edge of the cliff. The only thing he said was, 'That's her.' "

"After that, what did *you* do?"

"I put Sam in the back of the car and called the EMTs, on the off chance Marcie was still alive. Then I called our crime lab people and the county coroner, and went down to look at the body." Seed paused, his eyes still, as if he were remembering how Marcie Calder had looked. "As soon as I touched her, I knew she was dead. The EMTs came, and then the crime lab folks. I directed them to mark off the crime scene—on the cliff and around Marcie's body—and then I took him back to the station."

The way Seed pronounced "him," suddenly impersonal, seemed to reflect the moment, still clear in Jack Seed's mind, when Sam had moved from friend to suspect. "Did you ask him to give a statement?" Stella asked.

"Yes, on a voluntary basis; he wasn't in custody, and we didn't know what we had here. What we needed was whatever Sam could give us."

"And what was his response?"

"That he'd do anything to cooperate." Briefly, Seed's voice betrayed a trace of sarcasm. "Tell us *all* he knew. So we took him to the witness room, Carl and I, and turned on the tape."

Tony remembered it well: the eight-by-eight cubicle where, twenty-eight years before, the cops Dana and McCain had subjected him to what was at once so traumatic and yet so surreal that his memory, though vivid, was as hallucinatory as his new nightmare of Alison. Tony's skin felt clammy, and beneath this, he experienced a reflexive sympathy for Sam.

"And what," Stella asked, "was the defendant's demeanor?"

Seed glanced at Sam again. "Grief-struck, it seemed like, and stunned. All he wanted, I remember him saying, was to help us."

"And do you have the tape of that interview?"

Tony, who had listened to it many times, wished fervently that the answer could be "no." When Seed identified the tape, and Stella slid it into a cassette player, Sam turned away.

Sam's voice filled the courtroom, oddly hollow on tape, yet resonant with emotion. This, Tony thought, was another reason why today might be the last time the jury heard from Sam Robb: they would remember too well the sound of his lies.

"It was a mistake," Sam's voice told Seed. "A terrible, stupid mistake. But I didn't know what Marcie wanted, and she seemed—I don't know—secretive and kind of desperate. She said no one could know what we'd talked about, or even see us. . . ." Sam's voice trailed off, and he murmured, "God help me, Jack, I thought it might be drugs or something—or maybe anorexia, emotional problems. She'd been looking so skinny. . . ."

"So she just hadn't seemed right to you?"

Jack Seed's tone was sympathetic, accepting: Tony found that there was a certain fascination in listening to two liars feign credulity, and wondered if either man had ever believed the other. "Yeah," Sam told Seed. "She'd missed practice yesterday, too."

"So she came around when practice was ending?"

"Uh-huh. That was another thing that was weird—missing practice, then showing up. But there were other kids there, and Marcie had to get home for dinner, I guess. That was why she wanted to talk later. At night."

"But not in your office."

"No." Sam sounded chastened. "She said that would look bad, and this couldn't wait. I began to think about drugs again—maybe that she knew the kids who were dealing. We've had a problem lately; I guess you know that. . . ."

"Yeah, I do. . . ."

"Shit, Jack—I just can't believe she's dead." Suddenly Sam's voice was thick. "How could this have happened?"

"I don't know, Sam. I don't know. All you can do is help us." Seed paused a moment. "I guess you told Sue about all this?"

In the silence of the spinning tape, the beautician glanced at Sue; Tony imagined the woman wondering if Sue could yet believe in her husband's innocence. "No," Sam's taped voice murmured. "I didn't, really. Only that I was working."

When Seed said nothing, Tony imagined Sam, fidgeting across the table. "I *know* Sue," Sam finally added. "She'd tell me it was stupid, and she'd have been right. But Marcie had this urgency . . . all she'd said is meet her at the gas station. I never imagined she'd want to go to the park, to be alone."

Taut, Tony watched Stella Marz, listening with veiled eyes. The knuckles of Sam's folded hands were white.

"So you met her at the gas station?" Seed was asking.

"Yeah." On the tape, Sam's pause for breath was audible, and there was a tremor in his voice. "It was so weird, Jack . . . just so weird. Marcie said she couldn't talk unless we were really alone. The way she was— tense, insistent—I thought maybe that she *was* scared of someone. Almost like she was afraid of being followed."

As he listened, Tony's skin felt cold. What chilled him was less Sam's lies than the way he told them: the stunned pauses, the bursts of disbelief, the palpable emotion. But the emotion could be real enough—fear and perhaps guilt—just as the disbelief could come from innocence, not of an affair, but of murder. The best lies, Tony remembered Sam saying, are based on truth. Then it struck Tony that Marcie *might* have been afraid of someone following her—Ernie Nixon.

"So," Jack Seed said softly, "you drove Marcie to the park."

"Yeah."

"What happened then?"

"Oh, man . . ."

Seed's voice was gentle now. "What is it, Sam?"

"Jack, she made a *pass* at me."

"A pass?"

"No. It was more than that." Sam's voice was low, awed by the memory of where he had found himself. "As sweetly as you could imagine, this young girl I thought I knew said that she was in love with me and wanted to have an affair."

The faces of the listening jurors were hard—whatever they came to believe about the murder, Tony thought, for the rest of the trial they would despise Sam Robb. In the silence of the tape, Seed pondering his response, Tony saw Sue close her eyes. Jennifer took her mother's hand and, almost imperceptibly, Sam junior moved closer. Beyond them, Marcie's parents stared straight ahead, as if they could not bear to look at Sam.

On the tape, Seed asked, "What did you say to her, Sam?"

"God." It was the astonished voice of a man recalling his own shock. "I was so taken aback, I don't recall saying anything right away. So she took my hand and put it beneath her sweatshirt. She wasn't wearing a bra. . . .

"It was like an electric charge, and it woke me up to everything. I was in a car at night, touching the breast of a sixteen-year-old girl who wanted me. It was like suddenly I could see myself—how stupid I'd been, how much trouble this could be, that I'd never understood her." Sam's voice fell. "When I pulled my hand away, she said, '*No*—I want you.' "

Listening, Tony realized how close this was to a story only he had heard—Sam's version of his "seduction" by Marcie Calder, told with the same sincerity. But what unnerved Tony was not simply the question of whether this was another truth-based lie, borrowed with skill from Marcie's actual behavior, but whether, in the recesses of his psyche, Sam had a need for young girls to desire him.

"What happened then?" Seed was asking.

"I panicked. 'That's crazy,' I remember saying, and then got ahold of myself. 'Look,' I said, 'we can't do this. You're sixteen, and I'm responsible for you. It's not the kind of thing people should ever do.' Then I told her if she really cared about me, she'd think about the trouble this could be for me. *And* Sue.

"Marcie started crying. She just sobbed, couldn't even talk." Suddenly Sam's voice was swollen with regret. "I should have realized how troubled she was, Jack. But I was so scared for my own ass that I just waited for a minute and then put my hands on her shoulders and said, 'We have to go, Marcie. Really, we need to leave here. Before someone gets the wrong idea.' "

At last, Stella Marz caught Tony's gaze, eyebrows raised in an expression of weary disgust. Behind her, the grocer's face closed, and the warehouseman stared at his hands.

"How did Marcie react?" Seed asked quietly.

Sam's voice was tired, flat. "She pushed open the door. Before I could stop her, she was running away toward the lake. I started after her. . . ." The words trailed off.

"And then what?"

"I stopped, and got back in the car. I was too afraid of being seen." Sam's voice was nearly inaudible. "I let an upset, emotionally troubled girl run off into the night, alone. And now I can imagine her, stumbling over that cliff. . . ."

In the courtroom, tears began running down Sam Robb's face.

The nutritionist stared at him in bewilderment. Sam held his head rigid, not wiping the dampness from his face, as if he did not notice it.

Astonished, Tony watched him. If this was a simulation of grief, Tony thought, then Sam Robb was truly a man to fear. But other than his actress wife, Tony knew almost no one who could cry on cue. And this part of the story—Marcie vanishing—was exactly as Sam had told it to him: with respect to the charge of murder, it was the part that truly mattered.

"I drove off," Sam was telling Seed. "Just left her there. For a second, my front beams caught a car that had parked behind us, and then I saw a head above the dashboard. I can't tell you if it was a man's head or a woman's, or what kind of car it was. I just wanted to get away." Faltering, Sam's voice filled with grief and shame. "Marcie could get back to her car, I told myself. After all, it was only a quarter mile. . . ."

There was a long silence. Gently, Seed asked, "Have you told Sue now?"

"No." Sam's voice broke altogether. "No . . ."

As if Sue's name had awakened him, Sam wiped the tears from his face. And then Stella Marz switched off the tape.

Quickly, she was on her feet. "Shortly afterward, Detective Seed, did you visit Sam Robb's home?"

Jack Seed paused a moment, as though still reflecting on the tape, its damning portrait of a man Seed once thought he had known. "Yes. With Detective Talley."

"And what did you do?"

"We impounded the Volvo he'd been driving. To search for physical evidence."

"And what, if anything, did you find?"

Seed looked at Sam. "A smear of what appeared to be blood," he answered, "on the steering wheel."

"And did you send a sample to the county coroner's office for analysis? Along with a sample of Mr. Robb's blood?"

"Yes."

"Did the blood type of the sample from the steering wheel match that of the defendant?"

He could object, Tony knew. But the coroner would only confirm it, and Tony would appear to be another tiresome lawyer, quibbling about the truth. Silent, he watched Seed shake his head. "Mr. Robb's blood type was O. The blood in the car was AB."

Stella put her hands on her hips. "And what was Marcie Calder's blood type?"

"The same." Seed's voice was flat. "Type AB."

"And during your investigation, did you take anything else that belonged to Mr. Robb?"

Slowly, Seed nodded. "We took the clothes Sam told us he'd been wearing that night. And a pair of tennis shoes, to compare to the footprints we'd found by the edge of the cliff."

"What size were the footprints?"

"Size eleven."

Stella paused. "And Mr. Robb's tennis shoes?"

Tony knew the size. But the jury did not. And so, for the first time, Seed looked at them.

"Size eleven," he answered.

ELEVEN

Facing Jack Seed, Tony reflected that he seemed the kind of cop that Tony himself, were he living in a small town, would want—capable, straightforward, concerned. "Just for the record, Detective Seed, you knew Sam Robb prior to Marcie Calder's disappearance, correct?"

Seed nodded. "That's right. He's lived in Lake City all his life, I'm pretty sure, and he's been vice principal at the high school for years."

"Before Mr. Robb appeared at the police station, did

you consider asking him where Marcie Calder might be?"

Pausing, Seed glanced at Sam with puzzlement. "No."

"In fact, you were unaware of *any* connection between Marcie and Sam Robb."

"That's right. Except for his job, like with any student."

"Nor did you have any idea where Marcie had been that night."

"No."

"In fact, you found her body *when* you did because Sam Robb took you to Taylor Park?"

Seed frowned. "It was only a matter of time, and not very much time. But yes, that's true."

Tony made his voice slow and quite deliberate. "Since you found the body, Detective Seed, has anyone in Lake City—other than Sam Robb himself—come forward to connect him with Marcie Calder?"

Eyes narrow, Seed seemed to consider this. "No one has."

Tony glanced at the jury, noting their attentiveness, and then saw that Stella Marz was already poised to object. "So," he went on, "the only reason Sam Robb is sitting here, charged with Marcie Calder's death, is because *he* came to *you* when Marcie was reported missing."

"Objection," Stella said at once. "The question calls for speculation. We can only know what *did* happen—not what *would* have happened given a different chain of events."

Karoly nodded. "Sustained."

Tony was prepared for this: he had made his point with the jury and was ready with a question to which Stella could not object. "But you've found *no one* in Lake City who can link Sam Robb, by name, to the events surrounding Marcie's death?"

Seed slowly shook his head. "No, sir. We have not."

"No one else has even placed Sam Robb in Taylor Park that night, correct?"

"That's correct."

"So even now, you still have no other witness who could tie Mr. Robb to the events surrounding Marcie's death."

"No."

This was more than enough, Tony thought, to suggest Sam's candor with the police, and to belabor it created a problem: if Sam Robb was the only witness, he could imagine the jury wondering, should he not testify on his own behalf? Promptly, Tony moved to his next point. "Based on your knowledge of the law," he asked, "did you consider that by coming to you, Sam Robb might damage his career? Even lose his job?"

"Objection," Stella called out. "There's no foundation for assuming that this witness knows *what* the consequences might be. Also, it calls for speculation."

Karoly, Tony saw, looked curious. But the objection was a good one. "Sustained," he said to Tony. "Maybe you can ask some other way."

"Thank you, Your Honor." Tony turned back to Seed. "Sam Robb came to you, voluntarily, to tell you where and when he'd been with Marcie Calder."

"Yes."

Tony paused. "Doesn't it make sense to you," he asked, "that Sam Robb wouldn't want to admit to the kind of relationship which would end his career?"

"Objection," Stella said with asperity. "What makes sense to this witness might *not* make sense to Mr. Robb."

"Sustained," Karoly ruled. But this was what Tony had anticipated; once more he had made his point with the jury.

He faced Jack Seed again. "After Mr. Robb's voluntary statement, you asked him for a blood sample, correct?"

"Yes."

"And Mr. Robb also gave that voluntarily?"

"Yes."

"And, as you've already mentioned, let you visit his home."

"One or two days later, yes."

"At that time, Mr. Robb also gave you the clothes and shoes he'd worn that night."

Seed paused. "The ones he said he'd worn, yes."

"Until the time that *I* stepped in, Sam Robb had no lawyer, correct?"

"Not that we saw."

"And not until after you impounded his car."

"That's right."

"That period was roughly a week?"

"Yes."

"During that time, did Mr. Robb ever refuse any request for information?"

Seed's lips thinned. "No, sir. He did not."

"After you impounded his car, Mr. Robb told you he'd called a lawyer, right? Someone who also was an old friend."

"Yes."

"And, for the record, that lawyer was me."

"That's what he said."

"Did Sam Robb also tell you that I'd advised him that, in the future, I should speak for him?"

"He did."

Tony cocked his head. "As of that time, Detective Seed, were the Lake City police investigating any other suspects?"

Seed folded his arms. "We were considering any possibility that the facts suggested."

"Including suicide? Or accident?"

"Yes."

"But was there any other individual you considered to be a suspect should this become a murder case?"

Seed considered this. "What I'd have to say, Mr. Lord, is that no other individual ever *became* a suspect."

It was a skillful answer. For a moment, Tony hesitated, and then he saw his next question. "Isn't it true that once you found the blood on the steering wheel of Mrs. Robb's Volvo, and further found that Mr. Robb's shoe size matched that of the footprint by the edge of the cliff, you focused on Sam Robb as the *sole* suspect in a potential murder prosecution?"

Seed paused, and then Tony saw him decide on candor. "Certainly the primary suspect. But we also had his statement, placing him at the scene."

"Precisely. But based on your experience, *and* the files of your department, aren't there a fair number of people who pass through Taylor Park at night?"

"Yes."

"You've had a problem with drug dealers there, correct? As well as transients and homeless people who stay in the park at night?"

"That's true."

"In the course of investigating the death of Marcie Calder, did you make inquiries with respect to violent crimes in other nearby localities?"

"Not specifically."

"Or review records of sex crimes occurring in Lake City, or nearby, within the past few years?"

"We did not." For the first time, Seed sounded defensive. "From the evidence as it developed, we were satisfied that this was not a random event and that Sam Robb had motive, means, and opportunity."

Tony paused for a moment. "Are you familiar with the last homicide which occurred in Lake City? The murder of Alison Taylor?"

Tony felt a stirring in the gallery; to his side, the *Vanity Fair* reporter looked up sharply from his notes. Seed appraised Tony with open curiosity. "Not personally," he said at last. "The Taylor case was before my time, and there's no one still on the force who worked on it."

"But you're aware that no charges were brought?"

"Yes, sir." Seed's tone was dry. "Recent events have brought that to my attention."

"Then you must also be aware that one suspect in that case was a transient, Donald White, with a prior record of sexual assaults and *no* prior connection to the victim, Alison Taylor?"

"I'm aware of that, yes."

"Are you further aware that what first focused attention on Donald White was a search of police records in other jurisdictions?"

"Objection," Stella said. "There's no foundation that this witness has any personal knowledge." Pausing, she glanced at Tony. "Moreover, the facts of the Taylor murder—whatever they might be—are irrelevant to this one. Except in counsel's mind."

"The *facts* are irrelevant," Tony said to Karoly. "But the methodology is very relevant. My question, Your Honor, is whether the Lake City police considered the methodology used in the Alison Taylor murder to investigate the death of Marcie Calder. As we believe they should have."

Judge Karoly frowned at Tony, clearly befuddled by this flirtation with the facts of Tony's own life. "On that basis," he said finally, "you can have your answer." Turning to Seed, he asked, "Did you contact other jurisdictions for information about similar crimes?"

It could not be better, Tony thought—for the jury, the question now bore the imprimatur of the judge. "No," Seed answered. "Based on the facts of this case, we were absolutely satisfied that we knew who was responsible."

"So," Tony put in quickly, "you did not investigate anyone other than Sam Robb, whether known to Marcie Calder or not?"

"We certainly made inquiries about other people Marcie knew, including friends or boys she may have dated. But nothing resulted which gave us reason to suspect them."

"Including Ernie Nixon?"

Seed sat back, folding his hands. "We did not consider Ernie Nixon to be a suspect."

There was something missing in the answer, Tony thought; it seemed careful, considered. "Do you now?" Tony asked.

The answer "yes," Tony knew, would end the case in moments. Slowly, Seed shook his head. "We do not."

"When did you first meet Mr. Nixon?"

"Four, maybe five years ago. When Mr. Nixon came to run the rec center." Seed paused. "My kids go there a lot."

"When he came to tell you he'd seen Marcie Calder the night she died, were you surprised?"

Seed shrugged. "I can't say I was or wasn't."

"Is it fair to say, then, that your attention was focused on how Mr. Nixon's story fit the case against Sam Robb?"

"What *I'd* say, Mr. Lord, is that we were interested in whether what Ernie Nixon told us—that Marcie was pregnant, that she was going to see the father—might shed light on her death."

"Fair enough." For a split second, Tony paused. "At that time, were you aware that Marcie Calder was a frequent visitor to Mr. Nixon's home?"

Seed glanced at Stella Marz. "I was not."

"Did you ever search *his* house?"

"No."

"Or Mr. Nixon's car?"

"No."

"Or take any article of his clothing?"

"No."

"Or take a sample of his blood?"

"No."

Tony skipped a beat. The next question was a risk, he knew; not knowing the answer, he could be walking into a trap, set by Stella. But to set it, Tony knew, she would have to take a risk herself. Softly, he asked, "Or check his shoe size?"

Seed folded his hands. "At what time?"

He had been right, Tony knew—Stella *had* found out, but not until Tony had tried to implicate Ernie Nixon. "At any time," he said.

"Yes." Seed looked grim. "We did."

"And when was that?"

"Approximately three days ago."

Tony could feel his own tension. But there was no choice now; the questioning had gone too far. "And what," he asked, "was Mr. Nixon's shoe size?"

Seed's face became opaque. "Size eleven."

Tony felt relief course through him, overwhelming his ambivalence. He could sense the jury stirring with surprise. Confidence renewed, Tony asked, "So based on size, the footprints by the edge of the cliff could have been Sam Robb's, Ernie Nixon's, or someone else's altogether."

"Yes."

"All you know for sure is that the *tread* didn't match any tennis shoe you found at Sam Robb's home."

Seed hesitated. "That's true."

"Nor did you find any blood on Mr. Robb's clothes, or in his home."

"No."

Pausing, Tony shoved his hands in his pockets. "Wouldn't you expect to, judging from the nature of Marcie Calder's injuries?"

Seed paused, resistant now. "Not if Sam Robb, as we believe, got rid of the clothes he'd been wearing."

Then Sue Robb *would have noticed,* Tony thought. But this was not a point he could make without calling her as a witness—which, next to calling Sam himself, was the last thing Tony wanted. "But you have no idea, do you, when and how Mr. Robb could have disposed of what he was wearing?"

"Not at this time, no."

"And you never found any clothes with bloodstains—either *in* Sam Robb's house or at the school, where Mr. Robb told you he went after Marcie left his car."

"That's right."

"Or any traces of blood in his office?"

"No."

Tony stood straighter. "What *did* Sam tell you he was wearing?"

"A sweatshirt and sweatpants. The ones he gave us."

"Do you have any evidence that he *didn't* wear them that night?"

Seed gave him the measured gaze of a man trying to maintain his patience. "There *was* the blood on the steering wheel, Mr. Lord."

This was the answer Tony had hoped for. "Did you consider that an important piece of evidence?"

Seed shrugged. "Important? We didn't go right out and indict him." When Tony simply stared at him, silent, Seed added grudgingly, "At the time, we thought it could be significant."

Pausing, Tony framed his final question with care. "And at the time, did this trace of blood help persuade you that Sam Robb—and not someone else—was the potential murderer?"

Seed gave Tony a querying glance. At length, he answered, "Yes. It did."

"Do you have any notion how it got in Mrs. Robb's car? Based on personal knowledge, that is."

Again, Seed hesitated. "No, Mr. Lord. Not personal knowledge. But there's no way Mr. Nixon put it there, and I sure know *we* didn't."

Tony gazed at him a moment, silent. "Thank you," he said politely. "I have nothing more."

TWELVE

Walter Gregg, the Lake City crime lab specialist, had wire-rim glasses, a neat mustache, intense blue eyes, a thin, ascetic face. To Tony, he looked like either a scholar or a terrorist. But his voice and manner were a scholar's— dry and precise—even when Stella Marz took a color photograph of Marcie Calder's too-pallid face and pinned it to the bulletin board.

Marcie gazed at the jury, eyes frozen in death, the ribbon of blood purple on her cheek. For Tony, a moment passed before he could shake his instinctive recall of Alison Taylor. Then he glanced at Marcie's parents.

They were pale and motionless, their fixed gaze at the photograph an eerie replication of their daughter's. Next to Tony, Sam did not look at the photograph; at Tony's instance, Sue and her children were gone. Some of the jurors stared at Walter Gregg as though, like Sam, they found Marcie's face too painful. But no one, now, would forget the victim.

Yes, Gregg told Stella Marz, the photograph was his. So was the photo of footprints above the cliff, the peculiar scars in the mud beside them. This was the second of six photographs Gregg had taken, arrayed in a collage around Marcie's picture; with every photograph, the jury would be forced to look at her again.

Stella pointed to the third photograph. "And what is this, Detective Gregg?"

"It's a photograph of Marcie Calder's tennis shoes." Leaving the witness stand, Gregg stood next to Stella, placing a finger on the photograph. "What's important is the mud caked on the toe of each shoe, and nowhere else. According to our analysis, the composition of the dirt on these shoes corresponds to that in the marks running parallel to the footprints. Taken together, they suggest that the victim was dragged to the edge of the cliff and that the marks were made by the toes of her shoes."

"Where were the footprints and marks, Detective Gregg, relative to the location of Marcie Calder's body?"

"Directly above it."

Quickly, Stella moved to the next photograph; taken with Marcie's body at the foreground, it scanned the cliffside. "And what," Stella asked, "does Exhibit D-4 portray?"

"This shows the perspective from the victim's body, lying at the base of the cliff."

"Could you describe the geologic composition of the cliff?"

"Yes. It's almost entirely clay, and a little shale. Both the clay and the shale are quite soft."

"Would you describe the hill as rocky?"

"Not particularly. When I say shale, I mean slivers which crumble to the touch."

"And did you inspect the cliffside?"

"We did. In quadrants, four square feet at a time."

"What did you find?"

"We found a trail of crumbled shale and clay leading to Marcie's body. The fact that the mud found on Marcie Calder's jeans and sweatshirt were of the same composition confirmed that the trail was caused by the fall of her body."

"Did the clay or shale you describe contain any traces of blood?"

"We found none, no. That helped us conclude that Marcie's injuries were *not* caused by her fall."

Stella cocked her head. "Did you find *other* materials on the beach itself?"

"We did." Pausing, Gregg touched the fifth photograph. "A rock, shown here in Exhibit D-5."

"Could you describe the rock?"

Gregg nodded. "As this picture shows, it is oblong,

roughly the size of a football. It was smeared with blood and a few dark strands of hair."

"Did you subsequently weigh the rock?"

"We did. It was quite heavy, roughly ten pounds."

Stella touched one finger to her lips. "Where did you find the rock," she asked, "relative to the body?"

Gregg pointed toward the final picture. "The rock was situated in the sand, further from the base of the cliff. This photograph, Exhibit D-6, shows the distance between the rock and the body. When we measured it, the distance was over seven feet."

"Did you subsequently remove the rock and seal it in an evidence bag?"

"We did."

Slowly, Stella walked to her desk, reached into a storage box, and removed a glassine bag that contained an oblong rock. As she carried it toward Gregg, cupped in both hands to suggest its weight, the jury gazed at the rock. Even at a distance, Tony—whose own expert had inspected it—could see the red-orange stain.

"Jesus . . . ," Sam murmured. To the side, Tony saw Nancy Calder crying as her husband stared ahead.

"Is this," Stella asked softly, "premarked as Exhibit 6, the rock you found on the beach?"

Gregg made no move to touch it. Gazing downward at the rock, still cradled in Stella's palms, he answered, "Yes. It is."

"Your Honor," Stella said, "I would like to tender this exhibit to the jury."

One by one, the jurors passed the rock, sometimes quickly, always gingerly. The beautician, holding it, gazed from the rock to the photograph of Marcie.

Quietly, Stella resumed her questioning. "Did you subsequently submit this rock—Exhibit 6—to the county coroner's office for testing?"

"We did."

"What did the coroner report with respect to the rock?"

"The results of DNA testing. To which, I believe, the defense has stipulated." Gregg's voice remained clinical. "The coroner's office concluded that the blood on the rock was Marcie Calder's, that the strands of hair were Marcie Calder's, and that the surface of the rock had traces of skin tissue. The tissue was from Marcie Calder's scalp, the area where I observed the lacerations which accounted for the ribbon of blood on her face."

"Did your search uncover any *other* objects which, in your opinion, could account for those head wounds?"

"No. We found no heavy objects, or rocks of this size, whether on the cliff or closer to the body."

Gregg, Tony knew, was systematically destroying the defense of accident or suicide, and now Stella meant to drive this home. "Did you form an opinion," she asked, "as to how a rock with Marcie Calder's blood and hair and tissue on it wound up over seven feet from her body?"

"Objection." Tony stood. "We concede that Ms. Marz has qualified Detective Gregg as an expert with respect to the conduct of crime scene investigation. But there's *nothing* in his credentials or in the record to suggest that the 'opinion' Ms. Marz asks for is any better than anyone's guess."

Stella's gaze at Tony was ostentatiously unimpressed. "Your Honor," she said, "the witness can state the factual basis when he states his opinion. If the court considers the basis inadequate, it can so instruct the jury." Her voice took on a weary sarcasm. "As for expertise, I somehow think that this witness's extensive education and professional experience qualify him to opine on how a ten-pound rock managed to travel quite so far."

When Karoly, turning, raised his eyebrows, Tony knew that objection had been a mistake: the judge's expression was a silent comment on Tony's effrontery. "Overruled," he said in his flattest voice. "Do you have the question in mind, Detective Gregg?"

"Yes, Your Honor," Gregg answered. "My opinion is that someone took the rock from above the cliff, struck Marcie Calder on the head, and threw both her body and the rock off the edge of the cliff." Pausing, he gave Tony a brief sardonic glance. "As to how I reached that opinion, there are a number of factors.

"First, there are several rocks of a similar composition near the footprints above the cliff. We found no such rocks near the trail caused by Marcie's fall.

"Second, there were no footprints near the rock, or near the body. Marcie Calder didn't walk there, and no one walked the rock another seven feet.

"Third, Marcie Calder did not bludgeon herself to death with a ten-pound rock. She wasn't strong enough, and if she were, who threw it off the cliff?

"Fourth, it *is* a ten-pound rock. If Marcie's head had hit it in some accident, or in a fall, how could it travel so far from her body, *and* so far from the bottom of the cliff where the body ended up? Not plausible.

"Fifth, of course, are the marks above the cliff. They're almost four feet long. Even if she fell, the toes of her shoes—which I believe made those marks— wouldn't have made so long a trail. In my opinion, Marcie Calder was dragged to the edge of the cliff.

"Sixth, Marcie's body was heavier than a rock. Even someone with considerable strength could not have hurled a one-hundred-and-five-pound body very far out from the cliff. Ten pounds of a football-shaped rock is something else again. . . ."

Abruptly, Gregg stopped, as if he had lost track of the many reasons why his opinion was clearly right. When Tony looked to his side, the jurors were riveted.

"Oh, yes," Gregg added. "The rock was lying in a deep

indentation in the sand, as shown by"—he glanced over his shoulder—"Exhibit D-5. Like it had landed hard." He paused, as if aware that this was not his most compelling point; this hesitance made his demeanor, before somewhat robotic, suddenly quite human. It had been several trials, Tony realized, since he had seen a police department criminologist who seemed as credible.

"I guess that's all," Gregg finished abruptly.

Stella paused for dramatic effect. "When you found her, Detective Gregg, was Marcie Calder wearing a watch?"

"She was, yes. It was a blue Swatch—plastic and rubber."

Stella held out a glassine bag, containing a watch. "Is this the watch—premarked as Exhibit 7?"

Gregg turned the bag in his hands. "I believe so."

"And were you able to lift any fingerprints?"

"There were three distinct prints. One print, as you might expect, was Marcie Calder's. Another was unidentified."

"And the third print?"

"It belonged to the defendant, Mr. Robb."

Stella moved closer. "With respect to the smear of blood which the police found on the steering wheel, did you also submit a sample of *that* blood to the coroner's office?"

Gregg nodded. "I did. For DNA testing."

"And what, if anything, did the lab report to you?"

Once more, Tony was silent; to object would only worsen the inevitable. Gregg's gaze took in Tony and Sam, then the jury, their faces keen and attentive. "That the blood on the steering wheel was the *victim's*, Marcie Calder's."

In silent accusation, Nancy Calder turned to Sam Robb. "It's all right," Tony murmured to Sam. "It's all right."

"No further questions," Stella said.

THIRTEEN

During the recess, Tony asked the courtroom deputy to put away Stella's exhibits. When the jury returned, and Tony commenced his cross-examination, Marcie Calder's photograph was gone.

Keep it short, Tony told himself. *Get what you can get, and get out.* He was glad that Sue had not been in court to watch.

Rising, he faced Gregg with a look of puzzlement. "Did you test the *rock* for fingerprints?"

"Yes, sir. There were none."

"What about the third print on the watch, the one you couldn't identify? Did you run it through your own records, and those of other jurisdictions?"

Gregg nodded. "We did. We couldn't get a match."

"All right. You've already testified that the blood on the rock was Marcie Calder's, right?"

"That's correct."

"There was quite a bit of blood on that rock, wasn't there?"

"Yes, sir. There was."

"And *you* believe that all that blood got on the rock when someone—you don't know who—bludgeoned Marcie Calder."

Gregg smoothed a crease in his suit. "Yes. I do."

"But you're not an expert in forensic medicine."

"No, I'm not."

"So your opinion is not based on the injury itself, but something else. Like that the rock was seven feet from the body."

"Yes."

Tony put his hands on his hips. "The sand on that beach was packed down hard, wasn't it?"

"It was."

"So couldn't the rock have rolled there?"

"A rock that heavy? I don't believe so, and besides, there were no marks in the sand to suggest it had."

"Might not the rain account for that?"

Gregg hesitated. "It might."

"And if the rock were knocked loose by Marcie's fall, it would have a certain momentum as it went down the cliff, correct? Especially one that heavy."

"It *could*. But enough to roll an additional seven feet? I doubt that very much."

There was no more to be gained here, Tony thought. "If, as you believe, Marcie Calder was struck by someone standing above the cliff, that would have created a spray of blood, wouldn't it?"

"It might."

"And *did*, in this case?"

"It appears so, Mr. Lord. We found blood on both Marcie's sweatshirt and her blue jeans."

"Did you find any blood on the bluff itself?"

Gregg paused again. "No, sir. We didn't."

"Wouldn't you expect to?"

"Ordinarily." Gregg shifted his weight. "But by the time we found Marcie Calder, it had been raining—or drizzling—for at least seven hours. As you pointed out."

"But you *looked* for blood, right? On the mud, on the grass—in fact, in a fifty-square-foot area surrounding the footprints and what you refer to as the 'drag marks'?"

Gregg nodded; like any good expert, he knew when not to quibble. "We found nothing, Mr. Lord."

"And you also found no blood in Mr. Robb's home, or on the clothes and shoes he gave you."

"No, sir. We did not."

"Wouldn't the murderer, in the scenario you imagine, have a splatter of blood all over him? The same as Marcie?"

"I believe so, yes."

"And yet you found no evidence that Mr. Robb discarded any article of clothing."

Gregg adjusted his glasses. "At this time, we're aware of none."

"Where did you search for discarded clothing?"

"In the park, in the woods nearby, and, a few days later, at Lake City High School."

Tony paused, considering his next question. Softly, he asked, "Have you searched any private residence *since* Mr. Robb was indicted?"

Gregg gave him a cool look. "We have not."

"And with respect to Mr. Robb, the only evidence of Marcie Calder's blood was on the steering wheel of his car."

"Yes, sir."

Tony paused. "Apart from whatever theory you may have, you have no *factual basis* for knowing how Marcie Calder's blood could have gotten on Sam Robb's steering wheel?"

At the corner of his vision, Tony saw Stella stir, then reconsider, placing confidence in her expert. "My *theory* has a factual basis, Mr. Lord." Pausing, Gregg considered his further answer. "But no—I wasn't there. So I can't *know* how that smear of blood got there."

Abruptly, Tony's manner became more relaxed, discursive. "Let me ask you, as an expert witness, to assume for a moment that what I tell you is true. All right?"

Gregg hesitated. "All right."

"We'll keep assuming that this is murder, not something else. In fact, we'll assume practically everything that you *now* assume—that Marcie Calder was struck with this rock; that the murderer threw her body *and* the rock off the cliff where you found the footprints; that he or she got rid of blood-spattered clothes; and that the drizzle falling later that night washed away any blood on the ground. Still with me?"

"Of course."

"Let's change one simple fact. Just assume—for this purpose—that I've proven to you that there's an innocent explanation for that smear of Marcie Calder's blood on the steering wheel. It could be a cut finger; that really doesn't matter."

Gregg's face looked tighter, his cheeks more hollow. Softly, he answered, "All right. I'll assume that."

Tony cocked his head. "What does that do to the physical evidence that *Sam Robb*, as opposed to someone else, committed this hypothetical murder?"

Gregg grimaced. "Well, it weakens it. Assuming what you say—"

"*Weakens* it." Tony's voice rose in incredulity. "There *isn't* any, is there? Not a scrap."

"Not true." As Gregg paused, Tony watched him thinking. "There's the defendant's fingerprint."

"Ah, yes. The fingerprint. Of course, you've no idea how *that* got on Marcie Calder's watch, do you?"

"No, sir."

Pausing, Tony asked softly, "Or who the *other* print belongs to."

"No, sir," Gregg conceded. "I said that."

Tony moved closer. "All right. Let's get back to the smear of blood, then. When you sent the sample to the laboratory, did you ask them to test for foreign substances?"

"What do you mean? Like alcohol, or HIV?"

"No." Tony moved forward. "I mean any substance in the blood which is *foreign* to blood."

Gregg looked concerned; for once, it was clear, he did not see where Tony was going. "No," he said defensively. "I didn't specifically request that, and the lab did not report any 'foreign substances,' as you describe them."

Tony nodded. "Thank you," he said, and sat down, feeling the jury's puzzlement, knowing that, in the last two hours, Gregg had pushed him closer to a defense based on Ernie Nixon.

"Suicide looks bad," Saul said that night.

Tony stared out Saul's window at Steelton's skyline, the lights flickering and irregular, like a power outage. He must not let his thoughts dwell on what had really happened, he reminded himself, but only on what *could* have happened that would make his friend and client innocent of murder. "You're right," Tony finally answered. "A pregnant girl in despair is a tough sell now, and the jury will remember that I tried it."

Saul did not argue with him; among professionals, his look said, there was no point skirting the truth. "At least you had something going by the end."

Tony smiled a little. "So what would you give me, Professor? Maybe a C?"

Saul smiled as well. "A B-plus for cross-examination and a D for dumb objections." He sat back, serious now. "You were okay. But you're looking tired. More tired than a trial lawyer can afford."

It was true, Tony knew. During trial, adrenaline kept him going, but the nightly crashes were harder, longer, offering exhaustion without relief. "I'm not sleeping well," he said.

Saul frowned. "Is it this case? Or is that the usual?"

"No. It's not the usual." It was pointless, Tony thought, to talk about nightmares: in the early hours of the morning, when he finally slept, sleep did not last long. He took a deep swallow of Saul's single-malt Scotch.

Saul, Tony noticed, was not drinking. "Maybe I can help," Saul said at last. "Take a witness or two." There was compassion in Saul's eyes, Tony thought, and, more than that, a need to prove to himself, and perhaps to Tony, that he was not a burned-out case. "Of course,"

Saul finished, "speaking personally, I don't give a shit about our client. But maybe that helps."

This was so mordant, and so true, that it made Tony smile again. He gazed at Saul with real affection. "I'll hold the thought," he answered.

FOURTEEN

It was after nine when Tony returned to his hotel room, tired and hungry, meaning to order a sandwich from room service and outline his cross-examination of Stella's next witness, the coroner. Then he opened the door and found Sue Cash Robb sitting on the end of his bed.

She was dressed in a navy-blue suit, as though for court, and looked at him quietly before saying, "I hope this is all right."

Closing the door, Tony stood there, feeling the tingle of surprise and alarm, yet pleasure in seeing her alone and away from the trial. "Of course," he answered. "Are *you* all right?"

Almost imperceptibly, she shook her head. "I came back to court today. Without Sam and Jenn—I'm sending them home."

Tony put his hands in his pockets. "I didn't see you."

"I know. I sat in back, so nobody would."

"How much did you see?"

"Most of the prosecutor's questions. All of yours."

"Jesus, Sue." Tony walked across the room and sat next to her, taking her hand. "You've done enough. I didn't want you having to watch that."

"Do you think I haven't thought about her?"

"No. But *seeing* is different." Tony paused. "I've seen hundreds of pictures like the one of Marcie Calder's face, many much worse. But that one bothered me quite a lot."

She was quiet for a time. Though she still watched him, something in her gaze seemed inward, directed at her own thoughts; once more, Tony had the sense that she had come to tell him something that he did not wish to hear. But all that she said, finally, was, "Marcie Calder didn't kill herself, did she?"

Tony exhaled. "I don't think so, no."

"Then it comes down to Ernie Nixon." Pausing a moment, Sue finished softly: "Or a stranger."

Tony did not answer directly. "I think I can win this, Sue."

She turned from him, looking out his hotel window at much the same view, random lights in darkness, that Tony had watched from Saul's office. "We've asked so much of you, Tony. *I've* asked so much. Much more than I knew."

Tony smiled. *"De nada,"* he said.

"No. Not nothing. Too much."

She was plainly unsettled, Tony saw. "Does Sam know you're here?"

"Yes. I said I was going to buy you dinner, if I could. I'm still partial to the truth."

The last phrase, Tony thought, had an indefinable edge—what puzzled him was whether it was directed at Sam or at herself. "How has it been for you?" he asked. "We've hardly talked."

Sue got up, walking to the window. To Tony, she looked slender, small; it was the first time he had thought of her as fragile. "In a strange way," she said, "it's been like a lot of my life, like people are when they have kids they love and a marriage that isn't right enough to be really happy or wrong enough to change—you do what you need to do for the people around you, and try not to ask yourself too hard how you feel about it."

She paused, quite still now, as though staring out at

the city without seeing it. "For Sam and Jenny," she said
at last, "I'm still their mother. I ask questions about *their*
lives—the normal ones they have away from here—and
say hopeful things about the trial. And, like all families,
there are the subjects we avoid: they never ask, and I
never say, whether I think their father's innocent. They
just accept that I'm there, because that's what they
need—if I weren't there, this would be so much harder
for them. The only difference is how solicitous they are
with me." For an instant, her voice had a trace of dry
humor. "It's like this scary preview of what will happen
when I'm old and they think I'm not quite with it anymore."

She needed to talk, Tony realized, and he wanted to
listen, not just for Sue but for himself. For he had discovered that what had seemed in Sue at seventeen to be
deep empathy was something more: a particular acuity
once hidden by her sunniness, and obvious to him now.
"And Sam?" he asked. "How is that for you?"

She did not turn. "You mean, how is it to be in court?"
she asked. "Or to go home, almost as if nothing has happened, and then sleep next to someone who may have
murdered the teenage girl he was having an affair with."

The last sentence, less question than statement, jarred
Tony with its baldness. "To go home with him," he said.

Sue shrugged, the smallest movement of her back.
Still she did not look at him. "When you were married
the first time," she asked, "did you fight a lot? Or was
there this awful politeness, where you pretended not to
notice that you didn't want to touch each other, that it
was only safe to talk about your son or work. This kind
of quiet death."

He had never talked about this, Tony realized, except
with Stacey. "Marcia and I did both, Sue. First the politeness, then the anger. As much as I hate anger, it was
almost a relief."

For a moment, Sue was quiet. "For now," she told

him, "I keep the anger to myself. It's like fifteen years ago—don't fight too loud, the kids will hear. And there's no room for anger when your husband's on trial for murder. It just blots out everything else." There was a sudden change in her voice; when she turned, the tears on her face startled him. "I'm so damned alone, Tony. I lie there at night, listening to him breathe, both of us pretending to sleep. Afraid to move, because he may say something, or *I* may have to. So I just lie there, and wonder."

Tony hesitated, then he got up and put his arms around her, holding her close. She hugged him fiercely, wanting nothing more, Tony knew, than not to feel alone. "So," she murmured after a time, "had dinner yet? I promise not to cry."

There was humor in her voice again, meant now to reassure him. "I'm famished," he said. "But you and I can't be seen in public—I worry about what the press would make of it. So we'll have to stay here." Still holding her, Tony thought for a moment. "When was the last time you had pizza?"

"I think it was when Jenny left for college." Sue looked up at him. "Can we order a bottle of red wine?"

He smiled. "Sure."

Tony went to the phone and called room service. When he turned around, Sue was settled in a chair in the corner.

"Mind if I work a little?" Tony asked. "The pizza will take a half hour or so, and I need to write down some thoughts before I lose them."

Sue smiled, picking up a travel magazine. "Go ahead. I'll just be here. Dreaming of far-flung places."

Tony took a legal pad from the nightstand, loosened his tie, and propped himself against the headboard.

Ignoring Sue, he began scribbling questions. It was a comfort having her here, he realized: without Stacey and Christopher, he had felt quite alone, his only solace

Saul's friendship. And as with Stacey, he found that he could work with Sue in the room.

Once, he felt her watching him. When he looked up, there was a fond smile on her face.

"Work, Tony," she said. "It's no good if you notice me."

He smiled himself, and resumed writing. Sue was quiet until the pizza came.

They sat on the floor, the pizza between them, their wine bottle and two glasses on the open lid of the box.

"What does Christopher look like?" she asked.

"As a person, he's very much him. But he looks so much like my high school yearbook picture that it's silly. Fortunately, he doesn't seem to mind."

Sue smiled. "He shouldn't. I thought you were gorgeous."

"You were pretty quiet about it."

"I was taken." Her smile vanished, as though her awareness of the present had returned with a jolt. It was a moment before she asked, "Is Christopher like you in any other way?"

"I'm not sure. It's easier to say what *he* is." Tony sipped the Chianti, a ripe burst of flavor on his tongue. "He's bright, and very good-humored—he banters with me a lot, which I couldn't really do with my folks. He's a decent kid, I think, and a nice friend; not as ambitious as I remember being, probably because he doesn't need to be." Tony paused, reflecting. "The thing that Stacey notices is how wary Christopher seems—always watching, taking things in so quietly you almost don't see that he's doing it. That's the divorce, I think; though he never talks about it, I'm sure Christopher has an intense memory of conflict. It's given him an instinct for trouble, for things about to happen." Stopping to question himself, he looked at Sue. "Maybe that's also from me. All my life, I've worried for him, that something bad might happen. But I've tried not to let it show."

Sue considered him. "They sense things, though. Mine do—especially Sam junior. His father intimidated him, and I think he watched our marriage and identified with me. He is so *careful*—afraid to commit himself to a girl, or even to how he feels. God knows what he's thinking *now*." She paused, gazing at Tony with a gentle curiosity. "*You* try pretty hard not to look back at your life much, don't you? Sometimes I find myself thinking that this trial has made you do that."

Tony's instinct was to say that he was fine—not wanting to admit to himself, in the middle of this trial, how wearing it was *not* to feel, telling himself that to admit this was not fair to Sue. Then he looked at her, at the same clear brown eyes he had known at seventeen.

"I hate this case," he said.

Sue studied him. "Because of Sam?" she asked softly. "Or Alison?"

"Because of all that, and because of me." Tony paused, and then the words rushed forth, the things he had never said, even to himself. "Except for you and Saul, I never had any help getting through what happened when Alison was murdered. My folks didn't know what to do, and they thought that shrinks were for crazy people, even if they could have afforded to get me one. So my way of coping was to try to leave it all behind: the shock of finding Alison, the way the town saw me after that. Even who I was, the middle-class boy who'd believed that life would only get better and then the boy who felt so desperate and so scared—when I think of *him*, it's like holding my hand over a flame. Even then I didn't want to know that boy was me. So as soon as I could go to Harvard and get away, I pretended that he wasn't.

"I still do that. There've been times, sitting with

Stacey in that beautiful home, that I've barely remembered him at all. Like Tony Lord at seventeen is some other person, one I hardly knew. Except that I've always had these nightmares of finding Alison, and now—since the trial—a new one. Where she accuses me of killing her." Pausing, he shook his head. "It's all so fucked up, Sue. Sitting in court, I can't let myself remember the boy I was. Not just because I'm a lawyer. It's because when I try to believe Sam's innocent, I don't want to feel how scared he must be, how responsible I am for saving him from something he doesn't deserve. And when I wonder if he's guilty, I think about the seventeen-year-old boy whose girlfriend was murdered, and I'm damned sure that boy hates me. Even without what I may be doing to Ernie Nixon." Tony rubbed his temples. "It *is* screwed up. I don't even know what I'm saying now, and I'm afraid of saying it."

Sue was very still. "I knew that boy, and he was a very good person. He still is." She took his hand. "Oh, Tony, how badly hurt you were. How badly that whole town hurt you."

There was a tightening in his throat. "You never hurt me, Sue. Maybe I hurt you, not knowing what to do. I look at you now, and I wish I could go back—just for a moment—and change that."

Sue's eyes filled with tears. She shook her head, mute, and then slid across the carpet, resting her face against his chest. To Tony, it felt as natural as breathing.

Gently, he took Sue's face in his hands.

She gazed up at him. He was not sure whose head moved first. Only that their mouths were closer, an inch apart, and then that there was no distance at all.

Mouths touching, they rose together, Tony's hands on her waist. Their lips parted for each other, in a moment that seemed never to end, and then their kiss went deep.

As her hips pressed against him, Tony kissed her hungrily. This was not wrong, he told himself—this was

Sue, who was there first, who had rights to him that he had never acknowledged, who, in some past he had wished to hide from himself, he had loved more deeply than Alison Taylor. The woman who that same part of him, both boy and man, loved still.

Then their kiss ended, and Stacey Tarrant was his wife again.

This was all that stopped him. It would not change the beating of his heart, the wanting her, the sense of loss and sorrow. But Sue, his partner in this, felt all of it.

Their foreheads touched. "I know," she said softly. "You can't do this. You shouldn't." A tremor went through her body. "But God, how much I wanted you, and have for years. Even since our night together."

Our night, Tony thought. Their gift to each other, and their sadness. "That boy," he murmured, "is someone I just met again. And he loves you so much it hurts. Just like before."

Though her eyes were moist, she smiled a little. "That helps me, Tony. It helps a lot."

He felt himself breathe again, letting the passion go. "Then stay for a while. After tonight we can't be with each other like this. Even without Stacey, I'm Sam's lawyer . . ."

He did not have to finish. They sat together; without needing to speak, Sue leaned her back to his chest and, sitting between his outstretched legs, rested in Tony's arms. After a while she reached out for the Chianti and a wineglass; she filled the glass, and they took turns sipping wine, Sue still nestled there.

"You really love her," Sue said at last. "Stacey."

"Very much." Tony paused, reflecting. "She's smart, and she's honest, and yet there's this kind of tact—a sense of when to leave things alone. She's wonderful with Christopher, and she knows me as well as anyone can. Sometimes it strikes me how little help I've been with that." His voice softened. "I've said more to you, tonight, than I've ever let myself say to her."

Sue's voice was equally soft. "Thank you for that, Tony. Not for Stacey's sake, but mine. Even if it was just because I was here."

The tenderness Tony felt was painful now. "It was more than that, Sue. Just like it was more than that before."

Sue was silent again, seemingly reflective.

"I guess you recognized that piece of beach," she said at last. "The one where they found Marcie."

"Uh-huh. It was where the four of us built the bonfire. The night I fought with Alison."

She leaned back. "I think of Marcie Calder, Tony, and then us at that age. . . . Do you know Sam keeps a revolver by the bed now?"

"Why?"

"He's afraid that people want him dead—of Frank Calder, maybe." She paused. "God, I hate what's happened to us. And what we've done to you, reminding you of Alison."

Tony kissed the top of her head. "Lawyers hurt what's most human in them all the time—it's a professional requirement. So maybe it's best that I'm forced to face that, and what I started doing to myself well before." His voice was gentle. "Nothing you ever brought to me was bad. Only what I did with it."

Sue took a sip of wine, pensive. "Did you ever read *The Sun Also Rises*?"

"Sure. Poor Jake Barnes, impotent, with Lady Brett Ashley loving him hopelessly. I found it painful to think about, in more ways than one."

Sue smiled a little. "Remember what she says to him at the end? You were always a reader."

Tony thought for a moment. "Something like, 'Oh, Jake, what a fine time we could have had.' And he answers, 'Wouldn't it be pretty to think so.'"

Silent, Sue nestled closer.

After a time, the wine finished, she kissed him softly on the mouth, and left.

That night, Tony could not sleep; not, this time, because of nightmares, but because of thoughts too deep to avoid. He did not feel like a lawyer.

Finally, he phoned Saul at home. "I think you're right," Tony said. "I'm tired. Were you serious about helping?"

Saul could not conceal his surprise. "Sure . . ."

Hanging up, Tony found himself staring at the pizza box, the empty wine bottle, the empty glasses.

FIFTEEN

The next morning, in court, Tony felt the vibrations of the night before: Saul's new focus as he scribbled notes in the margins of the coroner's report; the heavy-lidded silence of the man next to him, his client and friend, whose wife Tony cared for; his own unsettling sense that he was headed toward some reckoning with himself. When Tony turned to look at Sue, she gazed back at him with a certain fond sadness, not looking away. Then Tony turned his attention to Dr. Katherine Micelli.

Kate Micelli was in her mid-fifties, with deep-set eyes, a beaked nose, and lusterless jet-black hair, which, Tony guessed, came from a bottle. Her lined face bespoke deep seriousness, and when she smiled, it was fleeting and preoccupied, a formal offering. It was clear that she found little humor in her work.

This was understandable. In a flat, unresonant voice, Micelli told Stella Marz that she had responded to the crime scene, and then described the intake process for Marcie Calder's corpse: combing her clothes for blood, hair, and fibers; inspecting her hands and nails for traces of skin; drawing a sample of her blood; undressing the body and taking oral, rectal, and vaginal swabs to determine the presence or absence of semen; carefully assessing the appearance of the body; taking X rays of Marcie's head; and finally, performing an autopsy to determine the cause of her death. Tony, who had seen several autopsies in his career, pitied Marcie's parents for what they were learning; he would never forget the sound of one human being sawing off the top of another's skull, the sight of gray-white brain matter being placed in a pan and weighed. To judge from Frank Calder's pinched eyes, the way Nancy Calder swallowed, the idea of their once living daughter being systematically disassembled was shocking, then devastating, then numbing. For an instant, Tony imagined Alison lying naked on the autopsy table, the same indignities recorded in the same sterile prose that Saul read now.

"And did you," Stella asked, "determine the cause of death?"

"We did." Micelli's expression was so grave as to appear angry, almost fierce. "Marcie Calder died of a cerebral hemorrhage which, in my opinion, was caused by multiple blows to the head with a heavy object."

" 'Multiple'?" Stella repeated pointedly.

"Yes. At least three."

"Could you describe the fatal wounds, Dr. Micelli, and explain how you came to that conclusion."

"Surely." Micelli turned to face the jury, a professor giving a grim but crucial lecture, which they must not fail to grasp. "Miss Calder's scalp displayed severe lacerations—a tearing through the skin. The skull itself was fractured and displayed three concentric rings of compression, indentations in the bone.

"These concentric rings reflected three blows, in

close proximity. We can tell this because the fracture pattern for a later blow—a series of irregular circles, almost like the rings of a tree—intersects with the pattern from an earlier blow, stopping the pattern from spreading. The three concentric rings met in this manner."

Narrow-eyed, Saul scribbled a note. The jurors listened intently. "Did you," Stella asked in measured tones, "form an opinion as to how Marcie Calder received these blows?"

"Definitely." Once more, Micelli surveyed the jurors, her hawklike eyes demanding their attention. "Marcie Calder died at the hands of another."

Today, Tony thought, Stella was methodical and undramatic; she would let the sheer weight of the evidence, cloaked in the mantle of science, stand on its own. "Did you consider, Dr. Micelli, the possibility that this trauma to Marcie Calder's skull was caused by a fall down the cliff?"

"I did, Ms. Marz, quite thoroughly. I rejected it."

"Why is that?"

Micelli folded her hands. "To start, because the three blows *were* in such close proximity. It would be a great coincidence to have a falling body suffer three blows so heavy and so close together. And *were* the body falling, it is difficult to understand how such blows could be caused by a single rock.

"In fact, I believe that the fatal blows were delivered by someone of considerable strength, on the ground above the beach, and that Marcie Calder was already dead by the time she was thrown off the cliff."

"On what do you base *that* conclusion, Dr. Micelli?"

"Several factors." Facing the jurors, Micelli began ticking off points with metronomical precision. "To start, internal brain injuries are different in a fall than when administered by another.

"This is a straightforward matter of physics. An

injury to the right side of the head, if suffered in a fall, would result in injuries to the opposite side.

"For example, an *external* injury to the forehead would cause an *internal* brain injury at the back of the head. This is because the force of a fall causes the brain to move to the opposite side; we call this a 'contre-coup injury.' Whereas with a blow to the head given by another, one would expect to see a 'coup injury'—an internal bruise to the brain which is on the *same* side as the external wound to the head—"

"And in the case of Marcie Calder . . . ," Stella interjected.

Micelli frowned at the interruption, then nodded curtly. "Both the internal and external injuries occurred on the right side of the head. Therefore, the medical evidence is inconsistent with injuries suffered in a fall and consistent with a homicide."

Watching the jury, Tony saw the professor leaning forward, intent. It seemed clear that the jurors understood Micelli and were impressed by her authoritative manner; Saul's job would be to crack this veneer and thus cast doubt on everything Micelli said. Saul had stopped taking notes; now he simply watched her.

"Are there further reasons," Stella asked, "why you believe that Marcie's death was *not* caused by a fall?"

"Yes," Micelli told the jurors. "On Marcie Calder's face we found several abrasions, scrapes to the skin. These injuries were orange in color, rather leathery to the touch, and involved no hemorrhage. That's what happens when a trauma to the skin occurs *after* the heart has stopped pumping."

Sam, Tony saw, had a veiled, reflective look, directed at the table. "Look at her," Tony whispered. "The jury watches that. . . ."

"How long," Stella was asking, "does it take after the heart has stopped pumping for injuries to have the appearance you describe—orange, leathery, lacking in any hemorrhage?"

"As little as two minutes."

Two minutes, Tony thought, for a murderer to drag Marcie's body from the place of death, her feet leaving skid marks as they dangled lifelessly, then throw her over the edge. "Did you form an opinion," Stella continued, "as to the approximate *time* of death?"

"I did." Turning, Micelli addressed the jurors directly. "My opinion is that Marcie Calder died at roughly ten o'clock on the night she disappeared."

In the momentary silence, Stella simply nodded: Marcie's death, if Micelli was right, occurred very close to Sam's estimate to the police of the time he had left the park. In the jurors' minds, Tony knew, a picture was forming: Sam Robb bludgeoning Marcie Calder; dragging her body to the edge of the cliff; throwing her over the side . . . This sequence had long since formed in Tony's own mind, like a silent film he could not stop. Glancing at Sue, he saw her downward gaze.

"Ten o'clock," Stella repeated. "On what do you base *that*?"

"When we arrived at the scene, rigor mortis had set in and the body temperature was cool—roughly that of the ambient air, sixty-five degrees or so. It was apparent that she'd been dead for hours." Micelli looked at several jurors, confirming their attention. "During the autopsy, we examined the contents of Marcie Calder's stomach. We found the remnants of a tuna sandwich.

"According to an earlier witness, Mr. Nixon, he gave Marcie Calder a tuna sandwich at roughly eight o'clock. This is consistent with our findings."

"And why is that?"

"It's based on the gastric emptying time." Pausing, Micelli spoke with didactic self-assurance. "A substantial meal will take four to five hours to empty from the stomach—that's how long it takes the acids found there to break down the food. By comparison, a meal of more moderate size will empty in roughly *three* hours. And a small meal—like a tuna sandwich—will empty in about two hours." Micelli paused, adding more softly, "Unless the process of digestion is terminated by death.

"In the case of Marcie Calder, traces of that tuna sandwich remained in her stomach. Meaning that she died within two hours after ingesting the sandwich. Or less." She faced the jury, her tone newly harsh. "If Mr. Robb was with her until ten, Marcie Calder had very little time left."

Next to Tony, Saul stirred but did not object. The damage was done, the relentless accretion of fact upon fact. Even Sam seemed sluggish, battered.

As for Micelli, she appeared more severe, a portrait by El Greco. "Were you able to determine," Stella asked, "what had happened to Marcie Calder in the hours before she died?"

"Yes." Micelli's voice was flat. "We determined that she'd had anal intercourse."

Stella was silent for a moment. "How did you conclude that?"

"There were lacerations in the anus and tears to the mucosa, indicating anal penetration. As did the blood on her external sphincter."

"Did the swabs show any semen in the anus?"

"No." Once more, Micelli faced the jury. "The swabs yielded traces of a petroleum-based lubricant found in a commonly used brand of condom. One with a ridged surface, called Adam's Rib."

Sam gazed at Micelli blankly, a flush coming to his face. Sue stared at her folded hands; the Calders had a bitter, sickened look.

From the bench, Karoly's eyes followed Stella. "Did you form an opinion," she asked, "as to whether this anal intercourse was consensual or forced?"

Micelli frowned. "That determination isn't easy. But I formed a definite impression, yes."

"And what is that?"

"From our examination, it appeared that Marcie Calder had little, or any, prior experience of such an act. Therefore, any penetration, even consensual, would cause trauma. Even the ridges of the condom might aggravate that." Pausing, Micelli gave Stella a narrow look. "If this were rape, Ms. Marz, I would expect to see more trauma. My impression is that this was consensual anal intercourse, involving a girl to whom this was new."

Stella folded her arms. Softly, she asked, "In the course of the autopsy, Dr. Micelli, did you make any other findings with respect to Marcie Calder?"

"One. She was pregnant."

With flickering quickness, the beautician glanced at Sam. "How did you determine that?"

Turning, Micelli addressed the jurors. "She was carrying a fetus," she told them softly. "At death, it was between one to two months in development. It had died with the mother."

The beautician seemed to wince; Tony sensed that for her, as for Stella and for Tony himself, the sadness of this was both personal and moral. "Was there sufficient fetal material," Stella asked, "to determine the probable father?"

"Yes. With the help of DNA testing."

"And did you direct that this testing be performed?"

"I did. By our office. I also asked the lab to run DNA testing on the blood sample taken from Mr. Robb by the police."

"What was the result, Dr. Micelli?"

Micelli's deep-set eyes were somber. "That the genetic material in the fetus reflected that found in Mr. Robb's blood." She paused, facing the jurors. "Within a probability of ten million or so to one, Mr. Robb was the father of that child."

Sam, Tony noticed, seemed not to breathe. Approaching Micelli, Stella appeared almost tentative, as if reluctant to break the silence. "Did you also, at the request of our office, attempt to determine whether there was any possibility that the father of this child was African-American?"

"Yes." Micelli's voice was flat again. "Based on the genetic material, there was *no* possibility."

Stella paused for a moment, eyes downcast, hands folded in front of her. Then she looked up at Karoly, quietly saying, "I have nothing more, Your Honor."

Karoly nodded and then, as if it were an afterthought, remembered the clock. "At this time," he told the jury, "we'll take our noon recess, until one-thirty."

A heavy half-silence ensued, the jurors rising with a look of preoccupation, little noise coming from the gallery.

Glancing at Saul, Sam turned to Tony. "I want to talk to you," he said. "Alone."

SIXTEEN

Tony and Sam sat alone in the witness room—small, cramped, and windowless, with a bare wooden table and hard wooden chairs. Even had the room not reminded Tony of the interrogation room of the Lake City police, Sam's demand would have made him edgy.

"What is it?" Tony asked.

Sam regarded him with open blue eyes. "Are you going to let that old man cross-examine her?"

So that was it—not Sue, or some last-minute confession. "I'm tired," Tony answered. "A tired lawyer makes mistakes—"

"Better your mistakes than *his*." Sam's voice rose. "That ugly bitch is full of shit, all right? I don't know when Marcie died, or how, but it was after I left. Micelli *crucified* me in there."

Tony tried to stay calm. "She didn't help you, for sure. But no one is going to take her apart—including me." His voice softened. "After all, she's right about the fetus, about the anal intercourse, even about the brand of condom you used. As for the rest, Saul's been doing this for years—"

"When was the *last* year, Tony? This may be a sentimental journey for you, but it's my life that's on the line here—my future, my marriage, everything." Sam stood abruptly. "I sit here, waiting to say I'm innocent until I want to fucking scream. And *you* sit here, cool as ever, and put me in the trembling hands of some prehistoric sot." Placing his palms flat on the table, he leaned toward Tony with his face red, his forehead damp. "It's because you think I'm guilty, isn't it? That all I deserve is a halfhearted effort by a lawyer who'll be fucking my wife the night after they ship me off for a lifetime of sex in the prison shower room. If you're not fucking her already."

Staring up at Sam, Tony felt his jaw work. "You're scared," he said softly. "I understand that. But try not to make losing quite so attractive to me. . . ." Abruptly, Tony stopped himself. "I didn't mean that. And you'd better not mean what you said about Sue. Because I am very, very tired of counting up all the things she doesn't deserve. . . ."

"Look—"

"No. *You* look." Tony's voice rose. "You're getting a goddamned good defense from me, pal—there may be better lawyers out there, but not many. So if I decide to take a break before my victory lap, *you* can take a moment to thank me. Instead of slandering your wife and reminding me of how pleasant *my* life was before that poor pregnant girl went off the cliff. However the hell *that* happened." Pausing, Tony mastered his own emotions. "As for Saul, I wouldn't sacrifice one friend to give another friend something to do. But before you open your mouth again, I'll thank you to remember that Saul *is* my friend. Just like Sue."

Sam stared down at Tony. "We're both tired," he said at length. Abruptly, he collapsed in the chair across from Tony, face buried in his hands, and emitted a deep breath. "I never sleep now. I just never fucking sleep. I lie there, watching the digits move on our alarm clock, and there's nothing I can say to her. Minutes, then hours, letting her pretend to sleep, and all I've got to hold on to is something I can't share with her. Because I'm the only person in the world who *knows* I'm innocent." Sam looked up again, and his face suddenly seemed haggard. "For me, innocence isn't a presumption, Tony, or a job. It's not about how good a lawyer you are. Try to imagine what it's like to know that I'm innocent and sit there, while all the mistakes I ever made—everything I'm ashamed of—makes me look not just disgusting but *guilty. . . .*" He looked down. "I guess you do understand that. Some of it, anyhow."

"Some of it," Tony said at last. "Except for whoever murdered Alison, I was the only one who knew. Almost everyone else thought it was me. So I can see why it matters to you. Just like it 'mattered' to me."

"*You* matter to me." Sam reached out, his hand covering the top of Tony's. "I'm not like that, Tony. Please, believe me."

Tony looked into Sam's light-blue eyes, silently pleading, and felt the cost of friendship, the incalculable ways, at first unimagined, through which one person's connection to another can alter the lives of both. "Then trust me," Tony answered. "We're going to get you out of this. No matter how it looks."

*   *   *

Watching Saul stand, then shuffle ponderously toward Kate Micelli, was painful to Tony. Saul was seventy, Tony guessed, and with a sudden sadness he knew that Saul would not reach eighty: the years of neglect, the drinking, the weariness of trial after trial, were like a weight he carried. Though he had a certain dignity, his voice was rough and quavery.

"Good afternoon, Dr. Micelli." Saul was quiet for a moment; Tony felt Sam tense, as if helplessly watching a once great actor forget his lines. Abruptly, Saul said, "Three blows to the head, right?"

"That's my opinion, yes."

"Wouldn't there be blood spatter?"

Micelli folded her hands. "Not from the first blow, I believe. That would simply break the skin. But probably from the second and third."

Saul listened, head cocked as if to hear. "All right. Now let me assume that the blows were administered by your hypothetical killer. Where would this blood spatter go?"

Micelli gave him a look of exaggerated patience. "In your question, Mr. Ravin, are you assuming that the killer is standing, holding the victim upright, or on the ground?"

Saul's smile was almost bashful. "That's a good point. Why don't we start with both killer and victim on the ground?"

Micelli frowned. "In that case, you'd have blood spatter on the ground, and on the victim's face and hair."

Saul put both hands in his pockets, fumbling for imaginary change. "What about your hypothetical killer?"

"Probably on *his* face and hair."

"This blood on the ground. Would it be substantial?"

"It could be, yes."

Slowly, Saul nodded. "But you don't think it happened that way, do you . . . ?"

"What way?" Micelli said with faint irritation.

The jury watched Saul in puzzlement, reflecting Micelli's apparent disrespect. "Oh," Saul said. "Sorry. I meant that you don't believe that the killer struck the victim while both were on the ground, do you?"

Micelli hesitated. "No. I don't."

Pausing, Saul gestured to the jury. "Could you share with the jury why that is?"

Micelli would not look at them. "There were significant blood spatters on Marcie Calder's sweatshirt and jeans."

Saul placed one hand to his face, so innocently pensive that, for the first time, Tony wanted to smile. "So your hypothetical killer was *standing*, holding the victim upright?"

"This is what I believe, yes. . . ."

"Then what do you believe the *victim* was doing?"

"I don't know."

Saul smiled. "I understand—of course you don't *know*. Let me put it this way, Dr. Micelli. During your autopsy, did you discover any evidence that Marcie Calder was struggling?"

"No."

"No skin beneath her fingernails. Or bruises on her neck or body, like those which might have been inflicted on a struggling victim by a person of considerable strength?"

Micelli frowned again. "No."

"All right. This hypothetical killer—if he was standing, what kind of spatter would he have on him?"

"There would likely be blood on his face and arms and upper torso."

"A lot of blood?"

"There could be, yes."

"Also blood on the ground?"

"Some."

Saul paused and took an audible rumbling breath, as if too many rapid questions had winded him. Tony wondered if this was true or an act—an attempt to distract Micelli, or to cover a pause for thought. But Tony took the moment to survey the room: the jury, engaged now; Stella, alert, her left hand poised over a legal pad; Karoly, looking curious for once. Abruptly, Saul said, "But there was no blood on the ground above the cliff— whether lying down, or standing up, no blood at all."

"It had been raining, Mr. Ravin."

Saul smiled again. "That may be part of your *answer*, Dr. Micelli. But it wasn't my question. So, again, was there any blood whatsoever on the ground? Or on the grass?"

"No. The rain could have washed it away."

"I see." Saul paused for a moment. "Just like it could have washed away blood on the cliffside if Marcie fell by accident?"

Micelli hesitated. "I suppose so."

"Or on a rock?"

"It could." Micelli's tone was condescending. "But you'll remember, Mr. Ravin, that the police found a rock with Marcie Calder's hair and blood. The lab confirmed that."

Saul looked abashed. "Sorry. I wasn't clear. I was talking about the *second* rock."

Micelli's brow knit. "I don't understand you," she said with faint annoyance.

"Okay. Let's suppose for a moment that—despite what you surmise—Marcie Calder fell down the cliff by accident. Can I ask you to assume that? Just for the purpose of my question."

"All right."

"You don't think, in that case, that Marcie Calder's head would have hit the same rock three times, do you?"

"Of course not."

"Indeed, her head likely would have had to hit three rocks."

"In your scenario, yes."

"Then there'd be no blood on the first rock, would there? Because, as you say, the first blow would tear the scalp without causing spatter."

"True."

Saul considered her. "What about the second rock, in my scenario."

"There would be blood on it, yes."

"Less blood than the third?"

"Yes. But the police found no such rock, you may recall. Indeed, there weren't any on the side of the hill."

"But there were at the bottom, right? Several rocks of a fair size."

"But none with blood."

Saul ignored this. "How did the rocks get there?" he asked.

"I don't know."

"Any chance they were knocked down the hill by Marcie's fall?"

"I don't know." Micelli grimaced, and then tried to look judicious. "There's always a chance, Mr. Ravin. But as to whether they caused injury, none had blood."

"Because of the rain? Isn't it true that the second rock, in my scenario, would have less blood than the last?"

"Yes."

"Which, during the rain, could have washed off."

Micelli sat back, answering at a staccato clip. "My opinion as to cause of death is a mosaic, Mr. Ravin— not a laundry list. The nature of the wounds, the absence of contre-coup brain trauma, and, yes, the single bloody rock seven feet from the body, *all* support my belief that Marcie Calder was killed by another above the cliff and thrown over the side already dead."

Turning from her, Saul walked to the defense table, pouring a glass of water as Sam looked worriedly up at him. Then Saul turned to Micelli, studying her as he sipped the water. "Dry throat," he said to her. "Tell me,

Ms. Calder must have fallen with considerable force, correct?"

"It would seem so, yes."

"And the blows to her head also required considerable force?"

"Yes. I said that."

Saul put down the glass. "Couldn't Marcie's head have hit the bloody rock you did find with *considerable force*, accounting for the blood on the rock and on her clothes, while causing the rock to roll down the hill another seven feet? It was round, after all, and about ninety-five pounds lighter than Marcie."

Micelli stared at him. "You've just given me *several* assumptions, Mr. Ravin."

Saul smiled. "Sorry. I guess my question was kind of a mosaic. Please let me break it down." Pausing, he walked toward her and asked, "The spatter could have happened when Marcie's head hit a rock, correct?"

"It's theoretically possible—"

"Particularly because the spatter is concentrated on her right sleeve and not the front of her sweatshirt."

Micelli paused. "True."

"In theory, the fall could have left blood on the second or third rock she hit."

"Theoretically."

"And the force of a one-hundred-five-pound girl, falling down a steep cliff and hitting a rock with her head, *could* cause that rock to continue down the hill at a greater speed. Enough to travel another seven feet."

"Possibly. But that's a lot of coincidences."

Saul folded his arms. "My only point," he said mildly, "is that you can't know *what* happened, can you? Just as you admitted earlier."

"No. I can't. All I can do is consider what the medical evidence, taken as a whole, tells me about the circumstances of Marcie Calder's death."

Saul nodded. "I understand. As I recall, another part of that evidence is the injuries to Marcie Calder's skin— the 'leathery' nature of the skin and the absence of blood on the surface."

Micelli gave him a guarded look. "Yes."

"Wouldn't rain have somewhat the same effect, causing the scraped areas of Marcie's skin to pucker?"

Micelli paused, gazing down; watching, Tony knew that she was reminding herself that she was a scientist, not a partisan. "It could," she allowed. "The exposed part of Marcie's skin was somewhat like that of a person who'd been too long in the bathtub. Especially her hands and fingers."

"All right. And rain would also tend to wash away blood, and alter the color of both wounds and normal skin. Particularly because Marcie Calder ended up lying on her back, with the surfaces of her skin exposed."

Micelli considered this. "Yes," she announced. "It obscured the nature of her injuries. But to me, they still appeared postmortem. Particularly the lacerations to her face."

Glancing at Frank and Nancy Calder, Tony saw that they were mute, still; their numbness seemed permanent now.

"But don't those very lacerations," Saul pointed out to Micelli, "suggest that she slid down the hill on the right side of her face, and thus could have hit the right side of her head on a rock or rocks? Causing three indentations quite close together?"

Micelli considered him. In a grudging tone, she said, "It could, yes. But in my opinion, Marcie would then have had contre-coup brain injuries."

Saul looked suddenly weary; the skin of his face looked dangerously pink, like that of a man who had overexerted, and he stopped to dab the sweat off his forehead with a white handkerchief. *Let it go,* Tony silently implored him. *You've done all you can.*

As if he had heard him, Saul said slowly, "Can we talk about the tuna sandwich?"

"Of course."

"How big was it?"

Micelli hesitated. "I don't know. An ordinary sandwich, I suppose."

"Know how much tuna Mr. Nixon put on the sandwich?"

"No."

Saul put away the handkerchief. "Wouldn't those things affect how long it would take Marcie Calder's stomach to completely absorb the sandwich?"

"They could. Not to any great degree, though."

"But you're not insisting that the tuna sandwich would empty from Marcie's stomach in two hours flat, are you?"

"Of course not. That's an approximate time."

Saul inhaled, his large frame shuddering. "Could have taken longer?"

"Somewhat longer. Though, if you'll remember, there was a residue of tuna in her stomach. Indicating that the digestive process was interrupted by death."

"But she could have died at ten-oh-five. Or ten-ten. Or ten-fifteen."

"Yes."

"Or at eleven?"

It was a bad question, Tony knew. "I'd consider that unlikely," Micelli said. "And the reverse of what you're asking is that Marcie Calder could have died at nine-thirty. Or nine-forty. Or nine-fifty. During which time the defendant told the police she was with him."

It stopped Saul for a moment. "But Mr. Robb also told the police that as he left, he saw someone in another car."

"That was what he said, yes."

"And it's possible that *this* person could have killed Marcie Calder before ten-oh-five, or ten-ten, or ten-fifteen."

Micelli stared at Saul. "In my opinion," she said coolly, "Marcie Calder was killed by another between nine-thirty at the earliest and ten-thirty at the very latest. I can also tell you that Mr. Robb was the father of Marcie Calder's child and that it was Marcie Calder's blood on the steering wheel of his car. But I have no personal knowledge of the events Mr. Robb described to the police *or* of the time he left the park."

This, Tony knew at once, was a devastating answer. He could see it on the faces of the jury.

"Shit," Sam murmured.

Saul drew himself up. "All that blood," he mused aloud. "And the only blood on Sam Robb's car on the steering wheel?"

"That's all we found, yes."

Saul slowly shook his head. "So how do you know the blood came from Marcie Calder's fatal injuries? I mean, all you know from your medical procedures is it's her blood, right?"

Micelli gave him a brief look of incredulity, then irritation, then tolerance. "As a matter of medical evidence, that's all I know."

Saul, Tony knew, was looking for a way to end this. "But that smear of blood," Saul asked slowly, "is, to your knowledge, the only medical evidence that *may* link *Sam Robb* to Marcie Calder's injuries? However she may have died."

Micelli paused to consider her answer. "Your question is limited to *medical* evidence?" she inquired pointedly.

"Yes. That's right."

"Then I would have to agree, with that qualification. The smear of blood is the only *medical evidence* which links Sam Robb to Marcie Calder's injuries."

Saul paused, lost in thought, letting his fleshy chin rest on his chest. "Thank you," he said at last, and walked back to the defense table.

"Nice job," Tony murmured, and meant it—there was nothing more to be done with Kate Micelli. But it was Sam who, when the jury was excused for the day, and Saul had slumped wearily in his chair, went to Saul and, with simple graciousness, thanked him.

With that, the case for the prosecution was over.

SEVENTEEN

That night, Tony took Saul to the steakhouse for dinner. Saul seemed so pleased that Tony did not mind the orange glob of dressing that sat there on his half head of iceberg lettuce, not moving, while he watched it with a kind of fascination.

"The record," Saul told him, "is forty-four minutes, seven seconds."

"Not anymore—that's my lettuce from the last time, I'm sure of it." Tony shook his head in wonder. "You'd think after a while the law of gravity would take over. Maybe you should give Kate Micelli a call—ask her what *she* thinks. 'Tell me, Kate, if a head of iceberg lettuce were rolling down a hill . . .' "

Saul gave a short laugh, and then his face turned curious. "How're you doing, Tony?"

Tony poured them both a glass of wine. "Oh, all right," he began, and then realized that more should be said. "You were *good*, Saul. Except that the defendant would have been me, I'm sorry I missed watching you take on those two Lake City cops. Dana and McCain."

Saul studied him, as if to ensure that this was not mere flattery. It must be hard, Tony thought, to wonder how far you've slipped, to question your ability to even know that much. "That was a long time ago," Saul said simply. "Too many years, too much booze. I'm not what I was."

"Then you must have been something, Saul. You must really have been something."

When Saul's smile reached his eyes, Tony knew that his friend believed him. "I was *you*," Saul answered. "Life is strange, isn't it."

"Very."

Saul was quiet for a moment. "You still in love with the missus? Is that what this is all about?"

Tony gazed at the table, trying to answer the question for himself. "If Sam were married to someone else, I still would have come. I guess some experiences are so essential they're always part of who you are. Sam's friendship was one. Alison's death was another. And so was Sue." He looked up. "Yeah, Saul, I still love her. I can't let that become a problem for Stacey and me, but in one way it's even harder. Because I look at Sue's life—what it's been and where it's going—and there's not a damn thing I can do for her. Sam's the only one I can help, and if we get him off, Sue will still have to figure out who he is."

"And you keep wondering."

"All the time."

Saul nodded. "He's a mixed bag, your friend. Sometimes when he acts decent, like he did today, it seems genuine and almost sweet-natured, if I can use that word about Sam Robb. At other times, it's the decency that feels like an act—like he's receiving instructions on an earphone, telling him how to behave, but something in his brain chemistry keeps him from getting it quite right." He looked at Tony intently. "Understand what I'm saying?"

Saul's perception made Tony smile in recognition, though the point was very serious. "Oh, yeah," Tony answered. "I understand."

Saul took a deep swallow of wine; he was drinking

more than he had in a while, perhaps out of relief from the burden of self-doubt, and it seemed to have loosened his tongue. "If I were you," Saul said at length, "I wouldn't dwell on your feelings for Sue. Her life might be a lot simpler if you lost, and pretty snarled if Sam's still free. She'll have to make a choice then. Just like you, she'll always wonder if he's a murderer. But you can at least go back to your wife and son, knowing you've done your job. *She'll* have to decide whether to go or stay, and Sam won't make that easy, especially for a woman like I think Sue is. No matter what, he'll always be the father of her kids."

It was true, Tony knew. "She *did* ask me to defend him, Saul. To give her an innocent man."

Saul emptied his glass. "That was before the trial, Tony. I wonder how she feels now."

The next day, the courtroom was dark. That afternoon, Sam challenged Tony to resume their game of basketball.

Grinning, Sam stood at half-court, the ball tucked beneath one arm. "Fifteen-fifteen, right?"

"Right."

Tony felt surprise that, despite the trial and all that was at stake, both of them recalled the score. There was the first touch of fall in the air; twenty-eight years had passed since this same crispness heralded the last season that had led Sam and Tony, friends and rivals, to the night of the Riverwood game. Yet the instinctive rhythms of that friendship, that rivalry, still seemed like second nature. It was just that Tony had been missing.

"Let's make a rule," Sam said. "One of us has to win by two buckets." He smiled again. "I want to be fair to you."

Tony rolled his eyes. "We could be here forever."

"Suits me. The trial's not that much fun." Sam tossed the ball to Tony. "Your turn, pal. I'd just tied the score by turning your behind-the-back trick around on you."

"Absolutely pathological," Tony said, and took the ball out of bounds. When Tony drove toward the basket, suddenly dribbling behind his back and leaving Sam frozen like a statue while he scored his sixteenth point, Sam whooped from the sheer joy of it.

"Too good," he said. But when Sam tried the same drive and Tony stole the ball, Sam stopped laughing. He tied the score after throwing a sharp elbow and knocking Tony aside. After that, they barely spoke.

Now time was marked by the sounds of panting and quick footsteps, the feel of sweat and two bodies shoving, the taut split seconds before Sam and Tony shot or drove the basket, when they simply watched each other. At twenty-three all, Tony shot and missed; when the ball fell toward an empty space beneath the basket, neither man gave way. Their bodies cracked into each other; Tony reeled to the side, crashing into the concrete post of the backboard; Sam fell to the asphalt.

There was a sickening pain in Tony's head and elbow, a momentary whiteness of vision. Then he saw Sam, rising from the asphalt to retrieve the ball. "Enough," Tony said.

Sam frowned. "How much time you need?"

"Five minutes," Tony answered, and realized that these were their first words in what seemed a very long time.

They sat in the middle of the asphalt, a few feet apart.

"You all right?" Sam finally asked.

"I'll live." Tony realized that he did not want to talk. He flexed his elbow, wincing at the way his temple throbbed.

Sam gazed out at Taylor Park and the lake beyond. "So how was Sue the other night?"

His voice was so emotionless, so studiedly devoid of feeling, that Tony turned to him. "I hope that question doesn't mean what it did two days ago."

Sam shrugged. "I was only asking how she was."

"Then maybe we should get something straight, once and for all—I don't know *how* Sue is, or what she'll do. My charm for Sue is that I'm not you or the kids, and that I don't live at your house. We're hardly 'fucking,' as you so elegantly phrased it."

Sam's gaze was probing, silent. "Not even before?"

Quite deliberately, Tony met his eyes. The best lies, as Sam had remarked, are based on truth; failing that, Tony told himself, they are accompanied by an unwavering stare. "Back in 1968," Tony said evenly, "I was too much of a mess to care for anyone. But you might not know that—seeing as how we stopped talking for a while. As I recall, it was something about whether I'd strangled Alison."

Sam's gaze broke, and then he looked down, leaving Tony with the sour aftertaste of his own manipulation. But he would not, could not, betray Sue Robb, any more than he could betray a client. "So let's play basketball," Tony said.

Silent, they got up and commenced the game again.

It was tense, as before. The only difference was a certain courtesy—tense and silent, punctuated by a nod or glance—and the careful way they held their shoulders and elbows in, as if the next blow would start something they could not stop. Tony felt this difference in the effort to make Sam what he tried to make any other opponent—a cipher for whom he felt neither love nor hate nor fear. For his strength in sport or as a lawyer, Tony had always known, was not to feel too much; in this he was the opposite of Sam, who, in his visceral immediacy, was like a copper wire exposed to heat. But with Sam, Tony felt the heat as well.

When he drove the basket, scoring his thirtieth point, Tony's head was pounding.

One point ahead. One to go.

Sam faced him now. The ragged sound of their breathing was like that of a single organism, united by sweat and desire and the fierce compulsive passion they could only create together. Tony watched Sam's eyes.

"Fuck you," Sam said softly, and drove toward the basket with a sudden propulsion, startling in its fury.

Desperately, Tony scrambled sideways, trying to block Sam as if this were all that had ever mattered to him. Sam stopped, face contorted with rage and need, then drove past, hip thrusting sideways to knock Tony from his path. Tony held his ground; they collided, Tony reeling backward, but not before he jolted the ball from Sam's hand. Desperate, Sam dived for it, landing chest-first on the asphalt as the ball dribbled out of bounds. When he looked up at Tony, his face was an opaque, unfeeling mask.

Silent, Tony reached out his hand.

"Break?" he asked.

Sam's eyes became veiled, thoughtful. "Break," he said.

Together, they walked to the side of the court. The breeze from the lake had picked up, cooling their skin; silent, they looked once more at Taylor Park in the distance, with its hedgerows, its oak trees, its profound and terrible memories.

"Have you seen Ernie Nixon?" Tony asked.

Sam shook his head. "The *Weekly* says he took a leave. No explanation."

Tony was quiet for a moment. "None needed," he said at last.

Sam turned to him. With a deliberate, accusatory calm, he asked, "So when do *I* say I didn't kill her?"

"Maybe you don't."

Sam folded his arms. "Maybe I *hide* behind you, you mean?"

"No." Tony's voice was cool, succinct. "Maybe we decide, like the rational adults that we are, that you don't need to 'win' this one. That I've established reasonable doubt by putting on our criminalist. That you don't need to run the risk of rationalizing infidelity, sodomy, and pregnancy to twelve solid citizens who may start to wonder where it is you drew the line." Pausing, Tony spoke more softly. "We'll do a practice run tomorrow, try it out."

Sam turned away, staring at the ground. In a flat voice, he said, "Let's finish this."

"The game? No, I think we should finish when the trial's over. I don't feel like winning today."

Sam looked at him askance, eyes narrowing. Tony hoped that Sam understood his silent message; that today, finishing would not be good for either one of them.

Quietly, Sam repeated, "I'd like to finish this."

Tony smiled, walking away. "That's the thing," he said over his shoulder. "It's like a trial. You can't play without me."

EIGHTEEN

On Monday morning, two weeks after the commencement of the trial, Tony at last made his opening statement.

The jury was still and attentive. Tony felt the weight of their expectations, the burden of Sam's tense watchfulness and Sue's unfathomable gaze.

"This is not a time for argument," Tony began. "It is a time for fact.

"The 'facts' offered by the prosecution are entirely circumstantial.

"There are no witnesses to Marcie Calder's death. Indeed, the only person who ever placed Sam Robb in Taylor Park that night was Sam Robb himself, and no one has offered a reason for that other than the one Sam gave when Marcie turned up missing—that he was concerned for her."

Pausing, Tony surveyed the two rows of jurors. "Ms. Marz," he said quietly, "has tried to give you reasons to dislike Sam Robb—that he had sexual relations with a teenage girl; that he was the father of her unborn child; that he concealed their true relationship from the police. Based on this, she then asks you to believe that Sam Robb must have *murdered* Marcie Calder to conceal it from everyone.

"But lying is not murder. As uncomfortable as this might be, I venture to say that everyone on this jury, and everyone in this room, has done things that they're ashamed of, and told lies that they regret. And the *facts* suggest that Sam Robb lied not to conceal a murder from the police he contacted voluntarily, but to protect his marriage, his livelihood, and his reputation in the town where he has spent his entire life." Tony's voice turned harder. "Just as Ernie Nixon tried to conceal his relationship with Marcie Calder from *you*—whatever it may have been—for whatever reason *he* might have had.

"As to either man, deception is not murder, and speculation is not proof. And I believe that, in the end, you must conclude that the prosecution has not even proved—beyond a reasonable doubt—that *anyone* murdered Marcie Calder.

"But let's assume for the moment, as you cannot do in your deliberations, that Marcie died at the hands of someone else.

"Your obligation as jurors is not to convict Sam Robb of *murder* because you disapprove of his conduct. Nor is it to decide whether he should teach in our schools—for by resigning his license to teach, Sam Robb has decided that himself. . . ."

Stella Marz stirred, angry. Sam's resignation was not a "fact" of record, and would not be unless he testified. But Tony had already moved on. "Your job—your *only* job—is to decide whether the facts require that Sam Robb spend his life in prison.

"That is, perhaps, the gravest judgment twelve people can render on another." Pausing, Tony looked at Sam, then Sue. "The judgment to take this man from his family, forever. Yet that is what the prosecution asks.

"Based on *what*?

"A fingerprint, and a drop of blood.

"A fingerprint. A drop of blood. I ask you to focus just on that. Because, before this day is over, I believe you will conclude that the prosecution cannot prove that Sam Robb is a murderer, or even that these two 'facts' suggest murder at all."

Pausing, Tony looked at each juror, a silent reminder of the compact they had made—to listen, and to be fair. Then he thanked them, and called the only witness he meant to call.

Peter Shapiro was a stocky man with salt-and-pepper hair and mustache, keen brown eyes, an air of evenness and good humor, and a plainspoken manner free of pomposity or cant. With degrees in medicine, criminology, and forensic science, all from Ohio State, he was one of the most expensive experts Tony had ever hired.

Quickly, Tony established Shapiro's credentials and then the scope of his assignment—to review the crime lab report, the autopsy report, and all physical and medical evidence that supported the prosecution case, but to do no original work of his own. In this way, Shapiro confirmed, he was able to review the exact evidence cited by Detective Gregg and Dr. Micelli, and to determine if his conclusions matched theirs.

"In your opinion," Tony asked, "does the physical and medical evidence support a homicide, as the prosecutor contends, or may it also suggest the possibility of accident or suicide?"

Shapiro nodded briskly, ready to tackle the question. "First of all, I don't question the competence of the Lake City police, and I have great respect for Dr. Micelli's experience and expertise. Are they right that this was a homicide? I'd have to say probably." Pausing, Shapiro turned to the jury. "But could Marcie Calder have died some other way? Yes, she could have."

It was a perfect opening, Tony thought: respectful, balanced, and credible—what Sam Robb needed was doubt, not certainty. "Why do you say that, Dr. Shapiro?"

"Let's start with the medical evidence cited by Dr. Micelli: first, the absence of contre-coup brain injury.

"It's a probable indicator that Marcie Calder did *not* die in a fall. But certain? Not to me.

"For over two centuries of trying, no one has ever been able to explain *why* the apparent correlation between falls and contre-coup brain injuries works the way it does. But it's not a 'straightforward matter of physics.' Take one example: the most serious falls, like from a building, may not result in contre-coup injury. Even though the skull may be totally fractured.

"Why?

"We *think* it's because the body falls with such speed that brain and skull accelerate at the same rate, and therefore no acceleration pressure develops within the skull prior to impact. So a fall from a chair can, in theory, inflict much more contre-coup damage than a fall from a cliff."

Scanning the jury, Tony saw that the nutritionist looked impressed, as did the English professor. It was just as well that they had not been there when Shapiro told Tony, "Micelli's probably right—odds are pretty high somebody threw the victim off the cliff, close to when your client says he was with her. But take Kate's reasons one by one, and there's a little doubt with each of them. It's the cumulative effect that bothers me."

"What is your assessment," Tony asked Shapiro now, "of Dr. Micelli's belief that the nature of Marcie Calder's skin abrasions suggests a postmortem fall?"

Once more, Shapiro spoke to the jury. "Well, it certainly *could*. But the point Mr. Ravin made with Dr. Micelli is a fair one—you'd like to see the body sooner, instead of after seven or so hours of rain. That could help account for the nature of the wounds, including the leathery appearance Dr. Micelli describes.

"You can go right down the list, Mr. Lord. *Could* the footprints and the marks on the cliff reflect someone dragging Marcie Calder's body? Yes. Could the footprints belong to someone other than Sam Robb—even to a jogger, stopping to look out on the lake? Sure, because we don't have a match."

"What about the so-called drag marks?" Tony asked.

"It could be from Marcie Calder's toes, yes. But she could have tripped or, to be blunt, jumped too soon. Just like the mud on the toes of her tennis shoes could have come from the fall itself." Shapiro stopped to wipe his glasses. "Look," he told the jury, "I'm not telling you that Dr. Micelli's wrong about a homicide. But I can't tell you she's right, and I believe there's a number of reasons why *she* can't tell you that, either. Every one of the factors she cites could mean something, nothing, or something altogether different than what the prosecutor suggests."

It was time to move on, Tony thought; the most Shapiro could do was leave some nagging questions. "Murder?" Shapiro had said to Tony several weeks before. "Yeah, I'd give you four to one in favor. So what's the ratio on reasonable doubt these days?"

Now, reaching beneath the defense table, Tony pulled out two separate charts—blowups of fingerprints. From the moment Tony clipped them to a bulletin board and saw Stella Marz look from one to the other, he knew that Stella understood.

Standing next to the bulletin board, Tony pointed to the blowup on the left side. "Can you identify defense Exhibit 1?"

"It's a blowup of the three fingerprints taken from Marcie Calder's watch. As Detective Gregg testified, one print is Marcie Calder's—that on the left. The second is Mr. Robb's. The print on the far right is the one Detective Gregg could not identify."

Stella watched with a studied blankness that Tony knew well; it was the face of a lawyer whose case was about to sustain damage and who did not wish the jury to see her dismay. "And what is Exhibit 2?" Tony asked.

"Those are blowups of two fingerprints taken from a black Swatch wristwatch."

Tony felt the stirring of anticipation. "And whose prints are they?"

Shapiro smiled slightly. "Well, Mr. Lord, one is yours."

"And the second?"

"It, too, is unidentified."

Tony paused, stringing this out. "And when did you first see this watch?"

"One week ago, the morning you first gave it to me. When I wiped it clean of prints, put it in a manila envelope, and gave it back to you before the day's proceedings."

"Do you know where it was after that?"

"Yes. Beneath the table where you've been sitting."

"How do you know that?"

Calmly, Shapiro folded his hands, playing the role of expert. "Because I was standing at the back of the courtroom."

From the bench, Karoly stared at Shapiro in belated understanding. "And what did I do with the watch?" Tony continued.

"In the course of cross-examination, you removed the watch from the envelope and handed it to the witness. Ernie Nixon."

"What happened then?"

"Mr. Nixon handled the watch for a moment." Shapiro glanced at Stella. "Then Ms. Marz objected, and you put it back in the envelope. When the cross-examination was concluded, you returned the watch to me."

"What were my instructions?"

"To see if I could lift any prints off the watch, and to make sure that no one else touched it."

Tony pointed to the second chart. "The result is shown on this chart?"

"Yes."

"My print is the one on the left?"

"Yes."

Tony glanced at the jury. "Then, by process of elimination, the second print must be Ernie Nixon's."

Shapiro looked solemn. "Yes. His right index finger."

"And with respect to Mr. Nixon's print, were you able to reach any other conclusion?"

"Yes." Facing the jury, Shapiro's voice was even. "It matches the unidentified print found on the watch Marcie Calder was wearing the night she died. Beyond any doubt, that print is also Mr. Nixon's."

Tony felt the reaction behind him—chairs moving, stifled coughs, the sounds of nervous attentiveness. At the corner of his vision, Tony could see that the beautician did not move at all. Facing Shapiro, he asked, "Do you have any opinion as to how Mr. Nixon's prints got on *that* watch?"

"Of course not." Shapiro's tone became puzzled, self-deprecating. "Any more than I, or anyone, can tell you how Mr. Robb's prints got there. Or what either print might mean."

"All right." Backing away from the bulletin board, Tony gave the jury a moment to absorb this. "Did I also ask, Dr. Shapiro, for your opinion as to whether Marcie Calder had anal intercourse the night of her death?"

"Yes, you did." Shapiro folded his hands. "I definitely agree with Dr. Micelli. Marcie Calder *did* have anal intercourse, and her partner *did* use a condom. I also agree with the coroner's assertion that the most likely brand is Adam's Rib."

"Did you agree, or disagree, with Dr. Micelli's belief that this act of anal intercourse was consensual?"

"Again, I agree. As Dr. Micelli stated, a rape should have caused more tissue damage. I believe that such damage as existed reflects prior inexperience but willing participation."

As with the jury, Tony saw, Sue had turned her gaze on Sam: it had the same unreadable quality that Tony had noticed on his return, so different from the gaze of the girl he once had known. Sam stared at his folded hands, unable to look at anyone.

It was time to end this, Tony thought. "Did you also examine," Tony asked Shapiro, "a sample of the blood smear taken from the wheel of Mrs. Robb's gray Volvo?"

"I did. And I agree that it's Marcie Calder's blood."

"Did you make any other determination?"

"Yes. At your request, I attempted to determine whether the blood sample contained traces of a substance not found in blood."

"Did you find any such substance?"

"I did." Pausing, Shapiro addressed the jury in a firm tone. "Two separate tests revealed that the sample contained traces of a silicone resin, called polydimethyl silicone, or PDMS."

"How do you explain the presence of PDMS in Ms. Calder's blood?"

"PDMS is the lubricant commonly found in Adam's Rib. That's the only explanation I can think of."

Tony nodded. "Does PDMS match the substance found on the anal swabs described by Dr. Micelli?"

"It does."

"Did you find any other foreign matter in the blood sample?"

"Yes." Shapiro looked at Tony now. "Both tests revealed traces of feces."

Softly, Tony asked, "Based on these results, Dr. Shapiro, what can you say about the blood found on the steering wheel?"

Shapiro folded his hands. "That it reflects the blood found on the exterior of Marcie Calder's anus and may well have gotten on the steering wheel after Mr. Robb removed his condom. Or, at least, touched it."

Tony moved closer. "In your opinion, what does the smear of blood tell you about whether Marcie Calder was murdered, or about the identity of the murderer?"

Shapiro looked grave. "In all probability, nothing at all."

Pausing, Tony saw the faces of the jurors, pensive and surprised. "Thank you," he told Shapiro, and returned to the defense table. Any relief he felt was canceled by the look on Sam Robb's face, suffused in shame and—for the briefest of moments—resentment.

NINETEEN

Appraising Shapiro with her eyes slightly widened, Stella Marz hesitated before rising, as though deciding which point to attack first. But her manner was calm and undismayed. "Let's start," she said bluntly, "with the possibility of accident or suicide. Is that what you really think happened here?"

Shapiro shook his head. "I was careful not to say that. What I *did* say—and all I said—is that the evidence cited by Detective Gregg and Dr. Micelli doesn't rule out the possibility."

"Then let's take the fatal injury. Marcie Calder had pronounced coup injuries, correct? Trauma to the brain on the side where her skull was crushed?"

"That's right."

"These suggest a blow administered by someone else, true?"

"Yes."

Stella placed her hands on her hips. "Ever seen a coup head injury this severe in a fall?"

Shapiro frowned. "No."

"All right. As I understand you, all you were saying is that the absence of contre-coup injuries does not rule out a fall."

"Yes. That's all I was saying."

"But combined with the presence of *coup* injuries, doesn't that strongly suggest death at the hands of another?"

Watching Shapiro, Tony saw the first signs of discomfort—an expert who fears that he is at the edge of his credibility. "It certainly 'suggests' a homicide, yes."

"And that's what you believe happened, isn't it?"

"More likely than not, yes."

Stella's long, silent look had the maternal contempt of a teacher who has caught a precocious student in a lie. "Then let's move on," she said. "You also suggested that rain obscured the evidence that the abrasions on Marcie Calder's face and hands were postmortem—that is, suffered in a fall after death. Do you remember that testimony?"

"I do, yes."

Already, Tony noted, Shapiro had begun to seem cautious, less voluble. "In a *pre*mortem injury," Stella pressed, "you would expect to find bleeding beneath the skin."

"I would."

"But not here."

"No."

"Isn't the likely reason that Marcie Calder's heart had already stopped pumping?"

"Yes."

"So, to use your words, it's much 'more likely than not' that these are postmortem injuries."

"Yes."

"And, of course, the rock *was* seven feet from Marcie's head."

"Yes."

"*And* there was no blood found on any other rock."

"No."

"So we have several factors which suggest that Marcie Calder was murdered before her fall: coup head injuries; likely postmortem abrasions; the absence of blood on the hill or on any other rock; and the fact that the one rock with blood on it was a fair distance from her head."

"Those factors exist, yes."

Stella paused. "You can quibble with any one of them, Doctor. But isn't this *combination* compelling evidence of homicide?"

"It certainly suggests homicide, yes."

"What about the footprints above the hill? Are you aware of any evidence of fall-like indentations made by someone's knees?"

"No."

Standing taller, Stella maintained her tone of calm relentlessness. "You would agree, then, that there is considerable physical evidence which affirmatively suggests a homicide?"

Shapiro pondered Stella's semantics for a moment. "Yes."

"Then please tell the jury what physical evidence, if any, affirmatively supports the notion of suicide or accident."

Shapiro folded his hands. " 'Affirmatively supports'?"

"That's right."

"I'm not aware of any."

Tony watched Stella hesitate, looking for a final question to drive the point home. Then, as Tony would have, she seemed to conclude that this was unnecessary.

"You mentioned, Dr. Shapiro, your belief that Marcie Calder engaged in a consensual act of anal intercourse, correct?"

"Yes."

"You assume, moreover, that Mr. Robb was Marcie Calder's lover?"

"Yes."

"Given this intimacy, wouldn't you expect to find traces of Marcie Calder's hair on the defendant's clothes?"

"Possibly."

"But there weren't any such traces on the clothes Mr. Robb claimed to wear that night, correct?"

"According to the criminalist's report, no."

"Doesn't that suggest that Mr. Robb wasn't wearing those clothes, and that he lied to the police?"

There was no need to object, Tony knew. "Not necessarily," Shapiro answered calmly. "It's entirely possible that he might not have Ms. Calder's hairs on his clothes. At the time of sexual intimacy, neither of them was necessarily dressed."

Sam shifted in his chair, trapped and restless. Tony's discomfort was different—the answer might remind the jury that Sam Robb had not testified.

Stella moved closer. "But the police *did* find Marcie Calder's hairs in the back seat of the car, didn't they?"

"According to the report."

"And on the headrest of the passenger seat?"

"That's what the report said."

"And there was no blood on the defendant's clothes, right?"

"Not according to the report."

"And yet you believe there was blood on his hands?"

"Yes."

"Doesn't *that* suggest that Mr. Robb had changed his clothes and lied to the police?"

"Not necessarily, Ms. Marz. Perhaps Mr. Robb simply didn't get any blood on his clothes."

Against his will, Tony imagined Sam in bloody clothes, desperate to get rid of them. But the image went black—there was no evidence that this was so. Next to him, his friend's face was vulnerable again, filled with shame and sadness.

"The police report," Stella prodded, "also noted gray-blond hairs on Ms. Calder's clothes, correct?"

"Yes."

"Those hairs matched the defendant's, right?"

"Yes."

"Doesn't that indicate that Marcie and the defendant achieved some degree of intimacy while she was dressed?"

"It does."

"And yet, Dr. Shapiro, none of Marcie's hairs are on the clothes *Sam Robb* says he was wearing."

"Yes. I said that."

"Did either you, or the police lab, find any hairs on Marcie Calder's clothes which appeared to belong to an African-American?"

"No."

"Wouldn't you expect some, if Ms. Calder were involved in a struggle with an African-American assailant?"

Shapiro shrugged. "That assumes too many facts, Ms. Marz. Was there a struggle? Where did the assailant touch the victim? Your question is impossible to answer."

This was a fair response, Tony knew, and the jury seemed to know it. They turned expectantly to Stella.

Stella stopped, frustration briefly crossing her face, and then she looked serene again. "Then let's turn to the tuna sandwich," she said. "Assuming that Marcie ate the sandwich at approximately eight o'clock, do you agree that she would have fully digested it by ten o'clock?"

"Only approximately. You have to allow a half hour either way, as Dr. Micelli conceded. So a homicide could have occurred as late as ten-thirty."

Stella tilted her head. "But not a homicide involving Mr. Nixon, correct? Assuming that his telephone records are correct and that he placed a call to his estranged wife at ten-eighteen."

"Assuming that, true. I have no knowledge, one way or the other."

"But you're also aware that Mr. Robb claims to have left Marcie Calder at around ten o'clock?"

"Yes."

"So this gives Mr. Nixon roughly eighteen minutes to find Marcie Calder in the dark, locate a rock, hit her on the head three times, drag her to the edge of the cliff without leaving any hairs on her clothes, throw her off, return to his car, drive two miles to his home, and call his wife in Chicago."

Shapiro looked faintly amused. "Assuming that Mr. Robb's ten o'clock estimate was right, yes."

"On that assumption, do you think Mr. Nixon—or anyone—could have done all this in eighteen minutes?"

Shapiro pondered his answer. "To start," he said finally, "the assumption about time is a big one. If Mr. Robb left the park at nine-thirty or nine forty-five, everything changes. And we have no indication that his statement to the police was precise, or that time was the biggest thing on his mind.

"But I'll assume for a moment that Mr. Robb's guess is right on the money. Could Mr. Nixon have done all that in eighteen minutes? I need more information. For instance, did Mr. Nixon stop to change his clothes, or did he run right home? And we've got no physical evidence with respect to Mr. Nixon, because the Lake City police never gathered any.

"But yeah—it's *feasible* that he could have done all that. Especially if he called his ex-wife as soon as he got home." Pausing, Shapiro faced the jury, finishing his answer. "I'm certainly not saying that's what happened. All I'm saying is that, hypothetically, it *could* have happened. I'm also saying, quite emphatically, that—if this is a murder—there's nothing to say that the murderer has to be Mr. Robb."

At the corner of his eye, Tony saw Saul regard the table, trying not to smile. Wounded, Stella tried to recover.

"Let's summarize where we are, Dr. Shapiro. There's no affirmative evidence to suggest that Marcie Calder fell over the cliff by accident?"

"Affirmative evidence? No."

"Or affirmative evidence that she killed herself?"

"No."

"Nor is there any affirmative evidence that Sam Robb was in the clothes he said he was wearing?"

"No."

"But there is affirmative evidence that he had anal intercourse with Marcie Calder, then lied to the police?"

"There seems to be. Yes."

"There is affirmative evidence that Sam Robb fathered Marcie's unborn child? And lied about *that*?"

"Yes."

"And Marcie Calder's body shows no signs of another assailant—no hair, no skin beneath her nails, nothing?"

"That's true. But as you point out, the only hairs on her clothes—Sam Robb's hairs—could have gotten there because of sexual intimacy. So there is *no* physical evidence—hair or skin—to suggest she was assaulted at all. Let alone that Mr. Robb assaulted her." Shapiro paused for a brief, lethal moment. "That includes the blood on the steering wheel, which I already explained."

It was the answer of the skilled expert; waiting for his moment, Shapiro had driven home the essence of Sam's defense.

"Isn't it quite possible," Stella rejoined, "that Mr. Robb murdered Marcie Calder and that the blood from the murder became commingled with material from the condom already on his fingers?"

Shapiro propped his elbow on the witness stand, head resting on the palm of his hand. "Possible?" he answered. "I can't rule it out. But I don't think it's likely that this would account for the amount of resin and fecal matter found in the blood smear."

"But you can't say, can you, that the blood wasn't derived from Marcie Calder's head injuries?"

"No, I can't. All that I can say is that there are compelling reasons not to *assume* that it *was*. Or that it implicates Sam Robb in a murder."

Stella paused, stymied for a moment. Leaning his head to Saul's, Tony whispered, "Have we done enough?"

Saul looked at the jury, then at Sam. "Yeah," he murmured. "I think we've done enough."

TWENTY

Tony and Sam sat alone in the witness room. "I want to rest our case tomorrow," Tony said.

Sam gave him a long, cool look. "*My* case, Tony. My case."

Tony sat back, tired. The first moments after adjournment had been spent thanking Peter Shapiro; stalling the bespectacled *Vanity Fair* reporter who wished to interview Tony about Alison Taylor; arranging a working dinner with Saul. When Tony glanced at Sue, her expression was one of deep preoccupation, and she did not see him. Then Tony's gaze was interrupted by a hand on his arm; turning, he saw Sam look from Sue to him. Tersely,

Sam said, "We need to talk," and Tony knew at once that there would be trouble.

Now, trapped with Sam in the witness room, Tony felt tense and claustrophobic. "Whoever's case it is," Tony answered, "*I* believe I can win it. I think we've got reasonable doubt."

Sam stared at him. "*They* think I did it. I've been watching their faces, and they think I'm guilty."

Tony drew a breath. "They may suspect that, but they don't *know* it. My job was never to make you look innocent, or even sympathetic. It's only to make you 'not guilty'—"

"To get me *off*, you mean. To get a guilty man acquitted because his lawyer's so fucking clever." Sam stood abruptly, voice rising. "They *hate* me, Tony. The people on the jury, and the people in my own town. I buggered a teenage girl and lied about it. I knocked her up and lied about *that*. I lied to my wife and Marcie's parents. Hell, I lied to just about everyone. . . ."

"True. You did. So now you want to testify? Have you forgotten our practice session the other day . . . ?"

"Dammit, they already *know* all that. What's to keep them from thinking I'm capable of murder? How could I make it any worse?"

"By having to *admit* 'all that' to the jury and then asking them to believe you're a swell guy. By seeming like someone who wants more than fairness—who wants their fucking *sympathy*. By looking like a liar who thinks they're gullible and stupid." Tony felt his temple throb. "Sam, we're talking about chemistry between you and twelve strangers who weren't sympathetic going in. Bad chemistry can overcome everything I've tried to do here. If the jury decides they hate you—that they don't want to believe you no matter what's true—it's over. Reasonable doubt won't do it."

Sam leaned forward. "Tony," he said softly, "I didn't kill her. If I can't stand up and say I'm innocent, then I can't live in Lake City. I can't win back Sue or face the kids. I've got no chance to ever put this behind me."

What Tony felt inside him, he realized, was the worm of his own fear—that his friend would be destroyed, then sent away to prison. "What if you're convicted?" he asked.

Sam's gaze was intense: in the hot, airless room, his forehead was stained with red. "Then I lose this half-life you want me to lead—Sam Robb, the guy who hid behind his lawyer." All at once, his voice was raw, accusatory, as if Tony's real motive had just struck him. "Is that what you want—for me to *hide* behind you, with some people doubting me about Marcie like they doubt you about Alison? How can you fucking *want* that for me?"

"I didn't put you here, dammit." Tony stood, face inches from Sam's. "You did, and you've got too much to explain."

Tony saw Sam's throat work, watched him struggle for self-control. Quietly, Sam asked, "You think I did it, don't you?"

Tony shoved his hands in his pockets, fighting his own temper. There was nothing left but the truth. "I don't know, Sam. I really don't. But on the evidence, you surely could have."

To Tony's surprise, Sam looked less angry than curious. "How do you live with that?" he asked. "Wondering if I killed her?"

"Not easily. And not well."

"I don't live with it so well, either. And if *you* think that, everyone does." Sam backed away, leaning against the wall with folded arms. "You never had your day in court, Tony. So some people, like Alison's parents, still think it was you, not that black rapist they shot—"

"Some people, Sam? Or you?"

Sam's eyes glinted. "No. Not me anymore. And I don't know whether fucking Ernie killed Marcie Calder, or if she fell off the goddamned cliff. All I know, like you told me about Alison, is that *I* didn't do it. But there's one difference between you and me. I got charged with murder. Which gives me the right to get up in front of God and everyone and *say* I didn't do it—"

"God and Stella Marz," Tony snapped. "She's damn near drooling—every few days she asks if I'll put you on. Do you need me to remind you of what she'll do to you?"

"*Do* to me? The fucking dyke's already done it." Suddenly, Sam's voice changed; it was low and measured, the voice of a man speaking a terrible truth. "You still want me to depend on you, don't you? To be the quarterback. We're still back in high school, and you're still telling me what the play's going to be, with the same cool blue eyes, the same cool voice, *so* cool it's like you're living in a different place than any of the rest of us, where nothing reaches you.

"Well, it's my play to call now, because it's my life. I can make them believe me, Tony. I *need* them to, *need* it—"

Sam stopped abruptly, as if the nakedness of his admission had frightened him. In the silence that followed, Tony said simply, "If you trip up, Stella may bring the second girl in on you. Jenny Travis."

As if deflated, his friend sagged against the wall; Sam was prepared for anger, Tony thought, but not for calm or reason. Perhaps this was the part of Tony that, for its self-control, Sam Robb had always feared and hated.

"I'm sorry," Sam said at last. "I didn't mean that stuff."

"Didn't you?"

Sam closed his eyes. "Maybe I did," he answered softly. "You've always been the sensible one, the one who never lost it. That was what always made you better than me—not talent or even smarts, but this *thing* you had that no one could ever take from you." He exhaled. "So yeah, maybe I did."

Opening his eyes, Sam looked straight at Tony. "But this isn't about sensible, pal. It's about—what would you Catholics call it?—redemption. The only way to redeem myself is to go through this. It's the only way I can face other people, face myself. To convince them that killing Marcie Calder isn't me."

"Killer, killer . . ."

In the silence, Tony felt himself transported to another time and place, a high school gym where catcalls echoed. . . .

Why don't you pretend the ball is Alison's neck . . . ?

At the school board meeting, accused of murder by John Taylor, Tony had sat silent as Saul spoke for him. . . .

Why are you being such a snob? Mary Jane Kulas had asked. *Like you don't care what people think . . .*

Tony had ached to say this was not so.

He says I shouldn't talk to anyone, he had said to Sam and Sue. *Even though I'm innocent . . .*

Tony rubbed the bridge of his nose. "Saul gave me a life," he said. "I want to give you yours back. That's all this is about, Sam. Not my vanity, not my needs. Not even about you and me."

"It *is*, though. You didn't do it, and I didn't help you. Now *I* didn't do it, and I'm asking for your help anyway." Sam sat across from Tony again. "They're waiting for me, Tony—the jury, everyone in the courtroom, the people in my town. They're waiting, and they're wondering: Does Sam Robb have the guts to face us and say he's not a murderer?" His voice became soft. "Maybe, when I do, they'll find me guilty. Then it'll be *me*, not you, sitting there in the Ohio State Penitentiary, waiting and maybe hoping to die. But if that's what has to be, and I don't testify, then I'll have a very long time to wonder what might have happened if I'd stood up for myself. And I *know* I'd rather die than live with that."

For once, there was nothing Tony could say. Quiet, Sam reached across the table and covered Tony's hand with his. "Stand behind me, Tony. Help me be as good a quarterback as I can be, as good a *man* as I can be. Then maybe you'll believe in me. Sometimes I think that would mean more to me than anything else."

There were tears in Sam's eyes, Tony saw. After a moment, Tony said, "Then we've got a lot to do."

TWENTY-ONE

Sam Robb sat on the witness stand, his striped tie carefully knotted, his gray-blond hair neatly combed. His candid blue eyes swept the courtroom; even amidst the tension, Tony sensed Sam's relief that, whatever the consequences, he would at last speak for himself. But faced with such disapproval, Sam also seemed taut, twitchy, unsure of where to look or how to act. It reminded Tony of one of the few times he had seen Sam in a suit, on the day of Alison's funeral, and Sue had rescued Sam from his own awkwardness. Tony himself felt tight; he did not want to be part of his friend's destruction, did not even care to watch.

Softly, Tony asked, "What was your relationship with Marcie Calder?"

Pretending to face his lawyer, Sam did not quite look anywhere, and there was a hollow sound to his voice. "At first, she was just a student, someone on my track team, then someone I was proud of. Six weeks before she died, we started a relationship. . . ."

To the side, Tony saw Stella watching Sam with a cold, unblinking focus. "How did that happen?" Tony asked.

Sam puffed his cheeks, blowing out a breath of air. "She was young and pretty . . . ," he began, then started over with a dogged air, his voice flat but under control.

"Marcie needed someone—me, she thought. For years I'd been watching these teenage guys be what I used to be, a hero. Now I was someone's hero again." Sam's throat worked, and he shook his head. "I mean, she was nothing like Sue. But she reminded me of when Sue and I were young. . . ." Startlingly, he looked up at the Calders. "I took advantage of her. If I hadn't been so selfish, none of us would be here. And now there's nothing I can do that's any good to anyone."

Tony realized that he could barely breathe. He did not know where this was going, what Sam would say, how Marcie's parents must feel, and when the harsh crack of Stella's voice would interrupt. But Stella was simply watching.

"You lied to your wife," Tony said. "Didn't you?"

"Yes. To Sue. To Marcie's parents. To the police." A sheen of tears appeared in Sam's eyes. "I was frightened and ashamed."

Tony felt as if he and Sam were encased in a cocoon constructed of a deep, pained silence. "You had sexual intercourse with her," Tony said flatly.

"Yes." Sam's fingers touched the bottom of his tie. "The first time was in Taylor Park. In a sleeping bag." His voice filled with shame and wonder. "Anytime, I could have stopped it. . . ."

Karoly stared at his hands; it seemed that, like Tony and the jurors, the judge wished he were not here. There are moments in the lives of others, Tony thought, that excite both our disgust and our shame, the fear of what we ourselves might do. The sole defense is to turn away, and Sam had now denied that choice to anyone here.

"Did you use birth control?" Tony asked.

"A condom." Sam paused. "The first time, it broke. . . ."

"But you didn't stop, did you?"

Sam shook his head. "I tried, but . . . I just wanted her too much—the newness, the excitement. Even this sickening feeling of tenderness about what this girl had given me, a middle-aged man. . . ."

Stop, Tony wanted to say. He felt a sour sickness of his own, the sensation of seconds passing too slowly. Sam's catharsis, if that was what everyone was witnessing, would leave him without dignity. The one possibility more terrible for Tony to contemplate was that he was witnessing a perverse act of contrition, performed with his assistance by a murderer, who now scanned the courtroom for sympathy from beneath a mask of self-abasement.

"Did you *ever* decide to break it off?" Tony asked.

"Yes." Sam licked his lips and took a quick, nervous gulp of water. "Because of Sue. Once you start lying to someone you love, it's like you're alone, watching them through a window you put there yourself. The night Marcie died, I wanted to tell her. . . ."

The last words had the bitter ring of guilt. Seemingly despite her own wishes, the beautician looked up at Sam.

"That night," Tony asked softly, "what really happened?"

Sitting back, Sam took a deep breath. His voice, newly raw, seemed to come from the back of his throat. "She was nervous—I thought she must know what I was going to say. Then we got to the park, and she said she loved me and wanted to do something special. So she whispered it in my ear. . . ."

"Anal intercourse."

"Yes." Now Sam could not look at anyone. "I'd given her one of my rubbers. She kept it in her purse for me. . . ."

Someone coughed. Other than Sam's voice, and his own, it was the first sound Tony had heard in moments.

"What happened then?" Tony asked.

"God . . ." Sam gave a disjointed shake of the head. "I wanted to. . . ."

"So you did. In the back seat of the car."

"Yes." Sam touched the water glass but did not drink. "When it was over, I felt so dirty. Then she asked me how it was, and I thanked her. . . ."

"After that," Tony asked, "did Marcie dress again?"

Sam drank the water in one long swallow. "I pulled up her underpants in the back," he finally said. "To cover her."

Tony felt himself wince. But the question was a necessary one; somehow Sam must account for where Marcie's blood was and why it was not on the back upholstery.

"What about the condom?"

"I'd started to take it off." For a moment, Sam's voice had the undertone of fear recalled. "Then there was this light in the window—headlights from a car at the rear of the parking lot. All I wanted was for us to get dressed. So we did, and then the lights went out. I figured that they'd just gotten there. . . ."

"Once you were dressed, what happened next?"

Sam raised his head. His next words were soft, astonished. "She asked me if I'd marry her."

"Were you surprised?"

"Yes." Sam's tone was ashen. "She said she could give me babies."

"Did she tell you she was pregnant?"

"No." For the first time, Sam looked at the jury—a sideways glance—then looked back. "If I hadn't panicked, I'm sure she would have. But I never gave her a chance."

"Why was that?"

"Because I was so shocked, I think. It was like I woke up and saw how far I'd let her go.

"I started blurting things. That Sue was still my wife; that we'd been married all these years; that we'd created a life together. That I was much too old for Marcie; that I didn't want her to throw her life away. I was trying to sound selfless, but I came off like this phony uncle on those kids' shows my own kids used to watch, talking down to the five-year-olds.

"Finally, I just broke down and asked her to protect me—" Sam caught himself. "A sixteen-year-old girl, and I wanted her to protect me, the vice principal of Lake City High. Protect me from what I'd done to her . . ."

Turning away, Sam fought back tears. But Stella's gaze had filled with a disgust so deep that, to Tony, she could barely contain it. Quite deliberately, she let the pencil drop from her hands, drawing the jurors' attention, then Sam's. They stared at each other across the courtroom, Stella's contempt reflected in the sudden redness of Sam's face.

Softly, Tony asked, "How did Marcie react?"

Sam turned from Stella. When he took a breath, his body shuddered with it. "I can still remember how she looked," he said finally. "The angriest expression I'd ever seen from her was more like determination, and only when she was running track. But now she was crying, and the look on her face was close to hate, and I could see how much feeling she'd invested in me.

" 'You want me to help *you*,' she said. 'I'll start helping you right now.'

" 'Wait,' I said.

" 'For what?' She was almost screaming, and I could see the pulse in her temples. 'For you to give me more precious memories? I'd die first. . . .' "

Pausing, Sam touched his throat. " 'I'd die first,' " he repeated slowly. "I've had three months, now, to think about that. To think about how I'd made her feel . . ."

I'd die first.

Caught in the middle of Sam's drama, Tony wondered why Sam had never told him this before. "What did you do . . . ?"

"Marcie got out of the car. Just like that, she was running into the park. Then I couldn't see her anymore. . . ."

Sam's voice broke, then recovered. "I was too afraid to follow her, afraid someone might see me, maybe the couple I imagined in the other car. So I just let her go. The next time I saw her, she was dead. . . ."

Sam turned, and his eyes met Tony's. Was he looking for distrust, Tony wondered, or disbelief? "And you never knew she was pregnant," Tony said.

Pausing, Sam writhed in the witness chair, and his voice became soft again. "Once she knew I didn't want to marry her, I guess she couldn't tell me. If she only had, I swear I'd have found a way to help her, even if I'd had to tell Sue everything. Instead it's like I killed her.

"But I *didn't*." Sam turned to the jury again, words filling with passion. "Not the way Ms. Marz says I did. Because I could never, ever take the life of a girl I cared for so much. Or *anyone's* life." Sam's voice became anguished, close to angry. "I'm not *like* that. I'm not the kind of person who would do that to protect myself. *That's* why I went to the police. Look at where it got me—*here*." Suddenly he looked away. "God help me, it's my own fault, and other innocent people have paid a far bigger price. But I didn't kill her, and when we found her body, I—"

In the stricken silence, Sam stopped, as if he had lost the thread. The courtroom was like a frieze: Karoly's expression of honest bewilderment; Stella's face, as hard as Tony had ever seen it, the almond eyes watching Sam with fierce avidity. But the jury, Tony noticed, no longer looked away.

"That night," Tony asked curtly, "what did you do next?"

Sam's face seemed rubbery, his eyes unfocused. "I left. That's all. I was afraid, so I just left her there. . . ."

"About what time?"

"I don't know." Pausing, Sam gathered himself, his tone becoming subdued. "I told the police about ten, but that was a guess. It could have been nine-thirty. . . ." Turning to the jury, Sam finished with terrible weariness. "I didn't know time was important then. I just wanted to find her, still alive."

Tony let the jury study Sam: twelve people watching a single man, his gaze imploring. "When you left," Tony inquired at last, "did you see anyone else?"

"In the car. I wish I'd looked closer. But I couldn't even see the make. All I remember is a head, ducking beneath the dashboard." Sam's face filled with shame and sorrow. "For a minute, I had this crazy fear—not for Marcie, but for me. Like the head was Sue, that she'd found me out . . ."

"After you left the park, what did you do?"

"At first, I went to school. Just sat in my office, wondering how I'd gotten here, what to do." Sam's hands gripped his knees now, and his stare was empty. "So I tried to call Sue, just to hear her voice. When she didn't answer, I felt lost.

"That's when I decided to rededicate my life to her. To remember how lucky I was. So I got in the car and drove home."

"And Sue was there."

"Yeah. Sue was there." Sam gave a fleeting, incongruous smile, as though remembering this last moment of hope. "She was watching TV, in bed. So I got in next to her, like I had a thousand times before. . . ." When Sam gazed past him, expression pleading now, Tony knew that he was looking at Sue. "But that night, I loved her more than I had in years. All I wanted was another chance. . . ."

Glistening, Sam's eyes did not move from Sue. The beautician's face, Tony saw, was curious, perhaps softer.

Quietly, Tony asked, "Can you explain your fingerprints on Marcie's watch?"

Sam was still for a moment. Then, with apparent reluctance, he turned from Sue. "When we were making love," he answered in a monotone, "I held Marcie's wrists."

Tony walked closer, as if to shelter Sam from his own shame. "The blood on the steering wheel? Can you explain that?"

Slowly, Sam nodded.

"I'm sorry," Tony said. "We need an audible response."

Sam folded his hands in front of him, head down. "At the high school, I went to the locker room. To flush the condom down the toilet. When I took it off, I saw Marcie's blood on it." His eyes shut. "I guess it got on my hands. . . ."

Silent, Sam began to weep. He would not hide his face.

Looking up at Karoly, Tony said, "No further questions," and, for once, was glad of this.

TWENTY-TWO

Stella Marz was out of her chair before Tony reached his.

Face tear-streaked, Sam braced himself. *Take your time,* Tony had said, *and don't ever lose your temper. She wants the jury to see that.*

"You lied to your wife," Stella snapped.

As Tony had instructed, Sam paused, to impose his own rhythm on her. "Yes," he said softly. "I lied to Sue."

"So you wouldn't get caught."

Sam glanced at Sue. "So I wouldn't *lose* her, yes."

"You misled Marcie's parents."

"Yes."

"You lied to the principal too. Told him you hadn't slept with her."

"I didn't want to lose my job—"

"Yes or no."

"Yes."

"You lied to the police about your relationship to Marcie."

"Yes."

"So you wouldn't get in trouble."

Sam folded his hands. "Yes," he said dully. "So I wouldn't get in trouble."

"And you lied to the police about what you and Marcie did that night."

Sam paused, looking down. "Like I said, I was embarrassed—"

Interrupting, Stella's voice dripped contempt. "Isn't it your pattern, Mr. Robb, to lie anytime the truth will get you into trouble?"

Sam crossed his arms now. "No. It isn't. Or I'd have never gone to the police."

It was a good answer, Tony thought, and an important one; Tony would not intervene, he had told Sam, unless Stella made it unavoidable. Sam liked this, he said—the jury must see him as on his own. But Tony's palms were already damp with tension, worse for his passivity.

"But you *lied* to the police," Stella prodded, "didn't you?"

"About some things—"

"Lied to the police, *and* to your wife, *and* to Marcie's parents, *and* to your principal. Every time the truth would hurt you, you lied."

Sam paused, the first flash of anger in his eyes. But he kept his calm. "Telling the police I was with Marcie didn't *help* me, Ms. Marz. Saying where I'd last seen her didn't help me. As near as I can tell, that's why I'm sitting here, answering your questions. . . ."

"Watch it," Tony said, under his breath.

Abruptly, Sam paused, as if hearing his friend's

voice, then added softly, "That, and my own mistakes. I'll never stop being sorry for that."

The jury, Tony saw, watched Sam intently, looking for cracks. Sam was walking the line that Tony had drawn for him—to neutralize Stella without appearing too clever.

Crisply, she asked, "Aren't you still doing what you've done ever since you slept with Marcie Calder—lying to this jury, to keep out of trouble?"

"No." Pausing, Sam turned to the jury, looking straight at the beautician. "No. I'm not lying now. . . ."

"But you only admitted the affair because DNA testing showed that Marcie Calder was pregnant with your child."

Slowly, Sam faced her. "I guess that's so. But I had a reason to be afraid. And, like my lawyer says, there's a difference between lying and murder. We *all* lie, Ms. Marz. But we don't all kill. *I* didn't kill."

"He's going too far," Saul murmured. Silent, Tony nodded.

Stella put her hands on her hips. "So you were just an innocent man, trapped in a bad situation."

Sam scowled at her. "I trapped myself, it seems like. By coming to the police—"

"By making Marcie Calder pregnant, you mean."

"That too, Ms. Marz. That too."

When Stella paused, the Calders stared at Sam with open hatred. Softly, Stella said, "Tell the jury how you seduced Marcie Calder."

Watching Sam, Tony felt himself tense. "It didn't happen like that," Sam answered.

"No? Did she seduce *you*, Mr. Robb?"

Sam looked down. "She came to my office and said she wanted to be with me . . . that way. I'm not saying it wasn't my responsibility. All I'm saying is that it wasn't my initiative."

Stella gave him a derisive smile. "I guess you'd never had sex with a student before—"

"Objection," Tony called out at once. "May I approach the bench, Your Honor?"

Karoly nodded. "Of course."

Heart racing, Tony crossed the courtroom; as Karoly leaned over the bench, Stella's level gaze met his.

"Nice try," Tony murmured, then said to Karoly, "Whether my client has, or has not, had sex with any other student is irrelevant to murder—"

"I disagree," Stella cut in. "And Mr. Robb is about to tell us the sad story of his seduction by Marcie Calder. I have a witness, Jenny Travis, whom Mr. Robb coerced into having sex when she was seventeen years old. That goes to his credibility. *And* to his predisposition to mistreat women."

"To *kill* them?" Tony retorted. "That's the issue here, and there is no evidence of any predisposition to violence—let alone murder." Staring at Karoly, Tony made his voice low and angry. "This isn't an academic debate, Your Honor. The proposed line of questioning *and* Ms. Travis's story are grossly prejudicial to the jury's attitude toward my client, without proving a thing about *this* supposed murder. If there's one more word about this, I'll demand a mistrial: if I don't get it here, I'll get it in the court of appeals." He turned to Stella. "You're losing, and you know it. You're trying to trap the judge in a mistake—"

"Bullshit," she cut in, and now her anger seemed quite real. "Your client has a pathological attitude toward women, and he's lying about it."

"So don't go out with him, Stella. But don't *ever* try to railroad him on a murder charge."

"All right," Karoly put in, moments later than he should have. He looked from Tony to Stella, indecisive but knowing that it was the defense, not the prosecution, that could appeal if it lost. Avoiding reversal was the first instinct of a cowardly judge; glancing at Stella, Tony saw this knowledge in her eyes.

"I'm sustaining the objection," Karoly said to Stella. "Any more, and I'll give Mr. Lord his mistrial, and hold *you* in contempt. Understood?"

Stella lowered her eyes, struggling to conceal her anger. "Yes, Your Honor."

"Thank you, Your Honor," Tony said promptly. Retreating back to the defense table before the judge could change his mind, Tony felt Sue's grave brown eyes.

"Another bullet dodged," Saul murmured.

Tony's heart was still racing; on the witness stand, Sam Robb breathed deeply, his eyes half shut. When they opened, it was to look at Tony with gratitude.

"Tell us," Stella asked with renewed calm, "how it was you first had sex with Marcie Calder."

Sam faced her again. "She came to my office and said she loved me."

"And then?"

Sam puffed his cheeks, but kept his eyes on Stella. "She said she wanted to go down on me."

Stella's eyes glinted. "As in oral sex, Mr. Robb? I just want to make sure the jury understands you."

"Yes. That's what I meant."

"What did you say to this offer?"

"Say?" Sam's words were mumbled. "Not much."

"Not even 'yes,' 'no,' or 'thank you'? As I remember, you thanked her for *anal* sex that night."

Sam flushed with anger. "I don't remember what I said—"

"You just *let* her?"

"Yes."

"Because she wanted to so much."

Sam looked down. "I wanted it too."

Stella gave him a cold stare. "So at least it wasn't too hard for you. . . ."

"No."

"Do you know if Marcie Calder had ever done anything like that before?"

"No." Sam's voice was quiet now. "She said she hadn't. . . ."

"But you didn't stop her."

"No."

"Did you achieve climax, Mr. Robb?"

Tony stood again. "Objection," he said. "No one wants to hear this, Your Honor. Least of all Ms. Calder's parents. And it's irrelevant to any issue in this case—"

"Nonsense." Stella's voice was crisp, confident. "It's the murder of *this* girl for which Mr. Robb is standing trial. The credibility of Mr. Robb's account, real or imagined, rests on his relationship to Marcie Calder, who he implies would have rather died than live without him. Mr. Robb has given that testimony voluntarily, and the state—which alone can speak for this dead girl— deserves some latitude in cross-examination."

Karoly pursed his lips, gazing out at Marcie's parents. "Overruled." He said to Stella, "Please re-ask the question."

Stella turned to Sam, her voice almost casual. "That first time, when you say Marcie Calder gave you oral sex in your office at Lake City High School, did you reach climax?"

Glancing at Tony, Sam folded his hands. "Yes."

"In Marcie Calder's mouth?"

Sam shut his eyes again. "Yes."

"Do you happen to know why this inexperienced girl found you so irresistible?"

"No." Eyes still shut, Sam shook his head. "No . . ."

"Did she have emotional problems, do you think?"

"No."

"No psychiatric treatment that you know of?"

"No."

"Her grades were good?"

"Yes."

"Her reputation at the school was good?"

"Yes."

"No rumors of promiscuity?"

"No."

Stella looked at him in open disbelief. "And yet this sixteen-year-old girl, without any prior warning, was suddenly so overcome by your appeal that she wanted to give you oral sex in the vice principal's office."

"That's what happened." Sam's face was suffused with new resentment. "Maybe *you* can't understand it, but that's what happened. . . ."

"No," Tony murmured under his breath. In the jury box, the nutritionist—the woman with two teenage daughters—looked startled and then stared at Sam with the same distaste and belief, Tony was certain, that he himself felt.

In a level voice, Stella said, "Explain it to me, Mr. Robb. Please, make me understand."

Sam's cheeks turned red. "I can't," he said. "She just wanted that with me. . . ."

"Uh-huh. Just like she wanted you to be the first to insert your penis in her anus . . ."

"Look," Sam started, then caught himself. "I was the responsible adult here, not Marcie. I knew we shouldn't have done those things, and still I took advantage, all right? I said that."

"So about anal sex, at first you were reluctant?"

"Yes."

"And *you'd* never, ever, done that, Mr. Robb? Not even once?"

"Objection." Tony tried to make his voice sound weary. "It's obvious what Ms. Marz wishes to do—to make everyone here squirm with such discomfort that it rubs off on Mr. Robb. But if she wants to humiliate him, she should at least choose questions that have some theoretical relationship, however tenuous, to Marcie Calder. *This* question has none at all, and to me and I'm sure to others, it's deeply offensive."

"If it is," Stella retorted, "then I regret offending Mr.

Lord. But the purpose of my question, Your Honor, is to test the credibility of this witness. When Mr. Robb claims that this sixteen-year-old girl initiated a sexual act as to which she had no prior experience, his *own* experience is relevant to whether this story deserves credence. Particularly when Ms. Calder cannot be here to answer for herself—"

"Relevant evidence goes to death," Tony snapped. "Not to her sexual reputation. Or experience."

"Your Honor . . . ," Stella began.

"Never mind, Ms. Marz. I'm overruling Mr. Lord. You can have your answer."

Promptly, Stella turned to Sam. "Had you, before that night, ever experienced anal intercourse with any-one? Man or woman?"

Face red with anger, Sam stared back at Stella. "No."

"No? So how did this eleventh grader get you to go along, Mr. Robb?"

Sam folded his arms. "I don't know. . . ."

"I mean, there you were in a car, just sitting in the lot at Taylor Park, and a sixteen-year-old girl from your high school is trying to get you to sodomize her? Didn't you stop to wonder if that was such a good idea?"

"I wasn't thinking. . . ."

"So how many times did Marcie have to ask you?"

"I don't *know*. . . ."

"Did you make her beg? Or were you more gracious than that?"

Sam sat straighter. "It just happened," he said be-tween his teeth. "I lost my head. . . ."

"You? Hard to believe." When Sam stiffened, in-sulted, Stella underscored this with an ironic smile. "So once you lost your head, how did you do it? You know, the act."

"Jesus," Saul murmured. But Tony did not move.

"Sam's on his own," he whispered. "If I break in ev-ery time he looks angry, the jury will hate us both."

Brusquely, Sam said to Stella, "What kind of question is that?"

"Okay, I'll break it down for you. Did Marcie bend over?"

Sam's voice filled with resentment. "Yes."

"And then you put on a condom?"

"Yes."

"It was in a foil packet, right?"

"Yes."

"And then you had to take off your pants?"

Sam folded his arms again, staring at Stella with open dislike. "Yes. I did."

"How long did all that take?"

Sam's eyes narrowed. "Maybe five minutes."

"And all this time, you were struggling with your conscience."

"I *don't know.* . . ."

"Did Marcie do anything to encourage you? Or was she just lying there, bottom in the air, obediently waiting?"

Sam took another deep breath. "She said that she wanted me."

"And you *always* did what this sixteen-year-old vamp wanted you to?"

"We *both* wanted to, Ms. Marz." Suddenly Sam's voice was rueful, as if Stella had held the mirror to his shame. "And that makes it my fault. . . ."

"How long did it take between the time she asked you and the time you decided to give anal sex a whirl?"

"I don't know. Five minutes."

"And another five or so minutes to put on the condom."

"Yes."

"So after you had the condom on, you put your erect penis between Marcie Calder's buttocks, right?"

Sam could no longer look at her—whether out of

shame, or fear of his own anger, Tony could not tell. "Yes," he said. "I did that. . . ."

"Did she tell you if that hurt?"

Sam swallowed. "I tried to take it slow."

Stella cocked her head. "How long, would you say, did it take to achieve full penetration? A couple of minutes, at least?"

"I don't know, Ms. Marz. I guess so."

"And after that, did you achieve climax?"

"Yes."

Stella paused, her expression curious. "How *long* after?"

Next to Tony, Saul smiled faintly at the table. "Clever," he murmured, and Tony knew that Saul, like him, could see where Stella was headed.

Sam looked down. "Four or five minutes."

"And then, afterward, Marcie asked you how it was."

Now the anger in Sam's eyes seemed close to hatred. "Yes."

"And you were nice enough to thank her."

"Yes."

"Were you still inside her?"

"Yes."

"How long did you stay inside her?"

"I don't know. Maybe another five minutes."

Stella gave him a cold smile: "So there you were, naked, lying on top of a sixteen-year-old with your penis inside her bottom. I hope at least it was dark out."

Sam took his water glass, sipping as he watched her with veiled eyes. "It was dark," he said.

"In fact, it must have been. Because, according to your testimony, you were startled by headlights."

"That's right."

Stella paused a moment. "I guess it was dark when you started lovemaking too. I mean, otherwise you'd have worried about someone recognizing you. Or Marcie."

"Yes."

"It was also dark when you met her, right? At the gas station."

Sam hesitated, and Tony saw comprehension cross his face. "I wouldn't say dark, Ms. Marz. I'd say dusk."

"How long did it take you to drive to Taylor Park? Five minutes?"

"Roughly."

"And was it dark then?"

Sam sat back. "Mostly."

"How long after that did Marcie Calder whisper in your ear that she wanted you to penetrate her anus?"

Sam scowled. "It was right away, almost."

"One minute, two minutes?"

"Soon." Sam's answer was grudging; to Tony, the distraught man the jury had seen on direct examination was gone. "Say two minutes."

Stella paused, eyes narrowing, as if there were something she wished to visualize. "So," she said, "it took at least five minutes to get to the park, one or two minutes for Marcie to proposition you, five minutes to wrestle with your conscience, at least five more to pull down your pants and get the condom on, a couple of minutes to achieve penetration, four or five minutes to orgasm, and, after that, roughly five minutes to thank Marcie politely before the headlights show up." She gazed at the ceiling. "That comes to a half hour, give or take a minute or two. Sound right to you, Mr. Robb?"

Sam folded his hands. "I don't know," he said coolly. "Maybe it didn't take that long, Ms. Marz. I never checked my watch."

It was too obvious, Tony thought, that Sam understood the question. From the nutritionist's skeptical expression, she thought this as well.

Stella returned to the prosecution table, picking up a document. "Your Honor," she said, "this is a certified copy of a report rendered by the National Meteorological Center in Steelton for Thursday, May twenty-third, the night Marcie Calder died. According to the survey, dusk occurred at approximately eight fifty-six. I ask the court to receive it into evidence."

Karoly looked at Tony. But before this jury, to challenge the meteorologic service was a losing proposition. Calmly, Tony said, "The defense has no objection."

In moments, the jurors were passing the report. Sam folded his arms again, defensive. "Would you agree, then," Stella said to him, "that at the time you saw the headlights, it was roughly a half hour—if not more—past the time you met Marcie Calder at dusk?"

Sam glanced at Tony. "Roughly."

"That would take us to nine twenty-five, at least. Do you have any reason to quarrel with that?"

Sam spread his hands. "I don't have any reason to say it's true, either. I just don't know, Ms. Marz, and neither do you."

Sam was tired, Tony saw: it was becoming difficult for him to maintain deference for more than a few questions. But what was more troubling was the difference in manner, caused by his antagonism to Stella: Sam no longer seemed contrite. Glancing at the clock, Tony made up his mind.

"Your Honor," he said to Karoly, "it's close to noon. If, as it seems, Ms. Marz has reached a convenient place to break, perhaps we should take the noon recess."

Stella was prepared for this. With a brief look of disdain at Sam for hiding behind his lawyer, she said calmly, "If Mr. Robb is tired, I'm willing to give him some time off. . . ."

"I'm fine," Sam shot back.

Tony gave Karoly his most pleasant smile. "I'm sure *Mr. Robb* is fine," he said. "But I'm hungry. So perhaps we should ask Ms. Marz how much longer she plans to take."

Stella paused. "At least two hours."

Turning to Karoly, Tony shrugged. "The rest of the day, effectively."

Karoly looked from Sam to Stella. "Let's take our break," he said. "We'll reconvene at one-thirty."

As Sam left the witness stand, clearly annoyed, Tony fooled with some papers, pretending not to look at him. Only when Sam was close enough did Tony say under his breath, without looking up, "Don't ever fucking do that to me again. For the next hour and a half, pal, you can damned well shut up and listen."

TWENTY-THREE

Fleeing reporters, Tony and Saul hurried to the witness room, Tony carrying a bag of roast beef sandwiches from the courthouse cafeteria. "God," Saul murmured. "I think I'm in love. Do you suppose Stella would go out with an old fat Jewish defense lawyer?"

Despite himself, Tony gave a thin smile. "Good, wasn't she."

"*Too* good," Saul answered, emitting a mock groan. "'Explain it to me, Mr. Robb. Please, make me understand.' Only a woman could get away with this." He stopped at the door of the witness room, pensive. "Maybe if I promise her I'll give up drinking . . ."

Tony did not smile now. "I hope the jury's not having the fun that you are."

"Don't bet the ranch, Tony. She's killing him."

Tony gave Saul his sandwich. "I'd better do this alone," he said, and entered the witness room.

Sam was waiting there, hands folded on the table in front of him. He looked wan, resentful, drained by Stella's attack, and his gaze at Tony was opaque. "You wanted to talk," Sam said.

"I wanted you out of there before you started calling Stella a 'cunt.'" Tony leaned forward, speaking more softly. "The woman's a professional, Sam, and she's doing her job. . . ."

"*Professional.* She fucking hates me—"

"Why wouldn't she?" Tony snapped. "Don't make that *your* problem, or it'll be the jury's." He paused for emphasis, looking into Sam's clear blue eyes. "The issue isn't Stella Marz; it's Marcie Calder. You're not nearly sorry enough about what happened to her, Sam, and you can take that any way you want. Because you're so busy resenting Stella that it even makes *me* wonder."

Sam sat back. "She's *humiliating* me."

"Humiliation is the price of admission here. Your job is to see that it's the only price." Pausing, Tony took the seat across from Sam, putting the bag of sandwiches between them. "Let me explain the game, pal. Stella's not just screwing up your time line. You're letting the jury watch you get pissed off at a woman, which is exactly what she wants. Every time you show a flash of temper, someone in the jury is imagining you crushing Marcie's skull with a bloody rock." Tony made his voice soft again. "Maybe she offended you by getting pregnant, they're thinking. Maybe she said she'd tell someone. . . ."

Sam sat back, eyes wider. With equal quiet, he said, "What are you saying, Tony?"

Tony drew a breath. "What I want you to do, every time you're getting mad at Stella, is to think of Marcie Calder and how very sorry you are."

Sam stared at him. "I didn't kill her, Tony."

For a moment, Tony was quiet. "I didn't kill Alison," he answered. "And there's not been a day in the last twenty-eight years I haven't felt sorry that she's dead. If you can't get back in touch with that same feeling, and within the next hour or so, *your* next twenty-eight years will be spent in prison."

Sam's mouth opened, soundless; suddenly he looked winded, dispirited, and his nod, when it came, was a delayed reaction. All that was left on his face was fear.

They still had an hour, Tony thought. "All right," he said. "Let's get a little food in us. Then we can talk about where Stella's going."

Taking the witness stand, Sam Robb was calm, composed.

"After you got dressed," Stella asked Sam, "what happened next?"

Sam gave her a reflective look, as though trying to remember. "The very next thing," he said at last, "was when Marcie said she wanted to get married."

"She just came out with it?"

Sam nodded. "I think the headlights spooked her too. And it must have been on her mind."

"How did you react?"

Sam shook his head in wonder. "I was flabbergasted—shocked. I remember that especially, but I know I felt guilty too."

"So you told Marcie you couldn't see her anymore."

Sam tilted his head. "Like I told Mr. Lord, it was a little more than that—things about Sue, about being wrong for Marcie. It sounded empty, and I guess it really was."

"How did Marcie react?"

"Upset," Sam said. "Outraged. I'd never seen Marcie like that. I'm sure it was that she knew about the baby."

"How long did this conversation take?"

"Not long. I'd say a couple of minutes."

"A couple of minutes?" Pausing, Stella looked incredulous. "Two minutes for Marcie to ask you to marry her, and for you to talk about your wife, your life, your twenty-four-year marriage, and all the reasons *Marcie* couldn't throw away *her* life for you?"

Sam placed a finger to his lips. "Maybe it was a little longer," he said at last. "Maybe it was four minutes, or five. But we were both upset, for different reasons. I mean, when people fight, they start blurting things out at warp speed. You never stop to think."

Next to Tony, Saul watched Sam with keen attention. "What did you do?" Saul murmured. "Sedate him?" As if to underscore Sam's change in manner, Stella gave him a considering look, ending in a smile so faint and so skeptical it was barely a smile at all. But Sam was behaving as Tony had ordered, and Tony's most fervent hope was that Sam not go too far.

"So here you are," Stella was saying, "scared to death, the vice principal of Lake City High School in a car with a sixteen-year-old girl who could cost you your job, your career, your marriage, and your family, and now she's terribly upset and angry with you, right?"

"Right."

"And you couldn't spare a few more minutes to try and calm her down?"

Sam gave a helpless shrug. "She was out of the car so quick—"

"Didn't you *follow* her, Mr. Robb? To make sure she didn't do anything rash?"

Sam looked down. "I was worried about being seen."

"Weren't you even more worried that she'd tell someone?"

"I don't know. . . ."

"*You don't know?* By your own admission you were one step from disaster, which is why you say you lied to everyone, and yet it never occurred to you that by rejecting Marcie Calder—as you say happened—you'd bring that same disaster right down on your head?"

For a moment, Sam was silent. Tense, Tony watched the jury study Sam expectantly. "I thought she wouldn't do that to me," he said in an embarrassed mumble. "Really . . ."

"Wait a minute, Mr. Robb. The Marcie Calder you describe was impulsive enough to give you oral sex in your office, aggressive enough to ask that you penetrate her anally, and it never occurred to you that this impulsive, aggressive, angry girl might tell someone you'd had sex with her?"

"I trusted her." Pausing, Sam briefly shut his eyes. "I was right to. All through this trial, witness after witness, Marcie never told a soul—" Sam's voice broke off; to Tony's astonishment, fresh tears were in Sam's eyes, as though he was suddenly moved by Marcie's loyalty.

Stella stared at him. "So you didn't go after her?"

"No." Sam touched his eyes. "I wanted to. But like I said, I was scared of being seen. . . ."

"If you were so scared of being seen, Mr. Robb, why were you in the parking lot?"

Sam blinked. "We were just going to talk."

"Well, you didn't just talk, did you?"

"No."

"You performed an act of anal copulation, which—if your story is true—could have been interrupted in a New York minute by someone parking next to you, right?"

Sam hesitated. "Like I told you, I lost my head—"

"Enough to have anal sex with a teenager in a semi-public place? Even though your prior act of intercourse was in a sleeping bag, hidden from view?"

Sam reached for the water glass, gaze averted. "Yes."

"No," Stella snapped. "Because you weren't *in* the parking lot, were you? You were parked in another part of Taylor Park, beneath some trees, where no one else could see you."

Slowly, Sam put down the water glass, staring at Stella Marz. "No," he said. "We were in the parking lot. . . ."

"Nonsense. No one saw you in the lot that night, and *you* didn't see any headlights. There was no one to keep you from getting out of the car, was there?"

Stunned, the jury watched Sam redden. "There *was*—"

Stella's voice rose in anger. "So you got out of the car and went after Marcie Calder. And when you caught up, you killed her with a rock, getting blood on your clothes, and then threw the rock and her body off the cliff."

Sam gripped the sides of the witness chair. Tony waited, taut. "No." Sam fought to keep his voice even now. "That's why I went to the police."

"Didn't you go to the police because—after you killed Marcie and started driving away—you *did* see a car? Didn't that scare you into trying to make up a story?"

"No."

"And when the facts kept changing, like Marcie's pregnancy, your *story* kept changing. Isn't *that* what happened, Mr. Robb?"

"No." Sam's voice was tight. "That is *not* what happened."

Pausing, Stella gazed at him with utter disbelief. "All right," she said. "Let's go on with your version for a while. After you saw the car, you were so scared you wanted to get out of there, right?"

Sam took a deep breath, calming himself. "Yes. That's right."

"Why didn't you just go home?"

Sam bit his lip. "I was just so shaken up—"

"About *what*? How to get rid of bloody shoes and bloody clothes before anyone saw you?"

"*No.*"

"Isn't that why you went to the high school? Because you had spare sweat clothes in your locker?"

"Objection!" Tony stood, his own tension becoming anger. "We've tried to give Ms. Marz some leeway here.

But there is no foundation for these questions anywhere in the evidence. Ms. Marz is offering her testimony—her *story*, more like—without a scrap of proof. All to prejudice the jury."

Karoly nodded, turning to Stella. "I'm going to sustain that one, Ms. Marz. You've made your point."

Quickly, Tony sat down. "Good story, though," Saul murmured.

Stella started in again. "Tell me, Mr. Robb, do you recall the tennis shoes you provided the police?"

Sam hesitated. "Yes."

"They were brand-new, weren't they? Never been worn."

"Just that night, Ms. Marz." Sam's voice was cool. "The athletic department has an arrangement with Reebok. They send us free shoes. So we don't keep old shoes around."

Stella stepped closer to the witness stand. "We can agree on one thing, can't we? That you went to the high school to get rid of evidence."

"No. I didn't."

"You got rid of the condom, didn't you? Because it was evidence of the affair?"

"Yes."

Stella placed her hands on her hips. "Wasn't Marcie Calder's *baby* evidence of your affair?"

Sam looked up at her. Softly, he said, "I didn't know about the baby, Ms. Marz. If I had, why would I go to the police?"

Stella looked at him askance. "Before this trial, what did you know about DNA methodology?"

"I don't know. . . ." Pausing, Sam appeared bemused. "A little from the Simpson case, I guess. That they can identify blood."

"Did you know they could establish paternity by analyzing fetal material?"

In the jury box, the nutritionist's brow furrowed in thought, as, in the witness chair, did Sam's. "I guess I did. But I'm not really sure."

"You weren't surprised when the tests established that Marcie's baby was yours?"

Sam looked down. "It was the baby that surprised me. I don't think the tests did. I mean, I knew it must be mine."

Tony stared at him.

And they think it's mine? Sam had asked him.

They're sure it is. With DNA, they can do that too. I guess you didn't know that. . . .

Silent, Stella studied Sam. "Tell me, Mr. Robb, do you believe that a fetus is a life?"

"Yes. I do."

"Did Marcie?"

Sam's eyes narrowed. "I don't really know."

"You didn't know that Marcie was a committed Roman Catholic, who believed that abortion was morally wrong?"

"I mean, I knew she was Catholic. We just never talked about abortion."

"You knew Marcie was Catholic, you were having sex, and you never talked about what would happen if she got pregnant?"

"No. We didn't."

"Even after the condom broke?"

Sam shifted his weight, uncomfortable. "I mean, we talked about what to do. She got a diaphragm—"

"Because for Marcie to get pregnant would be a disaster for you, right?"

"Yes. It would have." Looking up, Sam added softly, "It has been. On top of everything else."

Stella watched him, stymied for the first time. That he had helped make Sam a better witness, Tony was discovering, filled him with disquiet that kept growing, moment by moment. Though Sam had not directly answered him, Tony felt certain that he had not known about DNA.

"All right," Stella was saying. "You've testified that you wish Marcie had told you she was pregnant."

"Yes."

"What would you have done, Mr. Robb? Suggest an abortion?"

"Maybe."

"And what if she'd refused?"

Sam slowly shook his head. "I don't know," he finally answered. "Help her have the baby, I guess."

"But that would have ruined you, wouldn't it? Destroyed your career, your reputation, probably your marriage."

Sam wiped his brow. "I guess so, Ms. Marz. . . ."

"But that's not the choice you made, is it?" Stella's voice was quiet now. "You needed your baby to die, and so Marcie Calder had to die. Because that was the choice you gave her."

Sam's eyes filled with tears again. Blindly, it seemed, he sought out Sue. "No," he said softly, as if to her. "I'm not like that. Despite everything else I've done, I'm not like that."

Stella gazed at him and then slowly shook her head. To Karoly, she said simply, "I think I've seen enough of Mr. Robb."

Standing, Tony faced Sam again. *Just concentrate*, he told himself. *Be a lawyer.* But he felt empty to the core.

"We've heard testimony," Tony began, "that human life was precious to Marcie Calder. Is it precious to you?"

Slowly, Sam nodded. "Yes. It is."

"Including Marcie Calder's life?"

"Especially Marcie Calder's life."

"And why is that?"

"Because I was proud of her, as a coach. Because I

became close to her. Because she was a beautiful young woman with so many good things ahead of her—a marriage, a family. All the things that I've had, and maybe lost." Sam paused, swallowing. "Because, even though I betrayed everything I stood for, I've devoted my adult life to working with kids like Marcie."

Watch it, Tony thought reflexively. *It's too much.* He put his hands in his pockets. "And when you went to the police, Mr. Robb, did you really think you could keep yourself out of trouble?"

"No. It was from conscience—I was either going to be the person I used to be or let the bad things I'd done take over. Going to the police is the only thing I did that gives me any kind of self-respect." He paused, voice quieter yet. "I'd do it again, if they could find her still alive. . . ."

Sam's voice faltered, and then, quite suddenly, he lost all composure. He faced the courtroom, tears running down his face.

"We're through now," Tony said softly, and sat down. When he glanced at her, Sue's face was stiff, expressionless. From her table, Stella gazed at Sam with narrowed eyes.

At last, Sam stood, unsteady, giving a tentative glance toward Sue. Then he walked across the courtroom, to Tony, and put his arms around him, tears brimming again, just as he had on that spring day twenty-eight years before, carrying a trophy, applause washing over them both.

"We're still a team," Sam whispered hoarsely. "Still a team."

TWENTY-FOUR

Minutes later, after Tony had rested his case, Stella Marz declined to call rebuttal witnesses.

"All right," Karoly said. "We'll have closing arguments tomorrow morning. Nine o'clock."

As the courtroom cleared, Saul said to Tony, "No Ernie."

Tony nodded. "Which means she still can't account for his whereabouts between eight-thirty and ten-eighteen. Without that, I'm sure Stella figures that to have him simply repeat that he didn't kill her would dignify our defense."

Saul glanced at Sam. "Maybe," he said, and Tony understood at once: in Saul's view, Stella had decided to go to the jury with Sam's testimony fresh in their minds. Watching them as they filed out, eyes downcast, like strangers on an elevator, Tony could not tell what Sam had gained, or lost.

Sam himself sat in a wide-eyed stupor that, to Tony, mimed the sightlessness of someone in profound shock. Perhaps this was exhaustion, Tony thought, or that utter loss of dignity that separates the person who sustains it from all those who have watched. Or, perhaps, it was Sam's final, crushing acceptance of what his life had become. But the thought that troubled Tony most was that this torpor might be a clever self-portrait—another face Sam had chosen to present, which masked a perverse feeling of triumph. Whatever it was, Tony felt tired.

Gently, he patted Sam on the shoulder. "Let's go."

Looking up, Sam gave him a wan smile. "Thanks for helping me," Sam said. "No matter how bad it was, I needed to do this."

Then it was the right thing, Tony might have said in

other circumstances. His silence was the echo of his own disquiet.

Together, they turned to Sue.

Her gaze was not on Sam, Tony realized, but on him. Before he could interpret this, she flinched; at the corner of his eye, Tony saw a blur of motion.

Frank Calder came across the courtroom toward Sam, scalded face distorted by loathing. Sam looked at him in dull astonishment, making no effort to defend himself.

"You scum," Frank Calder said. As he raised his fist, Sam did not move.

Stepping between them, Tony grabbed Calder's arm, jerking him sideways. Their faces were inches apart; Tony could see the pain in Frank Calder's face as Tony twisted his arm, smell the man's breath. Over Calder's head, Tony saw a sheriff's deputy hurry toward them.

"You," Calder burst out. "You're as bad as he is."

Tony jerked his arm. There was something cold in Calder's hatred, Tony thought, a reptilian quality that must have always been there. But what Tony felt most was pity for all that this man had been forced to hear, and for the things that he would never understand.

"I'm sorry," Tony said, and then the deputy clamped Calder's arms and took him back to his wife. Nancy Calder stood there, pale, her expression one of grief, of estrangement from her husband. She could barely look at him.

"Jesus," Sam whispered.

His voice held a hint of awe, the recognition of human wreckage. "They'll never make it," Tony murmured. "They were on trial too."

Then he noticed Sue. Briefly, she touched Tony's wrist, then she told Sam in a toneless voice, "We should leave."

Taking Sam by the arm, she headed for the door of the courtroom, to meet the two deputies assigned to keep them safe. When Sam turned to her, speaking softly, she did not look at him.

That night, Tony tried to push everything else from his mind and review his final argument.

He had outlined it before the trial. Very little had changed, because very little had surprised him. It was the sign of a professional.

Lying on the bed, Tony put aside his legal pad. He had been a lawyer for twenty-one years: five years longer than Christopher's life, fourteen years longer than his marriage to Stacey. At this age, forty-six, he was older than Saul had been when he saved the seventeen-year-old Tony Lord and, by doing this, changed the course of Tony's life.

To defend those who might be guilty had always meant that he could not dwell on their presumed crimes, but on the need to make the government prove its case, to question its errors and assumptions, to ensure that it not convict on supposition. But that the defendant was Sam, and the victim a teenage girl, had made Tony face, and then inhabit, the gulf between the morality of the defense lawyer and that deeper morality, the layman's sense of right and wrong, which had been part of Tony since childhood. He envied Stella Marz this much—that her public beliefs and her private self were not in conflict here.

As for Tony the lawyer, he did not know that Sam was guilty. He was not even certain that he had lied on the stand.

Picking up the legal pad, he began scratching notes in the margin, and then he heard a knock on the door.

Tony half-expected Sue. When he opened the door, torn between worry and anticipation, Ernie Nixon was standing there.

"You going to invite me in?" Ernie asked.

Tony's surprise became alarm. But he nodded and stood aside.

Ernie crossed the room and sat near where, a week earlier, Sue had read the travel magazine. His thin frame was taut.

Watching him, Tony shoved his hands in his pockets. "What can I do for you?"

Though Ernie's gaze was level, Tony saw that he was fighting for self-control. "Not much now, Tony. Not much, now that half the folks who send their kids to me don't want to anymore. All that you can do is satisfy my curiosity." Pausing, Ernie looked up at him, his tight-lipped smile a grimace of repressed anger. "You really believe I killed that girl, Tony? Or were you just playing the 'race card,' as it were?"

Tony made himself be still, seemingly calm. "What difference would my answer make?"

"I'd just kind of like to know why I'm going through all this. And you're the only one who knows."

"No," Tony retorted. "You are. All *I* know is that you didn't use good judgment, and can't account for your time."

The bitter smile vanished altogether. "But what do you *think*, Tony? Are your palms turning sweaty 'cause you're locked in a hotel room with a murderer who's got every reason to hate you? Maybe you just think I was sleeping with her, or go around beating women? Or was all this another joke to share with your pal Sam?"

For a moment, Tony wondered if this was a trick—either on Ernie's own initiative or with Stella's collusion. Then he saw the Ernie he had known at seventeen, vulnerable yet contained, and felt again his own guilt. All that was left was to be honest.

"All right," Tony said at last. "Do I 'think' you killed Marcie? No. Do I think you were sleeping with her? Probably not, though there's room to wonder. Were you

emotionally involved with her? Damned right. And if
you think any of this is *fun* for me, you're out of your
mind.

"What I *know* is that Sam Robb is charged with a
murder you *could* have committed, out of jealousy and
anger, and that you shaded the truth about when and
how you saw Marcie Calder. Probably you're not guilty
of anything more than human weakness. But I don't
know that's all it was, and I'm not entitled to guess.

"But you already hate me, so I'll give you something
to take home with you. *Yes,* I'm perfectly aware, and
always have been, that some members of the jury may
be more likely to suspect you because you're black. And
when I repeated what your wife had said to you, I played
into that. It may even help acquit Sam Robb. But Dee
did say it, and you *did* hit her."

Ernie stared at him. "You know what's the worst
thing about you?" he finally said. "You don't believe in
anything. You don't believe your client's innocent, and
you don't believe I'm guilty. You're not even an out-and-
out racist. You're just a hired gun, and you remember
from Alison Taylor what worked for *you*."

Like any half-truth, Tony thought, the part that was
true hurt, the part that was unfair stung all the more for
that. But he was through with offering excuses. "So now
that you've figured me out," he said, "you can go home."

Ernie did not move. "What home, Tony? What home?"

Tony did not answer. Without resistance, the passion
seemed to go out of Ernie. What Tony saw now was a
hurt and loneliness that pierced him to the core. But
Tony could say nothing, for he himself was the cause; he
had damaged Ernie, for Sam's sake, perhaps as unfairly
as the Lake City police once had damaged him.

Slowly rising from his chair, Ernie stopped two feet
from Tony. "You know what's worst of all for me?" Ernie asked. "Having known Marcie Calder, and knowing
that Sam Robb killed her. Knowing that you've done all

this for a murderer." He paused, finishing softly: "That's what I wish for you, Tony. That you come to know it too. Although maybe *you* can live with it just fine, prick that you are. For you, winning is the only thing, isn't it?"

When Tony was silent, Ernie slowly shook his head, and left.

TWENTY-FIVE

When Stella Marz faced the jury, looking from one to the other, Tony knew at once that she had chosen her first words with care.

"This is the trial," she said with quiet contempt, "of a practiced—if not skilled—liar, who murdered a sixteen-year-old girl because lies could no longer protect him, and now asks you to accept his lies about *that*. And, when lies alone will not do, he asks you to accept coincidence.

"But there are far too many lies, and there is far too much coincidence."

As Stella paused, the jury watched with deep attention; for over two weeks, they had listened to the evidence, and now she would tell them what it meant. The beautician was still, her fingers tented in the attitude of prayer. Next to Tony, Sam Robb listened silently, his face as blank as Tony had instructed.

"This is not a single murder," Stella continued, "but two. The murder of an unborn child for the 'crime' of its conception, and of its teenage mother for the age-old 'crime' of any mother—to feel the growth of life inside her and to love.

"That this *was* murder there can be no doubt. The footprints on the cliff above where Marcie Calder lay;

the drag marks left by her toes; the triple fracture of her skull; the single rock covered with her blood and hair; the postmortem injuries suffered in her fall—each of these cry out murder, and taken together, they are overwhelming.

"And what is the positive evidence for suicide or accident? There is none. Not at the scene, and not in Marcie Calder's life. For it was this girl's commitment to the life of her child that brought Marcie to Taylor Park that night, to meet the child's father.

"And who was that?" Turning, Stella faced Sam across the courtroom. "Sam Robb.

"His path to that moment, and to that crime, is marked by a trail of lies—to his wife; to Marcie's parents; to his principal; to the police.

"Just as his account of that fatal night is now riddled with coincidence.

"It's just a coincidence that they were alone in the place that Marcie died.

"It's just a coincidence that she was pregnant with his child.

"It's just a coincidence that her blood was in his car and his fingerprint on Marcie's watch.

"And like all his lies, which, once discovered, each give birth to a new coincidence, Sam Robb's act of anal sex on Marcie Calder has now—incredibly—become his alibi." Standing straighter, Stella made her tone withering. "It was the coroner, not Mr. Robb, who revealed the sodomy of Marcie Calder. But—ever practical—Mr. Robb has made a virtue of necessity. So that now the fingerprint, and the smear of blood, are not evidence of murder but the residue of what Mr. Robb tells us was the final act of love performed by a forty-six-year-old assistant principal on the teenage girl in his care.

"This is what Sam Robb tells you *now*—now that he has been forced to admit their affair, her pregnancy, and the shameful things he did to Marcie Calder. A girl who, before this, was a good student, a loyal sister, a loving daughter—in every way, innocent.

"'I may be a liar,' Sam Robb says now. 'But trust me, I'm not a murderer.'

"Trust Sam Robb?

"This is a man who lied to his wife, the woman he lived with for twenty-four years, and deceived her *every* day of his affair with Marcie Calder.

"Every day he looked Sue Robb in the eye, lied to her, and got away with it. If he could fool this woman, who knows him so well, Sam Robb must surely believe that he can fool you too." Stella's voice vibrated with anger. "And so, awash in tears and righteous anger and unrelenting self-pity, he even asks that you pity him too."

Tony sneaked a glance at Sue. But she was as stoic as the jury, listening to Stella Marz, her expression less suffering than remote, almost neutral. Eyes lowered, Sam did not look at her, or anyone.

"Don't go for it," Stella said with sudden passion. "This man is a sneak, a cheat, a liar, and—he's now been forced to admit—a moral cesspool who broke the law, and violated his trust, by seducing a teenage girl, then lying about *that* until the truth caught up with him.

"He lied to save his job, his profession, his marriage, and his reputation. And when Marcie Calder told him she was pregnant, and lies would no longer do, he killed her. Killed her for the same reasons that he *lied* about seducing her—to save his job, his profession, his marriage, and his reputation.

"And now, of course, he has lied to you about *that*.

"In the course of this trial, Sam Robb professed to have learned a great deal about forensic science." Stella faced Sam again, her voice etched in irony. "He has even learned that, by virtue of a tuna sandwich, we can tell you that Marcie Calder was most likely dead by ten o'clock.

"That is why Sam Robb now claims that he did not

leave the park at ten o'clock, as he first told the police, but more like nine-thirty. Having rejected Marcie Calder's proposal of marriage, with all he says that entails, not in *thirty* minutes, but in five—which makes Marcie's death just another sad coincidence.

"Why? Sam Robb swears under oath that, despite the fact that Marcie Calder told two people—Dr. Nora Cox and Ernie Nixon—that she needed to see her lover that night to warn him she was pregnant, Marcie never got around to it.

"How handy for Mr. Robb—for if you believe *that*, then their conversation would take far less time, and Sam Robb loses his most compelling motive for murder.

"How handy, and how contemptuous of you.

" 'Trust me,' he says, 'the baby was just an excuse she gave to others. All she really wanted from *me* was a little sodomy, and maybe an engagement ring.'

"If you believe *that*"—here Stella paused, then softly repeated herself—"If you believe that, Sam Robb supposes, then he can ask you to believe that Marcie Calder was killed by someone else.

"If not Sam Robb, who?

"Well, Ernie Nixon, of course. I mean, it's so logical. Mr. Nixon has no credible motive. No one places him in the park. There's no evidence he was there. He *says* he wasn't there, that he was home the entire night. And we *know* he was home at ten-eighteen.

"Ernie Nixon has told you no lies here. We know who he is." Briefly, Stella turned to Tony. "And we know what this defense is. A callous attempt to smear an innocent man to save a liar and murderer.

"Of course, Mr. Lord suggests that the police should have checked Mr. Nixon's clothes, because *Mr. Robb*—that paragon of full disclosure and complete cooperation—gave the police what he *claims* were the clothes he wore on the night Marcie Calder died.

"Of course," Stella continued with sudden softness, "there was no trace of Marcie Calder on them. No perfume, no makeup, no hair—although, on Marcie Calder's sweatshirt, Sam Robb's hair was found. No blood—although on Sam Robb's steering wheel, Marcie's *blood* was found." Stella paused. "No blood, even, on Sam Robb's underwear, which had covered the supposedly bloody condom.

"Nothing, because these clothes, which Sam Robb did not wear that night, are another of Sam Robb's lies."

Stella moved closer to the jury box. "What happened that night is clear.

"Sam Robb learned that Marcie Calder was pregnant.

"Marcie Calder refused to take the baby's life.

"And for that, Sam Robb took a ten-pound rock and ended Marcie Calder's life with three crushing blows to the skull.

"He took the life of the child he'd seduced and the child he had left inside her, and then—as with everything to do with Marcie Calder—he lied about it.

"Perhaps his plan, such as it was, began when Sam Robb found that he had lost his control, that—this time—he could not bend Marcie Calder to his every wish.

"But that is planning enough. For you cannot then take a rock and shatter a girl's skull in three different places without *knowing* that she'll die, without *wanting* her to die.

"That, ladies and gentlemen, is the man whom all these lies were intended to conceal—a murderer. And when murder itself was not enough, Sam Robb came before you to tarnish the only thing he had left to Marcie's parents: her memory."

The Calders, Tony saw, were weeping now, though they did not touch each other.

"I ask you to do justice," Stella finished simply. "For Frank and Nancy Calder, and for their daughter Marcie, who cannot ask it for herself.

"I ask you to find Sam Robb guilty of the murder of Marcie Calder."

Stella returned to her table, gaze downcast, as though lost in her own thoughts and feelings. Sam was pale, silent.

"It's all right," Tony murmured, to Sam and to himself.

Rising, Tony saw faces that, for years or for months, had come to be a part of him—Sue, whom he had loved; the Calders, whom, perhaps, he had wronged; Saul, his friend, who had been to Tony what Tony was now to Sam. For Sam was not just the friend of Tony's youth but his client; whatever his private qualms, they were swept away by the lawyer's instinct to protect and defend, as Saul had once protected an innocent boy who—to almost everyone—had seemed guilty. So that it was Sam whom Tony looked to last.

His friend gave him a faint smile of confidence and encouragement, and then Tony faced the jury, speaking evenly and calmly.

"Ms. Marz has asked you to make a leap of faith," he told them, "and then, having done that, to perform an act of revenge.

"The leap of faith is that the evidence shows beyond a reasonable doubt that Sam Robb murdered Marcie Calder, when it does not.

"The act of revenge is to find Sam Robb guilty of murder, not because you know that he committed murder, but because he had an affair with a teenage girl and then tried to conceal it."

The beautician watched him closely, Tony thought—the sign of someone still willing to listen. "For *that* sin," he continued, "Sam Robb has already paid, and will continue to pay for the rest of his life—in guilt, in humiliation, in the damage to his family, in the loss of his profession and reputation, in the loss, forever, of anything resembling the life he once had. His mistake—abusing his relationship to a student—was a terrible one. And he will pay a terrible price: a life sentence, in the truest sense." This argument, Tony knew, flirted with impropriety; as Stella stirred, he finished it quickly. "That sentence must be served wherever Sam Robb goes. But the power to impose the added sentence of life imprisonment is in *your* hands, and you must act with justice.

"Consider, as you must, the prosecution's evidence."

Pausing, Tony envisioned Ernie Nixon, wounded and angry, then made himself go on. "Many men have size eleven shoes, including Ernie Nixon.

"Two men who have come before you cannot account for their whereabouts at the time of Marcie's death— and one of them is Ernie Nixon.

"Two men left fingerprints on Marcie Calder's watch, and one of them, yet again, is Ernie Nixon.

"There are two explanations for the smear of blood in Sam Robb's car: one is sinister; the other—and far more likely one—is not." Tony's gaze swept the jury now, and his voice grew stronger, harder. "But that one smear of blood was enough to get us here. Because the police never checked Mr. Nixon's car, or house—or story. They had their man, they thought—even though, we since have learned, it is Mr. Nixon, not Sam Robb, whose past suggests the potential for violence toward a woman.

"The police did not, and do not, have their man. They did not check out Mr. Nixon, or transients, or recidivists. And as professional as they are, Detective Gregg and Dr. Micelli cannot give us a murderer—they cannot even, to a moral certainty, give this jury a murder.

"Every scrap of evidence with respect to Marcie Calder's death is susceptible to multiple interpretations.

"On this evidence, it is possible to speculate that Sam Robb is a murderer, or that he is wholly innocent of murder. The only certainty is that you can never be certain. Because the killer—if any—could be someone else."

Tony extended his left arm, palm upward, toward Sam. "The only person who knows," Tony continued softly, "is Sam Robb.

"Sam Robb does not deny the wrongs he did to Marcie Calder, and to her family. The account he gave here was not a pretty one, nor was it pleasant for him to tell. It ends with yet another failure—Marcie Calder, filled with emotion, running from a man who she feels has used and then rejected her. But Sam Robb has plainly told you that—with respect to the crime with which he is charged—he is the innocent victim of his own belated act of conscience. Without which, beyond *any* reasonable doubt, he would not be forced to sit here amidst the wreckage of his life.

"Look at the price he's paid for that." Pausing, Tony injected his tone with irony. "And then look at *all* he's gained.

"To convict Sam Robb, you must not only disbelieve every word he says, but you must decide that the only way Marcie Calder could have died was as Ms. Marz imagines she did—you must accept, for example, the Alice in Wonderland notion that because Sam Robb's clothes contain no evidence of guilt, they must be evidence of guilt.

"Such is the prosecution's case.

"Accept it, and you may convict a man who has already endured so much, and yet nothing compared to what he *will* endure, for a crime he did not commit."

Tony paused, and then his voice became imploring. "Marcie Calder's death is a tragedy.

"Nothing can redeem it. Nothing can give Marcie

back to us—to her community or to her family. There is no redemption, anywhere, in placing the name of murderer on an innocent man."

Tony stopped, drawing the eyes of the jury. *"That,"* he finished, "would be a tragedy all its own."

PART FOUR
SUE ROBB

THE PRESENT

ONE

For three days, Tony waited for the jury to come back.

He called Sam at the end of every day, to report the lack of news. Increasingly agitated and anxious, Sam attempted to extract from Tony speculation about what the silence meant; all Tony could say was that some jurors must be finding the case quite difficult. Privately, he suspected a split in the jury, and worried about what this might mean.

As for Sue, when she answered Tony's calls, she was pleasant, somewhat distant, and—once Tony told her there was nothing to say—incurious. Tony stifled the impulse to keep her on the telephone.

So Tony killed time. He talked to Stacey, reviewed by fax, at Christopher's request, his son's essay for the admissions committee at Harvard. San Francisco seemed very far away; Lake City was terribly real now, and his past felt like his present.

At the end of the second day, he called Stella Marz. "Can I buy you a drink?" he asked. "I've been having separation anxiety."

Stella responded with a modest laugh and agreed to meet him at the hotel bar.

The bar was a plush, quasi-Victorian replica, half

filled with the usual depressed-looking assortment of commercial travelers and giving off that sense of unreality unique to instant fabrications of a bygone decor. Their server introduced himself by name, and when he brought Tony's martini in what looked like a brandy snifter, Tony rolled his eyes at Stella.

"You really *are* a snob," she said. "At least the drinks don't cost ten dollars."

Tony smiled. "Then they're on me," he said, and touched his snifter to Stella's wineglass. "Nice job. That was what I wanted to tell you."

Stella gave him an amused, somewhat skeptical look. "You too. And now that we're such good friends again, you're hoping I won't retry your other good friend, Sam Robb, if the jury just happens to hang. Which is a little easier decision to swallow when his lawyer's a gracious, humble man like you."

Caught, Tony laughed aloud but did not, thereafter, smile. "You have your heart and soul in this one, don't you?"

"Oh, yeah." Stella gazed at the table, her face hard, her eyes reflective. "He's a real bad guy, your friend. Watching him on the stand convinced me all the more." She looked up at Tony. "It's a tough prosecution case—I knew that going in. But when you put him on, I think, you let me back into the game."

Tony sipped his drink. "Not my idea," he said at last.

Slowly, Stella nodded, still watching him. "No. I didn't think it was."

Tony put down his martini, looking her in the face. "If it's any help, Stella, I don't know anything that makes him guilty. What he said in court two days ago could very well be the truth."

"Yes," she answered calmly. "But do you believe it?"

She did not expect an answer. "A lot of people," he said at last, "have been telling me I don't believe in anything."

Stella shook her head. "No, you believe in something. You and I even believe in some of the same things. When I worked my way through law school, I told myself it wasn't just to make my life better, but to make this place better. But that was *my* choice. When I judged you for leaving, I forgot that, or how many reasons you might have had, starting with what your parents wanted for you. My parents never wanted a thing for me, except that I be them. So Saint Stella the self-righteous is my very own creation." She picked up her wineglass, regarding him over the rim. "You're fair, Tony, and I did learn something. I watched you, and the trial played out the way you thought it would."

Appreciative, Tony smiled a little. "Except for the ending. I haven't a clue what that will be."

Stella finished her drink. "I may lose this one," she said. "Maybe I should. But God knows I don't want to."

Shortly afterward, she left. Tony watched her stop in the doorway of the bar, to brush back her hair with graceful fingers, then resume her determined stride through the swinging doors. Thinking of his client, Tony hoped that he would not be forced to admire her for winning.

The next day, at around four-thirty, the jury told Judge Karoly that it was hung.

The beautician was the foreperson. The nutritionist, with whom she had seemed friendly, would not look at her.

Standing beside Tony, Saul whispered, "Our foreperson is voting defense."

"I think so too," Tony whispered, and cursed himself for letting the nutritionist get past him. Next to Saul and Tony, Sam's shoulders sagged.

Stella, like Tony, scanned the jurors' faces.

"Madam Foreperson," Karoly said, "without telling me who the votes favor, could you tell me how the voting stands?"

The beautician glanced toward the nutritionist. "Nine on one side. Three on the other."

"How many ballots have you taken?"

"Four, Your Honor. The votes haven't changed."

Karoly's brow furrowed. "And do you think, with more deliberations, you can reach a verdict?"

The beautician shook her head, frowning. "The three won't budge."

Tony looked at Stella. There was a split-second decision to be made: depending on their guess as to whether they were winning, or losing, Tony and Stella would want—or would *not* want—more deliberations, which might end in a verdict. When Stella hesitated, Tony made his decision. "May I approach the bench, Your Honor?"

When Karoly nodded, Stella followed Tony, to huddle with the judge out of earshot of the jury. "Your Honor," Tony murmured, "three days of deliberations is not long in a complex case. I wonder if, in fairness to everyone, there might be some way the court can be helpful to the jury."

Stella shook her head. "I think we should take the jury at its word. *They* know what their situation is, and as disappointing as the lack of a verdict is, to force the jury through any more is to run the risk of coercion *and* an unjust verdict." Pausing, she glanced at Tony. "If necessary, the state is prepared to try this case again."

Karoly hesitated and then turned to the jury. "The court would like to thank you for your service," he began.

The vote was nine to three for acquittal.

Watching the jurors leave the courtroom, silent and unhappy, Tony patted Sam on the shoulder. Then he walked across the courtroom and shook Stella's hand.

"Good guess," he told her.

Her smile, fleeting and faint, did not hide the bitterness of her disappointment. "It's the same guess you made." She paused, studying Sam Robb, and then looked back at Tony. "Come by my office around two on Monday. After I've had some time to live with this."

Without waiting for an answer, she began clearing the table of her papers.

When Tony returned, Sam and Sue were talking quietly with Saul. "I'll try to catch some of the jurors," Saul said quietly to Tony. "Before Stella does. Find out what went on in there."

Tony nodded. "Thanks."

Stella, he noticed, was gone.

Sam and Sue were silent now. Sam had grasped her hand; Sue looked stiff, pale, weary. Suddenly Tony felt how tired he was.

"I'm sorry," he murmured. "I wanted to win."

Slowly, Sam nodded. "We nearly did, pal. At least I'm not in jail. You did everything you could—"

"You did," Sue broke in softly. "Everything."

Reporters were gathering behind them, waiting for a statement from Tony, a chance at Sam or Sue. "I'll talk to Stella," Tony said. "Monday."

Turning, he looked at the Calders.

They were frozen in their seats, shoulders barely touching. Frank Calder's eyes were empty, exhausted; tears ran down Nancy Calder's face. A reporter from the *Steelton Press* hovered behind them, blocked by an assistant from Stella's office.

Sue followed Tony's gaze. There was nothing for anyone to say.

That night, Saul called him. He had talked to most of the jurors.

"You know what I think happened?" Saul told Tony. "Our client hung the jury."

"How so?"

"My sense is, before Sam got on the stand, you had them—twelve people, unanimous in their unhappiness that reasonable doubt kept them from putting our man away. Sam polarized them: for nine, including the beautician, he either made no difference or helped them feel a little better about their vote. . . ."

"And the three?"

"Hated his guts and thought he was a liar. Their response to his testimony was absolutely visceral—especially our nutritionist, the mom. After these three women saw him, they just didn't want him walking around. Period."

Tony lay back on the bed, his headache a dull pounding in his temples and the back of his neck. "So," he said tiredly, "what you're saying is that Sam bought Stella another shot at him."

"If she takes it." Saul paused and, out of compassion, tried for fatalism. "You never really know, Tony—jury dynamics are funny. Maybe it would have hung anyhow."

For a moment, Tony was quiet, wondering. But this was pointless. "Monday," he finally answered, "we'll see what *she* thinks."

On Monday, at two o'clock, Tony went to Stella's office.

To his surprise, Stella was in a tennis dress, her wavy brown hair pulled back by an elastic band. "As soon as we're through," she explained, "I'm out of here. I'm taking a little time."

Tony nodded: decompression, the fatigue and lack of focus that follows a hard case, was something he understood. He was feeling it too.

"For me," he told her, "it's back to San Francisco. Tomorrow."

Stella studied him across the desk, a mess of files she had not bothered to straighten.

"Well," she said at last, "you probably won't have to come back."

"How so?"

Her face was calm, without expression. "You carried them nine to three. Next time, I figure, you'll shoot Sam

Robb before you let him testify." She paused, as though reluctant to finish, and then did. "I've told the chief I recommend against retrying it. Unless, somehow, the case gets better. More evidence—bloody clothes or something. Though I imagine Sam Robb got rid of *those* long since."

There was little to say. "I guess your boss agrees," Tony ventured.

"Yes. So you can tell your client."

She had done this quickly, Tony thought, and with as much grace as she could muster. "Thank you," he said.

Stella gave him the smallest of smiles. "Please. Don't."

She excused herself to play tennis. Tony went to call Sam, and Sue.

TWO

That night, at Sam's insistence, Sam and Sue took Tony for dinner at the country club.

"I'm free," Sam had said emphatically. "So I've got to start living like I am, or I can't live here at all. It'll be easier, the first time, if we have you for company."

To Tony, the "we" was optimistic; at their table in the corner, the same one where Tony had dined with Sue, she watched Sam and Tony as if she were a spectator. As though to compensate for her silence, Sam seemed heartier: maybe this wasn't a celebration, he remarked, somewhat defensive, but it was sort of a coming out. Halfway through the dinner, he had finished his fourth bourbon on the rocks, served by a young, slightly scared-looking waitress who was straining to pretend that she did not know who Sam was. Tony nursed his chardonnay and mostly listened; conscious of Sue's quiet scrutiny, he sensed that but for him, she would not be here at all. The minutes passed slowly.

Sam ordered another drink and then, swallowing half of it, settled back in his chair and looked about the room with a replete, satisfied look that, to Tony, was jarringly at odds with the realities of Sam's life. "Remember our prom night?" Sam asked. "The dance was right here."

Sure, Tony thought sardonically. *You drank too much then too. So I punched you out, helped Sue carry you home, and then made love with her, creating a memory so sweet that I can feel her, right now, thinking the same things I am.* Answering, Tony was careful not to look at her. "Sure, I remember. But do you?"

The remark, pointed beneath its lightness, drew a crooked smile from Sam. *He knows what he's doing*, Tony thought, and wondered if Sam would ever put the suspicion of Tony and Sue behind him. "I don't remember as much as you do," Sam answered. "You guys never really told me about the last part."

Tony heard Sue draw a breath. "Oh," she put in softly. "The part where Tony and I went to the grove of maple trees and made love until I climaxed for the first time. There really wasn't much more to it. Except that I fell in love with him, of course."

Her voice was so matter-of-fact that the remark could have been a deadpan joke or, more likely, an expression of deep weariness. But Tony felt the tingle of astonishment and danger; a flush spread across Sam's face, and his smile was the resentful one of a man who did not get the joke but knew he was the butt of it. He turned to Tony, his tone between jocular and accusatory. "Is that how you remember it, Tony?"

Tense, Tony looked at him, wondering what to do. Then he smiled at Sue and, quite casually, said to Sam, "Pretty much. I guess I'd have to say that Sue's the reason I came back here." Reaching out, he patted Sam on the arm. "You know, I'm really glad we've gotten to talk about this. I'm sure that Sue is too."

Tony watched Sam struggle with his choice—to believe them or to pretend it was all in fun. "You're drinking again," Tony said softly. "You shouldn't. It does things to you."

Sam's eyes widened; for a moment, Tony did not know what would happen next. Then, as if the circuits of his brain had reconnected, Sam said, "Yeah, I know. Knock off this one, and I'm through. It's just that I've been so scared, I don't know how to act anymore." He drained his drink in one deep swallow, shivering at the rawness of so much whiskey. Turning to Sue, he murmured, "Sorry, babe."

Sue did not answer. To cover this, Tony asked, "So what will you do now?"

Sam traced the rim of his glass, as though to taste the whiskey with his finger; Tony guessed that he wanted another drink quite desperately. "I don't know," Sam said. "I guess the first thing is whether we stay here. . . ."

His voice fell off. The first thing, Tony knew, was whether Sue would stay with Sam. She stared at the room with the abstracted look of someone who had internalized a great deal of pain and, perhaps, drunk more wine than usual. He would find a way to talk with her alone, Tony decided.

"I'd be tempted to take off," Tony said to Sam. "In fact, I *did* take off, when it was me. This town's too small."

Sam gave a bewildered shrug. "Where would I go, Tony? This place is all I know."

Anywhere Sue wants you to, Tony thought, *if that would make a difference.* Tony tried to smile. "Maybe near one of the kids, if they'll have you. In my own case, imagining Christopher in his twenties, I'm not so sure he would."

Sam did not smile back. "I don't know why mine *should*, pal. I really don't." He looked from Tony to Sue, hesitant. "Mind if I have one more, guys? Then we can hit the road."

There was a shamed, pleading note in his voice; for Sam Robb, Tony was certain, reality would be hard to face. Sue shrugged her indifference.

"I'll join you," Tony told Sam.

They drank their whiskeys in relative quiet, Tony telling harmless anecdotes about Stacey and Christopher, the things they had done in his absence. "Amazing," Tony said. "The kid may actually go to Harvard. As he pointed out to me, he's got an old man who can afford it. Christopher's world is a very different place. . . ."

It was, Tony realized, not the best thing to say. But Sam touched his glass to Tony's. "To your success, pal. And to all our kids. If they don't make it, the rest doesn't matter very much, does it?" He paused, his glance at Sue tentative but fond. "And if they do make it, maybe someone's done something right."

To Tony, the glance was a veiled plea for the value of their life together. But Sue did not look at Sam.

"Better go," Tony said at last. "I've got a plane out in the morning." He smiled again. "Besides, as they say, tomorrow is the first day of the rest of your life."

On the ride home, Sue drove. Sam slumped wearily in his seat, undone by whiskey and weeks of broken sleep. He looked less drunk than exhausted.

The living room lights were on. Entering, the three of them stood there, Sam facing Tony, Sue to the side. "I'm whipped," Sam said to Tony, then summoned the ghost of his old smile. "But I'll be great tomorrow. Sure you don't want to stay for one more day, finish our game? It's a tie, remember?"

Smiling, Tony shook his head. "A tie's good enough for me, Sam. Especially with you."

Sam studied his face for a moment. Then he stepped

forward, hugging Tony with fierce affection. "Thanks," he murmured. "Thanks for everything. It means more to me than I can say, and so do you."

"I know," Tony answered. "I know."

Sam leaned away from him, eyes glistening. Then he turned, climbing the stairs, glancing briefly back at Sue and Tony, as though to signal his hope that, soon, Sue would follow. "So long, pal," he said simply, gave Tony a casual wave, and was gone.

She turned back to Tony. "Can I pour you a glass of wine?" she said. "I'm having one."

She seemed weary, dispirited. But Tony wished to talk with her, and being her guardian was not the way. "Sure," he said, and sat on the sofa.

She returned with two glasses. "Let's go outside," she said. "It's a warm night, and I feel cooped up."

Silent, he followed her out the kitchen door to the rear yard, where, at fourteen, Sam and Tony had once thrown a football and, without seeming to acknowledge this, become friends.

Now Tony sat next to Sue on the hammock. For a moment, he looked up at the stars, remembering when they had laid Sam in the hammock and then spent the night alone. "I've been thinking about you," he said.

"Me too," she answered. But she seemed very far away.

"You asked me to give you an innocent man, Sue. I wish I could have."

"That isn't your fault." Her speech was slightly slurred now, and she paused before saying, "You did more than you know, I think. There's nothing left for you to do."

To Tony, the ambiguous remark begged the question of how Sue would cope. Softly, he said, "I just wish there were something I could do for *you*."

For a long time, Sue was silent, and then Tony felt her shiver. "There is, Tony. Don't come back here, ever. Not even if there's another trial."

Startled, Tony turned to her. "If I hurt you . . ."

"Oh, God, it's not that." Sue faced him. "Don't you understand?"

He touched her hand. "Tell me."

Sue swallowed, her face filling with anguish. "He's *lying*, Tony. He lied in court, and I think he's lied to you."

Tony stiffened; although this was a moment he had always feared, it took him by surprise. Quietly, he said, "About what?"

"The clothes." She fingered the sleeve of Tony's suit, her voice a taut, rushed undertone. "There's a pair of gray sweat clothes missing—Sam always kept an extra pair at school. After he testified, I realized it wasn't here. And it couldn't still be at school. The police would have found it."

The words jolted Tony. *Keep cool,* he told himself. *Think, don't feel.* "Memory's a funny thing, Sue. Sometimes we 'remember' what we're afraid of. . . ."

"It's more like I've been afraid to remember." Sue glanced up at the bedroom window. "Sam *did* have an old pair of running shoes. But they're gone."

Tony could feel the pulse in his own throat. "If Sam were lying, wouldn't he be afraid of what you know?"

Sue looked down. "If he were afraid of what I know," she said softly, "Sam wouldn't have said he'd never had anal intercourse. Trust me about this. Because I know what Sam likes, better than anyone, and he knows I know. . . ."

Gently, Tony pulled her close.

She was stiff for a moment, and then clung to him in silent desperation. "I'm not sure we can talk about this," Tony murmured. "Or anything about Sam."

"We have to." She pulled back from him, fingers resting on his cheek, as if to seek his forgiveness. Her voice quavered. "I think there's more. . . ."

"Much more," Tony cut in. All at once, he felt sick. "You're his wife, Sue. I'm his lawyer."

"You're not just his lawyer." She looked away, as though the sight of him were painful. "Can I ask you one question, Tony?"

Tony hesitated. His thoughts were a chaotic mix of dread and tenderness and obligation—his love for her, his duty to Ṣam, the fear of knowing that his friend and client, the husband of the woman he held, had murdered Marcie Calder. "What is it?"

For a last moment, she was silent, and then tears began running down her face. "When you found Alison's body," she asked, "what time was it?"

All at once, Tony understood. The breath he took made him shiver as Sue had. "You've always said Sam was with you. . . ."

"He was." Her eyes shut. "But no one ever asked how long, and I didn't want to think about it then."

Tony stared at her. In a voice not his own, he said, "Tell me what happened, Sue. Everything."

It was strange, Sue thought, how winning affected Sam. There were times when it filled him with elation; tonight, after his catch in the last football game he would ever play for Lake City High, she had seen that rapture she associated with much laughter and the desire to make love with her. But the separation from Tony and Alison seemed to change his mood abruptly. When they parked near the grove of maples, Sam made no move to touch her. Instead he drank, staring out the windshield at nothing.

"This stuff doesn't matter to him," Sam said at last. "I don't really matter."

She turned to him, puzzled. "Tony?"

Sam did not answer. "People do what he wants," he said. "And things turn out the way he expects them to. 'Nice catch, Sam; now it's time for me to fuck Alison. . . .' "

Alison, Sue thought. She watched Sam in the darkened

car, his profile a shadow with a whiskey bottle tilted to its lips. Evenly, she said, "How do you know that Tony even *is*? Has he said anything?"

"No. But *he* never would."

Sam was already drunk, she realized; that was when his conflicts, his feelings of confusion, crept to the surface. Suddenly Sue thought she understood: this was the biggest moment of Sam's life, one he and Tony had wished for, and now Sam felt excluded—the moment had come and gone, and to Sam's mind, Tony had barely noticed. What made it worse was that Tony was making love with Alison, and that Tony—though not, Sue suspected, Alison—was innocent of the feelings this might create in Sam.

"Are we any different?" Sue asked. "Do you talk with Tony about us?"

Sam took another swig. "No," he said in a flat voice.

Suddenly Sue felt an anger of her own. "Is *that* why you're so mad at him—because he never asks what *you* do with *me*? Or are you mad because *Tony* doesn't want to do it with *me*? I mean, that would make him more like you, wouldn't it? Or maybe it's *Alison*—"

Sue stopped herself, stunned at what she was saying, and that she had said it at all. Sam had frozen. For what seemed minutes, he did not speak or move.

Apprehensive, Sue tried to make a joke of this. "All right," she said. "Why don't we just sit here and imagine what Alison and Tony are doing in Taylor Park. Really, I hope it's great for both of them. At least it'll clear up the confusion for all of us."

Still Sam did not turn. "There's no confusion," he said.

His tone had an ominous quiet. Softly, she asked, "Then why are we having such a lousy night? I was so happy for you, Sam. All I want is for you to be happy with me."

Sam drank more whiskey. "Sorry," he said at last.

"Someone cracked my head with an elbow. My ears are still ringing." It was an excuse, Sue guessed: discomfited, Sam needed a reason for his distraction.

Pensive, she smoothed the pleats of her cheerleader skirt. "Maybe you should go home," she told him.

Sam slid down in the car seat. He took another deep swallow, sinking into unfathomable thought. Sue waited for him to speak.

He drank in silence.

"Sam?"

He appeared to shiver from the effects of the whiskey. "Yeah." His voice sounded thick. "Tomorrow I'll be fine. I promise."

Sue drew her shoulders in. She felt small, alone. They drove home without talking. Gently, she touched his wrist. But Sam seemed not to notice. When they reached Sue's driveway, he started, as though awakening from a trance.

"I'll be fine," he said again. "Tomorrow."

"I'll be fine too." She gave him a quick, firm kiss. "Congratulations. You *won*, you know."

"Yeah," he said. "I won."

Sue got out and walked up the driveway. Sam was already backing out when she reached the front door.

Sue went to her room, undressed, and lay in bed. The clock on her nightstand glowed in red numerals: 11:45. It made her think of Sam's taillights—heading, she thought, in the opposite direction from his house. She hoped that he was not too drunk to drive; for a moment, she thought about calling to make sure that he was safe. But this would awaken his parents, Sue realized, and so it was best to put her worries aside.

Naked, she tried to imagine Alison and Tony. But the image, to her surprise, was of Tony alone. Perhaps she was more like Sam than she cared to know.

Sue tossed, her thoughts confused, until she fell asleep.

* * *

The night had the first wet chill of dawn. Looking at Sue, Tony felt it to the bone.

"Alison?" he demanded. "You think there was something between her and *Sam*?"

Sue took his hands. "I don't know that anything went on. But for a while, Sam almost seemed obsessed with her—like *he* wanted to be the first, and couldn't say that." Her voice was quiet, shamed. "The week before she died, a slip of paper with a telephone number fell out of his binder. I recognized it—Alison's private line— the one her parents didn't want listed. When I asked Sam how he'd gotten it, he said it was from you. So Alison could help him with Spanish."

"No." Tony's own voice was flat; his emotion expressed itself not in words but as pinpricks on his skin. "He didn't get it from me."

Sue looked away. "You're sure. . . ."

"Oh, yes." Standing, Tony stared up at the darkened window, his voice soft with anger. "If I'd known Sam wasn't with you, I might have wondered just a little, even then. And how many seconds do you think it would have taken me to wonder once I heard about Marcie Calder? The *only* reason I didn't was because it never occurred to me he could have been in Taylor Park the night that Alison died. And only because *you* always told me Sam was with you." Suddenly he turned to her. "Why in God's name did you ask me to defend him? Because you didn't want to be alone with this? Or did you think that, somehow, I could answer all your doubts?"

Sue did not flinch. "I didn't *know* anything. But after Marcie Calder died, I began to question everything. . . ."

"Well, I'd have done a lot more than that. *If* you'd bothered to tell me before I became Sam's lawyer. And so would the Lake City cops, if anyone was left from 1967." His tone was savage, bitter. "But Sam's a lucky man, Sue. I always thought so. And now it's clear just how lucky he's been in *you*."

There were tears in her eyes again. She stood, grasping his shoulders, looking up into his face. "It was his *testimony* that did it. I haven't slept since then—worrying, hoping that I'm crazy. Not just because I'm scared to death, or because of the kids." Her voice lowered. "It tore me apart that I may have asked you to defend the man who murdered Alison. The man who changed your *life*. . . ."

Because of what I didn't know, I'm his *lawyer* now.

His voice was quiet again. "Oh, things are a little worse than that. No court would let me testify in a second Marcie Calder trial—I might as well be mute and paralyzed. And even if Karoly let Sam's *wife*—or maybe *ex*-wife—take the stand, which I'm pretty damned sure he wouldn't, there's how your *kids* would deal with that. As for Alison, nothing you've told me *proves* a thing." Tony paused and then, through his anger, saw Sue Cash as herself again. "Hope you're wrong, Sue. You still might be. Otherwise, Sam's killed twice."

Sue shook her head, as if to clear it. "So there's nothing you can do," she said dully. "I've put this in your mind, and now you have to live with it." She turned from him. "God, Tony, I'm so far past *sorry*. . . ."

She curled forward, hands over her mouth. The muffled sound of her keening, Sue's guilt and shame and anguish, blended in the chill night air with the chirr of crickets.

THREE

Stella sat with the accordion folder on the desk in front of her. "I didn't think I'd ever see you again," she said.

Tony remained standing. It was two o'clock in the afternoon; since he had left Sue two nights before, he had not slept. "I didn't think so, either. But I just kept wondering about this."

Stella studied his expression with a cool curiosity and, he thought, a touch of compassion. "They had to dig it out of the basement," she told him. "But before you came, I looked at the pictures. They aren't pleasant, and *I* didn't know her."

"They wouldn't show us the report, Stella. But I was the one who found her. I can still describe what's in the pictures."

Stella paused. "Not the ones they took at the morgue, Tony."

Tony was quiet. "Well," he said at last, "I'm not seventeen anymore."

Stella watched him for another moment and then stood, picking up the folder. "There's an empty office down the hall. I'll make sure no one bothers you."

Tony followed her through a green-tiled hallway to a room of bureaucratic bleakness, unrelieved by any signs of human habitation. Stella gestured at the metal desk. "Take your time," she said. "Just come back when you're through."

Tony turned to her. "I appreciate your help, Stella. Really."

Her eyes remained puzzled. Nodding, she closed the door behind her.

Tony sat on the hard wooden chair, the folder in front of him.

For some time, he did not touch the folder. When he

reached inside at last, his fingers felt clumsy, his stomach hollow.

The manila envelope, Tony knew, contained the photographs.

Inhaling, Tony reached inside. He did not yet look at the photographs. Beneath his fingertips, they were slick to the touch.

Tony spread the photographs in front of him.

"Alison." He said it softly, without volition.

Holy Mary, Mother of God, pray for us now and at the hour of our death . . .

She was as he remembered her. The nightmare did not lie.

The tears in Tony's eyes were those of a seventeen-year-old who had loved her. But they were also of the man, the parent, the criminal lawyer, who understood, as the boy could not have, what a terrible death this had been.

It was the man, now, who pushed the photographs aside.

The autopsy report was several pages long. "The decedent," Tony read, "was a Caucasian female approximately seventeen years old, five feet five inches in height, and weighing one hundred fifteen pounds. . . ."

"I want you," she whispered.

"Examination revealed the presence of seminal fluid in the decedent's vagina. . . ."

Alison began to move with him. She was everywhere now: in the clean smell of her skin; the thick softness of her hair; the warmth of her hips and thighs and stomach.

"The abrasions to the vaginal wall suggest a prior inexperience of sexual intercourse. . . ."

"I love you, Tony. You feel so good to me."

"Samples of fluid were taken from the vagina. . . ."

"Did I hurt you?" he asked.

Swallowing, Tony turned the page.

She raised her face to kiss him, and told him quietly, "I'm glad this was with you."

"Examination further revealed that the decedent had been anally penetrated. . . ."

Tony froze.

"The presence of semen in the decedent's anus was noted, and samples of seminal fluid taken. . . ."

"I'm not like that. . . ."

"The trauma to the decedent's anal tissue, including considerable hemorrhage, suggest that the decedent was forcibly sodomized. . . ."

"I know what Sam likes, better than anyone. . . ."

Tony sat back in his chair.

"The cause of death," Tony read, "was asphyxiation. The decedent had the deep bruises on her neck associated with strangulation, as well as burst vessels in her eyes and face. The medical evidence further suggests that death occurred in the course of forcible anal intercourse, during which the victim was held by the throat."

Tony stood. He forced his mind to go cold.

Hands on the desk, he stared down at the report. "The seminal swabs," he read, "were preserved on slides. . . ."

Tony placed the folder on Stella's desk. "Thank you," he said.

She looked at him. Quietly, she asked, "Did you find what you wanted?"

He made himself sit down. "They took semen samples, Stella. From Alison's body. In an unsolved murder, they should have kept them. Is that the procedure here?"

Stella folded her hands in front of her. "Yes. It is."

At four-thirty, Tony stepped into the darkened church of Saint Raphael for the first time in twenty-eight years.

He sat at the rear of the church, as he sometimes had as a boy, half conscious of the airy space, the light and shadow, the stained-glass windows. Father Quinn was long dead; there was no one left who remembered Tony, and he had nowhere else to go.

Head bent, Tony prayed to a God he no longer knew existed.

Faith extinguished, his world upturned, the Tony Lord who had left this church had turned first to a lawyer, then to the law. And under the law, his secular religion, his duties were to Sam alone.

But now the law, and his own life, had intersected once again, and this time the law held no answers.

Humbled by his limitations, shamed by his arrogance, Tony thought of the Calders, of Marcie, of Ernie Nixon and Jenny Travis, of Sue and, piercingly, of the Taylors and their daughter Alison.

Tony could not forgive himself or, devastated by what he might now have learned, forgive Sam Robb. If Sam was guilty, the betrayal was too terrible: justice had not been done in either case, and Tony, damaged by the first, had become responsible for the second.

What he felt now was beyond hatred. Beyond, even, the awesome, bitter knowledge that it was Sam Robb, not Tony himself, who might have defined Tony's life. For two women had died, and there was nothing to say, if Sam was the killer, that there might not be a third.

That was the sin for which Tony Lord would be to blame. The one for which, in his own heart, there could be no absolution from God, no balm within the law.

Mute, Tony prayed for the strength to do what must be done. Then he stood and walked from the church, to find Sam Robb.

FOUR

Sue opened the door.

Her lips parted, hand still on the doorknob. "Where is he?" Tony asked.

Her head twitched toward the stairs. "In the bedroom."

Tony paused in the doorway, touching her face. "Leave," he said softly. "Right now."

"What *is* it?"

"Alison." Tony brushed past her, turning at the foot of the stairs. "I don't want you here, Sue."

Sue was pale. "He has a gun, remember?"

Tony turned from her, walking slowly up the stairs.

He forced himself to take his time, to breathe easily. The ten feet to the bedroom seemed like a great distance.

When Tony reached the door, he held out his hand for a moment, to ensure that it was steady.

He pushed open the door.

Sam stood near the dresser, staring at his face in Sue's mirror. Tony's reflection seemed to startle him.

"Tony . . ." His voice held embarrassment, pleasure, wariness. Tony watched these feelings resolve themselves in a smile, which did not change his watchful eyes. "I thought you were gone."

Softly, Tony closed the door behind him. "I decided to stay. So I could read the autopsy report on Alison."

Sam blinked. "On *Alison*?"

"Yes."

Sam took three steps, resting his hands on the double bed between them, head down in a pose of thought. "Have you?"

"Read it?" Pausing, Tony wondered how he could sound so normal. "That's what I came to tell you, Sam. I think I can prove that I didn't kill her."

Sam raised his eyes. How many times, Tony thought,

had he gazed at this same face, seeing everything but what he should have seen. Perhaps what Sam saw, looking back at him, caused the flush to cross his cheeks like a stain. Softly, Sam asked, "How can you do that?"

"Alison was raped." Tony kept his voice as soft as Sam's. "The strangulation was to keep her quiet. So he could penetrate her anus."

Silent, Sam's mouth formed a small "o."

"They took semen slides, Sam. And murder has no statute of limitations."

Sam folded his arms. His face was calm, normal; for a moment, despite the tingle of his skin, Tony wondered if he was wrong. "DNA," Sam murmured. "They can run tests."

"It's a thought." Tony paused a moment, eyes boring into him. "Suppose Stella would care to help me?"

Sam's gaze at Tony turned narrow, hard. "Stella."

Tony's mouth felt dry. The room was silent now. Neither man moved.

At last Sam said, "You can't do this, Tony. But I guess you know that."

Tony felt his throat constrict. "You've always had strong feelings about loyalty, haven't you. It gives me something to live up to."

Sam blanched, wordless.

Where, Tony wondered, was the gun? "Cat got your tongue?" he asked.

Tears came to Sam's eyes now. His hand rose in entreaty. "You can't do this, Tony. It wasn't me—"

"Oh, I know. You're not like that, are you."

Sam flushed. "It was *her*. . . ."

Tony's head pounded. "Sue?" he said. "Or Alison?"

Sam stepped forward, clasping Tony's shoulders, staring desperately into his face. *"Listen to me. . . ."*

Alison sat in the love seat on the back porch. When her parents were out, she told him, boys could not come into the house.

Sam watched her face. In the afternoon light, it was strong, yet delicate, the dark eyes pensive, filled with mystery. Only the ankle of one crossed leg, jiggling slightly, showed the tension Sam knew he made her feel, the suppressed desire Tony could not quite touch.

She flicked back the long dark hair. Her fingers were pale, slender. "We shouldn't do this," she said.

"Do what?"

"Talk like this." Alison's gaze was level. "You're Tony's friend. I'm Sue's."

"So?" Sam's palms felt damp. "All we've done is talk. If I can help you out with Tony, maybe say something . . . I mean, it's no fun for anyone when you two are like this."

Alison did not look away. There was something challenging about the poise she seemed to share with Tony; sometimes, to Sam, they seemed almost the same person. "There's nothing much to say," she answered. "He wants me, and I'm not sure. When I see how much that hurts him, it hurts me too. . . ." She paused; her slender ankle, Sam saw now, still jiggled with the nervousness she tried so hard to hide. "You know," she said in a tone of surprise, "you're the last person I thought I'd talk to about this. Including my own mother."

Sam's heart swelled. The weeks of patience, foreign to him, were coming to fruition—the waiting for Alison near her locker, the small encouragements, the gestures of kindness, the offers to help. He was at last learning to be like Tony, to be a person people *came* to. "Your mother doesn't love Tony," he told her. "You do, and I do. The way guys can love other guys, I mean."

There was a sudden film in Alison's eyes. Softly, she said, "I *do* love him. I'm just scared. . . ."

She stopped abruptly; it was that moment, the flash of emotional defenselessness, which Sam, waiting, felt like a caught breath.

Leaning closer, Sam said, "I know, Alison. I understand. . . ."

She blinked, surprised at the nearness of her face to his, at the swirl of her emotions. "Sam . . ."

Swiftly he closed the distance.

Her lips were thin, trembling, neither yielding nor resistant. Sam felt the stirring of his penis, the beating of his own heart.

His tongue, licking her lips, slid inside Alison Taylor's mouth.

As if by reflex, her arms came around him. He kissed her desperately, hungrily, reaching for her breast, *his* now. As he felt it, small beneath the large palm of his hand, he imagined her unfastening the back of her bra, looking into his face the way he saw her look at Tony. . . .

"No." Her back arched, rigid, and she twisted angrily away, eyes wide and staring into his. "No, damn you . . ."

"Look . . ."

Alison stood, rigid. "How stupid I was," she said in anger. "It's my fault, all right? So leave."

Sam sprang up, grasping her wrists. "I don't *want* to. And you don't want me to. You knew what was happening. . . ."

"Maybe I did." Her tone was level now, and she gazed at his hands on her wrists. "Maybe that makes me a real tease. Maybe I don't deserve Tony at all. But at least you reminded me how much I really want him. . . ."

"You wanted *me*."

Her eyes rose to his, steady and cold. "Don't worry, Sam. I won't tell him. As long as you leave now."

Sam's fingers loosened. Slowly, firmly, Alison Taylor slipped her arms from his grasp.

She turned, silent, opening the screen door to escape inside. He stood there, enraged, irresolute.

Alison gazed at him through the door, suddenly still. Behind the wire gauze, she looked slender, beautiful, elusive. "I know you hate us both," she said softly. "But which one do you love?"

With a whisper, the door closed behind her, leaving Sam alone with his humiliation, his festering desire.

Sam was drunk. The image of Alison, the screen door between them, pulsed through the night.

He could feel the heat in his temples, the sweat on his forehead. As he drove toward Taylor Park, the trees by the road appeared from nowhere, the white line on the macadam unspooled before his eyes.

Jerking the wheel, he turned into Taylor Park. He could smell Sue's perfume in the car.

Slowly now, Sam eased into the parking lot, and stopped.

He cranked down the window, inhaling the cool night air. With the motor off, the park seemed vast and silent, a place of darkness, mystery, vague shapes, deep longings.

Somewhere in this cocoon, he imagined, Tony Lord and Alison Taylor wrestled with their own desires.

For what seemed quite long, Sam was still. The picture of two bodies, close but hidden, haunted him. He drank from the fifth of whiskey.

Driven by his imaginings, Sam stepped from the car, bottle clutched in his hand.

The park enveloped him—trees, shadows, the sliver of a cloud-swept moon. His forehead felt feverish, chill. His footsteps were whispers in the fall-stunted grass.

Where, he wondered, would Tony park? Sam and Sue had their grove of maples. But for Tony and Alison, Taylor Park was better, so close to her home that it gave them the last precious minutes before midnight, the last deep kiss, the last touch of a naked breast.

If it was more than this, tonight, Tony would need shelter.

Alone, almost soundless, Sam walked narrow-eyed across the open field. The only sounds were the deep rolling of the lake beyond, the rattle of wind through brittle leaves.

Leaves.

Tony, like Sam himself, would feel safest beneath a bower of trees.

Sam felt his mind open up, become a map of his memory. He walked toward images he could not see.

On the bluff above the lake was a grove of trees.

Blind, he approached it, guided by the stirring of leaves. Then Sam saw tree trunks, gnarled branches. Stopping, he drew a breath.

Amidst the trees was a darker shape, Tony's car.

Slowly, Sam stepped forward on the balls of his feet, shoulders hunched against the cold. Five feet from the car, he stopped.

The windows were fogged. Sam stood like a sentinal, outside the lovers' world, listening for their cries. He heard nothing.

The whiskey, raw in his throat, numbed his feeling of strangeness.

Tiptoeing, he stood beside the car.

A beam of light fell; the moon, breaking free of cloud cover, exposed childish lines amidst the vapor of the windows, backward letters.

"I love you," the lines said.

As Sam leaned forward, his own breath obscuring the "I," he read the line beneath it: "Me too." Then, in a second sprinkle of moonlight, he saw them through the lines of Alison's writing.

They were silver profiles, moving together. The silhouette of Alison raised her mouth to Tony's. Between her legs, for a fleeting instant, Sam could see the rise of Tony's buttocks.

He froze there, alone with the stirring of his body, the pain of his exclusion. He saw Alison's lips move, Tony's wrist as he raised it to his face, checking the time. Then the vapor of Sam's breathing concealed them again.

Slowly, Sam backed from the car. The luminous dial of his wristwatch read 11:42.

Torn by jealousy and confusion, Sam retreated behind a tree. He leaned against the trunk, feeling the rough bark against his cheek, the chill mist of air in his lungs. Only the whiskey kept him warm.

A car door opened.

Startled, Sam saw two shadowy figures hurry from the car. With bare hands they wiped condensation from the rear window—the film of their own breaths, and Sam's.

"Don't worry," Sam heard her say, "I can go home that way too."

"I'll go with you," he answered.

The shadows turned, hesitant. Then they slowly walked toward Sam. He dared not move, or make a sound.

Muscles taut, he watched them.

Five feet, four.

Suddenly they paused. Sam held his breath. Had they turned, they would have seen him; had Sam reached out, he could have touched them.

"Dark," Tony whispered.

Alison took his hand. "I know."

They started forward again, tentative. Two steps, then another.

Sam moved from the trees, behind them.

They stopped, as though they had heard his footsteps. Then they glanced at each other and began rushing across the open field toward Alison's house. Their footfalls echoed in the dark.

Drawn by the image of their lovemaking, Sam followed them.

He did not hurry. Without a plan, he knew only that his steps, unlike theirs, must be silent.

The sound of their footsteps faded.

Sam continued across the pitch-black field, catlike on the balls of his feet. Then the moon slipped through the clouds again, lighting Tony and Alison. They were facing each other, barely visible beneath the copse of trees that shrouded Alison's house, its roofline black and jagged against the muddy purple sky.

Silent, Sam stopped moving.

Though spoken softly, Alison's words carried in the night. "We should stop."

Tony kissed her forehead. "I'll wait for you here."

Alison shook her head. "It's cold out," she said softly. "You can keep the car warm."

Her voice was low, a woman's. It coursed through Sam like whiskey.

Alison kissed Tony deeply, longingly, her body pressed to his. And then clouds swept across the moon again, and there was nothing but her muted voice.

"We just used my final minute," Sam heard her say. "See you in about fifteen."

She was defying her parents for Tony Lord, sneaking from the house to open her legs for him again. Like Sam's mother did for Coach Jackson. The taste of whiskey on Sam's tongue was bitter now.

In the distance, he saw Alison.

She stood beneath the light of the back porch, waving. In his confusion, Sam felt she waved to him.

The light went off. The back door, closing, was a whisper.

Sam heard footsteps again, Tony's.

Sam stood there in the dark, bottle in hand. Perhaps if Tony saw him, Sam could offer Tony the drink he had refused.

But Sam could not see anyone. The sound of Tony's footsteps grew clearer, closer. The sweat chilled on Sam's face.

The footfalls faded, and there was nothing but emptiness. Sam was alone.

He tipped the whiskey bottle to his lips.

Fifteen minutes, and Alison would be out again. Sam wiped his mouth.

Approaching the house, his own footfalls were silent. He imagined sitting in her love seat, rocking ever so slightly, the creak of its frame startling Alison as she stepped out from the house. "My turn," Sam would whisper.

He stopped, gazing at the back porch, ten feet away.

It would be enough to watch her, Sam decided, to know what he could have done. The whiskey fantasies danced in his brain: Sam, watching two silhouettes move together, then taking the place of one of them.

The last swallow of whiskey burned his throat.

Walking toward the edge of the bluff, he hurled the empty bottle toward the water. He stumbled, caught himself.

As he felt her breast, small beneath the large palm of his hand, Sam imagined her unfastening the back of her bra, looking into his face the way he saw her look at Tony . . .

Perhaps he should leave, Sam thought.

Turning, he froze: framed in the screen door was Alison Taylor.

Behind the wire gauze, she looked slender, beautiful, elusive. "I know you hate us both," she said softly. "But which one do you love?"

The porch creaked beneath her feet.

Sam was utterly still. As she stepped from the porch onto the grass, he could no longer see her. Her footsteps made no sound.

It would be fate that decided for them, Sam knew suddenly. If she did not see him, he would let her pass, let her go to Tony. But if she found him in the night, it was because this had to be.

Her steps came closer.

Appearing, Alison was a slender form again, her face

not yet visible. She did not stop, or turn. In another few feet, she would reach him.

Five feet away, he guessed, now four. He felt his own desire stirring.

The sky opened, and moonlight fell again.

Sam heard the sharp intake of her breath. Then the light revealed her china face, the widening of her eyes.

"Hi," Sam said.

The cry died in her throat.

He could see everything so clearly now. Her relief, then the return of fear. The way, so much like Tony, that she tried to appear calm, unruffled. Her awareness, as she drew a deeper breath, of the whiskey smell that came from him. Even her decision not to question him.

"You shouldn't be here," Alison said.

Her voice was thin, but level. Softly, Sam answered, "I watched you in the car with him."

The simple words caused her to stare in fright. Sam could feel the racing of his own heart: the way that Alison straightened, head high to retain her dignity, insulted and excited him. "Then you know how much I love him," she said with equal simplicity. Voice quiet, so her parents could not hear, but shaking now.

She was still going to Tony, Sam realized. Even with his face inches from hers.

"Just imagine," he said softly, "that I'm Tony." Their breaths met in the air.

His tongue, licking her lips, slid inside Alison Taylor's mouth. . . .

"No," she said, turning her face. "I don't want you. . . ."

Her back arched, rigid, and she twisted angrily away, eyes wide and staring into his. . . .

Sam did not know what to do. He was paralyzed by his cowardice, his fury.

Alison opened her mouth, as though to scream.

Sam covered her mouth with his hand, the blood pounding in his head. It was too late, he told himself, too late. The fresh terror in her eyes ignited his excitement, his loathing of his own humiliation. She tried to bite his hand. . . .

Sam felt a spurt of pain. He saw a flash of light, and then rage broke through the last barriers.

"Yes," he insisted in a drunk's savage voice. "Yes . . ."

Jerking Alison's arm behind her back, he pushed her to the ground, one hand still across her mouth.

She was kneeling now, her back to him, writhing with anguish and her need to breathe. His palm was damp with her spittle; the rush of air through her nose grazed the back of his fingers. As he tried to turn her over, Alison lurched forward, sprawling face first on the grass. She lay there, stiff, refusing to give him what he wanted. His hand stifled her mouth.

Between his fingers, Alison gasped, "I'd die first. . . ."

His hand clamped her mouth and jaw. With a surge of hatred, he jerked her dress up with his free hand, then grasped the elastic border of her panties.

No stockings. Nothing in the way but nylon.

He wrenched the panties below her buttocks. As her pelvis pressed against the ground, resisting, he felt the round softness beneath his fingers.

"I know you hate us both," she said. *"But which one do you love?"*

His hand clutched her throat. "Don't move," he whispered. "Don't make a sound."

With the trembling fingers of one hand, he freed himself. He could feel the pulse in Alison's throat, hear the sound of her choking, air-depleted, too feeble to be heard.

Between her legs, Sam could see the rise of Tony's buttocks. . . .

"We'll do it this way," he told her.

When she felt him push against her, Alison stiffened, crying out. The sound died beneath his smothering hand.

She shivered as he pushed inside her, and then he stilled her with both hands, his hips thrusting harder, deeper. Her throat trembled with silent sobbing.

Sam's eyes shut, and the world went dark.

He clutched her tight, as if to save his life. Her deep, convulsive shudder became his; as he climaxed, filled with primal joy and terrible fear, his teeth clenched against the sound of his own outcry. Her tears were his as well.

She was still now.

Sam stared down at the joining of their bodies, overtaken by astonishment. The only sounds were his own ragged gasps.

Pulling himself free, he covered her with her skirt. "Alison," he whispered.

She did not answer. Then he rolled her on her side, and saw what he had done.

Nausea overcame him. Kneeling beside her, he writhed in agony, numbing shame.

He stood, staggering and stupid, zipping his pants. Alison lay at his feet.

Reeling, Sam stumbled back from her.

"Alison . . ."

Tony's voice came to him, as if in a dream. Turning, Sam had no sense of distance, place. The night was a morass.

A branch cracked beneath his feet.

"Alison . . ."

Sam began to run.

Ahead of him was a shadow. Sam knew the shape and size of it as well as he knew his own.

Sam felt his soul burst open.

He veered, running wildly through the dark, hoping that the shadow would not catch him. Sweat ran down his face.

Ahead, appearing as a mirage, was his car.

Pausing, he fumbled for his keys, got inside. The motor started. The drive home was sensory fragments—headlights, shadows, a siren in the distance, the scent of Sue's perfume.

His house was silent, dark. He climbed the stairs, to the room next to his parents', and crawled into his bed, still dressed. The night was surreal, a dream. . . .

In the morning, Sam awoke, his skull throbbing with whiskey, his stomach raw, his brain a swirl of doubt and horror. He reeled to his bathroom and threw up in the toilet. Amidst the sound of his own retching, there was one certainty Sam clung to.

It wasn't him.

FIVE

Tony felt too much to speak.

Looking into his face, Sam took one step backward, then another. "It wasn't me. . . ."

Alison's face was flushed, her mouth contorted. The eyes that had held such love for him were wide and empty, pinpointed with red starbursts. . . .

"No, Sam." Tony's voice was very quiet. "It wasn't me."

Sam flinched, and was silent.

Tony felt cold metal against his head, trembling with its own life. "You animal—what have you done to her?"

Were he holding a gun, Tony realized, he would kill Sam without thinking. He could feel the weight in his hand, the tension of his finger on the trigger, so sensitive to the touch.

"Nothing matters," Sam repeated softly. "It wouldn't matter to me if you'd killed her. . . ."

Sam's hand rested on the nightstand now. The drawer was slightly ajar.

"And it still matters," Tony said softly. "Even more. Because you murdered Marcie Calder."

Sam's fingers curled at the edge of the drawer.

Keep calm, Tony told himself. He watched the movements of Sam's hand, the nervous twitch of his fingers.

"Was it like with Alison?" Tony asked.

For a moment, Sam's eyes shut.

She had pale skin, straight black hair, which fell across her cheekbones . . . as she bent over the cinder track, Sam admired the sinew of her thighs, the tightness of her bottom. . . .

"No," Sam answered. And then he caught himself, his blue eyes cloudy with self-doubt. "Not until the end . . ."

On their last night, they drove to the park again. Filled with the glow of bourbon, Sam felt anxious, eager. Next to him, Marcie was quiet.

Tonight he would fulfill his deepest imaginings. When she had asked to see him, her voice taut with emotion, Sam knew that she remembered her promise to him. He had kept on drinking just to help the hours pass.

They parked in the grove of trees where Tony had parked with Alison. When she turned to him, mouth parting, Sam kissed her hard. She seemed to start at the whiskey taste of him. She looked irresolute, disconcerted.

"It's all right," Sam said softly. "I can make it all right."

Understanding crept into her eyes, and then they turned moist. "Does it mean that much to you?" she asked.

"Yes."

She looked down. "Everything's changing. My whole life . . ."

Sam put his arms around her to quiet her fears. "It's all right," he said again.

Head down, Marcie nodded her acquiescence. When

she silently undressed, then lay beneath him on her stomach, Sam was gentle. . . .

She shivered as he pushed inside her, and then he stilled her with both hands, his hips thrusting harder, deeper. Her throat trembled with silent sobbing. . . .

He was so careful that Marcie barely made a sound. . . .

Her deep, convulsive shudder became his; as he climaxed, filled with primal joy and terrible fear, his teeth clenched against the sound of his own outcry. Her tears were his as well. . . .

Pressed against her back, Sam shuddered with release. Marcie did not move or speak.

Slowly, he withdrew. "Marcie?" he asked.

She did not answer. Then he rolled her on her side, and saw what he had done. . . .

"I want to see your face," Sam murmured. When she turned, looking up at him again, tears came to Sam Robb's eyes.

"Thank you," he said. "Thank you."

Marcie dressed hurriedly, distractedly. "We need to talk," she said in a dispirited voice. "That's why I asked to see you. Not for *this.*"

Sam froze, feeling the sting of her dismissal. "What is it?"

Marcie touched his shoulder, looking down. "I'm pregnant." Her voice was sad, lost. "I'm going to have your baby."

Sam had no words. Suddenly he saw the tidal wave of consequence—the loss of Sue, his job, the respect he had worked so hard for.

Marcie seemed to sense his horror. "No one knows it's you. . . ."

Sam felt hollow. "Not yet. In the end, your father will beat it out of you. . . ."

"I haven't told *Janice.* What makes you think I'd tell *him?*"

The sound of her own anger seemed to deplete her. She laid her head on Sam's shoulder, clinging. "Just hold me, okay? I'm so scared. . . ."

Stiffly, Sam embraced her. "We'll get an abortion."

He felt Marcie shake her head. "I can't. I just can't. . . ."

"You *have* to." His voice rose. "What's more important to you—me, or a baby that will ruin things for both of us?"

Marcie pulled back, staring at him. "The baby didn't choose."

"Neither did I. I'm not a sperm donor, Marcie."

Marcie folded her arms. "You're the father of my baby," she said. "I came to say that I'll protect you. *Both* of you."

To Sam, her adamancy was slighting, then infuriating. "If you loved *me* . . ."

"If you loved *me*," she shot back, "you'd give me a little comfort." Her voice trembled with emotion. "You'd say, 'I love you, Marcie.' Just like you did when you were coming in my bottom."

Sam felt the blood rush to his face. "You wanted it. . . ."

"I *did* it for you." Suddenly each word was laced with contempt. "Because I thought I was special, and that you were a man. But you're acting like any selfish teenage boy, and now all you care about is that everyone will know about you. . . ."

Sam slapped her.

The crack of his hand across her face shocked him. Her head snapped back. Shaken, Sam gaped at her.

Sam heard the sharp intake of her breath. Then the light revealed her china face, the widening of her eyes. . . .

Marcie stared as though she saw right through him. Then she slid against the door, jerking it open. In a tremulous voice, she said, "Don't come near me. Ever . . ."

Suddenly she was gone, running into the night.

Sam ran after her.

The night was chill. In faint moonlight, filtered now by clouds, Sam saw Marcie Calder running toward Alison's house.

It would be fate that decided for them, Sam knew suddenly. . . .

If she had not done this, perhaps he could have let her go. But they could not know who he was.

Sam ran faster, fear and anger and whiskey racing through his brain.

Her footsteps whispered in the grass. He could see her lengthening strides, the speed that he had helped to give her. His chest and lungs heaved. . . .

She was closer now, to him, and to the Taylors'. . . .

"Marcie," he called out.

Turning, she stumbled, fell. Rolling on her back, she stared up, frightened and pale, as he approached. Sam slowed to a walk.

"Marcie," he said softly.

"Fuck you." Her voice was tight, scared, angry. "I don't care *what* happens to you now. This baby's more important—"

"No," she said, turning her face. "I don't want you. . . ."

At her feet was the rock she had tripped on.

Sam jerked her to her feet, grasping the rock with one hand.

"Don't move," he whispered. "Don't make a sound. . . ."

Marcie struggled in the crook of his arm. "You're crazy—" she began, and then he covered her mouth. . . .

He could feel the pulse in Alison's throat, hear the sound of her choking. . . .

In a spasm of fear and anger, Sam brought the rock down hard on Marcie's head.

Shock ran through his forearm. Her eyes popped open; slumped in his arm, she shuddered, twitched.

The next two blows were to stop this. Only with the last did he feel the blood touch his face, fine as mist.

Sam stood in an open field, gazing across the dark expanse of Taylor Park, Marcie Calder caught in his arms. In his shock and disbelief, he could not seem to move.

"Alison . . ."

Tony's voice came to him, as if in a dream. Turning, Sam had no sense of distance, place. The night was a morass. . . .

Sam turned toward the lake.

Beneath the moon, the lake, deep black, met the cloudy smudge of sky. Its sound was rolling, low.

Marcie's body twitched against him.

Shaken, Sam dragged her toward the lake, rock clutched in one hand.

The park felt vast and silent. At any moment, a car, pulling into the parking lot, might catch him in its headlights. Sam was damp with sweat; the sound of his panting breaths seemed to come from a great distance, as though from someone else.

Marcie did not twitch again.

Her body was awkward, heavy. Sam slung her against his hip, carrying her in the crook of his left arm. Her hand, spilling toward the ground, looked glossy in the moonlight.

At the edge of the grass was a patch of mud, the bluff. Sam dragged Marcie Calder the last few feet; staring at the darkened beach below, he felt the boulder in his right hand, the ache of his tendons as he clutched it.

Sam threw the boulder as far as he could. It made no sound.

Both hands beneath her arms, Sam lifted Marcie above the precipice, staring into her face, frozen in shock. His eyes shut; slowly, he bent his cheek to her mouth, listening for her breath. There was no sound, no warmth on his skin.

Moist-eyed, Sam looked into her face again, as if to be sure. Then he hurled her into the darkness. As she vanished, he could hear her body skidding down sheer cliffside, the victim, now, of a fall.

As if in a trance, Sam walked toward the bower of trees.

Kneeling beside the car, Sam wiped his hands on the moist grass. Then he peeled off his sweat clothes, turning them inside out, and put them on again. When he got in the car, it felt strange that Marcie was not next to him.

He could not go home, Sam knew.

He drove from the trees, headlights off, looking for other cars, or a transient like Donald White. As the car crept across the field, Sam's nerves tingled; only when he reached the macadam lot did Sam switch on his lights.

Turning, he headed for the mouth of the park.

Sudden headlights blinded him. Squinting, Sam slowed his car; as the sedan came closer, he saw the roof light of a Lake City police car, patrolling the park.

Sam's breath caught in his throat.

He drove slowly, fingers tight on the steering wheel. The patrol car slowed as well, perhaps to note the make of his car, his license plate, even his face. . . .

Passing, the police car was two feet away. Sam released a shuddering breath, watching its red taillights recede in the rearview mirror. Then his mind went cold.

Before anyone saw him, he must become Sam Robb again.

The teachers' lot was empty. Parking, Sam checked the digital clock. It was ten twenty-six. Marcie's parents would be waiting for her; Sue would be waiting for *him*.

Hurriedly, Sam left the car and went to the side door to the gym. Inserting his key, he hesitated, and then let himself inside.

The gym felt vast, dark. The hardwood floor creaked beneath his feet.

The basketball hoops, the wooden stands, were shadows. Somewhere on the wall above him, a banner recorded the names of those who had become the Athlete of the Year.

Beneath the basket, Sam turned toward the locker room. It felt strange for this place to be so dark, so silent. . . .

Like the gym, the locker room was dark. Fumbling his way to the sinks and mirrors, Sam switched on the light. In the mirror was a man with soft jowls, graying temples. There was blood on his face and hair.

He reeled to his bathroom and threw up in the toilet. Amidst the sound of his own retching, there was one certainty Sam clung to. . . .

Sam's retching echoed in the locker room.

Pale, Sam washed the blood and vomit from his face. His hands were trembling: this man, this stranger, could not be him.

The janitors would be working now, perhaps would hear him. Perhaps one might wander in to take a leak.

Hurrying to the shower, Sam stripped off his clothes and shoes, then washed the blood from his hair.

Inside his locker was a second pair of sweat clothes, a new pair of tennis shoes. Sitting on the bench, Sam dressed with clumsy fingers.

Tony stepped down from the bench before they could applaud, embracing the players who stood nearest him. But when he got to Sam, he said only, "Where are our girlfriends hiding?"

Panicky, Sam towel-dried his hair, stuffed the bloody shoes and sweat clothes and towel into his gym bag, and crossed the locker room to turn out the lights. Gym bag in one hand, he cracked open the door to the gym.

More lights struck his eyes.

The head janitor, Mike Griggs, was cleaning the floor with a mop. Heart racing, Sam shut the door. Its click was loud.

Fearful, Sam wheeled in the dark.

Half smiling, Sam spun the football on the end of one finger like a world globe, watching it with great concentration. "The parking lot," he answered, and flipped the ball back to Tony. . . .

Sam rushed to the other door. He pushed it open, and then the night air hit his face.

The public parking lot was beyond the football field. It was dark; Sam could barely see the goalposts. Blindly, he began running toward the lot.

As Sam reached the parking lot, he slowed, searching his memory.

The storm drain was at the corner of the lot, Sam suddenly remembered; after Tony had left him at the pier, he had driven here and sat beneath the goalposts, drinking, before he threw the empty bottle down the drain.

Stooping, Sam pushed everything between the slots of the metal drain: clothes, shoes, towel, the bag itself. It was beginning to drizzle; Sam could hear the water flowing through the hollow pipes below.

He was sober now, himself.

Rushing across the field, he got in his car and drove away. It was 10:55.

Composing himself, he stopped at a pay phone to call Sue. That she did not answer was both worry and relief. The four minutes to his home felt endless now.

His house was silent, dark. He climbed the stairs, to the room next to his parents', and crawled into his bed, still dressed. The night was surreal, a dream. . . .

Sam opened the bedroom door.

Sue was in bed, filing her nails, half listening to the eleven o'clock news.

"I tried to call you," he said.

She looked up at him, incurious. "I must have been in the shower," she said, and then frowned. "Broke another nail—my hands look like a washerwoman's."

Somehow this made Sam want to kiss her. But he stopped himself; he did not know what behavior might seem odd, or repentant. He changed into his boxer shorts and crawled into bed.

"I'm tired," he said, content to tell the truth.

Sue had noticed nothing.

Now she slept. Sam lay next to her in the dark, torn between horror and disbelief. Over and over, he saw a man in a car, caught in headlights. A man who could not be him.

Closing his eyes, Sam listened to the rise and fall of Sue's breathing, as if it were his own.

Tomorrow he would be himself again.

Perhaps, then, he should go to the police: when Sam was himself, people had always believed him. Even Tony.

SIX

Across the bedroom, Tony looked into the face of the man who had raped and strangled Alison Taylor, who had changed the course of his life, and then had used him, so many years later, to escape the consequences of killing Marcie Calder.

His voice was soft. "It doesn't matter, you said. I could tell you if I murdered Alison."

Sam's fingers still grazed the drawer. "You could have, Tony. But I could never tell *you*. . . ."

"Could I have murdered Sue, then? Would that have been all right with you?"

Sam drew himself up. "You slept with her, then lied to me, and I forgave you. Do you think I couldn't see what happened that night, or couldn't tell how different she was when I touched her? It made me crazy, but I let it go. For both our sakes."

Tony felt the slow, sick anger overcome him again. "I guess that made us even, didn't it. That made it all right for me to get you off when you killed a second girl. Especially if I slept with Sue again." Tony's voice quivered now. "What was the best part, Sam? Asking if I was 'fucking' Sue? Or manipulating your smart friend Tony, so blinded by being accused of killing Alison that I resolved all doubts in your favor?"

Sam was pale now. "You make it sound like a game. . . ."

"Alison, Sue, this trial—it was *all* a game we played, wasn't it. Except you were the only one who understood the rules." Tony paused, edging closer. "It must have been fun to have me back again. For one last round."

Sam slowly shook his head. "That was Sue's idea, not mine. I didn't *mean* for any of it to happen. Sometimes I felt like it never really had." His voice fell. "I competed with you, sure. But you were *part* of me. There were times—even now—when you were more important than anyone." Sam's face contorted in pain. "It wasn't easy to tell you, pal. When no one knew, it wasn't real. Now I look at you, and I know it's real. Because *you* do."

In the trapped silence, Tony forgot everything but the man in front of him, and what he had done to Alison. "It won't be just the two of us much longer, Sam. If Stella reads the report, she'll see what *I* saw." His voice was taut with anger. "Were I Stella, I'd charge you with both murders in a single trial. Which would make it pretty hard for you to blame Ernie."

Sam's eyes grew hazy; with a savage pleasure, Tony watched the knowledge of Sam's own ruin overtake him. Reflexively, Sam said, "You're my *lawyer*, Tony—"

"You mean there are *rules*?" Tony cut in. "That I can't do this to you? That it isn't *fair*? Then let me explain to you how the rules are going to work with Alison.

"I found her strangled. That makes me a *witness*, Sam. As well as a suspect." Driven by rage, Tony took another step forward. "But even if I weren't, there's nothing to stop me from asking Stella to run those tests. And you know what a clever woman *she* is."

Sam's eyes glinted with an anger of their own. All at once, Tony saw the humiliation, the sense of betrayal, that could drive Sam Robb to kill. "I can't let you fuck me over, Tony."

Tony fought for self-control. "You're a double murderer," he said softly, "and you're still saying you're not like that. This needs to end."

Sam reached into the drawer. Tony felt his mouth go dry. "It's too late, Sam. . . ."

Silent, Sam drew out a black revolver.

The reality of a gun aimed at his chest struck Tony like a blow. He thought of Christopher, of Stacey. Though Sam was flushed, his gaze was cold and level, as if the balance between them had been restored. Then Tony saw them in the mirror.

"Look at us." As he nodded toward the mirror, there was a tremor in Tony's voice. "Can you really do that, Sam?"

Sam glanced at them: two men—one with a gun in his hand; the other, perhaps, about to die. His hand trembled slightly. "I never thought it would come to this, Tony. You were my friend."

Tony watched the revolver. "If *you* were the 'friend' *I* used—twice—would you just let it go? Would *you* want to risk having another girl die, a third pair of parents on your conscience?" Tony could not keep the bitterness from his voice. "That is, if you were me."

Sam looked him in the face now. Quietly, he asked, "But what if *you* were *me*?"

Tony drew a breath. "I'd know that the game was over. That Sue will know, that the town will know, that everyone will know. That if you murder me, cold sober, *you'll* know. And you'll know that you made my wife and son suffer like the Taylors, or the Calders." Tony's voice was soft again. "Are you like that, Sam? Is that what you want me to die knowing?"

Eyes moist, Sam took two steps forward. "I can't let you turn me in, Tony."

Three feet separated them now: taut, Tony prepared himself to lunge at the gun in Sam's hand. "What about Sue?" Tony asked. "Do you want her to know *this*?"

Sam's face filled with anguish. "Don't talk about Sue," he said. "Don't use her on me anymore."

Tony swallowed. "Then you'll have to decide."

When Sam raised the revolver, gently placing it to Tony's forehead, Tony found that he was surprised, after all. He could not move. "Jesus, Sam. Jesus . . ."

Slowly, Sam nodded, tears running down his face. "It has to be one of us, Tony."

Feeling the gun to his head, Tony looked into the face of his friend; Sam's eyes were as filled with emotion as they had been in those first seconds in the end zone, the height of their time together, perhaps the height of Sam's life. Tony looked back at him, too afraid to speak.

"Can't let you win," Sam said quietly. "You know how it is."

Sam stepped backward, gun aimed at Tony, eyes locked on his face. "Bye, pal," Sam said.

Tony's voice trembled. "Sam . . ."

Smiling slightly, Sam put the gun to his own temple. "You lose," he said, and pulled the trigger.

Tony winced.

A piece of Sam's brain spat from the side of his head. Then he buckled, falling to his knees, still gazing up at Tony. He stayed there a moment, kneeling, his eyes glazed, unseeing, his arms at his sides. The gun clattered on the floor. Then Sam toppled sideways, and was still.

Paralyzed, Tony stared at Sam in some twilight of consciousness, unable to accept what had happened, what he was seeing now.

The door opened behind him.

Sue gasped. It was this that awakened Tony. He turned to her, and then, stricken, they stared at Sam together.

The bullet had not changed his expression, or much about his face. He lay there, still smiling, as if he had fallen asleep. A strange thought came to Tony: this was how they had watched him, lying in his hammock, on the night of the prom.

"Look at him," Tony said softly. "He'll probably die in his sleep . . ."

When Sue turned to him again, tears running down her face, Tony wondered if she had thought of this too.

Tony put his arms around her. He found that they both were crying: for Sam, Tony was certain; for Alison; for Marcie Calder; and for all the memories, forever changed, that each of them would have to face.

At last, Tony took Sue's hand and led her gently from the bedroom. Turning, Sue looked back at the man on the floor, her husband, Tony's friend, the murderer of two teenage girls.

SEVEN

Tony stayed on, to help Sue.

The day before Sam's burial, Tony made a statement to a room filled with reporters, photographers, and television cameras.

He spoke first for Sue Robb and for her children, expressing their shock at what they had learned, their deep sadness for the families of Sam's victims, their wish to mourn in private. Briefly, he described Sam's death: that Sam had admitted killing Alison Taylor and Marcie Calder; that he was torn by guilt and shame; and that—burdened by conscience—he had taken his own life. He did not mention the autopsy report or his role in confronting Sam.

Finally, Tony spoke for himself. The jury had been correct, he said. Based on the evidence, they should not have convicted; only Sam Robb knew the truth, and Sam Robb at last had told it. All that was left for Tony was to apologize to Ernie Nixon.

"I implicated an innocent man," he said, "without any real belief that Ernie Nixon was capable of murder.

"Mr. Nixon did nothing wrong. *I* did. Marcie Calder was Sam Robb's victim, and Ernie Nixon was mine. Everyone in Lake City should know that."

Tony left without taking questions, or addressing his own relationship to Alison Taylor. Anything further he had to say would be in private.

Sue and her children buried Sam quietly. Tony was not there.

Instead, as Sam was laid to rest, Tony completed his confession, begun twenty-eight years before. A soft-voiced priest, a shadow in the confessional, listened.

When he was seventeen, Tony said, he had made love

with Alison Taylor. He could not think this a sin. But this had led to other sins; perhaps, Tony said, he had misconceived the lessons he had learned. For he had abandoned his faith to make a religion of the law and then, faced with his arrogance and folly, had abandoned even that.

Perhaps he had done this for Ernie Nixon, or Jenny Travis. More surely it was for Sue, whom he still loved. But he had also faced Sam out of pride and, Tony was quite certain, the desire for revenge.

"Why do you say that?" the priest asked.

"I lied to him," Tony said simply, and then explained himself.

When he was through, the priest was silent for a moment, and then prescribed a penance.

For the sake of his soul, Tony performed it gladly. Then, still kneeling in the church of Saint Raphael, Tony prayed for the soul of Alison Taylor, for Marcie Calder, and, at last, for Sam.

He found Ernie Nixon in front of his garage, packing boxes. Bent over a box, Ernie looked up at him. His eyes were cool.

"Yeah," he said softly. "I thought you might come around."

Tony shoved his hands in his pockets. "What are you doing?"

Ernie considered him for a time. "Leaving," he answered. "Like you . . ."

A sense of hopelessness crept over Tony. "Look, I know I'm not the one to say this, but maybe you should stick this out."

Ernie stood, arms folded. "No, you're not the one to say that." He paused, face hardening. "I don't know what you want from me. But I have to live with this, and so can you."

For a moment, Tony was quiet. "I don't want anything

from you. I just thought I should apologize in person. That's how I did the rest of it—in person."

"And now you're doing the stations of the cross," Ernie said in a level voice. "You just can't help being the hero, can you. No matter what."

Tony felt a spark of anger. "You're right," he said. "That's how I am. But just for the hell of it, I wondered what you *are* going to do. Besides leave."

Ernie gazed at him. "Try to get Dee back," he said after a time. "She's willing to talk, and I'm going to start by saying she was right about *me*. But not anymore, Tony. So maybe I've got you to thank for that." Pausing, Ernie finished in a softer voice. "Stella Marz tells me I've got more to thank you for than that. But it's a little hard to get worked up about it."

"No," Tony said. "I wouldn't bother. But good luck, anyhow."

Silent, Ernie resumed packing boxes. Tony left.

It was close to five when Tony reached the cemetery. The afternoon light fell gently on Alison's headstone.

He had come, Tony supposed, to say goodbye to her. In the depths of his sorrow, he did that.

The nightmare, he was somehow certain, would not return. What would never leave him was deeper, surer—sadness, and a measure of comprehension.

At Sue's direction, Sam Robb had not been buried here: the Taylors had borne enough.

In the smaller cemetery near Taylor Park, Tony found his marker. "Samuel James Robb," it said simply. "Husband of Sue, father of Samuel and Jennifer."

"Athlete of the Year," Tony thought. *"Killer of Alison and Marcie."* The new headstone had already been defaced—someone, perhaps a teenager, had smeared it with blood-red paint.

"We both lost," Tony said to his friend.

* * *

For a long time, Tony stood on the Taylors' front porch. He was about to leave when the door cracked open, revealing John Taylor's seamed face, ravaged by time and tragedy.

There was a brief glint in John Taylor's eyes, some remaining spark of vitality. "What do you want?" he asked.

Tony's chest felt tight; he supposed that, with this man, he would never feel any other way. "I'm not sure. Maybe to reach some understanding, if we could. What happened, happened to us both." Tony paused. "At least now we know what that was."

John Taylor's eyes narrowed. "Happened to us both, you say?" His jaw worked, and his voice, when he spoke again, was rough. "You got him off, Anthony Lord. If it hadn't been for this strange attack of conscience—if that's what it was—Sam Robb could have killed again. What would you say then? I wonder. And who would want to listen?"

John Taylor did not know what Tony had done. But Tony suddenly saw what *John Taylor* had done: hating Tony had given meaning to his life, and he could not let it go. "When Alison died," Tony said at last, "you asked me for an answer. Now you have it, and you can hate me for what I *did* do. But, with all respect, it's a terrible waste of time."

John Taylor was silent, his face closed. Tony said goodbye, and left him with his bitterness.

Near his car, Tony stood for a time, gazing at the hedgerows of Taylor Park.

For almost thirty years, Sam Robb had defined the Taylors' lives as, in a sense, he had defined Tony's. All that Tony knew about his future, whatever it might be, was that Sam should not define it now. That was the lesson of John Taylor.

That night, Sue chose to be with her children. Tony had his last dinner with Saul.

They went to the steakhouse. At Saul's insistence, for old times' sake, Tony ordered the half head of lettuce with the gelatinous French dressing.

Content to be in Saul's company, Tony was quiet. Finally, Saul said, "Thinking about quitting, aren't you."

Looking at Saul's face—its strange combination of priest and cynic—Tony realized how well this man had come to know him. "It's just hard to imagine doing it again," he answered. "You need this ruthless objectivity, a kind of bloody single-mindedness. I don't know if I have that anymore. Or want to."

Saul nodded. "Rough times, my boy." Pausing, he took a swallow of red wine. "Of course, Sam could have been innocent, like you. The fact he wasn't doesn't change that."

Tony shook his head. "It also doesn't change what he did to Alison or Marcie, and could have done again. Or the fact that I made it possible." Tony paused for a moment. "Remember the story you told me? The child abuser you got off—the one who used the fireplace implements? Sam could have been mine."

Saul sat back, hands folded on his stomach, appraising Tony across the table. "How did you get him to do that, Tony? Kill himself."

Tony smiled a little, though his heart was hardly light. "I already went to confession. Why make a long day longer, when all I want is the pleasure of your company."

"Well," Saul said at last, "I'm sure Lady Justice would forgive you too. For whatever it was." Leaning forward, he touched Tony's arm. "You're a good man, and a good lawyer. After all this time, I've kind of gotten invested in you."

Tony smiled again. "What are *you* going to do, Saul?"

"I don't know. Maybe try another case—you inspired me." Saul's eyes were serious now, and his voice was soft. "Don't let your life come to *that*, either. *Have* a life. And when it's time to quit, quit."

Tony knew that and, he was sure, Saul knew that he did. But it was the last time for Saul to share whatever he could.

"I'll miss you, Saul."

"Me too." Abruptly, Saul looked out at the light and shadow of the Steelton skyline. "But if you ever come back here again, Tony, it really *is* your fault."

EIGHT

Neither Sue nor Tony wished to say goodbye in the house where Sam had died. And so, on a crisp fall morning, they met at the end of the Lake City pier.

They sat close to each other, feet dangling over the water. Sue leaned her head against his shoulder. "This is where we said goodbye the last time, remember?"

"Sure. I remember." Suddenly, to Tony, the passage of years was achingly sad. "I never imagined this, Sue. Any of it."

Sue was quiet for a moment. "I should have," she answered. "There were things I didn't want to know."

Tony took her hand. "Neither of us wanted to. And some of this we couldn't know. So we both took care of him, even if that meant not seeing him whole."

Sue looked down. "In an odd way, Tony, he loved you more than anyone. I always knew that. But the way it ended . . ."

"Was the way it had to end." Tony paused. "Otherwise, he'd have spent the rest of his life knowing what he was. I never thought he'd kill me, Sue. Except for the last few seconds."

She turned to him now, looking at him carefully. "You thought he'd kill himself, didn't you?"

Studying her face, once more so dear to him, Tony considered his answer. Then, at last, he chose the truth. "I didn't leave him any room, Sue. The alternatives were shooting me or letting me turn him in. Sam chose the way I thought he would."

Sue touched his cheek. Softly, she asked, "Is that why you didn't go to Stella Marz?"

Tony drew a breath. "I wanted peace for you, and justice for Alison. I got it the only way I could."

"What do you mean?"

Tony watched her eyes. "If Stella couldn't try Sam for Alison's murder, there would have been no conviction for killing Marcie Calder. Because I never could have testified, and the evidence still wasn't there."

Sue's fingertips had frozen on his face. "But Alison . . ."

Gently, Tony removed her hand. He did not look away. "Stella couldn't have charged Sam with Alison's murder. Sometime in the last twenty-eight years, moving old files from place to place, they lost the semen samples. Stella doubts they'll ever find them." Finishing, Tony spoke softly. "As any lawyer would have told his client."

Sue stared at him, the nature of what Tony had said washing over her. "My God . . ."

"So I guess I 'won,' Sue, after all. But Sam's not here to keep score."

Sue turned from him and was still for a moment. Then she stood, facing the water.

Standing behind her, Tony still spoke quietly. "For the last three days, I've told myself you were better free of him. It's the one excuse I can live with."

Sue did not move. "That decision was never yours to make."

In his pain, Tony felt the truth of this. Silent, he walked to the middle of the pier.

It was here, Tony remembered, that Sam had said that

it did not matter if Tony was a murderer. It was no comfort then—or now, when Tony was.

He heard Sue's footsteps behind him.

Tony found that he was afraid to turn. Then he felt Sue's hand on his waist, her face against his back.

"Am I forgiven?" he asked.

"Yes." Her voice was low, tremulous. "Am I?"

"God, yes." He turned to her and, for a long time, held her without speaking.

At length, he looked at her. Her eyes, tearless and steady, gazed back at him.

"Will you stay here?" he asked.

"For now. The kids have their own lives. I'll sell the house, and work, and see how that is. This is still my home, and I've got friends here. There's some comfort in that, even now." For the first time, she smiled a little. "If I win the lottery, maybe I'll travel. Go to Capri."

Her resolution, the absence of self-pity, pierced his heart. "If there's anything I can do . . ."

Sue shook her head. "That's probably not such a good idea. For either of us." She hesitated, and then her smile faded. "I'll always love you, Tony. It's a strange time to say that, I know. But there's never been a good time for us, has there."

Tony touched her face. "Maybe we just don't know, Sue. Maybe in some other life, where none of this ever happened, Alison is forty-five, with two nice kids and a man her parents adore. And you and I are married."

Gently, Sue kissed him. Then she leaned back, her eyes moist, looking up at him. "Wouldn't it be pretty to think so," she said.

He flew to San Francisco under an assumed name, to avoid reporters. Landing, it was better than he had hoped, for Stacey and his son were there.

Christopher hung back. So that it was Stacey who

came up to him, ignoring the stares of onlookers, and kissed him.

"I thought I'd appear in person," she said. "Just in case you'd forgotten me."

Tony smiled. "I never did."

On the ride home, Stacey was quiet, thoughtful. Once they arrived, she gave him time with Christopher.

To Tony, his son seemed older. The initial pleasure of Tony's return was replaced by a watchful curiosity, concern with what his father had been through. To Tony, the risk he had taken seemed beyond his power to forgive himself.

They sat together in the living room. "What happened?" Christopher asked.

As completely as he could, Tony told his son the story of his seventeenth year and realized that, for the first time, the story had an ending. Christopher said almost nothing—the empathy was on his face.

When Tony was finished, Christopher said, "It explains a lot, Dad."

"Yeah. I guess it does."

For several hours, they talked about that. When, at last, Christopher went to bed, Tony stood on the rear balcony, looking at the bay, the lights, the stars.

After a time, Stacey was next to him. "What will you do now?" she asked.

"I have no idea."

She touched his wrist. "Well," she said, "we've got time to talk about it. Now that you're home."

He *was* home, Tony realized. This city. This woman. The life they shared, and the boy they loved in common. He had never known this so completely and, for now, this was enough. The rest would come in God's own time.

Turning, Tony Lord looked into the face of his wife, his lover. "Yes," he answered. "I'm home."

ACKNOWLEDGMENTS

Silent Witness could not have been written this way without the help of others. In San Francisco, I received advice from those experts I've begun to think of as my criminal law board of directors: Medical Examiner Dr. Boyd Stephens; Homicide Inspector Napoleon Hendrix; Detective Hal Lipset; and defense attorneys Hugh Levine and Jim Collins. As usual, Assistant District Attorney Al Giannini gave me critical advice before I wrote the novel, and then reviewed the manuscript for atmosphere and authenticity.

Because the starting points for Lake City and Steelton were the suburb of Bay Village and the city of Cleveland, the locations where I lived more or less continuously from ages ten to twenty-four, I should reemphasize what I hope is already obvious—that this is a work of fiction and that the places and events are imagined. Fairness also impels me to add that Bay Village and Cleveland are considerably nicer than Lake City, which I envision as more rural and isolated, and Steelton, a rust-belt amalgam whose grimness owes much to other models. But revisiting both locales helped me create the milieu I wanted for this novel, and a number of people helped as well. Carmen Marino, chief of the

Criminal Division of the Cuyahoga County Prosecutor, laid out possible prosecutorial tactics in a fascinating way. Defense lawyer Jerry Gold provided good advice, fine company, and some great suggestions for cross-examination. And County Coroner Dr. Elizabeth Balraj, forensic expert Linda Luke, former assistant county prosecutor Jack Hudson, and my friend and law school classmate Jerry Weiss all assisted my research. (An addendum: those familiar with procedures in Cuyahoga County will be aware that, unlike many jurisdictions, the coroner's office grants relatively liberal access to coroner's reports. The restrictions reflected in my story are those commonly used elsewhere.)

Similarly, a number of people reacquainted me with various aspects of life in a smaller midwestern community, including Fred Drenkhan, Jim Tomkins, Eric Eakin, Mary Slama, Joe Loomis, and George Serb. Special thanks go to my oldest friend, Dick Penton, who helped me relive the time in which Tony Lord grew up.

The psychology of a character like Sam Robb is quite complex. Psychiatrists Dr. Rodney Shapiro and Dr. Ken Gottlieb explored with me the possible components of Sam's pathology, and helped to put it in a fictional context. Nor was the life of Tony Lord uncomplicated: my friend Mike Robe helped me re-create the role of a star athlete in a small town; and Father Tony Sauer graciously outlined the possible differences in the relationship of Tony Lord to the Catholic Church between the 1960s and the present, a time during which the evolution of the Church might enable Tony to reexamine his disaffection.

Several important people supported me throughout the writing of *Silent Witness*. My literary agent and friend, Fred Hill, and my dramatic rights agent, Richard Green, lent their usual fine assistance. My wife, Laurie; our dear friend Anna Chavez; and my wonderful assistant, Alison Thomas—who gets better with each book—gave me painstaking feedback on every section of this novel. My friends Philip Rotner and Thelton Henderson kindly commented on various aspects of the manuscript. And my publishers at Knopf, including Sonny Mehta and Jane Friedman, encouraged me as always.

Finally, there are Linda Grey and Clare Ferraro. As president of the Ballantine Publishing Group, Linda inherited me a few books back. In the process of helping me reach millions of readers, she has become my friend and good-humored guide to the sometimes arcane world of paperback publishing. Clare Ferraro, publisher of Ballantine, is—however inartful the phrase—my oldest friend in publishing, and her splendid company and consistent support have been one of the real blessings of my career. With the help of George Fisher, Kim Hovey, Woody Tracey, Jean Fenton, and many others, including the dedicated Ballantine sales force, they have helped bring me the writer's ultimate reward: thanks to them, even my kids know who I am.

Read on for an excerpt from

IN THE NAME
OF HONOR

by Richard North Patterson

Available in hardcover from
Henry Holt and Company

The phone call awakened Paul Terry from the dream of his father.

Disoriented, he sat up in bed, staring at the wall of the hotel room. In the dream, he was thirteen, the age at which the image had first come to him. His father had just died; reappearing in Paul's sleep, Frank Terry assured his son that he was fine, just living in a different place. Relieved, Paul would awaken, and then feel more abandoned and alone. Even now, at thirty-one, the dream left tears in Terry's eyes.

His cell phone rasped again. Beside him, Jenny stirred. Groping, he found the phone on a nightstand and flipped it open.

"Captain Terry," he said in a sleep-stunned voice.

"Paul. It's Colonel Dawes."

"Morning, sir." Glancing at the drawn curtains, he detected no light. "Is it morning?"

"Six A.M. Where are you?"

"D.C. I'm spending the weekend here."

"Not anymore, I'm afraid." Dawes's southern-tinged voice was soft. "I guess you haven't seen the papers. There's been a shooting on the post. A captain's dead."

Terry tried to process this. "Are they preferring charges?"

"Not yet." The colonel's voice lowered. "The shooter is Lieutenant Brian McCarran."

Terry was instantly alert. "The general's son?"

"Yes. He's in need of a lawyer, Paul. Hopefully not for long."

At once Terry understood his superior's undertone of caution and regret. "I'll be there in an hour and a half," he promised.

When he turned the phone off, Jenny was awake, blond hair falling across her forehead. "I'm sorry, Jen. There's been a shooting at Fort Bolton—one officer killed another. I have to go."

Jenny switched on the bedside lamp. The disappointment he read in her pretty, intelligent face was mingled with resistance. "Don't they have other attorneys? Why you, Paul?"

"The colonel didn't explain himself. Just sounded worried."

She shook her head. "I thought you were leaving the service. I mean, isn't a Wall Street firm about to pay you a ton of money?"

Terry paused to assess her mood. Six years after a law school romance had revealed them to be unsuited as life partners, they had become lovers of convenience, who connected only at the end of her sporadic business trips to Washington. For the odd forty-eight hours, they would always rediscover their shared sense of fun, their enjoyment of verbal combat, the luxury of sex without anxiety or inhibition. It was too bad, Terry often thought, that their differences prevented more. Now Terry grasped that their scattered weekends meant more to Jenny Haskell than she let on.

"They are," he told her. "But for another month I can't debate an order." He gave her a lingering kiss, then added gently, "However much I'd like to."

He sensed her regret becoming withdrawal. "I think I'll stay here for a while," she said in a subdued tone. "Order room service, read the paper. Maybe I'll call friends in Bethesda."

Terry felt his own regret, both at leaving and, as with other women, that leaving did not matter more. He kissed her again, this time on the forehead, then reluctantly headed for the shower.

Shortly before seven-thirty, dressed in the uniform of a JAG Corps captain, Paul Terry passed through the main gate at Fort Bolton, headquarters of the Seventh Infantry and, for one more month, Terry's home.

Over twenty miles square, Fort Bolton was sequestered amid a wooded area of northern Virginia, an enclave sufficient to itself: shopping centers, athletic facilities, offices, a hospital, apartments, town houses, and, for senior officers, commodious colonial-style houses dating back to the fort's establishment eighty years before. Turning down its principal thoroughfare, McCarran Drive, Terry was reminded of the three generations that preceded Brian McCarran. That Brian had killed a fellow officer, whatever the circumstances, would reverberate all the way to the Pentagon, where the family's most revered member, Anthony McCarran, served as the chief of staff of the army. Parking at the headquarters of the regional defense counsel, Terry felt edgy.

The aftershock of the dream still muddied his thoughts. But by this time, at least, he resembled the officer Lieutenant Colonel Dawes expected to brief. He had taken a large black coffee for the road, and the mild hangover he had earned through a bibulous dinner with Jen was fading. Fortunately for Terry, his life circumstances had lent him an air of near-perpetual alertness, accenting the swift intelligence reflected in his penetrant blue eyes. Jen sometimes teased him that he looked like an officer whether he meant to or not: tall and fit, he had jet black hair and strong but regular features accented by a ridged nose, which, broken during a high school basketball career based largely on determination, added a hint of ruggedness. That Terry had never fired a shot in anger did not detract from the success he'd had in the courtroom.

Taking a last swallow of lukewarm coffee, Terry went to meet Harry Dawes.

Colonel Dawes sat behind a desk so orderly that, Terry often thought, even the piles of papers appeared to be standing in formation. For Terry, this thought was a fond one: a soft-spoken Virginian, the colonel treated Terry with an avuncular regard enhanced by the military courtesy that governed their relationship. As Terry entered, a brief smile crossed Dawes's ruddy face. "Sit down, Paul. Sorry to get you out of whatever bed you happened to be in."

The remark was delivered with quiet humor; a committed Christian and devoted husband of twenty-five years, Dawes never concealed his belief that Terry's rotating cast of female friends suggested an attenuated adolescence that could only be cured by marriage. "A warm one," Terry responded. "But even in my sleep, I grasped that this case is special."

Without asking if Terry wanted coffee, Dawes poured him a cup and handed a Washington Redskins mug across the desk. "It is that," Dawes concurred soberly. "In the last twenty-four hours, the media's been all over this. You must have been living in a cave."

"When I take time off, sir, I commit myself. Please catch me up."

Pensive, Dawes ran a hand through his dwindling gray-brown hair. "To say the least, the relationships surrounding this shooting are complicated. For one thing, the victim, Captain Joe D'Abruzzo, was married to General McCarran's goddaughter, Kate Gallagher—"

"Hang on, sir," Terry interjected. "The general's *son* killed his goddaughter's *husband*?"

"Yes," Dawes answered unhappily. "It seems that her father was General McCarran's classmate at the Point. After he died in Vietnam, the families remained close. So Kate's relationship with Brian McCarran predated her marriage to D'Abruzzo by many years. To top it off, D'Abruzzo was Brian's company commander in Iraq. Whatever *their* relationship, this tragedy leaves two kids— an eight-year-old boy and six-year-old girl—without a father."

Terry found himself squinting; the summer sunlight, brightening, hit his face through Dawes's window. For a painful moment he imagined the children's shock at learning their father was dead. "Tell me about the shooting, sir."

Even in difficult circumstances, Dawes was the most considerate of men; noting Terry's squint, he stood to lower the blinds. "It happened in McCarran's apartment," he began, "between seven and eight on Friday evening. Sometime before eight, Lieutenant McCarran called the MPs and calmly advised them that he'd shot Captain D'Abruzzo. The MPs and paramedics found D'Abruzzo on the floor of the lieutenant's apartment. There were four wounds, including one in the dead man's back. Despite this, when two men from the Criminal Investigation Division questioned him, McCarran claimed self-defense."

Terry put down his mug. "He gave a statement to CID?"

"A fairly comprehensive one, I'm told. It also seems that McCarran's the only witness."

"What do you know about the gun?"

"It was a semiautomatic—a nine-millimeter Luger. What's odd is that it's D'Abruzzo's gun."

"So he brought it to McCarran's apartment?"

Dawes grimaced. "Apparently not. According to both Brian McCarran and D'Abruzzo's wife, Brian took it from D'Abruzzo's home after he threatened her with it. Brian's story is that D'Abruzzo came looking for the gun. The shooting followed."

Terry took a sip of coffee. "Do we know anything more about the relationship between Lieutenant McCarran and the widow D'Abruzzo?"

"Just that they still had one. At the least, it's clear that their families have been intertwined over many years."

As Terry took out a pen, Dawes handed him a legal pad across the desk. "What else do we know about Brian McCarran?" Terry asked.

"Only good things. He was third in his class at West Point, a leader among his classmates, and a first-class soccer player. He graduated in 2003 and turned down a Rhodes scholarship in favor of serving in Iraq. By early 2004, Brian was a platoon leader in Sadr City, one of the most dangerous assignments in the war. He's got a scar on his neck—three months after his arrival an RPG came within inches of removing his head. But he served out his year there without missing any time. By all accounts, he was an outstanding combat officer." Dawes's tone was respectful. "He certainly isn't cruising on his father's reputation. Even in a family of decorated soldiers, Brian has more than held his own."

Terry nodded. "What's he doing now?"

"He's the executive officer of Charlie Company, his outfit in Iraq. Once again, his fitness reports are excellent."

"And D'Abruzzo?"

"Not as stellar, clearly. He didn't go to the Point, and his early record lacks McCarran's glitter. But he comes across as capable—he's been serving as a battalion operations officer, in line for promotion to major. There's nothing on the surface that suggests any real problems."

"Including domestic violence? That's starting to show up among Iraq War vets, and it certainly fits with the story about the gun."

"All I can tell you," Dawes responded cautiously, "is that there were no reported incidents. At least before he died."

Terry scribbled a note: "Check out DV." Looking up, he said, "What's happened since McCarran reported the shooting?"

Dawes gazed at the desk, organizing his thoughts. "The MPs taped the call, of course. The paramedics were there in minutes, at which point D'Abruzzo was pronounced dead. The CID man secured the apartment, called in the crime lab team, and requested that the county medical examiner come out. Then CID started questioning McCarran."

"What do we know about that?"

"Other than what I've told you, very little. Nor do we know anything more about what Kate D'Abruzzo told them."

"So where does this stand?"

Dawes's forehead creased with worry, no doubt reflecting the level of scrutiny each step in the case would receive. "As you can imagine, it's being handled by the book. On the recommendation of the staff judge advocate, General Heston has ordered a formal inquiry, to be carried out by CID and the office of the chief trial counsel, Colonel Hecht. In turn, Hecht has designated Major Mike Flynn to monitor the investigation and, if necessary, prosecute the case as trial counsel."

"No surprise," Terry remarked. "By reputation, Flynn's the best. Where are they keeping McCarran?"

"Not in the brig. On the recommendation of General Heston's chief of staff, Brian is living at the bachelor officers' quarters. On Monday he'll continue his normal duties." Dawes grimaced. "Outsiders may feel he's getting special treatment. But this is an officer with an unblemished record who claims self-defense. Your job will be to help him."

"I gather that, sir. But this assignment raises a number of questions."

Dawes's eyebrows shot up, a sign of irritation that betrayed the pressure he felt. "Such as?"

Unfazed, Terry responded, "Why me? For openers, the McCarrans can have anyone they want, including the top defense lawyers in America—"

"Few of whom understand the military, and none as well as we do. The McCarran family knows that. And if this one comes to a court-martial, the court would have no doubt about the integrity of military defense counsel. That is *not* an assumption granted to civilian lawyers."

Fair or not, Terry knew that this was true. With the smallest of smiles, he responded, "It's true that our integrity is unique, sir. But not unique to me."

Dawes was unamused. "There are other considerations—beginning with my own. Lieutenant McCarran has requested a lawyer. As regional defense counsel, it falls to me to detail one. Given that he's from a notable military tradition, and that his father is odds-on to be the next chairman of the Joint Chiefs, everything we do must be beyond reproach."

The same skeptical smile played on Terry's lips. "At least for the next month. As you'll recall, sir, there's a law firm in New York expecting me to show up."

Caught, Dawes allowed himself a rueful smile. "To my regret. But Anthony McCarran seems to prefer you, nonetheless."

Terry laughed in astonishment. "Me? I've never met the man. How does he even know I exist?"

Dawes steepled his fingers. "The general has been very decorous—as chief of staff, he has to be. But there was nothing to keep him from visiting his neighbor in the Pentagon, the judge advocate general. General Mc-

Carran made it clear that he didn't wish to exercise un-
due influence. He merely expressed the hope that his son
would have the help of an able lawyer. Meaning, General
Jasper assumed, the best defense counsel at Fort Bolton."

"In all modesty, sir—"

"Naturally," Dawes continued, "General Jasper responded that *all* our lawyers are highly qualified. It was
then that General McCarran said that he had heard that
a certain Captain Terry was particularly able.

"The judge advocate general did not inquire as to
where he had gotten this information. He merely assured
the general that his son would be well represented, and
then made his own inquiry of me." Dawes's voice became softer. "What I told him, Paul, is that you were the
best young lawyer I've ever seen. And that if Brian Mc-
Carran were my own son, I'd want you to defend him."

Though touched, Terry smiled yet again. "You're a
devious man, sir."

"There's no wind so ill," his mentor answered
blandly, "that it can't serve someone's purpose. In this
case, mine. I assured General Jasper that, as a short-
timer, you wouldn't mind breaking a little china if it
served young McCarran's interests. And if it came to a
trial, God forbid, I hoped you might be willing to extend
your tour in the army. I generously promised not to
stand in your way."

As Terry framed a droll reply, the seriousness in
Dawes's face stopped him. "You know I'd like you to
stay, Paul. But if this goes to trial, it could be the high-
profile case of a lifetime, with all the human challenges
and opportunities that involves. No matter what awaits
you in your Wall Street firm, you'll likely be a better
lawyer, maybe even a better man. That's part of what
I'm trying to do."

Absorbing this, Terry nodded. "Thank you, sir. Unfortunately, the firm has already assigned me an investment

banker to defend, with more to follow. Whatever Brian
McCarran's problems, I don't think the firm will wait.
But I'll go to see him, of course."

Briefly, Dawes frowned. "There's someone else you
should meet first. Brian McCarran's sister."

Terry gave Dawes a puzzled look. "No doubt she's
concerned," he answered. "But I should meet my client
first."

"Meg McCarran's more than a concerned sister. She's
a lawyer, and she came here from California to help her
brother. She's also quite insistent on 'helping' you."

Terry felt himself bristle: he did not want to deal with
an anxious relative standing between him and his client—
or serving as a conduit to her father, the general. "Is
there anything I can do about this?"

"Meet her and see." Smiling faintly, Dawes glanced
at his watch. "It's eight-forty. I told her to be in our reception area at nine o'clock. If she's as businesslike as
she sounds, she's already here."

As Dawes had predicted, Meg McCarran was waiting
outside his office.

She stood, briskly shaking hands with Terry as the
colonel introduced them. Her looks surprised him. En-
countering her at random, Terry might have seen an
Irish beauty, a fantasy from his Catholic youth: glossy
auburn hair, large blue eyes, softly glowing skin, a button nose, and a wide, generous mouth, which, parting
for a perfunctory smile, exposed perfect white teeth.
But her suit was the pin-striped carapace of the courtroom, and the skin beneath her eyes was bruised with
sleeplessness. The effect was somewhere between trial
lawyer and the vigilant older sister of a juvenile facing
trouble, and her swift appraisal of Terry combined a
palpable wariness with an air of command worthy of
her father.

Standing to one side, Dawes offered them the use of

an empty office. "Mind talking outside?" Terry asked her. "I could use some fresh air, and there's a park across the street where we can sit."

Meg gave a fractional shrug. Opening the door, Dawes reminded Terry of an anxious parent watching two recalcitrant teens embark on a blind date. Instinctively, Terry wished that the occasion were as trivial as a high school dance, and would be over with as quickly.

They settled on a bench beneath a cluster of oak trees, set back some distance from McCarran Drive. Terry reminded himself that less than two days ago, this woman's brother had called her to report killing a man she must have known well. "I understand how worried you must be," he ventured.

"Clear-eyed," she amended. "I know the army. Because of our father, they'll bend over backward not to show Brian any favoritism. So whoever we engage to help him, I need to be here."

Briefly, Terry weighed his response. "No matter whose son Brian is, there's an orderly process. CID will investigate; Major Flynn will make recommendations; ultimately General Heston will determine whether to refer charges for trial. What Brian needs right now is an advocate."

Meg faced him. "What Brian needs," she said with quiet urgency, "is for the army to comprehend what it's done to him. I'm absolutely certain that Brian acted in self-defense. But the man who shot Joe D'Abruzzo is different from the man they sent to Iraq." Her voice slowed, admitting a first note of entreaty. "Sadly, Captain Terry, Brian's not very trusting anymore. He's not likely to trust you or any lawyer but me. That's another reason I'm here. Of all the people in Brian's life, I'm the one who knows him best."

Terry contemplated the grass at their feet, dappled with light and shade. "How long do you plan to stay?"

"Until Brian's out of trouble. Whether that's days or weeks or months."

"What about your job?"

"I'm a domestic violence prosecutor in the San Francisco DA's office." She bit her lip. "I love my work, Captain Terry. But the DA can't have a prosecutor from his office acting as a defense counsel. If Brian's charged with Joe's death, I'll have to resign."

Even under the circumstances, the depth of her resolve struck him. "We're not there yet," he reminded her. "Even if we were, I'm not sure Brian will need that kind of sacrifice."

Meg shook her head. "He's my brother. I won't let anything happen to him."

Something in her fierce insistence suggested the conscientious child she might have been, charged with protecting a younger brother. "Are there just the two of you?" he asked.

"And my father," she said. "My mother's dead."

The flatness of her tone deflected further questions, let alone any rote expression of sympathy. After ten minutes of acquaintance, it was hard for Terry to imagine Meg McCarran seeking sympathy from anyone. She had a quality of independence as striking as her beauty, suggesting both intelligence and a considerable force of will. But Terry also intuited a trait he understood all too well—the instinct for self-protection. Facing him on the bench, Meg said in a neutral manner, "I know my father made inquiries. But I don't know anything about you, or much about the JAG Corps."

"It's pretty straightforward. Every major installation has JAG offices, including a legal adviser to the commanding officer, judges, prosecutors, and defense lawyers. The Trial Defense Service, my unit, has its own chain of command. The purpose is to ensure that our superiors don't punish us for winning—"

"That's reassuring," Meg interjected tartly. "How, specifically, was Brian assigned to you?"

Terry was determined to maintain his equilibrium. "In any case occurring at Bolton, Colonel Dawes details a defense counsel. As you suggested, your father also made inquiries. I'm the result."

Meg regarded him closely. "No offense, Captain Terry, but you're obviously young. Don't you think Brian might do better with an experienced civilian lawyer?"

Briefly, Terry had the thought that if he were to be relieved of this case, and this woman, his departure from the army would be far simpler. "It's not my call," he answered. "I can tell you the pros and cons. A JAG lawyer knows the military justice system and the psychology of the potential jurors. Most people don't trust defense lawyers; military people trust them less. If you asked the average army officer, odds are he'd say that many civilian lawyers are ethically challenged or just in it for the money.

"A defense lawyer in uniform avoids that bias. On the other hand, a civilian lawyer is less inclined to be deferential, and the talent pool is larger." Terry paused. "Military or civilian, what a court-martial comes down to is how good the lawyer is. Hopefully, you won't need one. Right now the idea is to persuade the army not to prosecute."

A light breeze stirred Meg's hair. She pushed her bangs back from her forehead, her intense blue-eyed gaze still focused on Terry. "Why did you choose the JAG Corps?" she asked.

Terry decided to be direct. "First, my family had no money, so a ROTC scholarship to college helped get me where I am. Second, I don't like taking orders.

"That may sound strange coming from a JAG officer. But a number of my law school friends wound up as gofers in big corporate firms, shuffling papers miles from the courtroom. To have the career I wanted, I needed to try cases—hard ones, and a lot of them."

"Have you?"

"Over a hundred twenty in the last six years, the first ninety as a prosecutor. I didn't always get the sentence I wanted, but I never lost a case."

" 'Never'?" Meg repeated skeptically.

In the face of Meg's challenge, Terry stopped resisting the sin of pride. "Means never. When the Trial Defense Service got sick of losing to me, they asked me to switch sides."

A first sardonic smile appeared at the corner of her mouth. "At which point you started losing, too."

"Rarely."

This stopped her for a moment. "What about homicides?"

"I've defended five. Three acquittals; one conviction on a reduced charge; another on second-degree murder. In that case, the victim was a six-year-old boy, my client's prints were on the knife, and he confessed to CID *and* the victim's mother. Clarence Darrow couldn't have saved him." Terry's speech·became matter-of-fact. "I'm getting out next month, so I hope to wrap this up by then. But I chose defense work on principle—too many prosecutors lack a sense of justice. Temperamentally and professionally, I'm more than capable of helping your brother."

She gave him a considering look. "Why do you think you've been so successful?"

"Simple. I hate losing." Terry paused, then decided to finish. "Since the age of thirteen, no one has given me anything. I got here by sheer hard work, the only asset I had. Lose a case, and I'm haunted by what I might have done better.

"There may be smarter lawyers. But no one hates losing more than I do, or works harder for their clients. I've defended thirty cases; I've lost four. I still can't shake them."

Meg sat back, her eyes meeting his in silence. "I think I understand," she said at length. "At least for now, I'd like you to represent my brother."

For some reasons he could identify, and others that eluded him, Terry felt both satisfaction and a deep ambivalence. "Then let's go see him," he answered simply.

Tony Lord — hero
Sam Robb — coach
Gina Belfonte — killed husband
Stacey — Tony's wife
Kilcannon — killed by Harry Carson
Chris — Tony's son
Allison Taylor — early girlfriend died